Mercycle

PIERS ANTHONY

D0012206

ACE BOOKS, NEW YORK

This Ace book contains the complete text of the original
hardcover edition. It has been completely reset in a typeface
designed for easy reading, and was printed from new film.

MERCYCLE

An Ace Book / published by arrangement with
the author

PRINTING HISTORY
Tafford Publishing, Inc. edition published 1991
Ace edition / August 1992

ISBN: 0-441-52562-8

Ace Books are published by The Berkley Publishing Group,
200 Madison Avenue, New York, New York 10016.
The name ''ACE'' and the ''A'' logo
are trademarks belonging to Charter Communications, Inc.

10 9 8 7 6 5 4 3 2 1

CONTENTS

CHAPTER 1

DON

Proxy 5–12–5–16–8: Attention.
Acknowledging.
Status?
Four locals have been recruited and equipped. They are waiting for the signal to commence.
They are ignorant of their mission?
They believe they have missions, but none know the true one. They have been given a cover story relevant to their interests. By the time they realize that the cover story is irrelevant, they should be ready for the truth.
Contraindications?
One is an agent of a local government.
Why is this allowed?
The recruitment brought the response of this person. It seemed worth trying. That one can be eliminated if necessary. Such involvement might prove to be advantageous.
With the fate of a world at stake?
We do not know what will be most effective. It is no more risky than the exclusion of such persons might be.
It remains a gamble.
Any course is a gamble.
True. Proceed.

Acknowledged. I will start the first one through the phasing tunnel.

Don Kestle pedaled down the road, watching nervously for life. It was early dawn, and the sparrows were twittering in the Australian Pines as they waited for the picnickers, but nothing human was visible.

Now was the time. He shifted down to second, muttering as the chain caught between gear-sprockets and spun without effect. He still wasn't used to this multiple-speed bicycle, and it seemed to be more trouble than it was worth. He fiddled with the lever, and finally it caught.

He bucked the bike over the bank and into the unkempt grass, moving as rapidly as he could. He winced as he saw his thin tires going over formidable spreads of sandspur, though he knew the stuff was harmless to him and his equipment. That was because, as he understood it, he wasn't really here.

Soon he hit the fine white dry sand. He braked, remembering this time to use the hand levers instead of embarrassing himself by pedaling backwards, and dismounted automatically. Actually it was quite possible to ride over the sand, for it could not toss this bike—but anyone who happened to see him doing that might suspect that something was funny. A bicycle tire normally lost traction and support, skewing badly in such a situation.

In a moment the beach opened out to the sea: typical palm-studded Florida coastline. Seagulls were already airborne, raucously calling out. A sign warned NO SWIMMING, for there were treacherous tidal currents here. That was why Don had selected this spot and this time to make his cycling debut; it was least likely to harbor prying eyes. He had been given a place and a time to be there; his exact schedule was his own business.

The tide was out. Don walked his bicycle across the beach until he reached the packed sand near the small breaking waves. Myriad tiny shells formed a long low hump, and he realized that early-rising collectors could appear at any moment. Why hadn't he thought of that before? Yet when else could he enter the water, clothed and on a bicycle, by daylight? He simply had to risk it.

Beyond the shell ridge, the sand was wet and smooth. He looked carefully, both ways, as if crossing a busy intersection. Was he hoping that there would be someone, so that he would have to call it off?

No, he *wanted* to do it, Don reassured himself. In any event, his timing was such that he could not spare the hours an alternate approach would require. He had chosen dawn at this beach, and now he was committed. He had been committed all along. It was just that—well, a bit hard to believe. Here he was, a healthy impetuous fair-complexioned beginning archaeologist with a bicycle—and a remarkable opportunity. What could he do except grasp it, though he hardly comprehended it?

Don remounted and pushed down hard, driving his machine forward into the flexing ocean. The waves surged through the wheels, offering no more resistance than air. He moved on, feeling the liquid against his legs as the force of gentle wind. He didn't really need more power, but he shifted into first anyway, bolstering his confidence. It remained hard to believe that he was doing this.

The bottom dropped, and abruptly he was coasting down into deeper water. Too fast for his taste. Now he did backpedal, futilely. There was no coaster brake on this machine!

The water rose up to his thighs, then his chest, then his neck. Still he coasted down. In another instant it was up across his face, and then it closed over his head. Don did not slow or float; he just kept going in.

He could see beneath, now. There was a rocky formation here, perhaps formed of shell. He would have investigated the local marine terrain more carefully, if only he had had time. But the whole thing had been set up so rapidly that he had barely had time to buy his bike before going through the tunnel. Now here he—

He realized that he was holding his breath. He forced himself to breathe, surprised in spite of himself that he still could do it. He had tested it by plunging his head into a tub of water, but somehow the surging sea water had restored his doubt. He applied his handbrakes.

The bicycle glided to a halt. Don braced it upright by spreading his legs, and rested in place for a moment with his eyes closed. This way he could breathe freely, for he couldn't see the surrounding water.

Don found himself cowering. He knew he was not physically courageous, but this seemed to be an overreaction. In a moment he realized why: it was the noise.

He had somehow imagined that the underwater realm was silent. Instead it was noisier than the land. Some was staccato sound, some was whistling, and some was like the crackling of a hot frying pan. Grunts, clicks, flutters, swishes, honks, rattling chains, cackling hens, childish laughter, jackhammers, growls, knocking, whining, groaning, mouse squeaks—it all merged into a semi-melodious cacophony. He had no idea what was responsible for the assault, but was sure that it couldn't all be inanimate. The nearest commercial enterprise was twenty miles away!

Could fish talk? Probably he would soon find out. It would be no more fantastic than the other recent developments of his life.

He was way under the water, standing and breathing as if it didn't exist. How had he gotten into this?

"Well, it all started about twenty three years ago when I was b-born," he said aloud, and laughed. He was not unduly reflective, but he did stutter a bit under tension. So maybe it wasn't really funny.

Don opened his eyes.

He was down under, all right. He could see clearly for perhaps twenty feet. Beyond that was just bluegreen watercolor wash. Above him, eight or ten feet, was the restless surface: little waves cruising toward ruin against the beach. Beneath him was a green meadow of sea grass, sloping irregularly down.

Now that he was stationary, he did not feel the water. He waved his hands, and they met no more resistance than they might have in air. It was warm here: about 88° Fahrenheit according to the indicator clipped to his bicycle. The temperature of subtropical coastal water in summer. He would be able to work up a sweat very quickly—unless he chose to descend to the deeper levels where the water got cold. He did not choose to do so, yet. Anyway, he was largely insulated from the water's temperature, as he was from its density. That was all part of the miracle of his situation.

A small fish swam toward him, evidently curious about this weird intruder. Don didn't recognize the type; he was no expert on marine biology. In fact he didn't know much about anything to do with the ocean. It was probably a nondescript trash fish, the kind that survived in these increasingly polluted waters. This one looked harmless, but of course even the deadliest killer shark was not harmful to him now. He was really not in the water, but in an aspect of reality that was just about 99.9% out of phase with what he saw about him. Thus the water had the effective density of air.

In impulse, he grabbed at the fish as it nosed within reach. His hand closed about its body—and passed through the flesh as if it were liquid foam. The bones of his fingers hooked into the bones of its skeleton without actually snagging.

Don snatched his hand away. Equally startled, the fish flexed its body and shot out of range. There had been a kind of contact, but not one that either party cared to repeat. No damage done, but it had been a weird experience.

It was one thing to contemplate a reality interaction of one part in a thousand, intellectually. It was quite another to tangle with a living skeleton.

Well, he had been warned. He couldn't stand around gawking. He had a distance to travel. The coordinate meter mounted beside the temperature gauge said 27°40′—82°45′. He had fifteen hours to reach 27°0′—83°15′. He had been told that a degree was sixty minutes, and a minute just about a mile, depending on location and direction. This sounded to his untrained ear like a mish-mash of temperature, time, and distance muddled by an incomprehensible variable. It seemed that he had about thirty miles west to go, and about forty south, assuming that he had not become hopelessly confused. The hypotenuse would be fifty miles, per the three-four-five triangle ratio. Easy to make on a bicycle, since it came to only three and a third miles per hour average speed.

Of course he probably wouldn't be able to go straight. What was his best immediate route?

He didn't want to remain in shallow water, for there would be bathers and boaters and fishermen all along the coast. His depth meter showed two fathoms. That would be twelve feet from bike to surface. Entirely too little, for he must be as visible from above as those ripples were from below. How would a boater react if he peered down and saw a man bicycling blithely along under the water?

But deep water awed him, though he knew that pressure was not a significant factor in this situation. Men could withstand several atmospheres if they were careful, and he had been told that there were no depths in the great Atlantic Ocean capable of putting so much as two atmospheres on him in his phased-out state. He could ignore pressure. All of which somehow failed to ease the pressure on his worried mind. This business just wasn't *natural*.

He would take a middle course. Say about a hundred feet, or a bit shy of seventeen fathoms. He would stick to that contour until he made his rendezvous.

Don pushed on the left pedal—somehow that was his only comfortable starting position—and moved out. The seagrass reached up with its long green leaves, obscuring his view of the sloping floor. But his wheels passed through the weeds, or the weeds through the wheels, and so did his body. There was only a gentle stroking sensation that affected him with an almost sexual intimacy as plant collided with flesh. The grass might be no denser than the water, but it was solid, not liquid, and that affected the contact.

He didn't like it, this naked probing of his muscle and gut, but there was nothing he could do about it. Except to get out of this cloying patch of feelers.

At nine fathoms the grass did thin out and leave the bottom exposed. It needed light, and the light was dimming. Good enough. But this had a consequence for Don, too. Just below the surface things had looked normal, for the limited distance he could see. Now the color red was gone. It had vanished somewhere between three and four fathoms, he decided; he hadn't been paying proper attention. He had a red bag on his bicycle that now looked orange-brown. The effect was eerie and it alarmed him despite his awareness of its cause.

"S-steady," he told himself. "The water absorbs the red frequencies first. That's all there is to it. Next orange will go, then yellow, then green. Finally it will be completely dark." He found his heart pounding, and knew he had succeeded only in bringing out another fear. He just didn't feel safe in dark water.

He had somehow supposed that the ocean floor would be sandy and even, just like a broad beach. Instead it was a tangled mass of vegetation and shell—and much of the latter was living. Sponges grew everywhere, all colors (except red, now) and shapes and sizes. His wheels could not avoid the myriad starfish and crablike creatures that covered the bottom in places.

But at least he was getting his depth. The indicator showed ten fathoms, then fifteen, then twenty. Down far enough now to make headway toward the rendezvous.

But he had to go deeper, because the contour would have taken him in the wrong direction. He had been naive about that; if he tried to adhere strictly to a given depth, he would be forced to detour ludicrously. The ocean bottom was not even; there were ridges and channels, just as there were on land.

The medley of mysterious sounds had continued, though he had soon tuned most of it out. Now there was something new. A more mechanical throbbing, very strong, pulsing through the water. Growing. Like an approaching ship.

A ship! He was in the harbor channel for the commercial ships using the port of Tampa. No wonder he had gotten his depth so readily.

Don turned around and pedaled madly back the way he had come. He had to get to shallow water before that ship came through, churning the water with its deadly screws. He could be sucked in and cut into shreds.

Then he remembered. He was out of phase with the world; nothing here could touch him. He had little to fear from ships.

Still, he climbed out of the way. A ship was a mighty solid artifact. The hull would be thick metal—perhaps solid enough to interact with his bones and smash him up anyway. After all, the bicycle's wheels interacted with the ocean floor, supporting him nicely. Could he expect less of metal?

The throbbing grew loud, then terrible. There was sound throughout the sea, but the rest of it was natural. Now Don appreciated the viewpoint of the fish, wary of the alien monsters made by man, intruding into the heart of their domain. But then it diminished. The ship had passed, unseen—and he felt deviously humiliated. He had been driven aside, in awe of the thing despite being a man. It was not a fun sensation.

Don resumed his journey. He followed the channel several miles, then pulled off it for a rest break. The coordinate meter said he had traversed only about four minutes of his fifty, and he was tiring already. He was wearing himself down, and he had hardly started. Cross-country underwater biking was hardly the joy that travel on land-pavement was.

Wouldn't it be nice if he had a motorcycle instead of this pedaler. But that was out of the question; he had been told, in that single compacted anonymous briefing, that a motor would not function in the phase. So he had to provide his own power, with a bicycle being the most efficient transportation. He had accepted this because it made sense, though he had never seen his informant.

Something flapped toward him. Don stiffened in place,

ready to leap toward the bike. He felt a chill that was certainly not of the water. The thing was *flying*, not swimming! Not like a bird, but like a monstrous butterfly.

It was a small ray, a skate. A flattened fish with broad, undulating, winglike fins. All quite normal, nothing to be alarmed about.

But Don's emotion was not to be placated so simply. A skate was a thing of inherent terror. Once as a child he had been wading in the sea, and a skate had passed between him and the shore. That hadn't frightened him unduly at the time, for he had never seen one before and didn't even realize that it was really alive. But afterwards friends had spun him stories about the long stinging tail, poisonous, that could stun a man so that he drowned. And about the creature's cousins, the great manta rays, big as flying saucers, that could sail up out of the water and smack down from above. "You're lucky you got out in time!" they said, blowing up the episode as boys did, inventing facts to fit.

Don had shrugged it off, not feeling easy about taking credit for a bravery he knew he lacked. But the notion of the skate grew on him, haunting him retrospectively. It entered his dreams: standing knee-deep or even waist-deep in a mighty ocean, the long small beach far away, seeing the devilfish, being cut off from escape, horrified at the approach of the stinger but afraid to wade out farther into that murky swirling unknown. But the ray came nearer, expanding into immensity, and he had to retreat, and the sand gave way under his feet, pitching him into the abyss, into cold smothering darkness, where nothing could reach him except the terrible stinger, and he woke gasping and crying.

For several nights it haunted him. Then it passed, being no more than a childish fancy he knew was exaggerated. He never had liked ocean water particularly—but since he didn't live near the shore, this was no handicap. For fifteen years the nightmare had lain quiescent, forgotten—until this moment.

Of course the creature couldn't get at him now, any more than it could have in the dream. Not when its body was phased out, with respect to him, to that one thousandth of its actual solidity. Or vice versa. Same thing. Let it pass right through him. Let it feel the brushing of bones.

The skate veered, birdlike—then came back unexpectedly. It was aware of him. Without conscious volition Don was on the bike and pedaling desperately, fleeing a specter that was only partly real. The thing's flesh might be no more than a ghost to him, but that very insubstantiality enhanced the effect. The supernatural had manifested itself.

Adrenaline gave him strength. By the time he convinced himself that the skate was gone, he was miles farther along. He had never been overly bold, but this episode had certainly given his schedule a boost.

Next time, however, he would force himself to break out his camera and take a picture. He couldn't afford to run from every imaginary threat.

He had lost track of the channel. The meter now read eight fathoms. He had moved about three minutes west, and would have to bear mainly south henceforth. But he could use some deeper water, as patches of weed still got in his way.

But deep water was not to be found. Sometimes it was nine or ten fathoms, but then it would shrink to six. He had to shift gears frequently to navigate the minor hills and dales of this benthic terrain, for he was tired. The wind—really the currents of the water—made significant difference. Some spots were hot, others cool, without seeming pattern. Some were darker, too, as if polluted, but this could have been the effect of clouds cutting off the direct sunlight.

Don was tired of this. The novelty had worn off quite

quickly. His time in the water had acclimated him; what could there be in the depths more annoying than this? He cut due west again, knowing that there had to be a descent at some point. The entire Gulf of Mexico couldn't remain within ten fathoms.

His legs protested, but he kept on. Miles passed—and gradually it did get deeper. When he hit fifteen fathoms he turned south, for he was now almost precisely north of his target area.

There was still enough glow for him to see by, which was good, because he didn't want to use his precious headlamp unnecessarily. Actually this objection was nonsensical, he realized, because it had a generator that ran from his pedaling power. But he was still having trouble overcoming his lifelong certainties: such as the fact that one could use a flashlight only so long before the battery gave out. Besides, a light might attract larger creatures. He didn't care how insubstantial they might be; he didn't want to meet them.

Don had thought it ridiculous to enter the water fifty miles from his destination, and doubly so to do it alone. What did he know about the ocean? But now he was able to appreciate the rationale. He had a lot of mundane edges to smooth before he could function efficiently in this medium. Better to work it out by himself, and let the others do likewise; then they would all three be broken in and ready to function as a team, minus embarrassments. That was the number he had guessed; each would have a relevant specialty for the mission. Strangers, who would get along, perforce.

Reassured, he stopped for lunch. Actually it was only nine a.m. and he had been under the water about three hours. But it seemed like noon, and he needed a pretext to rest.

There was a radio mounted within the frame of his

bicycle. It was not for news or entertainment, but for communication with his companions, once he had some. He didn't see the need for it, as sound crossed over perfectly well. But of course there could be emergencies requiring separation of a mile or two. The radios would not tune in the various bands of civilization, he had been told; they were on a special limited frequency. But they should reach as far as necessary.

Idly, he turned the ON switch. There was no tuning dial or set of station buttons; all he would get from this thing would be an operative hum.

"Hello," a soft feminine voice said.

Surprised, Don didn't answer.

"Hello," she repeated. Still he was silent, having no idea what to say, or whether he should speak.

"I know your set is on," the voice said. "I can hear the sea-noises in the background."

Don switched off. There wasn't supposed to be anybody on the line! Especially not a woman. Who was she, and what did she want?

By the coordinates, he had come barely ten or twelve miles. It was hard to figure, and not important enough to warrant the necessary mental effort. Three or four miles an hour, average. On land, the little distance he had gone, he was sure his rate had been double or triple that. He could have walked as fast, down here. And with less fatigue.

No, that was not true. He had to be honest with himself. He was carrying considerable weight in the form of food and clothing and related supplies. He even had a small tent. Then there was the converter: portable plumbing. And complex miniaturized equipment to keep the humidity constant, or something. His instrumentation was formidable. That coordinate meter was no two-bit toy, either. He had not known that such things existed, and suspected their cost would have been well beyond his means. Regardless of their miniaturization, they weighed a fair amount. His bicycle weighed about forty pounds, and the other things might total a similar amount. Half his own weight, all told. He would have felt it, hiking, and would not have been able to maintain any four miles an hour.

Naturally the bike was sluggish. Even the quintuple gearing could not ameliorate weight and terrain and indecision. Once he found a good, smooth, level stretch without weeds or shells, he could make much better time.

Even so, he was on schedule. Fortunately he was in good physical condition, and recovered quickly from exertion. How good his mental state was he wasn't sure; small things were setting him off unreasonably, and he was hearing female voices on a closed-circuit radio.

He unpacked the concentrates, having trouble finding what he wanted. These were supposed to be packages of things that expanded into edibility when water was added.

He had a bulb of water: a transparent pint-sized container. There was a second pint in reserve. After that he would have to go to recycled fluid, a prospect he didn't relish.

There were a number of things about this business that did not exactly turn him on. But two things had overwhelmed his aversions: the money and the chance to be involved in something significant. The mission, he had been told, would be done within a month, and the pay matched what he would have had from a year with a good job in his specialty. And if he did not agree that it was a mission he was proud to be associated with, that pay would double. The money had been paid in advance, in full; there was no question about that. So he had been willing to take the rest on faith, and to put up with the awkward details. They were, after all, necessary; he could not drink the water of the sea because it was both salty and phased out, and he could not eat the food of it either. He had to be self sufficient, except for the supplies which would be found in depots along the way.

Don inserted the syringe into the appropriate aperture of his food-packet and squeezed. The wrapping inflated. The principle was simple enough; he could have figured it out for himself if he had not been told, and there were instructions on the packets. He kneaded it, feeling the content solidify squishily. He counted off one minute while it set. His meal was ready.

He tore along the seam, exposing a pinkish mass. Cherry flavored glop, guaranteed to contain all the essential nutrients known to be required by man, plus a few good guesses. Vitamins A, B, C; P and Q; X, Y, and Z? It looked like puréed cow brains.

Don brought it cautiously to his nose and sniffed. Worse. Had he done something wrong? This smelled as if he had used urine as the liquid ingredient. He would never make his mark as a chef!

He suppressed his unreasonable revulsion and took a bite. After all, what could go wrong with a prepackaged meal? He chewed.

He spat it out. The stuff was absolutely vile. It tasted like rotten cheese laced with vinegar, and his stomach refused to believe it was wholesome. He deposited the remains in the converter, for even this must not be wasted.

Now he had sanitary needs. The hard labor of travel had disturbed his digestion. Or was it the experience with the foul glop? No, neither; it was the emotional strain of traversing the ocean floor in this remarkable phase state. He had practiced breathing in that tank of water, just after tunneling through, so that he had known it was feasible. But that had hardly prepared him for the psychological impact of pedaling a bicycle under the heaving sea.

He had to admit that this was an interesting adventure, even in its bad aspects. He knew already that he would not be demanding double pay. He had not been told he would *like* every aspect, just that it would be significant, and *that* it was.

He wound up with a plastic bag of substance. He hesitated, then reluctantly deposited it, too, in the converter. This stuff was in phase with him, and there was not much way to replace it; it must not be wasted. The unit would process it all, powered by a spur from his pedaling crank just below, reducing the solids to ash and filling another pint container with potable water.

Water, water, everywhere—how odd that he should be immersed in it, yet have to conserve it rigidly lest he dehydrate. There was a dichotomy about this phaseout that he wasn't clear about. The sea was like air to him, yet it remained the sea to its denizens. Fish could and did swim right through him and his bicycle without falling or gasping for gill-fluid. So it wasn't air at all, merely water at one one-thousandth effective density. *So how was he able to breathe it?* That little matter had not, in the rush, been clarified.

Don was no chemist, but he knew that H_2O did not convert to—what was it? N_4O? No, air wasn't that kind of combination, it was just a mixture of gases. Anyway, the O, for oxygen, in H_2O could not be asssimilated for respiration. He knew that much. Water vapor wasn't breathable. Even the fish had to sift their oxygen from the air dissolved in water, not the water itself. Yet even if he could have breathed the water, he would have been getting only one thousandth of the oxygen it contained, or maybe one five-hundredth what he was accustomed to. That was extremely slim pickings.

He was wasting time. He had perhaps forty miles to go

yet—a good four or five hours even on a decent surface. Twelve hours at his present rate. Which left him no time at all to rest or sleep. He had to keep moving.

Maybe his contact was expecting him. Was he in radio range? He flicked the radio switch.

"Now don't turn me off," the female voice said, "before I—" But he had already done so.

Now as he rode he tried to analyze his motive. Why did he object to hearing from a woman? So maybe she had somehow tuned in on this private band; that did not make her a criminal. She evidently had some notion where he was. What harm would there be in talking to her?

He got under way and tuned out the scenery. Not that he had paid much attention to it so far. What had he seen, actually? Fish, sponges, a blur of water, the shift of digits on the meters, and the irregular terrain of the sea floor.

Somehow the radio voice seemed one with the scenery. Both needed to be tuned out. Yet he knew that this was nonsensical. The scenery was already over-familiar, but the woman was a stranger. Why wouldn't he talk to her?

He realized that he couldn't blame it on the secrecy of the mission, because he knew no secrets yet, and was not responsible for radio security. It was the fact that she had caught him by surprise, and that she was a sweet-voiced young woman. That voice conjured a mental image of an attractive creature—the kind that paid no attention to a studious loner like him. So he had tuned out immediately, rather than get involved and risk the kind of put-down that would inevitably come. It was a virtually involuntary reflex.

So now he understood it. That didn't change it. He was afraid to talk to her.

He moved, he rested, he moved less, he rested more, he ground on, he tried another meal—and quickly fed it into the converter. It *couldn't* be his imagination! That food was spoiled. Fortunately his appetite was meager.

Don woke from his travel-effort oblivion to see to his dumbfounded joy that he had picked up on his schedule and could afford an hour's break. So he propped his bike, lay down on the strangely solid sand, and sank into a blissful stupor until the alarm went off. The world outside his little sphere became as unreal as it seemed.

Just so long as he didn't miss his rendezvous. He thought of himself as a loner, but that was mainly with respect to women. He had been alone more than enough, in this odd region on this strange mission.

He made it. He was on 83°15′ west longitude already, and bearing down on 27° north latitude. It was a few minutes (time, not distance) before nine in the morning. Nothing was visible, of course. It was dark above, and even with his headlight on he could not see far enough to locate anything much smaller than an active volcano. Water in his vicinity might feel like air, but it still dampened vision in its normal fashion. Except that the lamp restored full color, blessedly. Even if he could have seen for miles, the problem of pinpoint location would be similar to that in a dry-land wilderness. His meter was not that precise.

As his watch showed the moment of scheduled contact, Don stood still and listened. The ever-present noises of the sea crowded in annoyingly. Sound: there was the key. Here in the ocean, sound traveled at quadruple its speed in air, and it carried much better. Light might damp out, and radar, but sound was in its element here. Make a noise in the sea and it would be heard.

Don heard. It was the faint beep-beep of a signal no marine creature made—he hoped. It was Morse Code. And it had an echo: the slower arrival of the impulse through the air of the phase?

When it paused, he answered. He did not know Morse himself, except as a typical pattern of dots and dashes, so he merely sounded three blasts on his whistle. After a moment the same signal was returned.

Contact had been made.

CHAPTER 2

GASPAR

Proxy 5–12–5–16–8: Attention.

Acknowledging.

Status?

The first three recruits have been sent through the phase tunnel and the fourth alerted. The mission is proceeding as designed.

Contraindications?

The first recruit refuses to hold a radio dialogue. This may indicate an intellectual problem that did not manifest itself on the initial screening. He is otherwise normal, and seems to be pursuing the mission in good faith. The second recruit is more assertive, and may override this attitude or incapacity in the first. This foible does not appear to pose a threat to the mission.

There are always peculiarities of local situations. If this is the extent in your case, you are well off. 5–12–5–16–9 has a suicidal recruit.

That world may be lost!

Not necessarily. A suicidal person may be in a position to understand the loss of a world.

And may not care.

True. But what we offer does seem preferable to complete destruction.

"Gaspar Brown, marine geologist," the man said. He was short and fairly muscular, dark-haired and swarthy and looked to be in his mid thirties.

"Don Kestle, archaeologist," Don responded. "Minoan."

The bicycles drew together and the men reached across to shake hands. Don was phenomenally relieved to feel solid flesh again. He found himself liking Gaspar, though he had never met the man before. At this stage he liked anything human. The specters of his loneliness had retreated immeasurably.

"S-so you know about the ocean," Don said, finding nothing better as conversation fodder at the moment. He had never been much for initiating a relationship, and hoped Gaspar was better at it.

"Almost nothing."

"W-what?"

"I know almost nothing about the ocean," Gaspar said, "compared to what remains to be discovered. I can't even identify half these fish noises I'm hearing. They're much louder and clearer and more intricate than normal."

Don smiled weakly. "Oh. Yes."

"That's why I welcome this opportunity to explore," Gaspar continued, warming. "This way we don't disturb the marine creatures, so they don't hide or shut up. Think of it: the entire ocean basin open to us without the problems of clumsy diving suits, nitrogen narcosis, or the bends."

"N-nitrogen—?"

"You know. Rapture of the deep. Nitrogen dissolves in the blood because of the pressure, and this makes the diver drunk. This can kill him faster than alcohol in a driver, because it's himself at risk, not some innocent pedestrian. So he comes up in a hurry, and that nitrogen bubbles out of his blood like the fizz in fresh soda, blocking blood vessels or lodging in joints and doubling him up like—"

"You're right," Don agreed quickly. "Nice not to have to worry."

"Hey, have you eaten yet? I've been so excited just looking around I haven't—"

"W-well, I—" Don was abashed to admit his problem with the food, so he concealed it. "I haven't eaten, no." Gaspar was carrying the conversational ball, and that was a relief. Don was happy to go along, letting his compliance pass for social adequacy. Once he knew a person, it was easier.

"Great." Gaspar hauled out his packages and chose one. "Steak flavor. Let's see whether it's close."

Don dug out a matching flavor from his pack, not commenting. If Gaspar could eat this stuff . . .

They squeezed the bulbs and the packages ballooned. Gaspar opened his first and took a bite. He chewed. "Not bad, considering," he said. "Not close, but not bad. Maybe it would be closer if it didn't have the texture of paste. Better than K-rations, anyway."

Don got a grip on his nerve and opened his own. The same rotten odor wafted out.

"Hey, is your converter leaking?" Gaspar inquired.

"Not that I know of. Why?" As if he didn't know!

"That smell. Something's foul. No offense."

Wordlessly Don held out his package.

Gaspar sniffed, choked, and took it from him. In a moment it was in the converter. "You got a bad one! Didn't you know?"

"They're all like that, I thought. I was afraid—"

"They can't be! These things are sterile. Let me check."

"B-be my guest."

Gaspar checked. "What a mess! I can tell without having to use the water. Did you actually eat that stuff?"

"One bite."

Gaspar laughed readily. "You've got more grit than I have. What a rotten deal! Have some of mine."

Don accepted it gratefully. Gaspar's cherry glop tasted like cherry, and his steak like steak. Texture was something else, but this wasn't worth a quibble at this stage.

"H-how do you think it happened?" Don asked as his hunger abated.

"Oh, accident, I'd say," Gaspar decided. "You know the government. Three left feet at the taxpayer's expense. We'll share mine, and we'll both reload at the first supply depot. No trouble, really."

The man certainly didn't get upset over trifles. But Don wondered what kind of carelessness would be allowed to imperil this unique, secret mission, not to mention his life. For a man had to eat, and they could only assimilate food that had been phased into this state.

"Is it a government operation?" Don asked. "I thought maybe a private enterprise."

Gaspar shrugged. "Could be. I wasn't told. But somebody went to a pretty formidable expense to set us up with some pretty fancy equipment. If it's not the government, it must be a large corporation. This looks like a million dollar operation to me, apart from what they're paying us. But you're right: the big companies get criminally sloppy too. It could be either. Let's hope their quality control is better on the other stuff."

That reminded Don about the female voice on his radio. Had it been mistuned, so that it connected to someone not with this mission? If so, he had been right to cut off contact, though that was not why he had done it. Obviously that person wasn't Gaspar. Did she speak on both their radios, or only his own? Or had he imagined it? Should he ask?

Yes, he should. "D-did you t-turn on your—?"

"Say, look at that!" Gaspar cried.

Don looked around, alarmed. It was a monstrous fish, three times the length of a man, with a snout like the blade of a chain saw.

"Sawfish," Gaspar exclaimed happily. "Isn't she a beauty! I never saw one in these waters before. But then I never rode a bike here before, either. My scuba gear must have scared them away. What a difference that phase makes. Not that I'm any ichthyologist."

"I thought sea-life was your specialty."

"No. The sea *bottom*. I can tell you something about rock formations, saline diffusion, and sedimentary strata, but the fauna I just pick up in passing. I know the sawfish scouts the bottom—see, there she goes, poking around—and sometimes slashes up whole schools of fish with that snout, so as to eat the pieces, but that's about all. Relative of the rays, I believe."

That ugly chill returned. The fish was horizontally flattened, with vaguely winglike fins. It did resemble a skate, from the right angle.

"Y-you know, w-we aren't completely apart," Don said. "The bones—they interact—"

"Oh, do they?" Gaspar asked, as if this were an interesting scientific sidelight. As of course it was, to him. "I suppose they would, being rigid. There has to be some interaction, or we would sink right through the ground, wouldn't we? In fact, I'm surprised we don't; it isn't that solid, normally. Sediment, you know."

The sawfish vanished, and Don was vastly relieved. "You're right! If we intersect the real world by only a thousandth, why don't we find the sand like muck? If anything, it's harder than it should be. My tires don't sink into it at all. And how is it we can see and hear so well? I should think—"

"I'm no nuclear physicist, either. I have no notion how this field operates, if it is a field—but thank God for its existence."

"Maybe it isn't exactly a field," Don said. He was glad to get into something halfway technical, because it was grist for conversation, and he was curious himself. "Why should we have to ride through that tunnel-thing—you did do that?—to enter it, in that case? But if we were shunted into another, well, dimension—"

"Could be." Gaspar considered for a moment. "Maybe one of the others will know. I'm just glad it works."

"Others? I thought this was a party of three."

"Oh? Maybe you're right. I wasn't told, just that there would be more than one. I thought maybe four." Gaspar seemed to sidestep any potential disagreement, inoffensively. "Do you happen to know his specialty?"

"Me? That official was so tight-lipped I was lucky to learn more than my own name. And we're not supposed to tell each other our last names, I think."

"Necessary security, I suppose," Gaspar said. "I clean forgot. Well, you just forget mine, and I'll forget yours. Did you get to see anyone?"

"No, it was just an interviewer behind a screen. A voice, really; it could almost have been a recording."

"Same here. I responded to this targeted ad on my computer, and the pay and conditions—I was about ready for a job change anyway. I still don't know what the mission is, but I'm already glad I'm here." He glanced at Don. "How'd you get into this project, anyway? No offense, but archaeology is mostly landside, isn't it? Digging trenches through old mounds, picking up bits of pottery, publishing scholarly reports? There can't be much for you, under the sea."

"That's a pretty simple view of it," Don said, glad to have a question about his specialty. His reticence faded when he was in his area of competence. "But maybe close enough. The fact is, a great many archaeologists have combed through those mounds and collected that pottery, on land. They've reconstructed some fabulous history. If I could only have been with Bibby at Dilmun . . ." He sighed, knowing that the other would not comprehend his regret. No sense in getting into a lecture. "But I came too late. Today the major horizon in archaeology is marine, and the shallow waters have been pretty well exploited, too. No one knows how thoroughly the Mediterranean Sea has been ransacked. So that leaves deep water, and I guess you know better than I do why that's been left alone."

"Pressure," Gaspar said immediately. "One atmosphere for every thirty four feet depth. A few thousand feet down—ugh! But I was asking about *you*. I don't want to seem more nosy than I am; I just think we'd better have some idea why and how we were picked for this mission. Because the sea is formidable, even phased out as we are; make no mistake about that. The depths are a greater challenge than the moon. So it figures that the most qualified personnel would be used."

Don laughed, but it was forced. "I—I'm the *least* qualified archaeologist around. My only claim to fame is that I can read Minoan script, more or less—and there's precious little of that hereabouts."

"I'm not the world's most notable marine geologist, either," Gaspar agreed. "Any major oil company has a dozen that could give me lessons. But what I'm saying is that for this project, they should have used the best, and they could have, if they cared enough, because they evidently do have the money. Instead they placed little ads and hired nonentities like us, and maybe we aren't quite even in our specialties. You're—what was it?''

"Minoan. That's ancient Crete.''

"And I specialize in marine impact craters. Want to know what there're none of, here in the Florida shallows? If they had taken us down to the coast of Colombia, as I had hoped—'' He shrugged.

"What's there?'' Don asked.

"You don't know? No, I suppose that's no more obvious to you than Crete is to me. That's where we believe the big one splashed down: the meteor that so shook up the Earth's system that it wiped out the dinosaurs.''

"The extinction of the dinosaurs!'' Don exclaimed.

"Right. But the site has about sixty five million years worth of sediment covering it. So it will take an in depth—no pun—investigation to confirm it, assuming we can. But instead of sending me there, they sent me here. We'd have to bike across the Puerto Rico Trench to reach it, which is pointless and probably impossible. So either they have some lesser crater in mind for me, or they don't care whether I see a crater at all. I'm out of specialty, just as you are. See what I mean?''

Don nodded soberly. "Maybe we're expendable.''

"Maybe. Oh, I'm not paranoid about it. This phase thing is such a breakthrough that I'd sell my watery soul for the chance, and I think I mean that literally, to explore the ocean floor at any depth, unfettered by cumbersome equipment— that's the raw stuff of dreams. But why *me?* Why *you?*''

"I can't answer that,'' Don said. "All I can do is say how I'm here. I wasn't the bright boy of my class, but I was in the top quarter, with my main strength in deciphering. The lucrative foundations passed me up, and anyway, I wanted to go into new territory. Make a real breakthrough, somehow. Too ambitious for my own good. The prof knew it, and he made the contact. Swore me to secrecy, told me to buy myself a good bicycle and ride it to the address he gave me—well, that was two days ago, and here I am.''

"You're single?''

"All the way single. My father died about five years ago, and my mother always was sickly—no s-sense going into that. I've got no special ties to this world. Maybe that's why the ancient world fascinates me. You, too?''

"Pretty much. Auto accident when I was ten. Since then the sea has seemed more like home than the city. So nobody is going to be in a hurry to trace down our whereabouts. I think I see a pattern developing. We must have had qualifications we didn't realize.''

"Must have," Don agreed. "But you know, it's growing on me too. I don't know a thing about the sea, or even about bicycles, but I do know that the major archaeological horizon is right here. Not that I have the least bit of training for it. I guess I just closed my mind to the notion of going to the sea. But now that I'm *in* it—well, if I have to risk my life using a new device, maybe it's worth it. All those ancient hulks waiting to be discovered in deep water—''

"Sorry. No ancient hulk is in the ocean," Gaspar said. "Not the way you're thinking, anyway. Ever hear of the teredo?''

"No.''

"Otherwise known as the shipworm, though it isn't a worm at all. It's a little clam that—''

"Oh, *that*. I had forgotten. It eats wood, so—''

"So pretty soon no ship is left. Modern metal hulks, yes; ancient wood hulks, no.''

"What a loss of archaeology," Don said, mortified. "I could wring that clam's neck.''

Gaspar smiled. "Of course the ship's contents may survive. Gold lasts forever underwater, and pottery—"

"Pottery! That's wonderful!" Don exclaimed.

For the first time Gaspar showed annoyance. "I'm just telling you what to expect."

"I wasn't being sarcastic. Pottery is a prime tool of archaeology. It breaks and gets thrown away, and so it remains for centuries or millennia, undisturbed, every shard a key to the culture that made it. Who wants broken pottery—except an archaeologist? There is hardly a finer key to the activities of man through the ages."

Gaspar gazed at him incredulously, or so it seemed in the fading light of the headlamps, whose reservoirs were running down now that the bikes were stationary. "It really is true? You *do* collect broken plates and things? You value them more than gold?"

"Yes! Gold is natural; it tells little unless it has been worked. But pottery is inevitably the handiwork of man. Its style is certain indication of a specific time and culture. Show me a few pottery shards and let me check my references, and I can tell you where and when they were made, sometimes within five or ten miles and twenty years. It may take time to do it, but the end is almost certain."

Gaspar raised his hands in mock surrender. "Okay, friend. If we find a wreck, I'll take the gold and you take the broken plates. Fair enough?"

"I'll have the better bargain. You can't keep the gold, by law, unless it's in international waters; but the shards could make me famous."

"You archaeologists may be smarter than you look!"

"I should hope so."

Gaspar smiled. "Let's sack out. We've got a long ride tomorrow, I fear."

"What's the position?"

"The coordinates for the next rendezvous? I thought you had them."

"N-no. Only this one. The same one you had, it seems, so we could meet."

Gaspar tapped his fingers on his coordinate meter. "What a foul-up! They should have given one of us the next set."

Don's eyes were on Gaspar's fingers, because he couldn't meet the man's eyes. "I guess I should have asked. I just assumed—" He paused. Next to the meter was the radio. He had been about to ask Gaspar about that, when they had been interrupted by the sawfish. "Maybe the—did you check your radio?"

Gaspar snapped his fingers. "That must be it. I just came out here, gasping at the sea-floor and fish, never thinking of that." He flicked his switch.

"Leave it on!" the female voice cried immediately.

Startled, Gaspar looked down. Unlike Don, he was not dismayed, and he did not turn it off. "Who are you?"

Don kept silent, relieved to have the other man handle it. Maybe he should have had more confidence in his own judgment about both this and the bad glop, but he couldn't change his nature.

"I'm Melanie. Your next contact. Why haven't you answered before?"

"Sister, I just turned on my set for the first time! What are your coordinates?"

"I'm not going to give you my coordinates if you're going to be like that," she responded angrily.

"M-my fault," Don said, "I—I heard her voice, and thought—no one told me it would be a woman."

Gaspar looked at him, comprehending. Then his mouth quirked. "Give with the numbers, girl," he said firmly to the radio, "or I'll turn you off for the night. Understand?"

She didn't answer. Gaspar reached for the switch.

"Eighty one degrees, fifty minutes west longitude," she said with a rush, as if she had seen him. "Twenty six degrees, ten minutes north latitude."

"That's better," Gaspar said, winking at Don. "What's the rendezvous time, Melanie?"

"Twenty four hours from now," she said. "You did make it to the first rendezvous point?"

"Right. We're both here. Just wanted you to know who's in charge. Don, turn yours on so we can all talk."

Don obeyed. Gaspar had covered nicely for Don's prior mismanagement of the radio, and he appreciated it. Why hadn't he realized that the woman could be one of their party? He had simply assumed without evidence that it was to be three males. Maybe he just hadn't wanted to face the prospect of working with a woman, especially a young one. He wished he could do something about his shyness.

"A day," Gaspar said. "Ten miles an hour for twelve hours, cumulative, and we can sleep as much as we want. That's in the vicinity of Naples, Florida, you see."

Don hoisted up his nerve. "Are—are you—have you gone through the tunnel already? You're in phase with us?"

"Yes," she replied. "I'm still on land, but I'll come into the water at the right time to meet you there."

"D-do you have the coordinates for the next one?"

"Yes, for all of them. I'm your coordinate girl. But I'm allowed to tell only one rendezvous point at a time. You just be thankful you've got company. I'm alone. That is, alone in phase. It's weird."

"Wish you were here," Gaspar said generously.

"Did they tell you what the mission is?" Melanie asked him.

"Nope. They told us no more than you. I answered an ad, believe it or not, and they checked my references—which were strictly average, and sent me out to get a bike. Same as you, probably.''

"Yes," she agreed.

"I think this secrecy kick is overdone."

"It certainly is," Melanie agreed. "I never even applied, actually. But here I am."

"There must be some rationale," Don said. "I'm archae-ological, you're geological, she's—"

"Hysterical," Melanie said.

"The next member is mechanical, I hope," Gaspar said. "Suppose the phase equipment breaks down when we're a mile under? Do you know how to fix it?"

"N-no." Don shuddered. "I wish you h-hadn't brought that up."

"We're going to click out for about five minutes, Melanie," Gaspar said. "Nothing personal. Man business." Before she could protest, he turned his set off, gesturing Don to do the same.

"Your stutter," Gaspar said then. "Does it affect your decision-making ability in a crisis? I wouldn't ask if I didn't suspect that my life may be subject to your ability to act, at some point."

Don could appreciate why Gaspar had an undistinguished employee record. He was too blunt about sensitive issues. "N-no. Only the v-vocal cords. Only under stress."

"No offense. Ask *me* one now."

"Not n-necessary," Don said, embarrassed.

"Well, I'll tell you anyway. My friends—of which I have surprisingly few—all tell me I'm nice but stubborn and sometimes insensitive. The less tenable my position, the worse I am. They say."

Don shrugged in the dark, not knowing the appropriate response.

"So if it's something important, don't come out and tell

me I'm crazy, because if I am I'll never admit it. Tell me I'm reasonable, jolly me along—then maybe I'll change my mind. That's what they say they do.''

"Okay!" Don didn't laugh, because he suspected this was no joke. Gaspar had given him fair warning.

They turned on their radios again. "Okay, Melanie," Gaspar said. "We're turning in now. No point in leaving the sets on; might run 'em down, and anyway, all you'd hear would be snoring.''

"Oh," she said, sounding disappointed. "I suppose so. I need to sleep too. I've been hyper about listening for the contact, but now it's done. They *do* run down; you have to keep the bike moving, for the radio, too. Check in the morning, will you? I do get lonely.''

Don felt sudden sympathy for her. She sounded like a nice girl, and Gaspar was treating her rather callously. Did he have something against women?

"Good enough," Gaspar said, clicking off again. Don reluctantly followed suit. Now that the ice had been broken, he would have liked to continue talking with Melanie. But of course he would be meeting her tomorrow, and they would be able to talk without the radio. If his nerve did not disappear in the interim.

It was hard to sleep, though he was quite tired. Don had never cycled such a distance before, and the muscles above his knees were tense, and the rest of his body little better off. The tiny ripples against his face that were all he could see or feel of small fish swimming disturbed him by their incongruity and made him gasp involuntarily. The temperature bothered him as well; he was accustomed to a drop at night, but here it still felt about 80°F.

"Are you as insomniac as I am?" Gaspar inquired after a while.

"Dead tired and wide awake," Don agreed. "I'm afraid

I'll poop out tomorrow and miss the rendezvous, and that doesn't soothe me much either."

"I was thinking about your inedible food. I said it was an accident, but now it strikes me as a pretty funny mistake. Now I wonder whether there are any other mistakes." He paused, but Don offered no debate. "Tell me if this is paranoid: we both have the same kind of food packs. They should have come from the same batch. Could yours have been deliberately spoiled?"

Don's jaw dropped. He was glad he could not be seen. "That does seem farfetched. What would be the point?"

"To test us, maybe. See just how resourceful we are."

"Why should anyone care? We're just ordinary folk."

"White rats are selected to be absolutely ordinary. That's the point. How would regular folk survive in a really strange, isolated situation?"

"B-but that would be—be inhuman!"

"What do we really know of the motives of our employer?"

"B-but to just assume—"

"So it's paranoid."

"But m-maybe we should keep a good watch out," Don said. He had been shaken by Gaspar's conjecture; it had a horrible kind of sense. If there were dangerous new conditions to test with uncertain equipment, how would a company get volunteers? Maybe exactly this way.

"That's my notion. I don't think it's the case, but there's this ugly bit of doubt in my mind, and I thought I'd discuss it with you in private before we join the lady."

"Th-thanks," Don said without irony.

After that he did drop off to sleep, as if the awful notion had actually eased his mind. Maybe it merely gave his fears something more tangible to chew on.

* * *

In the dark morning they ate again and moved out. They
gradually ascended, but the slope was generally slight and
Don found himself moving better than he had. Gaspar's
presence seemed to give him strength; perhaps he had been
dissipating some of his energy in nervous tension, and now
was more relaxed. Or maybe it was that Gaspar seemed to
have a knack for picking out the easiest route. That made
sense; the man was conversant with the sea, after all.

As the day ended, they were back in the offshore
shallows, having traveled a hundred and twenty miles in
about ten hours of actual riding time.

Now it was time to rendezvous with Melanie. Don felt his
muscles tightening. It had become excruciatingly important
to him that she match his nebulous mental image of her. He
might be riding hundreds of miles with her. Suppose—?

Gaspar turned on his radio. "You there, Melanie?"

"Yes," she replied immediately. "Are you close?"

"Close and closing," Gaspar said.

The next contact was upon them.

CHAPTER 3

MELANIE

Proxy 5–12–5–16–8: Attention.
Acknowledging.
Status?
Situation developing. First recruit has discovered his defective food supplies, and the second recruit conjectures that this was an intentional lapse. They suspect that it is a test of their survival skills. They are now linking with the third recruit.
Each recruit has a liability?
Yes. The third recruit's liability is inherent; I did not need to interfere with her situation.
This seems like a devious way to convert a world.
The direct approach has been known to fail.
Apology, Proxy; it is your show. Proceed as you see fit.
I have no assurance that this approach will work. Only hope. Much depends on the interaction of the recruits, and how they react when they learn the truth.
True.

They zeroed in on Melanie, proceeding from radio range to voice range, until she came into sight. She was a figure in a blouse and skirt, standing with a loaded bicycle.

A skirt, under the sea? But Don realized that his reaction was mistaken; a skirt was as sensible as any other clothing, here in this phased state.

As they came up, he saw that not only was she female, she was quite attractively so. She was not voluptuous, but was very nicely proportioned in a slender way. Her face was framed by curls so perfect they could have been artificial, and was as pretty as he had seen.

All of which meant that it would be almost impossible for him to talk to her. This was exactly the kind of woman who had no business noticing a man like him.

"Well, hello Melanie!" Gaspar said without any difficulty. "I'm Gaspar, and this is Don."

"I recognize you by your voice," she said. She turned her eyes on Don. They were as green as a painting of the sea. "Hello, Don."

He tried. "H-h-hel—" He gave up the effort, chagrined.

She smiled. "Were you the one who kept cutting me off?"

Don nodded, miserable.

"Because you were shy?"

He nodded again.

"That's a relief! It makes me a whole lot less nervous about meeting you. I thought maybe you had a grudge."

"N-no!" Don protested.

"You're like me: single, unemployed, no prospects?"

"Y-yes." She had answered a question he had been too timid to ask, while seeming to ask one. But Don was unable to follow up on the conversational gambit.

"What's the coordinate for the next person?" Gaspar asked when a silence threatened to develop.

"Twenty four degrees north latitude, thirty minutes," she said immediately. "Eighty one degrees, fifty minutes west longitude. Twenty four hours from now."

"Key West," Gaspar said. "We'll have to move right along, but we can do it." He looked around. "That's just about due south of here, but it should be easier riding downhill. Why don't we coast out to deep water where it's cooler? That way we'll make some distance, even if it isn't directly toward Key West, and we can sleep when we can't stay awake any more."

Melanie shrugged. "Why not? As long as you know how to find the way. I memorized the coordinates, but I don't have much of a notion what they mean."

Don was glad to agree. His earlier fear of the deeps seemed irrelevant, now that he had company. Gaspar would not have made the suggestion if he had thought there was any danger, and the man did know something about the ocean.

"Of course we're a good distance from the edge of the continental shelf," Gaspar continued as he started moving. Melanie fell in behind him, and Don followed her. It was easier to hear him even at some distance, because of the carrying capacity of the water. "Too far to get any real depth. But we might make it forty or fifty fathoms. Extra mileage but easier going. Worth it, I'd say."

That reminded Don of something. "Key West—how did you figure that out? Do you have a map?" He was able to speak more readily to Gaspar than to Melanie.

"I know the coordinates of places like that. Same way you know types of pottery, I suppose. Nothing special."

"Oh." Stupid question.

"You know pottery?" Melanie asked.

"Y-yes. I-I'm an a-arch-archaeologist."

"I envy you. I have no training at all. I don't know why they wanted me here."

Ahead, Gaspar turned on his headlight. They followed suit. The trend was down, and it did make the cycling easier,

which was a relief. Melanie might be fresh, but Don wasn't.
The temperature did seem to be dropping.

She had spoken to him, and Don wanted to answer. But
it remained difficult. What could he say about her lack of
training?

Gaspar saved him the trouble. "I'm a marine geologist,
and he's an archaeologist, but we're both out of our
specialties here, so we're essentially amateurs. We thought
we were selected for our skills, but that may not be the case.
Maybe we just happened to be available. Were you out of
work, Melanie?"

"Yes. But I didn't even apply. I just got a phone call
telling me that there was a job for me that would be
interesting and challenging and paid well. I was suspicious, but it did seem to be an opportunity, and the more
I learned about it, the more intriguing it seemed. So here I
am."

They rode twenty miles southwest before quitting. Don
felt ashamed for looking, but he admired Melanie's form
during much of that travel. It was easy to watch her, because
she was right ahead of him. He wondered why she had been
both out of work and unmarried. She should have been able
to get work as a receptionist readily enough, and any man
she smiled at would have been interested.

Gaspar called a halt at what he deemed to be a suitable
location. Then they broke out the rations, and Melanie
learned about Don's bad food and expressed sympathy, and
shared hers with him. She was very nice about it, not
prompting him to talk.

They took turns separating from the group in order to
handle natural functions. This was in one sense pointless, as
each person was self contained in this respect, but the
protocol of privacy seemed appropriate to accommodate the
two sexes.

Then they lay down beside their bicycles for sleep, in a row of three, Melanie in the middle. Don lay awake for a while, appreciating the proximity of the woman though he knew her interest in him was purely that of mission associate. Then he slept, for suddenly the night-period passed.

They proceeded to a point seventy five miles west of Key West, moving well. "To avoid the coral reefs," Gaspar explained. "We'd have to cross them, otherwise, to get to the rendezvous, and it's a populated area. No sense scaring the fish there, either. Also, it's cooler and less cluttered here in deeper water."

"You're the geologist," Melanie agreed.

Indeed, he was. Their depth had, in just the past few miles, changed from forty fathoms to two hundred, and the coasting had allowed Don to recover some strength in the legs. He had seen the colors change from orange to green to blue-black, and the headlights were now necessary at any hour. The fish, too, had changed color, whether by the dim "daylight" or the headlamps. First they were multicolored, then two-tone—black above, light below—and finally silvery.

Camouflage, he decided. Near the surface all colors showed, so color was used to merge with the throng. Farther down only the silhouettes showed from below, so the bottoms were light to fade into the bright surface, and the tops dark to fade into the nether gloom when viewed from above. In the truly dim light, color didn't matter much.

But the crawling crustaceans had become bright in the depth, and he saw no reason for that. Unless they used color to identify themselves to each other, like women with pretty clothing. Maybe they were not easy for fish to eat, so did not have to hide.

"However, we should keep alert," Gaspar said. "There aren't many dangerous things on the Gulf side of Florida, and you can't fall off the shelf. But here below the Keys we'll hit deep water."

"I noticed," she said.

"I mean five hundred to a thousand fathoms—on the order of a mile. We're still fairly high."

"D-dangerous things?" Don managed to inquire.

"Living things can't touch us, of course. But rough terrain might."

They didn't talk any more, because now they were climbing, gradually but steadily. Don shifted down to second, then to first, and that gave him plenty of power. Melanie had only three gears, and was struggling. Gaspar, who had just the one ratio, stopped.

"Tired?" Don called, surprised, for Gaspar had seemed indefatigable despite his lack of gearing. Don had survived only because of those five speeds.

"Broken chain," Gaspar said.

So it was. "Too bad," Don said. "But not calamitous. You have a spare chain, don't you?"

"Do. But I want to save that for an emergency."

"This is an emergency. You can't ride without a chain."

"I'll fix this one."

"But that will take time. Better to use the spare, and fix the other when there's nothing to do."

"No, I'll replace the rivet on this one."

"But you don't have t-tools."

"I have a pen knife and a screwdriver and a bicycle wrench," Gaspar said, taking out these articles and laying them on the ground beside the propped bicycle. "Haven't done this since I was a kid, but it's not complicated."

"B-but it's unnecessary."

Gaspar ignored him and went to work on the chain.

Belatedly Don remembered the warning about stubbornness. He had been arguing instead of thinking, and now he was stuttering, and Gaspar had tuned him out. His first "but" had probably lost his cause, and he wasn't certain his cause was right. Why *not* fix the chain now? They did have time for that, and he needed a rest. The muscles of his legs were stiff again.

He saw that Melanie was being more practical: she was lying beside her bicycle, squeezing in all the rest for her legs she could. Her skirt had slid up around her full thighs. Oh, her limbs looked nice!

Don returned his gaze to Gaspar's bicycle, before he started blushing or stuttering worse. He tried a new approach. "A chain shouldn't break like that. It must have been defective, or—"

"Oh, it can happen. Stone tossed up—"

"Here?"

Gaspar laughed. "Got me that time! Stone couldn't do much unless it was phased in. But this is an old bike—I never was one to waste money, even if Uncle Sam or whoever pays the way. Ten dollars, third hand. Got to expect some kinks."

Ten dollars! A junker would have charged that to haul the thing away! Yet it was now loaded with what might be a hundred thousand dollars worth of specialized equipment. "S-so you don't think that anyone—" But it sounded silly as he said it. How could anyone sabotage a third-hand bicycle that hadn't yet been bought? And what would be the point? It was obvious that it could readily be fixed, so that was no real test of the man's survival skills.

He walked his own bike back to where Melanie lay, wishing he had the courage to start a dialogue with her. He turned around so that he would not be peering at her legs when he lay down, though he wished he could do that too.

"I heard," she said, though he had not spoken to her. "What's this about something happening?"

Don managed to get his mouth going well enough to explain about the possibility of sabotage. "But it was just a conjecture," he hastened to say. "Probably p-paranoia."

"I'm into paranoia," she said, surprising him.

"You are? Why?"

"Maybe some time I'll tell you. For now, just take my word: I'm more diffident about people than you are, for better reason."

"You?" He was incredulous.

"Oh, I shouldn't have said that. Let's change the subject."

"I—I can't find a subject."

She laughed, tiredly. "Then I'll find one. It's nice talking to you, Don. So much better than waiting around for the radio to sound, with a pile of books and packages of ugh-y food."

He chuckled, surprised that he was now able to do that in her presence. She was making him feel more at ease than he had a right to be.

He glanced at Gaspar. The chain was still off, and the man was doing something with the little screwdriver and pliers. It would be a while more before the job was done.

"Y-you were just waiting?"

"For you, yes. Two days. But my life was much the same before that, mostly alone. Books are great company, but I would have enjoyed them more if I'd had live companions. So when I took this job, hoping my life would change, and then for two days it was just more of the same, well, I had to do something."

"I-I can't believe you were alone!"

"I could make you believe, but I don't want to." She rolled to her side and angled her head to face him. "You're really interested, aren't you?"

"Yes."

"I'll try to explain. When I was just waiting for you, I walked down to the beach."

"The beach?"

"In the early morning, when no one was around. I didn't want anyone to see me, because of the phase."

"I know. I came into the water at dawn."

She laughed again. "Here I'm telling you something that's not meant to be understood, and you're understanding."

"I—uh—"

"Don't apologize! It's not meant to be understood, just felt. But you feel it too, don't you?"

"Yes." This conversation was becoming odder and more comfortable. He could lie here forever, talking with her like this, his shyness ebbing.

"I enjoyed the beach," she continued. "It was raining. Just a little cool. There was a stiff wind—I couldn't really feel it, but I saw the sea-oats leaning. I just had to go out and walk along the surf a way. Right near the edge of the water. In my bare feet. Except there wasn't anything to feel, it's just sort of neutral in phase, and I had to walk the bicycle right along. You know—so I could breathe. That's one thing that doesn't wind down when the bike stops moving: the oxygen field. Lucky thing, or we'd never be able to rest or sleep. Batteries, I guess, that recharge for that. I tried to breathe away from the bike, and couldn't. I'm married to the bike, now. We all are.''

"Yes."

"So I had to pretend. I had the whole beach to myself with only the gulls for company. They stood on the sand facing the wind. I saw a horseshoe crab, and I tried to pick it up—it was the first horseshoe crab I had ever seen.''

"They're not crabs," Gaspar said without looking up from his work. That surprised Don; he had thought the man had tuned them out. "They're related to the scorpions and are the only living members of a large group of extinct animals. They've survived unchanged for two hundred and fifty million years.''

"All the more wonderful to behold," Melanie said. "The beach has a powerful internal significance for me that I've never quite been able to understand. This one I experienced was wonderfully dramatic. They all are. I never just have seen a beach. It's a total experience. The sand under my feet, warmth, wind, smells, sound, and motion. The beach just is. And I am there walking along looking for seashells and somehow I feel that I belong there. For the moment. It feels like something I can always come back to. Something almost unchanged in a sea of change.''

Like the horseshoe crabs, Don thought. Unchanged since the dinosaurs. Perhaps man, when he gazed upon the beach, remembered his ancestor who fought the extraordinary battle to free himself from the grip of the sea, and this was that battleground.

"My life so easily slips into things and experiences with labels," Melanie said. "But the beach somehow for me always slips the compass of a label and asserts the primacy of existence." She paused. "If that makes sense to you.''

All he could say was "Yes." It wasn't just her perspective on the beach, it was the fact that she had presented it to him as a fellow human being, as if he deserved to have this insight. What a wonderful experience!

Gaspar completed his repair, and they resumed riding. The difference between a slight decline and a slight incline was enormous, when they were pedaling it. But they could not go down forever. Don had been pleased at how well he was keeping up, but now he wondered whether there was something wrong with his own bicycle. He pushed and pushed on the pedals, but the machine moved slowly, and he was out of breath doing a bare five or six miles per hour. Melanie was struggling similarly.

Gaspar abruptly stopped again. This time his rear wheel was loose, so that it rubbed against the frame with every revolution. *Thank God!* Don thought guiltily, offering no argument about repairs. He dropped to the ground and let life soak back into his deadened limbs.

Gaspar was tough. If he was tired, it didn't show. Don had never been partial to muscle, but would have settled for several extra pounds of it for this trip.

Melanie dropped beside him, almost touching. Even through his fatigue, he felt the thrill. "Talk to me, Don," she murmured.

This time he was able to perform. "You know, Gaspar and I are both only-survivors in our families. We think that's because our employer selected for singleness. Maybe they don't want people wondering where we are. In case— you know. Uh, you said you're single, but otherwise—is it the same with you?" He had even asked her a direct personal question!

"Almost," she said. "My father died ten years ago. He married late. My mother was thirty five when I was born. I haven't seen her for a couple of years. So it's the same, I guess. I'm uncommitted. But I'd be uncommitted even if I had a massive crowd of relatives.''

"You keep saying that," Don protested. "But you're such a lovely young woman—"

She looked at him. "I guess I'd better take the plunge and show you. Get it over with at the outset. That's maybe better than having it happen by chance, as it surely will otherwise."

"Show me what?"

"Look at me, Don." She sat up.

He sat up too, uncertain what she had in mind. He tried to keep his eyes from the firm inner thighs that her crossed legs showed under the skirt, but that meant he was focusing on her evocative bosom. He finally had to fix on her lovely face.

Melanie put her hands to her head and slid her fingers in under her perfect hair. She tugged—and her hair came off in a mass. It was a wig—and beneath it she was completely bald.

Don simply stared.

"I'm hairless," she said. "All over my body. My eyebrows are glued on, and my eyelashes are fake. It's a genetic defect, they think. No hair follicles." She lifted one arm and pulled her blouse to the side to show her armpit. "I don't shave there. No need to. No hair grows." She glanced down. "Anywhere."

Don was stunned. She had abruptly converted from a beautiful young woman to a bald mannequin. She now looked like an alien creature from a science fiction movie. Her green eyes shone out from the face on the billiard ball head, as if this were a doll in the process of manufacture.

"So now you know," the mouth in the face said.

Don tried to say something positive, but could not speak at all. Her beauty had been destroyed, and she had been

made ludicrous. It might as well have been a robot talking
to him.

Gaspar righted his bicycle. "Ready to go," he said. "We
shouldn't use up the batteries unnecessarily." Then, after a
pause: "Oh."

"Oh," Melanie echoed tonelessly.

"I wasn't paying much attention when it counted, it
seems," Gaspar said. "Disease? Radiation therapy?"

"Genetic, from birth," she said.

"Why show us?"

"Because Don was starting to like me."

He nodded. "Hair is superficial. We know it. Now all we
have to do is believe it."

Melanie put her wig back on, and pressed it carefully into
place. It was evident that it had some kind of adhesive, and
would not come loose unless subject to fair stress. She
resumed her former appearance. But now, to Don's eyes,
she looked like a bald doll with a hairpiece. She had set out
to disabuse him of his notions of her attractiveness, and had
succeeded. Evidently she didn't want to be liked ignorantly.

They resumed travel without further comment. The
coordinates were 24°20'–82°30'. Forty minutes west of their
rendezvous, ten south. Depth was one hundred fathoms.
They must have been traveling well, indeed, downhill,
before starting the laborious climb. Don was amazed to
realize that they were now beyond their target, and he had
never been aware of their passing it. They had time, plenty
of time, thank the god of the sea.

They had climbed six hundred feet in the past two miles,
and it didn't look steep, but it was grueling on a bicycle.
Now he was glad for the continued struggle, because it gave
him something other to think about than Melanie's hair. She
had figured him exactly: he was getting to like her, because
she was pretty and she talked to him. And now his building

illusion had been shattered. He should have known that there would be something like this.

Twenty miles and seventy fathoms east and up, with a break for another bicycle malfunction—this time Don's, whose seat had come loose and twisted sideways—the way abruptly became steep. Gaspar, in the lead, dismounted and walked his bike up the slope. Don and Melanie were glad to do the same; it was a relief to change the motion.

Suddenly Don saw a rough wall, almost overhanging. Jagged white outcroppings and brown recesses made this a formidable barrier, and it extended almost up to the surface of the sea.

"This is it," Gaspar said with satisfaction as they drew beside him.

"But how can we pass?" Don asked. "What is it, anyway?"

Gaspar smiled. "Coral reef. Isn't she a beauty!"

Don, not wanting to admit that he had never seen a coral reef before, and had had a mental picture of a rather pretty plastered wall with brightly colored fish hovering near, merely nodded. It looked ugly to him, because he couldn't see how they were going to get across it. There might be a hundred feet of climbing to do, scaling that treacherous cliff—and how were they going to haul up the bicycles?

He glanced at Melanie, who had not spoken since her revelation. Could she be likened to a coral reef? His mental image suddenly disabused by the reality? Unfortunately, it was the reality that counted.

They did not have to scale the reef. Gaspar merely showed the way east, coasting down the bumpy slope to deeper water. This was why they had come this way: to go around the reef instead of across it. Don was now increasingly thankful for Gaspar's knowledge of the geography of the sea. When they struck reasonably level sand they picked up speed. They went another ten miles before he called a halt.

"We're within a dozen miles," Gaspar said, breaking out the rations. "I guess we'd better get inside the reefs, next chance. Rendezvous is only a couple miles out of Key West."

"Get inside the reefs?" Don asked, dismayed. "I thought we already went around them."

"No, only part way. But this is a better place to cross them, I think."

"Why is the rendezvous so close to civilization?" Don mused. "Can this next person know even less about the ocean than I do?"

Melanie remained silent, and Gaspar discreetly avoided the implication. "The reefs are rough—literally. The edges can cut like knives, and the wounds are slow to heal. It's no place to learn to swim, or ride. So we'll have to guide him through with kid gloves. He probably *does* know less than you—now."

A left-footed compliment! "So how *do* we get through?"

"Oh, the reefs are discontinuous. We'll use a channel and get into shallow water. Have to watch out for boats, though; we'll be plainly visible in twenty foot depth." He considered briefly. "In fact, as I recall, there's a lot of two fathom water in the area. Twelve feet from wave to shell in mean low water, which means barely six feet over our heads. That's too much visibility."

Don agreed. He would now feel naked with that thin a covering of water. He was tired, and wanted neither to admit it nor to hold up progress, but here was a valid pretext to wait. On the other hand, he was increasingly curious about this close-to-land member of the expedition. If the man were not knowledgeable about the marine world, why was he needed at all?

But Melanie wasn't knowledgeable either. What was her
purpose here? Unless this really was a testing situation, a
maze for average white rats. How would those rats find their
way through? How well would they cooperate with each
other? He remembered reading about a test in which a rat
could get a pellet of food by striking a button. Then the
button was placed on the opposite side of the chamber from
the pellet dispenser. Then two rats were put in the same
chamber. When one punched the button, the other got the
pellet. That was testing something other than wit or mechanical dexterity. Could this be that sort of test?

They cut into the reef. This time Don observed the myriad
creatures of this specific locale, and the reef began to align
better with his former mental image. The elements were
there, just not quite the way he had pictured them. The fish
in the open waters had generally stayed clear of the odd
bicycle party, probably frightened by the lights and machin-
ery, so that he had ignored them with impunity. But this
stony wall was well populated. Yellow-eyed snakes peeped
from crevices, teeth showing beneath their nostrils, watching, waiting.

Beside him, Melanie seemed no more at ease. She tried to
keep as far from the reef as possible without separating from
the human party.

Gaspar saw their glances. "Moray eels," he said. "No
danger to us, phased—but if we were diving, I'd never put
hand or foot near any of these holes. Most sea creatures are
basically shy, or even friendly, and some of the morays are
too. But they can be vicious. I've seen one tackle an
octopus. The devilfish tried to hide, but the moray got hold
of a single tentacle and whirled around until that tentacle
twisted right off. Then it ate that one and got hold of
another."

"Why didn't you *do* something?" Don asked. He had no

love of octopi, which were another group of childhood nightmares, but couldn't bear the thought of such cruelty.

"I did," Gaspar admitted. "I don't like to interfere with nature's ways, but I'm not partial to morays. Actually the thing took off when I came near. Good decision; I would have speared it."

"The-the octopus. Did you have to—kill it? With two arms off—"

"Course not. Tentacles grow back. They're not like us, that way."

"I guess not," Don agreed, looking again at the morays. They might not be quite in his phase, but he would keep clear of them regardless. Certainly there were prettier sights. He spied zebra-striped fish, yellow and black (juvenile black angelfish, Gaspar said), red fish with blue fins and yellow tails (squirrelfish), purple ones with white speckles (jewelfish), greenish ones with length-wise yellow striping—or maybe vice versa (blue-striped grunt), and one with a dark head, green tail, with two heavy black stripes between (bluehead wrasse). Plus many others he didn't call to Gaspar's attention, because he tended to resent the man's seemingly encyclopedic nomenclature. Melanie seemed similarly fascinated, now that they had gotten among the pretty fish instead of the ugly eels.

"Good thing you didn't ask me any of the difficult ones," Gaspar said. "There's stuff in these reefs I never heard of, and probably fish no man has seen. New species are discovered every year. I think there are some real monsters hidden down inside."

But the surface of the coral reef was impressive enough. They passed a section that looked like folded ribbon (stinging coral–stay clear), and marveled at its convolutions.

Then the reef rounded away, and they pedaled through. Melanie almost bumped into a large ugly green fish and shied away, still not completely used to the phaseout. But that reminded Don of something.

"We ride on the bottom because that's inanimate," he said. "The living things are phased out. But aren't the coral reefs made by living creatures? How come they are solid to us, then?"

"They're in the phase world," Gaspar said. "They're part of the terrain. They may not be the same reefs we see, but they're just like them. So we have to take them seriously. Otherwise we could have ridden straight through them, and saved ourselves a lot of trouble."

Of course that was true. Don was chagrined for not seeing the obvious.

They climbed into the shallows, passing mounds and ledges and even caves in the living coral. For here it was not rocklike so much as plantlike, with myriad flower-shapes blooming.

Gaspar halted as the ground became too uneven to ride over. "Isn't that a grand sight?" he asked rhetorically. "They're related to the jellyfish, you know. And to the sea anemones."

"What are?" Don asked, perplexed.

"The coral polyps. Their stony skeletons accumulate to form the reef—in time. Temperature has to be around seventy degrees Fahrenheit or better, and they have to have something to build on near the surface, but within these limits they do well enough. They strain plankton from the water with their little tentacles—"

"Oh? I didn't see that," Melanie said, finally speaking. Apparently her revelation of her condition had set her back as much as it had Don, and she had withdrawn for a time. Now she was returning, and maybe it was just as well.

"They do it at night, mostly," Gaspar explained. "We're

seeing only a fraction of the fish that live on the reef; night
is the time for foraging.''

"You certainly seem to know a lot about sea life,"
Melanie said. "Are you sure you're a geologist?"

Gaspar laughed. "You have to know something about the
flora and fauna, if you want to stay out of trouble. Sharks,
electric eels, poisonous sponges, stinging jellyfish—this
world is beautiful, but it's dangerous too, unless you
understand it.''

"I believe it," she said.

"And there are practical connections to my specialty,"
Gaspar continued, gazing on the coral with a kind of bliss.
"I could mistake coral for a limestone rock formation, if I
didn't study both. Actually it *is* limestone—but you know
what I mean. It tells me about historical geology, too.
Because of the necessary conditions for the growth of coral.
If I spy a coral reef in cold water, and it's five hundred feet
below the surface—''

"Say!" Don exclaimed, catching on. "Then you know
that water was once seventy degrees warm, and that the land
was higher.''

"Or the sea lower. Yes. There are hundreds of things like
that. Fossils in sediments, for example. They account for an
entire time scale extending through many hundreds of
millions of years. Check the fossils and you know when that
material was laid down and what the conditions were.''

"Like pottery shards!" Don said. "Each one typical of a
particular culture. Only your shards are bones and shells.''

"You're right," Gaspar agreed, smiling. "Now I understand what you do. You're a paleontologist of the recent
past.''

"Recent past! I wouldn't call several thousand years
exactly—''

"Geologically, anything less than a million years—''

"Maybe we'd better make our rendezvous," Melanie suggested.

They moved on, drawing nearer to the surface. The water inside the reef was barren in comparison: pellucid, with a flat sandy bottom. Don did spy a number of swift-moving little silvery fish scooting across the floor, and once something gray and flat flounced away as his front tire interacted with its bones.

Then they hit a field of tall grass—except that it wasn't grass. Some was green and flat, some was green and round. The stalks offered little effective resistance to the bicycles, but Don still had the impression of forging through by sheer muscle. It was amazing to what extent sight, not knowledge, governed his reactions.

He glanced covertly at Melanie. She looked perfect: still slender and feminine. Had she not shown him her bald head . . .

Finally they came to the "patch" reefs that marked their rendezvous. Between these little reeflets and the shore he knew there was only more grass flat.

"Maybe if someone comes—a boat, I mean," Melanie said, "we could lie down and be hidden by that grass."

Gaspar nodded. "Smart girl. Keep your eye out for suitable cover."

They drew up beside a great mound of coral, one of the patches. All around it the sand was bare. "So much for my smarts," Melanie said ruefully.

This section was as bald as her head, Don thought, and wished he could get that matter out of his mind.

"Grass eaters," Gaspar explained. "They graze, but don't go far from their shelter. So they create this desert ring by overgrazing."

"I would never have thought of that," she said. "But it's

obvious now that you've pointed it out. Penned barnyard animals do the same."

"Yes, the absence of life can be evidence of life," Gaspar agreed.

The two were getting along together, Don noted with mixed feelings. He had talked with Gaspar, and he had talked with Melanie, but so far there had not been a lot of interaction between Gaspar and Melanie. Yet why shouldn't there be? It was evident that Gaspar, though surprised by her hairlessness, had not really been put off by it. He had broader horizons than Don did, and greater tolerance. Why should Don be bothered by that?

"Rendezvous is at dusk," Gaspar said. "To let him slip into the water unobserved, probably. We're early, so we can rest a while. Out of sight, if we can. Should be an overhang or maybe a cave."

"Is it safe?" Melanie asked. "We aren't entirely invulnerable."

"Not much danger here, regardless," Gaspar said confidently. "Why would the little fishes use it, otherwise?" He began pedaling slowly around the reeflet. The others, disgruntled, followed.

There were several projecting ledges harboring brightly colored fish who scattered as the bicycles encroached. Then a large crevice developed, and they rode between sheer coral walls. These overhung, and finally closed over the top, and it was a cavern.

The area was too confined for riding, and the floor was irregular. They dismounted and walked on inside, avoiding contact with the sharp fringes. Don was reminded of the cave paintings of Lascaux: the patchwork murals left by Upper Paleolithic man some fifteen thousand years ago, and one of the marvels of the archaeological world. Primitive man had not been as primitive as many today liked to suppose.

But this was a sea-cavern, and its murals were natural. Sponges bedecked its walls: black, brown, blue, green, red, and white, in dabs and bulges and relief-carvings.

There was life here, all right. The smaller fish streaked out as the men moved in, for their eyesight was keen enough to spot the intrusion even though its substance was vacant. One man-sized fish balked, however, hanging motionless in the passage.

"Jewfish," Gaspar remarked—and with the sound of his voice the fish was gone. Sediment formed a cloud as the creature shot past, and Don felt the powerful breeze of its thrust. He appreciated another danger: just as a stiff wind could blow a man down on land, a stiff current could do the same here in the ocean. If his position happened to be precarious, he would have to watch out for big fish. Their bones could tug him if their breeze-current didn't.

"Looks good," Gaspar said. "I'm bushed." He lay down beside his bicycle and seemed to drop instantly to sleep.

Don was tired, but he lacked this talent. He could not let go suddenly; he had to rest and watch, hoping that sleep would steal upon him conveniently. It probably wasn't worth it, for just a couple of hours.

"I envy him his sleep, but it's beyond me," Melanie said, settling down to lean cautiously against a wall.

"Me too," Don agreed, doing the same. The real wall might be jagged, but the phase wall wasn't, fortunately.

"You're not stuttering now."

"Maybe I'm too tired."

"Or maybe you know I'm no threat to you."

"I didn't say that." But it might be true. Before, there had been the frightening prospect of social interaction leading into romance.

"You didn't have to. Now you know why I read books. They don't look at you."

"But people don't—I mean, they don't know—"

"*I* know."

"Well, I read too. Mostly texts, but—"

"I read fiction, mostly. Once I fell asleep during a book, and dreamed the author had come to autograph my copy, but we couldn't find him a pen."

"You like signatures?" he asked, not certain she was serious.

"Oh, yes, I have a whole collection of autographed books, back home." She spoke with modest pride.

"Why? I think it's more important to relate to what the author is trying to say, than to have his mark on a piece of paper."

She was silent.

After a moment he asked, "You want to sleep? I didn't mean to—"

"I heard you. I wasn't answering."

"Wasn't what?"

"Maybe we'd better change the subject."

"Why?"

"You couldn't expect me to agree with you, could you? I mean, I collect autographs, don't I? So what am I supposed to say when you say you don't think they are very much?"

What was this? "You could have said you don't agree."

"I did."

"When?"

"When I didn't say anything. I think that should be obvious."

"Obvious?"

"Well, you seem to use different conversational conventions than I do, and it's unpleasant to talk to someone who doesn't understand your silences."

"Why not just say what you mean? I have no idea what's bothering you."

"No more than I did, when you kept cutting me off."

Oh. "I'm sorry about that. I just had this notion it was all men on this circuit, and I thought something had gone wrong, the way my food did. I would have answered if I had realized."

"Well, then, I'll answer you now. I don't want to be placed in the position of having to defend something I know you don't like. I mean, if I answered you there would be all kinds of emotional overtones in my voice, and that would be embarrassing and painful."

"About *autographs*?" he demanded incredulously.

"Obviously you didn't mean to be offensive," she said, sounding hurt.

"What do you mean, 'mean to be'? I wasn't offensive, was I?"

"Well, I shouldn't have said anything about it."

"Now don't go clamming up on me again. One silence is enough." He was feeling more confident, oddly.

"I was trying to hint that I didn't agree with you."

"About meaning being worth more than a signature?"

She was silent again.

"Oh come *on*!" he snapped. "What do you expect me to say to a silence?"

"I've already told you why I don't want to talk about it any more. You could at least have apologized for mentioning it again."

"Apologized?"

"What kind of unfeeling barbarian culture did you grow up in, anyway?"

"Primitive cultures are *not* unfeeling!"

There was no answer.

"You're right," he said with frustration. "We do have

different conversational conventions.'' Sane and insane, he was tempted to add.

And so they sat, leaning back against the spongy coral wall, watching the little fish sidle in again. Don wondered what had happened.

CHAPTER 4

ELEPH

Proxy 5–12–5–16–8: Attention.

Acknowledging.

Status?

Three recruits are in motion, with the fourth incipient. The liability of the third has been established, with what impact is uncertain. The group seems to be melding satisfactorily.

Such melding is a two-edged tool. If they unify against the mission, it will be lost.

I mean to see that they react properly. They will not be advised of the mission until the time is propitious.

And if that time does not manifest?

This group must be abolished and another assembled.

You are prepared to destroy them?

No.

Though the alternative is to lose their world?

I will abolish the group without invoking the mission. The individual members will return to their prior lives.

And if you invoke the mission, and they oppose it?

Then we shall have a problem.

"There it is!" Gaspar cried. "Right on time."

Don jolted awake. It was night, and the rendezvous was

63

upon them. He had slept when he hadn't expected to, and it seemed that Melanie had done the same.

They scrambled up and walked their bikes out to catch up with Gaspar, who was standing at the mouth of the cave. Then, together, they advanced on the lone figure beyond.

The third man was Eleph: perhaps fifty, graying hair, forbidding lined face. There was a tic in his right cheek that Don recognized as a stress reaction similar to his own stuttering. Don would have had some sympathy, but for the cold manner of the man.

Gaspar tried to make small talk, but Eleph cut him short. He let it be known that he expected regulations to be scrupulously honored. Obviously he was or had been associated with the military; he would not bend, physically or intellectually. There was an authoritative ring in his voice that made even innocuous comments—of which he made few—seem like commands. Yet he also telegraphed a formidable uncertainty.

Don decided to stay clear of the man as much as possible. Gaspar, undaunted or merely stubborn, used another approach. "Look at that bicycle! How many speeds is that, Eleph?"

Eleph frowned as if resenting the familiarity, though they were on a first name basis by the rules. He must have realized that it was impossible to be completely formal while perched on a bicycle anyway. "Thirty six," he replied gruffly.

Don thought he had misheard, but a closer look at the machine convinced him otherwise. It had a thick rear axle, a rear sprocket cluster, three chainwheels, and a derailleur at each end of the chain. The triple gearshift levers augmented the suggestion of a complex assortment of ratios. The handlebars were turned down, not up or level, and were set with all the devices Don had, plus a speedometer, horn, and

others whose functions Don didn't recognize. What para-
phernalia!

"Don here's an archaeologist," Gaspar said. "I'm a
geologist. Melanie knows the coordinates for our various
encounters. How about you?"

Eleph hesitated, oddly. "Physicist."

"Oh—to study the effects of this phaseout field under
water?"

"Perhaps," Eleph vouchsafed no more.

It was shaping up to be a long journey, Don realized.

"Melanie, where next?" Gaspar asked.

"Twenty five degrees, forty minutes north latitude," she
said. "Eighty degrees, ten minutes west longitude."

"Got it. Let's get deep."

Gaspar led the way through the shallows, pedaling slowly
so that there was no danger of the others losing sight of his
lights. Eleph came next, then Melanie, and Don last. That
put the least experienced riders in the middle, out of trouble.

All four of them would have to douse their lights and halt
in place at any near approach of a boat. So far they were
lucky; the surface was undisturbed. Once they reached
deeper water there would be no problem unless they
encountered a submarine. That was hardly likely.

The barren back reef had come alive. Great numbers of
heart-shaped brown sea biscuits had appeared. Delicate,
translucent sea anemones flowered prettily. Fish patrolled,
searching for food; they shied away from the beams of light,
but not before betraying their numbers. Some were large;
Don recognized a narrow barracuda, one of the few fish he
knew by sight.

The outer coral reef had changed too. The polyps were in
bloom, flexing rhythmically, combing the water with their
tiny tentacles, just as Gaspar had said they would. In one
way they were flowers; in another, tiny volcanoes; in yet

another, transparent little octopi. What had seemed by day to be forbidding rock was by night a living carpet.

Now Don observed the different kinds of coral in the reef. Some was convoluted but rounded, like the folds of a—yes, this had to be brain coral. From it rose orange-white spirals of fine sticks: yet another kind of flower that Don was sure was neither flower nor even plant. He swerved toward one, reaching to touch it though he knew he couldn't. As his hand passed through its faint resistance, the flower closed and disappeared, withdrawing neatly into a narrow tube-stem.

Yet there were dull parts, too. In some regions the coral featured little or no life. It was as if tenement houses had been built, used, and then deserted. But surely the landlords hadn't raised the rent, here!

"Pollution is killing the reefs," Gaspar remarked sourly. "Also over-fishing, sponge harvesting, unrestrained memento collecting, the whole bit. The sea life here isn't nearly as thick as it used to be, and species are dying out. But the average man doesn't see that, so he figures it's no concern of his."

"They are wiping out species on land, too," Melanie pointed out.

"You think that justifies it?" Gaspar asked sharply.

"No! I think it's horrible. But I don't know how to stop it."

"There are just too many people," he said. "As long as there keep being more people, there'll be fewer animals. It's that simple."

Don gazed at the barren sections of the reefs. Was it that simple? He distrusted simple answers; the interactions of life tended to be complex, with ramifications never fully understood. Still, it was evident that something was going wrong, here.

The moray eels were out foraging. One spied Don and came at him, jaws open. Don shied away despite his lack of real alarm, and it drifted back. Melanie, just ahead of him, was veering similarly.

Then, remembering his own initial reactions, Don looked ahead to see how Eleph was taking it. This was a wise precaution, for Eleph reacted violently. Two eels were investigating him, as if sniffing out the least secure rider.

Both Eleph's hands came off the handle bars to fend off the seeming assault. The bicycle veered to the side and crashed into the sand.

Don and Melanie hurried to help the man, but Eleph was already on his feet. "The phase makes the predators harmless," Don explained reassuringly. "All you can feel is a little interaction in the bones."

"I am well aware of that!" And Eleph righted his machine and remounted, leaving Don and Melanie to exchange a glance.

Angry at the rebuff, Don let him go. For a physicist specializing in this phase-field, Eleph had bad reflexes.

"And they say that pride goeth *before* a fall," Melanie murmured.

Don had to smile. Then he seized the moment. "Melanie, whatever I said before, I'm sorry. I—"

"Another time," she said. But she smiled back at him.

Then they had to follow, orienting on the lights ahead.

Lobsterlike crustaceans were roving the floor, making free travel difficult. Swimming fish were easy to pass, and living bottom creatures, but inanimate obstructions could be every bit as solid as they looked. When a living creature obscured a rocky projection or hole, and the wheel of the bicycle went through the living thing, it could have trouble with the other. Successful navigation required a kind of doublethink: an object's position and permanence, not its appearance, determined its effect. More or less.

They coasted bumpily down past the outer reef and into deeper water. But more trouble erupted.

A blue-green blob with darker splotches rose up from the sand in the wake of a scuttling crab. Gaspar's light speared it—and suddenly the green became brighter as tentacles waved. It was an octopus, a large one.

Gaspar slowed, no doubt from curiosity. Don caught up, while Melanie remained behind. But Eleph, in the middle, didn't realize what they were doing or what was there. He sped straight on—into the waving nest of mantle and tentacles.

Ink billowed. Eleph screamed and veered out of control again, covering his head. Meanwhile the octopus, who had been traversed and left behind, turned brown and jetted for safer water. Each party seemed as horrified by the encounter as the other.

For a moment Don and Gaspar stared, watching the accidental antagonists flee each other. Then a chuckle started. Don wasn't sure who emitted the first choked peep, but in a moment it grew into uncontrollable laughter. Both men had to put their feet down and lean over the handlebars to vent their mirth. It was a fine release of tension.

When at last they subsided, Don looked up to find Eleph standing nearby, regarding them sourly. Melanie stood behind him, her face straight. Abruptly the matter lost its humor.

Gaspar alleviated the awkwardness by proceeding immediately to business. "We're deep enough now. Eleph, do you have the instructions for our mission? We have been told nothing."

"I do not," Eleph replied. The episode of the octopus had

not improved his social inclinations. "Perhaps the next member of the party will have that information."

Don had thought there would be three members, and Gaspar had guessed four. Evidently there were five.

Gaspar looked at Melanie. "How long hence?"

"Sixty hours," she replied. She had evidently known, but had kept silent, as it seemed she was supposed to.

Gaspar grimaced, and Don knew what he was thinking. Another two days and three nights before they caught up to the final member of their party and learned what this was all about. Maybe.

"Well, let's find a comfortable spot to turn in," Gaspar said. "Maybe we'll find a mound of gold ingots to form into a camping site."

"Gold?" Melanie asked.

"From sunken treasure ships. There are a number, here in the channel between Florida and Cuba, and they haven't all been found by a long shot. Whole fleets of Spanish galleons carried the Inca and Aztec treasures to Spain, and storms took a number of them down. That cargo is worth billions, now."

"Maybe that's our mission," Don said. "To explore this region and map the remaining treasure ships."

"I'd be disappointed if so," Gaspar said.

"Yes," Melanie agreed. "We have to hope that something more than greed is responsible for us."

"We can best find out by getting on with the mission," Eleph said. That damped the dialogue.

Gaspar led the way to the more level bottom and located a peaceful hollow in the sand. There was no sign of gold. This time they pitched their tents, which they had not bothered to do before: one for Eleph, one for Melanie, and one formed from Don and Gaspar's combined canvas.

This really was more comfortable than sleeping in the

open, though the difference was more apparent than real.
There was nothing to harm them in their phased state
anyway. But Don liked the feeling of being in a protected,
man-made place. Appearances were important to his emotions. Which brought him back to the subject of Melanie.
Her appearance—

He shoved that thought aside. The emotions were too
complicated and confused. That business about the
autographs—where had he gone wrong? Suddenly he had
run afoul of her, and he didn't quite understand how it had
happened. So it was better to let it lie, for now.

"That wig," Gaspar said.

So much for letting it lie! "You noticed it too," Don said
with gentle irony.

"I want to be candid with you, because it might make a
difference. Melanie is one attractive woman, and I'd be
interested in her. Except for that wig. If she meant to see
whom it fazed, she succeeded."

Fazed. A pun, since they were all phased? Evidently not.
"But there's more to a woman than hair," Don said,
arguing the other side.

"I know that. You know that. Everybody knows that. But
I have a thing about hair on a woman. I like it long and
flowing and smooth. I like to stroke it as I make love. My
first crush was on a long-haired girl, and I never got over it.
So when I first saw Melanie I saw a nice figure and a pretty
face, but the hair didn't turn me on. Too short and curly. But
hair can grow, so if she was otherwise all right, that could
come. But then she took off that wig, and I knew that her
hair would never grow. A wig won't do it, for me. The hair
has to be real, just as the breasts have to be real. I don't
claim this makes a lot of sense, but romance doesn't
necessarily make sense. Melanie is not on my horizon as

anything other than an associate or platonic friend, regardless of the other aspects of our association.''

Don was troubled. ''Why are you telling me this?''

''Because I can see you are shy with women. You wouldn't want to go after one actively. You sure wouldn't compete with another man for one. Well, maybe you don't have the same hang-up as I do. In that case, I just want you to know that there's no competition. If you can make it with Melanie, I'll be your best man. The field is yours.''

''B-but a woman can't just be p-parceled out!'' Don protested.

''There's a difference between parceling and non-commitment. I think Melanie needs a man as much as you need a woman. In fact I think you two might be just right for each other. If you were with her, you'd keep her secret, and she'd love you for it, and other men would wonder what she saw in you, and she would never give them the time of day. Ideal for you both, as I see it. I can see already that she's got her quirks, but is one great catch of a woman. But matchmaking's not my business. I'll stay out of it. Just so you know that no way am I going to be with her. She lost me when she lifted that wig, and she knows it. You are in doubt. I mean, she doesn't know whether you can handle the business of the hair. When you decide, that will be it. I won't mention this again.''

''Th-thanks,'' Don said. His emotions remained as confused as ever. He knew that the best thing he could do was to put all this out of his mind and let time show him the way of his feelings and hers. He would just relax.

Yet sleep was slow, again. He told himself it was because of his recent nap in the patch-coral cave, but he knew it was more than that. There was a wrongness about this project, and not just in spoiled rations or breaking bicycle chains or undue secrecy. Gaspar seemed to be the only one qualified to do anything or learn anything here. Don himself was a misfit, as was Melanie—and what was a man like Eleph doing here? Not a geologist, not a biologist, not even an undersea archeologist—but a physicist! His specialty could have little relevance here. A mysterious mission like this was hardly needed to check out the performance of the phase-shift under water—if that were really what Eleph was here to do. The man wasn't young and strong, and certainly not easy to get along with. He could only be a drag on the party. At least Melanie wasn't a drag.

"It's Miami," Gaspar said, startling him.

"Who?"

"Those coordinates. Offshore Miami. Must be another inexperienced man."

Don shook his head ruefully. "I wish I had your talent for identifying places like that! I can't make head or tail of those coordinates."

"It's no talent. Just understanding of the basic principle. The Earth is a globe, and it is tricky to identify places without a global scale of reference. On land you can look for roads and cities, but in the sea there are none. Think of it as an orange, with lines marked. Some are circles going around the globe, passing through the north and south poles. Those are the meridians of longitude, starting with zero at Greenwich, in London, England, as zero, and proceeding east and west from it until they meet as 180 degrees in the middle of the Pacific Ocean at the International Date Line. The others are circles around the globe parallel to the equator; they get smaller as they go north and south, but each is still a perfect circle. Thus we have parallels of latitude. Since we happen to be north of the equator and west of England, our coordinates are in the neighborhood of twenty five degrees north latitude and eighty degrees west longitude. Just keep those figures in mind, and you'll know how far we go from where we are now.''

It began to register. "Twenty five and eighty," Don said. "Right here. So Miami is—"

"Actually those particular coordinates would be about ten miles east of Miami, and fifty miles south of it," Gaspar said. "We're on the way there. I meant our neighborhood on a global scale."

"Just as all of man's history and prehistory is recent, on the geologic scale," Don said wryly. "Fifty miles is pinpoint close."

"Yes. Our bicycle meters give us our immediate locations."

"Still, I'll remember those numbers. It will give me a notion how far we are from Miami, and that's a location I can understand. Southern tip of Florida."

"Well—"

"Approximately!" Don said quickly. "In geologic terms."

"Approximately," Gaspar agreed, and Don knew he was smiling.

Don returned to the matter of their next group member, glad to have company in his misgivings. "What do you think he is? An astronomer? An electrician? A—"

"Could be a paleontologist. Because I think I know where we're heading, now. The Bahamas platform."

"What?"

"The Bahamas platform. Geologically, a most significant region. It certainly made trouble for us in the past."

Don would have been less interested, had he not wanted someone to talk to. "How could it make trouble? It is whatever it is, and was what it was, wasn't it, before there were geologists?"

"True, true. But trouble still, and a fascinating place to

explore. You see, its existence was a major obstacle to acceptance of the theory of plate tectonics.''

"Of what?"

"Drifting continents."

"I've heard of that," Don said. "They're moving now, aren't they? An inch a century?"

"Faster than that, even," Gaspar agreed wryly.

"But I don't see why those little islands, the Bermudas—"

"*Bahamas.* The thesis was that all the continents were once a super land mass called Pangaea. The convection currents in the mantle of the earth broke up the land, spreading the sea floor and shoving the new continents outward. North and South America drifted—actually, they were *shoved*—to their present location, and the Mid-Atlantic ridge continued to widen as more and more lava was forced up from below. But the Bahamas—"

"You talk as if the world is a bubbling pot of mush!"

"Close enough. The continents themselves float in the lithosphere, and when something shoves, they have to move. But slowly. We could match up the fractures, showing how the fringes of the continental shelves fitted together like pieces in a jigsaw puzzle. All except the Bahamas platform. It was extra. There was no place for it in the original Pangaea—yet there it was."

"So maybe the continents didn't drift, after all," Don said. "They must have stayed in the same place all the time. Makes me feel more secure, I must admit."

"Ah, but they *did* drift. Too many lines of evidence point too firmly to this, believe you me. All but that damned platform. Where did it come from?"

"Where, indeed," Don muttered sleepily.

"They finally concluded that the great breakup of Pangaea started right in this area. The earth split asunder, the land shoved outward in mighty plates—and then the process halted for maybe thirty million years, and the new basin filled in with sediment. When the movement resumed, there was the half-baked mass: the Bahamas platform. Most of it is still under water, of course, but it trailed along with the continent, and here it is. The site of the beginning of the Atlantic Ocean as we know it.'' The man's voice shook with excitement; this was one of the most important things on Earth, literally, to him.

But Don wasn't a geologist. ''Glory be,'' he mumbled.

''*That's* why I find this such a fascinating region. There are real secrets buried in the platform strata.''

But Don was drifting to a continental sleep. He dreamed that he was standing with tremendous feet straddling Pangaea, the Paul Bunyan of archaeologists. But then it cracked, and he couldn't get his balance; the center couldn't hold. The more he tried to bring the land together, the more his very weight shoved it apart, making him do a continental split. ''Curse you, Bahama!'' he cried.

CHAPTER 5

PACIFA

Proxy 5–12–5–16–8: Attention.
Acknowledging.
Status?
Four members introduced, final one incipient. Progress good. Group is melding. They are as much concerned with interpersonal relations as with the mission, but unified in their perplexity about it. The likelihood of success seems to be increasing.
That is good. We have lost another world via the straightforward approach. If your experiment is effective, we will try it on the remaining worlds.
But the outcome is far from assured. Human reactions are devious and at times surprising.
How well we know!

Offshore Miami: the continental shelf was narrow here, but they could not approach the teeming metropolis too closely. The rendezvous was just outside the reefs, thirty fathoms deep and sloping.

Gaspar tooted on his whistle. The answer came immediately. Before they could get on their cycles the fifth member of the party appeared, riding rapidly. Don noted the turned-

77

down handlebars and double derailleur mechanism first: another ten-speed-or-more machine, perhaps an expensive one.

"It's a woman," Gaspar said.

Don and Melanie peered at the figure. It was female, but neither buxom nor young.

She coasted up, turned smartly, and braked, like a skier at the end of a competition run. "Pacifa," she said. Her hair was verging on gray, obviously untinted under the hard helmet.

The others introduced themselves.

"Well," Pacifa said briskly. "If I had known you would be three handsome men and one pretty girl, I'd have sent my daughter. But she's all shape and no mind and this is business not pleasure, so we're stuck with each other for the duration. Any problems with the bikes?"

They assumed that this was small talk, so demurred. Don saw Melanie react at the reference to "pretty girl," but she did not speak. He wasn't sure whether it was the first word or the second that bothered her.

"No, I'm serious," Pacifa said with peppery dispatch. "I'm your mechanic, in a couple of ways, and I can see already that none of you except Gaspar knows the first thing about cycles, and he doesn't know the second thing. Three of you have insufficient and the fourth too much. Can't be helped now, though. Who has the coordinates?"

"Twenty four degrees, fifteen minutes latitude," Melanie said. "Eighty four degrees, fifty minutes longitute."

"But that's—" Don started, trying to figure it out.

"Right back the way we came," Melanie said. "Eleph was at 24°30′, and this is 24°15′."

"But farther along," Gaspar said. "In fact, offshore northern Cuba."

"We're picking up a Cuban?" she asked.

"Unlikely," Gaspar said. "If there was supposed to be another person, he should have joined us at the same place Eleph did, not close by. Now I think we're complete. A larger party would be unwieldy. So it's more likely the site of our mission—or a supply depot." He sounded disappointed. It seemed they were not going to the Bahamas platform.

"Let's go," Pacifa said. She mounted and moved out with such smoothness that the three were left standing.

Gaspar filled the leadership gap again. "Don, you catch her and make her wait. Eleph, I saw a map in your pack. Let's you and I check it and find out more specifically where we're going, because Cuba just doesn't make sense to me. Maybe there's something in the Gulf of Mexico I'm missing."

Don took off. But Pacifa was already out of sight, lost in the vague dark background wash that was the deep ocean at dawn. There were not tire tracks, of course. It was hopeless.

"Fool woman," he muttered.

"Whistle for her," Melanie called. He hadn't realized that she was following him, and indeed she wasn't very close, but it was a good suggestion. He blew his whistle.

Pacifa answered at once, just a short distance to the side. "Are you lost, young man?" she inquired solicitously as he drew up to her.

"No. You are—were. Wait for the rest of us!"

"Why?"

"W-we have to operate as a p-party," he said, annoyed.

"I'm glad that's settled. Let's get on with it."

They returned to find Gaspar and Eleph poring over the paper held before one headlight. Gaspar lifted his bike and spun a wheel by hand when the headlight began to fade, to keep the light bright. There were a number of sections of the map, each overlapping the boundaries of the next, so that they could travel from one to another without interruption. It looked to Don as if the entire Gulf of Mexico was covered, and perhaps more.

Gaspar looked up. "It's in an American explosives dumping area," he said.

"A what?" Pacifa demanded. "That can't be right."

"It's the location Melanie gave us," Gaspar said evenly. "Got any other?"

"Do I understand correctly?" Eleph demanded. "Must we venture into a munitions dump?"

"I have no knowledge of munitions dumps," Pacifa said. "I don't know anything about undersea coordinates either. It does seem strange, but if they want to keep our ultimate destination secret, this is as good a waystation as any, I suppose."

"That must be it," Don said. "For some reason they don't want us to know our mission any sooner than we have to. But it must be far enough away so we'll have to reload on supplies." He would be glad to get good rations to replace his bad ones; so far there had been plenty for the others to share with him, but it made him feel as if he wasn't carrying his own weight.

"But an explosives dump!" Gaspar said.

"Can't hurt us," Don reminded him. "We're out of phase."

"I'm not so sure about that. Our weight is still real, and if we were to ride over an old live depth bomb—"

"They do not dump that way," Eleph said. "Those weapons are sealed in."

"How do you know?"

Eleph hesitated. "I have had military experience."

So there *was* a military background, Don thought. That explained the man's military bearing and attitude. But it still didn't explain his presence here.

"Probably it was easier to dump supplies on a regular run," Gaspar said after a moment, evidently not wishing to appear unduly negative. "But it's a good three hundred and fifty miles from here. And if that's only half way to our goal—"

"Our goal may be even farther," Don said. "Because we've been riding back and forth with our initial supplies."

"Of which we still have plenty," Melanie said. "Even sharing."

"Sharing?" Pacifa inquired alertly.

"Don's are bad," Melanie explained. "We don't know if it's poor quality control or what."

"Or what?" Pacifa asked.

"Or intentional," Gaspar said.

"Whatever for?" Pacifa demanded.

"We don't know," Don said.

"Regardless, it seems odd to start us far from the site of our mission," Gaspar said. "It's been bad enough, having to ride all around just to assemble our party. Now to have to go farther yet—"

"Maybe it's that crater off South America," Don suggested. "The one with the dinosaurs."

Gaspar brightened. "Could be. They could start us here, so that no one could guess our destination from our initial motions."

"But what's the point of secrecy?" Don asked. "If that crater is sixty five million years old and has no military value—"

"Never underestimate the secrecy of the military mind," Eleph said.

"Still, that's a thousand miles!" Gaspar said.

"That's why we have our bicycles, isn't it?" Pacifa asked.

"A thousand miles!" Don said, horrified. "That'll take weeks!"

"Days," Pacifa said. "What's wrong with that?"

Eleph regarded her with severity. "Madam, have you any notion how far that is on a bicycle?"

"I ought to," she said, smiling. "I have traveled ten thousand miles in the past year on this bicycle, and I didn't ride much in winter."

The other four stared at her.

"That's my business, after all," she said. "Checking touring paths for bicycle clubs. Terrain, hazards, accommodations available along the way—I earn a few dollars a mile, plus expenses, for doing what I like best. Being independent."

Don didn't comment, and neither did the others. Who wanted to be the first to inform an old lady that she was off her rocker?

Eleph finally broke the silence. "This route takes us in an unexpected direction."

Pacifa shrugged. "So?"

"It's more than we bargained on," Don said. "I thought this mission—well, maybe down off the continental shelf to investigate a sunken ship, not that I wanted to—"

"Or to check the configurations of the terrain beneath the Gulf Stream," Gaspar said. "And the Bahamas platform—"

"To field test the phasing apparatus," Eleph said. "Which requires no great amount of travel, and is not antipathetic to the other—"

"Or to see how well a group of strangers can get along under the sea," Melanie said. "Male, female, young, old, with different—"

"Fiddlesticks!" Pacifa snapped. "This tour will obviously give you all your chances to look at the bottom and search for ships and test your equipment and get along together or quarrel incessantly, whatever direction we go. There must be something special at the end—something more important than any of our separate little specialties. The sooner we get there the sooner we find out what that is."

She was making sense. "But food—water—we can't survive indefinitely under the sea," Don said, feeling the dread of the unknown.

"We certainly can," Eleph said, surprisingly. "These concentrates we carry are pure nourishment. All we need is water—and the recycling system insures the supply. The only really crucial external commodity is oxygen, and the diffusion field takes care of that."

"So there is a field," Gaspar said. "I wondered. We seem to be riding in an alternate realm, where there is ground but no water and perhaps no air. What do you know about it?"

"This is within the province of my specialty," Eleph replied stiffly. "The solid material, animate and inanimate, with which we associate, has been shunted into an alternate framework. That's what that 'phase tunnel' is: the shunting device. That material, which includes our living bodies, will remain in that state until reprocessed. But it is not feasible to recycle oxygen, so within each bicycle is a generator supported by batteries that creates a temporary partial phase, permitting a certain interaction between frameworks. In this manner oxygen is diffused in, and carbon dioxide is rediffused out, enabling us to breathe."

That explanation relieved one of Don's main concerns. But only one of them.

"My, my," Pacifa said. "If one of those generators fails—"

"That is unlikely," Eleph said.

"But you said that Don's supplies are bad. Why not some of the equipment too?"

Don found that question painfully on target.

"I am conversant with the mechanism," Eleph said, "and should be able to repair most malfunctions."

Gaspar whistled. "You must be some physicist."

"I'm sure each of us has his particular area of expertise." Eleph's tone discouraged further comment.

Melanie, nevertheless, made one. "So carelessness or poor quality control may have wiped out Don's food, but anything else can be fixed."

"Precisely," Eleph agreed.

"I'll make a note," Don said. He rummaged in his pack and brought out his pad of paper and pen. Melanie smiled and Gaspar laughed. Don appreciated that.

Pacifa was studying the map. "I see where we are and where we are going. Now must we follow the exact route, or do we have some leeway?"

"What difference does it make?" Eleph demanded.

"Now if we start out grouchy, we'll never get along," she snapped back.

Don had to turn away to hide a smile, and he caught Gaspar doing the same. Neither commented directly.

"Because if we do have leeway," Pacifa continued, "and it seems we have to, because we're the ones who have to do the job, whatever it is, and you can't ride a bike from some fat-bottomed swivel chair—it seems to me that we ought to get off the coral shelf and get down under the Gulf Stream—it's going the wrong way for us, isn't it?—and coast down around here into the Gulf of Mexico. We have to get down there anyway, and according to this map it is sixteen hundred fathoms deep at our depot—what's that in real terms, Gaspar?—and the drop-off doesn't get any—"

"About one and three quarter miles deep," Gaspar said.

"Don't interrupt," Pacifa told him. Don exchanged a glance with Melanie. "The drop-off doesn't get any easier down beyond the Keys, from the look of this."

"No, it doesn't," Gaspar said. "But don't go thinking of the continental slope as a sheer cliff. It may have cliffs and canyons in it, and overall it represents a more formidable climb than any mountain we know on the surface, but it is a slope. We can manage it on the bicycles, if we watch where we're going."

"You're the geologist," she said dubiously. She had caught on to all their names and specialties astonishingly quickly, but it was evident that she was as ignorant as the others about the nature of the sea floor. "Let's slant down it and be on our way."

Gaspar shrugged, out of arguments. Pacifa suited action to word, evidently being a person of action. This time Don and Melanie fell in behind her, and Eleph followed them. Gaspar, most familiar with the depths, was this time at the rear.

They dropped down to two hundred feet, three hundred, four hundred. The terrain became more even, though it was hardly the smooth slope Don had pictured from Gaspar's description. Of course the man had not claimed it was smooth, only that it was a slope. Only flat beds of sand seemed smooth, and there weren't many of them here. They reached a hundred fathoms, and Don gave up converting to feet. It was easier to go along with his depth meter.

Pacifa abruptly slowed. In a moment Don saw why. A tremendous and weird-looking fish was pacing her. It had a vertical fin like that of a shark, but its head terminated in a horizontal cleaver.

"Hammerhead shark," Gaspar murmured, coming up. "Average size, maybe fifteen feet. The eyes and nostrils are at the edge of the spread, helping it to triangulate on prey. Very efficient.''

"A science fiction monster!" Pacifa exclaimed, shaken.

"Nothing to worry about," Eleph said, just as if he had never been frightened by a marine creature. "Only one tenth of one per cent of its mass can affect us, and vice versa."

The hammerhead looped gracefully, circling them. "You know that," Pacifa said. "I know that. But does *it* know—''

The shark charged. All five people leaped for their lives. The wide-flung nostrils and open mouth passed through the party, stirring it further, feeling like a harsh gust of wind. The tail caught Don, and he felt again that disquieting interaction of substance.

They all looked at each other, tumbled unceremoniously. "Well, it is a man-eater," Gaspar said, apologizing for them all. "Our conditioned reflexes still govern us. That may be dangerous, because they don't apply in this situation. Maybe I'd better take the lead, now."

Pacifa, momentarily chastened, acquiesced.

Gaspar moved ahead, and Don took the end spot, and travel resumed. Don was privately satisfied to be following Melanie again; his headlight played at intervals across her well proportioned backside. He liked her body and her personality. If only she didn't have that condition with the hair!

At a hundred and fifty fathoms the dawn of the near-surface had become the deepest blue-black of unearthly night. It was cooler, too; the meter said the temperature had dropped almost fifty degrees, and was now approaching what he thought of as the freezing point.

The pace slowed as they navigated a devious stretch, and Don took the opportunity to pull abreast of Eleph. "Should we stop to put on heavier clothing?" he asked.

"The temperature is a function of the heat of the

converter, modified by very limited external factors, such as the caloric content of the incoming oxygen,'' Eleph said curtly.

"Limited, my foot!'' Don said. "My meter says—''

"That meter is oriented on the oxygen, as a guide to conditions in the other framework,'' Eleph said. "Surely you are not cold.''

Don was embarrassed to realize that he wasn't. All this time he had been reacting to the meter, instead of reality. Naturally he couldn't expect the bicycle temperature to be controlled by that one-thousandth transfer across the phase.

But it did make him wonder again just what the phase world was. Didn't it have temperature or weather of its own? Why couldn't they see it? They could feel it, because that was what their tires rode across. Invisible mass?

There were fish about, but not many. Increasingly Don felt alone, though Melanie's taillight remained in sight ahead of him, and Eleph's ahead of hers, bumping over the irregularities. Don thought he saw another shark feeding on the bottom, and there were a number of unidentifiable glows. But no vegetation at all, at this depth.

The path turned, until they were going southwest, parallel to the reefs, not away from them. Then Don saw why: the drop-off did become steep. Gaspar was making it easier by descending on the bias.

But it wasn't easier. The roughness of the ground increased. Large sponges, grotesquely shaped, loomed out of the gloom to force detours. The land seemed formed into irregular rocky ridges which had to be portaged across. No erosion here to smooth things. Finally Gaspar stopped, letting the others catch up.

"This is messier than I figured,'' he said as they clustered together, pooling their lights. "We're riding along an outcropping—Oligocene deposits, I'd say—of rock, and it probably parallels the coast for a hundred miles.''

"Why not check the map?'' Don asked.

"Map doesn't show it; too general. There are sharp limits to what they can do by echo-sounding, anyway—which is why we need people down here to do the job properly. There's no erosion to speak of at this depth, so every jagged break is as sharp as it ever was. From what I know of this shelf, I'd guess this interruption isn't broad; two or three miles should traverse it, crosswise. Then it's fairly easy coasting on to the foot. But here it's a rough two miles. We're probably better off going straight across it, then riding the trough—but we may have to go mountain style. Who's game?''

Pacifa grinned. "Good idea. We have rope, pitons—''

"Rope and pitons!'' Eleph exclaimed. "Madam, these are not the Alps!''

"Nor the Himalayas,'' Gaspar said. "They're worse, in places. The greatest mountains on Earth are under the sea.''

"Now don't exaggerate,'' Pacifa said.

"No exaggeration. The great mid-ocean ridge runs forty thousand miles around the globe. The largest single mountain of the world, Hawaii, is far larger than Everest, as an entity. Just be thankful we're not trying to navigate a fracture zone. As it is, we'll be seeing moon landscape and Mars landscape before we're through.''

"Goody,'' Pacifa said with almost girlish gusto. "What a marvelous guided tour that would make. Moon and Mars under the sea.''

It occurred to Don that he'd like to meet her daughter— the one who was all shape and no mind. Was her personality like this? But of course he would go into a terminal stuttering attack if he did encounter her, so the fancy was pointless. Better to wrestle with the problem of Melanie's hair. Melanie just might be attainable, if—

"Guided tour," Eleph muttered with disgust.

They unlimbered the rope. "Now we'll have to stay on foot while we're tied," Gaspar said. "I don't know what effect a sharp rope-jerk would have on a rider. No sense risking it."

"No sense at all," Pacifa agreed. "We're a long way from the hospital."

"But we have to hold the bicycles," Don pointed out. "How can we climb and hold on to ropes at the same time?"

It turned out to be less of an obstacle than he had supposed. Pacifa looped the rope firmly but not bindingly about each person's waist and knotted it in place with quick competence. This linked them securely without occupying their hands. She connected the bicycles to short offshoots. The hike would have been more convenient without the bikes right at hand, but of course this was out of the question; the oxygen went with the machines.

Cautiously they proceeded on down the continental slope. A pass opened in the projecting ridge, and they made their way through without difficulty. The steepness leveled off into a smooth, steady, undemanding decline. For miles they trekked downward when they could have been riding, their lights spearing into drab mundane waters, reflecting from harmless sponges and innocuous fish.

At last, embarrassed, Gaspar called another halt. "Wouldn't you know there'd be a break right when I geared us up for a real climb!"

"Security before convenience, always," Eleph said with his normal stiffness. Don was beginning to appreciate that the man was fair, if taciturn. Gaspar had erred on the safe side, and that certainly was best.

"Might as well unhitch now and go on down," Gaspar said. "Should be no more trouble. 'Course we don't want to get reckless. There is always the unexpected."

They unhitched. "I'm glad it *wasn't* bad," Melanie confided as Don helped her. He had to agree.

Gaspar led the way southwest, picking up speed—and dropped out of sight.

It was a depression in the ocean floor resembling a sinkhole. A spring of water issued from a hole at its base. Gaspar had held his seat, and the bicycle straddled the hole, making his clothing billow up and out. "Must be a freshwater well," he remarked. "I had forgotten they were here."

No harm had been done, but the episode served as a sharp reminder. This was unknown, largely uncharted terrain; no one had ever mapped it in fine detail. Anything, geologically, could be here, and they would have no more warning than that provided by their scant headlights.

They made it down safely. Hours had passed, and Don's waterproof watch claimed it was afternoon. The depth was 380 fathoms: a scant half mile. It seemed like a hundred miles, with the phenomenal weight of all that water pressing down. The very fact that they could not feel that weight made the experience vaguely surrealistic. This was indeed an alien horizon.

They stopped and ate and rested, but were soon on their way again, because it was cold when they stopped, whatever Eleph might say about imagination. There was something about the depths and gloom that chilled Don from the mind outward.

Gaspar led them another thirty miles in the next four hours, then halted at a partial cave in a hillside. "Let's camp here," he suggested, knowing that no one was about to argue. "We have had a good day."

"We have indeed, considering," Pacifa agreed, though she looked as fresh as when she had started. "Suppose we join our shelter-canvases together and make one big tent and heat it?"

"Sounds good," Don agreed eagerly. "But—"

"Now I won't tolerate any sexual discrimination," she said briskly. "I'm an experienced camper and I know more than the rest of you combined about setting up. I'll prove that right now."

And she did. Her nimble fingers fashioned the tent much more efficiently than the others could have, even working together. She also set up a separate minor tent for sanitary purposes, a refinement the others had not thought of. That eliminated the need to take individual hikes into the gloom. She detached each person's converter from the bicycles and carried them into that tent, since each person's ecological balance depended on that recycling system. This amazed Don, and evidently the others; they had not realized that this could be done. She set four bicycles inside the tent, bracing the walls, and the fifth beside the privy.

"Now you'll have to hold your breath to cross between tents, because there'll be an oxygen shortage," she warned. "But the one bike will provide for one person in the sanitary tent. You will have to carry your own converter with you to use; that can not safely be shared. Don will have to contribute bad food packages to the other converters at the same rate he borrows good food from the others, to keep the approximate balance. Right, Eleph?"

"There is some oxygen in the alternate framework," Eleph said. "But this is insufficient without supplementation by the field, yes. And it is true that the converters must remain virtually sealed systems."

Some oxygen in the other realm. Don wondered about that, but couldn't quite formulate a specific question. What kind of alternate was that? He wished he had a better notion.

Pacifa set the five converters in the main tent on "high." The heat wafted through the tent as the accelerated chemical composting proceeded within each unit, processing the wastes of the day. It became a thoroughly pleasant place, walling out the gloom, almost making this seem like a chamber in some civilized city on land. Don felt his fatigue and tension melting away.

"But it will be necessary to relocate periodically," Eleph warned. "The oxygen dissolved in sea water is limited, particularly at this depth, and unless refreshed by current—"

"You're right!" Gaspar said, snapping his fingers. "I should have thought of that. We could suffocate in our sleep."

"I did think of it," Pacifa said imperturbably. "We are camped in a slight but steady current that should provide fresh oxygen as we need it. Now for supper." She took the food packages from each supply except Don's, squeezed water into them, and set the result on top of the center converter. Its surface was now burning hot. In a few minutes she served them a hot meal that seemed vastly superior to what they had had before, even though it had to be the same stuff. "Seasoning," she confided with a wink.

Don basked in the warm tent and ate his hot food. Yes, the selection of personnel was starting to make sense. A man did not live by archaeology alone; he required the minimum comforts of life. Pacifa had provided them, and at this moment he would not have traded her for anyone. Not even her shapely daughter, even if his stutter did not exist.

That reminded him of Melanie. He was sitting beside her in the tent, hip to hip, but it was as if she were far away. "You've been quiet. How are you doing?"

She turned her face to him and smiled. "You are interested?"

It became as if the two of them were alone. "Yes."

"I was imagining myself on land. While we were riding, and now."

"While we were plunging to the dismal depths, risking our very lives?" he demanded facetiously. One thing her revelation of her condition had done for him was to distance her enough emotionally to make her approachable socially. This was not a paradox so much as an eddy-current; he could talk with a woman who was not a romantic prospect, just as he could talk with a man who was not a rival. "What if something had happened?"

Gaspar half-smiled and lay back comfortably. Pacifa had eaten her serving quickly and was quietly cleaning up. Eleph seemed to be falling asleep. It was Don's conversation to carry, if he chose.

"What could I have done if it had?" Melanie asked reasonably. "I'd be better off far away."

He played the game, beginning to enjoy it. "Where did you go? To the beach again?"

"No, this time I rode around town."

"Around town!" he exclaimed, evoking a small smile from Pacifa. "In the daytime? Didn't people see you?"

"No. At least, not exactly."

He was beginning to see it himself: her riding her bike as he had at the outset, on land. "This is a secret mission. If you—"

"I couldn't stand being alone anymore!" she cried with the edge of hysteria.

Don felt a wash of sympathy. He saw Gaspar nod, and Pacifa paused for a moment. But still they stayed out of it, letting Don talk to Melanie alone, as it were.

He had never held a dialogue like this before, and was afraid he would muff it. At the same time, he was profoundly grateful for it. He would try to calm her down, not merely because it might help her, but because it felt good to be trying to help her. This was on one level a flight of fancy, an escape from the emotional pressure of this fatigue and mystery in a strange dark, cold place. But on another it was personal truth.

"I can't blame you," he said. "This whole project is weird. What did you see?"

Her eyes were closed now, and she seemed to be truly in her vision or memory. "I rode right along the downtown streets." Now she sounded almost breathless, as if she were active instead of passive. "Beside the cars, through crowds of people, in the middle of the day. I obeyed all the traffic signals and gave pedestrians the right of way. It was all so ordinary I nearly cried."

"Like the beach," he said. "When you walked on the sand and saw the seagulls in the wind. I didn't have the nerve to go out among people. After being phased out, I mean." Or before, really, he realized. He had always been a stranger, as much when in the city as when in his home neighborhood.

"I guess so, pretty much," she agreed. "But then I got so hungry for some kind of interaction I—"

Because she too had always been alone: without family support, and with that stark lack of hair making her a freak—

He brought himself up short. "Yes," he said gently. "It's hard to be alone." He was discovering that no artifice was needed, just identification.

"I started breaking the rules," she confessed. "I'm basically a social creature. I—I rode right through people, to see what they'd do. And—"

This was getting too real. Don was afraid to ask, but afraid not to. Was this truly invention, or had she done this while waiting for the rendezvous? "And—?"

"And they never even noticed. Any more than the sea did. No contact."

"Not even the bones?"

"I—I didn't know about that, then. There was a—but I don't want to talk about that. It's too much like violation. I meant there was no personality contact. They just shrugged and apologized and went on. They—they never realized what it was."

"Never realized they had had a ghost on a bicycle ride through them? How could they miss it?"

"Well, I guess in a crowd you get banged quite a bit anyway, so you don't notice things. Maybe you don't want to. And all the world's a crowd, today. They never really looked at me."

"That's incredible."

"No it isn't," she said sadly. "When I thought about it, just now, I realized that it was no different from the rest of my life. Being alone, no matter how big the crowd, no matter how different I think I am, no one notices. The mind, the personality, I mean. All they notice is the other."

Now Pacifa spoke. "What other?"

For answer, Melanie swept her hands up and dragged off her wig. "Just a little physical interaction," she continued. "Like that gruesome meshing of bones, but no awareness of what's inside, what's beyond the label, beyond the . . ." There were tears now, flowing from the doll's eyes in the doll's bare skull.

"Oh, my," Pacifa murmured.

Melanie seemed oblivious. "It reminds me of a song that was popular before my time. I had it on a record. 'Nobody loves me 'cause nobody knows me.' It was called 'Single Girl.'" She hummed the tune.

She was feeling sorry for herself. But Don could not deny she had reason. Those who blithely disparaged the state tended to be unfeeling louts, he felt. He had not liked his own lonely first section of this mission, and that had been for less than a day. Melanie had been isolated longer, waiting. But for her, as it was for him, this was only an episode in a life of similar isolation.

What could he tell her? Her problem was real, and it would be hypocritical to pretend that it wasn't. Don found himself tongue-tied, when he least wanted to be.

"May I?" Pacifa inquired.

Don looked at her. She came to kneel before Melanie. Melanie's eyes opened. "What?"

"I am one of those who does not know you," Pacifa said. "How could I? I am new to this group. But perhaps I know your type."

"My type?"

"And you do not know me. But this much can be rectified. I can tell you in a few minutes what is relevant."

"N-now wait—" Don started.

Gaspar lifted a hand, signaling peace. Don took the hint and was quiet.

"We are all of us alone, I think," Pacifa said. "That seems to have been a requirement for this mission, which is not the most comfortable thought. It may mean that we're expendable. But it could mean instead that we are fragments capable of uniting into a kind of family. Then none of us would be alone."

Melanie's eyes widened, but she did not speak.

"About me," Pacifa continued. "I oversimplified. I could not have sent my daughter here. I was once part of a reasonably typical family. My husband was fifteen years older than I and a good man. But he did not take care of himself. He smoked—too much, drank—too much, ate fatty foods, did not exercise, and had a high-stress job. He led, in general, the conventional unhealthy lifestyle, and it took him out with a heart attack at age sixty. I had taken a job which absorbed my attention, and somehow had not seen his demise coming. My daughter was beautiful, but she ran off with an alcoholic who finally beat her to death. That I saw coming, but she wouldn't listen. Had I my life to live over, I would address both situations in time and save my family. But I was wise way too late. I disavowed it all, their parts and mine, and focused thereafter on a totally healthy lifestyle, maintaining economic and emotional independence. Yet satisfaction eluded me. I signed up for this mission in the hope that it would offer me not only a challenge but—'' She paused.

"I understand," Melanie murmured.

"You are in a way like my daughter. I realize that this is artificial, and there are no quick fixes—''

Melanie lifted her arms. The two embraced, awkwardly but tightly.

Don closed his eyes. Why couldn't he have done something like that?

CHAPTER 6

MYSTERY

Proxy 5–12–5–16–8: Attention.

Acknowledging.

Status?

Group is complete and melding is proceeding. There should be further progress as they encounter the next group challenge.

When will they learn the mission?

When melding is complete.

Do they know that one of them is an agent of a local government?

The others do not know.

Or that you are a member of their group?

They do not know.

You run the risk of destroying the group and with it the mission, when they learn.

Yes. I hope the risk is less than that of the direct approach.

We hope so too. A world is at stake.

As they progressed, the differences between bicycles became more obvious. Gaspar was in the best physical condition of the men, being muscular and accustomed to strenuous activity. Yet he seemed to tire the most rapidly. Pacifa, a woman in her fifties, was indefatigable. Don and Eleph and Melanie fell in between, with a slight advantage going to Eleph. It had to be the bicycles.

Don watched, working it out. Gaspar had a one-speed machine without fixtures, apart from those attached for the phase trip. Up hills he panted; down hills he used the coaster brake. When the way was steep, he had to walk because he could not put out his feet to steady himself in emergencies in the way the others could—not without sacrificing his necessary braking power. Thus his muscle was inefficiently employed, and it cost him.

Melanie had three speeds, and they seemed to help her a lot. She was young and trim; her lack of weight surely helped her keep the pace, because it took less work to haul that weight upslope. But she was structured in the fashion of a woman, not a man, and simply lacked the muscle mass to do a lot.

Don himself had five speeds. Ordinarily he remained in third or fourth gear, but on a sustained climb he shifted down to second. A smooth decline allowed him to speed along in fifth. The range seemed quite suitable, and he had no complaints, though he certainly felt a day's travel. He was hardening to it, as they all were, but he did wish the sea floor was both smoother and more level.

Eleph, who was of Pacifa's generation, had all of thirty six speeds. He seemed to use only a few—no more than Don did, perhaps—but he could choose them precisely, and could take advantage of the best ratio for any situation. Those turned-down handlebars looked awkward, but they caused the man to assume an efficient riding position: head down, body hunched so as to reduce wind (water) resistance and allow the most effective use of the leg muscles. The whole body was positioned in line with the thrust of the

pedals: therein might lie the real key. Don tried to imitate
the position, though his higher handlebars forced his elbows
out awkwardly, and it did seem to help.

Pacifa's bicycle had only ten speeds, and the same
turned-down handlebars. She was no more muscular than
Melanie, and a generation older. Yet she moved effortlessly,
it seemed. What advantage did she have over Eleph?

The differences seemed small. Pacifa wore gloves, not
the dressy kind or heavy protective ones, but a kind of open
webbing with the fingers cut off. They seemed useless, a
pointless affectation. Until he noticed how sweaty his hands
became on the hard rubber grips. Her gloves removed the
palms from the rubber—actually she had black tape
wrapped around the bars instead, for some reason—just
enough to ensure ventilation, and they also provided friction. That could count for a lot, after eight or ten hours of
arm-muscle twitchings. She had loops over her toes, fasten-
ing them to the pedals. This looked clumsy and dangerous
at first; what if she took an unexpected spill? But Don soon
saw that the straps did for her feet what the gloves did for
her hands. Furthermore, she could actually pull-up on the
pedals as well as push-down, using different muscles
while increasing power. As if that weren't enough, her
shoes were cleated, and seemed to have metal-reinforced
soles to protect her feet from battering. Don's own feet felt
as if someone had been hammering on them, the soreness
extending right into the bone.

Even so, it didn't seem to account for her stamina. She
was in good physical health, but so was Gaspar. She wasn't
muscular, yet she seemed to have the endurance of a woman
twenty years younger. Don resolved to talk to her about it at
the next opportunity.

When that chance came, he was surprised. "Ankling,"
she said. "Cadence."

"What-ling?"

"Ankling. That's half my secret. You men just push on the balls of your feet; I use my ankles. Like this." She positioned one foot in the stirrup. "At the top of the stroke, my toe points up. As I complete the stroke, it angles down, until at the bottom—"

"But that makes your ankle do all the work of pedaling, instead of the large muscles," Don protested.

"No, the entire body participates. Ankling merely increases the effectiveness of the stroke, letting me use every muscle to advantage. You can't put the whole load on one part of the leg and expect it to stand up."

Don tried it. "Seems awkward."

"For you, the first time, yes. But so is a baby's first meal with a spoon. Here, let me raise your saddle; you can't operate effectively unless your bike is adjusted to your leg-length."

She loosened a bolt with her wrench and raised the seat about an inch and a half.

"I can barely reach the pedals now!" Don protested, trying it.

"Nonsense. Any change feels strange at first, even when it's for the better. In the long run—"

"Maybe so. I'll practice ankling tomorrow, if I don't fall over. But why didn't you tell me about it at the beginning?"

"Why didn't you tell me about hammerhead sharks?"

"That's not the same."

"It will do."

"I suppose we all have to learn by experience. But at least they could have had us standardize on bicycles. Experience won't change our problem of equipment. Poor Gaspar—"

"There will be adaptation equipment at the first supply depot," she said with a smile.

"How do you know that?"

"We women are not so amiable as you men about the finicky details. I put conditions on my participation in this venture. I knew someone would foul up on the hardware, as it seems they already have on your food."

"I never realized bicycles were that different," Don said sheepishly.

"Oh, they are. Wait till you try a lightweight tourer, instead of that milk wagon you're on now. Ten speeds, rat-trap pedals—"

"Rattletrap pedals!"

"Rat-trap. Like this." She showed one of her pedals. Don was amazed; with all his comparison of the bicycles, he had not picked up on this detail. The thing was empty. There were only two strips of metal paralleling the main bolt. It did look like the jaws of a rat trap.

"Cuts weight, provides a better grip for the foot," she explained. "The true racing pedals have saw-tooth edges for real friction. But I'm not racing."

Don would never want to race her, however, "About those ten gears. Eleph has—"

"Thirty six speeds. Talk about overkill! Trust the military mind to squander resources. But it is a good machine, for all his ignorance. Once he learns how to use it, he'll be all right."

"Why is it you have only ten speeds, instead of—"

"Ten's all I need. The point of gearing is not to give you different speeds, in the manner of a car, but to enable you to maintain a suitable cycling rhythm. That's cadence. A steady turning of the crank arm at constant revolutions. Find what's most comfortable for you—say sixty turns a minute—and stick to it. Your forward speed may vary, but not your cadence. That way you'll last longer with less fatigue."

Don shook his head. "If I didn't see you standing there all peppery while I'm beat, I'd figure it was quibbling."

"That's right." She started off to see about camping arrangements.

"Uh, one other thing," he said, suddenly feeling awkward. "Last night—what you did for Melanie—that was a g-generous thing."

"Don't give me credit that isn't due," she snapped. "I did it for me."

"For—?"

"Your turn will come, when you get over this nonsense about appearances." She moved off.

Bemused, Don went about his own business.

They traveled a hundred miles a day, under the Gulf Stream. However warm the water might be above, it remained cold here, for they were in the region of deep-water circulation. The cold current was opposite to that of the warm one, giving them an effective tailwind. Though only a thousandth of the water temperature affected him, Don was very glad for the protective warmth of the converter unit.

At the end of the first day of full bottom travel the depth was over six hundred fathoms. At the end of the second day it was one thousand fathoms. On the third day they reached fourteen hundred fathoms and encountered the vast sedimentary plains of the Gulf of Mexico. As far as their headlamps would show, which was not any great distance, the sea floor was flat and featureless except for spider-like brittlestars and occasional sea cucumbers. Some few glass sponges stuck up in clusters, and some fanlike sea fans. Ugly two-foot-long fish, which Gaspar identified as rat-tailed grenadiers, scouted here and there, as well as spindly-legged crustaceans. But the overall impression was that of a desert.

A desert under water! Could this be the result of man's pollution? Actually it was a swamp. Don imagined the muck giving way beneath the weight of the bicycles, scant as the effect might be with the phaseout. If they slowed, would the thin tires sink?

The answer was no. The phase world's surface was hard. Don mused again about that, without effect. The full nature of that other realm remained a mystery.

On and on, for hours, unvarying. There was no danger here, merely boredom. Yet this region was tiny compared to the great abyssal plains of the main oceans, according to Gaspar. The Bearing Plain was supposedly about as large as the entire Gulf of Mexico.

"*Abysmal* plains," Pacifa retorted to that statement. "Not much for tourists here."

"You'll just have to bus them over this stretch," Gaspar said with a smile. The seat of his bike was higher now, and the level terrain helped too, so that he was doing better.

"Impossible," Eleph said, taking him seriously. "No motor will operate within the atmospheric conversion field."

"Oh?" Don was interested. "I thought it was just electricity that got fouled up."

"Ignition is required for a motor."

"How about a diesel?"

"That might operate, if allowance is made for continuous oxygenation in the chambers. But the exhaust would foul our limited environment very quickly and asphyxiate us. The same is true for almost any flame. Human usage is the reasonable maximum the infusion of oxygen can sustain."

"But our radios work," Melanie said. She too had her seat higher, and was doing better, but Don thought the bike

was only a small part of the reason. For one thing, she was
no longer wearing her wig. She had packed it away, and was
going openly as she was. That had bothered Don at first, but
he discovered that after the first few hours it didn't matter.
She was herself.

"The radios are shielded," Eleph said. "The current they
use is minor."

"Still, if electricity does—" Don began.

"Of course electricity functions," Eleph said sharply. "I
never said it didn't. Our own nervous systems are electrical.
But the heavy-duty applications involved in a motor become
complex."

"So we use bicycles," Pacifa said. "They always did
make more sense than cars, anywhere, and are mighty
handy if you want to sneak up on something."

"Sneak up?" Eleph demanded, frowning.

"Cuba is a hostile foreign nation," she said. "Our
mission may be to circle it, spying out its secrets. We
couldn't do it if we made a lot of noise."

"I hope it's not that," Melanie said. "I don't want to spy
on anyone."

Don agreed. Exploration was fine, but not spying.

"We should know, when we are informed of our mission," Eleph said.

"Aren't we getting close to that depot now?" Don asked.
"My meter says so."

"Close," Pacifa agreed. "The depot is right in these
flats, or we wouldn't be here at all. I've been watching for
dud shells, or whatever. How's the ankling?"

"Doesn't seem to help much."

"Oh, come on. Get your toes up, and don't push with the
middle of your foot. If you had proper gear, you wouldn't be
able to do that. We'll have to lift your saddle a bit more.

Lean forward; get your weight where it belongs. You aren't tricycling around the city block, you know."

Indeed he wasn't. The resistive muck had sapped his scant strength, though he knew that resistance was largely in his imagination. Oh for a good long rest.

Melanie cycled close. "Mothers are like that," she said.

They rode on for another half hour. Pacifa pulled up to talk with Gaspar. Then the two called a halt.

"We're past the spot," she announced. "Anybody hear a beacon?"

No one had. "A beacon is a visual indication, not a sonic," Eleph muttered. "You must have misunderstood."

"It's supposed to be the same whistle we use to find each other," Pacifa said. "But mechanically generated. Check it yourself."

"Madam, I shall." Eleph led the way back, watching his locator closely. There was a slight difference between units, so that when Eleph's read exactly 84°50′ west longitude, Don's read 84°49′, and the others varied similarly. That represented a divergence of a mile, and the whistle was limited to about a mile. No one on the surface, a mile and a half above, could pick it up, theoretically. Don questioned the validity of any claim that a sound could be completely damped out by distance, but he wasn't going to question a physicist on that. Perhaps the phase had something to do with it.

They checked the exact coordinates as interpreted by each of their meters, then circled the entire area at one mile and two mile radii. There was no whistle, and no sign of the depot.

"We appear to have inaccurate coordinates," Eleph said gravely.

They knew what that meant. No supplies. It would be impossible for them to find the depot without knowing its precise location, for the Gulf of Mexico was a thousand miles across. An error of as little as twenty miles would reduce their chances to sheerest accident.

"Cuba?" Don asked, remembering Pacifa's suspicion. "If they knew—"

"They do not control these waters," Eleph said. "They would have no clue to the location, even if they were aware of the mission."

"Must be a simple mistake, then," Gaspar said. "Melanie, are you sure you remembered the coordinates correctly?"

"I'm sure," she said. "I wish I weren't."

"Mistakes of this nature are not made," Eleph insisted, the tic in his cheek beginning to show again.

Pacifa began unpacking the tent sections. "If it isn't a mistake, and no one took away the depot, it must be deliberate. Do you really think we would be set up for nothing?"

"Of course not!" Eleph said. "The depot is here, somewhere. The coordinates must have suffered a change in transmission."

"Hey, are you saying I—" Melanie demanded.

"No. I am saying that you must have been given the wrong coordinates. Such information is routinely transferred from one office to another. Someone in the chain must have changed it, to strand us here."

"Who?" Pacifa asked.

"A representative of anyone who wanted this mission to fail."

Gaspar shook his head. "The simplest explanation is most often correct, correct? These government bureaucracies make a living from fouling things up. Some dolt put spoiled food-powder in Don's pack and never checked it, and another dolt must have misquoted the coordinates. No mistake is too idiotic for a bureaucrat to make, especially when lives are at stake. Remember all the boo-boos over the years in the space program! Tying down delicate equipment with baling wire, putting faulty wiring in an oxygen chamber, sending up a manned mission when there were icicles on the rockets—''

"Icicles?" Eleph asked.

"Remember when the Challenger exploded? Because the cold had stiffened the O-rings? That mistake cost seven lives. And the Hubble orbiting telescope—two billion dollars, and then they discovered they'd put in the wrong shaped mirror."

Eleph frowned as if confused, but rallied in a moment. "Those were isolated incidents in an operation of unparalleled complexity. Still, I fear that something of that nature is the case here."

"We shall have to go backward to land—or forward to the mission," Pacifa said. She had been working all along, and now had the tents assembled and was starting on supper. "We do have access to the location of the next depot, fortunately."

"No certainty of that," Eleph muttered.

"For someone who's as pro-government as you are, you're mighty suspicious!" she snapped at him.

The tic was rampaging now. "Madam, I am merely being realistic. We are already short of food, and further complications—"

"If this was an accident," Pacifa said evenly, "the next depot may be all right. But if someone deliberately changed the number, he could just as readily have changed all the numbers. So we had better guess right."

"Maybe if we knew what the mission is, we could tell

whether it's an accident," Melanie said. "I mean, who cares if we're just riding around? But if we're spying—"

"I don't see why anyone should try to abort undersea geology," Gaspar said.

"Or archaeology," Don said.

"Or a new kind of tourism," Pacifa said.

"Or a mere testing of equipment," Eleph said. "But—"

"But our specialties may be just a cover for what we're really supposed to do," Pacifa concluded. "So we really don't know and can't guess. But it occurs to me that our smartest move, if this trouble is deliberate, might be to get on with it in a hurry and catch them by surprise. They'll be expecting us to turn back at this point, and if something is going on under the ocean, that reprieve may be all they need to cover it up."

"Precisely my sentiments," Eleph said.

"If those two agree, they must be right," Gaspar said with a smile.

"B-but if we don't find the s-second depot—"

"Then we'll simply blow the whistle," Pacifa said. "Ride up on the nearest land and make a scene that'll bring our bureaucrats scampering. They may have ignored Melanie, in her vision, but I suspect that if we made a concerted effort, we would not be ignored."

Melanie clapped her hands. "How beautifully simple!"

Indeed, Don liked the notion too. No one could hurt them in their phased out state; they would be pedaling ghosts. The fearful hullabaloo would publicize the whole business. A drastic step, and not one to be taken short of necessity—but still a realistic alternative that would ensure prompt action. It would have to be prompt, if they ran out of food.

And probably there was no conspiracy anyway. But then

he thought of one more thing. "B-but suppose no land is near?"

"Well, let's find out," Pacifa said. "If there's nothing, we'll just have to plan ahead. Save enough food to make it to land. Melanie?"

"I'm not supposed to give out the new coordinates until—"

"Until we're at the prior ones," Pacifa finished for her. "As we are now. Satisfied?"

"Yes, I suppose so," Melanie agreed. "Twenty one degrees, fifty north latitude, eighty nine degrees, thirty west longitude."

"The Yucatan," Gaspar said promptly. He showed the relevant map segment. "North coast, about here."

Don stared. "Dzibilchaltun," he breathed.

The others looked at him.

"Dzibilchaltun," he repeated. "Fabulous ancient city of the Mayans, and before. That's the area. I don't know it from the coordinates, but I could never forget that spot on the map."

"I thought you were a European archaeologist," Gaspar said, not unkindly.

"I am. I know almost nothing about the new world. But who hasn't heard of Dzibilchaltun?"

"Who, indeed," Pacifa said wryly. It was obvious that the name meant nothing to the others. "But at least it gives you something to work on."

"Yes!" Don said. "Dzibilchaltun was contemporary with the Minoan culture, though of course there was no connection between them. Certainly I'll want to compare—"

"Maybe we'd better save the exploration for when we get there," Pacifa said. "We have a long hard ride on short supplies. At least it *is* near land—quite near. Right now we'd better sleep.'' She served up reduced rations, and they turned in.

But Don, as always when under stress, could not get the rest he needed. The entire project had taken on new meaning. He strove to remember what he had picked up about the Mayan culture, but there were only inconsequential fragments. The Mayans had had what some reckoned to be the world's finest calendar, and much fine handiwork in metals and cloth, and superior art—but what of their considerable history? Dzibilchaltun dated from about 3000 B.C., as did the Minoan civilization, but the Mayans hadn't built that city. They had come later. That was all he could remember, if he had ever known more. He had been too narrow a specialist, engrossed in the wonders of his own specialty, poring over the language and script of the ancient Cretans until these seemed almost as familiar to him as his own people. He had neglected the other side of the ancient world almost completely. If only he had known of the opportunity that was coming!

As he wrestled with his uncertainties and frustrations, an unpleasant truth emerged. Pacifa was correct: their specialties were only a cover for their real mission, which had nothing to do with anything they had studied. Otherwise Gaspar would have been sent to the Bahamas platform, and Pacifa would have had a feasible tourist route to clarify. There would have been a Mayan scholar along, instead of a Minoan one. And Eleph—what was he doing, anyway? He said he was a physicist, and that he knew how to repair the breathing field, but probably that would never have to be put to the test.

If Don and Gaspar and Melanie and Pacifa were merely along for appearances, with Eleph doing the dirty work—it *had* to be dirty, with secrecy like this!—why had the government bothered? There *were* no appearances on this mile-deep tour.

The more he thought about it, the less he liked it.

Melanie was lying beside him. "You're not sleeping, Don," she murmured. "And I don't suppose it's because of frustrated passion for me."

He had to laugh, but it was forced. "I'd rather be honest, and just admit that your hair has severely shaken my romantic notions," he said. "But you're a good enough person, Melanie, and—"

"Don't belabor it. What's really on your mind?"

"Do you ever get the feeling that we're penned in a madhouse?"

"All the time," she agreed.

"I mean here/now. The group of us on this mission."

"Oh, you're not mad," she said. "Not really. I've seen much worse."

"Worse than a militaristic physicist or a bike-toting grandma?"

"He's not as bad as all that. And she's not a grandma. Just—I do like her, Don. I do need her."

"Sorry. That business between you two—"

He broke off, but Melanie didn't respond.

"Hey, did I say something to—?" he asked, concerned.

"Oh, no," she said quickly. "I was just thinking. About worse people. I knew some real characters at—at another place. One woman was a farmer, slaughtering and butchering her own hogs—do you have any idea how much blood—?"

"I don't care to," Don said quickly, not from squeamishness, but because it was an oblique way to support her. She was doing him the kindness of talking to him now, and he wanted it to last a little longer.

"And once I met a couple of young men at a John Birch meeting. I wore the wig, of course; they didn't know. One had a gun collection—"

"John Birch?" Don demanded, surprised. "Isn't that the far right group that—*you* went to—?"

"I do try to listen to everyone's viewpoint," she said defensively. "When I get up the nerve to go out among people. Anyway, he collected guns. About twenty rifles, eight pistols, three submachine guns, and two bazookas, with ammunition. He said he was a monarchist. He had a bottle he'd picked up in Turkey, he said—full of enemy eyeballs. Turkish enemies—I don't know where the eyes came from originally, but they were awful. Maybe it was some other country; I don't know whether I can believe him. But those eyeballs certainly looked real. He talked about impaling the Supreme Court justices on the front steps of the Court Building, the slow way."

"Impalement!" Don exclaimed. "I didn't know there were fast and slow ways."

"Neither did I. In fact, I didn't know what impalement *was*. But he explained. In detail. I think I got sick."

"But how—?"

She was silent.

Don decided not to push the question. He was beginning to remember how the Assyrians had done it. The sharp point of a long stout pole was inserted in the subject's posterior, and he was thereby hoisted into the air, his own weight completing the impalement, in the course of agonizing hours. Melanie *had* known worse people!

"I guess we're pretty well off, here, after all," he said.

"Yes. Despite all the doubt, it's sort of nice. In its way. We're together, all of us, perforce. Holding hands, as it were. I haven't felt that sort of thing in a long time."

He pondered briefly, and decided to take a plunge. "M-may I?" he asked.

She laughed. Then her hand came to him in the darkness, and he took it.

Then, holding hands, they slept.

CHAPTER 7

CREVASSE

Proxy 5–12–5–16–8: Attention.

Acknowledging.

Status?

The members of the group are coming to terms with their situation. They realize that something is wrong, and that it may be because of external malice, but have resolved to proceed regardless. This is an excellent sign.

Are you sure of them now?

No. There remain too many complex currents. They are for the moment united in a specific effort, but are not melded. They need more time. Progress is being made, and the young woman is forming attachments to two of the other recruits. The outcome looks positive, but cannot be presumed. We need four attachments.

How will you achieve this?

I will continue putting challenges before them, as planned. The next one is natural: a crevasse which will be difficult to pass rapidly.

We hope you know what you're doing.

I hope so too.

"Now we'll have to set up rationing," Pacifa said. "We're already short because of that spoilage. No trouble stretching the food of four between five people; we each have more than enough. But we have five hundred miles to go with no refills, and that's a rough haul. We'll make it because we have to, and because perhaps some other party doesn't think we can—but we aren't going to enjoy it much.''

Don felt guilty, because it was the failure of his food supply that intensified the squeeze. He knew it wasn't his fault, yet it bothered him.

"Now I'll ration it out with strict impartiality," Pacifa continued in her brisk way. "You will all carry your own, but we shall do a count now. You'll get suspicious when you get tired and hungry and short of sleep—and believe me, you'll be all three!—and that's natural. So I want you to check the count now, so we all know exactly how many packages there are."

There were sixteen.

"Each package is supposed to be good for one meal," she continued. "At three meals a day for all five of us, that's about one day. At our normal progress, we have five days travel coming up." She paused, making sure they all understood. "So we'll have to speed up. Our limit is food, not strength. We've toughened up the past few days, warming up for this effort. We'll do it in two and a half days. And we'll make the food stretch to cover that. Five meals a day."

"Five meals a day!" Eleph exclaimed. "Madam, we haven't enough for three, let alone—"

"Small ones, Eleph," she said. "Eat often, and you eat less. You never get really hungry, so never have to compensate. And your system processes the small amounts efficiently. Especially when you're exercising."

Gaspar caught on. "We'll split one package between the

five of us, each time. Five times a day, two and a half days—and—"

"Almost," she said. "I believe we need more than that; one quarter of a package at a time should be about right. So we shall quarter them, making sixty four quarters in all. We shall eat twenty five quarters a day, for two and a half days, or a total of sixty two and a half quarters. That's nonsense, of course; no one will eat half a quarter. But the point is, we shall have a slight reserve, which we can dispense as necessary. If one of us is required to do heavy work—" she glanced at Gaspar—"he will get an extra ration. We can not safely assume that the way will be completely without challenge."

"That's for sure!" Gaspar agreed. "We'll have to climb the continental shelf to reach the Yucatan peninsula, and that in itself will be a formidable task. If there are any obstructions—"

"Precisely," she agreed seriously. "We need that emergency reserve. We all have some fatty reserves; we can put out some energy without killing ourselves. But if we go too slow, we can starve before getting there. Now let me brush you up on riding technique. First, posture. Eleph, you ride like an old woman—and even old women don't do that, if they want to get anywhere. I ought to know."

She went on to give them all the information she had given Don before, while she adjusted saddles and handlebars and checked each bicycle quickly for problems. Eleph and Gaspar were shaking their heads dubiously, but Don knew she was right.

"We must make two hundred miles a day," she continued. "Roughly fourteen miles per hour, average. That may not sound like much, and it isn't—for me. It'll kill *you,* in this terrain. But not quite as dead as hunger will. At least you know what the deep sea is like, and won't stop to gawk at the fish.'' She smiled briefly. ''Are you ready?''

Of course they weren't, but there was no choice.

They rode, paced by Pacifa. Gaspar led, followed by Eleph, then Melanie and Don. Pacifa changed positions, riding parallel to each of the others in turn, making sure they were all right. Her stamina was amazing; she really did have far better ability than any of the others, in this regard.

On the level it wasn't bad; the hunched posture did seem to diminish the watery resistance. But then they crossed low hills rising out of the abyssal sediment, and Don quickly felt his leg muscles stiffen. As time passed, it got worse. From knee to crotch, the great front muscles tightened into dull pain. His breath came fast and sweat ran down his forehead despite the minimum setting on the converter. He shifted from fifth to fourth, and then to third; this eased the immediate strain but increased his rate of pedaling. Just as much energy was being drawn from his body, but in a different manner, and his cadence was being sacrificed.

He saw that Melanie was having similar trouble. Fortunately she had good legs, and she was keeping the pace. She had a small advantage because her bald head presented less resistance to the current-wind.

Don concentrated on the techniques Pacifa had described, leaning forward to put his weight over the pedals instead of into his posterior, utilizing his torso as well as his legs, and ankling. The higher saddle no longer felt strange. He saw the others doing the same, looking worse off than he felt. That was gratifying. As the grueling pace robbed his leg muscles of their capacity, these other actions did come to fill the power vacuum, and he gained a second wind that was much more durable than the first. He was moving!

But when they clocked 120 miles and stopped for the fourth meal of the day and Don stepped off his bike, his

knees buckled and he sprawled ignominiously on the
ground. There was no gumption left. Gaspar and Eleph were
no better off. Melanie was standing as if both knees were in
casts, afraid to bend them at all.

Pacifa remained distressingly spry. "Eat hearty, folk,"
she said as she divided a package of fish-flavored glop.
"We'll be doing some riding, soon."

Don ate, and she was right: it was enough, for his hunger
was as small as his fatigue was large.

They struck the continental slope of the Yucatan Peninsula of Central America. In the space of ten miles they
climbed a thousand fathoms, and were still deeper than they
had been in the straits of Florida. A rise of one part in ten
was a killer. When it became steeper than that, they
dismounted and trudged, leaning on their machines for
support. No fourteen miles per hour here!

The terrible climb went on and on, dragging at the last
vestiges of bodily strength. Here even Pacifa suffered, for
she was a cyclist, not a hiker. But no one would give up, and
when at last the land leveled into the continental shelf, about
six hundred fathoms deep, four of them dropped without
eating into the troubled collapse of exhaustion. Only Pacifa
remained on her feet.

They had not made their mileage quota, but they were
well over the hump.

"Here, Gaspar, I'll give you some ease," Pacifa said. She
sat and took one of his legs and kneaded the muscle. He
sighed with dawning bliss.

"That looks good," Melanie said. "Trade?"

Don sat up and took one of her legs. He watched what
Pacifa was doing and tried to do the same to Melanie. She
smiled rapturously. His arms were merely tired, not knotted;
he was working with the part of his body that had some

reserve energy. But even in his fatigue, he noticed how nice her legs were. At any other time, he would not be able to handle them like this without getting seriously distracted. Did hair really matter? He could feel his doubt growing. A wig could emulate hair, but what could emulate flesh like this?

But soon she insisted on taking her turn and doing his legs. Her hands were marvelously healing. It was a wonderful feeling which had nothing to do with sex; his legs started to relax. If he had been bringing this feeling to her, he had been doing right. Did her thoughts drift as his had?

"One thing really impressed me about taking birth control pills," Melanie said as she kneaded. It was her way: to embark on some remote subject that nevertheless related in some manner to whatever was going on in the foreground. It seemed that her thoughts *did* drift. "They impaired my ability to follow abstract arguments. I had been working my way through Henri Bergson's book *Time and Free Will.* I don't know how the pills did it, but the results were too obvious. The most direct was indirect: how much more readily I could follow the arguments after I stopped taking the pills. That kind of thing always brings to my mind the specter of chemical control. A subtle, insidious thing. Control of the higher faculties. Maybe it was all due to a mild induced anemia or some such, but whatever it was, it was most effective. It robbed me of my spark, or inner drive or whatever, which was about all I had going for me."

Don's leg muscles were relaxing, but his mind was not. Melanie was supposed to be a shy single girl. Why was she taking birth control pills?

Why, indeed! Was he hopelessly naive? She had wanted social interaction, and if she didn't remove her wig, a short-term relationship was feasible. Sex could be quite short-term.

"I consider myself more a complete determinist than Bergson is," she continued. "But my final conclusions about free will are very close to his. To me it has always seemed as if all these arguments are aspects of an inner drive that is trying to assert itself. A drive toward higher abstraction. Something I consider to be characteristically human.''

Don wondered what kind of a drive accounted for talking about birth control pills while massaging a male companion's legs. He also wondered irrelevantly why she had shown him and the others her bald state. The one could almost be taken as an oblique sexual come-on, while the other was the opposite. He had never heard of Bergson and had not thought much about free will.

''Human beings greatly desire to be free,'' Melanie continued. ''But freedom as experienced by the self is not the absence of prior determining experiences, but rather the opportunity to act in accordance with one's innermost drives. So that if one assumes that physical determinism is all-pervasive—that the combination of one's past history and one's physical reality completely determines one's choices—even then there is no absence of freedom. Because no matter how completely one's choices have been predetermined, there always remains complete inner freedom. I can make any possible choice as long as I am willing to suffer the consequences of my actions. If a person says 'I can't do that' about anything it is physically possible for him to do, he is saying in effect 'I am unwilling to suffer the consequences of that action.' ''

Don wondered morosely whether she thought that taking birth control pills was an evasion of the consequences of her actions. Here she was talking about freedom, but all he could think of was what she was planning to *do* with that freedom. Why had she been thinking about those pills, right now?

Then it came together. Melanie was chained by her circumstance: any man who saw her bald would be turned off. So whatever she might have done while on the pills was not relevant, because it could not last. Now she was being open about her liability, and taking the consequence. But apart from that, she was a human being, and a lonely one, like him.

He sat up. "I-I'm going to exert *m-my* free will," he said. "And take the consequence." Then he caught her shoulders, drew her in, and kissed her. He had been massaging her legs, right up to the buttocks, and the buttocks too, but that had been a necessary courtesy without special significance. This was personal, and therefore more intimate.

She neither returned the kiss nor withdrew. She seemed not quite surprised. "I shall have to think about this," she said. Then she lay down beside him, taking his hand.

Whatever consequence there was was not apparent. Except that it had shut her up. Perhaps that was just as well. He had done what he had done, but he had perhaps surprised himself more than her. In the darkness her baldness had not been apparent. Could he have done it in daylight? Or was he merely testing the waters, as it were, to see whether a romance between them was possible?

If only that hair—

Don had forgotten, in the deep-sea interim, how much life teemed in the shallows. He woke to find fish nibbling at him curiously, or trying to, supposing that they had free will in this matter. Starfish were easing through his territory.

But a good distance remained across the wide continental shelf, and Pacifa gave them no time to lie about. She allocated two and a half full food packages, making up for the missed meal. "We'll make it," she said.

Don's muscles seemed to have coagulated during the night, despite the massage. Every motion was agony. Melanie looked drawn. Suddenly her decision made sense:

to make no commitment when she was dead tired. He wasn't sure whether he had offered any commitment. The kiss had somehow seemed appropriate after the pseudo-intimacy of their handling of each other's legs. But it might have been a mistake. Certainly it seemed remote, now.

He climbed aboard his bicycle and bore down on the pedals, and lo! the machine moved. Melanie started off similarly, somewhat unsteadily. The other men were no better off. Grimly they followed the ever-sprightly Pacifa across the sandy slopes, working the adhesions out of their sinews.

They had overestimated the total distance by about a hundred miles. The result was that they were slightly ahead of schedule despite the slow climb. But their slowly growing optimism was abruptly squelched.

Less than a hundred miles from the depot—they all maintained the firm fiction that there was a depot—they encountered a crevasse. It was not the scope of the Grand Canyon, but it was quite enough to halt the five cyclists.

They verified the depth only by tying a package of tools to a rope and letting it down until it bumped. The near wall dropped into a plain below. How broad it was they could not know; Gaspar tried for a whistle-echo, but came to no conclusion.

"What," Eleph demanded severely, "is a canyon doing *under the sea?*"

"Mocking us," Melanie said dully.

Pacifa smiled through her frustration. She was tired too, and the extra muscles the males carried were beginning to tell in their favor. Melanie had the advantage of youth. "Obviously there is a river on land. It continues as a freshwater current for some distance over the shelf, cutting away the ground."

"No such luck," Don said. "Fresh water is less dense

than salt water, so it would tend to float. It takes a *land* river to cut a canyon. No doubt it was a land river, in the ice age when so much water was taken up by the glaciers that the sea level dropped several hundred feet. This canyon must have been carved then, then covered up when the sea level rose again.''

''I thought Gaspar was the geologist,'' Pacifa said.

''Well, I run into such things archaeologically,'' Don said. ''Many of the old civilizations were shoreline cultures, and some were buried by the slowly rising waters. In fact, civilization itself had a hard go of it until about 3000 B.C., when the ocean level finally stabilized. How could you maintain an advanced cultural exchange when your leading seaports kept sinking under water? It was no coincidence that the Minoans and Egyptians developed only when—''

''I hate to interrupt,'' Gaspar said, ''but we're talking beside the point. We have to get across this detail of the landscape, and a detour may be too long. Our food is almost gone. Any ideas?''

''What about the map?'' Pacifa asked. ''Let's assess our handicap. There may be a better place to cross.''

''Our general map doesn't show it. Probably there was a detailed map at the first depot, but—'' He shrugged.

''Better not gamble, then,'' she said. ''We'll rope it.'' She unlimbered the long cord. ''Now we have a logistical problem. We can get people down, and we can get bicycles down, but both together is tough.''

''Not at all,'' Eleph said. ''The problem is physical, not logistical. Merely rig a pulley and use one mounted rider as counterweight for another.''

''Pulley? Good idea if we had one!''

''Remove the tires from one bicycle. String the cord through the rims.''

Pacifa nodded. ''Eleph, I hate to admit it, but you do have

something resembling a brain on you. We can even hitch a loop to the pedals to serve as a brake. But how do we get that bike down afterwards—and how do we get it up the other side, to haul us *up*?"

"One problem at a time, woman," he said curtly. "We need a suitable location."

"And we'll have to select a bike," she agreed. "Let's see. The multiple-speeders are better constructed, but they all have hand brakes. We need a coaster brake, and good heavy construction."

Gaspar had anticipated her. He was already unloading his machine.

Eleph, meanwhile, scouted the canyon, riding perilously close to the stony brink. "This will do," he called. "An outcropping. We can suspend the bicycle over this, and rig a trip-wire to drop it down afterwards."

"Is that safe?" Melanie asked, gazing at the brink with dismay.

"Safe enough," Eleph replied.

Don had thought of Eleph as a grouchy desk scientist, but now the man was displaying considerable practical finesse. This challenge was evidently bringing out the best in him.

They rigged it. Gaspar's stripped bike was tied to the rock spur by the safety rope, and the rear wheel hung down below. The cord fitted neatly within the bare rim, both ends dropping down into the depths.

Pacifa, the lightest member of their party, went down first, complete with her bicycle. Gaspar and Don paid out the line according to Eleph's terse instructions. Eleph straddled the bike with his foot on one pedal, using the coaster brake to prevent slippage. The whole procedure looked awkward and dangerous, and it was—but it worked.

In a surprisingly short time Pacifa reached bottom and the line went slack.

"No trouble," she called after a few minutes. "Smooth and flat. Far wall's two hundred feet off. Little squid, crayfish, sponges, and maybe a sea monster or two. Send down the rest."

Eleph was the next. He and his bicycle were tied to the upper loop, while Pacifa herself, below, served as the counterweight. As Eleph went down, she came up. Braking was hardly necessary, as there was only a twenty pound differential. Don had not realized that Eleph was so light, but part of it could be a difference in the bicycles and other gear.

Then it was Melanie's turn. Pacifa served as the counterweight again, because it had to be lighter than the one who was descending. As it was, it was close; Melanie had the fuller flesh of youth, but nothing more. In her case, it *was* her heavier bicycle that made the difference.

After that Don went down. He mounted his bike and hung on as he dangled over the seeming abyss, slowly rotating. He tilted to the right, and automatically turned his front wheel to compensate, though this was useless in the circumstance. His second reaction was to haul on the suspending rope, and this righted him promptly.

Down he went—and up came Pacifa from the murk, burdened with extra items to increase the mass of the counterweight. "Fancy meeting you here!" she called with a cheery wave as she passed. "If you jump off and let me drop, I'll never speak to you again."

Macabre humor. In a moment she disappeared above.

The descent slowed as he neared bottom. Melanie was waiting for him. Don knew that Pacifa had come into sight above, giving warning, so that Gaspar had applied the brake.

Then he touched down. His line did not go slack, for

Pacifa's counterweight maintained tension. "Okay!" he called.

There was a jerk, and then the line did slacken. Pacifa had grabbed hold of the pulley wheel, relieving the rope of most of her weight, and Gaspar had braked hard to hold her there.

Don unhooked quickly. "Off!" he shouted.

Slowly the loop moved up. Slowly Pacifa came down. This was the dangerous part; if Gaspar slipped or if the bicycle chain broke—don't even think it!—she would plummet. She had confidence in her handiwork and in her companions, and she had courage.

"Next time we'll have to use rocks for counterweights," she said, smiling. "Then we can send someone down with every shift."

"We shall," Eleph agreed.

Pacifa gave a short laugh, but the notion made sense to Don. What did she see wrong with it?

The rope slackened. "All right—get off," Gaspar called from above. Pacifa unhooked.

Then the rope jerked upward, halted, and jerked again. Gaspar was handing himself down, using both ropes. No—he was tying the other end, for the doubled strand would reach only half way.

Down he came, handing it along the single rope without his bicycle. Don was amazed. Gaspar had nothing to breathe!

Gaspar dropped the last few feet and jumped into Don's field. He took a tremendous breath. He had been holding it! "Cold out there," he exclaimed.

"Must be nice having muscle and wind like that," Eleph remarked, a bit wistfully.

"Just conditioning," Gaspar said. "A diver has to keep in shape. I'd have been in trouble if I'd had to depend on my worn-out legs! Got a counterweight?"

"Here," Pacifa said with a chuckle, indicating a rock.

"But that's phased out!" Don protested, suddenly realizing why she had found the matter humorous. "I mean, *we* are."

But Eleph was serious. "It still weighs the same," he said. He brought out a tiny cylinder, opened it, and drew forth an almost invisible fine thread. He strung this around and within the open tire casing that had been removed from Gaspar's bicycle. Then he folded the tire about the rock and tied it in place with the rope.

The others watched silently. Don could make no sense of the procedure. The moment any pull was exerted on the rope, the whole phased tire would slide through the unphased rock without significant effect. Only if the rock also existed in the phase realm could it be used, and they had encountered no loose fragments there.

"Will you two healthy specimens carry this over to the hoist, please?" Eleph asked.

Don looked at Gaspar. Pacifa hummed a merry tune. Melanie looked studiously neutral.

Gaspar shrugged. He walked to the rock, and Don followed. Gaspar took hold of the rope and yanked, one-handed.

Then he looked down, surprised. "It resists!"

Don tried it. The stone did resist. It was heavy. He poked his finger into it, and found only that whipped-cream semi-solidity. He hauled on the rope again, hard—and the stone budged.

"Let me see that," Pacifa said, no longer laughing. She repeated the experiment, while Gaspar took her place at the hoist-rope so that his bicycle would not crash down. Then: "Eleph, you sphinx—what have you done?"

Melanie was smiling now, appreciating the interplay.

"Merely another facet of the phasing," Eleph said as if it

were unimportant. "This thread they gave me has been passed only half way through the phasing tube, so represents a compromise between the two frameworks. It interacts with both, partially. It is a very dense, very strong alloy, I understand, so that it can withstand the double load. See, it does not penetrate the surface of the rock."

"But our own interaction with the sea is only one part in a thousand," Gaspar said. "If this is twice that, or one part in five hundred—"

"It seems the phase does not operate in a linear manner," Eleph explained. "We are standing on another world, not the Earth we know. This one is without an ocean and with very little oxygen in the atmosphere. This half-phase thread, if I may employ an inexact term, seems to occupy both worlds, and to act in each with equivalent effect."

"I see," Gaspar said thoughtfully. "Not one five-hundredth, but one half. So we can use it to lift this rock."

"But the rock itself—" Don began, then reconsidered. The rock was real. His notion that what he could not directly touch was unreal—that was the fallacious concept.

"That thread must drag against you when you're carrying it," Pacifa said shrewdly. "The friction of the water—"

"Normally this is minimal, for the wire is very fine," Eleph said. "I also carry it so that the narrow side of the coil is forward, decreasing the effect. However, I admit the effect can be awkward when I encounter a solid object."

Gaspar's mouth dropped open. "That little octopus—you were knocked out of your saddle, when—"

Don remembered. So Eleph had not been reacting foolishly when marine creatures approached. They really could strike him, via that little spool of thread.

"Lord grant that I may walk a mile in the other fellow's shoes before I . . ." Gaspar muttered, embarrassed.

They carried the rock and tied it to the dangling hoist

rope. They let go. The rock traveled upward at a moderate pace. "If it jams now, we've lost a bike," Gaspar said.

It didn't jam. Gaspar's bicycle, rigged this last time as a counterweight, came down. How the man had anchored it firmly enough for a man's descent, while leaving it free to be lowered like this, Don could not imagine.

Melanie's brow wrinkled. "If the bike is down here, where's the pulley?" she asked.

Don stared up into the gloom. She was right: the bicycle had been the pulley.

"I put a loop over the smoothest projection of the ledge I could find," Gaspar said. "And hoped that the lighter weight of the bike wouldn't cause it to chafe too much. Then I handed myself down. The rock-counterweight allowed us to lower the bike slowly, instead of bringing it crashing down. Thanks to Eleph."

"But Pacifa could have gone up again—"

"Ha!" Pacifa exclaimed.

Then Gaspar jerked hard, so that the rock was pulled up over the ledge. They stood back as it came crashing down. It was expendable; Pacifa wasn't. Now he understood the last of it. They had done a nice job of maneuvering.

Once this mission was over, Don wondered, would he ever be able to swim without feeling as if he were flying? To a swimmer, this entire hoist would have been unnecessary.

But a swimmer would never have been able to traverse the mile-deep bottom, camping out among the living fish. He would know the difference immediately.

Gaspar carried his bicycle across the canyon, not bothering to reassemble it until they knew their next move. Don followed, expecting to find a stream of water down here, until he reminded himself again that the whole atmosphere was water. The hazard of the cliff made it hard to credit, emotionally.

"Here it is," Pacifa said. "Vertical cliff again. How do we string the rope this time?"

"I have been thinking about that," Eleph said. "I hope we can borrow from a principle of flotation. Gaspar—how do divers lift substantial objects from the bottom?"

"Shipboard winch, mostly. Or do you mean balloons?"

"I understood they used canopies similar to parachutes."

"Oh. Yes, the archaeologists have a system."

Don perked up. This was new to him. Of course the entire field of underwater archaeology was new to him. That was one of the incongruities of this assignment. Even had this been near the island of Crete, he would not have been much help in any practical way.

"They fill these little parachutes with waste air from their scuba rigs, and after a while the flotation is enough to lift almost anything," Gaspar said. "Pretty neat system, but tricky, if the chute slips or tilts. A current could make havoc."

"Hey, that's smart," Don said appreciatively. "Using their bubbles to do the hard work. Trust an archaeologist to figure that out."

"But we don't have bubbles," Pacifa said. "Just an oxygenating field that *doesn't* float. How can we use that?"

"By interfering with the carbon dioxide rediffusion, and capturing the resultant accumulation."

Pacifa looked around. "Anybody understand that?"

"Sure," Gaspar said.

"No," Don and Melanie said simultaneously.

"Oxygen filters in for us to breathe," Gaspar said. "Otherwise we would suffocate. The molecules are the same, regardless which world we're in. The problem is getting them across to us. But we have to get rid of the spent air, too. The carbon dioxide. So that moves out while the oxygen moves in, right, Eleph? Like scuba—''

''Self Contained Underwater Breathing Apparatus,'' Eleph said. ''The principle differs, but for the sake of analogy—''

''Fair exchange, no loss,'' Gaspar said. ''Actually, the scuba isn't exactly self-contained either, because the bubbles do go free. But if we can save our own lost air, we might fill balloons.''

''Correct in essence,'' Eleph said. ''We are not actually inhaling air as we know it. We are inhaling oxygenated nitrogen. The field—''

''Fill balloons,'' Pacifa said. ''That much I follow. But A Number One, we don't have any balloons. B Number Two, how can we fill them when they're phased out? The bubbles would pass right through, just as we pass through water and fish. C Number Three—''

''Not if the balloons were filled with our air,'' Gaspar said. ''Normal air would pass through, but not matching-phase air.''

''C Number Three,'' Pacifa repeated, ''we've got to use non-phased balloons, because only that kind can provide any lifting power in natural water. Obviously our own air won't lift us very high in a gaseous medium—which is what natural water is to us. Mouth-blown balloons don't float in air; only the helium or hydrogen-filled ones do that.''

''Precisely, Madam. We have the enormous advantage of being in a liquid medium. Tremendous flotation is available, provided we are able to invoke it. Fortunately we came prepared.'' He rummaged in his pack. ''We do have balloons, half-phased in the manner of the thread. They will proffer similar resistance to water that a normal balloon might to air.''

Eleph brought out the balloons and passed them around.

Each member of the party began to blow. Soon each had a bobbling sphere a foot or more in diameter.

"This is hard work," Don said. "And it feels funny. As if I'm not really blowing."

"That's the water filling the shell, in the other world," Gaspar explained. "It's passing right through your head to squirt into the non-phase aspect of the balloon, that is a vacuum there."

Don shook his head, not following the reasoning.

"They aren't floating," Pacifa pointed out. "In fact, they're shrinking."

"Naturally. The carbon dioxide is phasing through, while the nitrogen remains. You will observe a bubble of gas trapped in the water of the other world, within the balloon."

"Yes, I see it," Don said, peering through the transparent material.

"Now we shall have to squeeze out the water, that corresponds to our nitrogen. Save only the bubble, and keep the nozzle down, so the gas can't escape."

They did so, intrigued. They were actually witnessing the operation of their breathing fields.

"Now refill the balloon, so that more carbon dioxide can phase through."

Soon the trapped bubbles were larger.

"But what about the oxygen phasing through the other way?" Don asked. "Wouldn't it balance and cancel the effect?"

"No," Eleph said patiently. "Only the transfer of gas from here to there, within the balloons, is significant. For this limited purpose."

Don gave up trying to understand it all. It was hard enough just to keep blowing.

It was a long job. Only a portion of the exhaled breath was carbon dioxide, and only that portion they actually breathed into the balloons could be used. Eleph had calculated that each person should be able to fill a balloon to serviceable dimension in two hours, provided that all his carbon dioxide was utilized. This proved to be impossible. The phasing through normally occurred throughout the volume of the breathing spheres, and the rate was adequate for the need. The much smaller volume of the balloon allowed only a portion of the field to operate. Thus it was several hours before the balloons swelled into real instruments of flotation, though each person worked on three simultaneously.

In one way this was good, because they all got needed rest for their legs. But their food supply was diminishing. This balloon device had to work, now, or they would not make it to the depot.

But finally the upward tug became strong, and they knew that success was incipient.

"Keep the lift under control," Gaspar warned. "We don't want to float right to the top. When you're rising too fast—and you'll tend to accelerate, because the balloons will expand as pressure decreases—let a little gas out of one. When you reach the brink, get hold and ease yourself over onto ground." He showed the way by making the first ascent.

It worked. Don was amazed at the hauling power of three medium balloons. He watched Gaspar go up, and then Melanie. He felt guilty for looking up under her skirt, but did so anyway. He had massaged those legs; they were nice ones. But somehow this illicit peek was more evocative than the direct handling had been.

When his turn came he puffed a last burst into his third one and waited while it diffused into full strength. His front wheel came up, then his rear, and he was waterborne.

It seemed precarious, and he decided that he preferred the rope and pulley method. What if a swordfish took a poke at his balloons? They were vulnerable now. Or a shark, taking an experimental bite.

But he had more immediate concerns. His rate of climb, slow at first, was now swift. The balloons were ballooning alarmingly. One atmosphere less pressure for every thirty-three or thirty-four feet, and now he was above the rim, but too far out.

Fortunately his problems had a common solution. Don angled the snout of one balloon and let out a jet. This did not provide the propulsion he had hoped for; the bubbles rose toward the flexing surface of the sea, now so near. But at last his ascent slowed, and he had to cut off the valve lest he commence a descent that would speed up the same way.

The last bubble passed through his hand as he tied off the balloon. Then he breast-stroked his way across to the ledge, tediously. He didn't have much leverage, because it was like paddling in air, but he didn't need much. He landed and deflated his balloons, hating to see that hard-won gas escape. But its job was done.

Eleph, the last to start up, had arrived before Don, having managed his ascent better. The crevasse had been navigated.

"Why didn't you tell us about this before we climbed down?" Pacifa demanded of Eleph. "We could have floated down, or even straight across. Much less effort."

"Horizontal travel is hazardous, because of the time consumed," Eleph said. "A few seconds are reasonably safe, but a few minutes multiply the opportunity for inquisitive sea creatures to come. Descent is not recommended, because of its accelerative nature."

"Hard bump at the bottom," Gaspar agreed. "Can't let
out gas to stop it, going down."

Whatever the merits of the case, it had provided them
with a needed change of pace. It was now too late to
complete the trip to the depot this day, but they proceeded
with renewed vigor and optimism.

CHAPTER 8

CITY

Proxy 5–12–5–16–8: Attention.
Acknowledging.
Status?
The crevasse has been navigated in good order. Melding is proceeding. The next three challenges may complete it.
These are natural or unnatural challenges?
Both. They are works of man, but of unusual nature. I routed the travel to include them. It is not safe to interfere any further with their supplies; they have no remaining food, and will march onto land and give up the mission if further denied.
This seems like unity of purpose.
Yes. That is why I am optimistic. They could have turned back, but did not. This group is integrating, and I think will become what we need.
We hope so. Two more worlds have been lost since we last communed.
This one we shall save, I think.

As they lay in the joint tent at night, Melanie remained uncommunicative, so Don entertained himself by sketching Minoan symbols on his note pad, analyzing them for new

meanings. The writing had been largely deciphered, but
some obscure aspects remained, and these were his special
challenge. It occurred to him that it was a similar case
with Melanie; much of her was coming clear, especially
when she spoke so freely about her memories and impressions, but some of her was opaque. He had kissed her,
perhaps surprising himself more than her, and she was
taking time to consider her reaction. The thing was, he
had done it while she was bald. His first shock at her
state had faded, and increasingly he was becoming
aware of her other traits. There was a lot about her that he
liked, both physical and mental. Maybe she thought he
was teasing her, but he wasn't; he was coming to terms with
her. He knew that if he could truly accept her bald, it would
be all right if she wore her wig again. But he was not yet
sure of his deepest feeling about that. So he focused on
symbols, as if their interpretation was also the key to
Melanie.

"May I inquire what you are doing?" It was Eleph, also
slow this night to sleep. Extreme fatigue did that; the body
had to unwind somewhat before it could relax enough for
sleep. His tone was carefully courteous, and Don was
flattered to realize that this was the first friendly overture
the man had made to any of the rest of them. So Don
explained.

"I do not mean to be offensive," Eleph said, and it was
evident that he was not used to being inoffensive. It was not
because he tried to be offensive, but that he was unschooled
in nonmilitary courtesy. "But I had understood that Cretan
writing has never been deciphered."

"So how can I read it?" Don asked rhetorically. "That's
a good question, and as with most good questions, the
answer is not simple."

Eleph actually smiled. "I appreciate a complex answer."

MERCYCLE 141

Amazing how simple it was to get along, once the effort was made! Don liked talk about his specialty. "All right. First, you have to understand that what we think of as Cretan writing is fragmentary and inconclusive, and much of it isn't Minoan. It's Greek."

"That's a fair start," Eleph agreed wryly.

"We call this 'Linear B.' It appears to date from the Mycenaean occupation of Knossos, the latter half of the fifteenth century B.C. This has been deciphered, but it turns out to consist entirely of routine palace records. Inventories, receipts, accounts. No chronicles of kings, no literature. Thus it is of limited value to the historian."

"Linear," Eleph said thoughtfully. "Does this mean that it was written along straight lines, like our own script?"

"No. The name is to distinguish it from true hieroglyphic writing, the little stylized pictures such as those used by the Egyptians, where the word for 'man' is a stick-figure man, and 'walk' is a pair of legs beside the man. Such pictogramic or ideogramic representation is cumbersome at best. The linear form is much superior, because a few stylized strokes replace the picture, as in the Babylonian cuneiform, done entirely by wedge-shaped imprints on clay. Not only is this faster, it is far more versatile."

"I can see that. But if your linear writing is not Cretan—"

"I'm coming to that. 'Linear B' derives from 'Linear A,' which in turn appears to be the true Minoan writing. But it seems to be restricted to the Phaistos area of Crete, while Linear B appears at Knossos, the capital. Linear A is largely undeciphered; progress is being made, but there is no uniformity of interpretation. So some would say it remains obscure."

"I see. But what, then, do you read?"

"Well, Linear B, of course. But my real interest is in
Linear A. A number of characters are common to both, so
we do have a starting point. Many scholars have assumed
that because Linear B is cumbersome, omitting many
middle consonants among other things, that Linear A
can be no better. I believe, in contrast, that B was a bastard
offshoot used by the barbaric Mycenaean conquerors, therefore representing only a crude fragment of the potential of
the original. It is in Linear A that we shall find the real
literature of the Minoan culture—and indeed, we are finding
it."

"Do you have extensive manuscripts in Linear A?"

Don grimaced. "No. I theorize that the Mycenaeans
destroyed Minoan libraries and literature in their venge-
ful fury. No doubt most of it was on paper or parchment,
so it would burn, and King Theseus was a bookburner.
Natural calamity was responsible for a great amount of
loss, too. But these things can't have eradicated it *all*.
Someday we'll excavate some official's private library, and
then—"

Eleph smiled. Don relaxed—and was abruptly asleep.

The final miles seemed like nothing. The depot was there,
exactly where indicated. The sonic signal was clear.

They pulled up and listened, tangibly relieved. Don had
not appreciated how worried he had been until he felt the
load depart. They would have food again.

He also felt the fatigue of three hard days' travel, as if it
had been stored for this occasion. What a journey they
had made, crossing the Gulf of Mexico on short rations!
That canyon had wiped out their schedule and their reserve,
and they had finished the last food package four hours
before.

As they paused, listening, Melanie moved next to him. "I

am still thinking,'' she said. Then she caught his shirt and drew him to her, and kissed him on the mouth. That was all. It was enough.

They resumed their ride toward the depot, their feelings toward each other intensifying with their relief from concern about their supplies. It was as if there was a certain charge of emotion which had to find a new object.

''Hey—isn't this your department, Don?'' Gaspar asked suddenly. ''Hard to tell, because of the sediment, but aren't these buildings?''

Don looked, startled. He had been paying no attention to his surroundings, just driving onward, and had been distracted by the sonic signal and then by Melanie. But now he saw clearly that they were on the verge of a submerged ruin—perhaps even a sunken city.

''Dizzy Choo-choo,'' Melanie said.

''Dzibilchaltun,'' Don corrected her, having to laugh. ''Yes, I suppose it has to be. No telling how much of that fabulous city was drowned. The depot must be right in the middle.''

Now Eleph and Pacifa exchanged glances. ''Don, tell us about the city,'' she said.

''Glad to—what little I know. But first let's get on to the depot. I just want to fill my belly and flop down.''

''No, we shall have to wait,'' Eleph said. ''I believe I have read about Dzibilchaltun or some similar Mayan city. Weren't there impressive sacrificial wells?''

''Sacrificial wells?'' Melanie asked, frowning.

Gaspar scratched his head. ''I'm curious about that too. But I'm with Don: let's nail down the supplies before we gossip about past civilizations. We've missed one depot, remember.''

''Gaspar,'' Pacifa said with motherly gentleness.

"Doesn't it seem providential that the depot is right here, inside a famous old city?"

"It was obviously set up this way," Gaspar said. "To give the archaeologist a good crack at it. This must be Don's mission."

"That is plausible," Eleph said. "As is no doubt intended. But if exploration of this city is the object, why did we have to travel underwater from Florida? Why wasn't a Mayan specialist assigned? Why have there been so many problems? They didn't have to route us across that crevasse. I think we need to consider."

"But what is there to consider?" Gaspar asked. "The depot is here, we've found it, and we need it. This is the one time nothing is wrong."

"That's what's odd," Eleph said meaningfully. Now Don realized what the two were driving at.

"Don, is there anything *about* this city?" Pacifa asked.

"Well, as you know, I'm out of my specialty. But I understand that Dzibilchaltun is unique in the western hemisphere. For one thing, it was large—probably the largest city in the ancient world. For another, it's old: continuously inhabited for about four thousand years, until the Spanish Conquistadors destroyed the native culture. It must have been a mighty seaport, and the pinnacle of the old Mayan civilization. That's about all I know. I think the old Mayan script has now been deciphered, but I'm not sure there are texts relating to the history of the city."

"So it may be a mighty good place to visit," Pacifa mused. "Especially underwater, where it presumably hasn't been touched by looters."

"Oh, plenty of looting goes on under the sea," Gaspar said.

"Indeed it does," Don agreed. "The Mediterranean—"

"But why us?" Pacifa continued. "That sticks in my craw. Do you think it's a trap, Eleph?"

"Perhaps. I seem to remember human sacrifices. But there shouldn't be any Mayans here now."

"That was part of their religion," Don said. "But the Mayans were basically peaceful. Mostly they sacrificed precious objects. Golden artifacts, handicrafts, things like that. I think it was the Aztecs who made a wholesale business of human sacrifice. They were comparatively recent and barbarian."

"The city may be a decoy," Eleph said. "It is hard to believe that our real mission concerns the ancient Mayans. Our government is generally more pragmatic."

"There's nothing wrong with surveying a Mayan city," Don said defensively.

"By a Minoan scholar?" Melanie asked. "And the rest of us, who are really ignorant about archaeology?"

Don couldn't answer. It was making less sense.

"Could someone have substituted these coordinates and planted a fake beeper to bring us in?" Pacifa asked.

"After entirely losing the first depot?" Eleph asked in return. "That's unnecessarily circuitous, considering that we surely weren't expected to make it here. And it doesn't account for the selection of this unique spot."

"You're right again," Pacifa said, and it seemed to Don that she had raised the point for the sake of having it refuted. "It's so fouled up it must be the way the bureaucracy planned it. A Minoan scholar sent to an old Mayan city. They both begin with M, don't they?"

Don laughed and the others smiled. "That's reasonable. The bureaucrats didn't know the difference. And I *will* want to look at these ruins closely. I don't mind expanding my horizons. Let's get on to the depot."

The others agreed, though with less enthusiasm. The party rode on—cautiously.

The arrival was anticlimactic. The depot was there, almost hidden by a mound of rubble that turned out not to be real—to them. The phased-in supplies could and did occupy the same region inhabited by real-world material. A very neat hiding place for a foreign shore. No local fishermen or incidental looters would have spotted it. Even though they could not touch it, such a discovery could have spread an alarm.

"That bothers me," Pacifa said. "But I don't know why."

"There is no need for us to remain in the vicinity," Eleph said. "We can ferry the supplies out to deeper water and make our own depot, that no one knows about except us."

That they did, quickly, leaving only their surplus waste. There were limits to what the converters could do once the water was recycled, so they had to be emptied periodically. Once safely clear of the city they pitched their joint tent and ate ravenously and slept. The pressure was off, for the time being.

Melanie slept beside Don, and held his hand, but said no more about herself or their relationship. Evidently she was still considering her response. That was just as well, as he was still considering his feeling. If only she had hair!

"Okay, Melanie," Gaspar said after breakfast. "How about the next coordinates?"

"Wait a minute!" Don cried before she could answer. "I'm not leaving before I take a good look at this city!"

"You saw it yesterday, didn't you?"

"No. I had a passing glimpse of the cover. Now I want to read the book."

"That city is buried in silt," Pacifa pointed out. "The cover is all you can see, so long as it's phased out."

"What about Eleph's thread and balloons?" Melanie asked.

"These should not be expended spuriously," Eleph said.

Don saw his prize slipping away. The others just did not understand archaeology.

"We don't actually know what our mission is," Gaspar said thoughtfully. "From what Don says, this is a significant location. Maybe we're supposed to investigate, lending our skills to support his skills."

"That's not true," Eleph said.

"How do you know?" Pacifa inquired. "Did Melanie give you the next coordinates?"

Melanie smiled at this teasing.

"No, of course not," Eleph said stiffly. "But the very fact that there are further coordinates—"

"*Are* there?" Gaspar asked.

"You yourself were asking for them a moment ago."

"But I didn't get them—and now I wonder. This place is beginning to make sense to me as a destination, and not just archaeologically."

Now Pacifa was interested. "How do you mean, Gaspar?"

Then, oddly, Gaspar backed off. "I'd rather think about it some more. Why don't we let Don have his look? We're ahead of schedule now, surely, and we can use the rest."

"Why don't we just find out?" Pacifa asked. "Melanie, are there more coordinates?"

"Yes," Melanie said faintly, with an apologetic look at Don.

"How many? You don't have to give the figures. Just tell us how many numbers you have."

"I suppose that's all right," Melanie agreed uncertainly.
"Three."

"And are they near or far?"

"I-I think they're far."

"So maybe we'd better get on with it, in case we have
more trouble," Pacifa said.

But now it was Eleph who demurred. "We must be fair.
I suggest we give Don two days, since we may not return
once we go on. Possibly later there will be things important
to the rest of us, and the Golden Rule—"

Pacifa threw up her hands, literally. "They talk about
women changing their minds!"

"But it will be nice to relax," Melanie said. In that she
spoke for them all.

The city was huge. Don and Gaspar rode for miles along
patterns suggesting wide boulevards and rubble-clogged
streets though their tires encountered only the rolling
sea-floor of the phase world. Everywhere they passed the
ruins of what might have been ancient monuments and
colossal buildings.

Don shook his head, amazed at the remaining grandeur.
"These may seem like mere wreckages to you, but to me
they're foundations. I'm beginning to see the structures they
supported. They're inherent. I—"

"No, I'm impressed too," Gaspar said. "On a couple of
levels."

"You mean you're getting interested in archaeology?"

"No such luck. My interest is geological and practical."

"Geological?" Don asked, surprised. "Look at this: a
corbelled arch. See how the columns project sideways, with
a capstone across? Not a true arch; I don't think that was
known in the New World. What has this to do with
geology?"

"Think about it and you'll see."

Don shook his head, suspecting Gaspar of mocking him. "I *am* thinking about it. You can see how this is one of several arches that formed a pattern. See those broken columns there, and the mounds across this court. This silt hides them, but obviously these were entrances to a royal garden or amphitheater. Maybe an outrider to a palace. Can't you visualize it rising around us, perhaps decorated with splendid murals?"

"Oh, some," Gaspar said tolerantly. "But let me show you my vision. We really are riding on a different world, and why we can't see it bothers me more and more. Because if these ruins were in our phase, we'd be able to walk on them and bang into them. We thought only the life was different, because it moves, but the buildings are different too. This proves it. It's the first time we've been able to pass through stone."

"No, there was that counterweight stone in the chasm," Don said. "But I see what you mean. There never was any question, was there? How can there be a city without life, and how can there be life with no real air or water?"

"It wasn't obvious to me until I saw this city," Gaspar said. "These worlds are awfully close. Remember how we rode across the abyssal plain?"

"Sure. But that has nothing to do with—"

"No? How can you form a sedimentary flat—without water? Without erosion and settling? And that canyon—if water didn't cut it in this phase world, what did?"

Don was stunned. "You're right! Our world is water-formed, and the phase world duplicates it. There *has* to be water here. And air. We rode over those coral reefs, and there wouldn't be any coral without—"

"So if there was water in our phase world, what happened to it?" Gaspar asked. "And the life. Things certainly changed, and not very long ago, geologically. That's convenient for us, but alarming.''

"Yes." Don tried to visualize how a world might be deprived of air and water in one quiet operation, with inert nitrogen substituted for both, and could not. "H-how long ago?"

"Within the past hundred thousand years, I'd say. But not within the past six thousand."

"W-why not *one* year ago?"

"Because then this city would be in the phase world too," Gaspar said. "Assuming the history of this world was as similar to our own as it seems. And this city dates from 4000 B.C.—six thousand years ago."

"Y-you're guessing! Y-you're no archaeologist."

"It wasn't built under water, was it?" Gaspar demanded, waiting for Don's reluctant nod. "It was built on land. No earthquake sank it, or it would have been shaken apart, instead of just weathered and buried, right? So the water came in slowly—and that means the end of the ice age. The level didn't stabilize until about five thousand years ago, so this must be older."

There it was: the obvious situation that Don's mind had balked at. A fine city, six thousand years old. "B-but then it c-can't be Dzi-Dzi—"

"No, of course not. This is a good twenty miles out from the present shore, and Dzibilchaltun was onshore or inshore. This city was submerged before the Mayans even appeared in the Yucatan."

And Dzibilchaltun was now inshore, Don remembered. The shoreline had changed, in effect pushing it inland. He had gotten it reversed, thinking the ruins would be out under the sea instead of inland, as the shore silted up. The revelation was so vast that it threw him into a new mental framework, and his stuttering stopped. "You're right! Who could have built it?"

"You're the archaeologist. Pretty nice material for a scholarly paper, eh?"

"But this must predate Egyptian and Sumerian civilization! Nothing in the Old World has this level—"

"So?"

Don shook his head. It was not credible that the American Indians could have built elegant cities before the Mesopotamians. But how could he argue that fine point with a skeptical geologist?

Pacifa had been sure there was something about this region. She had been right. Don had been misled by his blind assumption that this was Dzibilchaltun and his confusion about his assignment, as a Minoan specialist, to a Mayan region. A Mayan specialist would have known instantly that this was not Dzibilchaltun, but would have been no better off. In fact, there might be no archaeologist in the world really qualified to excavate these phenomenal ruins.

Nice material for a scholarly paper, yes. Schliemann had discovered his Troy, Bibby his Dilmun, Mellaart his Catal Huyuk. Would Don Kestle join these illustrious leaders? No, that was a foolish dream. The credit belonged to whoever had come across the city first—or to whoever actually excavated it and unraveled its marvelous secrets. Don was only a visitor, here to look and sigh.

Gaspar was watching him. "What would you give to bring a competent crew here, in the real world?"

"My soul."

Gaspar nodded understandingly and moved on.

The street they were on became narrow and crooked. It was as if they were entering a denser, older inner city. Large structures remained, but they were set much closer together.

"Hey—steps," Gaspar said.

He was right. Their street had become a walkway, with twenty or thirty broad steps, each about thirty feet from side to side, fashioned of—what? Fine marble? He could not tell through the smothering sediment. They led up to the remains of a labyrinthine palace. Don made out the shells of what must have been spacious, shady courts, with elegantly drained lavatories. The few standing columns were tapered downwards, narrower at the base than the apex.

"Typical Minoan architecture," Don murmured professionally.

"What?" Gaspar asked sharply.

"The hygienic sanitary facilities," Don explained. "The Cretans were virtually alone in the ancient world in their fastidious insistence on personal cleanliness. They had the most sophisticated system of water supplies and drainage, with pipes designed on correct hydraulic principles. See, that's the fundament of a flush toilet, I'm sure, even through the silt. The configuration—"

"What kind of architecture?" Gaspar repeated.

"Minoan, of course. I've seen many examples of—" Don stopped. "Minoan! What am I saying? *Mayan!* I mean—"

"You sounded as if you knew, just as clearly as I know metamorphic from igneous."

"Ridiculous! I'm just used to saying—" But he had to stop again. "Damn it, these *are* Minoan configurations, essentially. I don't care how crazy it is. This is my specialty."

"I don't see that it's crazy," Gaspar said. "When did your Minoan civilization develop?"

"About three thousand B.C., or a little later. They appeared suddenly; they must have had a high culture

before they came to Crete. But we have no tangible
evidence of them before; it's just conjecture.''

"So let's say the waters encroached here after 4000
B.C.,'' Gaspar continued carefully. "It was slow but sure.
So wherever they were, they had to move, and they didn't
like the barbarian mainland, so they went to Crete and set up
shop there.''

Don stared at him. "You mean to suggest—they were
here? They crossed the Atlantic?" Don shook his head,
bemused. "Even if—no, they would have chosen a closer
island. Like Cuba.''

"Too big. They wanted something the size of Crete.''

"Jamaica, then. Why didn't they move to Jamaica?''

Gaspar shrugged. "Got me there. But there must have
been some connection. Or could the architecture be coincidental?''

"It must be,'' Don said. "Crete is six thousand miles
from here by water, and even today that's a fair piece. For
an Amerind canoe—''

"How about the other way, then? Maybe your Minoans
developed earlier than you think. Two thousand years
earlier. Maybe *their* main cities were submerged, so most of
them set up colonies elsewhere. They had ships, didn't
they? They could sail the oceans?''

"They were the leading maritime culture of the ancient
world,'' Don said warmly. "The Phoenicians developed
only after the Minoan civilization perished—and the early
Phoenicians were afraid to lose sight of land, because they
couldn't navigate by the stars. The Minoans were true
sea-voyagers.''

"Just a moment. If the Minoans were so strong, what
brought them down? Maybe *there's* our real city-builder!''

"Two things,'' Don said. "There was the explosion of

the volcanic island of Thera, which devastated Crete, leveled their palaces and probably wiped out their fleet. It was one of the worst eruptions known to man, many times as powerful as Krakatoa. It literally buried Crete in ash. But that was not the end; they did rebuild. But they needed an enormous supply of wood, for their ships and buildings, and the rebuilding used it up at a faster rate. Their civilization flourished even more after the eruption than before it, but in the end they ran out of wood and had to leave the island. Lesser cultures, with virgin forests, expanded to take their place.''

"Oh. Well, back to the sea. I still think there could have been a connection. Didn't some guy cross from Egypt to America in a reed craft?"

"That was Thor Heyerdahl. Yes, he reconstructed an Egyptian papyrus vessel and crossed the Atlantic in 1970, demonstrating that it could have been done in ancient times. He had a similar venture some years before, crossing from South America to the Polynesian Islands. The Kon-Tiki.''

"Right. He discovered new species of fish and had an adventure with a whale shark."

"But he knew what he was doing, or thought he knew. Even so, it was an extremely risky business. The Egyptians would hardly have set out voluntarily to cross the Atlantic in a sinking reed craft.''

"Maybe they didn't," Gaspar said. "Maybe they set out to reach some port on the western coast of Africa, and were stormblown toward America. The prevailing winds and currents favor that, you know. If it's possible with a reed craft, it's more than possible with a full-fledged Minoan seaworthy ship.''

"In four or five thousand B.C.? The Minoans can't have had such good ships that far back.'' But Don was wondering, for it could have been the Palace of Knossos he saw here, with its tremendous inner court and interminable surrounding walls and passages and cubicles. The court was oblong, about fifty feet across and a hundred long, quite flat and completely walled in. Even through the rubble he could make out the enormous complexity of the surrounding corridors, stairs, terraces, and halls, that crisscrossed and dead-ended and right-angled bewilderingly. A stranger would soon have been lost within the living building.

"What a maze," Gaspar remarked.

"That's the point," Don said. "According to legend, Theseus fought the bull-man, the Minotaur, within just such a labyrinth. Then he needed help finding his way out. God, I wish I could trench this."

"Do what to what?"

"Dig a trench. Excavate. The vast majority of artifacts are well buried in silt. But if I could cut a trench through the middle—"

"You can't do that," Gaspar said.

"I know. That's the frustrating thing about this phaseout. My inability to interact with the substance of the world when I need to. But if I could dig, I'd mark off the most promising mound here, and excavate a narrow trench across it, very carefully, and note the exact position of every artifact I located. I'd make the sides exactly vertical and smooth them off so I could observe the precise layering, because there are apt to be a number of layers of occupation—"

"You don't understand, Don! You can't do that here. Even phased in. You can't dig a trench underwater. Not the kind you want."

"Why not? Are there laws against it?"

"The law of nature. Start digging, and your trench will

immediately fill in from the sides. Silt doesn't pack the way dirt does on land; it's always partly in suspension. Touch it and you stir up a cloud of stuff so that you can't see. You get nowhere."

Don looked at him, appalled. "But how can an archaeologist excavate?"

"Not the way you do it on land. You have to suck up the sludge, then let the water clear, and see what you have."

Don sighed. "It's unnatural."

"But I'll bet we can find you some artifacts right now."

"F-forget it," Don said with disgust. He had glimpsed marvelous visions, but in the end he was impotent.

"I'm not joking. Consider: when you grab a fish, you feel the bones, right? Because they're just a bit more rigid than flesh. Well, what are your artifacts made from?"

"Anything is an artifact. Pottery, statuary—"

"Anything made of gold?"

"Yes, of course. Much of the finest Minoan handiwork—"

"Gold has a density of about twenty-two times that of water. You could almost pick it up through the phase, couldn't you?"

"I suppose I could. But—"

"While this rock must be no more than four or five times as dense as water. And the silt is little thicker. So—"

"So I could feel the gold under the silt!" Don exclaimed.

"Of course you couldn't actually move it. But you could get a pretty good idea of its shape. That would help, wouldn't it?"

"Yes!" Don cried.

"So why don't we get up a team of five tomorrow and feel through a likely spot? Maybe we'll find something to unriddle Atlantis."

* * *

"Why is it so important to explore this city?" Melanie inquired when they got back together. She had spent her day resting, and looked refreshed. "I heard you say it was six thousand years old, but you can't really see it, under all that mud. Or do anything, because of the phase. So it's all sort of pointless, isn't it, holding up the party?"

For a moment Don was irritated. But he realized that it was an honest question. How could she comprehend the drive of archaeological zeal? It was not enough to claim that a mountain had to be climbed merely because it was there; a more rational answer was required. But Don's head was spinning with the irrational notions forced upon him during the day: a city with apparent Minoan affinities that predated the known Minoan culture by a thousand years or more. A mysterious alternate world, Earth's almost perfect duplicate, except that it had lived and then died. Recently. Geologically. His mind still balked at such concepts. And she wanted to know why he had to investigate this city! What answer could he give her?

"Hey, are you doing it to *me*, now?" Melanie asked, smiling. "The silent treatment?"

Don had to laugh, really appreciating for the first time the kind of mood that dictated silence as the best answer. In a year he might explain it all to her, if ever. Had she felt that way about her autographs, that first time she had hit him with a silence? If so, he had been a boor.

"Why do you collect autographs?" he asked.

"Uh-oh. You mean it's that way?"

He didn't answer.

"Well, all right, then. I guess I asked for it." She took a breath. "As I remember, you said something to the effect that you were more interested in what an author said, and that autographs and such were relatively unimportant. But books are printed by a very mechanical process, and in such a way that one must accept on simple faith that they are written by any one particular person at all. Not that all books are, of course. But we are used to dealing with particular individuals, and it seems somehow proper that a book should have been written by an individual. But if we consider society to be a network of human relations, the believability of the existence of an 'author' back there somewhere becomes rather attenuated. Writing is in some sense a form of sharing. We can all sit at the feet of and listen to whomever we like. Sort of like the university lectures in France. Some of the lecturers have small audiences and some have very large audiences. There the important thing is passing the exams at the end of the four years or so of study, and attendance *per se* is not as important as it is in the system here. But we all long to be recognized for ourselves. To receive some token, however small, of the uniqueness of the relation between ourselves and the author. An autograph is one such token. It all seems to be a striving for affection and attention. For recognition of the uniqueness and value of the individual self. Readers and reviews give recognition to an author, although the relationship is sometimes painful. But authors in their turn give recognition to readers. By writing, of course—but also by standing still for pictures, smiling, saying things and autographing. The relationship between an author and his readers can be very much strained by the very large number of the latter. So—''

''Enough!'' Don exclaimed. ''You've made your point, I think. And I guess if it could be turned about, you've made mine too. Because the books I read, archaeologically, are the record of an entire culture, and the physical artifacts are like personal autographs that some living hand has shaped and used. When I study a city such as this one, even under the mud, I am relating to living human beings of the past, just as you relate to the author of a novel. That's very important to me. I can never actually come to know them better than this, though I long to. If I could actually *visit* that past—"

"Yes, I understand!" she said warmly. "I suppose it *is* the same. Now I see why you want to find a real artifact tomorrow. And I hope you do. I'll help you look."

Did that mean she had completed her period of considering their relationship? What was his own conclusion about it?

"You know, if you *could* visit the past," she remarked, "well, maybe it wouldn't mean so much."

She had surprised him again. "How can you say that? An actual look at—"

"Because I did visit a writer once. Not settling for just an autograph. If the parallel holds—"

"You-you visited the past, in effect?" He was intrigued. They had had a breakthrough in mutual understanding; was another on the way?

Then he thought: was that when she took the pills?

"I had been hinting to Mother now and then that I would like to go on a trip," she said blithely. "Partly to make a pilgrimage to the ocean—that was before I came to Miami on my own—and partly to see something, some place, besides home. I guess I just get the urge to travel a little, every now and then. Maybe expecting to find something better on the other side of the mountain. If I could afford it I would travel around the world a few times, I am sure. But the thing that most immediately precipitated my trip was reading Shirley MacLaine's *Don't Fall Off the Mountain.* Have you—?"

"No, I never heard of it," Don said. Where did she dig up these obscure books?

"Oh. Well, for one thing it made me jealous. For another it is a tribute to the admissibility of a woman wandering around on her own. The voices of conformity sound strongly in my head, and to some extent I live in fear." She paused again. "I shouldn't be saying this."

"I shouldn't be listening," Don said comfortably. "Go on."

"I have always been somewhat of a disappointment to my mother," she continued faintly. "I mean, not just because of the hair. Because she always wanted someone who was level headed. So I try to pretend to be. And quite frankly it is a very painful pretense. Somehow I have learned, rightly or wrongly, to keep silent on many kinds of things."

Was he about to wish that she had kept silent on this? Here he was getting jealous of someone she had visited before he ever met her. But maybe that was a sign: why should he feel that way, unless he cared about her?

"Anyway," she continued after a moment, "I went to visit this writer. He'd published a couple of novels I liked, and there'd been some correspondence. Nothing much—I don't mean to make it sound like more than it is—just some fan letters and a polite acknowledgment. I sent him clippings, too. That sort of thing."

She valued an autograph as a personal touch. How did the things she sent to the writer relate? Did they make the personal touch mutual?

"So when I decided to meet him, one of my reasons was simple curiosity. To see if he looked anything like my mental picture of him. So I glued on my wig and went."

And she took pills, just in case. Damn her!

"And you know, he did," she said. "Close enough."

Don would have hit her with a silence, had he not already been silent.

"Not that it made a great deal of difference. What he looked like, I mean. At least I had a better image to orient on when I thought of him. I have been meeting some people in the flesh always, and some people always through the medium of the written word, and the curiosity is about the similarities or dissonances between the possible views."

"Now you're meeting people under the ocean."

"Yes. I like being with you, Don. I've thought about it, and I like it. Even if it doesn't last." She met his gaze, and smiled.

Suddenly Don regretted his silent objects. She wanted to be with him! Had she brought her pills? But he couldn't say that. "How did your visit go? W-with the writer?"

"Oh, it was nothing, really. That's why I used it as an example. He'd come out with opinions—that's what writers do, you know—and I'd be silent. You know."

"Yes." *Good.* He was still jealous of that writer, and wished the man ill. Yet he remained quite curious about the event.

"I talked with his wife, too. And I played with his little girl. She was about four. She liked to climb. On people. I thought he might invite me to stay to supper, but he didn't. He was locked up in his family. So I took some pictures and went home. It was raining."

So the writer had been married, with a child. Don had visualized a lecherous bachelor. Now he felt ashamed. "I see," he said, because he had to say something. A silence at this point could give him away.

"So that's what I mean," Melanie said. "Really, that writer was just another person, in person. I wouldn't have known he had written those novels, just by meeting him. I can't say it was a disappointment. I mean, people are what they are. But it wasn't exactly a revelation, either.''

''So you think that if I traveled into the archaeological past, it might be like that,'' Don said musingly. ''Mundane. I wonder.''

Melanie nodded. Then she rummaged in her pack and pulled out her wig. She put it on, working it carefully into place and pressing it down so that it stayed.

''You look strange,'' Don said.

''Thank you.''

Apparently she had made her point, and now was satisfied to resume the illusion.

They settled into sleep.

''I'm no historian or archaeologist,'' Eleph said as he walked his bicycle through the waist-deep silt of what Don hoped was a temple storeroom. ''But I seem to remember something about a unique Indian tribe in North America, racially and linguistically distinct from the norm, with a legend of arrival from the east. Do you suppose they could have—?''

''Oh, yes,'' Don said, sweeping his hand through the slight resistance of the mud. ''I remember now. The Yuchis. They wound up in Oklahoma, I think. From Georgia. But we can hardly rely on such scant evidence as legends. We'd have to believe that some peoples descended from the sun, and others from human miscegenation with animals.''

''Well, the sun *is* the ultimate source of our life,'' Pacifa said. ''A legend could reflect this. And man, paleontologically, does derive from the animal.''

''That's still a long way from making sense of our expedition,'' Don said, and they laughed.

Eleph had wandered into another chamber. ''Don, would you check this? Possibly a blade.''

Don got over there, wading through waist-deep stone-work, and Melanie followed him. She still looked odd in her hair, as if it were a pointless affectation. There was no question now: he could take it or leave it. It was Melanie herself he cared about.

There was a blade: large and curved. It tapered into a narrow stem, then expanded again. There was a swelling in the middle. "That's a double axe!" Don exclaimed, hardly believing it. "A golden decorated double axe!"

Eleph looked pleased. "That is significant, archaeologically?"

Don kept running his fingers through the hidden pattern, his arms elbow-deep in the visible muck. "It's the labrys, the double axe of Minoan Crete. Our word labyrinth derives from it. It's one of the religious symbols."

"So this is a Minoan city," Gaspar said.

Don shook his head. "I told you, the first typical Minoan palace was built after 2000 B.C. This predates it by two millennia."

"But that architectural ability had to come from somewhere," Gaspar said. "It didn't slowly evolve on Crete, you said."

"Yes, it seems to have emerged full-blown on Crete," Don agreed. "But two thousand years—!"

"Perfectly mundane, I'm sure," Melanie murmured.

"Is this city really that old?" Eleph inquired. "Isn't this one of the fracture zones? It could have subsided."

"Not really," Gaspar said. "Continental drift seems to be occurring in six major plates and a few minor ones, with the midoceanic ridges and trenches marking the fringes. The Puerto Rico and Cayman trenches represent one such fringe, but it's relatively inactive now. That's several hundred miles from here, anyway."

"But that's not far at all, geologically, is it?" Eleph persisted.

"Far enough." It was a matter of opinion, and Gaspar was not about to give way. But Don recognized it as a reasonable alternative: if subsidence rather than a rising ocean level had submerged this city, the date of its demise could be much more recent. That made a great deal more sense, archaeologically.

Don and Eleph and Melanie spent some time searching the storeroom for more objects of gold, but found only three small cups. Only? They were fabulous too. They were very thin, but had pictures on the sides in high relief. Don licked his fingers repeatedly to make them tender, trying to pick up every detail by touch. If only he were able to *see!* He was tempted to ask for Eleph's threads and balloons, to haul this up out of the muck and into view. But he didn't want to disturb it; that could ruin its seeming authenticity when a real archaeological crew came here.

The first cup had people marching in a procession around the sides. One figure seemed to be carrying a lute, another a small calf, and the others unidentifiable objects. The second cup had the figure of a man and a tree and some animals, perhaps cattle. The man seemed to be holding one of the cattle by a rope tied to its back leg.

But it was the third cup that astonished Don. It had two men performing acrobatics with bulls. Could Don's imagination be leading his fingers?

"Melanie, I want you to feel this," he said. He guided her hand to the hidden cup. "Can you make out the embossed picture?"

She concentrated. "One animal, a cow—no, bull. A man being thrown from its back. Another man holding on to the bull's horns. Something like that."

Confirmation! Their readings of the illustrations on the

cups could be grossly mistaken, but even so, they represented stronger evidence of the city's association with the Minoan culture. The ancient traders of Crete, or of the culture preceding it, *had* crossed the Atlantic!

CHAPTER 9

GLOWCLOUD

Proxy 5–12–5–16–8: Attention.
Acknowledging.
Status?
The group has encountered the evidence of the lost city, and begun to appreciate its nature. This has taken the members a significant step toward melding, though they are not aware of it.
What evidence is there for this?
They elected to delay two days to provide time to explore it, though this exploration benefits only one of their specialties. They worked together in harmony, making discoveries cooperatively and discussing them. And they are starting to care for each other on a personal basis.
How so?
The older and younger women are deepening a relationship similar to that of mother and daughter. The young woman and young man are developing a romantic attachment.
They are having an affair?
No. But she put on her hair.
Proxy, you have lost us.
The young woman is bald. She has been rejected in the

167

past when this was discovered, so is introspective and tends to be diffident about commitments beyond the superficial. She removed her wig so as to cause any rejection by this group to occur at the outset. When the group, and particularly the man, accepted her, she restored the wig. It has become cosmetic rather than substantive. She is now ready to make a romantic commitment.

We must defer to your judgment in this respect. When will you reveal the mission?

After the remaining two challenges have been navigated. They are sufficiently remarkable to cause serious reflection by the group. If it melds instead of breaking up, then it will be ready to handle the reality.

We hope you are correct.

"Eighty-eight degrees west, fifteen degrees north, approximately," Melanie said.

Gaspar worked it out. "Gulf of Honduras."

"Closer to the trenches?" Eleph asked.

"Yes. Cayman. It projects southwest right into the Honduras. In fact there's a valley in the corner there on land, probably an extension. If we find any underwater cities *there,* I'll consider subsidence."

A passing reference to a passing difference of opinion. Yet it had a remarkable effect on Don as the party cycled on around the Yucatan peninsula. Gaspar was his friend, and Eleph an annoyance—but it was Eleph who had made the decisive suggestion that had given Don two days in the ruins, and Eleph who had found the *labrys* and cups. Those were perhaps the most significant New World artifacts ever, and they would make Don famous when he finished this mission and led a party to discover the city and them. Now it was Eleph who was pursuing the archaeological probabilities. Eleph was not only doing Don favors, he was demonstrating the more resilient intellect.

No, that wasn't fair. Gaspar had worked out geological prospects that were as significant as the archaeological ones. Gaspar certainly had preoccupations of his own. Both men were more important to Don's interests than he had thought at first.

"Maybe we are after all heading down to that dinosaur crater," Don said.

"Let me tell you, that would give me the same thrill you just got," Gaspar said. "But it's still a long way there, and I won't hope until I see its coordinates."

They decided to skirt the eastern Yucatan close to shore. Gaspar said the typical depth of this region was five hundred fathoms—three thousand feet, over half a mile— extending almost to the brink of land. They could travel this deep water safely, completely hidden from human perception. "But farther out it drops to twenty five hundred fathoms," he cautioned.

"Two and a half miles!" Melanie exclaimed.

"That's nothing compared to the trench," Gaspar said, checking the map. "It reaches a depth of over five miles. But no point going way down, when we'll only have to climb out again. Anyway, the sea floor's irregular. Used to be a land bridge from Cuba to the Yucatan."

The others were glad to agree about keeping to moderate depths. The climb from the abyssal plain to the continental shelf had worn them out, and only the two-day exploration of the city had allowed them to recover.

Even so, it wasn't easy. In places the continental slope was so steep it resembled a cliff rising to their right, forcing them not only to walk, but to rope themselves together, just in case. Don knew that if they could only see it clearly, it would be the most impressive mountain any of them had experienced.

"That's the trouble," Pacifa remarked, affecting distress. "Here I'm supposed to survey potential scenic routes—and they aren't scenic. It doesn't do a tourist much good to know that he's passing near the most remarkable view, only it's invisible."

Don had grown accustomed to the continuing night of the deeps, and to the ocean bottom animals. But there were surprises yet. One day they bore down on a giant squid, who was so startled that it emitted a cloud of glowing ink and disappeared. That horrified Don, for some reason that he decided was more instinctive than rational.

"Makes sense," Gaspar said. "Where there's light, darkness conceals, so the inkfish makes it dark. But where it's dark, maybe light conceals."

"Pretty smart," Don agreed, shuddering as that ghostlike nimbus drifted through him. Melanie closed her eyes so that she couldn't see it, which was perhaps a better reaction.

"They are smart," Gaspar said. "Cleverest animals in the ocean."

"Except for the dolphins?" Pacifa asked.

"I wouldn't except the dolphins," Gaspar said, getting that stubborn tone again. It seemed harder than ever to avoid this attitude. "Everybody talks about them, but what are dolphins, really? Friendly mammals. Overrated."

"Don't they help ships?" Pacifa demanded. "Imitate human sounds? Do tricks?"

"So do birds," Gaspar said. "I don't despise the dolphin or the other intelligent cetaceans. But I think we'd profit more by studying the squid. He's more versatile, and as I said, probably smarter."

"Well, we have a good chance now," Pacifa said. "Old Glowcloud is back."

"I'm not surprised," Gaspar said. "They're curious creatures. See, his skin is green. I think that's his curiosity color."

"Don't tell me they're chameleons!" Melanie said, becoming interested.

"A chameleon is unworthy of the name, compared to this. Here, I'll show you." Gaspar rode up to the slowly moving squid and waved his arms violently.

The mollusk turned white and jetted away, backwards. The color shift was so sudden and complete that the other four of them gaped. One moment the squid was green; the next, pale watery white.

"How—?" Melanie asked, amazed.

"There isn't any light down here, normally," Eleph said. "Why should it change color?"

"Squids are versatile," Gaspar said with satisfaction. "They inhabit all levels. Probably this one has fed in surface waters at another season. And of course there are some natural sources of light. Anyway, it has different color pigments in tiny sacs all over its skin. Muscles attach to elastic walls, opening these sacs, pulling them into star shaped patches of color. There are several layers, so the squid can blend colors like paints. Because the effect is muscular, not chemical, it happens instantly, with every change of mood. Hey, he's back again."

The squid was swimming tentacles-first, slowly flapping broad fins near its rear. Don tried to conceal his automatic apprehension. It was hard to tell how long the creature was because Don didn't know where to measure from, but the tentacles seemed to be twelve or fifteen feet from base to tip. The body was now light green.

"Watch," Gaspar cried, and charged it again.

"Don't tease it!" Melanie cried, her fear of the monster becoming sympathy. But she was too late.

This time the squid did not blanch or retreat. Black stripes flickered over its body. Its tentacles reached forward in a mass and grabbed at Gaspar, who was of course untouched.

"Octopi are timid," Gaspar said. "But squid are bold, and the larger they are, the fiercer. The biggest ones will fight small whales. I'd never try this in real life."

It looked none too safe even in phase. Startled at the lack of contact, the squid flashed black spots and grabbed again. It brought one huge eye to bear, trying to comprehend this thing that it could see but could not hold. It moved up and opened its massive, horrible parrot beak to take a bite. When this also failed, it turned reddish brown and waved its tentacles angrily.

"It's furious," Melanie said. "Justifiably."

Gaspar laughed. Then the squid quit. It faded to a neutral gray and jetted away smoothly, its long arms trailing behind.

"See, he learns from experience, and controls his emotions," Gaspar said with a certain pride. He had evidently decided the creature was male. "He won't try to grab me again, you can be sure."

But to Don it was macabre sport. Had they been on the same plane of existence, the monster could have devoured them all.

They rode on, but several hours later Glowcloud was back. He checked each rider over, refusing to be dissuaded by shouts or action. Don was irrationally terrified, and even Pacifa looked quite uncomfortable as the tentacles passed through her. But Eleph had the most reason to take evasive action, because of his half-phased thread and balloons. If the squid discovered these, he would have leverage, and would surely use it.

Perhaps to forestall this, Melanie nerved herself and tried to distract Glowcloud. "Hello, you gorgeous monster," she said, trying to pet a tentacle. "How many colors can you make, when you feel artistic?"

The squid's reactions were extraordinarily rapid, and his manner disquietingly purposeful. He surely wanted to understand the nature of these little intruders, so as to consume them, and he intended to keep after them until he had solved the riddle.

In fact, Glowcloud followed them. He would disappear for hours, but always reappear, no matter how rapidly they moved. His water-jetting mode of swimming was beautifully effective, and he could—and did—swim rings around them. Perhaps it was imagination, but the squid did seem to prefer the company of Melanie, and she was definitely warming to him. Was it because Glowcloud was hairless?

"Beauty and the beast," Pacifa remarked.

Melanie, flustered, demurred. "I'm no—"

"*He's* the beauty," Pacifa clarified with a smile. "Look at that color."

"B-but you are too," Don added. Melanie seemed not to hear.

"Good thing Glowcloud's not one of the large ones," Gaspar said merrily. "They grow up to over fifty feet, with tentacles over thirty feet, and maybe much larger yet."

"In horror magazines," Eleph muttered, again avoiding the creature's advances.

"There's pretty good evidence," Gaspar insisted. "Sperm whales like to eat squid, and tentacles over forty feet long were found in a whale once. That squid must have weighed over forty tons, alive. But even that's small compared to the ones that get away."

"From the sperm whales?" Eleph demanded. "How can you judge what the whale doesn't catch?"

"Maybe they tell squid stories," Melanie suggested.

"By the sucker marks," Gaspar said. "You see the

suckers on Glowcloud, here? All down his arms? Well, when a whale goes after a big squid, that squid fights, and his suckers make imprints on the whale's hide. A fifty footer leaves scars four inches across. But some sperm whales have been caught with scars eighteen inches across.''

"Talk of the kraken!" Pacifa exclaimed, awed.

"They *do* tell stories," Melanie said, tittering. " 'Hey, Joe, you should have seen the sucker that got away!' ''

"If the ratio holds true," Eleph said, "eighteen inch suckers would indicate a squid over two hundred feet long, massing over a thousand tons. That would be the largest creature ever to inhabit our world."

Gaspar shrugged. "The ocean has secrets yet."

All of which did not make them feel easier about Glowcloud. But the squid was gone again, rocketing smoothly into the murk. Any notion any of them might have had about clumsiness of such creatures had been abolished. Octopi might be awkward and slow when traveling, but squid were sleek and fast.

They rode on down a narrowing valley, breathing hard.

"I can't catch my breath," Pacifa complained. "Eleph, will you check the field generator on my bike?"

They stopped, and Eleph checked. Don also felt out of breath, and Gaspar's chest was pumping. Melanie's bosom was heaving in a manner Don would have found interesting at another time.

"The field is in order," Eleph said. "But I must admit—"

"Uh-oh," Gaspar said. "I know. We're in a valley that's low on oxygen. Some of these exist in the ocean, if the water doesn't circulate enough. See—almost no life around here. Turn and go back in a hurry."

They retreated with alacrity, but the breathing did not

improve. Even if there were more oxygen in the water, the field would take time to phase it through.

"Up!" Gaspar said. "Got to get out of the trough, into richer water."

"The map shows a steep rise to your west, as I remember," Melanie said, trying to help.

"Thanks!" Gaspar bore west immediately. "The rest of you—keep alert for Glowcloud. Where he is, there's oxygen, sure."

They found the rise, but it was too steep to climb. Pacifa reeled visibly, the first sign of physical weakness she had shown, and Eleph was almost collapsed over his handlebars. Don felt like lying down and sleeping, and knew he dared not.

"Glowcloud—where are you?" Melanie gasped.

Gaspar found a discontinuity in the impassible face of the cliff, and scrambled up, hauling his bicycle along. The others followed, helping each other up. This was mountain climbing, for the path was narrow and the walls bare. Still there was little life.

On they slogged. When Melanie seemed about to fall, just ahead of him, Don simply put the top of his head against her rear and pushed, and she made it to the next ledge. This was no place for niceties. He lost track of the others, concentrating on getting himself and Melanie to the higher ground.

A tentacle passed through his face. Don blinked—then shouted. "Glowcloud! Glowcloud! He's here!" Indeed, it was almost as though the giant squid were trying to pull Melanie upward. They struggled a few more feet, until their heads were buried within the body of the monster, and collapsed. Oxygen!

When they resumed the climb they were roped again. This time there was no question of the necessity; a misstep could mean a fall of hundreds of feet. Where the way became narrow, they anchored front and rear while the middle proceeded. Gaspar was the front, Pacifa the rear, with Eleph, Melanie and Don not ashamed to admit their incompetence in the center.

And it was not so bad. Much of the climb was gentle, and some was downhill, for the continental slope was by no means regular. They were neither rushed nor hungry now, and they had become experienced at this sort of thing. Just so long as there was some current in the water, and some animal life.

"I heard that," Melanie said during one of their pauses for anchorage. "You think I'm beautiful?"

It took Don a moment to orient. She was referring to the "Beauty and the Beast" exchange. "Yes."

"Physically?"

"Th-that too."

She looked startled, but pleased.

Then it was time to move the anchor along.

At the next stop Don looked around. "Where's Glow-cloud? Never thought I'd miss the sight of his ugly beak, but—"

"We're changing depth pretty rapidly," Gaspar said. "Few creatures can handle substantial and rapid pressure differentials. We aren't being subjected to them, phased out, or we'd be in real trouble. By the time he adjusts, we'll be gone again."

"Too bad," Melanie said. "But not worth going back down into that deadly valley!"

Near the top—fifty fathoms—Gaspar gave a cry. "Hey! There's a cave."

There was. "We need a safe place to spend the night," Pacifa said. "Let's check it out. I don't want to roll off any ledges in my sleep."

Her given reason was spurious; she had no fear of ledges. She merely liked to explore. But so did the others. They were all adventurers, now that they had the means.

They moved in cautiously, Don staying close to Melanie, or perhaps the other way around. There was no concern about wildlife, of course, except to make sure that it was present, but a gap in the floor would be every bit as hazardous to them as to land dwellers in a land cave. They remained roped.

The passage wound about, going first up, then down. The floor was irregular, so that they would have to walk. Then the way opened into a large cavern.

"Stalactites!" Don exclaimed. "This was once a land cave!"

"Why not?" Gaspar called back. "You said yourself that the water receded this far during the ice age, and I agree."

"Stalactites," Eleph repeated. "They hang from the top?"

"And stalagmites rise from the floor," Don said. "Remember it mnemonically: C for ceiling, G for ground. Stalac, stalag."

"Strange they have not dissolved away," Eleph said.

"They may, in time. They must have been millions of years in the forming, while the sea has been here for only a few thousand."

"Was the sea level down for millions of years?"

"Well, no, but this cave could have been sealed off with air in it."

"Maybe cave men used it," Pacifa said half facetiously. "They cut this passage in, little dreaming that the sea would return."

"I'm not sure the Amerinds used caves," Don said. "Certainly, they did not paint on the walls the way the Reindeer People did in Europe."

"How do you know?" she asked.

"Well, they—" He stopped. "You know, I *don't* know! Maybe they did, at that."

"If habitable caves were available, they would have been stupid not to utilize them," Eleph said. "Man is not stupid."

"Man's an idiot," Pacifa retorted. "Look at what he's doing to the world!"

"I can only draw a parallel to the European situation," Don said. "Certainly caves were used there, from time to time—but not by all men, and seldom by civilized ones. There is evidence that many of the caves that were used, were not used for residence."

"What else would a cave be used for?" Eleph asked. "Storage?" He seemed to be fascinated by this region, though he evidently knew little about it.

"Religion. Or some similar ceremony. The golden age of stone age man was probably the Magdalenian culture, about fifteen thousand years ago. They hunted reindeer and other animals during the ice age, and used sympathetic magic to help overcome these creatures. They painted pictures of them on the walls and ceilings of deep grottoes, some of the finest naturalistic art ever rendered. But then the glaciers receded, the reindeer migrated north, and the Magdalenians declined."

"The glaciers," Gaspar said. "That was an ice age culture."

"You haven't been paying attention," Pacifa said.

"Very much an ice age culture," Don said sadly. "In some ways man's civilization was shaped by the ice. It gave him a real hurdle to overcome, for it overran his choicest residential areas and reshaped the land. To survive he had to develop clothing—"

"And that killed him," Melanie said. "It stopped the sun

from striking his skin, and Neanderthal man was wiped out by rickets, the Vitamin D deficiency disease.''

Don stopped short. ''Where did you hear that?''

''I read it somewhere. Isn't that what you were saying?''

''No. It may have been Cro-Magnon man who developed civilization as we know it, and he wore clothing too. We can assess its approximate coverage by noting the places where our own bodies lack heavy hair. We have light hair all over our bodies, of course. Possibly his skin was lighter, so that he could adapt better to the scant sunshine of the northern latitudes, but that alone could hardly have wiped out Neanderthal. He lived in the tropics as well, after all.''

''Ah, well,'' she said with cute resignation. ''But then what happened to Neanderthal man?''

''We're still not sure. He overlapped modern man by eighty thousand years or so, so it seems unlikely that he was conquered. There is evidence that Neanderthal was truly robust, physically, capable of feats that our champions can't match today. He had the same braincase and tools as Cro-Magnon. But it may have been his diet.''

''No Vitamin D enriched milk?''

Don had to laugh. ''Vitamin D isn't even a vitamin! No, he seems to have become a vegetarian, perhaps living on fruits and nuts. He may have driven Cro-Magnon man out of the good forests and forced him to become a scavenger, taking the leavings of hunting animals. Finally modern man became a hunter himself, his system adjusting with difficulty to the wholesale consumption of flesh. Then the climate changed and the dense forests shrank—and Neanderthal man was starved out, because he could not eat the foods of the savanna. It may be that he had never developed truly organized hunting techniques, and it was too late for him to change. When modern man did, he started hunting game species of animals to extinction—and perhaps used those same techniques on his longtime rival Neanderthal, exterminating him at last. Cro-Magnon man was better equipped to survive, being less specialized. It's a common theme, paleontologically.''

"You mean we're murderers?" Melanie asked, distressed.

"As Cain slew Abel, perhaps. It's all conjecture.''

"But the glaciers," Gaspar said again. "There's the connection.''

"Between Neanderthal and Cro-Magnon man?" Don asked.

"No, between the Minoans and the Mayans. Your finest cave culture was the result of the ice age. Well, the ice age was worldwide. Why couldn't there have been fine cave cultures over here in the Americas, too?"

"And when the world warmed up," Melanie added eagerly, "and the waters rose, those cultures didn't just expire, they went elsewhere. Maybe they kept their civilization alive for thousands of years, building great cities, until—''

"Hunter-gatherer societies do not build cities," Don said, laughing. "How many reindeer do you see roaming the streets of New York?"

"Well, small cities, then," she said. "Villages, maybe. Rome was not built in a —''

"Something strange ahead," Eleph said, and they broke off. This spared Don the onus of debating against more amateur theories of civilization.

Strange it was. A horizontal sheet of something crossed the entire top of the next cavern, cutting it off. The demarcation was so level and regular that it had to be artificial. A sheet of clear plastic?

"That's the surface!" Gaspar cried, laughing.

"At forty five fathoms?" Eleph demanded.

"An air pocket. Come on, we can ride up out of the water for a change."

But they couldn't. The surface was twenty feet above their heads, and the cavern walls were vertical. They could only look.

"Do you suppose there are cave paintings remaining in the dry portion?" Eleph asked.

"I doubt it," Don said. "But I'd sure like to look."

"We're wasting time," Gaspar said. "Let's find a place to set up our tents."

This callousness to archaeological potential irritated Don, but he knew Gaspar was right. The man wasn't really uninterested; he merely wasn't going to worry about reaching an inaccessible spot. He was being practical.

"Perhaps if we used the balloons," Eleph murmured.

"Yes!" Don agreed. It was becoming difficult to dislike the man.

Gaspar and Pacifa set up camp, anchoring the tents to the rising spires of old stalagmites. Don and Melanie and Eleph blew up balloons, waiting for them to achieve sufficient flotation. Working together, they inflated six balloons in somewhat over an hour, and hitched them to Don's bicycle. In time Don lurched to the surface and whipped his lamp around.

There was nothing. The walls were completely natural.

A small blind fish nosed up. "Get out of here!" Don shouted, bashing through it with one fist.

But the disappointment was minor, compared to what had been discovered before. As they settled down for the night, Melanie took his hand again. "But suppose you found a girl with real hair?" she murmured.

"What is hair?" he asked rhetorically. "It's just dead cells. It's superficial. I can take it or leave it, now."

"Can you? I think you should meet such a girl, and see."

He laughed. "Here?"

"Well, after the mission. Then you'll know."

She didn't want to be hurt. He understood that. He knew that if he met a pretty girl in the regular world he would be tongue-tied anyway. Part of the appeal of Melanie was that he had seen her shorn, and gotten to know her without romantic pressure, and now there could be romance, if she wanted it. Evidently she did want it, if she could only be sure of him. He had accepted her without hair, but that was only half way there. He had to show that he would not change his mind when he encountered a woman with body and hair. That he did not see her as a Neanderthal, to be discarded in favor of Modern. So it was necessary to play it through. Once she saw him with anyone else, she would know that hair had nothing to do with it, anymore.

In the morning they completed their preparations and moved out, single file. Don hated to leave this cave without exploring it more thoroughly, for the discussion of the evening before had taken hold of his fancy. Suppose man had lived here? This cave was three hundred feet below the present surface of the ocean. Its entrance could have been exposed only when the water was low enough—if, indeed, someone had not cut the passage into it, as Pacifa had suggested. Ludicrous, yet not impossible. Either way, that would have been 15,000 years ago, at the height of the ice age—the same time as the European Reindeer culture. A fantastic notion, but tempting.

Yet hardly more fantastic than the idea of a mighty city off the coast of the Yucatan, dating back perhaps six thousand years and containing Minoan artificats. But with the sea washing off any pictures that might have been on the walls, and the fish consuming any bones, and the sediment covering whatever remained, this quest was hopeless. If only he had the facilities to investigate thoroughly!

Don sighed. That was the nature of archaeology. The breakthroughs were wonderful, but most of it came to nothing significant. Some other man would have to discover the wonders of pre-Mayan cave cultures, if any were to be found.

The trip along the continental shallows was more difficult than Don had anticipated. While the Yucatan was hardly a modern center of commerce, it was populated. Small boats plied its waters, fishing and hauling. Several times the cyclists had to hide, to prevent possible discovery. But the shelf here was so narrow that they had either to remain quite close to shore, or negotiate the descending slope to rejoin Glowcloud and perhaps the valley of death.

It was hot. Maybe the ambient temperature was governed mainly by the converter and the nitrogen atmosphere of the phase world, but when Earth was warm, *Don* was warm. Their terrain was not smooth, and he sweated steadily with the exercise. So did Melanie; her blouse was plastered to her skin. He knew she would not appreciate him staring, so he tried not to. Hair? Who cared about hair!

The problem was that the mountainous inland features were duplicated near the water, forcing repeated gear-shifting and portages, with occasional use of the safety rope. At one point they actually had to cross overland in order to avoid an ocean canyon that would have forced an unreasonably long detour.

But they made it in good order to the third depot. There was plenty of food there, and spare wheels for their bicycles—most of which did not fit, since it had been presumed they would be in the better ten-speed machines that had supposedly been waiting at the first depot.

"Eighteen degrees, thirty minutes north latitude," Melanie said. "Seventy eight degrees, ten minutes west longitude."

"I don't know coordinates, but I know that's toward Cuba," Pacifa snorted.

"Maybe," Gaspar said, sounding disappointed. "It's not toward South America, for sure. Let me work it out. Eighteen, nineteen—no, that's Jamaica. Northern coast, I think."

"Port Royal!" Don exclaimed. "We're going to see Port Royal!"

"That doesn't sound like a stone age culture, or even an old Mayan city," Pacifa said.

"It isn't. Port Royal was an English town of the seventeenth century, notorious for its illicit trade and rich living. It suddenly sank beneath the sea, around 1690 I think. Its enemies thought it was divine retribution. But for my purpose a quick burial is much better than a slow decline, because all the common artifacts of daily existence remain."

"You archaeologists are ghoulish," Melanie said, smiling.

"I remember the story," Gaspar said. "That's a legitimate case of subsidence along the fault. It does happen. But wasn't Port Royal on the south of the island? We're going to the north of it."

"I don't remember," Don said, disappointed. "The New World just isn't my specialty. You're probably right."

"It's as if whoever set this up is teasing you," Melanie remarked. "Sending you close to something really important to you, then turning away."

"What would be the point of teasing us?" Gaspar asked.

"I don't know. I don't understand what's going on at all."

"You and the rest of us," Pacifa agreed.

"The spot is very near the trench, isn't it?" Eleph asked. "It may be several thousand fathoms down. What could be so important there?"

"Maybe an eight-thousand-year-old pre-Minoan city," Gaspar said with half a smile. "Complete with television sets."

Don did not deign to respond.

They proceeded. The great Cayman trench coincided almost exactly with the Honduras shoreline in this region, forcing them to hew to an even narrower margin than before. Here they could not avoid a canyon, so they used rope and balloons in combination and followed it down . . . and down.

"Just how far did the waters recede during the ice age?" Pacifa demanded.

"Three hundred feet," Don said. "Four hundred at the most."

"Do you realize that we are down to two hundred fathoms? Twelve hundred feet, and no sign of the end?"

"I can't explain it," Don said.

"Fortunately I can," Gaspar said. "You were right about the cutaway on the Yucatan shelf. But the really large canyons are below that level. Some go right to the ocean floor, three miles deep."

"How can they be formed, with the water always there?" Pacifa asked.

"Turbidity currents. A function of that same sediment you see all over the ocean floor. The large rivers deposit a lot of silt, and a lot remains suspended in the water. Periodically it builds up to the point where it must come down, especially when the motion of the river is lost within the mass of the sea. So it overturns, and the loaded water drops. That forms some pretty formidable currents—up to forty miles per hour. With that sort of motion, you can cut canyons anywhere. They still have trouble with undersea cables getting snapped that way. Any natural tremor can set off a mud slide, and once it starts, it's like an avalanche. That has a similar effect."

"Ocean currents and mud slides cut this?" Pacifa asked, gesturing about. "This is like the Grand Canyon!"

"Makes you respect mud, doesn't it," Gaspar said, smiling. "We'd better move on, because even in our phased-out state we could be in trouble if some such action occurred around us."

There was no argument, though Don was sure they would have to wait years for a mudslide. Why take any more of a risk than they had to? And suppose their passage did set off such a slide? He tried to suppress his nervousness.

They rode and hauled and climbed vigorously, searching for safer waters. But it was more than a hundred miles before there was room to diverge freely from the trench's edge. Even then there was not much improvement, because the sea floor became mountainous. Progress was slow.

"Maybe we should just drop down to the center of the trench," Pacifa suggested.

"I wouldn't," Gaspar said. "The trench is not your ordinary innocent sea floor. Remember what I said about the Bahamas platform?"

"No."

"How it filled in at the beginning of the great continental crackup? Well, the Puerto Rico-Cayman trench runs right under it, cutting off the bottom part. That makes it especially hazardous for us."

"You talked about the trench, but not about any platform," Pacifa said.

Melanie broke in. "You weren't there, Pacifa. That was just before you joined the party."

"Now wait a minute," Don protested. "Why should a

crack in the platform or under it or whatever—why should
that be bad for us? Worse than any other crack, I mean?''

''Because the great trenches of the ocean are not just
cracks. They are stress points of the globe. They are where
the spreading ocean floor pushes down under the land mass,
because it has nowhere else to go. They are in motion,
swallowing mountains. Such regions are deep and jagged,
and always the raw material for volcanism and earthquakes.''

''Volcanoes and earthquakes,'' Melanie said morosely.
''And I thought this trip might be fun.''

''I just don't see that,'' Pacifa argued. ''A volcano is an
eruption of lava and ash, while an earthquake is a shaking of
the ground. This is just some ground going slowly down,
you say. Maybe an inch a century?''

''I can't go into the whole of sea-floor spreading right
now,'' Gaspar said, exasperated.

''You don't need to. I know about the magma coming up
and pushing apart the sea floor and continents. There is
surely some violence there! But why should there be
earthquakes and volcanoes here at the other end?''

''Because when the leading edge of one plate collides
with another above a certain speed, one plunges under the
other to make room. It descends into the asthenosphere—
that is, deep down—and is destroyed by pressure and heat.
That impact and that action are responsible for both the
local quakes and the local volcanoes.''

''You are beginning to make sense,'' Pacifa admitted.
''Does that mean we'll get sucked into the crevice if we
aren't careful?''

Gaspar smiled. ''Unlikely. These are the processes of
many millions of years. Sea floor spreading occurs at the
rate of a few inches per year, average.''

''Inches a year,'' she said. ''That's certainly faster than

an inch a century. But you made it sound like a ravening maw."

"It is, geologically. A few inches is plenty, when you consider the masses of the material involved. The Caribbean is a twisted area, and the heart of that twist is that trench, because it is at right angles to the nominal direction of spreading. I think one of the Pacific plates has crossed over the continent and ridden sideways across the Atlantic plate. Now it's coming up against the Bahamas platform, which is a considerable mouthful even for this process. We don't know what we'll find down there."

"You really want to see it, don't you," Melanie said.

"Not as much as I want to see the dinosaur crater. But yes, the whole ocean is interesting, and this especially so."

"Just as Don wants to excavate New Atlantis on the Yucatan," Gaspar agreed. "But I don't want to travel the length of this crevasse. Better to make our next depot, then make forays from there at our convenience."

"So you won't be tempted to stop at every sexy outcropping on the way," Pacifa said. "I know the problem. All right, why not travel the rim to the next depot? Then we'll see."

"You are assuming that simple exploration is our mission," Eleph said. "I remind you that we do not yet know what we are getting into."

Pacifa nodded. "Good, grim point. Well, let's travel."

Easier said than done. The rim of Cayman was knifelike in places, with an overhang on one side and a precipice on the other, and cut into segments by transverse cracks yards or miles across. The rope and pulley were too tedious, so they kept the balloons inflated just under the necessary amount of air needed for full flotation, and added to them when a bad section had to be traversed. This was tedious, as the balloons had to be dragged at other times, making

progress extremely slow. But the terrain was so jagged they
had to take what precautions they could.

One section was terraced like a contour farm, the individual ridges seeming to continue indefinitely. They deflated the balloons and cycled along the broadest ledge,
making better time. Here too there were cracks, but most
were less than a yard across, and negotiable. Occasional
breaks in the wall gave access to the more regular ocean
floor beyond the trench—but that was such a wilderness of
crosshatched ridges that they stayed on the terrace. It was
somber and impressive and rather peaceful.

That peace was suddenly to end.

CHAPTER 10

DECOY

Proxy 5–12–5–16–8: Attention.
Acknowledging.
Status?
The party is approaching the next challenge. It is integrating well. I believe it will accept the mission.
Why not acquaint it with the mission now, in that case?
Because it will be more certain after the last two challenges. I do not wish to risk loss by premature presentation.
They still are not aware that one of them is a local government spy and another is an agent from another world?
They do not know. I will acquaint them with this information when the challenges are done. Then they should be ready for it.
Yet if they are ready now, and you delay, you risk the interference of some outside factor.
I believe this is a risk that must be taken. It seems slight at the moment.
Even a slight risk is unwise, if it is unnecessary.
I deem the risk of rejection at this point to be greater than the risk of random interference.
That is your assessment to make. Continue.

*   *   *

"What's that?" Melanie cried, alarmed.

They all looked. A light was coming through the water, floating over the abyss.

"That couldn't be Glowcloud," Pacifa said.

It was huge and bright, reminding Don of a Cyclops: a giant with a single glowing eye in its forehead. Fantasy, surely—but whatever was coming was surely trouble.

"That's not natural," Gaspar said. "That's—"

"A submarine!" Eleph cried. "Douse the lights!"

In a moment the five bicycle lamps were off. Now they could make out the big machine's outline: a monstrous barrel with small bulging ports and large fins. It was absolutely silent.

"Why no sound of engines?" Pacifa inquired from the darkness.

"Don't talk!" Eleph cried with dismay.

Too late. As they spoke, the great headlight rotated, orienting on the sound. The machine's listening devices were sophisticated, evidently distinguishing their faint noises from the background cacophony.

Don threw himself down and hauled his bicycle after him, seeking the cover of the nearest stone. Where was it? If only he had made a note before turning off his light!

The sub's beam swept near, splashing across the jagged rock and highlighting two stages of the terrace wall. Don saw to his relief that he was sheltered behind an upthrusting ledge, and was hidden from the sub. Melanie was almost behind him, similarly sheltered. Gaspar and Pacifa were not in sight, so must also have found concealment. But Eleph—

Eleph stood frozen, and the beam had already picked him out. Don cursed the man's ineptitude—then saw that Eleph was stranded on a narrow platform. He could not move without falling into the trench. It was the luck of the draw.

"Who are you?" Eleph shouted suddenly. "You're not native to these waters!"

Why was he calling attention to himself? Don was tempted to run over and haul the man back out of the light. But how could he manage it on his bicycle? That pause gave him time to realize the foolishness of such a gesture. He could only expose himself. And the sub could not actually harm Eleph, considering the phase.

"So you have found me!" Eleph continued, doing something with his bicycle. "But I'm going to lose you!" Then he pedaled on.

Now Don saw that Eleph had unhitched the safety rope. He was going off by himself!

That was it, of course. Eleph had been spotted, and knew it. He had nothing to lose, and might find out something that would help the others, while they stayed hidden. He was serving as a decoy, so that the main party could escape undiscovered. He had spoken aloud to cover Pacifa's blunder; the sub oriented on sound, and knew that *someone* was there.

This must be a foreign sub; an American one would not have been sneaking about silently. No—perhaps it was a bathyscaphe, a research diver, checking for life in the trench, quiet so as neither to disturb the fish nor to foul its own auditory receptors with mechanical noise. But Eleph had said it wasn't native, and Don had a feeling the man would not make a mistake about such a thing. Not with his military background.

Whatever the truth, Eleph had demonstrated intelligence and courage in a crisis, and perhaps self-sacrifice. How could they know the intention of that submarine? If it represented a foreign power, it might seek to eliminate anyone who saw it. It would have trouble doing anything directly to a man who was phased out, but if it managed to shove him into the trench, that would do it.

The spotlight followed the moving man, the sub gliding smoothly after, still silent. The decoy was working.

They waited for several minutes. Then Gaspar stood up. Don saw the glow of light from the man's covered lamp, and felt the tug of the rope. That was what Eleph had been doing: detaching himself from the rope, so he could travel alone. Don stood himself, and carefully walked his bike over.

The four of them met by that faint glow. Gaspar pointed back the way they had come, one finger limned against the headlight. Away from the sub.

They moved, quietly. Gaspar seemed to have a good memory for the terrain, for he proceeded with greater confidence in the dark than Don could have.

They diverged from the rim of the canyon at the first opportunity, climbing to the upper levels and thence through a mountain pass. Only when they were well clear of the great trench, concealed by myriad and labyrinthine projecting stones, did they stop to confer.

There were no recriminations. They all understood what Eleph had done. They had let him do it because there was no better choice. The less the enemy sub knew, assuming that it was hostile, the better off they were. They had to preserve their privacy for the sake of their as yet unknown mission. Perhaps it concerned—submarines.

"Suppose we split," Gaspar said. "Each look for him alone, keeping out of sight. He'll slip the sub all right; it can't touch him and can't possibly follow where he can go. But he'll probably lose himself in the process, and we can't use the whistle while the sub is near. So we'll have to locate him visually. Rough job."

"What about the radio?" Don asked. "We're all on the

same private circuit—'' He stopped, appalled. ''The radio! Can the sub intercept it?''

''I don't think so,'' Gaspar said. ''We're transmitting in the phase world, and it shouldn't cross over.''

''Light crosses over,'' Don said. ''Sound crosses over. How can we be sure the radio doesn't?''

''Good question,'' Melanie agreed.

''Eleph's the only one who can answer that,'' Gaspar said.

''And he's maintaining radio silence,'' Pacifa said, snapping off her radio. The others jumped to do the same.

Now they were cut off from their missing member. If anything happened to him, such as a fall into the chasm, they might never be able even to verify it. They had not been using the radios much, once all of them were together, but had known that they could not get truly separated as long as the radios were functional. Now Don felt a bit naked.

''What is a foreign sub doing here?'' Pacifa asked.

''When we know that,'' Gaspar replied slowly, ''we may know our mission. That's a deep-diver.'' He paused. ''Now suppose we meet here in four hours? We can't afford to get permanently separated.''

Don and Pacifa agreed, but Melanie looked doubtful.

Gaspar glanced at her. ''No offense, Mel, but maybe you shouldn't go alone. Why don't you go with Don?'' She nodded gratefully. The notion of being separated in the deeps evidently appalled her. She might have been emotionally isolated all of her life, but this was a rather special physical isolation. She lacked both the muscle of the men and the expertise of Pacifa, and with radio silence she would be even more alone.

They split up. Gaspar took the trench, because he was most familiar with its hazards. Pacifa took the encircling approach, because she could make the best time. She would be trying to intersect the trench ahead of Eleph, and work back. If Gaspar and Pacifa met, they would know that Eleph was not on the terraces. Don and Melanie took the mazelike periphery.

Four hours deadline: in his present toughened condition, Don might have done eighty miles in that time, on a decent level surface. But he would have to reserve half his time for the return, and the surface was anything but decent. His effective range—the most distant spot he could check—was probably about twenty miles. He would use up much of that winding about the interminable projections. It didn't matter; he wasn't going anywhere, he was searching for a lost man.

But with Melanie along, they could double the width of the search path. They could ride parallel, keeping each other in sight while extending their range. That would help not only in effectiveness, but because they were keeping each other company. Because Don didn't like the notion of being alone in this dangerous murky region either. It was indeed lonely, being alone. He understood the ocean much better than when he had first entered it, but its dark immensity still cowed him when he became aware of it. He was aware now.

". . . when I was in college," Melanie was saying.

Don realized that she had been speaking, and he hadn't been hearing. She must have started quietly, really talking to herself, when they were at a farther separation, and then he picked it up when they veered closer to each other. So he listened. He doubted that the sub could pick up on this, if it were even in the vicinity; only because he had become accustomed to picking a human voice out of the constant background noises was he able to hear her at all.

"I liked my favorite very much," Melanie continued equably. "Mostly he just listened. Most of the time he just looked as if he were going to sleep. I guess he wanted me to start thinking aloud about some of the important things in my then-current life. He would just prod me now and then. After a while I noticed that he seemed to give quite a number of compliments. Sometimes they were strange. One day he said that I had erected one of the most formidable barriers around myself that he had encountered in all his years of practice. In fact that was my favorite of all his compliments.''

"That was no compliment!" Don snorted. "He just wanted to seduce you."

"What?" She seemed confused.

"That dumb writer you visited. Telling you about barriers. That was just his l-line."

She choked and made strangled sounds. It dawned on Don that she was suppressing laughter.

"It's not funny," he said. "A man like that—you didn't tell him about your hair, did you? So—"

"That was my psychiatrist," she said. "Long before I visited the—"

Oops! Don felt his face burning. He had gulped his foot to his knee that time.

"You're jealous," Melanie said.

"I—I—" Damn that stutter! He couldn't get anything out.

"I'm thrilled and flattered," she said, sounding pleased. "I don't think anyone was ever jealous on my account before. You really do care."

"Of *course* I care!" he snapped. "Y-you visiting s-strange men, and taking p-pills, and—"

"Pills? I never—"

"B-birth control pills. You told me—"

She laughed again. "Oh, that. Don, I only took those pills because my mother insisted. Just as she insisted about the psychiatrists. While I was in college. She wanted me to be a normal, extroverted girl. Not to be afraid of foolish little things. Like pregnancy.''

''Your mother!''

''She was pretty domineering, in her fashion.''

''But that's white slavery. To make you—''

''Oh, Don! I took the pills. That was all. The only thing they ever did for me was to foul up my analytical ability. As soon as I got out on my own, I dropped them. It seemed pointless to waste the money any more. Even with the pills, I could analyze things to that extent.''

He had definitely blown it. ''I—I'm sorry. I a-apologize.''

''Oh, don't be! I'm reveling in the feeling. You know me as I am, Don. Words I never quite know whether to believe, but jealousy I believe.''

Then maybe his miscue hadn't been as bad as it could have been. ''Okay.''

''You know, Don, I've been thinking. It seems to me that I was told that the radio has no crossover. Otherwise we'd be getting Earth broadcasts, interference, and—''

''So the sub can't intercept!'' Don said, hugely relieved. ''And since we had our radios on before, and the sub didn't seem to know about us until it spied Eleph, probably it wasn't following any radio signal. But why isn't Eleph talking, then? He knows more about the equipment than we do.''

''I don't know. Maybe he turned his radio off automatically, as we did, before thinking it through, and then forgot to turn it on again.''

''*Him?* He'd be the first to remember it.''

''Or he might be hurt.''

''Hurt too bad even to talk?''

''I don't want to guess,'' she said.

''Well, we have to find him. Where do you think he is?''

"Maybe we should think like a fifty-year-old conservative physicist with a military background," she suggested. "Where would he go?"

Don thought. "Into a cave!" he exclaimed. "He showed real interest in that Yucatan coastal cave. I'll bet it wasn't for the archaeological or geological prospects, but because it served as a secure retreat. Agoraphobia, not claustrophobia—fear of the heights."

"That's acrophobia," she said. "I know, because I've got it too. A little."

"I mean fear of the open spaces," he said.

"Are there caves, here? There can't be any erosion as we know it. How would caves form?"

"Only a geologist knows for sure. Maybe a freshwater spring could do it. I don't know. But if there's one, that's where he'll be, maybe. For one thing, the sub couldn't follow him there."

"We'll just have to look," she agreed. "For cave openings."

"Um."

They rode on, looking for cave openings, but saw none. There were fish here, but not many, and they seemed to be blind. The cousins of the starfish were far more common, and snails and clams were abundant.

This was mountainous country, and the constant steep climbing and fierce coasting were wearing. A man could readily lose himself here, and it would certainly be hazardous for a submarine to maneuver too close to these jagged rocks.

They searched for another twenty minutes, looking carefully into every recess, but it was apparent that they were needles looking for another in a haystack. The ground was too rough; there could be a hundred caves, and they could miss them all unless they dropped a wheel into one. They needed an overview, and even then, the opacity of the water would severely restrict their scope.

"At least we know the sub probably didn't keep him in sight, once he decided to shake it," Melanie said.

A shape loomed near, long and oval and glowing slightly. "Speak of the devil!" Don cried, throwing himself to the ground. Melanie peeped and did the same.

But even as he barked his shins, Don realized that it was a huge squid, some twenty feet long. As if they didn't have troubles enough!

The squid glided up, light green in the beam of light Don angled at it. Its monstrous eye contemplated him. "Go away!" he cried.

The squid jetted in a circle around them.

"It's Glowcloud!" Melanie cried. "He must have been trailing us all the time, and finally homed in." She stood, lifting her hands to the creature. The squid extended a tentacle. That was identification enough; obviously Glowcloud remembered.

"Well, at least it's not the sub."

"What determination," Melanie said, her hands playing a game of touch and dodge with the tentacle. "It must be almost impossible to locate anything in this expanse, as we've been discovering."

"Trust Glowcloud," Don said. "He always did know how to find us, as long as we're in his depth. Hey!"

"What?" She was almost shaking hands with the tentacle. "You're not getting jealous of a squid, now, are you?"

"I just thought, maybe Glowcloud can find Eleph."

"Oh, Don, now you're dreaming! A *mollusk?* He may be cute, but—"

Cute? This twenty foot monster with ten tentacles and a huge hard beak? How her attitude had changed! "Worth a try, anyway. Gaspar said they're the smartest creatures in the sea. Glowcloud!"

The squid rotated gracefully to bring the eye to bear on him. Probably he was reacting to the sharpness of the sound. "Where's Eleph? Eleph! Take us to Eleph. Eleph!"

"Eleph!" Melanie echoed with less conviction.

The squid circled twice more in a climbing spiral, then shot off at a tangent.

"Do you really think—?" Melanie asked. "I mean, he is a wild creature, and can't be expected to—"

"No. But what better chance do we have?"

"Well, we can't follow where he's going, so we'd better keep looking."

They kept looking, with no better success than before.

Ten minutes later Glowcloud was back. "Hey, did you find Eleph?" Don asked facetiously. Yet he did wonder: the squid certainly seemed responsive. Was it possible that Glowcloud understood their need—or cared?

The squid jetted slowly north, low enough for them to follow. They did so, knowing that one search pattern was as good as another, in this water wilderness. If . . .

But they didn't find Eleph. Eleph found them. "Don!"

Glowcloud looped around them, then took off after a careless fish.

The bicycles almost collided, for Eleph was riding crookedly. "Eleph!" Don cried. "I thought you were lost."

"How could I be lost, with the coordinates plainly visible on the meter?" Eleph asked sourly. "I was merely doubling back to rejoin the company. Why didn't you wait?"

"Why didn't you call, once you were alone? We assumed—"

Eleph looked embarrassed. "There was a slight mishap in transit." He indicated his radio.

"Small mishap!" Don exclaimed. "The whole thing's stove in! And you—you're—"

"I was in too much of a hurry," Eleph admitted, glancing down at his red-stained shirt. "I took a fall."

Some fall! The man's forbidding front had deceived Don, but only for a moment. Eleph's left arm was tucked inside his shirt, and blood soaked the entire length of it. A bruise showed on his cheek, and his trousers were torn. He must have rolled over, with a jagged spike of rock smashing both arm and radio.

The pain had to be phenomenal. Don was no expert in medicine, but his first-aid briefing had familiarized him with the general nature of a compound fracture. One surely rested inside that shirt. Yet Eleph had roused himself and ridden on, one-handed, actively mastering his destiny. Don had not suspected that the man had that kind of courage. It was a thing he admired tremendously, and it transformed his attitude toward Eleph. Yet nothing in the man's manner suggested that he sought sympathy, so Don didn't proffer it, verbally.

But Melanie did. "You poor man! You're all bruised."

"It happens," Eleph said.

"We broke up to search for you," Don explained. "We agreed to meet again in four hours. More than two to go, still. Pacifa has the—the medication."

"Excellent."

"Are you all right, Eleph?" Melanie asked. "Why is your hand out of sight?" Evidently she hadn't caught on to the extent of it, yet.

"Scratches and bruises," Eleph told her firmly. "Do not concern yourself further, my dear."

Don, to his own surprise, was suddenly overwhelmed. Eleph had such courage in adversity, yet was no more expressive than he had been at the outset. This was another silent person, whose speech and overt actions only partly reflected his true passions. He was familiar in an illuminating, *déjà vu* fashion, yet completely strange. Don had wronged him grievously by thinking him to be a stuffed shirt, and now he couldn't even apologize without alerting Melanie to the extent of the problem. If Eleph preferred to keep it private, Don had to honor it. But he had to express himself somehow, because he was really not the silent type, just shy in new situations.

So Don held out his hand. It seemed inane, but his conscience refused to stand aside. One token handshake had to say it all.

Eleph understood. He let go of his handlebar—and the wheel flopped sideways, almost dumping him. Don jumped to support him—and banged the injured arm. Eleph winced, and a small strangled cry escaped him.

White-faced and red-faced, respectively, Eleph and Don shook hands. Then they rode on, Melanie leading the way.

Depot #4 was tremendous. "There's enough here to last us a year," Pacifa said. "We must have arrived at our major base of operations."

So it seemed. Another set of coordinates was waiting— 19°30′N, 77°0′W—but that location was so close it was obviously an offshoot from this site.

They repacked their supplies and rested for a day, only scouting the immediate vicinity. "These are bad," Pacifa said, indicating one box of glop packages. "See, the serial matches that on Don's old supply." She was right. But there were twenty good boxes as well.

They held a business meeting. "This has to be it," Gaspar said. "The next are Melanie's last set of coordinates, and they're close—within sixty miles, as the fish swims. Maybe we should come at the site cautiously. After all, if it is all this secret—''

"And with an enemy craft patrolling the vicinity," Eleph said. "We must consider the possibility that we did not lose that submarine. If it realized that Glowcloud was accompanying us, and oriented on the squid—"

"If it's tracing anybody, it's Eleph," Pacifa said. "The sub never saw the rest of us."

"We *think* it never saw us," Gaspar corrected her.

She sighed. "You have a suspicious mind, but you're right. We can't take the chance. How about this, then: you and Eleph decoy Glowcloud south, while Don and Melanie and I maintain radio silence and sneak a peek at whatever is there? We'll meet back here when we can."

"But that's giving them the risk while we take the prize," Don protested.

"We're not going to steal it, Don," Pacifa said. "We're a group. We'll finish this mission together. But we are learning caution."

"Actually Gaspar and I would be running no risk we haven't run all along," Eleph said. "While you have no idea what awaits you."

Don could not argue with that.

"Also," Gaspar said, "the sides of that trench can be steep, and Eleph can't climb. So he can't go anyway."

Which clinched it. Pacifa had doused Eleph with a pain killer from her supplies and supervised the resetting of his arm, no simple task for the squeamish. She had to rummage in all their packs to obtain material for splint and bandage. Don knew it would be weeks before the member healed, and a fair length of time before the man recovered from his loss of blood. The trench was certainly no place for the wounded. Not until they knew there was a safe route there, and what their mission was.

"Actually, I could go with Eleph," Don said.

"No need," Gaspar said easily. "It isn't as if it's a chore. In fact, I'd like to see Jamaica and Port Royal. We can loop clear around the island, and the sub'll think we have a rendezvous there, if it's tracking Eleph. We'll even take pictures."

For a moment Don was jealous. He, the archaeologist, should be going to Port Royal. But the others all seemed satisfied with the arrangement, so he stifled his ire. He knew it was a device to make it easier for Eleph and keep him out of danger.

Eleph distributed his supply of balloons among them, in case they had an emergency requiring flotation. Don put three in his pack. They would exert some drag, but they just might be his lifeline in a crisis.

Gaspar and Eleph packed up and departed, Gaspar leading the way so as to pick out the easiest route. They moved slowly, for Eleph, stiff though his lip might be, was obviously not up to strenuous activity.

Pacifa made them wait four hours before they set out toward the final coordinates. "Just in case," she said. "We don't know exactly how far toward the surface Glowcloud can come right now, or how far he ranges while we're out of reach. We want to be sure El and Gas pick him up before we go down. We need our decoy in order."

There was a great deal of light rope in stock, and they packed several thousand extra feet, knowing they would need it for the canyons. Don did not feel easy about this trip, but didn't care to admit it. He wished that they could have gone as a full group, instead of fragmented. Odd that he should be so glum, when they were so near their destination.

They moved north, directly into the trench. Almost immediately they had to break out the rope, tying a length to a spur of rock, climbing down it, and leaving it there for the return trip. A submarine might discover it, but that risk seemed small, in this craggy wilderness, and they might have to return in a hurry. Without the ropes, they might have to ride a hundred miles out of their way—if any alternate avenues were even available.

It was a fear-of-heights nightmare. In the first five miles they descended a thousand fathoms. The site wasn't close at all, in terms of their effort! Then the ground evened out somewhat, and they rode down irregular slopes another five hundred fathoms.

The scenery was breathtaking, not pleasantly. Bare rock projected everywhere, forming overhanging cliffs, with rifts packed with boulders. Barnacles studded the surfaces, combing the water with their little nets, and sponges bulged wherever they chose: black unenterprising masses. There was little of the beauty of the coral reef, here.

But, aided by Pacifa's energy and expertise, they covered sixty miles in one day. Sixty horizontally, plus three vertically, and not directly toward their objective. They were now in the center of the Cayman trench proper: as grim a region as Don cared to experience. Fortunately there were steady currents of well oxygenated water, so breathing was no problem.

"About ten miles to go," Pacifa said. "Let's hold it until morning. That spot is about twenty five miles south of the coast of Cuba, and that's too close. We may need our strength."

Don agreed. The closer they got, the less he liked it. Geographically and politically, this was a dangerous region. And what *was* it they were supposed to find? All would soon be known, but he feared that it might better remain unknown. Certainly it wasn't any archaeological structure, this deep.

Melanie smiled at him as they settled for a meal. "I'm worried too," she murmured.

"Melanie—" he started, drawing her hand in toward him.

She shook her head. "Not yet, Don. We must tackle our mission. That's what we're here for."

After a few hours rest, they resumed the quest. Now they were exceedingly careful, watching for anything at all. But there was nothing except the rocky, slanting, evil bottom of the trench.

"Half a mile," Pacifa whispered. She was nervous too, though she contained it well.

Suddenly they were struck by a current of warmth. They stared at one another. "Am I going batty, or are you?" Pacifa inquired.

Don squinted at his temperature gauge. "Eighty degrees!" he exclaimed. "Our converters can't account for that! Where does it come from?"

"Only two reasonable guesses. A hot spring, or a nuclear reactor."

"A nuclear reactor!" Melanie exclaimed, horrified.

Don choked. "H-how do you—I mean, would they send us out like this to investigate a h-hot spring?"

That needed no answer. "This close to Cuba," Pacifa murmured. "A nuclear plant. Thermal pollution—but no one would notice, this far down. But what's it *doing?*"

"Nuclear subs," Don said, working it out. "Like the one we saw. Their port of Cienfuegos is just a decoy. The real stuff is here. Maybe hardened missile sites, too. They're not making the same mistake they made before, putting bases in sight of spyplane overflights."

"But things are peaceful now!" Melanie protested.

"There are a number of nuclear powers," Don reminded her. "Any one of them could be doing this, secretly."

"Now it all makes sense," Pacifa agreed. "And I wish it didn't."

"Y-yes." Don felt very tired. "B-but we'd b-better make sure. Get p-pictures."

"Afraid so. We're the spy-plane, this time. A group of folk no one would ever suspect of undertaking a mission like this, in a fashion no one would ever dream. Riding bicycles under the sea!" She shook her head. "We have to nail it down with absolute proof."

"But what about radiation?" Melanie asked.

"I think I was trying not to think about that. There's sure to be radioactive wastes. That may affect us. Maybe already have."

"N-not if we s-stay in the c-cold water?" Don asked with wan hope.

"Why should it be restricted to the warm? No need to shield, down here. They could saturate the entire area."

"B-but their own p-personnel! They wouldn't—"

"Probably automated."

"Even the s-subs?"

She considered. "You're right. That doesn't make sense. If they had completely automated submarines, they wouldn't need a base. Not this close, anyway. It's men that need all the attention, not machines or supplies. And if they're manned subs, there's got to be radiation shielding. Actually, they can't let too much escape, because those rays pass through water even more readily than we do, and you bet Uncle Sam has telltales to pick it up. Especially around here! So probably it's all safe. Nothing but thermal pollution."

Don nodded. He wasn't really reassured, but realized that if there was radiation, and if the phase didn't nullify it, the three of them had no way to escape it except to run for home immediately—and might already have received a lethal dose. Unless the phase protected them from this, too. Better to pretend that the threat did not exist, and accomplish the mission regardless.

"Still, I can see why nonentities were selected for this mission," Melanie said. "We're expendable."

"We don't know that there's r-radiation," Don reminded her ineffectively.

"What's it going to do to me anyway—make my hair fall out?"

Neither Don nor Pacifa saw fit to respond to that.

They turned their bikes and pedaled upstream, grimly tracing the moving water to its source. Their mission no longer seemed as intriguing as before.

They did not have far to go. The water issued from a vent in the rock.

They stared at it. "I wish Gaspar were here," Pacifa said. "I just can't tell whether that's natural or manmade."

"Natural," Don said.

"Oh, that's right! You're an archaeologist. You should have had practice. Perhaps they wanted you for that reason: your specialty didn't matter, just your general background. But suppose someone went all-out to make it *seem* natural. Could you still call it?"

"N-not outside of a laboratory," Don admitted. "You think they're trying to h-hide the p-plant?"

"Maybe." But then she changed her tack. "Seems like an awful lot of trouble, though. Think of the job of construction! And to make a naturalistic outlet aperture like this, when chances are no one will ever see it—do you suppose we're wrong?"

"No atomic plant?" Melanie asked, brightening.

"It *could* be an artesian well, couldn't it? A hot spring?"

"Then maybe there's weird life around it," Melanie said. "Things that live only in permanent deep hot wells."

Don looked. There were encrustations on the rock, and odd natural tubes clustering around the vent, but he had no idea how to classify them, or whether they were alive or dead.

"It didn't make sense the first time round," Pacifa said. "But my female intuition says that there's something fishy here. Suppose we just look around, and if we don't find anything else, we'll bring in the geologist and the physicist to tell us for sure about hot springs and nuclear outflows. Obviously our full party is equipped for this mission; we just happen to be the wrong part of it."

Don agreed, moderately relieved. Pacifa had a sharp mind, and he preferred not to have to argue anything with her unless it was directly in his area of competence. The other two would certainly be equipped to settle the matter. If only that sub hadn't spotted Eleph, forcing their decoy ploy!

They rode on, and abruptly left the warm water. The near-freezing cold of the normal deeps was a shock even though it was more apparent than real, considering the protective environment of phase and field. But soon they were back in the warmth, in a current that spread across and upward, gradually cooling but remaining much warmer than the normal water.

Three quarters of a mile from the assigned coordinates, on their way back toward their original destination, they saw a fish. That was not in itself unusual; though fish were much less common at this depth than at the surface, they remained present. But this was a strange one.

"It has legs!" Pacifa cried, astonished.

They oriented their lights on it, but the strange fish moved out of sight, stirring up a cloud of silt. "Downward pointing fins, I think, to stilt over the bottom muck," Don said. "We saw that on the abyssal flats."

"Uh-uh! Do you think I don't know the difference? I saw real lizard legs."

"There it is again!" Melanie cried, catching the fish with her beam.

"Look," Pacifa said. "You can see the articulation of the bones as it walks. But it's a *fish,* with fishtail and fish gills. Not an amphibian muck-wallower at the edge of land."

Don peered more closely at the elusive creature. He had to agree.

"I'm no naturalist," Pacifa said. "But this is odd."

"Prehistoric," Don agreed, thinking of ancient life. "Premammalian."

"No doubt," she said dryly. "But what I mean, Don, is how can a normal cold water fish survive within hot water, legs or no?'"

"And fresh water!" Melanie cried. "It can't be salt, coming from the ground!"

"It could, if it's from a nuclear plant," Pacifa said. "Regular ocean water, run through sluices for cooling the equipment."

"Wouldn't the heat evaporate it?" Don asked. "The salt would solidify and gum the works." But he wasn't sure; they probably had ways to handle that sort of thing. Maybe a series of cooling stages, with special sealed-in fluids for the really hot parts. It was probably elementary, for a nuclear power specialist.

Pacifa wasn't sure of her thesis either. "Fish living in this water would not have evolved here, if it's artificial. They couldn't just move from cold to hot. Not in just a few months or years. Or from salt to fresh. These barriers are very strong to sea life, I understand."

"Gaspar will know," Melanie said.

"You think this fish means the springs are natural?" Don

asked, hardly daring to hope. "But maybe they stocked the region with laboratory breeds. To fool us."

"Decoy fish," Melanie suggested.

"If this is f-fresh," Don said, arguing a case he hoped would be refuted, "why doesn't it look different? Without the salt—"

"Salt in solution is transparent, isn't it?" Pacifa asked. "You can't see far in any kind of water, because of the refraction."

Don lacked the information to refute her, though he remained doubtful. "If this is what we're supposed to investigate, why isn't one of our number a biologist? Or chemist?"

"I think someone spotted the thermal flow," she said. "They must have ways to chart such things. Vaguely, at least. Maybe their echosoundings are affected by the temperature of the water. So they had to send in a team to verify—"

"But that doesn't explain *me,*" Melanie said. "I know less than anyone."

"Cover," Pacifa said. "Same as me. They could have trained Gaspar or Eleph how to repair a bike or pitch a tent, after all. But by adding us and extending the route to take in that city of yours—who would suspect the real mission?"

"It's ironic that the least qualified members of our group were the ones to come here," Melanie said.

"Just Eleph's bad luck to be spotted by that sub. But don't forget the two of them will see it; we're just doing the preliminary scouting, and finding a route Eleph can navigate, while they decoy the pursuit, if there is any. But we still aren't quite at the coordinates. Maybe it's something completely different."

Don shrugged. Melanie spread her hands. They went on.

They were not, after all, quite at the base of the trench. A new canyon developed, a mere fifty feet deep where they intersected it but possessed of a strong current that seemed to be seeking deeper recesses. They were so close to the specified location that they could not avoid this gap; their objective well might lie within it.

Another descent placed them on the rough but ridable floor, with an uncomfortably stiff wind-current at their backs. As they progressed, the walls rose higher and drew nearer at either side. The narrow valley curved and recurved like a monster snake, and the breeze accelerated. Don and Melanie no longer pedaled; they coasted, blown along, hands nervously near the brake levers.

They rounded another turn. Here the canyon narrowed into a crevice only a few feet across: treacherous terrain for swift-moving bicycles. But Don abruptly forgot that concern.

Melanie made a sound halfway between awe and disbelief.

Straddling the crevice was an ancient ship. Intact.

CHAPTER 11

SHIP

Proxy 5–12–5–16–8: Attention.
Acknowledging.
Status?
Doubtful. Mischance struck, and the success of the mission is now in peril.
Details.
A submarine associated with the final challenge happened to come upon the party, and one member of the party was not in a position to conceal himself. So he acted as decoy, leading it away from the others. This diversion was successful, but in the process he fell and broke his arm, and was unable to continue immediately. As a result the party split into two, and one section proceeded to the next challenge. But that fraction of the party may not be sufficiently competent to handle the challenge appropriately.
There is danger?
Not physical. But with the full group not present, the challenge may have a divisive instead of a unifying effect. Therein is the peril to the mission.
But the mission is not yet lost?
Not yet lost. Indeed, it is possible that melding has pro-

ceeded far enough so that this hurdle will be overcome. But
the issue is in doubt.

*Even a failure can have its benefit. We may learn from it
a better way to approach the next world.*

But a success could offer more of that benefit, as well as
salvaging this world.

True. Handle it as you must, Proxy.

They stared at the ship. Not only was it intact, it seemed
to be in perfect condition. And it was ancient.

"But the teredo—" Don protested, his belief unwilling to
take hold lest it be dashed. "The destructive worm. There
can't be—"

"But this is fresh water, isn't it?" Melanie asked. "So
the clam can't live here . . ."

"That must be it," Pacifa agreed. "Since we all see it,
this can't be a mirage or hallucination, so it must be a
genuine wreck. But what a strange one! I never saw a ship
like that before."

While they spoke, the larger import was filtering into
Don's consciousness. This was no Spanish galleon. This
was a beaked craft, curiously high in the prow, about fifteen
feet across, with a single mast broken off about ten feet up.
That was about all he could make out, for they were
approaching it endwise. Even so, his pulses were racing. It
might have been Roman, but wasn't; Greek, but wasn't;
Phoenician . . . no. Certainly not Egyptian. By elimina-
tion, it had to be—Minoan.

Minoan. A ship of the isle of Crete, at the time of its
greatness. Right in Don's specialty. He could not imagine a
brighter dream of discovery.

"Right at the coordinates," Melanie said. "This is our
mission. What a relief!"

"No accident," Pacifa said. "Our party has an Old

World archaeologist. And this is Old World, isn't it, Don?''

"Yes," he answered absently as they braked.

"But what's it doing *here*?" Melanie asked.

They came to a stop almost under the hulk, where its base formed a crude triangle with the canyon, leaving five or six feet for the water to pass below.

"A storm-blown stray—what else?" Pacifa said. "What matters is that it's here—and so are we. No nuclear plot, no radiation. All we have to do is help Don study it."

Don hardly heard them. He was in a private rapture, gazing at the ship. A virtually complete, preserved ship of one of the greatest civilizations of the ancient world. This could be anything up to four thousand years old: a phenomenal bonanza for archaeology. A set-group of functioning Minoan equipment. If the teredo hadn't been able to rifle it, who else could have?

"So now we know what they spotted," Pacifa said. "An old Roman ship."

"Minoan," Don said. "Notice, it is carvel, not clinker built, and the configuration of the—"

"And the fresh water preserved it. How old would you say it is, Don?"

"Between 3,500 and 4,000 years, perhaps even more. We should be able to date it more precisely once we really check it over. And later, with laboratory verification of the wood—" He was talking as if the matter were routine, when actually his mind was partially numb. This was the find of the century!

"How can you check it?" Pacifa asked.

"Why, climb aboard and—uh-oh!" He had forgotten the phase again. He couldn't touch this exquisite ship!

Melanie rode slowly to it and lifted her hand, evidently finding it difficult to believe that so remarkable an object could be a ghost. She was just able to reach the keel. She froze in place, the current blowing out her skirt. "Don!"

"Might as well ride through it, if we can get up there," Don said, disappointed. "Maybe we can see inside the hold. It's certainly not a total loss."

"It certainly isn't," Melanie said. "Don, come here."

This time he picked up on her tone. He pedaled over. The ship loomed above, seeming absolutely solid. He could not resist reaching up to put his hand through its hull, as she had.

His hand banged.

He stared at his finger, then up at the ship. Unbelievingly he extended one digit to touch the wood. It met a hard surface. "It's *here*!" he exclaimed.

"And it shouldn't be," Pacifa said, coming to test it herself. "Because, according to Gaspar, this phase world was denuded at least six thousand years ago, and this ship isn't that old. According to you. And you should know your business. But here it is."

"But the sunken city wasn't—isn't—here!" Don protested. "How can—?"

"Makes you suspect something is wrong with our theory," she said.

"Terribly wrong!" Don's head was spinning again. "Unless this ship *is* older. Surely ships preceded the city, or it could not have been built. Unless the Minoan culture originated here. But then the ruins would be solid for us too." Nothing seemed to make sense.

"At any rate," she said, "it does suggest that this warm fresh water is natural. A nuclear plant would date from no more than a generation past, not several thousand years. Unless someone planted this ship to make us think—?"

"In both phases?" Don demanded. "If they could do

that, they wouldn't be mucking about in the deep trench! They'd have conquered us long ago.''

''Who says they want to conquer us?'' Melanie asked. ''We don't know anything about them.''

''True, we don't,'' Pacifa said. ''We'll have to accept the phase aspect as definitive. Which puts it right back in the archaeological pot. Obviously you're here to check it out. If it is genuine, it's highly significant archaeologically. If it isn't, it's significant scientifically, and politically. And I'll be someone who wants very much to know.''

''Well, let's get on with it!'' Don cried, his excitement growing as his shock abated. The ship might have been here for thousands of years, but it seemed as if it would vanish in a minute if he didn't get busy.

The tight hull curved up to the deck, about twenty feet above the ground, overhanging the three of them. Pacifa assessed the situation in a fashion only an objective non-archaeologist could. She noted the manner the ship was supported by the impinging crevice walls, checking the contacts with her hands.

''It's secure,'' she reported. ''The this-world and that-world ships are identical. Except that the one in our phase sits a little lower, and its sides are stove in a bit.''

''There's no water to support it,'' Don said. ''We're just lucky it was so well jammed in that not even the removal of the water in the phase world could drop it far. I'm surprised it didn't collapse entirely, in those thousands of years.''

''That is strange,'' she said. ''Though I suppose with no spoilage—even so, steady pressure should have warped the wood.'' She paused. ''Wood? Don, do you realize that this phase ship *isn't* wood?''

''Isn't wood?'' Don asked absently, still staring upward with awe as the current tugged at his body.

"Feels like stone. The same stuff we've been riding over."

Don remembered the touch. This had bothered him before, about the landscape. But *wood?* "That makes no sense at all! This is a wooden ship; it wouldn't have floated if it was stone."

"It *has* to make sense," she said. "Everything does. We just haven't unriddled it yet. But it does grow intriguing. I'd like to know too why we don't see anything in the phase world, though we're ninety-nine-point-nine percent in it."

"I think that's because it has less in it," Melanie said. "Its rocks are all bare or absent, while Earth's are covered with silt and life. So we see that outermost layer. We might see the things of the other phase if they didn't exist also in the regular world."

"Feel that hull," Pacifa said. "Isn't that a good inch lower than it looks? The phase hull extends beyond the real hull."

Don felt. "I—I can see it now. I—it must have been psy—psycho—mental blindness. Not believing—"

"I know what you mean," Melanie said. "We're so used to seeing Earthly things that something completely outside that framework disappears, even if it's in plain sight. Subjective. It's powerful." She tapped her wig. "But I'm going to start looking at phase objects from now on, even if it gives me a headache."

Meanwhile, Pacifa wheeled her bike a short distance upcurrent, propped it solidly, and hitched a rope to its frame. Then she swung a length up over the projecting bow and pulled it taut. "I'll haul you up as much as I can, and Melanie can help."

Don was so eager to board the ship that the problem of hurdling the hull seemed academic. He tied the other end of the rope to his own bicycle, balancing the weight as well as he could.

Pacifa hauled on the rope, and so did Melanie. There was no pulley, so this was inefficient, but the rope did slide, and he went up.

"Heave!" Pacifa gasped, and the two heaved together, drawing him up another notch. It was hard work, even with the three of them cooperating, but there was only about fifteen feet of actual rising to do, and he was able to put his feet against the side of the ship and walk on it, to an extent, as if rappelling. Or at least to brace his feet near the top, while the bicycle banged him. He nudged the prow and caught hold before his strength gave out. Now he could have used Gaspar's muscle! The bike dangled on the rope, jerking up as his weight came off.

Don held his breath and swung his feet up. He scrambled over the edge and landed on the deck. He stretched back far enough to catch the bicycle, bringing it and its atmosphere back to his lungs. He had had much recent practice in similar maneuvers, descending into the Cayman trench. But going up was three times as hard as going down.

The deck was firm, though his feet stood about two inches below the visible level. The settling of the phase ship, obviously. Disconcerting, but a useful reminder that what he saw was not necessarily what he felt. The planks were tight. The support strong. This was a well made ship, in both worlds.

He turned and looked down. He waved at the two women who were looking up. "I'm fine," he said. "But I'll be going into the interior of the ship, so you might as well take a rest. I'll report every so often, if you're interested."

"I want to explore some," Melanie said. "I'll go on down the cleft a way and see where it leads, and how far the

222 Piers Anthony

fresh water extends. I can't get lost, here. Pacifa can stay in touch with you.''

"But to go alone—"

"I've got to learn to do it sometime," she said. She rolled her bicycle under the ship and moved on beyond.

He realized that she was disciplining herself to eliminate her own weaknesses. This was as good a place and time as any, since she had nothing to do. If it built up her confidence, good.

"Get to work," Pacifa told him. "I'll pitch a tent."

Don tried to absorb it all at once, greedy for information. The timbers of the hull were mortised together with precision, and the whole was extremely well insulated with what appeared to be tar. No doubt it had been on the outside too, but the current had washed it away. The Romans, later, had even impregnated their ships with lead, for protection against such things as the teredo; but this ship predated such sophistication. There were portholes along the sides for oars—ten or twelve pairs. Later the Cretans were to distinguish between war galleys and merchant ships, with the former carrying oars and the latter only sails. This particular ship was evidently a compromise between the two developing types, lacking the cargo space of the fat wind-driven vessels, but also lacking the sleek power of the warships. Not that the Minoans ever had been much for war; peace was their normal course.

The hatch to the interior had what seemed to be a watertight covering, so that storm waves could not swamp this ship unless a hole had been bashed in. But the hatchcover had been removed; it lay to the side, and his hand passed through it. Near the stern stood several cages, built into the deck. Those would have been for pigeons, those invaluable aids to ancient navigation.

Don took a deep breath. This was Minoan, all right!

There were markings on the base of the mast and on the inside of the bulwarks: script "Linear A," the writing of the Cretan heyday. These were mainly cautions about the care of the equipment, as nearly as he could tell without more careful analysis. Probably marked by the manufacturers and of course ignored by the illiterate crewmen.

The ship was about seventy five feet long, and fifteen wide across the mid-deck: in the middle range for seagoing craft of the period. And it *was* seagoing, despite the oars; in all its appointments and arrangements it spoke of the long haul.

"What do you see?" Pacifa called from the ground.

Don was jolted out of his preoccupation. He flashed his light around again, organizing his thoughts for a coherent reply—and saw a mermaid.

She had just floated up out of the open hatch. Her hair hung about her in a dark cloud, and her black eyes were piercing in a pale face. She had two splendid breasts, a narrow waist, and overlapping scales that gleamed irridescently from naval to flukes. She carried a small, dim lantern that highlighted her remarkable characteristics.

"S-splendid!" Don breathed idiotically.

"Say, are you all right?" Pacifa called.

The mermaid spun around at that, orienting on the sound of the voice. But immediately she returned to Don, shielding her eyes against his bright beam.

She was real! On top of all the other incredible developments, this fish-girl was alive!

"Don, answer me!" Pacifa called more urgently.

But he couldn't answer. That dazzling female torso, so abruptly phased into piscine anatomy. That fantasy amalgam of woman and fish. If the mermaid were genuine, what was she doing here, four miles down, far below normal light and warmth? It was nonsensical.

Which meant that he was having a vision. Too much or too little oxygen must have saturated his field, affecting his brain. He wasn't sure which way led to hallucination.

"Knock once if you can hear me," Pacifa called.

Numbly, Don knocked his heel against the deck.

The mermaid turned, lithe and sleek as any living fish, and swam rapidly away from him. Her tail worked powerfully, so that she used her hands only for course corrections. Her luxuriant hair streamed behind her as she disappeared over the rail.

Now Don was able to speak. "Splendid!" he repeated.

After a moment Pacifa spoke again, hardly loud enough. "Don—did you see that?"

"I—I—yes!"

"I declare, I thought for a moment it was my idiotic daughter, reincarnated as a sylph. Until that tail—"

"I—I thought it was—brain damage," Don admitted, walking his bike across the deck to peer down at her. He didn't know whether to be relieved for the state of his brain, or apprehensive for the state of reality. A live mermaid!

"You realize, of course, that this is ridiculous," Pacifa said matter-of-factly. "The real mermaids were dugongs—and you'd never find any of those down here! They're air breathers."

"B-but she didn't have g-gills," Don pointed out.

"Yes, of course. She's mammalian. You must have noticed."

Don had noticed.

"Here's my speculation," Pacifa said. "See what you make of it. A bathyscaphe was photographing this region of the trench, looking for geological features of stray foreign fusion plants, and it caught one shot of this preserved sunken ship with a mermaid on deck. Later the analysts went over the material and called their experts, and the archaeologist said 'That's a 1723 B.C. Minoan craft of the Zilch II class from the shipworks of King Tut-Tut!' and the artist said 'That's a statue of a mermaid by the hand of Artisan Smut-smut!' and the archaeologist said 'Impossible, you dolt, the Minoans didn't *make* any statues of mermaids that year!'' and the artist said 'Oh, yeah? Then it must be a *real* mermaid, stupid!' and the psychiatrist said 'Tut, smut, calm down, boys, what you need is another picture.' But the next time the bathyscaphe stopped at that station, the mermaid was gone. And the artist said 'See, it's all your fault! You didn't believe in her!' and the archaeologist slugged him.''

"Archaeologists don't slug people!'' Don protested, laughing.

"So they packed up a bicycle party with a nonslugging Minoan scholar on board, but they didn't want to prejudice the case by mentioning the mermaid . . .''

Don had to smile. ''Must be. We had no idea what to expect! But what do we do now?''

"Maybe it's time to break radio silence.''

"Yes. We've found what we were sent for, obviously.''

"Then again, we don't *know* that either ship or mermaid are genuine. Maybe we should make quite sure before we say much. If we make a wrong report—''

"Somebody might slug *us!* I'd like nothing better than to stay here and study this ship in detail,'' Don said fervently. ''But we have to rendezvous with the others, or contact them by radio, so they won't—''

"Yes,'' she said thoughtfully. ''But if we'd reported as we went along, we'd have had them depth-bombing the trench for that atomic plant. There are still enough incongruities so that we know we have only part of the story. We've kept our noses clean so far by being cautious; let's hang on a little longer.''

"I agree. But still—"

"Look, Don. You're the expert, here. I could prowl around this ship for the rest of the year and never find out anything worth knowing. So I'm expendable, as far as this part goes. I could go back—"

"Alone?"

"Don't look so horrified! I'm no tender violet. I can rejoin the others faster by myself than with company."

Surely that was the truth. Don thought ruefully. "But Melanie—"

Pacifa nodded. "It would be difficult at best to get her up there with you, though you will be able to let yourself down by the rope when you're through. I'd better take her back with me. You should be safe here, and you won't be going anywhere soon."

"That's for sure! I could stay here a year and never notice the time. The things I can learn here—"

"And maybe it's best if she doesn't see that mermaid, right now. All that hair, you know."

Don hadn't thought of that. "It could be awkward, yes. That mermaid is not of our phase; still—"

"All right, we must act with dispatch. Let's compromise: you can turn on your radio and keep company with Melanie that way, while she and I travel back. We'll have quite a climb to make, even with the ropes in place. Just don't give away any details on this situation. There's no danger of Glowcloud zeroing in on you here—not in this hot fresh-water. But anything you broadcast just might be intercepted by parties unknown. Not worth the risk of giving away anything of substance. Meanwhile I'll tell Melanie not to mention me, so no one knows where we are, and when we get back we'll acquaint the other two with what we know so far. If Gaspar or Eleph tunes in, you just pretend I'm here with you."

"But—"

"Because we're really not sure that that sub can't pick up our radios. It may know we're here, but it doesn't know what we're doing or where we're going. Best to play it safe."

Don mulled this over. He did not like the deception entailed, but there seemed to be considerable merit in her caution. There was indeed so much they didn't know! Meanwhile, he could study the ship with complete freedom and without distraction, and Melanie on the radio would be a comfortable hedge against the specters of isolation. It would only be for a while, after all, until the entire group returned here, or he returned to the base camp to rejoin them.

Still, he argued. "Yet with the phase—there's been no evidence that there's any other party on our radio circuit."

"Do you think we're the only ones ever to go through the tunnel? They could easily have a man sitting just this side, monitoring everything we say. They'd be fools not to."

"Oh." Ever the practical mind! "But what if the mermaid comes back?"

"For God's sake, don't blab on the radio about that! Gaspar would think you're crazy, and Melanie would be insanely jealous."

"Melanie jealous of a *mermaid?*"

"Imagine Melanie in the husky arms of a handsome triton."

"Triton?"

"Merman. Man with a fish tail. Picture him kissing her and running his slippery hands over her torso—"

"The bastard!"

"See? And *you're* not in love with her."

"W-what?"

"You wanted to know about jealousy, didn't you?"

"N-not that much!"

"Well, if that mermaid comes back, study her too. We have to ascertain the truth, and that's part of it. Just don't talk about it on the air, because another misunderstanding—"

"That sub might fire torpedoes!"

"Or something. All through your nice Minoan artifact. Want to gamble that men like Eleph *aren't* running this show?"

Men like Eleph. How cunningly she planted her barbs. This one was misdirected, for Eleph was a fine man under his crust. But no, Don didn't want to gamble on the militaristic mind, and there was surely one in that mystery submarine. Silence was a mandatory virtue, here.

It was done with dispatch. Soon Pacifa and Melanie were on their way back, leaving Don at the ship. They had never pitched their tent; the appearance of the mermaid had given them reason to change plans immediately.

Don explored the ship plank by plank. This was not as easy as he had expected. He could not leave his bicycle; he needed its field to breathe, and its light to see. There was not enough oxygen in the water inside the ship for his purpose. He had to haul himself topside regularly, lest he be asphyxiated. He could not conserve oxygen by sitting still, because the bike had to be in motion for the generator lamp to function more than a few seconds. In addition, he took a surprise tumble over a heavy beam that crossed the hold. It was invisible until he concentrated; it existed only in the phase world. He decided that it had been placed deliberately, to brace the ship against the outside pressure of the canyon walls, and it felt like metal. Which meant that someone had been here, in phase, before him—a lot less than four thousand years ago. Highly significant—but that was one thing he was not going to discuss on the radio.

There were no amphorae, those large two-handled point-bottomed jars used for the transport of grains and liquids in ancient times. Ordinary folk wondered why big jars should be pointed at their bases, so they could not stand up; the reason was that those points were wedged into pegboards, so that they were firmly planted and could not be dislodged by the heaving of the ship. Only a few pottery sherds remained, the kind that were so valuable archaeologically for the identification of cultures—when there was no chance to save the complete urns.

But far in the stern, in a nook in the galley section, stood a greater treasure: two intact *pithoi,* the monstrous ornate wide-mouthed storage jars typical of the Minoan society. Each had eight small handles, hardly large enough for a fingerhold, arranged around the top and near the base. No doubt these eyelets had held rope, so that the jars could be securely anchored as the ship heaved. But the rope itself had long since dissolved away.

Don peered inside, but could not bring his headlamp to bear conveniently. His hand passed through the jar without effect. They existed only in the other world: another frustrating dichotomy.

What had happened to the cargo? A ship this size might have had a capacity of several hundred tons, and carried a thousand amphorae. All the sherds remaining could not account for more than a dozen. They would not have been washed out when the ship sank, for the hull remained tight. In fact, the ship should not have sunk. Yet here it was, with a phase-world beam supporting it.

Was it a plant, after all? A manufactured artifact, placed within the past few years or months? All his experience with Minoan artifacts told him no, that the ship was genuine—but these logical incongruities were weighing heavily.

"You've been quiet too long," Melanie said on the radio. "Don, what are you up to?"

"I'm short of oxygen, I think," he said. This was true enough. As he spoke, he remembered what Pacifa had said of Melanie, indirectly: *And you're not in love with her.* That spoke volumes! But it wasn't necessarily true.

"Well, get yourself into a better current," she said, her concern coming through. Yes, she was perhaps in love with him, but that did not mean that he did not return the feeling. Why had Pacifa suggested otherwise?

He hauled himself up to the main deck again, short of breath. He was glad he had some physical justification for his discomfort, because with every discovery he made, his intellectual certainties took another battering. It was becoming difficult not to blab something on the radio that would give away more than was wise.

On the deck, walking the bike for oxygen and light, Don blinked. The mermaid was back.

CHAPTER 12

SPLENDID

Proxy 5–12–5–16–8: Attention.
Acknowledging.
Status?
Complicated. Dissension is occurring, and I fear that this is going to be difficult. The mission is in peril. I cannot make a proper report at this time.

Still dizzy from his interior explorations and the effort of getting himself and the bicycle clear of the hatch, Don nevertheless had the presence of mind to snap off the radio. "Splendid!" he exclaimed. There really seemed to be no better name for her, considering her attributes. That cloud of hair surrounding her head in the water . . .

She retreated with a graceful flexing of torso and tail. Her natural swimming motions only accented the flair of her wide hips. Don realized that she was afraid of him. That gave him confidence. He was as strange to her as she was to him!

The remaining mysteries of the Minoan ship could wait for a bit. Right now there was the living mystery of the mermaid.

He studied her carefully. She was beautiful, from hair to

waist; he could imagine no more perfect attributes in the female of the species. Her breasts in particular stood out, being full-bodied and supported by the water so that there was absolutely no sag. "Splendid," he said once more.

Actually, her nether portion was beautiful too. The smooth green scales began as her narrow waist expanded into what would have been a remarkable derriere of a normal woman. From there her body tapered into a strong, sleek tail, with only a suggestion of thighs near the origin.

Why had she returned, if she feared him? Where had she come from, really? She was mammalian, not piscene; there were no gill slits in her neck, and he could see her handsome chest expanding and contracting as she breathed.

Yes, breathed. Through her nose and mouth.

Was she phased?

No, for she swam. She had to be breathing water.

Okay, he thought. *Accept her as she is. And find out* WHAT *she is.*

"Come here, Splendid," he said. "Let's talk."

She heard him. But she seemed not to understand. She hovered off the edge of the deck, beyond his reach, and surveyed him nervously. At least she did not swim away, this time.

"Are you as curious about me as I am about you?" he asked her, pleased to note that he had no stutter. "Is that why you're h-here?" Oops.

She surveyed him a moment longer, then upended attractively and swam swiftly to the ground.

"Don't go away!" he cried. "I won't hurt you. I only want to know—"

But in a moment she was back, carrying something flat. It was a slate, like those once used for school lessons. ENGLISH? she wrote.

"American!" he exclaimed. "You *do* understand!"

Then, again, he wondered whether his mind had been affected. Fresh water under the sea; a preserved Minoan ship; a mermaid—who comprehended his own language. The stuff of dreams!

WHY DO YOU COME? she wrote.

And to her, *he* was the stuff of dreams! "I'm an archaeologist," he said.

Her eyes widened, I, TOO, she wrote.

A mermaid archaeologist? How far could credulity be stretched?

More and more, this reeked of a setup. Someone had been expecting him. Yet the problems of technique and motive remained. Who could do such a thing—and who would bother?

Which suggested again that the principle error lay within his own brain.

National security be damned, if that was what it was! If he was inventing all this, talking about his delusion could not hurt anyone but himself. If it wasn't all in his mind, the others needed to know. He needed to discuss it with someone.

He turned on the radio. "Melanie?"

There was a pause, and he thought she wasn't going to answer, but then she did. "Don, I wish you wouldn't just cut off in the middle—I mean, I'm afraid that you're hurt or—"

"Melanie, something came up."

Abruptly she expressed concern. "Are you all right? Say you're all right, Don!"

"Yes. I hope so. I—" But what could he say now?

RADIO, Splendid wrote. WHO?

"That's Melanie," Don explained. "I—"

"What?" Melanie asked.

"I—I'm all confused." Lame apology for what Melanie could hardly understand. But with the mermaid right here, what was he to do? "I'm not sure I'm quite sane at the moment. Too little oxygen—though I have enough now."

"I knew I shouldn't have left you alone! But you can tide through, Don. As soon as—" Then she evidently realized that she was breaking the rule herself, because she was supposed to pretend that Pacifa was with him.

Her voice was reassuring, because it was so familiar. But Splendid remained before him, observing and listening. It was evident that she understood the nature of the radio, and heard it. Don's headlamp had faded, so he saw her by her own lantern. Of the equipment that required power, the light went first, then the radio, and finally the battery-operated oxygenation field. He lifted the front of the bicycle and spun the wheel with his hand, to keep the radio going.

"Listen, Melanie," he said urgently. "I—when you're alone, do you ever *see* things? That don't make sense?"

"You're hallucinating? Oh, Don—"

WIFE? Splendid inquired on her slate.

"No, I'm single!" Don said. Then, to the radio: "I mean, Melanie, I'm not alone, exactly, and—" But how could he explain, without saying too much? He had made a bad tactical mistake, calling Melanie in the presence of the mermaid. "I'm—I'm just not sure I—I think the sea is—"

"You're seeing things, you mean? And you're not sure whether they're real?"

Splendid things—and they looked completely real. "Well, I—that is—Melanie, suppose I met another archaeologist?"

"In the *sea?*"

"Yes. Right here. In the trench."

"Another archaeologist—under the sea?" She was having understandable trouble with this.

"I'm trying not to say anything, until we—we muddle this through. Let's make it hypothetical. If I met—"

"Would you be seeing things?" she finished. "Not necessarily. There could be another party with the same mission. That makes as much sense as a sub with an eavesdropping radio. More bicycles starting from another point."

"Not on a bicycle," he said, eyeing Splendid's tail. The mermaid, catching on to the problem, flipped a fluke.

"Well, I suppose they could walk. It would be slower, but the phase would still—"

"Not phased." Fortunately?

"That submarine!" she exclaimed. "You mean it's ours? With archaeologists aboard? And they can't get out to check what's at the coordinates, while you can, so—"

"Not exactly. The sub's not here."

Melanie paused. "What are you trying to tell me, Don?"

"I'm trying *not* to tell you! It's just that I—"

"Oh, forget all the secrecy! I'm not going to blab. Tell me."

"Well, all right. I'm where you left me, only there's a mermaid here."

"A what?"

"A mermaid. A woman with the tail of a fish. She's hovering about fifteen feet away, and she's an archaeologist."

"Don, are you serious?"

"Afraid so," he said dubiously.

"You didn't fall and hit your head or something?"

"That's why I'm talking to you. It seems so crazy I hardly believe it myself, but here she is."

"Right there? Physically?"

"Completely." Splendid laughed silently, her breasts heaving. "Except for the phase, of course."

"Can she talk?"

"No, I don't think so. At least she hasn't, so far."

"Then how do you know she's an archaeologist?"

"She wrote it. With slate and chalk, or the equivalent."

"In English?"

"Yes."

There was a short silence. "Don, I hate to disappoint you. But I do think you're cracking up. Maybe you'd better talk to—to Pacifa." She was trying, belatedly, to pretend that Pacifa was with him.

"I did. She saw Splendid too."

"She *what?*"

"Saw Splendid. The mermaid, I mean. While you were exploring."

"What do you call it?"

"I don't know her real name."

"Splendid?"

"Well, I—"

"What's so splendid about her?" Melanie demanded.

"She—" Don looked nervously around, hesitant to mention breasts and knowing that hair would be disaster. His eye caught that of the mermaid, who was smiling above her splendors, her hair spreading out like a cape. That made it worse. But it gave him the inspiration of desperation. "Maybe you can talk to her!"

"Oh, now she talks!" Melanie said coolly.

"Through me, I mean. I'll read you what she writes."

"Don, this is—" Then she reconsidered. "All right. Ask her how she breathes."

He looked at Splendid, but she was already writing. Obviously she had grasped enough of the situation to participate, and her fear had dissipated. How could anyone be afraid of a man as bumbling as he was proving to be?

OUR LUNGS ARE ADAPTED TO ABSORB OXYGEN FROM WATER.

Don read it off to Melanie.

She did not sound convinced. "Where did she learn English?"

I STUDIED IT WHEN YOUNG.

"Don," Melanie said. "I can't keep ahead of your subconscious invention. These answers prove nothing."

Splendid frowned. It seemed that she did not appreciate being doubted.

"Melanie, she's really here! I'm not inventing this. I hope. Ask her something I can't answer."

"What color is George Washington's white horse?" she inquired sarcastically. "Look—did she study any other languages? Where is she from, anyhow?"

FROM CHINA. STUDIED SPANISH, GERMAN.

From China! Now he realized that part of what he had taken to be mer-features were actually the oriental cast, especially the eyes. He remembered that the orientals had adapted to the rough climate of their region with slightly different patterns of the distribution of fat, and flatter faces. These might also help in the rigors of the deep sea. They in no way diminished Splendid's beauty.

"Well, now," Melanie said. "It happens I know some German. Do you, Don?"

"No. Nothing except nein."

"And that's probably a number to you."

"No, I—"

Melanie fired off a paragraph in what sounded to Don's untrained ear like German. He was amazed: he had had no idea she knew any foreign language.

Splendid blushed. Splendidly. Then she looked angry.

"What did you say to her?" Don demanded.

Melanie sounded smug. "If I told you, you'd know. I want her answer, not yours."

"She's blushing. I didn't know mermaids could blush."

"They're female, aren't they?" Melanie inquired with satisfaction.

Now Splendid was writing furiously.

"I can't read her answer to you," Don said. "It's German, I think."

"That's all right," Melanie said. "Just spell it out. I'll copy down the letters and read it here. Then we'll know."

"Know what she says? Or that I'm not imagining—?"

"Yes."

Don sighed and began spelling out letters. "D-A-S M-Ä-D-C-H-E-N . . ." When he had spelled out the slateful, Splendid erased the tablet and started over. The transcription seemed interminable, because Don wasn't familiar with the alphabet, which had some funny squiggles, and had to read or describe each letter with extraordinary care. For example, there were two dots over the A in MÄDCHEN. The nipples of breasts? ". . . D-E-M A-B-O-R-T. H-A-B-E-N S-I-E V-E-R-S-T-A-N-D-E-N?"

"You bitch!" Melanie exclaimed.

"What?" Don asked, startled.

"Not you, dope. Her. With the splendid bosom."

"You mean you b-believe in her now?"

For an answer, Melanie let out another torrent of German. Her fury was manifest. This was an aspect of her Don had not encountered before. But this time Splendid merely turned her back, not deigning to respond. Don noticed that she had buttocks shaped under her scales, and there was a stronger suggestion of bifurcation, rear-view.

And he realized something else: the mermaid resembled a Cretan court lady, with her terraced skirts (scales) and generously open bodice. That was one reason she had been so appealing to him at first glance. A Minoan ship, with a Minoan lady? That sense of visiting the past . . .

"Well, what does she say?" Melanie demanded. There

was a sharpness in her voice that he had not heard before, in all their long conversations. It did not become her.

"Nothing. She's just facing away. I think she's ignoring you."

"Of all the nerve!" Melanie cried, and clicked off.

Now Splendid turned to face him. There was a new look of confidence on her face. She had evidently had the best of it, despite the initial setback. It no longer seemed so strange to be talking to a mermaid on an ancient ship, in the depths of the deepest trench in the Atlantic Ocean. "What were you two *saying*?"

WOMAN TALK, she wrote noncommittally. HOW DID YOU COME HERE?

How much could he afford to tell her? He hardly knew her! On the other hand, how could he learn about her, if he didn't exchange information? She was a tough bargainer. "I rode my bicycle. How about you?"

She looked at his bike, and her eyebrow lifted as she noted the way the tires sank beneath the visible deck when he rode it, picking up oxygen and recharging his headlamp. Then she looked at his feet as he stopped, for they also sank. Some of her confidence dissipated. She had to admit he resembled a ghost in this respect.

WE ARE AN EXPERIMENTAL COLONY, ADAPTED TO LIVE UNDER PRESSURE IN WATER. HOW DO YOU SURVIVE THIS?

So she was willing to trade information. "I'm phased into another framework," Don said, making sure his radio was off. "I'm not subject to pressure, and the water's like air. You say you're adapted. You mean you were born on land? With—with legs?"

YES. I STILL HAVE LEG BONES, FUSED AT THE BASE ONLY. FOR FLEXIBILITY. She rotated her nether portion, switching her tail. It was remarkably supple, and the motion reminded him vaguely of a hula dance. It certainly accentuated her anatomy provocatively. HOW CAN I PERCEIVE YOU, IF YOU ARE NOT HERE?

"Well, I am here—in a way. I am of this world. But I'm not very solid, as far as this world goes, right now. Here, I'll show you." He walked his bicycle toward her.

Splendid backed off, then reconsidered and propelled herself forward by means of little swimming motions that accentuated her various attributes intriguingly. She put out a hand to touch his.

The two hands passed through each other with that odd temporary meshing of bones. Splendid's mouth opened, and she catapulted herself backward with a grand flip of her tail.

"It's just the phase," Don said reassuringly. "I'm not a ghost." Then he remembered to ask his question. "If you're Chinese, why are you here? In the Western hemisphere?"

WE NEED TO MATCH THE PRESSURE OF JUPITER'S ATMOSPHERE. THIS IS ONE STAGE. BUT FIRST WE MUST HAVE WARMTH AND FRESH WATER, AND THERE IS NONE THIS DEEP NEAR CHINA. CAN YOU SURVIVE ANYWHERE?

Jupiter's atmosphere! Were the Chinese planning a colony there? Don had no idea whether the pressure of four miles of water on Earth came anywhere near approximating that of the atmosphere on monster Jupiter; it probably depended on how deep in that atmosphere they went. It did seem reasonable that what could be adapted to survive in the one medium, could also be adapted to survive in the other. A fish tail here; wings, there?

"Pretty much," he said, answering her question. "But it has its limitations. I can't do anything much in the real world, and I can't leave my bicycle. And I have to keep moving around, to pick up oxygen, unless there's a good current." Was this too much information? American relations with China varied through the years, and changed as the administrations of either country changed. No, she couldn't use the information against him, because she couldn't touch him. He had told her nothing that wouldn't be evident if she watched him for any length of time. "And are you studying this ship?"

It turned out that she was. She was part of a mer-colony whose main object was mere survival at this depth. Pressure *per se* was not the greatest hurdle to overcome, for anyone could live at any depth provided there was a life support system and no sudden or extreme pressure flux. But it was a convenient starting place, and much had to be learned about the long-term complications of such existence before the sophisticated aspects of alternate-medium colonization could be explored. Later there would be other adaptations, to compensate for the cold, and the methane atmosphere, and turbulence of liquid Jupiter. Meanwhile, the hot fresh water enabled the human beings to survive naked without osmotic dehydration—and also preserved remarkable artifacts, such as this ship. That was an unplanned bonanza! So Splendid, an amateur archaeologist, had expected, before being selected for this experimental mer-colony, to specialize in one of the pre-Columbian American Indian cultures and to trace the connections between it and the prehistoric Mongolian cultures from which the Amerinds derived. She had given up her first dream to realize the second: mankind's exploration of a really new world. Now she was making herself useful by returning to her first specialty, recording the ship's anomalies to the best of her abilities. She knew little of Minoan culture, to her regret, but did recognize this as an Old World vessel of considerable antiquity. She had cleaned up much of the interior and had taken all but two of the unbroken *pithoi* jars to her village for transshipment to China by submarine.

"But that's plundering!" Don protested. "The relic should be preserved intact!"

WE DID NOT EXPECT ANY OTHER PARTY TO HAVE ACCESS TO IT, she explained contritely. WE DARE NOT REMOVE THE WOOD, FOR IT MIGHT DISINTEGRATE ON LAND. BUT THE AMPHORAE ARE GOING TO OUR BEST ARCHAEOLOGICAL MUSEUMS. THERE ALL THE PEOPLE WILL SEE AND LEARN AND BENEFIT, INSTEAD OF ONLY THOSE FEW WHO DWELL IN THE DEPTH OF THE SEA.

What could he say? The Chinese were perhaps the most culturally aware people in the world; they would not be hawking invaluable ancient relics on the streets. The deep reaches of international waters were open to any party for salvage—anyone who could manage to reach them. It would be a criminal waste not to recover as much of the ship and its contents as possible.

"I'm sorry," Don said after a bit. "You're right. Except about the amphorae. They're *pithoi*—wide-mouthed, flat-bottomed jars. But I don't think it's fair to remove everything before I have a chance to study it. This entire ship represents an artifact of my specialty, Minoan Crete."

Splendid drifted toward him excitedly. She opened her mouth as if to speak, but no sound came. Obviously she had once talked, and still tried to do it when she forgot herself. Probably her vocal cords had been exchanged for some liquid filtering device. But he needed no words to grasp what was on her mind.

"Yes. That's why I'm here. I—"

But it wasn't that simple. Splendid tried to take his hand, and failed. But this time she did not recoil. She beckoned to him as she swam across the deck.

Perplexed, Don followed, walking his bicycle. She dived down into the hold, but he balked at the access hole, fearing that there was not yet enough oxygen. The water changed slowly, here. But he did crank up his light and shine it down inside so that he could watch her.

She passed through the cross-timber as if it did not exist, which was true for her, then drew up to the two remaining *pithoi*, and reached inside one. There was something there. She lifted it and carried it back, breathing rapidly.

Don realized as she angled up through the hatch that she, too, suffered from lack of oxygen. Her chest was heaving strenuously. This was impressive for an irrelevant reason, as he tried to remind himself.

As she recovered her breath in the fresh water topside, she offered him the object she had taken from the jar. It seemed to be a flake of stone, rectangular and flat.

"Sorry—the phase won't let me touch it," Don said regretfully. He passed his hand through it by way of illustration.

Disappointed, she held it up so that he could see the face of it. It was a tablet of some sort: clay, not stone. At least it had a ceramic coating. He cranked up his light again and flashed the beam across the surface.

There was writing on it! Don recognized the typical configuration of Minoan Linear A or B: the lines, boxes, and slashes. It was an ancient manuscript!

He had thought that the discovery of the ship was the ultimate in his career desire. Now he knew he had been too conservative. A document relating to the ship and its business, perhaps dated, putting things into context—it was probably the A script, considering the age of the ship. Ideal!

Smiling, Splendid turned the tablet away.

"Wait!" Don cried. "I can read it!"

She wrote on her own tablet. BUT I CAN'T.

"You don't understand! I can read some of the Minoan

signs—but you have to hold it up, because I can't touch the tablet myself. I need your cooperation!''

She nodded affirmatively, her hair flaring in the trace currents the action made, but did not expose the face of the tablet.

''What do you want?'' he demanded, frustrated.

She wrote: IT MUST BE SHARED.

''You mean you want to know what it says? I certainly don't object to that.''

TRANSLATE ALOUD.

''But that's a long, tedious task! Nobody can decipher such a document at a mere glance! When I said I could read it, I meant—given time. A day, a week, perhaps more, depending on the clarity and dialect. There'll probably be many symbols I can't make out at all, so the narrative will be fragmentary.''

She nodded as she wrote. BOTH JARS ARE FILLED WITH SIMILAR TABLETS—ALL DIFFERENT.

It was like being informed of victory in a million dollar sweepstakes. A sizable cache of narrative Minoan Linear A! His single glance had told him that this was no list of accounts; he could recognize numbers instantly, and this contained few. It was text!

But she had a stiff price. ''That will take months,'' he exclaimed with mixed concern, intrigue, and greed. It didn't seem feasible to commit himself to such a long period of shared labor, that would certainly be complicated by involved explanations of nuances. He didn't know when Pacifa and the others would return to cut it short.

On the other hand, this might be his only chance to really study the tablets. That was an opportunity it was inconceivable to squander. He did need her assistance, and it would not be exactly boring, considering her body and exposure. Too bad he couldn't touch her.

Touch her? What was he thinking of? What of Melanie, with whom he was developing a significant relationship. Why should he be distracted by a creature who was both out of phase and of a different, if newly-created, species? It was nonsensical.

Yet those breasts, that hair . . .

So he was a voyeur. As was any man who watched what was paraded on television or motion pictures. Just so long as he didn't confuse the vision with the reality. Meanwhile, he had a vital job to do, that he might never be able to do at another time.

"All right," he said at last. "I've got to see those tablets. You handle the hardware; I'll translate. Aloud."

She clapped her hands noiselessly and dived down the hatch with marvelous grace. Her tail now seemed to be a natural part of a lovely creature.

Splendid had not exaggerated about the number of tablets. It took some time to bring them all up, and she was breathless and tired. She had been holding her breath while working in the hold, to avoid the oxygen-depleted water there, but that hardly added to her comfort. Don became concerned, watching her game struggle. She was doing her part, certainly.

How fortunate that the tablets had been in the last remaining *pithoi*. No, not fortune, but design, for the huge jars were normally used for liquids and grains, not ceramics. Splendid must have found the tablets elsewhere in the ship, and hidden them. Why? Surely not in the hope that a phased-out American archaeologist would ride up on a bicycle.

Now the tablets were all present, and minor reservations were forgotten in the excitement of incipient discovery. Already he could see that there were numerical designations in the corners of each tablet, probably representing dates and order. That suggested a single coherent narrative spanning the tablets as if they were pages of a book. Nothing like this had been found on Crete itself, as far as he knew.

Splendid put her hands over the nearest, warningly.

"Okay, okay!" Don said. "Aloud. I was just getting organized. See those symbols in the corners? The simplest ones are in the upper left, here. These are numbers. These four little lines | | | | stand for the number four. The Minoans didn't have separate signs for each, as we do, but they did use the decimal system. This has to be a serious document, and this is page four. The first thing to do is put them in order."

Comprehension lighted her face, and he was reassured that she really did have serious archaeological interest. She soon located the little sun-circle ° that stood for number one, then the stacked circles °₀ that were two, and the ⁻_⁻ that was three. The first four pages were intact.

Their luck could not hold forever. Tablet number 5 was missing, as was number 11, of an original total of twelve or more. Even so, Don was gratified that the all-important opening tablet was present, because he saw that it contained some truly remarkable material: lines of symbols in different scripts.

"Another Rosetta Stone!" he exclaimed. "Column One is Linear A; Two looks like Ugaritic, and Three is Sumerian cuneiform!"

DO YOU READ THEM ALL? Splendid inquired, amazed.

Don laughed. "N-not really. But I have studied many ancient forms of writing in the course of my attempts to decipher Minoan, so I am familiar with a number of the common symbols. See, here's a column of Egyptian hiero-glyphs, too, but they aren't as important as the Linear A here. See this insect-form? We can trace it right along . . ."

Because the text was extensive, consistent, and straight-forward, and because he was aided immeasurably by the key-code of parallel languages, Don found the text much easier to decipher then he had feared. There were still a number of terms he didn't recognize, as the tabulation was representative rather than comprehensive, but the context made many of them clear, and his own knowledge of Minoan culture offered hints for the remainder. This was a narrative like none other known of this culture. He could not vouch for place names, but was sure his general rendition was reasonably accurate. Splendid turned out to be far more help than hindrance, industriously running down word-repetition and offering alert conjectures for unintelligible symbols.

They had a story—and what a story it was!

CHAPTER 13

MINOS

Proxy 5-12-5-16-8: Attention.
Acknowledging.
Status?
Remains difficult. Two members of the group have developed a suspicion, and are trying to verify it. One is holding me captive, and I am unable to tell of the mission for fear it will only be misunderstood. I must wait for the assembly of the remainder of the group, and hope I can then persuade it. The final two challenges have become passe.
Then it will be better to abort the mission. We can recover you—
No! There remains some hope. I will remain with it. I am convinced this method can be effective. I must see it through.
Your insistence may cost you your life.
And it may salvage this world!
It remains your prerogative. Signal us at need.

You who peruse this printed clay, I charge you by the name of the Great Earth Mother, and by the Sacred Leaf of the Tree of Life, and most particularly by our common bond of scholarship: honor the foible of a kindred spirit.

Grant to me the favor I ask herein, or relegate this manuscript unread to that place from which you recovered it, that one after you may honor it instead.

Don exchanged glances with Splendid as they shared this opening injunction. "Can we be bound by that?"

She thought for a moment, then wrote: BY EARTH MOTHER, NO. BY TREE OF LIFE, NO.

"But by 'our common bond of scholarship'? He really covers everything!"

WHAT IS HIS SPECIFIC REQUEST?

Don glanced ahead at the partly blocked out text. "He doesn't seem to say, here. Maybe he's saving it for the end." He moved toward the final tablet, but Splendid swam to block him. Their bodies passed through each other with a complete meshing of skeletons: hip against hip, rib against rib, skull against skull. His open eyes stared through the fog of her brain. It was as close as he would ever be to a woman, but he did not find the experience exhilarating.

Splendid emerged from his back with a startled expression, but quickly recovered and flashed around him to the tablets. She covered the last with her tail, so that he could not see the script.

"But you asked—" Don said, still assimilating impressions from their momentary merger. Had he actually felt her living heart beating?

She shook her head, recovering her slate, and explained: HE WANTS US TO DECIDE FIRST.

"Yes, certainly. But we *can't* commit ourselves blindly, whatever his conventions may have been. Maybe he wants us to commit ritual suicide so we can't pass on the secret. Considering how long he's been dead himself—"

NO. HE WANTS IT KNOWN. ONLY A SCHOLAR

COULD READ EVEN ENOUGH TO RETURN THE
TABLETS TO THE SEA.

"That's the point! An illiterate is not bound. He can do
anything he wants with the manuscript, but he'll never know
what it says. A scholar must either return it unread, or bind
himself to an unspecified commitment. Which may be to
forget that he ever read it."

AN UNSCRUPULOUS SCHOLAR WOULD IGNORE
THE STIPULATION. HE IS ADDRESSING THE PER-
SON OF INTEGRITY. WHY SHOULD HE COMMIT
ONLY THAT ONE TO SILENCE OR DEATH?

Don began to see it. "Only a really honest man
would—" He paused as she wrote emphatically on the slate.

PERSON.

Oh. She objected to usage which seemed to exclude her.
Melanie would have approved that sentiment! "Only a
really honest person would comprehend certain niceties.
Would understand the necessity of doing—whatever is
requested. And he'd have to read the full manuscript first, to
get the background. But maybe the thing is difficult, so he
has to be committed first, and not depend on his own first
reactions."

Splendid nodded agreement.

"I really don't care what the price is," Don said. "I must
find out what this manuscript says. Now more than ever."

I AGREE IF YOU DO.

Don sighed. "I agree to our Minoan's terms. I hope I
don't regret it."

I am Pi-ja-se-me, appraiser for Minos by vocation,
antiquarian by avocation. To me it has fallen to record the
termination of civilization.

Surely no parchment can survive the eons until mankind recovers the cultural level of the Thalassocracy,

even were that document not to reside beneath the restless turbulence of this phenomenal and distant ocean. Therefore I have fashioned this stylus and this tablet of clay, and I shall fire it well in the hearth of the ship's galley until it has the permanence of fine pottery. A tedious task, but I have nothing if not time, until the wine runs out.

I append here a glossary of signs, that my manuscript may be intelligible for the eye of whatever national who at length recovers it. I regret I can do no more, but I am not expert in all the myriad written variants of the world, even had I the space to render them here. Perhaps even this token is wasted, for who but the gods can say what shall arise from the depths of the unknowable future. Yet must I essay it.

Our merchant fleet of five fine ships was bearing south after engaging in profitable trading with the Megalithic cities of the far west as we knew it. We exchanged pithoi of fine Cretan olive oil for equal measure of their special stone pigments. Our sophisticated gold ornaments for their rare ores. The Megalithics seem less cultured than we, but this is deceptive; their knowledge is confined largely to their priesthood, and they are unexcelled builders and astronomers. In fact, I suspect their culture goes back farther than ours, for some of their most impressive monuments are ancient by our standards, and we still could learn from them were their priestly hierarchy less canny about the disposition of their arts. But I diverge; it is the wine. Yet must I imbibe what offers, or thirst interminably. This salty sea . . .

It was at [indecipherable place name—north coast of Iberia?] that Admiral Su-ri-mo and I first had word. We had been at sea five months, and I was eager to return to villa and concubine. My villa: none quite like it on all [Thera], though never was I a wealthy man. Situated high on the side of the holy mountain, provided with fiercely hot water by duct from the sacred spring: few in all our empire possess rights to such overflow, but I, as royal antiquarian/appraiser was favored by the priesthood. I do not mean to exalt my own importance, which is not great; I seek only to explain in part the kindly favoritism extended to me by a monarch who values cultural studies. All about my residence perched the artifacts of my life's collection: ancient identification seals of baked clay from [Anatolia—Turkey]; faience from the orient, distinct from ours; a fine flint dagger from a burial mound in [Arabia]; and of course many varieties of decorative pottery, each representative of a vanished culture. For years my concubine, otherwise a very fine woman if a trifle tight about the waist-ring, was jealous of the attentions I paid these objects, not understanding how a man could see as much value in a discolored sherd as in a living woman. In truth, I was at times grateful for that jealousy, for it prompted her to ever-greater imagination in her calling.

Don could not restrain a smile at this point. Splendid, after due consideration, decided to smile too. How little some things changed!

This amount of translation had taken two days. But it was time well spent, and the remainder promised to move more rapidly as the last difficult symbols yielded their meanings.

It seems I cannot hew precisely to my theme; my mind insists upon revisiting those things that were dear to me. Must I then ramble, however pointlessly, and hope to cover the essence in whatever fashion I can manage.

The omens were ill. The sky turned drab, and the sunset was like a stifled inferno. A hideous odor suffused the air. Yet there was no storm. We put into a local port and made inquiries, and received a story brought by runners, of a disaster unlike any known.

Neither Admiral Su-ri-mo nor I believed it at first. We supposed Greek enemies had spread the foul story in an effort to dismay us and force us to divulge our technical secrets. But within a few days one of our own ships hailed us and confirmed the disaster in all its awfulness.

Terrible fire and storm had ravaged all Crete. Our cities had been destroyed by waves taller than the mast of this ship, our crops buried under a thick mass of choking hot dust. Of our mighty fleet, the finest ever to rule the [Mediterranean] sea, only that fraction at sea and far from home escaped. The land itself, buried in noxious mud, was unlivable.

Now those far-flung ships were summoned home. Our people needed them for migration to unspoiled lands, lest our power be dissipated entirely. Vain hope! The strength of our civilization lies not in our ships, but in the extreme fertility of our land, the density of our great timber forests, and the unexcelled craftsmanship of our artisans. We must rebuild our palaces, as we have in the past, if we are to maintain any portion of our national well-being.

"But what of our own fair city?" I cried. "Our isle is not Crete, our homeland is not Knossos. Surely we, at least escaped the holocaust?"

"Your city is no more," our informant said. "We sailed by it, checking all our cities. The fire consumed [Thera] utterly. Not even the island remains, merely a burnt shell."

Still we could not believe. But if we went home to verify this horror directly, and it were true, we would become subject to this makeshift government and have to give over our fine ships to the transport of women and cattle, and our treasures to usurping tyrants. No way to salvage our culture, this! Yet if we did not go back, and this report were false, what then of our loyalty?

The Admiral and I discussed the matter at length, the crushing hand of calamity gripping us both. We professed not to believe, we reassured each other repeatedly, but at the root we withered. At length we decided to detach two ships, who would return to ascertain the truth, while the remainder stayed clear. One ship at least would come back to us to make report. This was a cumbersome procedure, but it seemed the best strategy, given our divided belief.

I remained aboard one of the three. I would have gone home, but Su-ri-mo chose to keep me with the bulk of the merchandise, for only I knew its precise value and the details of its inventory.

For a time we continued to travel the coast of the [Atlantic] ocean as if seeking more trade, though we had little remaining for barter. At night we found safe anchorage and sent the men ashore to gather driftwood and make a fire to cook the main meal. The crewmen would grind grain and bake the morrow's bread over the embers, and the wine would circulate. They slept on the sand, the smoke from banked fires driving off the nocturnal pests. The Admiral and I had to remain aboard our respective ships, guarding the cargo, for not all the impressed hands were trustworthy. I made do with the ship's galley, learning by scorching my fingers on the inadequate hearth. How I envied the landed crew, and how I cursed my isolation here! Yet it would seem that the Great Earth Mother destined this, for now I have need of this hearth.

Time hung heavy as we awaited confirmation of the fate of our land. The men shaved each other with the few precious iron blades available, with much cursing and scraping of skin. Perhaps not all of the cuts were accidental. They wagered interminably. I completed the inventory of cargo of all three ships, and started it over, for want of other diversion.

Winter came, harsh in these hinterlands, and it was impossible to continue at sea in the treacherous weather and waters. We docked at [another Megalithic city?], paying an exorbitant harbor tax. Now at last I could depart ship, for our wares were secure. But it was scant improvement. This was no Knossos.

Knossos! I had visited there often, in my official capacities, and though I would not have cared to reside in that crush, it was a splendor. Four and five stories high, with the magnificent reception hall on the second girt by the massive, artful pillars—would you believe it, I have seen pillars elsewhere that actually contract toward the apex, making the entire structure appear inverted. Any refined eye must readily perceive that a decorative column must expand toward the apex—which shows little aesthetic hope, for example, for the [Mycenaeans— Greeks].

But this Megalithic port: the houses were all separate, none possessing even a second story, and all without proper sanitary facilities. These people hardly believed in bathing, and the odor inside became appalling. Their men were thick-bodied, wearing waist-clasps only to support their rude garments. They even had the effrontery to remark on our own style, calling our narrow waists unnatural. Unnatural! How could I ever forget my pride when I donned the metal belt of adulthood at the age of ten, wearing it to preserve that aesthetic slenderness of torso that so befits the physically fit. I wear it to this day, and no man of this expedition can lay claim to a smaller or more manlier waist than I, despite the fact that my gaming days are long past. To watch Island-born Cretans laying aside their clasps of honor and allowing their bodies to grow gross with dissipation—that is unnatural!

Yet I must admit they had some cause. The semi-savage women of this town were alluring in their very primitiveness. If a man must put aside his belt in order to enjoy the favors of such—well, I would not do it myself, but I can not entirely blame the younger males who never had relations with a competent concubine. It was a long, bitter winter, and the women were warm-bodied.

I did find some solace. Not far distant was one of their great monuments, not of stone, unfortunately, but still impressive in wood. Impressive architecturally, that is to say; to my way of thinking, the man is far more important than any monument, and needs no wood or stone to bolster his glory. He is the ideal. Hence we have few actual monuments in [Keftiu] or any of the islands. For foreigners seldom comprehend. There, again, is the distinction between the civilized and the pseudo-civilized. Consider, if you will, the extremes of the [Egyptians]. Yet, in fairness, I must say that the Mega-lithics do put their edifices to marvelous uses, and I understand their astronomical data are the most precise in the world. It is always a folly to take too narrow a view. Even clumsy cultures have their points.

I found a number of significant artifacts about the premises. Enough to satisfy me that the Megalithics have, indeed, had a long history, and may even have declined from prior greatness. Of course I have no absolute way to date any given sherd of pottery, but I believe it is safe to assume that those excavated from deep in the ground are of greater antiquity than those near the surface. I was extremely fortunate in discovering a clay seal in good condition that I suspect is several hundred years old. That is especially gratifying, because of the symbolism of my own seal. As a matter of information, I shall imprint it here. [Imprint of an oval scene, a representation of a pottery sherd, on which is a mazelike pattern.] Note the design on the sherd: it is a precise duplicate of an actual decoration on a sherd I recovered from a cave on the [Syrian] coast. But the linkage between seal and design is more than this. I have reason to believe that this particular pottery design is itself emulative of the pattern on a fabric, perhaps a hanging tapestry. And that, in turn, the design was imprinted on the fabric by a large clay seal. So the complete symbolism on my own seal, of which I am justly proud, is that it completes the circle. It is a seal bearing a representation of a design copied from a tapestry imprinted by a similar seal! I suspect that this was, in fact, the original purpose of seals, and that only later did they evolve into personal signatures. Whatever the truth, I believe my own seal captures a portion of it. Alas, no one else appreciates this meaning, yet it sustains me now. I speculate endlessly: in my collection is a seal recovered from a mound in [Anatolia], that I once toured with a [Hittite] scholar. Our own Cretan origins, according to legend, are there. Certainly there are similar bulls there, and similar plants, and I saw the ruin of an ancient city there that was very like one of our own. Foreigners consider our palaces to be mazes in their complexity—and there in [Anatolia] are maze patterns. Yet in opposition I must say that our legends also speak of a seafaring tradition extending very far back and covering an even wider scope than at present, so that our ancestors could have traveled by ship from much farther ports than [Anatolia]. How dearly would I like to know the answer!

* * *

Don pushed away the tablets, and naturally his hands passed through them instead. "I like that man!" he exclaimed. "He's a real archaeologist!"

Splendid looked thoughtful. HE IS MUCH LIKE YOU, she wrote.

Flattered and embarrassed, Don changed the subject. "I've hardly been aware of time! Do you realize we've used up two more days? But at the rate this is accelerating, we'll finish it tomorrow. This is obviously the mission for which I was sent, and it's the greatest experience of my life. And you are making it possible, you gorgeous creature."

She smiled, touched her hand to her lips, and put it to his mouth.

Don, fatigued from his strenuous intellectual labors and intoxicated by the combination of Minoan revelation and lack of sleep, was moved. Splendid had kissed him! He had spoken to her with the camaraderie of their intense recent intellectual association, without stuttering, and she had responded. How things had changed! "Watch that," he told her facetiously. "Old Pi-ja-se-me relaxed with his jealous concubine after a hard stint of business."

Splendid smiled again and opened her arms invitingly to him.

"God, no!" he exclaimed, shocked now. "You're— I'm—I was joking. I mean, the phase—"

She drifted up to him and put her arms about him, barely touching. He could feel that fringe contact of flesh through flesh, and it was very like the feather-gentle caress of a real woman. Her face came up to his, and he could not resist meeting her lips. It was like kissing a wisp of fog, yet it had considerable impact on him.

Don backed away, guiltily. "What are you trying to do?"

She only shook her head, still smiling.

Don turned away. What would she be doing, except playing with a man she knew could not touch her? Both because of the phase, and because she was a mermaid. Was that why mermaids had such fascination for men, mythologically? Because, anatomically, they were genuinely unobtainable?

Still, he was tired and he did envy Pi-ja his jealous concubine. Who could say what he might do, given the ability actually to touch a female like Splendid?

When he turned again, she was gone. Nothing exceptional about that; she departed regularly to fetch food and take care of natural calls. However she performed them. She would return, as decorative and helpful as ever. She had left the remaining tablets face down on the deck, so he could not cheat; this remained a business association, with safeguards.

Jealous concubine. That reminded him of Melanie, perhaps unkindly. He had been severely distracted these past few days, but down below his consciousness he had not forgotten her, or Pacifa's remark about her. Melanie loved him? How would he feel about Melanie in the arms of a virile merman, or even merely alone with one for several days, unchaperoned?

It was time to check in with her. He turned on the radio. "How are you doing, Melanie?" he inquired, not sure her set was even on. It had been off the other times he had tried calling her.

She was waiting for him this time, however, her hand evidently on a figurative detonator. "Why don't you go make out with your paramour, instead of wasting my time?"

Taken aback because this so baldly reflected the lascivious thoughts he had just entertained, Don could only stutter. "I—I—"

"I, by God, am a human being," Melanie informed him wrathfully. "A female only to the extent I choose to be."

She couldn't know about Splendid's seeming invitation! The radio had not been on for any dialogue for four days. What had set her off, aside from that tiff with the mermaid?

What else but jealousy! Hell had no fury. Yet it was baseless, because Splendid simply was not obtainable, and he understood that on both the intellectual and emotional levels. What good was the most impressive body known—and Splendid had that—when it might as well have been an untouchable hologram? Melanie, in contrast, was real for him, and not merely physically. He had to reassure her about that.

"Melanie, you don't un-understand—" he started lamely.

"I am quite certain that you have conscious control over the specifically male aspect of your life—sexual inter-course—but I am much less certain that you have much conscious awareness of your internal myths concerning sexual roles."

She certainly wasn't tongue-tied! But what was this about having sex? She knew the phase made that impossible. "I d-don't know what you're t-talking about," he said, never-theless feeling guilty. Suppose it *had* been possible? What would he have gotten into—bad choice of words—then?

"You mean you haven't tried the balloons yet? How considerate of you." Her tone was cutting.

"B-balloons?"

"Oh, you're impossible!" She clicked off.

Don shook his head. She was furious, all right. But what was responsible? This seemed like more than mere irritation because of his necessary association with another woman.

Then he began to see. The balloons were about the only way the phase world could interact with the real world, since they were half-phased. Gas trapped in the balloons made them rigid in both frameworks. If they were put on the fingers like gloves, they would make it possible to handle something, and to feel it fairly firmly. Even human flesh. A balloon was a lot like a condom.

In his naivete he had never thought of this in connection with Splendid. Obviously Melanie had. Maybe she did have grounds for jealousy.

Yet that could not be the whole of it. Even if Melanie assumed that he, as a man, would take whatever offered— why should she think that Splendid would offer? The mermaid had a community of her own kind. Her interest here was archaeological, and it was genuine, as was his.

Don had a question for Splendid when she returned: "What did you tell Melanie, that made her so mad?"

The mermaid shook her head negatively. She wasn't telling.

"Uh-uh," Don said. "Y-you tell me, or I'll s-stop translating!" It was a bluff, for he knew nothing could keep him away from the tablets after he'd had a few hours of sleep. But it was important to unravel this personal matter too.

Splendid elected to yield to the threat, though she doubted that she took it seriously. She took up her slate. ONLY WHAT SHE ASKED.

"Then what did she ask?"

There was just a hint of that blush. HOW WE DO IT.

Um, yes. How *did* mermaids reproduce, etc.? There simply seemed to be no apparatus in the nether section of her body. "And what did you t-tell her?"

THAT I WOULD SHOW YOU.

Brother! Every day of his radio silence must have been new evidence to Melanie that Splendid was, well, showing. And that he was using the balloons in a new way.

"I—I wish you would apologize to her. She's furious!"

Now Splendid looked stubborn, with a heightening of the blush. I HAVE NOT YET SHOWN.

"You don't *need* to show!" he yelled. "Melanie's jealous because she thinks—never mind. Just tell her what we've really been doing. She refuses to believe *me*."

SHE WOULD NOT BELIEVE ME EITHER.

Probably true. But it was necessary to make the effort. "Look, Splendid, this—she—I—it's important."

The mermaid cocked her head, evidently catching on. YOU LOVE HER?

"I—I—yes, I guess I do."

SHE KNOWS WE CANNOT TOUCH?

"There might be a way."

She nodded. I WILL TELL HER.

Don felt a wash of relief. "Thank you! I—" He gave up trying to express himself, and turned on the radio.

It was no use. Melanie's radio remained off. It might remain that way for some time.

He sighed. She would just have to stay mad for as long as it took. At worst, until they got together again, and communication between them could not be cut off.

Right now he had to sleep.

Our two vessels never returned. By spring we were assured the story was accurate, and we had a fair notion what had occurred. I have seen volcanic action upon occasion, and know how devastating such blasts from the deep earth can be. I also know that the fumeroles and hot springs that made our islet warm and fertile had to stem from similar forces. It was surely a volcanic eruption near or at [Thera], and the fire and stone from it, and the waves it made in the sea, and the dust and gases of its murderous exhalations, that ravaged our world and brought our very civilization to its knees.

But that is the lesser of two *mysteries*. The greater is not how, but *why*. Surely our priests were well aware of the propensities of the mighty Bull of the Earth, and surely they propitiated it regularly and generously. Every sacrifice, every spectacle of bull-leaping, every intoned prayer—all these tokens, and indeed our cultural outlook, have been dedicated to the pacification of that shuddering Power. Had we been remiss in our worship, then might such retribution have been justified. But I am certain that we were not; the rites were maintained faithfully right up until the moment of the holocaust. Why, then, did the monster turn on us?

I have no answer. I must instead face the reality, as Admiral Su-ri-mo and I faced it then. What should we do with our treasures, so laboriously acquired? They became meaningless when our homeland ended. Our king was dead, our homes destroyed. The barbarians who had seized titular power in our misfortune were not worthy of our allegiance. We should not, could not, go home. But neither could we endure another winter in a pagan city. It was necessary to get our men away from such influences, lest we lose our identity along with our culture and our wealth.

After much consideration we plotted course for [Africa]. Because many of our men on all three ships had become corrupted by the life among the Megalithics, and were almost openly rebellious, we were forced to voyage far out to sea, planning to make landfall only in the direst emergency. For this reason we loaded our holds with a tremendous volume of supplies, though we had to sacrifice the goods for which we had already traded. What use were ores and pigments, now?

Yet even to me, the sheer volume of wine and grain seemed excessive. I tried to caution Su-ri-mo, but he assured me that [Africa] was farther distant than I realized, and that we needed a good margin in case of delays. We would be traveling shorthanded, for we could not hope to recruit enough oarsmen to fill the seats of the defectors. But with good winds it would not matter as much. One sail is worth all the oarsmen, when the wind is right.

Thus I bowed to his judgment, for he was much experienced on the sea and the responsibility was his. Certainly I had little cause for misgiving on this score, since too much food is far less burdensome than too little.

For a month we journeyed south, impeded by adverse winds and contrary currents. It seemed that our store of misfortune had not yet been expended. Discipline among the men, never good since the disaster, became ragged, for they sought surcease from the toil of rowing through still seas and wished to return to the pleasures of the city. Also, they did not like such a long period out of sight of any land. But the Admiral held firm, and after several troublemakers had been quartered the noise subsided somewhat. I was glad that harsh measures had not been required. We remained far out to sea, however, for fear of mutiny should the men catch sight of land and know their bearings.

Still, I knew that navigation entirely by sunstone was precarious, and I feared the Admiral himself lacked precise knowledge of our whereabouts. Yet he seemed assured, even confident. First I supposed this was a false front, so as not to show weakness before the crew; then I suspected that he was deluded. But in no wise did he play the role of delusion, apart from this foolhardy westward drifting. I am a fair judge of men, necessarily, and I knew the Admiral well. Gradually it came upon me that he had a destination—and that it was not [Africa]. I braced him one day when I caught him privately during a routine inspection of my ship.

"Admiral, I must know the truth if I am to function effecively," I said with some asperity.

He attempted to evade. "Do you doubt my bearings?"

"Not at all, except as they pertain to [Africa]. Our homeland is gone; what use are secrets now?"

He understood my reference. "Yes," he said slowly. "There is no proper home for us in [Africa]. It is the far port we voyage to."

"It is forbidden!" I cried, shocked by this bald confirmation of my dark suspicion.

He was unmoved. "As you have so eloquently pointed out: what are secrets, what are prohibitions, when we have no one to answer to? It is for us to carry the news, and to make a new life for ourselves. Surely we can not do so among the savage Greeks or land-hugging Canaan-ites."

"[Atlantis]!" I breathed, uttering the forbidden name.

"Atlantis!" Don repeated, as amazed and excited as ancient Pi-ja-se-me had been. The fabulous continent intro-duced to historic mythology by Plato, who had it from Solon, who had it from an Egyptian priest. The story had been that Atlantis, a rich and powerful and happy island continent, had suddenly sunk in a day and a night. It had been most generally supposed by scholars that Atlantis had in fact been Minoan Crete, ravaged by the phenomenal eruption of Thera in the fifteenth century B.C. The ignorant had spun grandiose stories of a continent in the Atlantic Ocean, for which no justification was offered. Of course Plato had said that Atlantis perished nine thousand years before his time, and was ten times the size of any ruins found at Thera, but this was readily explained by postulating an error in translation of one decimal place. That brought the capital city of Atlantis right down to the size of the settlement on Thera—Pi-ja's home city—and the time lapse to nine hundred years, which was a close match to the geological record of the eruption. Thus Don had hardly concerned himself with the legend of Atlantis, knowing it to be extrapolation from a clerical error. True, Plato had placed it beyond the Pillars of Hercules. But that was standard practice for the Greeks, who were too familiar with the Aegean to accept such mysteries there.

Now it seemed that the Atlantis legend predated Thera. Don went over the symbol on the tablet again and again, trying to discover whether he had misinterpreted, but it stood firm as the best guess. If the concept were not Atlantis, it was similar. To Pi-ja, as with the later Plato, Atlantis was a tremendous island across the great ocean.

Yet who would know the source of the legend better than the Minoans, the foremost seafaring people of the ancient world? If they had had a legend of Atlantis, that land must have existed!

Actually the eruption of Thera had not ended Minoan civilization. They had suffered terribly, but soon enough had reasserted themselves and driven off the marauding Greeks and gone on to greater heights. Their power had not faded until they depleted the natural resources of their island, and had to shift their bases elsewhere. But the eruption had been remembered. Thera had been something like four times as great an explosion as the later Krakatoa. Surely the gods had never spoken with greater authority than that! So the Cretan captain, far distant, had misjudged the situation, understandably. Many others had done the same.

Abruptly a new conjecture opened like a fragrant flower.

CHAPTER 14

ATLANTIS

Proxy 5–12–5–16–8: Attention.
Acknowledging.
Status?
Dismal. I dare not tell the truth for fear of sacrificing the mission, yet I cannot prevail otherwise. I think I can accomplish it only by the intercession of one member of the party, and I am unable to contact that one. I must bide my time, and hope.
Then terminate it.
No. Not until all hope is gone. Sufficient time must come for the one to be ready. Then if I can manage contact, I can still succeed.
In view of the risk, we feel that greater judgment than yours should be invoked. Obtain our acquiescence before presenting the mission to your group.
I will do so.

"Atlantis," Su-ri-mo agreed. "It is at least a civilized port."

A few days later a terrible storm formed, and for two days we rode before it, and two more within it, hardly knowing day from night. All our hatches and oar-ports were sealed, lest we be swamped; we rode blindly.

Just when the winds were worst, they abruptly abated, and we sailed serene in sunshine. But the Admiral allowed no relaxation, and drove us all on all three ships to batten down even more firmly than before, with no sail and every oar-port closed. The men thought him moon-struck, and even I had my doubts—but suddenly a frightening wall of cloud swept over the horizon, and almost before we could fetch down our heads and cling to the beams the wind struck again, fully as fiercely as before. It was another storm—blowing from the other direction!

Surely this ocean was cursed by the gods, to have such incredible storms. How was it that the first storm had not crashed headlong into the second, and so dissipated both? But the gods are not limited by such considerations; they do as pleases them, and it was evident that our presence here did not please them. For three more days we cowered before the awful wind, the huge waves striking our ship as if to sunder it in twain. The crewmen prayed valiantly to one god or another, but the elements seemed almost beyond the control of divinity.

When at last the weather eased, we were alone and completely lost. Our sail was in useless shreds, our mast stripped bare. The admiral's ship was gone, as was the third vessel; we could not ascertain their fate. We ourselves were helpless before the currents of the sea, for our oars had all been broken off.

The ship's captain supervised repairs, but there was no new tackle to mount and no new sail. Our hull at least was tight, for our own guild of shipwrights at Thera was ever the finest, and after bailing out the bilge and the wash from the storm waves we floated as high as we had before. We had a fair supply of food and wine, because of the staples the Admiral had laid in for the voyage to

Atlantis, though we seemed unlikely to arrive there now.
And of course we fished.

Now fish is fit for kings, but seawater is not. As for
imbibing the discolored juices of crushed fish in lieu of
water, and drinking bilge salvaged from rain—well, then
we really appreciated the hardships of existing on a
derelict. I suspect that had we had good Cretan wine we
might have endured even so without complaint, but what
filled our supply jars was Megalithic Mash, as the cynical
crewmen put it.

The captain of our ship consulted with me, as I was
now the ranking remaining officer of the fleet, but I could
tell him nothing. It was not that I chose to preserve the
secret of our destination from him; it was that it was
pointless to tantalize him with it when we had no hope of
achieving it. Even had I said it, no one had the bearing of
Atlantis. Only the Admiral had that.

On we drifted, ever father from our homeland, for the
seas were moving west. Illness broke out among the
crewmen, and we had no proper physician to attend to it.
I suffered pains in my own bones, at times so pervasive
that I lay in my cabin unable to move, seeking to alleviate
my discomfort by consuming bad wine and dreaming of
diversions of the past. I saw in my mind a gallery of our
sprightly island ladies, with their long gaily colored skirts
tiered with five and six bands of flouncing, bright
bracelets on their wrists and ankles, their puffed sleeves
and lush breasts standing behind thin gauze, their elabo-
rate jeweled headdresses over curly black hair, a snakelike strand bobbing in front of each ear, large dark-etched
eyes—ah, ah! Who can lay claim to knowledge of beauty,
who has not gazed on such as these!

At other times it seemed I was traveling down a street
in my palanquin, passing well-kept houses flush with the

edge of the pavement, their windows filled with taut oiled parchment panes. I would enter one, my slaves waiting outside. The sweet smell of cooking-smoke tantalized my nostrils, and I knew that a fine repast was in the making. I would sit on a red cushion on a fine stone bench in the pale blue chamber, awaiting invitation to the central patio. I do not know whose house it was; not my own. Just an average domicile in a better neighborhood. Perhaps that was the point of vision: its reassuring suggestion that such houses and such neighborhoods still existed, when I feared they did not. The life I had known lingered wistfully within me.

Sometimes I recovered enough to sit on the open deck, and then my gaze fixed on the steady waves and I dreamed of the sea-ancestry of our culture. If our origins lay in Anatolia, yet we had been sea-faring before achieving fair Crete and fairer Thera—could these legends be reconciled? As I now analyzed them, two thousand years ago we were part of an empire of all the seas, whose ports touched on every shore. But slowly the waters rose and those fabulous ancient cities were drowned, and lacking the means to hold back the waters the empire fragmented, leaving pieces of itself scattered across the world like broken pottery sherds. One fragment became the Megalithics, another the Kingdom of Meluhha, yet others Egypt, Makan, Ubaid, and Dilmun. Even farther spread were the enclaves in southern Africa and eastward beyond the farthest reaches of the Sumerian trade routes—and of course Atlantis. Crete was only a minor refuge, then. Or so I conjecture, making allowance for the inflation of our own importance in our legends.

I myself have visited a number of the old sites that produced such material as obsidian, that volcanic glass once so valuable for tools and weapons. Now we prefer bronze, of course, and iron when we can obtain it. But still the extent of that old empire is suggested by the ores it mined and the technologies it disseminated. If I could go back to learn the full history of that golden age of . . .

At this point the first missing tablet manifested. Damn! Any loss from the narrative was painful, but when the discussion was on ancient history as seen by an ancient scholar, what a loss!

Disgruntled by the insuperable interruption of the story, Don took a break. Splendid was glad to relax, too; she had been making notes on small waterproof sheets, recording this for her community.

Don turned on the radio by force of habit, but Melanie still would not answer. Splendid noticing, smiled.

Don's frustration at the double balking by tablet and woman abruptly focused on what was available. "What are you laughing at?" he demanded.

The mermaid was unperturbed. WHY NOT LET ME SHOW YOU, she wrote. WHILE THE MINOAN DRIFTS AND FRETS.

"Show me what?" Then he remembered: how mermaids reproduced. She was teasing him, secure in the barrier of phase. Or was she trying to tempt him into some sexual attempt, that had to fail embarrassingly? Revenge for what Melanie had said to her?

That reminded him of what Melanie had said about the balloons. All this time, he could have handled the Minoan tablets himself! Instead he had had to bargain with the mermaid, and compromise, translating only in her presence. That had not been a bad experience, actually, but he cursed himself for not thinking of the balloons before. Now she was cocksure, and his frustration found a way of expression.

He brought out one of the balloons. It was very fine and

flexible, and felt as if he were moving it through the resistance of water. As he was, now that it was no longer balled up. He stretched it carefully over his clumped and stiffened fingers, clamping it in place with his thumb. Hardly a perfect glove, but serviceable.

"Come here, Splendid," he said.

She swam forward with enticing undulations, ready to play the futile game. She expected him to make a pass, literally: a sweep of his hand through her body without contact.

He poked her left breast with the gloved fingers. Her flesh was firm and resilient, a genuine delight to poke. Splendid was laughing silently, enjoying her invulnerability.

Then she realized that the touch was real. With one phenomenal thrust of her flukes she shot straight up a good two fathoms.

Don's *pique* dissipated, but he maintained a straight face. "Please *do* show me how," he suggested as she leveled out and peered down.

She touched her breast herself as if verifying what had happened. Now it seemed she was not so eager. She looked at the sheath on his hand, realizing that it did not have to be restricted to a finger. Her bluff had been called.

"While the Minoan drifts and frets," Don added encouragingly.

Splendid glanced westward, as if debating whether to flee back to her village. He would not be able to pursue swiftly enough to keep her in sight, because of the difficulty of getting off the ship with his bicycle or out of the chasm the ship was in. Even on the level she could lose him, merely by swimming upward until gone.

"If you go home, I shall continue translating on my own," he said.

That got to her. She was as eager as he to read that manuscript. Now he had possession.

Then she dived purposefully for the tablets. She was going to carry them away!

"No you don't!" he cried, diving for them himself.

They collided. This time flesh and bone passed through flesh and bone as before, but the balloon-glove got hung up against her torso just where flesh merged into scales. Don tried to yank back his hand, but his arm actually passed through her abdomen, leaving the hand at her rear, and he goosed her royally. Her mouth opened in an outraged O as she jackknifed, inadvertently showing him a bottom that resolved the long-standing question of "how." It was all there in normal human order when the legs folded clear and the scales parted.

Don had to roll away, finally managing to disengage, and go back to his bicycle for a breath of air. Splendid used the opportunity to pick up two of the tablets. Don, now aware of her liability, charged back balloon-first and tickled her under one raised arm, just where the breast began.

She shrieked silently, squirming away, and dropped the tablets to the deck. One cracked apart.

Appalled, they both broke off hostilities and stared. The damage was not total, as the tablet had split into two major portions rather than shattering. But had it not been buoyed by the water it would have been another matter. The look on Splendid's face showed that she was as chagrined about the accident as he.

She recovered her slate and wrote. I WILL NOT GO. I WILL MAKE IT RIGHT WITH YOUR FRIEND.

Don merely nodded, putting away his balloon. Too bad it had taken this near disaster to straighten them both out. Yet now he realized that this was the first time he had had an interaction like this with a woman; his shyness had not gotten in the way. Ordinarily the mere thought of poking, grabbing, or goosing a woman would have made him flee, stutter-bound.

Splendid wrote a treatise in German, and Don spelled it out over the unresponsive radio. He didn't inquire what it said, and he had no evidence Melanie was listening, but it was the best he could do. He planned to broadcast it again in a few hours, and then yet again, until she picked it up.

They returned to the manuscript, picking up the text after the missing tablet.

. . . snake. Certainly we have many legends, and the serpent, as an aspect of the earth, is commonly worshipped in Crete. I use that term advisedly. Actually we worship no animals, as that is a practice for barbarians. We merely use them as adjuncts of the ritual in the worship of that divinity we may not approach directly. Yet this is difficult to justify to foreigners, and I have fallen out of the habit of trying. I myself have offered incense before the altar of the lovely Snake Goddess. And our regard for the bull as another aspect of that same Earth Spirit is too well established to warrant repetition here. Yet there are elements that do not entirely jibe, and the legend is in many ways alien to our comprehension. I shall present it here only in summary:

Three thousand years ago—they are specific, as they possess a marvelously accurate calendar, but I round it off for convenience—there was an upright priest king who was identified with the Bull God for his strength and determination. No woman could resist him, and thus he attracted the romantic attention even of his sister, identified with the Bird God. She it was who nursed him when he was stricken ill as his penance for neglecting the Snake God, and in this case the Bird prevailed and she cured him. He was so joyous to be well again that he celebrated for forty days—some say four hundred. A ritual figure, subject to interpretation. She then tempted him with wine, making him intoxicated, and disguised himself so that he did not know her, and thereby seduced him. When he recovered equilibrium and realized what he had done, he built a great pyre and threw himself on it, ascending to the Heaven of the Bulls. But she endured alone and in due course gave birth to the Feathered Bull: a creature at once ferocious in animal aspect while well-favored in human aspect. He was both beast and god, but at the same time a man, with mannish appetites. This entity in due course became king, and set out to rule all the world of men. He discovered how to grow plants, how to sail a ship, and how to work with metal. His reign was long and glorious, extending over all the islands of the world and all the lands bordering on the sea. But in his old age, when he was five hundred years old—perhaps fifty, allowing for the rituality of figures—he became savage, for he was simultaneously a child of incest and miscegenation. He attempted to destroy what he had wrought, and at last his subjects had to confine him in a massive temple. For many years they fed him sacrifices of living flesh, but then they neglected him, and slowly he weakened. When he expired, the earth shuddered and groaned with the rage of a bull, and the sky whipped itself into a tremendous storm signifying the rage of the birds, and the sea came up in the rage of the Snake of the Water and inundated all the great cities of that kingdom, which was the original Atlantis. It fell apart and was no more.

That, at any rate, is the legend. I have heard it in many variants, but all agree in essence. How strikingly it concurs with ours of the ancient sea-empire! Elements do seem contradictory, such as the father of the Feathered

Bull becoming intoxicated by wine, when plant cultivation—surely including that of the vine—was discovered only later by his son. And I question the capacity of his subjects to imprison this powerful, god-imbued, man-bull-bird, however old he became. But as I noted before, legends of this nature must be taken allegorically, and the seeming errors analyzed for the more subtle truths they hint. What intrigues me primarily is the presence of the bull, for I have found no evidence of this animal existing in contemporary Atlantis.

"So they made it Atlantis after all!" Don said, satisfied. "I rather thought they would."

BUT THEY WERE ADRIFT AND LOST, Splendid protested.

"Haven't you figured out where Atlantis is? The winds and currents naturally carried the ship there—which has to be the way the Minoans discovered it in the first place."

Her face lighted. AMERICA!

"Certainly. It meets all the criteria. It is far across the sea to the west, beyond the Pillars of Hercules; it is larger than all of the Mediterranean lands combined—as far as they could tell, anyway, since they could not get around it either to the north or south; and it possessed great wealth and high civilization. Probably it was the major remnant of that worldwide maritime culture both legends speak of—a culture in its prime about 4000 B.C., before the celebrated Flood. But by 1500 B.C. only the Minoans maintained contact, as far as we or they knew. The Megalithics had declined and were no longer a significant maritime empire, despite their residence all along the European Atlantic coast. The several highly advanced cultures around the Arabian peninsula and India—Dilmun, Makan, and Meluhha, of which we have archaeological record—were blocked from it by the huge mass of Africa. The Chinese—your civilization—were balked by the sheer immensity of the Pacific. When the Cretan contact was severed by the eruption of Thera, it didn't destroy the Minoan culture, but did end that contact with Atlantis. Atlantis became a myth.''

BUT WHAT REALLY DESTROYED THE ORIGINAL MARITIME EMPIRE? she was writing.

''The rising of the seas, of course. The melting ice of the glaciers of the ice age caused the water to cover much of the prior shoreline. The worldwide legends of the great flood may derive from—''

THIS SHOULD NOT HAVE DESTROYED CIVILIZA-TION. IT WAS VERY SLOW IN TERMS OF MAN'S HISTORY.

Don hesitated. ''I suppose not. Certainly we owe much more to the ice age than it can ever have cost us, for the Magdelanean cave art culture derived from ice-age conditions. In fact, I'm sure those reindeer people migrated to the Near-East when conditions changed, building cities in Anatolia like Catal Huyuk of 6500 B.C. in which the cave motifs were transferred to house walls and ceramics, and metalworking first developed. But remember, two and a half thousand years elapsed between that civilization of 4000 B.C. and Pi-ja's time. It could have atrophied, as all civilizations have well within that span, and the rising waters then covered up most of its architecture, leaving little evidence but legends. After all, consider how knowledge of the Minoan culture itself was lost for millennia, surviving only in that passing reference to Atlantis and such things as the Theseus legend.''

She considered. YES, I SEE IT NOW. AND THE MAYAN LEGEND OF QUETZALCOATL, THE FEATH-ERED SERPENT.

Don was electrified. "The feathered *serpent*? In American legend?"

She looked askance. YOU ARE NOT FAMILIAR WITH THIS FAMOUS STORY?

"I—I've concentrated pretty much on Crete," Don admitted. "I guess I have heard of it, but I'm hazy on the details."

She provided them, and his wonder grew. The American Indian legend, common in many languages and variants in both north and south continents, told how the goddess Coatlicue gathered white feathers, placing them in her bosom; but she swallowed one and thereby became pregnant. She gave birth to Quetzalcoatl, whose name was a combination of *Quetzal*, a special green-feathered bird; *Co*, a snake; and *Atl*, water. Thus he represented air, earth, and water, and was a complex symbol of man's condition and possibilities. He was the Feathered Serpent.

Quetzalcoatl grew up tall, robust, handsome, and bearded. He loved all living things, and would not kill a bear or pick a flower. Then an enemy showed him his image in a distorting mirror, and he saw himself as wasted away. He was shocked, and went into seclusion so that his people would not see him. But then his enemy dressed him well, painted his face, and gave him a fine turquoise mask, making him appear so handsome that he had to celebrate. He was then tempted with wine: first just a sip, then more, until he became intoxicated. His sister Quetzalpetlatl was similarly tempted into inebriation, and in this carefree state the two indulged in an act of incest. Later, in remorse, Quetzalcoatl immolated himself on his own funeral pyre.

"That derives from this legend on the tablet!" Don exclaimed. "The symbolism, the elements of illness and incest—only the bull has been eliminated!"

Splendid nodded, eyes bright.

"And the bull—that carried on through the Minoan culture," Don continued, seeing whole sections of the puzzle fall into place. "The Greek legend of Theseus—it derives from the same source! According to it, King Minos controlled the seas, but his wife became enamored of a bull, and finally concealed herself inside a wooden cow in order to couple with the bull. Then she gave birth to the Minotaur, a man with the head of a bull, who fed on human flesh. He was confined to the Labyrinth—the Greeks' notion of the complex Minoan palace, in whose center court the bull-leapers performed. But the Greeks transferred his hero-properties to their prince Theseus, who slew him. The mythic lineage is plain, now. A forbidden sexual act that spawns a man-creature with godlike properties who finally dies ignominiously, in both the Mayan and Minoan/Greek versions."

AND SO WE VERIFY ATLANTIS, she wrote.

"*And* the ancient sea empire," Don agreed. "It explains so much. Like that fabulous sunken Yucatan city, that Pi-ja apparently didn't know about—and the later Dzibilchaltun, whose source of culture was such a mystery."

Then he had to explain about that, for of course Splendid hadn't known of the submerged city. She knew about Dzibilchaltun, though, and was fascinated by the apparent connection.

At last they returned to the manuscript. New horizons had opened, and Don was in a hurry to assimilate the remainder, for the rest of his group was overdue to return. He would have been more concerned about what was delaying them, had he not been so distracted by the Minoan manuscript.

I conjecture this: our bull and snake honoring ancestors of many thousands of years past emerged from the coastline of Anatolia, becoming a great seafaring nation.

Soon they spread even to Atlantis, perhaps under some
great king whose birth was clouded: illegitimate, possibly, the result of covert incest. Thus his identification as
the anomaly of the feathered bull. The wealth to be
derived from wide-spread trade would account for this
basic initiative, and there would be a powerful civilizing
effect wherever this trade touched, as there has been in
the case of our own missions about the Aegean and other
islands and peninsulas. The case of the Greek tribes may
seem hopeless, but even there there are signs of promise.
But under poor kings even the soundest empire becomes
weak, and there may have been extensive natural catas-
trophes. Again, as we know from bitter experience. So the
empire that spawned all the present cultures of the world
at length passed, and was almost forgotten.

But I could discourse interminably on the ways and
legends of these people. It must suffice to establish that
they differ in many ways from our own culture, but not so
completely that we would not accommodate. And that is
the problem. For if we adapt too amicably to their
customs, and marry their women, and become absorbed
in their culture—then we shall surely lose their own
identity. We were not spared the holocaust of our island,
we did not survive the ferocity of the ocean storm, we did
not endure the mutiny of the hungry crew merely for this!

So I did what I had learned with such difficulty when
the captain died at sea, and I assumed once more the
leadership of our remaining group. There was some
strenuous resistance, but I performed as necessary, even
to distasteful bloodshed, and we won free and set sail by
night. Northward across the round sea, bearing toward the
place we understood there was a colony of kinsmen. If we
could join these, our situation would be better.

* * *

"Don! Don!"

Don jumped, startled. It was as if Pi-ja-se-me had called to him directly! But it was the radio, which he had left on in the hope that Melanie would respond to one of the Germanic spelling broadcasts.

"I'm h-here," he said, reorienting. "What—?"

"Don, return instantly! And be careful! I cannot—"

There was a click, and Don was unable to get further response. The other radio was off.

Splendid was evidently annoyed by this abrupt interruption of the Minoan narrative. HER VOICE HAS CHANGED.

"That's not Melanie! It's Eleph! And something's wrong. He's not one to play games—" He paused. "He doesn't even have a radio, now. He must have been using Gaspar's, or one of the others. And someone must have stopped him. Why?"

THERE MUST BE TROUBLE IN YOUR PARTY.

"Yes! I should have been suspicious about this long radio silence. I have to get back. When Eleph cries for help—" But again he paused. "The translation! I may never have another chance. I can't go without finishing that!"

I CANNOT GO WITH YOU, Splendid wrote. THE COLD AND THE SALT AND THE PREDATORS OF THE MARINE—

"And Pi-ja's request! I agreed to honor it—but I don't know what it is. But if I keep Eleph waiting—I know I can't afford to waste any time!" Don was not a man of decisive action in a crisis; he felt himself falling apart. What should he do?

Splendid looked at him compassionately while her hand printed her message. COMPROMISE. PROMISE TO SPEAK WELL OF US TO YOUR PEOPLE, AND I WILL HELP YOU RETURN SWIFTLY.

"You can't help me! The phase—"

But she was still writing. THE OLD WOMAN TOOK AWAY YOUR ROPES. WE CAN SHOW YOU A BETTER ROUTE.

Don was aghast. "Pacifa wouldn't take away the lines! I need them to climb out of this trench! The cliffs—"

"She did, you know," Melanie said suddenly on the radio. "She told me we might need the rope, and it seemed to make sense at the time. I never thought—"

"Melanie! Where have you—?"

"Something *is* wrong," she said. "Nobody else has used the radio since we split into two parties. Except you and me. And now Eleph. I—"

"You refused to t-talk to me!"

"I was in a jealous snit. Because—well, never mind. I thought the radio silence was just to keep from alerting the sub to the locations of the others. But Eleph wasn't fooling. I can tell."

"Why didn't you say something before? I never realized—"

"And interrupt your charming relationship with that fishwife? You can go to hell for all I care! But not Eleph. You've got to go back!"

Don caught a movement, and turned to see Splendid swimming swiftly away. "Wait!" he cried. "I agree to your compromise! I—"

Then he saw that her tablet was filled with writing. He moved over to read it.

"*What* compromise?" Melanie demanded.

"The mer-people will show me a fast route back to the depot, if I agree to speak for them when I get back. I really don't know much about them—"

"*Don't* you?"

"I think they're afraid of the U.S. reaction to their

presence here. You know, the depth-bomb psychology. They mean no harm; they're practicing for colonization of Jupiter. But Splendid just took off. She left a message—"

"Well, read it!"

Don read aloud: IT WILL TAKE ABOUT AN HOUR TO GET THE INFORMATION FROM OUR PERIMETER GUARD. I WILL RETURN WITH A MAP YOU CAN COPY. MEANWHILE, TRANSLATE THE END OF THE NARRATIVE. YOU CAN KEEP BOTH PROMISES.

"*Two* promises?"

"Melanie, the author of the tablets made a condition for anyone who reads them. Splendid and I have been translating the whole time. Didn't she explain that in the German?"

"Yes," Melanie admitted. "She also said you goosed her."

"Well, she deserved it! And if you don't stop being so cynical, I'll goose *you*, first chance. I tell you, we never—"

"That's three promises," Melanie muttered.

"So you know you don't have reason to—"

"Well—"

"Melanie, I love you! I—"

She was evidently startled. "But—"

"But Splendid has a glorious head of hair. So I've been exposed to that, now. And I know. So if you—"

"If you repeat that when we get together again, I'll say it too. But that's personal. Right now you have to get on that translation."

"Yes. I—I'll see you soon, Melanie. I hope. Then—"

"Then," she agreed. She clicked off. He knew this was to guarantee him the undistracted time he needed.

Don pored over the remaining tablets, picking out those symbols he could read easily so as to get a rough gist before settling down to the final one. He was pegging in meanings with a facility that amazed him. He could almost read the text straight, now!

Pi-ja, it seemed, had directed the ship north toward the American Gulf coast, searching for the settlement whose descendants would be known as the Yuchi Indians. But another storm, or perhaps an arm of the Gulf Stream, carried them east and south, at last brushing the north shore of Cuba. There his men jumped overboard and swam for shore, for what reason Don wasn't clear. But Pi-ja-se-me seemed to be an extraordinarily capable and hard-nosed leader, despite his literary background. He had invented magic to cow the superstitious, and perhaps had over-done it. But he was suffering again from debilitating illness, possibly nutritional deficiency symptoms.

At any rate, only one loyal slave remained. The two attempted to sail the ship, but lacked the ability to do more than keep it clear of the shoals. It was in poor condition, with its repairs haphazard after the hurricane that had sunk the other two ships, and a tattered partial sail on the stripped mast was all they could muster. Mostly it drifted, while Pi-ja wrote his long memoirs, baking each finished tablet in the galley hearth. Apparently the ship passed all around Cuba and between it and the island of Haiti, losing its mast in another storm, and was progressing back toward the Yucatan when Pi-ja called a halt. His augurs had identified this particular spot as most propitious for his purpose. He had his slave bail water *into* the ship, already half swamped by the storm, until it sank. The implication was that ship and passengers went down together.

Then the final passage:

I have considered carefully the destruction of my own world. We were a prosperous, carefree people, much given to pleasure, but we knew our gods and took them seriously. I remain satisfied that in no way did we renege on our rituals prior to the calamity. In fact our religious exercises had become more detailed as our wealth and power waxed, and many more youths of either sex were sacrificed in the bull-leapings than had been done in prior centuries. Almost every year we had a champion who performed so well as to complete the leap uninjured and in perfect form. Had the Earth Mother chosen to rebuke us, she should have done it long ago, before our faith and technique were perfect. Almost, it seems, our very closeness to our subject was our undoing, for the farther away any given city was from Thera, the less it suffered.

So I am forced to a conclusion that counters the faith of my lifetime: *Our Gods do not care.* Our worship was vain, not because the object was false, as it demonstrably was not, but because of our conceit that anything we might offer could have any conceivable ameliorating effect on that arrogant Power. We are as ants before the hoof of the bull: neither our love nor our hate can mitigate the weight and placement of that deadly tread. We were fools ever to think otherwise, and we have paid the ultimate price.

Oh, scholar, honor then my charge: Build not on the flank of the Bull. Delude not yourself about the propensities of the Beast, by whatever guise it manifests. Imagine not that you can propitiate it by dances or offerings or prayer, lest that monster heave without reason or warning and destroy all that you have wrought.

CHAPTER 15

CRISIS

Proxy 5–12–5–16–8: Attention.
[No answer.]
Status?
[No answer.]

Don looked up. Splendid was back. He had continued translating aloud, from habit and for Melanie's benefit (if she tuned in), and knew that the mermaid had heard enough.

"Do you know," Melanie said after a moment, "we have already built on the flank of the bull. We call it the Bomb."

Don nodded, though she could not see him. "It's a bigger bull than that. Nuclear power has enormous advantages and equivalent liabilities. But it's only one facet of the danger to our species and world. We are overrunning the planet, enslaving or destroying all other species. The climate is changing, deserts are being made, the sea is dying. Maybe we are the bull, this time. The world is too small for us. But we have no way to get off. Nowhere to go."

EXCEPT TO GO TO JUPITER, Splendid wrote.

"Maybe so," Don agreed after reading her words to Melanie. "I'll do what I can—for Eleph and Jupiter." Yet he suffered a background doubt. Could this be all of it? Just to come here and read the Minoan warning? Meet the mermaid? These things somehow seemed incidental to whatever mission might have been set up. Who had set it up? And what had gone wrong? Why had Pacifa seemingly arranged to isolate him here, by taking the ropes and not returning? Where was Gaspar, and why was he maintaining radio silence in the face of this situation?

Pi-ja's story might be over, but Don's wasn't. And it might not have any happier ending. Key pieces were missing.

Splendid swam to the edge of the deck, then hovered, waiting for him to let himself down. By the time he was ready to ride from the ship, she had another message:

ONE STRANGE THING. WE FOUND TRACES IN THE SHIP. NO BONES, BUT METAL BELTS AND JEWELRY. IT SEEMED TO US THAT THE ARTIFACTS NEAR THE CACHE OF TABLETS WERE FEMALE.

For a moment Don was stunned. Then he shook it off. "That narrative was written by a man."

She paused to write again. THERE IS TROUBLE IN YOUR CAMP. WE DON'T KNOW THE MOTIVES OF THE OTHERS, BUT TRUST YOU.

"Well, thanks, Splendid. But I have no idea what's going on."

YES, YOU ARE INNOCENT.

That, it seemed, was his prime recommendation.

Splendid swam ahead, and he followed, riding rapidly across the rocky floor of the sea. She led him down the trench below the ship, then up out of the canyon by a winding path and onto a broad plain. In a surprisingly short time they arrived at the mer-colony.

The artifacts were not impressive. A cluster of cylindrical tanks evidently deposited by submarine and camouflaged so as to be difficult to spot from above. Several vertical nets, perhaps intended to strain fish out of the moving current—or possibly a kind of defense, as there weren't many fish in this freshwater enclave. And the mer-people themselves: seven or eight women and about a dozen men. All were well proportioned, the women running to large breasts, the men to powerful chests. Don realized that this might not be a matter of mammary or muscle. They probably needed extraordinary lung capacity to make use of the meager oxygen in the water, and a padding of fat to protect their vital organs, accounting for their notable attributes. The men had no visible genitals, but did have a kind of codpiece effect in the arrangement of their scales. Streamlining, of course.

Then he saw the submarine. Similar to the one they had encountered before. Don felt an apprehensive chill. It was coming clear how the mer-people had known about the status of the ropes. The sub had indeed kept track of the party. Had it found a way to mess up the other members, perhaps taking them captive one by one? Was this a trap for one more? "They have a sub," he murmured to Melanie.

Splendid tried to reassure him. WE KNOW YOU SAW ONE OF OUR PERIMETER GUARDS. THE MACHINE IS HERE TO HELP YOU. ONLY IT CAN LEAD THE WAY OUT OF THE TRENCH. TRUST US AS WE TRUST YOU.

Well put! Of course they had submarines; how else could this colony be supplied! It was now to the interest of the Chinese to assist him—or to kill him. If Gaspar or Pacifa had gotten away and could not be stopped, then only Don or Melanie could speak in favor of this mer-project. But his intuition told him that these folk were not hostile to his mission; they were coincidental to it. Splendid seemed like a fine creature. He had to trust them. They only wanted to be left alone to complete their project. He hoped.

Then he realized what Splendid meant. "Oh—to hitch a ride!" For the submarine could go where the mer-people couldn't, into the cold salt water. The cliffs of the trench would be no barrier to it.

Splendid laughed in her silent way, then looked thoughtful. The other mer-people did not understand English; at least they did not react. Had Splendid told them about the phase?

THE GLOVE—Splendid wrote.

"The balloons. Of course. If I can have a handhold, and carry my bike too—"

"Is that safe?" Melanie asked. "I was always warned against hitching rides on trucks—with a bike, I mean."

"Safer than climbing those cliffs without anchored ropes! The sub could cut my time in half!"

"But if it dropped you—"

"I'd smash. I wish you hadn't brought that up, Melanie. But I have to trust them. And I do. Just from knowing Splendid, I'm convinced they're—"

"Oh?" Melanie interjected with a certain emphasis. He'd have to stop mentioning the mermaid!

"I wish I could stay and really study their c-culture," he said a bit lamely. "There are mer*men* here too, you know. Tritons. It's a whole v-village."

"So I gather." She seemed mollified.

HERE ARE CHARTS, Splendid wrote. THEY WILL HELP YOU. CAN YOU CARRY THEM? COPYING WOULD TAKE A LONG TIME.

"Can you fold them tight and put them in a small packet? I could carry that wrapped in a balloon."

"So you *did* use a balloon," Melanie said accusingly.

"N-not the way you th-think!"

"N-no?" she mimicked. "Just how do you think I *think?* And you were being so upset about my being on the pill!"

Splendid, meanwhile, went to one of the mermen to explain, using sign language Don could not follow. The man's face was expressive. First he nodded agreeably. Then his brow furrowed. Then he looked angry.

"Uh-oh," Don murmured to Melanie. "I think that triton she's talking to is her mate, and now he has a notion about the balloon too."

"Serves you right," Melanie said gleefully. "Hey, merman! Let me tell you about—"

Don hastily snapped off the radio. As if he didn't have problems enough! Melanie might be teasing him, since Splendid had already explained things, but such words could be dangerous.

Soon the job was done, despite the glower of the muscular triton. Don was glad to see the sub lift, so that he could tie on firmly to the rail at its base.

Splendid waved good-bye, one breast heaving in unison with her arm, as sub, bike, and man rose into the sea. Don didn't wave back, as he had to hang on and the triton still looked extremely ugly.

The journey itself was almost disappointing. The submarine lifted high, so that the opacity of sea water closed in and fogged out sight of land. Don soon lost his bearings, and had to depend on the changing coordinates on his meter. His head brushed the bottom of the sub, and passed through it, reminding him distressingly how slight his support was. If even one balloon gave way—but of course it wouldn't.

He looked ahead, but there was only the great light spearing out, now and then impaling stray fish. That made Don wonder where Glowcloud was. He missed the giant mollusk.

He had underestimated the capacity of the sub. It plowed through the water at phenomenal velocity, though with almost no sound. It felt like fifty miles an hour, but was probably closer to twenty five. The Chinese had to know more about the construction of such machines than the other nations suspected. He was glad that he saw no evidence of missile or torpedo ports. He wanted to believe this was a peaceful project.

In just two hours they glided to land in the shallows just north of Jamaica. They had agreed to stand by for two days in case he needed more help. A slate was provided for messages. It turned out that the sub had not been able to tune in on the phase radio; their communications had been private all along. But it could pick up the sounds of their travel, so had known their whereabouts. It was amazing the cooperation Splendid had been able to arrange. "An apple a day keeps the depth bombs away," Don muttered a bit cynically.

He disengaged, took down his balloons, used them to tie the charts low on the bike frame, and pedaled through the base of the sub. His fully-phased upper section encountered only trace resistance, and the balloons and charts were now below the sub, experiencing only the drag of the water. He was curious about something. Yes! Regular human beings were manning the sub, not tritons. Their faces turned to him in amazement as he waved and coasted out the far side.

Now, abruptly, he was nervous. What *had* happened to Eleph? What *were* Gaspar and/or Pacifa up to?

He stopped after a couple of miles, waiting silently to see whether the sub was trailing him. Meanwhile he used the balloon-gloves to fumble open the package of charts. It made an uncomfortable resistance as he rode, because the charts were of the same phase as the water. But they were remarkably detailed, much better than the maps they had been using. The colony must have supervised a really thorough survey.

Two routes were marked through the complex trench

terrain, calculated to avoid cliffs of more than six foot elevation. Either would have cut many hours off his journey.

As it was, he would arrive less than four hours after Eleph's terse call, instead of fifty. That was very good.

The sub did not seem to be following. Reassured, Don resumed his ride, centering on the depot coordinates. He slowed again when within a mile. Eleph must have had good reason for advising caution, before that abrupt cutoff. Yet Gaspar and Pacifa were nice people, under their sometimes crusty exteriors. Why should either make trouble?

But when he moved quietly to the depot, there was only one figure there. "Melanie!"

"Don! How—?"

"The mer-folk gave me a lift, so I'm back much sooner."

She waited for him to draw close, then stepped into his embrace. "I'm sorry I was so bitchy," she said. "This business—"

"That mermaid—there really wasn't—"

"I know. I was so lonely for you, and then when I had you on the radio, all I did was quarrel with you. I've never been in—I mean, I don't know how to handle emotion like—"

"I have a notion," he said. He hugged her tight.

Then they kissed. Maybe it was the excitement of his fast, unusual trip back, or maybe the heightened emotions of their argument, or maybe just her. It was like the discovery of the Minoan Manuscript.

But there was pressing business. "What's been happening? Where are the others?"

"I don't know. I don't think Gaspar and Eleph ever came back here, and Pacifa must have gone to join them. She told me to wait here while she checked around, and then she was gone. I've been going crazy, worrying."

"Do you think their radio silence means anything?"

"It must. But what?"

"I don't think it has anything much to do with the mer-colony," he said. "They seem innocent."

"How would you know?" she asked sharply.

He spread his hands. "I guess I don't."

"Well, I believe it. They helped you return here in record time, and that's a monstrous relief to me. And your splendid fishwife—with nerve like hers, why should she bother lying to an innocent like you?"

"But if it's something else—some other crisis—why the radio silence? I mean, if someone got hurt, they'd call for help."

"I don't know," Melanie said, frustrated. "But there certainly is something, and it has to involve Pacifa, because she deliberately stranded you there at the ship, she thought. Maybe Gaspar is in on it too. So Eleph tried to warn us."

"But Pacifa is a good person! She wouldn't—"

She laughed somewhat bitterly. "Men of any age aren't very smart about women of any age. *Women* aren't dumb about women. Though how I managed to fall for that business about taking up the ropes—"

"But if all of you were planning to come back, then the ropes would have been placed again."

"Only that evidently wasn't the plan. I'd have had to do it alone, and I'm not competent. I was isolated too, except for the radio, and I didn't dare blab my suspicions there."

"So what do you think—?"

"I think Pacifa had a mission from the start, and separating us had something to do with it, and now she's completing it—and we'd better find out what it is and stop her, before—"

He nodded. "All we can do is look for them—carefully."

She looked at his bicycle. "What is that?"

"Oh, the mer-folk gave me some charts of the area, so I can find my way around. They were going to show me the best routes, but then they gave me the lift on their sub, but I took the charts anyway, because they know something's wrong and want to help. They said I would need them. I—I made a deal. They're just testing how adaption works under pressure, so they can adapt people for colonizing Jupiter. Now that their presence here is known, they want America to know that's all there is to it. I promised to do my best to—"

"Yes, of course. Let's take a look."

He used the balloon-gloves and opened the charts again. They were indeed detailed; they were contour maps with special sites marked, such as the mer-colony, the Minoan ship, and the extent of the freshwater region. Also the supply depot.

"They didn't need to follow us," Melanie said. "They knew where we were going, all the time."

"And they didn't interfere," Melanie said. "Unless that other depot—?"

"We didn't see any evidence that anything had ever been there," he reminded her. "I think that was our own foulup—I mean, whoever set up this mission."

"Yes. We still don't know who hired us, or for what." She peered more closely. "What's that?" She poked her finger through the chart without touching it.

He looked. "Two dots. Not far from here, by bike. Another supply depot?"

"That's not the depot symbol."

Now he saw something else. "Look—there's one dot at the ship. And one here. Where we have been."

"Those dots are *people!* One for you. One for me. And two others."

"Where's the fifth?" he asked.

They looked, but could not find a fifth dot. "They marked every member of our party by location, and kept it right up to date," she said. "But one of us is missing."

"Eleph?"

"He couldn't have been alone, because he didn't have a good radio. And someone cut him off. So he must be one of the two."

"Then that's where I have to go. Since I'm two days faster than anyone expects, my arrival may be a surprise. Maybe I can learn from him just what's going on."

"I'm coming too!" she said.

"But there may be danger."

"What safety is there in being alone? I've had more than enough of it, these past two days."

"Glad to have you with me," he agreed.

They set off for the two dots, radios remaining off. Don wasn't sure whether to be glad for the murky water; it prevented him from seeing far ahead, but also shielded him from the view of others. He took care to make no noise as they approached the place marked, and hooded his light. But he had to have some light to see, as the site was low enough to be dark.

He gestured to Melanie to stay back. Then he moved directly to the dots.

A tent was there, pitched onto a slope as if to allow for drainage. Don felt about himself—then realized with a shock that he was actually searching for some kind of weapon! What would he do with a weapon? If he had a gun, he wouldn't know at whom to point it, and wouldn't have the nerve to shoot it. He was just here to find out what was going on.

Still, if Gaspar were in on it—the man was powerful and stubborn, and experienced under the water. Don was very poorly equipped to tangle—

This was ridiculous! Don nerved himself and hailed the tent. "Hello!"

There was no response. But he saw the wheel of a bicycle. Eleph's, by the look of it.

"Eleph!" he cried, going in.

Eleph was there—but he was unconscious. Don tried to shake the man awake, but had no success. Apparently he had been drugged.

There was no sign of the other person. Who had done this? Had Eleph been left here to die? No, the tent had been carefully pitched, open on both ends to channel the gentle current through, providing oxygen. Food packages and water were in easy reach. When Eleph woke, he would have no trouble getting along. He had merely been put out of the way for a few hours. Just as Pacifa had tried to isolate Don and Melanie.

Don cast about for an antidote, but realized that without specific knowledge of the drug used, it would be dangerous for him to tamper. Pacifa had had something that lasted for about four hours; she had used it to put Eleph out, so that they could set his arm. This was probably the same. The man seemed to be resting comfortably.

Don went out and signaled Melanie in. He explained the situation. "One of them must have drugged him, after he called me. That was about five hours ago, so the drug should be wearing off soon."

"They never expected you back this fast," she said. "Or that you'd have a chart that gave you this location. So he must have been drugged to prevent him from taking off while the other person went on some errand. This is our chance to do something."

"Yes, but do what? By the time he wakes, the other will be back."

"Unless we wake him sooner." She knelt by Eleph and patted his face.

"That won't work. I shook him, and—"

"He's coming to!" she exclaimed. "Come on, get him up on his feet. Time is critical."

Don obeyed. He hauled on Eleph, forgetting about the man's arm, while Melanie helped from the other side. They got him into a sitting position. Eleph groaned and opened his eyes.

Slowly he recognized Don. He smiled. "Get me to my feet," he said with difficulty. "That will make it wear off more rapidly. My head is spinning—it seems like only hours since I called you."

"It was," Melanie said. "What happened, Eleph?"

But the man was holding his breath to keep from crying out with pain as they struggled to get him up. It was complicated because of the confined space and the three bikes and the man's injury. But soon they were tramping back and forth between parked bicycles.

"Who drugged you?" Don asked.

"Gaspar. But do not blame him. He was trying to give Pacifa time."

"What did I tell you!" Melanie exclaimed. "What's she up to? Is it the mer-colony?"

"He doesn't know about that yet," Don reminded her.

Eleph winced, but not from physical pain. "I am sorry, Don. I *do* know. I have not been candid with you."

"That is the understatement of the mission," Gaspar said behind them.

Don whirled around, inadvertently yanking Eleph. If he had had any notion of catching anyone unawares, the initiative had now been reversed. Gaspar was unencumbered, while Don and Melanie had to support Eleph. Not that either would have been any match for the man, physically, under any circumstances.

"What are you talking about?" Melanie demanded.

"Why did you drug this man?" Don asked almost at the same time. "Why have you been keeping radio silence, when the sub couldn't intercept it?"

"We had reason," Gaspar said, maintaining a distance of about six feet. "Pacifa and I knew something was up. Both of you were straight, obviously. But we suspected that Eleph wasn't what he seemed. So we arranged to isolate him."

"So Pacifa *is* in on it," Melanie said. "And she's fooled Gaspar."

"Why did Pacifa remove my return ropes?" Don demanded. "The two of you have been acting a lot more suspiciously than Eleph ever did!"

"She had to be sure you stayed put, until we had a chance to work this thing out," Gaspar said evenly. "We would have preferred to have Melanie stay with you at the ship, but the mermaid complicated that, so Pacifa brought her back."

"Work *what* thing out?" Don was getting angry now.

"The fact that Eleph represents a foreign universe."

"*What?*" Don and Melanie said together. Don wasn't sure which of them was more vehement.

"Not exactly foreign," Eleph said. "And not inimical."

"Will you tell the truth now?" Gaspar asked him.

"I must have appropriate clearance. Give me my communicator."

Gaspar shook his head. "And let you call in an alien strike? No way."

Don could hardly believe this. Eleph was some kind of agent?

"Where's Pacifa?" Melanie inquired urgently.

Don realized that this was relevant. Pacifa had every

reason to be here, and her absence was as ominous as Eleph's admission.

"I know," Eleph said, looking at his watch. "She departed twelve hours ago for your home base on land. We have to stop her!"

"You can't stop her," Gaspar said. "You could never keep up with her, let alone make up that hundred mile head start. None of us could."

Don thought of the waiting Chinese submarine. He could catch her—if he had to. But he was hardly going to advertise that to Gaspar now! "Why is she doing that?"

"Because someone has to notify our government that our world is being infiltrated by alien agents."

Don would have laughed had he not been so concerned. "You sound the way I thought Eleph did, once! And Pacifa was the one always talking about Cuba. But now you're both accusing Eleph! What evidence do you have—for anything?"

"This," Gaspar said. He brought out a small object. "Do you recognize it?"

"A locket," Melanie said. "Eleph's; he wears it on a chain around his neck."

"But it's phased," Gaspar finished. "Otherwise I could hardly handle it like this, could I! He has had it all along."

"A phased locket," Melanie said. "Of course it is; it went through the tunnel with him. What's wrong with that?"

"Watch." Gaspar touched a finger to the little locket, and it sprang open. "Merely a ruse, you see. A tiny transceiver, not the kind we carry. Do you know what it is tuned to?"

No one answered. Gaspar turned it on.

"No, I'm afraid that won't work," a woman's voice was saying faintly. *"They have electronic guards. If I try to phase through, the alarm will sound."*

"But there is a world at stake!" a gruff man's voice responded. *"You* have *to get through!"*

"There are a million *worlds at stake,"* she retorted. *"Do you mean to risk them all for the sake of this one?"*

There was a pause. *"Sorry, I'm overtired. Near the end of my shift, and we lost three more during it. Very well, you're on the spot. Better your way. Off."*

There was another pause. Then: *"Proxy 5–12–5–16–12: Attention."*

"Acknowledging."

"Status?"

"Extreme doubt. They have sought to imprison me."

"But your mission was going well!"

"This was illusory. I now realize that they were playing me along, hoping to capture my technology. They refuse to heed my message."

"Then we must terminate your mission."

"I'm afraid this is the case. I regret my failure."

"Stand by for recovery."

There was another pause. Then another call for a proxy, by a different number.

Gaspar clicked it off. "That goes on continuously," he said. "That's the net that Eleph is on. Always different, always the same. Crisis to crisis. Worlds blowing up. A real alien invasion. If they don't subvert a world, they destroy it."

"No!" Eleph cried. "That's not it at all!"

Don looked at him, appalled. "The city! The ship! You set this all up! Why—?"

"Something we'd all like to know," Gaspar said. "But he won't talk."

"Now, wait, give Eleph a chance," Melanie protested. "He said he would explain, if he gets clearance."

"Tell me how you make contact," Gaspar said.

"Let me sit down," Eleph said. "I am not in good form at the moment."

"Of course," Melanie said solicitously. She and Don helped him get comfortable.

"I am of Earth," Eleph said. "I am human, and of this culture. You can verify this by the language: it is the same on my communicator. But not *this* Earth. I have come to save your world. That is all I can tell you, without clearance."

"You are not getting your hands on this radio!" Gaspar said.

"Maybe you can answer for him," Melanie suggested. "For the clearance."

Gaspar was surprised. "Eleph?"

Eleph nodded. "It will have to do. It is difficult to distinguish individual voices on this circuit. Turn it on, and when you hear this world's number, acknowledge."

"Number?"

"Proxy 5–12–5–16–8. I am the proxy for this alternate world, which is one of twenty in this frame."

"What's that number again?"

"Perhaps the mnemonic will help. If you number the alphabet, with the letter A being the number one, and B number two, and so on, it spells out E L E P H. 5–12–5–16–8."

"Got it," Gaspar said. "And how do I report?"

"You will be asked for your status. Then simply say that you request permission to clarify the mission for the locals. It will be granted. Then I can tell you."

"If you know it will be granted," Melanie asked, "why not simply tell us now?"

"We have to coordinate. Central must know the status of each mission constantly, especially when one is in trouble."

Gaspar shrugged and turned on the special radio.

". . . *political situation here is deteriorating, and I'll need central guidance, if I haven't blown it already. The president will not be moved on this issue, and unless I reveal myself—*"

"*No! You know that is out of the question, in this situation.*"

"*But there is a diminishing chance that—*"

"*OVERRIDE!*" a man's voice cut in. "*I have failed. The alternate faction has launched a full strike.*"

"*Phase out!*"

"*No. It was my miscalculation. I must remain. Just put a prohibition for all remaining—*"

There was a ghastly sound that abruptly cut off. Eleph winced.

In a moment the first man's voice resumed. "*GENERAL OVERRIDE: Option fifty twenty one demonstrated ineffective. Proxy lost. Prohibition for that course for all alternates within—*" Unintelligible gabble followed. Then the man resumed normal transmission. "*Attention, 16–19. Word from Central: appeal to his vanity. Do you require detail?*"

"*Not yet. Off.*"

Gaspar looked at the others. "This can continue forever!"

"No; they check each proxy frequently," Eleph said.

Sure enough, a few minutes later the number came.

Proxy 5–12–5–16–8: Attention.

Gaspar jumped. "Acknowledging."

Status?

"Permission to inform locals of mission."

"*16–8, why have you not acknowledged recent calls?*"

"The locals made me captive," Gaspar said with a straight face. "Now I must explain the mission if I am to have further access to this radio."

Do so. We shall call again. Off.

Gaspar looked at Eleph, who nodded. "The essence is simple," he said. "There are a seemingly infinite number of alternate worlds, the adjacent ones very similar to each other. But a considerable number of them face a life-destroying threat. It is a particular type of meteor that—"

"A calcium meteor?" Gaspar asked.

"Why yes. It—"

"It grazes the atmosphere and fragments, interacting with the water of the planet, forming calcium oxide. Not too much damage to the physical features, if it powders thinly enough, other than crusting them. But most or even all of the water could be gone."

"What are you talking about?" Don asked.

"The phase world," Gaspar said. "I've thought about that quite a bit. It's just like ours, only without water, therefore without life. If a meteor with a dark shell came, the telescopes could miss it until too late, and we couldn't stop it anyway. We don't have the technology to intercept something that massive and fast. But there's one thing I can't figure. That world should be buried in ash, especially in the ocean basins. Miles deep, perhaps. That's obviously not the case here. Calcium oxide is fierce stuff. Touch it and you're burned."

"The ash is there," Eleph said. "The phase takes care of that, too. The ashes are phased out, leaving only the stripped world for us to relate to."

"The phase," Gaspar agreed. "Of course. And the weight of that ash prevents the sea-floor from rebounding, so it still matches our world almost exactly."

"I thought you were against him," Melanie said to Gaspar.

"I just want to know the truth," Gaspar replied evenly. "He brought us on this wild chase. There has to be a reason."

"You mean you're the one who set this up?" Don asked, surprised.

"I am," Eleph said. "This is another world facing the disaster of the comet. But this is not the normal type of collision, such as generated the waves of extinctions including those of the dinosaurs. This is a fluke that will extinguish all life on Earth. Indeed it has done so, on countless worlds, and is proceeding to others."

"Wait," Don said. "If it has already happened, where it's going to, then we're out of danger, right?"

"Not so. The worlds differ slightly in time as well as substance. The meteor has already struck some, is striking others, and will strike the rest, in this sector of the spread. We know this, because we are seeing it happen. It is my mission to warn your world of this threat, so that it can expend its effort and resources to save itself."

"Why not just tell our leaders?" Gaspar asked. "Why go through this convoluted business of exploring under the ocean? We aren't significant people! We can't do anything about it."

"That is the crux," Eleph said. "We have been trying, literally, to save worlds, with a poor record for success. The true leaders of the world are generally inaccessible, both physically and intellectually. In America, a man cannot simply walk into the president's office and tell him to change his policies to save the world. The same is true in other parts of the world. Since considerable short-term sacrifice is required, even if the politician understood the need, he would be unlikely to act, because his first concern is the security of his office. We did try this route, and got nowhere, as our ongoing reports from other worlds demonstrates."

"Well, then, why not be more direct?" Melanie asked. "I

mean, if you have the technology, land in the capital city in a shining space ship, or something.''

"I can answer that," Gaspar said, smiling. "Such a ship would get blasted out of the air before it landed."

"It has happened," Eleph said. "We have also tried sending messages to key figures. So far these have either been ineffective, or have destabilized the political situation so that mischief results."

"Such as nuclear warfare!" Don exclaimed, remembering part of the radio sequence of reports.

"Precisely," Eleph said. "While such events are not the disasters they may seem, in view of the coming total destruction by another cause, they do represent failures of our policy. It is our purpose to save worlds, not to hasten their destruction. So I am trying a completely different route. I am attempting to demonstrate the reality of the alternate world framework to a select group of ordinary residents of this world. If I can convince them, then they may be able to convince their world. That is, you can convince yours. Your world may listen to you, when it would not listen to me."

"But what has archaeology to do with this?" Don demanded.

"You, as an archaeologist, are able to appreciate the reality of the knowledge I was able to draw on, from my contact with the larger framework of worlds. I routed the party to the Yucatan ruins, and then to the Minoan ship. You know how the phase works, and that the information it provides is genuine, not cobbled together. You believe. Also, you are in a better position to understand the cultures of other worlds that are not virtually identical to this one."

"But I have no power to influence anyone!" Don protested.

"Yes you do. You can convince Gaspar."

"But Gaspar can't influence anyone either!"

"Yes he can," Eleph said. "He is an agent of your government. They will give his report credence. Especially when he shows them the ruins and the ship, and you publicize your interpretation of the manuscript. When the four of you together speak in a way that I could not. They will see that the government takes my message seriously. In that may be the salvation of your world."

Melanie was aghast. "What a roundabout route!"

"Yes," Eleph said. "I knew you would reject it if you didn't learn much of it yourselves. So I specified the coordinates, and arranged other challenges whose purpose was to make you interact and learn to rely on each other and to trust each other. This process we call melding. It seemed to be working—until it abruptly went wrong."

"It was working," Melanie murmured, glancing sidelong at Don.

"But there are holes in it," Gaspar said.

"Holes?" Don asked. "You didn't see that ship!"

"I didn't need to. Consider this, Don: if the calcium meteor destroyed all the water and wiped out life and in the process even leveled those ruins off Yucatan so that we could walk right through them—why did it leave your ship? That wooden vessel would have been completely destroyed, and certainly no documents would have survived."

Don was stricken. That was true!

"The ruins were not destroyed by the meteor," Eleph said. "That world was further advanced archaeologically than this one. Both ruins and ship were excavated. But for this purpose, we arranged to have a similar ship phased back in from a third world, complete, to match the one here. The ship is genuine—but the one in the phase world is not from *this* world. It is merely a prop to enable you to explore the real one. The manuscript is genuine too, as you can tell."

CHAPTER 16

MISSION

Gaspar frowned. "If what you say is true, we must cooperate with you to save our world."

Eleph nodded. "This is the case."

Now Don remembered how Eleph had hesitated when they had discussed governmental foul-ups, including the exploding shuttle and the wrong-shaped mirrors on the telescope. Eleph had not known of these episodes—because he was not from this world! His world would have had different episodes.

"But first we have to believe you," Gaspar said. "And I'm not sure I do. There are too many oddities. Such as the mermaid Pacifa described."

"Splendid," Don said. "She helped me translate the tablets."

"And he goosed her," Melanie said.

"What's a mermaid doing there?"

"They are Chinese," Don said. "Learning how to colonize Jupiter. The sub is theirs—bringing supplies, protecting them. They mean no harm to us, and should be left alone."

"How do you know?" Gaspar asked.

Don shrugged. "I have no reason to doubt. They helped

me get here quickly. They could have dropped me and killed me, if they wanted to stop me. I did get to know Splendid somewhat, and I believe she's sincere.''

''But the chances of their being right there by that ship—''

''That was not coincidence,'' Eleph said. ''The freshwater outflow is ideal for both the colony and the ship, and they were interested in the ship anyway. And Jupiter is part of the answer.''

''Answer?''

''The mer-colony was to be the last challenge for this group, before you learned of the mission. Once you saw that it is possible for man to adapt for residence on another planet, and understood how much can be done when there is dedication. Then, I believed, you would be ready to grasp the greatest of all: the saving of your world.''

''How can it be saved?'' Melanie asked.

''Any living things that are to be saved will have to depart Earth, and it is not possible to build enough spaceships for the whole population of human beings, animals, and plants. But Jupiter could serve as a substantial base for adapted creatures. Ordinary ocean denizens could be adapted more readily. They could be ferried there by the shipful.''

''Couldn't everyone be put through the phase tunnel to a safe alternate?'' Melanie asked.

''No. The phasing is an extremely limited resource, to be used only for those who are trying to save worlds. I was the only one to cross to this world, with my equipment for the recruits.''

''Why not simply blow up the meteor?'' Gaspar asked.

''That is another possibility. But it would require a phenomenal unified effort, because your technology is barely at the necessary level. It would be better to transfer as many people, animals, and plants to other sites as possible, in case that is not effective.'' Eleph took a breath. ''The point is, your world can surely be saved—if it makes a concerted effort. But first your leaders must believe in the necessity, and organize the effort.''

''And other worlds have not made that effort?'' Gaspar asked.

''They have not. So the worlds are being lost.''

''Because they don't believe,'' Don said.

''Or don't choose to,'' Melanie said. ''I read about a girl, once. She was grabbed in a shopping center and hauled into a car, and no one objected. Later she managed to get away, and ran screaming down the highway, half naked, and no one stopped to help. Two days later they found her raped and strangled body in a ditch. She was ten years old.''

There was a silence. What better comment was there on the nature of man? Knowledge of trouble was not enough. There had to be leadership. *Would I have stopped to help?* Don asked himself, and did not know the answer.

''Nobody will stop to save a world,'' Melanie said.

''How much time—before the meteor?'' Gaspar asked.

''For this world, ten years.''

''It couldn't be done in that time, even if everybody believed and acted,'' Gaspar said.

''It could—with technological advice from more advanced worlds. But it will be extremely close.''

Gaspar shook his head. ''I can't say I believe you, Eleph. But I don't think I can take the chance. Will you talk to my superiors if I take you to them? Will you open your communications to them? Show your technology to our experts?''

''Yes, if the rest of this party will speak for my sincerity and tell what you have seen.''

''Then we'd better intercept Pacifa before she reaches

Florida and makes a report that brings a force to arrest or destroy us," Gaspar said. "We thought that you were working with the Chinese subs to establish a base here to compromise American interests. You won't be able to persuade anybody of your mission, once she reports that and they send a military force to take out the colony."

"No!" Don cried. "That's what the mer-folk are afraid of. I promised them—"

"How well I know," Eleph said. "My whole effort was to persuade the four of you first, so that you would help me to persuade your world. Other approaches are failing, but I hoped that this personal approach would provide me that necessary channel. I need exactly the right key to alert the right people in the right way. Then it becomes possible."

"It's an odd device," Gaspar said. "I agree with your radio contacts there."

"Well, it worked for me," Melanie said. "I believe Eleph, because I've come to know him. If you hadn't been so paranoid—"

Gaspar smiled. "I was infiltrated into this mission because my superiors were paranoid."

"I can intercept Pacifa," Don said. "The sub will help me, and I can get to the tunnel she used before she does, and stop her." Then he hesitated. "It is still there?"

"Yes," Eleph said. "It is a single unit, left there for our return."

Melanie was perplexed. "Now wait. I can see how you handled the interviews and all, with your fuzzed-up voice. You could have taken your tunnel-generating unit to Don and then to Gaspar and then to me. But you were the fourth person through. How did you get it to Pacifa?"

Eleph smiled. "I wished to conceal my nature, in case of suspicion, until the group had proper chance to meld. That was evidently ineffective, as my present situation demonstrates. So I went to Pacifa and sent her through with instructions to practice her phase technique, until the designated time for rendezvous several days later. Then I went through myself and rode down the highway to my own coordinates. It was a simple ploy.''

''Which Pacifa saw through, when she reflected on it,'' Gaspar said. ''So she knew the tunnel was still there.''

Eleph nodded. ''She is an intelligent woman. I deeply regret—'' He did not finish.

Gaspar smiled. ''She likes you too, Eleph. She was sorry to learn of your alien involvement. But her first loyalty is to her own world.''

''Which I am trying to save.''

''I'll have to load up on supplies, though,'' Don said. ''I don't want to be caught hungry.''

They went as a group to the depot. ''Your direct route is to cut east of Cuba, while Pacifa circles it to the west,'' Gaspar said. ''She won't go to the Yucatan, but will ride up into the Cuban coastal water if she has to. Once she intersects our prior route north of Cuba, she'll be sure of her destination. Unless that sub takes you to the Bahamas platform, you'll still have trouble beating her there.''

''I'll do what I can,'' Don said.

''And your bike may fail. Your rear wheel is warped.''

''Yours is no better,'' Don said.

''Mine is available,'' Eleph said. ''It should not be difficult to adjust it to you.''

Don considered the offer. ''I'd feel more comfortable on my own bike. Thirty six speeds would just confuse me.''

''Now *you're* being stubborn,'' Melanie said. ''I'll bet Eleph's bicycle weighs half yours, and so does Pacifa's. You're an idiot if you race her using your old rattletrap.''

Don had to concede the merit of the case. ''Okay. Eleph's bike.''

Eleph instructed Don on the proper use of the various mechanisms, while Gaspar selected and loaded supplies. They set the seat and handlebars and adjusted the pedal straps. The taped metal in lieu of handgrips was disquieting, as was the narrow saddle, and it all felt ludicrously off-center, forcing him to hunch way over. The toe straps made him fear for his equilibrium should he need to put out a foot suddenly, and the reversed handles seemed impossible to use effectively. The entire machine felt strange, with everything not quite where it should be and with a different feel to the action. How was he going to steer this thing, let alone ride it? He regretted allowing himself to be browbeaten into the change.

But before he could formulate an effective resistance, he was on his way. Once the bike was in motion, it seemed to make much more sense. He *was* able to ride, and that was what counted. He concentrated on cadence and ankling and shifting gears and guiding it with his hands set in near the stem, so he wouldn't have to lean over quite so far. He practiced pulling up on the pedals as well as pushing down, a trick impossible without these toestraps.

It seemed he had only started, but he looked up to find himself already at the submarine. He slid two fingers over each brake lever and coasted to a beautiful stop, even remembering to disengage his feet from the straps in time. He was becoming a pro! The feel of this bicycle was growing on him.

There was a language difficulty, compounded by the phase. Don tried to explain that he needed a ride across the trench and as far around the island of Cuba as possible. They did pick him up and move—only to deliver him instead to the mer-colony.

Don simmered while the tritons stared at him contemptuously. He was trying to save the colony too, as well as to save the world, if only they would comprehend.

In due course Splendid appeared, swimming in from elsewhere. She must have been at the ship, making further notes from the tablets. She had been picking up on the Minoan Linear A, evidently having a ready mind for interpretation. He had been wrong to see her as mainly a creature of myth and sex appeal.

Don explained the present-day situation to her, stressing the need for speed. Pacifa had a one day start on him, and she could travel faster, but his route would cut the distance almost in half. If Pacifa averaged two hundred miles per day, she would reach the base in nine or ten days. If Don averaged a hundred and fifty a day, he could do it in seven or eight, and just catch her. If the trench didn't stop him.

OUR MACHINES ARE NOT PERMITTED BEYOND THE ENVIRONS OF THE TRENCHES, she wrote. ESPE-CIALLY NOT NORTH OF CUBA, WHERE AMERICAN PATROLS ARE HEAVY.

This made sense. Relations between America and China were chronically mixed, with minor thaws and re-freezes occurring periodically. A Chinese submarine there would be asking for an Incident.

Yet his need was urgent. "If I don't catch that woman, the Americans will learn about your colony, which she thinks is part of a conspiracy to build a military base of some bad sort within ready range of the continent. My situation turns out to have only coincidental connection to yours, and I hope to avoid mention of your presence here, or to clarify its beneficial nature if it must be told. I know she will be persuaded, but I must catch her before she reaches the base in Florida and gives an alarm that could be very bad for you."

Splendid conferred with the mers. Don reminded himself

that these were carefully selected and modified and trained people, but somehow his errant eyes kept centering on the women, with their phenomenal breasts and clouds of hair around their heads. Superficial characteristics, perhaps the largess of the same surgery that had formed their tails and modified their lungs and metabolism, but impressive regardless. The eye of the human male was fashioned to lock onto such things, and it was hard to resist this imperative. In all the time he had worked closely with Splendid, he had never become inured to the sight of her. Melanie's jealousy had been justified to that extent.

But a woman was more than body, and a man's interest was in the long run governed by more than that. Splendid had in her fashion proved to Don that such a body, even had it been fully human through to the feet, was not what he sought for a permanent association. It wasn't that Splendid's mind was bad, for it was excellent; it was that the peculiarities of Melanie's personality were a better match for the peculiarities of Don's own.

So why hadn't he said that to Melanie? Well, he would do so, the first chance he had. He had his good radio installed on Eleph's bicycle, and it was a private circuit.

Splendid swam toward him. YOU ARE CORRECT, she wrote. WE MUST ASSIST YOU DESPITE THE DANGER. THE SUB WILL TAKE YOU TO THE THOUSAND FATHOM DEPTH IN THE OLD BAHAMAS CHANNEL, HERE.

She showed him on the map. It was well around Cuba, about a third of the way along his route, and beyond the trench. From there the channel was comparatively level all the way up to Florida. That might well cut his time in half, and provide him an ample margin.

"Yes!" he exclaimed, giving her a misty kiss that made the jealous triton clench his fist. "That'll do it."

So the sub-lift resumed, though the mers were uneasy. It seemed that the danger from foreign military patrols was formidable, there in the Windward Passage between Cuba and Haiti. But the colony's supply route came through there, along the entire length of the Puerto Rico trench, so Don suspected that their apprehension was exaggerated. Splendid might trust him, but the others did not.

For an hour he passed through the nebulous reaches of the middle ocean levels. It was dull and hypnotic, and he was tired, and he nodded off to sleep astride his bicycle.

Melanie stood before him, trim and pretty. She removed her blouse, showing her bra, and then opened the bra to reveal her breasts. "How do these compare to the fish-wife's?" she asked.

"Not as large," he said. "But that's not the point. I—"

"Then how does this compare?" she asked, drawing down her skirt and stepping out of it.

"Well, her, uh, she—the scales of her tail cover—but the point is—"

"She can't exactly spread her legs."

"The body doesn't matter!" he exclaimed. "I mean, not that much. She has hair, you have legs. The point is, you have all your hang-ups, and I have mine, and they make a good fit. The—the bodies—any two bodies fit, when you come down to it, but any two personalities don't mesh. I like you when you're sweet, and I like you when you're angry, and if we were two hands of cards, I think we'd make a winning combination. Maybe that's not exactly commitment, but it's a solid base for it, and if you agree I'd like to try it."

"Well, here is my body. Try it."

"That too. But I mean love. Marriage. The long term. Whatever I'm doing, I want you with me. Your body—oh, yes, I'll take it with or without the wig, and it'll be great.

But your convoluted, elliptical, deviously logical mind—that's what I love.''

"Is that a proposal, Don?"

"Yes! Marry, me, Melanie, after we save the world."

"After we save the world," she agreed.

"Is that an elliptical yes?" he asked, excited.

"An elliptical yes," she agreed.

That shocked him awake. He was still riding beneath the submarine. "Damn it! I was dreaming!"

"No you weren't," she retorted.

He glanced down. His radio was on! He must have done that in his sleep. "You mean I was talking in my sleep?"

"You mean you didn't mean it?"

"I meant it! If I said what I dreamed I said."

"You said the mesh of personalities was more important than the mesh of bodies. I gather there was some body-meshing going on."

"Not yet. But if you care to repeat what you did there, outside my dream—"

She laughed. "With or without the wig?"

"Yes!"

"Then it seems we have a date."

"Date, hell! We have an engagement."

"That, too," she agreed.

His radio was fading. It lasted only a few minutes when he wasn't riding. He reached down to spin the wheel, cranking it up again. "Oh, Melanie, why couldn't we have had this dialogue when we were together?"

"My, you *are* eager to mesh!"

"That, too." They laughed together, and it was great. Maybe their physical separation had enabled him to be bolder. He hadn't stuttered at all. The luck of his dream, and of the radio being on—

No, they had to be linked. He had unconsciously turned it

on, and gone into his fancy—and she had joined it and
accepted. He had been able to do in partial reality what had
balked him in reality, and then it had turned real, and now
it was wonderful.

He was jolted by a sudden change of course. He grabbed
onto his bike and fought to maintain equilibrium. "Hoo!"
he exclaimed.

"What's happening?" Melanie cried faintly, for he was
no longer spinning the wheel.

He grabbed it and turned it vigorously. "The sub is
maneuvering wildly! It's going down. I'm straining at my
balloon-moorings."

"But why?"

"Wish I knew!"

But in a moment he figured it out: the sub had passed
close to the American naval base at Guantanamo, an action
which begged for trouble. There had been no choice,
because the trench passed that region. So an American sub
had fired first, asking no questions.

Then a shark-shape swam in from behind, following the
sub unerringly, and he understood. A homing torpedo. The
threat of this region had not been exaggerated!

A smaller fish shot out of one of the sub's ports and
moved to intercept the torpedo. There was an immense
explosion.

Don was not directly affected, because of the phase. But
the sound was deafening, and the bucking of the sub seemed
about to tear him and his bicycle loose. It seemed that the
sub was not defenseless.

"Don! Don!" Melanie cried desperately.

"I'm here," he gasped. "Torpedo—they stopped it—but
we're going down."

Now the vibration of the sub's motor was gone, and the
machine was drifting as if dead. Don wondered why, since

it hadn't been hit. Then he realized that this was part of its defensive strategy. Whoever had fired that torpedo would record the blast, spot the descending hulk, and maybe assume that the job had been done and move on. If they were tuning in on the faint motor, that was gone, with the obvious implication.

Don hoped the ruse worked. What would happen to *him* if the sub were blown up? He was attached to it, and even with the phase he doubted that he could survive that kind of shock. This whole business was his fault, too; the sub was trying to do him a favor, and had gotten into real trouble.

No other torpedo came. The sub kept dropping. The radio was silent, and he didn't dare spin the wheel for fear that the motion or the sound of the radio would be picked up by the enemy. He hated to have Melanie worry, but stillness was necessary now.

Down, down. This was a deep-diver; it could handle the depths of the trench, as perhaps the attacking sub could not. Probably it would go all the way to the bottom and lie there until it seemed safe to resume. Hours later, or even days.

In which case Don's mission was doomed.

But there was a much more immediate and personal danger. His bike was firmly tied to the bottom rails. If the sub struck the ocean floor, the balloon fastenings would transmit its entire weight to the bike beneath, crushingly. Don himself could walk through the sub and escape, but what good would that be without his bike?

Feverishly Don tried to untie the knotted balloons. But they were under the stress of his own weight and that of the bicycle, and would not budge. Two loose balloons were in his hands, so that he could also hold on directly, but he could free those hands only by putting his full weight on the bike.

Then he had a second and worse realization: the sub was

sinking at moderate speed, its fall restrained by the resistance of the water and its own calculated buoyancy. If he let go, he would fall at his own rate, as if through air, and smash to death below. He couldn't afford to desert the submarine!

He was trapped. His choice was between dooms: crushing or smashing. And he had no idea how soon. The murk blocked any sight of what was below.

He put his hand to the wheel to recharge the radio, so that he could tell Melanie. She might have a clearer head in this emergency, and figure out his best course. But the enemy sub might still be watching, with sonar or radar or whatever sophisticated devices it possessed, and his activity could still bring ruin. He had to remain silent, so that he wouldn't inadvertently endanger the friendly sub more than he already had.

Don knew he was on his own, for this crisis.

Then, as if his brain clicked into a new mode, he knew what to do. He took out his pencil and pried at the balloon anchoring the front of his bicycle to the rail. The graphite snapped off, but slowly he worked the taut knot loose, until it gave way and snapped free. The front wheel sagged, forcing him to support it by hand, with his other balloon-gloved hand clenched over the rail. Now he really appreciated the extreme lightness of the bike; it was no trouble to hold.

The second bike balloon was too much for him to untie this way, so he got out his penknife, hooked his elbow over the rail with balloon-padding, and hooked both feet into the chassis of the bike. Then, laboriously he cut the balloon. It parted with extreme reluctance, because of its half-phased condition, but finally the rear wheel also hung loose.

Now he carried the entire bicycle on his legs, hanging onto the rail with left hand and right elbow. But he could not rest. He let go with his left hand and brought it down to his mouth. He used his teeth to wrench off the glove. His small packet of maps was tucked inside that same balloon; he hoped they would be legible after taking this beating. He cupped both balloons under his elbow, his sole support, and got ready to tackle the last connection, his right hand still gloved. The sub might be drifting relatively slowly through water, but his own weight was excruciating, because his full weight was hanging by that one arm.

The ocean floor came into view. Don snapped at his right hand with his teeth. He bit painfully into his own fingers, cursing the awkwardness of his position, but the balloon refused to come.

There was no time! Don let go, dropped the last eight feet, hauled the bike up over his head as a kind of counterbalance to break his fall, and landed running.

The sub came down on top of him. Its substance could not touch him or the bike, but it caught his balloon-hand with a glancing blow and shoved it down irresistibly. Don was felled as if clubbed, but momentum carried him forward. He spun free of the bike and rolled.

In a moment the world settled. All was still.

Don took stock. He was lying under and within the resting sub, but his outstretched gloved hand lay just outside. He had made it.

He got up, pulled off the glove, dropped the balloons to the ground and walked back through the sub to carry out his bike. "Thanks for the lift," he told the crew. "I know you did the best you could, and risked your lives on my account. Now I'll do the best I can. So long." He felt a bit like a carefree hero, dismissing severe wounds with cheer.

But maybe the others saw him that way too. A couple of them waved back as he walked on.

Three balloons and the maps were lost, pinned somewhere under the sub. He picked up the fourth, rolled it into a tight ball, attached a length of string, and pocketed it. If he had any further trouble with the real world, he would dangle the balloon behind him. Better that than getting himself crushed or knocked around.

He checked his position. North latitude 20°30′; west longitude 73° even, approximately. Now he could have used the maps! But his recollection showed his position as north of Haiti and east of his projected route. The sub had gone far astray during its evasive action, not that he blamed it. The Chinese were lucky to have survived.

Now he had a doubt about his prior conjecture. Who had really fired that torpedo? An American submarine—or some other? He hoped American, because that would be less of a threat to him.

The depth was twenty two hundred fathoms, or about two and a half miles. He wished the sub hadn't sunk so far; he would be exhausted long before he made it to the shallows, but there was no choice.

Fortunately he had a fair notion of his route, even without the maps. All he had to do was follow the Puerto Rico trench west until it branched into the Old Bahama Channel, then bear north along the Santaren Channel until he reached the vicinity of Florida. Most of that would be between 250 and 450 fathoms—deep enough to keep well out of sight, shallow enough to keep him out of serious trouble with the terrain. He hoped. If he had to surmount a cliff, he would inflate the balloon. It would take a long time to fill it full enough, and he hoped it wouldn't burst, but it was better than nothing.

Time, time! That was his constant enemy, now. The sub had helped him on his way, but not enough. His easy interception of Pacifa had become chancy.

He rode on. He was learning to respect this bicycle. The

narrow seat had grown uncomfortable for sitting upright during the sub ride, but for serious pedaling it was superior, because it did not interfere with his thighs the way a broad seat would have. He was making better time with less effort than normal. There was a gear ratio to accommodate his slightest whim, and this did save him energy. And it was a much lighter machine; even fully loaded, it moved along more readily than his old one ever had. No wonder Eleph had kept up so well, even after his injury.

Where could Eleph have gotten it? Not from a regular shop! Perhaps not from Earth at all. From another alternate?

Was he riding a machine from another universe?

That intrigued Don deviously. His mind seemed to be racing right along with his pedals, and he moved at quite respectable velocity. What would it be like to visit an alternate world?

"Don."

He jumped. His radio had recharged, and Melanie was paging him. How could he have forgotten her?

"Here, Mel. Sorry I damped out. Someone fired a torpedo at the sub, and it had to drop and play dead. I lost the maps, but I'm on my way now. It'll be close, but I think I can still intercept Pacifa."

"Oh, Don, I'm so relieved! I was afraid—"

"So was I, for some moments there. But I squeaked through. It's wonderful to have your company!"

"I'll stay with you all the way. Maybe I can help you by checking our maps, if you get lost."

"That will be nice."

Then he saw light. How could that be, this deep? Was it a beam from a sub, and if so, which one?

Then he saw it more clearly. "Glowcloud!" he cried.

But it was not Glowcloud. It was a monster, so large that he could see only a small section of any given tentacle at one time in the haze of water. The thing had to be a hundred feet long!

"Are you sure?" Melanie asked. "You're a long way from here."

Don snapped off his headlamp and swerved aside, hoping the squid had not noticed him. Glowcloud he knew and could get along with, he was even company of a sort. "You're right; it's another squid, a huge one. I'm steering clear."

But the giant mollusk's curiosity had been aroused. It changed colors in rapid sequence and put forth the great tentacles to investigate. Don could see them because they glowed in the gloom. He pedaled desperately, trying to avoid their snakelike approach. If one snagged on the balloon—

The bicycle dropped into a hole, and Don took a spill as he came to a stop. His arms bashed into rock, and he pulled up his legs to disengage them from the bicycle. He pushed off, as he had from the dropping sub—and plummeted into the blackness, finding no ground.

He flung out his arms, catching hold of a smooth rim of rock, breaking his fall. But the slope was convex, providing no purchase, and his hands slid down. He dropped upright into an aperture like a well.

He landed hard. It had felt like a drop of ten feet, his hands scraping all the way, and his right foot had twisted as he landed. Now the pain was starting. He was in real trouble.

Actually, the squid had been no threat. He should not have reacted so precipitously. Had the balloon snagged on a tentacle, it might have alarmed the squid as much as Don. Now, through his folly of riding blind, he had gotten himself into a hole, literally.

He tried to climb out, but the sides were almost slick. He

felt the breeze of flowing water; this was another small freshwater spring, and the constant current had worn off all the rough edges, reaming out the vertical tunnel. Below him, by the feel, it curved and continued on down. No escape that way!

"Don! What's happening?" Melanie called from above.

Don looked up to see the faint glow of the passing squid, obscured by something over the hole. The bicycle! It must have straddled the aperture—about six feet out of reach. The rope was on it, looped and securely fastened. He could not haul himself up.

"I'm in a hole!" he called back. "I can't reach the bike. The radio will fade out in a moment."

"Oh, Don!" she cried despairingly. Her voice was already fading.

A tentacle reached down, searching for him. Don ducked away, avoiding it—and ran out of breath. He was standing at the fringe of the oxygenation field, and had to count himself lucky that the straight section of the hole had been no deeper. He could have suffocated immediately.

He swept his hand through the groping tentacle. "It's your fault, sucker!" he said angrily.

He tried to climb again, this time bracing his feet against the opposite wall. Pain flared in his right ankle, forcing him to desist. That injury was worse than he had thought.

The balloon tugged at its string, borne upward by the current. Of course! he could blow up the balloon and let it haul him up out of here. It would take time, but it was sure. And if the squid annoyed him thereafter, he could let the balloon go as a decoy, leading the monster in a futile chase upward.

He hauled the package in and opened it. He exhaled with vigor, inflating the balloon. Of course there was no real lift

yet, as his breath was mere water in the real world. He had
to wait for the carbon dioxide to phase through.

Gradually the balloon shrank—but no bubble formed. He
gave it another lungful, and another. Still nothing. The gas
was going somewhere, but not into the balloon of the other
phase. Was there a leak?

But he should be able to feel little bubbles escaping, in
that case. There were none. What was wrong?

"I'm a fool!" he exclaimed as another tentacle felt
through him. "Carbon dioxide is compressible! At this
pressure, it must liquefy!"

His emergency lifting balloon was useless in deep water.
He couldn't even use it as a decoy.

Don swept his hand through the tentacle again, furiously.
This time the member withdrew.

Then the weight of despair bore down on him. Don sank
down—but gasped for air and had to stand again, his ankle
hurting. He couldn't even give up gracefully!

The squid was gone and his radio was dead and he was
alone. He felt dizzy; the steady current was washing his
oxygen up and away, even as that current renewed the
supply.

It wasn't only his mission that was drifting away while he
languished here; it was his own life. He had no food or
water on him. It was on the bicycle. In time he would grow
too tired or sleepy to stand, and then he would suffocate.
Unless he chose to end it sooner by diving down into the
airless lower tunnel.

He thought of Melanie. They had been on the verge of
such joy, having discovered each other. Now their love
would be lost, along with the world. Damn!

And the story of the Minoan ship—would that be told,
now? Splendid knew it, but Pacifa's report might get the
mer-colony wiped out too. Everything he cared about—and

he did care about Splendid and her people—was doomed. Somehow these things seemed almost worse than the destruction of the world, because they were more immediate.

He woke, and realized after the fact that he could sleep standing up. But his ankle was swollen and hurting, and he was increasingly thirsty.

What was one ankle, compared to life? All he had to do was grit his teeth and brake against that wall and shove himself up and out.

He tried it. Pain overwhelmed him, and he fell hard. He gasped again for oxygen, struggling upright on one foot.

He could not do it. Perhaps eventually he would have what it took. Eleph certainly did. The kind of physical determination that took no note of pain or frailty. Don admired it enormously, but he was made of different and inferior stuff. He could not just walk into that amount of agony, though his world hung in the balance. He would pass out from the pain first, and be lost. And with him, the world. When the meteor came, and the world was not ready.

Build not on the flank of the bull . . .

Good advice! But add this to it: trust not in a weakling, lest he fall in a hole and not climb out.

Eleph had done everything he could. He had phased through to this world with his limited equipment, and set up the mission and almost made it work. But for the bad break of Gaspar's suspicion, he would have persuaded them, and they would be on the way to saving the world. Now he depended on Don, and Don was failing him.

For that matter, the Minoan scholar Pi-ja-se-me had done everything he could, and also failed because of the inadequacy of others. So at last he had resigned himself to his fate and left his message for the future.

If only he could get out of this hole and ride to intercept

Pacifa! Yet at this stage, even that was a lost hope. He had lost hours here, and it had already been a close thing; he was probably already too late. Even if not, how could he ride well, with his right ankle unable to sustain any significant weight? And if he could ride, by maybe fixing some kind of splint to brace his ankle and staying on a level route—how could he find that route, without his maps?

Well, maybe he had a map, in the form of his depth meter. The thousand fathom contour was a reasonably straight line passing north of the entire Greater Antilles chain, only recurving well up the channel. He could cut due south to intercept it, then stay right on it, and his route would be level all the way, by definition. Any mindless lout could follow that route, ankle or no.

Maybe it wasn't lost quite yet. Pacifa, expecting no pursuit, might not be rushing; she didn't want to blunder carelessly into any holes either. So he might yet catch her at his slower pace. Certainly it was worth trying. If she turned on her radio to check with Gaspar, he might tell her to wait for Don. So it remained possible to save the world, barely. Except for one thing.

Don Kestle, genius world saver, who couldn't lift his posterior from a hole in the ground to save his life, let alone the world.

He drifted into a daze. Insufficient oxygen, or maybe nitrogen narcosis, because it was almost pleasant. He really didn't know anything about either condition. This was what it felt like to die.

"So it has come to this at last for you too," Pi-ja-se-me said.

Don was not surprised to find the Cretan scholar with him, or to hear him speaking intelligibly. "Yes. But I am neither as bold nor resourceful as you. I simply fell in a hole."

"We all fall, eventually. Are you hallucinating? I did, at the end."

"I must be. But I can think of no person I would rather meet in a hallucination than you."

"Thank you, Don-kes-tle. Have you prayed to your God?"

"No. I don't believe in that sort of miracle. If I can't figure out how to save myself, then maybe I deserve to die."

"I agree. The Gods care nothing for our convenience. But is there a way to save yourself?"

"Well, if the sides of this hole weren't so smooth, I could climb out. Or if I had something to stand on, I could reach or jump to catch hold of my bike. Or if someone found me, and let down a rope I could use. It is really a simple thing, getting out."

"That glove you used to handle the mermaid—could that help?"

Don brought out the balloon. "If I had something to grab with it, yes. But I don't." He jammed it back into his pocket.

"I am sorry, my friend. I would help you if I could, but words are all I have."

"I would help you too, Pi-ja, if I could. Let me shake your hand."

The man looked confused. "Do what?"

"It is a simple clasping of right hands. By this we signal our appreciation of each other, and our agreement."

Pi-ja nodded. He extended his hand. Don took it.

Then Don thought of something else. "There were female things by your tablets, jewelry, but you mentioned no woman on the ship."

"Of course. They were mementos of my lovely concubine. She had her odd ways, and was jealous, but I loved

her, and I kept the things she gave me always close. They
were a comfort in my time alone.''

Such an obvious explanation! Why hadn't he thought of
it himself?

He was awakened again by a tentacle passing through his
face. He had lost another two hours, according to the
glowing hands of his watch. Not that it mattered, since he
couldn't go anywhere anyway. Old long-arms was back
again, making a second round investigation after several
hours. Damned mollusk curiosity!

The tip of the tentacle hung up momentarily on the
useless balloon wadded into Don's pocket.

Don-kes! The glove!

Don snatched the limp rubber out and cupped it in the
palm of his hand. Then he clapped that hand to the dangling
tentacle, squeezing tightly. He put his other hand over the
first, locking it in place.

The squid felt it. The giant limb yanked up—and Don
hung on, coming up with it.

His head cracked into the bicycle. Involuntarily he let
go—and grabbed the crossbar of the bike. His feet dropped,
but he had hold of what he needed.

He saw the startled squid jetting high and away, flashing
colors. ''Get lost, monster!'' he called after it. ''Thanks for
the lift!''

He heaved up his feet, getting them onto the bike. He
fought his way to the side, crawling to land. Then he pulled
the bike after him.

He mounted it and pushed off. His right foot hurt, but he
could pedal with his left. Inertia kept him moving. So it was
possible. But it would be better with a splint, so he could use
both feet.

But you are free. Perhaps your concubine can help.

''Melanie,'' he said, as the radio recharged. ''I'm out.''

"Oh, Don! I was so worried! All this time with no word from you—"

"But my right ankle is hurt. I have to fix that before I can go on. I don't suppose Pacifa has opened radio contact?"

"No, nothing from her."

He came to a stop and dismounted. Pacifa would have been expert at this, but he was clumsy. How was a splint made? Or could he just somehow fasten something to his knee, to push at the pedal? He had to be quick about it, whatever it was.

There was another light. "Go away, squid," he said.

What is that? There was never a ship like that!

Then he realized that it wasn't squid glow. It was artificial light. A submarine!

Ah, now I have the concept from your mind. What a strange world you have, Don-kes-tle!

Had the Chinese sub come to take him the rest of the way? In that case, the mission had been saved.

But as the think loomed closer, he saw the markings on its tower. It was American!

Ordinarily this would have been good news, but right now it was bad news. The Chinese sub understood his situation, but the American sub did not. It might think he was some kind of enemy agent. Better to let it pass without noticing him. It had no reason to suspect his presence here; it was only the luck of his fall into the hole that had prevented him from being far away.

Your friend may be your enemy?

"What's happening, Don?" Melanie asked.

A beam of light speared out from the sub, orienting on the sound. It must have heard his prior dialogue, and come to investigate; now it had him pinpointed. In a moment the light illuminated him, making him avert his gaze from its brilliance. Beyond, the sub settled slowly to the ground, and into it, as nearly as he could tell. The sea-floor here was evidently a bit lower than in the phase world, or mushier because of the sediment. He hadn't noticed, but since he automatically attuned to what was in the phase world, now, that wasn't surprising.

Pointless to try to hide, now. "American sub," he said. "Probably the one that fired the torpedo. It must be casting around for the other, to be sure it's dead."

"But they mustn't fight!" Melanie exclaimed.

"I'll try to talk to it." He waved into the blinding light. "Hi! My name is Don Kestle and I'm American!"

The light dropped to cover his feet. There was a metallic squawk. Then a bubble formed on the front deck and something poked out of it. Don couldn't make out any further detail because of the light.

Beware!

Something shot through the water at him. It was past him before he realized what it was: a harpoon. A spear with a line attached. This was evidently a dual-purpose sub, with torpedoes and fish-spearing equipment. It would normally be used to nab specimens for study: when the fired spear lodged, the line pulled it and the fish back.

"They're firing spears at me!" he told Melanie.

Either the sub wasn't equipped to receive and interpret his words, or it didn't believe him. It thought him a hallucination or strange creature, and it was going to spear him, pull him in, and examine him. That shoot-first mentality was in evidence again.

"What's the matter with them?" she demanded.

"I guess they don't understand men riding bicycles on the floor of the ocean."

He could not be hurt by the spears, but this wasn't helping him communicate. How could he get the sub to stop and listen, as the Chinese sub did?

You must surprise it.

Don threw himself to the side as a second harpoon was fired. He wasn't quite fast enough, and it passed through his shoulder.

"That does it!" he said. He picked up his bike, got on it, winced as his right foot hit the pedal, and started moving. He got up speed, then turned to charge the submarine. He rode right into it.

Then he was passing through its nether portion. Because it was sitting several feet lower than his phase surface, he was passing through its second level of compartments. In fact he seemed to be traversing the crew's quarters.

Amazing! Can you talk to them?

Maybe this was what he needed! He turned off his radio, so that there would not be confusion. "Hey, fellows!" he cried, stopping his bike and gesturing.

There were several crewmen there. Their eyes bugged as they saw him among them. "What the hell is this?" one burly sailor demanded, jumping off his bunk.

"I'm Don Kestle," Don said quickly. "I'm sort of like a—a hologram. You can't touch me. But I need your help."

"Get the Officer of the Day!" the man said over his shoulder. Then he came to lay his hand on Don's shoulder. It passed through. "You're a damned ghost!"

Then what am I?

"A hologram," Don repeated. "I'm not really here. But listen to me! I need a lift to Florida, or—" But he knew it would be no good trying to tell them about the end of the world. He got off the bike, waiting.

In what must have been record time, an officer appeared. "It's the same manifestation that was outside!" he exclaimed.

This is the man you want. Address him forthrightly. Show no doubt, Don-kes-tle. Take the initiative.

"I hailed you and you fired harpoons at me!" Don retorted angrily. "What kind of trigger-happy idiots are you? Now listen to me: I have a vital mission. I must get to Florida immediately. You can help me."

The officer looked as if he wanted to freak out, but could not afford to do so in front of the men. "Identify yourself!" he snapped.

"I'm Don Kestle, archaeologist. I—"

"Prove it."

He is recovering the initiative. Do not let him!

Don realized that he could hardly expect to be taken on faith. Any papers he had might be forged, and they couldn't be handled by the officer anyway. But he had a bright idea.

He dived into his pack and pulled out his notepad and pen. "Photograph this and fax it to the American Archaeological Association," he said, quickly printing out the equivalent of a sentence in Minoan Linear A. It incorporated some of the new signs whose meaning he had had to glean from the context. "Tell them to contact Dr. Evans Green immediately. He's the leading contemporary Minoan scholar. This is a matter of life and death."

The officer looked as if he would have preferred to throw Don in the brig. But he elected to play it cool. "Camera," he snapped.

Got him.

By the time they had the camera set up, Don had written enough of a message in Linear A to make any competent Minoan scholar's jaw drop. If such a scholar was reached in time. If he believed. It was a gamble, but the best he could think of at the moment.

They photographed the pages of the notepad. Then they waited while the picture was sent to Naval headquarters, and that office attempted to contact the archaeological association. If this failed, Don knew that he would have no chance to intercept Pacifa; he had lost too much time, and still couldn't move well with his injured ankle. The fate of the world really did lie in the balance.

But the officer was concerned with something more immediate. "What is your connection to the Chinese submarine?"

Trouble! Should he tell, or refuse? The one could result in torpedoes in the mer-colony; the other torpedoing his mission.

Demur. He can not make you say what you do not wish.

"I am not free to say."

The officer frowned. But since it was evident that Don could depart the same way he had come—through the hull—he did not push the matter.

Suddenly the word came back: "Can you contact Gaspar Brown?" the officer asked, after reading the message.

Who was a government agent! "Yes!" They had checked far enough to verify that they had a man on the job.

Don turned on the radio; there would be power enough for a few sentences. "Melanie, I'm in the sub. Is Gaspar there?"

"Here," Gaspar's voice came back immediately.

"Talk to the man here." Then Don lifted his bicycle and spun the wheel by hand, so as to keep the radio going.

Gaspar's identification was evidently good, because soon the officer turned his attention back to Don. "We will take you back to your base near Jamaica."

"But I have to go to Florida!" Don protested.

"No. That has been taken care of."

Then Don realized that he had missed the obvious. The moment Gaspar had gotten in touch, Pacifa's message had become inoperative. Whatever Gaspar had decided, the government was acting on.

You have won the day, Don-kes-tle.

But Don wasn't clear what Gaspar had decided. The dialogue had not gone that far.

They let Don tie onto the sub with his remaining balloon. It was a precarious perch, but it held, and in due course he was back with Gaspar, Eleph, and Melanie.

"Oh, Don!" Melanie cried, hugging him. "You got through!"

Your concubine is lovely.

"Yes, in a way. But what did Gaspar—?"

"Eleph kept talking to him, and now he's satisfied that this needs a formal investigation. We will all have to testify, but I think they are going to take Eleph seriously."

"So his mission to save Earth is a success," Don said, starting to be relieved.

"It probably is. And the mer-colony is safe. We're going to need that adaptation technique to get our own people to Jupiter. We'll be cooperating with China."

"I'm glad."

"In fact, it looks as if we've done about as much as we can, here," she continued. "After we testify, we'll be free to go."

"To go?"

"On our honeymoon. Where would you most like to visit?"

Remember our agreement, Don-kes-tle. We squeezed hands, and I helped you as I was able.

Don laughed. "To Minoan Crete!"

"That's what I thought. Eleph says it's possible, if we join the mission."

"The mission?"

"To save other planets. Now that we're melded. A close-knit group. Pacifa's part of it. She didn't like having to blow the whistle on Eleph; she likes him, and she loves

exploring. So we know she'll be with us. We were supposed
to convince each other that the threat to our world was real,
and go as a unit to convince the authorities. That was
Eleph's notion, and maybe it seems farfetched, but they're
going to try it on other worlds now. Eleph has talked with
the proxies on his radio. But Gaspar is shortcutting that, so
we won't need to spend much time here. There are a lot of
worlds still in doubt, and more knowledgeable folk are
needed to phase into them and convince them of the danger.
Gaspar has decided to go, and I want to, if you—"

"Yes!" The thrill of the notion was second only to that
of his rapport with Melanie. "But what's this about—"

"The worlds are separated in time as well as phase, but
their cultures are similar. The languages. So there are
futuristic ones, and ancient ones, and there is one where the
Minoans—where your fabulous underwater city is above
water and thriving—it's a lot like what your tablets
described—"

*And I am there, my friend. The culture of those who are
now saving worlds derives from mine, and from that of
Atlantis. From a world where the ships were not lost, and
the broader empire was restored, and grew to dominate
nature in much the way I see yours has. Those people never
forgot to be wary of the Bull! Help me as you are able. I
desperately want to return to my concubine.*

Don intended to. He hoped he wasn't merely suffering
from a lingering hallucination. But it was too much to
assimilate all at once. So he cut it short. He kissed Melanie.

She was ardent. Then she drew back, as if uncertain
whether to laugh or snap. "Concubine?"

So when I got time in edgewise, I did a full revision of the novel, revamping both the characters and the plot. In the process I added 25,000 words. So though this started as an old novel, it's a new one now. My agent placed it, and here it is for you, twenty years later. I hope you enjoyed it.

I did have some credits to give for help on this novel, in 1971. I am long out of touch with those folk, but their contributions remain real, so I shall credit them here and hope that they happen to see it. One is Phyrne (I love that spelling!) Bacon who is responsible for much of the way Melanie thinks. Another is Harry M. Piper, who has done underwater exploration. He had been written up in a newspaper article, and I got in touch and asked for his advice, and he gave it, making my water scenes more authentic than they would have been. Another is Joanne Burger, who helped with advice on the technical end: density of water at different depths, chemistry, and such.

You may be wondering just what changes I made in the original novel. Well, Melanie was then named Melody, but I had subsequently used that name in *Chaining the Lady,* so had to modify it. She never appeared physically in the novel; she was a radio contact only. The story developed slowly, then suddenly everything broke loose with so many complications that it was difficult to follow. So this time I added heavy foreshadowing, in the form of Eleph's reports to his frame supervisor, so that that element did not seem to come from nowhere. And I simplified the ending, trying to give it more clarity and force. Some things I wasn't sure about, so I let them be, such as the reference to the Yuchi Indians. I was later to do a whole lot more research on American Indians, when writing *Tatham Mound,* but did not verify any strange origin for this tribe. But who knows? I must have had a reference, when I first wrote this novel. It was as if I were collaborating with a promising writer who couldn't quite get it all together; I saw what was necessary and did it. It's the first time I've collaborated with myself, and it was about as difficult as collaborating with another writer. Which is to say, not too bad, when I have the last word.

Two later notes: after I completed the revision of the novel, and it was published in hardcover, the geologists changed the location of the Dinosaur Meteor strike. Now it is in a region my characters crossed, the north coast of the Yucatan. Ouch! My folk could have looked at it, had they realized. And those who are looking for a source of all my novels and my quarterly Newsletter can call 1-800-HI PIERS to get on our mailing list.

Tales of
Redwall

❖

BRIAN JACQUES

❖

MATTIMEO
A Tale of Redwall

Illustrated by Gary Chalk

RED FOX

A Red Fox Book

Published by Random House Children's Books
20 Vauxhall Bridge Road, London SW1V 2SA

A division of Random House UK Ltd

London Melbourne Sydney Auckland
Johannesburg and agencies throughout
the world

First published by Hutchinson Children's Books 1989

Red Fox edition 1990

15 14

Text © Brian Jacques 1989
Illustrations © Gary Chalk 1988

Printed and bound in Norway by
AIT Trondheim AS

RANDOM HOUSE UK Limited Reg. No. 954009

Papers used by Random House UK Limited
are natural, recyclable products made from wood grown in
sustainable forests. The manufacturing processes conform to
the environmental regulations of the country of origin.

ISBN 0 09 967540 4

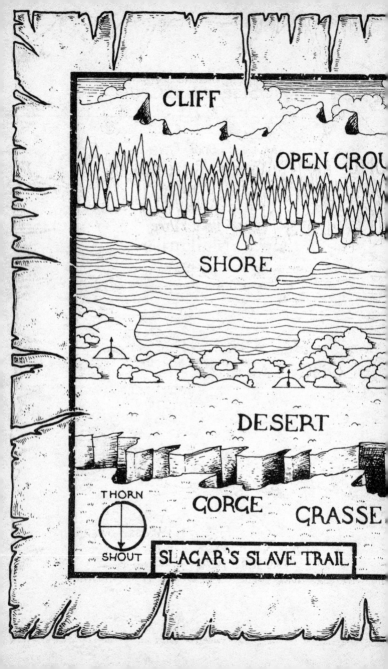

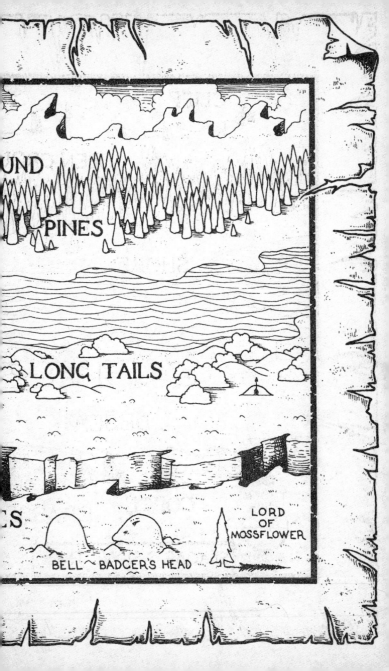

High noontide sun beat down on Orlando the Axe.

The mighty badger strode the far reaches of the western plains, blind to the beauty of the flower-carpeted grassland which had turned green to gold.

Orlando the Axe was following the fox.

The badger wiped a huge dusty paw across his eyes. Sun glinted off the massive double-headed battle-axe slung over his shoulder. His home lay plundered behind him; there was nothing left there except desolation and loneliness.

Orlando the Axe was following the fox.

Two sunrises ago he had passed the strange fox and his band. They had given him a wide berth as he trudged to the foothills of the mountains, seeking food and the small rock plants which his little daughter Auma loved so much. Orlando feared no living creature. He had passed by the fox, not thinking that he had left a clear trail back to his den. The following morning he had returned home, laden with food and rock flowers. Auma was gone, his home was smashed and broken.

Orlando the Axe was following the fox.

Three winters ago his wife Brockrose had died, leaving him to rear their little badger cub. Auma was the most precious thing in Orlando's life. He taught her of the seasons, the plains and the mountains. Now he had turned his back on those same mountains and plains with only one thing in his mind: to find his daughter and the creature who had taken her.

Orlando the Axe was following the fox.

Striding the wide spaces, the badger let a fearsome rumble start to build deep within his cavernous chest, a terrible sound that grew into a howling roar of pent-up rage and anger. It rebounded to the mountains across the sunlit plain as he shook the battle-axe aloft with one paw, his eyes narrowed to red bloodshot slits which changed the whole world crimson in front of him.

Orlando the Axe was following the fox!

BOOK ONE
Slagar the Cruel

1

From the diary of John Churchmouse, historian and recorder of Redwall Abbey in Mossflower country.

We are close to the longest day of this season, the Summer of the Golden Plain. Today I took up my ledger and quill to write. It was cool and dim in the quiet of my little study indoors. With a restless spirit I sat, quill in paw, listening to the merry din outside in the sunlit cloisters of our Abbey. I could no longer stand the solitude, that happy sound of revelry drew me outside, yet there was still my recorder's duties to catch up with. Taking ledger and quill, I went out, up the stairs to the top of the outer wall, directly over the Warrior's Cottage, which is the gatehouse at the threshold of Redwall Abbey.

What a glorious day! The sky, painted special blue for the summer, had not a cloud or shadow anywhere, the hot eye of the sun caused bees to drone lazily, while grasshoppers chirruped and sawed endlessly. Out to the west, the great plains stretched away, shimmering and dancing with heat waves to the distant horizon, a breathtaking carpet of kingcup and dandelion mingled with cowslip; never had we ever seen so many yellow blossoms. Abbot Mordalfus named it the Summer of the Golden Plain. What a wise choice. I could see him ambling round the corner by the bell tower, his

13

habit sleeves rolled well up, panting as he helped young woodlanders to carry out forms for seating at the great feast, our eighth season of peace and plenty since the wars.

Otters swam lazily in the Abbey pond, culling edible water plants (but mostly gambolling and playing. You know what otters are like). Small hedgehogs and moles were around the back at the east side orchard. I could hear them singing as they gathered ripening berries or collected early damsons, pears, plums and apples, which the squirrels threw down to them from the high branches. Pretty little mousemaids and baby voles tittered and giggled whilst choosing table flowers, some making bright posies which they wore as hats. Frequently a sparrow would thrum past my head, carrying some morsel it had found or caught (though I cannot imagine any creature but a bird eating some of the questionable items a sparrow might find). The Foremole and his crew would arrive shortly to dig a baking pit. Meanwhile, the bustle and life of Redwall carried on below me, framed at the back by our beloved old Mossflower Woods. High, green and serene, with hardly a breeze to stir the mighty fastness of leafy boughs, oak, ash, elm, beech, yew, sycamore, hornbeam, fir and willow, mingled pale, dusty, dark and light green hues, the varied leaf shapes blending to shelter and frame the north and east sides of our walls.

Only two days to the annual festivities. I begin to feel like a giddy young woodlander again! However, being historian and recorder, I cannot in all dignity tuck up the folds of my habit and leap down among the merrymakers. I will finish my writings as quickly as possible then, who knows, maybe I'll stroll down to join some of the elders in the cellar. I know they will be sampling the October ale and blackcurrant wine set by from other seasons, just to make sure it has kept its taste and temperature correctly, especially the elderberry wine of last autumn's pressing. You understand, of course, that I am doing this merely to help out old friends.

John Churchmouse (Recorder of Redwall Abbey, formerly of Saint Ninian's)

2

Afternoon sunlight slanted through the gaps in the ruined walls and roof of Saint Ninian's old church, highlighting the desolation of weed and thistle growing around broken, rotted pews. A small cloud of midges dispersed from dizzy circling as Slagar brushed by them. The fox peered through a broken door timber at the winding path of dusty brown which meandered aimlessly southward to meet the woodland fringe on the eastern edge.

Slagar watched silently, his ragged breath sucking in and out at the purple-red diamond-patterned skull mask which covered his entire head. When he spoke, it was a hoarse, rasping sound, as if he had received a terrible throat injury at some time.

'Here they come. Get that side door open, quick!'

A long coloured cart with rainbow-hued covering was pulled into the church by a dozen or so wretched creatures chained to the wagon shaft. A stoat sat on the driver's platform. He slashed at the haulers savagely with a long thin willow withe.

'Gee up, put yer backs into it, me beauties!'

The cart was followed by a rabble of ill-assorted vermin: stoats, ferrets and weasels, garbed the same as their comrades who were already waiting with Slagar.

15

They wore broad cloth sashes stuffed with a motley assortment of rusty daggers, spikes or knives. Some carried spears and curious-looking single-bladed axes. Slagar the Cruel hurried them along.

'Come on, shift your hides, get that door back in place quick!'

The driver jumped down from the cart.

'They're all here, Slagar,' he reported, ''cept fer that otter. He wasn't strong enough to carry on, so we finished 'im off an' chucked his carcass in the ditch, then covered it with ferns. The ants an' insects'll do the rest.'

The hooded fox gave a bad-tempered snort. 'So long as you weren't spotted by any creature. News travels fast in Mossflower. We've got to stay hidden now until Vitch gets back.'

The twelve captives chained to the wagon shaft, mice, squirrels, voles, a couple of small hedgehogs and a young female badger, were in an emaciated condition.

One of them, a squirrel only a few seasons old, moaned piteously. 'Water, please give me water.'

The stoat who had been acting as driver swung his willow cane viciously at the unfortunate squirrel.

'Water? I'll give you water, you little toad. How about a taste of cane, eh? Take that!'

Slagar stepped on the end of the cane, preventing the stoat swinging it further. 'Halftail, you idiot, what d'you want, slaves to sell or a load of dead flesh? Use your brain, stoat. Give the beast a drink. Here, Scringe, give 'em all a drink and some roots or leaves to eat, otherwise they'll be fit for nothing.'

The ferret called Scringe leapt to do Slagar's bidding.

Halftail tugged at the willow cane to free it from Slagar's paw. The hooded fox held down harder so the stoat could not budge it.

'Now then, Halftail, me bucko, I think you're getting a bit deaf lately. I thought I told you to keep inside the woods with that cart?'

Halftail let go of the cane. 'Aye, and so I did, wherever

possible,' he said indignantly. 'But have you tried hauling a cart and twelve slaves through that forest out there?'

Slagar the Cruel picked up the willow cane, the hood coming tight about his jaws with a sharp intake of breath. 'You forget yourself, stoat. I don't have to try hauling carts, I'm the boss around here. When I looked up that path a short time ago, I saw you coming up the centre of the road as if you hadn't a care in the world, bold as brass in broad daylight. Do you realize that a sentry could have seen your dust from the top of Redwall Abbey?'

Halftail failed to recognize the danger signals. 'Yah, what's the difference,' he shrugged. 'They never saw anything.'

Slagar swung the cane furiously and Halftail screamed in agony. He huddled down against the side of the cart, unable to avoid the rain of stinging cuts showering on his head, shoulders and back.

'I'll tell you the difference, slimebrain. The difference is that you don't talk back to me. I'm the leader. You'll learn that or I'll flay your hide to dollrags!' Slagar's voice grated harshly with each slash of the whipping willow.

'Whaaah mercy, ooh owow! Please stop! No more, Chief!'

Slagar snapped the cane and threw it scornfully at the stoat's heavily welted head.

'Ha, your hearing seems a little better now. Cut yourself another switch. That one's worn out.'

The masked fox whirled upon his band of slavers. They sat in cowed silence. The silken hood stretched around his face as he leaned forward.

'That goes for all of you. If anyone ruins my plan, that creature will wish he'd taken his life swiftly with his own paw, by the time I'm through with him. Understand?'

There was a murmured growl of assent.

Slagar climbed up into a ruined window frame. He sat gazing in the direction of Redwall Abbey.

17

'Scringe, bring me some decent food and a flask of wine from the cart,' he commanded.

The servile ferret ran to obey his master.

'Threeclaws, station yourself outside at twilight. Keep an eye peeled for Vitch coming back.'

The weasel saluted. 'Righto, Chief.'

The afternoon wore on, peaceful and golden. Now and then a small dust devil swirled on the path with the summer heat.

Slagar ran a paw tenderly over the silk harlequin-patterned hood, smiling beneath it as a plan of revenge against Redwall revolved slowly in his twisted mind.

Vengeance had kept him going for a long time now. Sometimes he actually savoured the burning lances of pain that coursed through his face, knowing the day was approaching when he would pay back those he considered responsible for his injuries.

A beetle trundled out of the pitted, rotten woodwork of the window frame. Slagar the Cruel pierced it neatly with a single claw, watching the insect writhe in its death throes. 'Redwall, heeheeheehee!' The fox's laughter sent shudders through every creature present.

3

'Mattimeo, Mattimeo!'

Cornflower wrung her paws distractedly. She took one last look around Cavern Hole before climbing the stairs to Great Hall. It was quiet and cool in the Abbey's largest room. Shafts of sunlight, multi-coloured from the stained-glass windows, lanced downwards, etching small pools of rainbow-hued light on the ancient stone floor.

The mouse wandered outside, murmuring beneath her breath as she bustled along, 'Where has the little snip gone this time, I wonder? Oh, Matti, you'll have me grey before my time.'

John Churchmouse was climbing rather stiffly down from the west wall stairs with his book and quill. He almost bumped into Cornflower as she crossed the grounds.

'Afternoon, ma'am. My, my, you look busy.'

Cornflower sat upon the bottom step and heaved a huge sigh. She fanned her whiskers with her paw. 'Busy isn't the word for it, Mr Churchmouse. I've spent the last hour looking for that son of mine. You haven't seen him, by any chance?'

The kindly recorder patted Cornflower's paw. 'There, there, don't you worry your head, ma'am. If your little

Matti is anywhere, he'll be with my Tim and Tess. Young rips, they were supposed to be helping Brother Rufus to write out place names for the table. Ha, there he is now. Hi, Rufus, seen anything of Tim, Tess or young Matti lately?'

Brother Rufus strode across, shaking his head. He waggled a scroll of birchbark parchment at them both.

'Ruined!' he exclaimed. 'Just look at this list they're supposed to have written. I can't possibly use any of this for place settings. Look, Abbot Mordalfus, spelt with one "b". Basil Stag Hare, you'd think that was simple enough. Oh no, they've spelt Basil "Bazzerl" and put an "e" on the end of Stag!'

John Churchmouse pulled forth a kerchief. He blew his snout loudly to disguise the laughter that was shaking him. 'Hmm, yes, ahaha. 'Scuse me, well, that wouldn't have been my Tess, you know. She's quite good at the spelling.'

Brother Rufus rolled the parchment tightly. 'It's that little Mattimeo, he's the ringleader. I know you may not like that, Cornflower marm, but it's the truth!' His voice was shrill with frustration.

Cornflower nodded her head sadly. 'Yes, I'm afraid I must agree with you, Brother Rufus. Matti is becoming a real problem. I daren't tell his father half the things he gets up to.'

John Churchmouse peered sympathetically over the top of his square eyeglasses. 'Maybe it'd be better to do so if you'll excuse me for saying, but young Matti will have to start growing up sometime if he ever hopes to become the Warrior of Redwall like his father Matthias. Mattimeo will have to start behaving responsibly instead of going about like a spoilt brat, if you'll pardon the expression, ma'am.'

Cornflower stood up. 'I know exactly what you mean, Mr Churchmouse, but we may be judging Matti a little unfairly. After all, he does have quite a lot to live up to, being the son of Redwall's Warrior. Besides, practically every woodlander within our walls has spoiled him since the day he was born.'

Both John and Rufus nodded their heads in agreement.

The awkward silence which followed was immediately broken by a band of small creatures headed by a young mole who waved his digging claws wildly.

'Cumm yurr quickly, gennelmice, 'asten ee. Li'l Matti be a-slayin' Vitch. Do 'urry!'

Even though the little creature was speaking in the quaint and complicated molespeech, they understood the urgency of his message.

'Where, where?' they cried. 'Take us there quickly!'

The group dashed around the south Abbey gable, taking the shortcut to the east grounds.

Cornflower picked up her skirts, narrowly avoiding collision with a baby hedgehog. Brother Rufus was out in front.

∽

Jess Squirrel was first on the scene. She had been up an apple tree in the orchard with her son Sam when they heard the screams. Travelling from bough to bough, swift as a bird in flight, Jess dropped to the ground and set about trying to separate the two creatures locked together on the grass. They rolled, kicked, spat and bit furiously. Sam dropped down to his mother's aid. They grabbed one each and held them apart. As they did, the crowd arrived.

∽

Mattimeo was panting heavily. He tried to break free, but Jess shook him soundly by the scruff.

'Be still you little ruffian, or I'll tan your hide!' she warned him.

Sam held tight to the other mouse, Vitch, who looked more like a rat, small though he was. Vitch was not struggling. He looked quite relieved that the fight had been stopped.

John Churchmouse strode firmly between them. 'Now then, what's all this about, eh?'

'He called me a skinny little rat.'

'He said I was not a warrior's son.'

'He pulled my tail and he jumped on me and bit me an—'

'Silence!'

Every creature present froze at the booming growl of a huge grey female badger. Constance, the mother of all Redwall, stood high on her hind legs, towering above them. Folding her front paws judiciously, she glared down at the two small miscreants.

'Vitch, is it? Well, Vitch, you are a newcomer to our Abbey, but that is no excuse for fighting. We are peaceable creatures at Redwall. Violence is never the answer to a quarrel. What have you got to say for yourself?'

The ratlike mouse wiped a smear of blood from his snout.

'It was Mattimeo,' he whined piteously. 'He hit me first, I wasn't doing anything, I was just. . . .'

Vitch's faltering excuses faded to a whimper under the badger's stern gaze. She pointed a blunt paw at him.

'Go to the kitchens. Tell Friar Hugo that I sent you. He will set you to sweeping floors and scrubbing pans. I will not have fighting in the Abbey, nor whimpering, whingeing and trying to put the blame upon others. Brother Rufus, take him along, see he delivers my message to Friar Hugo properly.'

Vitch looked as if he were about to dodge off, until Brother Rufus caught him firmly by the ear and marched him away.

'Come on, young Vitch, greasy pots and floor scrubbing will do you the world of good.'

'Owowooch, leggo, you big bully,' Vitch protested. 'You're pulling my ear off!'

When Vitch had gone, Constance turned upon the other culprit. Jess had released Mattimeo. He stood shamefaced, kicking at a clump of turf, looking down at his paws. He did not see the nod which passed between his mother and Constance. Cornflower was giving her silent permission to the badger; Mattimeo was in for a dressing-down.

'Son of Matthias the Warrior, look at me!' Constance commanded.

Sheepishly the young mouse gazed upward until he was staring into Constance's unblinking dark eyes. The onlookers stood silent as the matriarch gave the young mouse a piece of her mind.

'Mattimeo, this is not the first time I have had cause to speak with you. I am not going to ask you for an explanation because in this case I do not think you could justify yourself. Vitch is a newcomer, hardly arrived here. You were born at Redwall, you know the rules of our Abbey: to live in peace with others, never to harm another creature needlessly, to comfort, assist, and be kind to all.'

Mattimeo's lip quivered, he looked as if he were about to speak, but the badger's stern gaze silenced him.

'Today you took it upon yourself to attack another creature who is a guest in our home,' Constance continued, her voice an accusing knell. 'You, the son of my old friend Matthias the Warrior, who fought to bring peace to Mossflower. Mattimeo, I will not give you any tasks to do as a punishment. The sorrow and worry you cause your mother and the shame you bring down upon your father are the penalties that will rest on your own head. Go now and speak with your father.'

Mattimeo's head drooped low as he stumbled off.

Tess, Tim and Sam Squirrel kept silent. They knew that every word Constance spoke was the truth. Mattimeo's middle name should have been trouble.

4

The new moon was up. It hung like a fresh-minted coin in a still, cloudless sky of midnight blue. Moths fluttered vainly upward, only to drift spiralling down to the grass-carpeted woodland floor. The trees stood like timeless sentinels. Somewhere a nightjar serenaded the soft darkness.

Threeclaws was alert at his sentry post. He spied the figure of Vitch approaching and gave a low whistle.

The undersized rat looked up. 'Where's Slagar and the others?' he asked.

Threeclaws pointed with his dagger. 'Inside the church. What've you been doing to yourself?'

'Keep your snout out of my business, fatty,' said Vitch, dodging nimbly past Threeclaws into the church.

Weasels and a few ferrets and stoats lay about sleeping on the floor. Slagar sat with his back against the painted cart. He scowled at Vitch.

'You took your time getting here, what in the name of the fang kept you?'

Vitch flung himself wearily on a tattered hassock. 'Washing dirty pots and greasy pans, scrubbing floors and generally getting meself knocked about.'

Slagar crouched forward. 'Never mind all that. I put you in there to do a job. When is the feast to begin?'

'Oh that. One more moonrise, then the early evening following.'

'Right, did you fix the bolts on the small north wall-gate?' asked Slagar.

'Of course. That was the first thing I attended to. They're well greased and fit for a quick getaway. You can keep that Redwall place, Slagar, I'm not goin' back there again.'

'Oh, why's that, Vitch?' The fox's voice was dangerously gentle.

'Huh, it was hard enough tryin' to pass meself off as a mouse. That young one, wotsisname? Matty something – he smelt a rat right away. I had a fight with the little nuisance. He's strong as an otter. Then I was pulled up by a big badger. She gave me a right old tellin' off. Peaceful creatures, my front teeth! I was lugged off and made to scrub dirty pots for some fat old cook. He had me up to my tail in greasy dishwater, standin' over me and makin' me scour and cl—'

'Ah shut your trap and stop snivelling, rat. This little mouse, was he called Mattimeo, son of Matthias the Warrior?'

'Aye, that's him, but how do you know?'

Slagar touched the red silk skull cover, baring his fangs viciously. 'Never mind how I know. He's the one we'll be taking away with us, him and any others we can lay our paws on.'

Vitch brightened up. 'Maybe I'll get a few minutes alone with Mattimeo after we make our getaway, when he's chained up good and proper.'

Slagar watched the small rat's face approvingly. 'Ha, you'd like that, wouldn't you?'

'Heehee, like it, I'd love it!' Vitch's eyes shone malevolently.

The fox leaned closer. 'Vengeance, that's the word. I tell you, rat, there's nothing in the world like the moment when you have your enemy helpless and you can take revenge.'

Vitch was puzzled. 'I can't imagine a little mouse like that being able to hurt you, sly one. What did he do that you seek revenge upon him?'

Slagar had a faraway look in his eyes and beneath the mask his breath hissed roughly.

'It was his father, the Warrior, that big badger too – in fact, it was all the creatures at Redwall who hurt me. The little one was not even born then, but I know how they all dote on him. He is the son of their warrior, the hope of the future. I can kill a lot of birds with one stone by taking Mattimeo. You couldn't imagine the agonies they'd go through if he went missing. You see, I know the woodlanders of that Abbey. They love their young and they'd rather be made captive themselves than have anything happen to their precious little ones. This is what will make my revenge all the sweeter.'

Suddenly Vitch stretched a paw towards Slagar's masked face. 'Did they do that to you, is that why you have to wear a mask over your head, why don't you take it o— Aaaarrrggghh!'

Slagar seized Vitch's paw and bent it savagely backwards. 'Don't you ever dare put your grubby paw near my face again, or I'll snap it clean off and make you eat it, rat! Now get back to that Abbey and keep your eyes open. Make sure you know exactly where that young mouse is at all times, so that I can put my paw on him when the moment arrives.'

He released Vitch and the small rat huddled on the ground, sobbing. Slagar spat on him contemptuously. 'Get up, misery guts. If you're still lying there in a moment, you'll feel my sword. That really will give you something to moan about.'

Vitch picked himself up slowly and painfully. Next moment he was sent hurtling by a kick on the behind from Slagar.

'Garn! Get yourself out of my sight, you snivelling snotface.'

Vitch departed hastily, leaving Slagar to take his ease

once more. The Cruel One lay back, all thoughts of sleep banished by one word which echoed around his twisted mind like an eerie melody.

Revenge!

5

Matthias the Warrior of Redwall stood with his back to the empty fireplace. Cornflower had gone out early to help with the baking. Golden morning sunlight streamed through the windows of the small gatehouse cottage, glinting off the dewy fruit piled upon the table. There was a pitcher of cold cider, some cheeses and a fresh-baked loaf set out for breakfast but Matthias lacked the appetite to do it justice and stared miserably about the room. It was neat and cheerful, which did not reflect the Warrior's mood.

There was a knock on the door.

'Come in please,' he called, straightening up.

The Foremole entered, tipping the top of his black velvet furred head with a huge digging claw. He wrinkled his button nose in a wide smile that almost made his bright little eyes vanish.

'Gudd morn to you'm, Mattwise, yurr. Uz moles be diggen a cooker pit t'day. May'aps you'ud loik to 'elp?'

Matthias smiled fondly. He patted his old friend's back, knowing the mole had come to cheer him up.

'Thank you for the offer, Foremole. Unfortunately I have other more serious business to attend this morning. Hmm, that sounds like it in the next room, just getting out of bed. Will you excuse me, my friend?'

'Hurr hurr, ee be a roight laddo, yurr young Mattee. Doant wack 'im too 'ard naow,' Foremole chuckled, and left to join his crew.

Matthias had been far too angry to deal with his son on the previous afternoon, so he sent him straight off to bed without tea or supper. Now the Warrior stood facing the bedroom door, watching the tousled head of his son peer furtively round the door jamb.

Seeing his father, he hesitated.

'Come in, son.' The Warrior curled a paw at him.

The young mouse entered, gazing hungrily at the laden breakfast table before turning to face his father. Sternness had replaced the previous day's anger on the Warrior's face.

'Well, what have you got to say for yourself, Mattimeo?'

''m sorry,' Mattimeo mumbled.

'I should hope you are.'

''m very sorry,' Mattimeo mumbled again.

'Foremole said I should whack you. What do you think?'

''m very very sorry. 't won't happen again, Dad.'

Matthias shook his head, and placed a paw on his son's shoulder.

'Matti, why do you do these things? You hurt your mother, you hurt me, you hurt all our friends. You even get your own little pals into trouble. Why?'

Mattimeo stood tongue-tied. What did they all want? He had apologized, said he was very sorry, in fact, he would never do it again. Jess Squirrel, his mother, Constance, they had all given him a stern telling-off. Now it was his father's turn. Mattimeo knew that the moment he set paw out of doors he would be spotted, probably by Abbot Mordalfus, and that would mean another stern lecture.

Matthias watched his son carefully. Beneath the sorrowful face and drooping whiskers he could sense a smouldering rebellion, resentment against his elders.

29

Turning to the wall over the fireplace, Matthias lifted down the great sword from its hangers. This was the symbol of his rank, Warrior of Redwall. It was also the only thing that could command his son's total attention. Matthias held the weapon out.

'Here, Matti, see if you can wield it yet.'

The young mouse took the great sword in both paws. Eyes shining, he gazed at the hard black bound handle with its red pommel stone, the stout crosstree hilt and the magnificent blade. It shone like snowfire, edges sharp and keen as a midwinter blizzard, the tip pointed like a thistle spike.

Once, twice, he tried to swing it above his head. Both times he faltered, failing because of the sword's weight.

'Nearly, Father, I can nearly swing it.'

Matthias took the weapon from his son. With one paw he hefted it then swung it aloft. Twirling it, whirling it, until the air sang with the thrum of the deadly, wonderful blade. Up, down and around it swung, coming within a hair's-breadth of Mattimeo's head. Turning, Matthias snicked a stalk from an apple, sliced the loaf without touching the table and almost carelessly flicked the rind from the cheese. Finally Matthias gave the sword a powerful twist into the warrior's salute, bringing the blade to rest with its point quivering in the floor.

Admiration for the Warrior of Redwall danced in his son's eyes. Matthias could not help smiling briefly.

'One day you will be the one who takes my place, son. You will grow big and strong enough to wield the sword, and I will train you to use it like a real warrior. But it is only a sword, Mattimeo. It does not make you a warrior merely because you carry it. Weapons may be carried by creatures who are evil, dishonest, violent or lazy. The true Warrior is good, gentle and honest. His bravery comes from within himself, he learns to conquer his own fears and misdeeds. Do you understand me?'

Mattimeo nodded. Matthias grew stern once more.

'Good, I am glad you do. I will not whack you. I have

never laid a paw on you yet and I do not intend starting now. However, you attacked little Vitch and you must pay for that, one way or another. At first I thought I should refuse you permission to attend the celebrations. . . .'

Matthias watched the shock and disbelief on his son's face before continuing.

'But I have decided that you may go, providing you run straightaway to the kitchens. There you will ask Friar Hugo to allot you double the tasks he gave to Vitch yesterday. When you have finished working for the Friar you will offer to help your mother with the gathering of flowers until such time as she decides to free you of your task. Is that clear?'

Mattimeo's face was a picture of disbelief. He, the son of the Redwall Warrior, working! Never before had he been asked, much less ordered, to carry out Abbey tasks. The young mouse considered himself the inheritor of his father's sword and duties. As such, he was firmly convinced that he was above any type of pan-scrubbing or daisy-gathering. Even Constance knew that. She had sentenced Vitch to hard labour, but even she did not dare tell the future Champion to dirty his paws with menial chores. Besides, Vitch would be finished his tasks by now. He could stand about and gloat at the sight of his enemy ordered to perform double the work and more.

Matthias watched his son's face. Now was the testing time. Would he behave like the spoilt little creature who had been indulged all his life by the Abbey dwellers, or would he show a bit of character?

The young mouse swallowed hard, nodding his head. 'I'll do as you have asked, Dad.'

Matthias clapped him heartily on the back. 'Good mouse. That's the mark of a Warrior in training, obedience. Off you go now!'

Morning sunlight stencilled the high window shapes in soft pink relief on the sandstone floor of Great Hall as

31

Mattimeo passed through on his way to the kitchens. He felt the fur on his shoulders prickle slightly, as if some beast were watching him from behind. Turning slowly, he faced the west wall. No creature was there. The hall was empty, save for the picture of Martin the Warrior upon the Redwall tapestry. Mattimeo often had this same experience when he was alone and near the large woven cloth. He drew closer, standing in front of the magnificent armoured mouse's likeness. Martin the Warrior looked big and strong. He held the famous sword easily in his right paw, a smile upon his broad honest face, and behind him the images of bygone enemies fled in fear as if trying to escape from the tapestry. The young mouse's eyes glowed in admiration of his hero. He spoke to Martin, not knowing that his father Matthias had done the same thing when he was young.

'I could feel you watching me, Martin. I'm just on my way to do penance in the kitchens, but you probably know that. I didn't mean to disobey my parents or cause them unhappiness. You can understand that, can't you? I had to fight Vitch because he said things about my father. He thought I was scared of him, but I am the son of a warrior and I could not let him insult my family. If my father knew the truth of it all he would not have punished me, but, well, he's my father, you see. I can't explain things properly to him. You're different, Martin, you understand how I feel.'

Mattimeo shuffled his paws on the stones beneath Martin's never changing expression.

'You know, sometimes you're just like my father. Look, I'm sorry, I'll try to be a better mouse. I promise not to fight or get into any more trouble or worry my parents again.'

He turned and shuffled sulkily toward the kitchens, muttering as he went, 'I wish there was another Great War, then I'd show 'em. Huh! They'd be glad of young mice that could fight then. I wouldn't be sent off to scour pans. They'd probably have to give me a medal or something like that.'

The smile upon the face of the tapestry warrior seemed to be gentler as the immobile eyes watched the small habit-clad figure descend the steps of Cavern Hole.

∽

Friar Hugo was absolute ruler in the vast kitchens of Redwall. He was the fattest mouse in the Abbey and wore a white apron over his habit. Hugo always carried a dockleaf in his tail, which he waved about busily, fanning himself, rubbing it upon a scorched paw, or holding it like a visor across his forehead as he peered down into steaming, bubbly pots. Mattimeo stood by, awaiting orders, whilst Hugo checked his lists, issuing instructions to his staff of helpers.

'Mmmm, let me see, that's six large raspberry seed-cakes. We need four more. Brother Sedge, quickly, take that pan of cream from the flames before it boils over. You can add the powdered nutmeg and whisk it in well. Sister Agnes, chop those young onions and add the herbs to the woodland stew. Er, what's this? Ten flagons of cold strawberry cordial. That'll never do, we need twice that many. Here, young Matti, nip down to the cellars and fill more flagons from the barrels. Ambrose Spike's down there, so you won't need the keys.'

Though the cooking smells were extra delicious, Mattimeo was glad to be out of the steamy heat and bustle of the kitchen for a while. He saluted the Friar smartly and ran off, dodging mice, hedgehogs, voles and squirrels, all carrying trays, pots, platters and bowls.

∽

The Abbey cellars were peacefully dim and cool. Unwittingly Mattimeo surprised old Ambrose Spike. The cellar keeper was pouring a bowl of October ale, blowing the froth from the top before he drank. As he dipped his snout, Mattimeo said ''scuse me please, Friar Hugo said I was t—'

The ancient hedgehog choked and sneezed, spraying

Mattimeo with ale as he whirled around.

'Pahcoochawww! Don't sneak up on me like that, young Matti. Hold still a moment, will you.'

Ambrose drained the bowl. Regaining his composure, he stared at the froth lying in the bottom of his sampling bowl.

'Harr, wunnerful! Though I do say it meself, no creature brews October ale like the Spike family. Now, what can I do for you, mousey?'

'Friar says I've got to fill more flagons of strawberry cordial, sir.'

'Oh, right, barrels are through in the next section,' Ambrose told him, 'the ones marked pink, flagons against the wall as y'go in. Careful now, don't disturb the little casks of elderberry and blackcurrant wine or they'll go cloudy.'

As Mattimeo wandered into the next section, he was hailed.

'Psst, Matt, ssshhhh, over here!'

It was Tim and Tess and Sam Squirrel. Mattimeo tippawed over.

'What are you three doing down here?'

Tess Churchmouse stifled a giggle. 'We slipped past Ambrose while he was dozing. Come and have some cold strawberry cordial, it's scrummy.'

The trio had prised the bung from a barrel that lay on its side. They used long hollow reeds as drinking straws, dipping them down into the liquid and sucking up the sparkling ice-cold strawberry juice.

Tess gave Mattimeo a straw, and he could not resist joining them.

∽

Cold strawberry cordial becomes sickly when drunk too freely. Matt, Tess, Tim and Sam soon found this out, and they lay back awhile and rested. Later, the two churchmice and the young squirrel helped Mattimeo to fill the flagons. Together they bore them up to the kitchens.

Ambrose Spike raised his snout from a bowl of nutbrown beer as they passed through his cellar.

34

'Mmmm, 's funny, there was only one of 'em here before,' he muttered.

∽

Friar Hugo was working flat out now. There was still more than enough to be done before the feast.

'You there, Billum Mole, can you dig me a nice neat tunnel through the middle of that big marrow?'

'Hurr, gaffer, oi serpintly can. Pervidin' oi can eat it as oi goes along.'

'Righto, carry on. Oh, there you are, young Matti. Now take your friends along to the larder. I want two small white cheeses flavoured with sage, two large red cheeses with beechnut and rosemary and one of the extra large yellow cheeses with acorn and apple bits. Be very careful how you roll the extra large yellow, don't go knocking any creature down or breaking furniture.'

The four chums dashed off whooping, 'Hurray, we're going to roll the cheeses!'

∽

Abbot Mordalfus cut a comical sight for so dignified a figure. He was up to his whiskers in fresh cream, candied peel, nuts and wild plums.

Friar Hugo dusted off the Abbot's face with his dockleaf as he passed. 'Ha, there you are, Alf. Well, how's the special Redwall Abbot's cake coming along?'

Old Mordalfus chewed thoughtfully on some candied peel. 'Very well, thank you, Hugo. Though I still suspect it lacks something. What d'you think?'

Hugo dipped his dockleaf into the mix and tasted it. 'Hmmm, see what you mean, Alf. If I were you, I'd put some redcurrant jelly in to make it look more like an Abbot's cake. Doesn't hurt to cheat a little. After all, you're only going by Abbot Saxus's recipe, and that's a matter of taste. Yes, put more redcurrant in and we'll name it Redcurrantwall Abbot Alf cake.'

The Abbot dusted flour from his paws, smiling proudly. 'What a good idea. Hi there, Matthias, where are you off to?'

The Warrior of Redwall was carrying two fishing lines and bait. Dodging a pair of moles who scurried past with a trolleyful of steaming bilberry muffins, he called across, 'Don't you remember, Abbot, we were supposed to be going fishing in the Abbey pool for our annual centrepiece?'

Mordalfus clapped a floury paw to his brow. 'Goodness me, so we were. I'll be right with you, my son.'

Matthias peered about in the activity and bustle. 'Friar Hugo, have you seen Mattimeo?'

'Indeed I have, Matthias. The young feller's a great help to me. Haha, I've sent him and his pals to roll cheeses out. That'll keep them busy. Constance Badger is the only one large and strong enough to deal with a big yellow cheese, and I've told them to roll one out, hahaha. I'd love to see how they do that.'

Matthias winked at the Friar 'Don't laugh too soon, Hugo. I've got news that'll wipe the smile from your whiskers. Basil Stag Hare has just arrived. I let him in the main gate not a minute ago. He says that he's been on a long patrol over the west plain and hasn't had decent food in three sunrises. Oh, he also said to tell you he's appointed himself official sampler.'

Matthias and Abbot Mordalfus left the kitchens with all speed. Friar Hugo was speechless at the news, but only momentarily. His fat little body puffed and swelled with indignation almost to bursting point. As they hurried across Great Hall, Hugo's outraged squeaks followed them.

'What? Never! I'm not having any retired regimental glutton feeding his face in my kitchens. Oh no! Why, the skinny great windbag, he'll eat us out of storeroom and larder before sunset, then, fur forbid, he'll meet up with that Ambrose Spike and start sampling the barrels. We'll have to tell the young ones to cover their ears when those two get to singing their barrack-room ballads and wild woodland ditties. Oh my nerves, I don't think I'll be able to stand it.'

Cornflower and Mrs Churchmouse were carrying a bundle of roses across the Abbey grounds. The blooms ranged from white, right through the shades of yellow, intermixed with lilacs, pinks, carmines and crimsons, to the rich dark purples. Suddenly they were confronted and relieved of their burdens by a lanky old hare whose patchwork-hued fur defied description. His swaying lop ears twitched and bent at the most ridiculous angles as he bowed, making a deep elegant leg to the two mice.

'Allow me, laydeez, wot wot? Two handsome young fillies totin' all this shrubbery, doesn't bear thinkin' about, eh,' he said gallantly. 'Basil Stag Hare at y'service, gels. Hmmm, my my, is that cookin' I smell? Ha, old Hugo burnin' somethin' tasty, I'll be bound. I say, d'you mind awfully if I leave you two ravin' beauties to carry all these lovely roses, charmin' picture. Must go now, investigatin', doncha know. See you later, after tiffin, p'raps. Toodle pip now!'

Cornflower and Mrs Churchmouse collapsed in tucks of laughter as the odd hare shot off in the direction of Friar Hugo's kitchen.

'Oh hahaheeehee! Good old Basil, ohoohoohoo! There'll be fur flying in the kitchens soon. Hahaha-hohoho!' Cornflower gasped.

'Heeheehee! Oh my ribs, did you see the way he dropped the roses when he smelt food. Haha, he's a stomach on four legs, that feller,' Mrs Churchmouse chortled.

∽

Foremole and his crew looked up from the roasting pit they were digging. Wiping paws on fur and blowing soil from their snouts, they chuckled and slapped each other's backs.

'Hohurr hurr, ee be a champeen scoffer that un, oi never seed narthin so 'ungered atop or below soil. Ee Froiyer'll wack 'im proper wi' ladlespoon on m'ead, you'm see if ee doant, hurrhurr.'

6

Slagar sorted the odd jumble of performers' clothing from the bed of the painted cart, throwing appropriate outfits to the chosen actors of his travelling troupe.

'Fleaback, Bageye, Skinpaw, you'll be the tumblers, share that lot out between you.'

'But Chief. . . .' Fleaback protested.

'And no complaints, d'you hear!'

'Here, give me those yellow pawsocks, you.'

'Huh, you can have 'em, they look daft.'

'They're supposed to look daft, thickhead,' Slagar explained. 'I said no complaints. Come over here, Hairbelly. You'll be the balancer. Try this on. Oh, and don't forget to put the ball sticky side down on your nose, otherwise it'll fall off. Let's see how you look.'

'Arr Chief, I was the balancer last time. Can I do the rope tricks this time?'

'No you can't. Leave that to Wartclaw, he's best at it.'

'Oh, I'm fed up with this already,' Hairbelly grumbled. 'Look, this tunic doesn't fit me. Besides I can't sing.'

Slagar was upon the unlucky weasel, dagger drawn. 'You'll sing a pretty tune if I tickle your eyeballs with this blade, bucko. Listen, all of you, one more moan from

39

anyone and I'll dump the lot of you back out upon the road, where you came from. You can go back to being the starving tramps and beggars you were before I took the trouble to form you into a proper slaving band. Now is that understood?'

There was a subdued mutter. Slagar dropped the knife and grabbed a sword. 'I said, is that understood?'

There was a loud chorus of ayes this time, as the silken hood was beginning to suck in and out rapidly, denoting Slagar's mounting temper.

Hairbelly was a little slower than the rest, still unhappy with his role as the balancer.

'It's still not fair though, Chief,' he piped up. 'You'll probably only be standing about, watching, tomorrow night while we do all the work.'

Slagar seemed to ignore him for a moment. Turning to the cart, he whipped out a swirling silk cloak. It was decorated with the same design as his headcover, and the lining was black silk, embellished with gold and silver moon and star symbols. Twirling it expertly, he threw it around his body, leaping nimbly on to a row of pews. Then Slagar spread his paws wide in a theatrical gesture.

'I will be Lunar Stellaris, light and shadow, hither and thither like the night breeze, presiding over all. Lord of Mountebanks, now you see me. . . .' He dropped out of sight behind the pews, calling, 'And now you don't!'

The audience strained forward to see where he had hidden himself. Slagar was gone from behind the pews.

Suddenly, as if by magic, he reappeared in the midst of his band. Right alongside Hairbelly.

'Haha, Lunar Stellaris, Lord of light and dark. But to those who disobey my word I am Slagar the Cruel, Master of life and death.'

Before Hairbelly could blink an eye, Slagar had run him through with his sword. The stricken weasel stared at Slagar in surprise and disbelief, then he looked down at the sword protruding from his middle and staggered as his eyes misted over.

Slagar laughed, an evil, brutal snigger. 'Take this fool outside and let him die there. We don't want his blood in here. Now, any one of you scum that wants to join him, just let me know!'

 ∽

The morning of Redwall's feasting dawned misty at first light. Abbot Mordalfus and Matthias had fished since the previous afternoon. Having had little luck in daylight, they elected to continue until such time as they made a catch. Tradition dictated that a fish from the Abbey pool must grace the centre of the festive board. In bygone years they had been lucky enough to land a grayling, but this year there were few. Out of respect for the graylings, they had let two fine big specimens slip the lines, fishing doggedly throughout the night. In the hour before daybreak they struck a medium-sized carp. It was a fine battle. The small coracle-shaped boat was towed round and round the waters, ploughing through rushes and skidding across shallows. Mordalfus was an experienced fishermouse, and he plied all his skill and guile, remembering the time when he was plain Brother Alf, keeper of the pond. Helped along by Matthias's strong paws, the carp was fought and tackled, diving and tugging, leaping and backing, until it was finally driven into the shallows, blocked off by the boat, and beached on the grassy sward.

 ∽

Warbeak the Sparra Queen was up early that day. She roused the sparrow tribe who lived in the roof of the Abbey when she spied the activity at the pond.

'Warbeak say Sparras help Matthias and old Abbotmouse.' Matthias and Mordalfus were glad of the assistance. Tired, wet and hungry, they sat breathing heavily on the bank.

'Warbeak, whew! Thank goodness you've arrived,' Matthias saluted his winged friend and her tribe. 'The Abbot and I are completely tuckered out. What d'you think of our fish?'

The fierce little bird spread her wings wide. 'Plenty big fishworm, friend Matthias. My warriors take um to fatmouse Friar, he burn um fish good. Sparra like fishworm, we eat plenty at big wormtime.'

As the Sparra folk towed the carp off in the direction of the kitchens, Abbot Mordalfus turned, smiling, to Matthias.

'Good friends, our sparrow allies, though why everything is worm this or worm that I'll never know. Can you imagine Hugo's face when Warbeak tells him to burn fishworm good?'

Matthias shook pond droplets from his paws. 'It's just their way of talking, Abbot. Sometimes I wonder who is the harder to understand, a sparrow or a mole.'

Mordalfus glanced up. The sun was piercing the mists, casting a rosy glow over the world of Mossflower with the promise of a hot midsummer day. From the bell tower the sounds of the Abbey bells pealed merrily away, calling the inhabitants of Redwall to rise and enjoy the day.

Constance the badger ambled down to the pond and beached the coracle with one mighty heave.

'Whoof! It's going to be a real scorcher,' she remarked. 'My word, little Tim and Tess are certainly energetic. Listen to them ringing the Methusaleh and the Matthias bells. Still, we mustn't waste the day, there's so much to do before we can sit down to feast this evening.'

Matthias yawned and stretched. 'Well, I'm for a swift forty winks and a bath after all that night fishing. D'you realize, the Abbot and I have been stuck in that boat since yesterday noon? Right, Mordalfus?'

Constance held a paw to her muzzle. 'Ssshhh, he's fallen fast asleep. Good old Alf.'

The Abbot was curled up on the grassy bank, snuffling faintly, still tackling the carp in his dreams.

Matthias smiled, patting his friend gently. 'Aye, good old Alf. I remember him taking me on the pond for my first fish. It was a grayling, as I recall. Hmm, I was even younger than my own son then. Ah well, none of us is getting any younger as the seasons pass.'

'Huh, I'm certainly not,' the badger snuffled. 'Neither is Alf. But I'm not sure about you, Matthias. Sometimes I wonder if you've aged at all. You go off and get your rest now, and I'll see to our angling Abbot here.'

Constance quietly scooped the slumbering Mordalfus up on to her broad back and trundled slowly off in the direction of the Abbey dormitories.

⌒

On his way over to the gatehouse cottage, Matthias spied Cornflower and Mattimeo carrying flower baskets and pruning knives. He waved to them.

'We landed a beautiful carp. I've got to have a nap and a bath.'

Cornflower tied her bonnet strings in a bow. 'Oh I'm glad you caught a good fish, dear. I've left your breakfast on the table, we'll see you later. Mattimeo is so kind, guess what? He's promised to help me all day with the flowers.'

Matthias winked cheerily at his scowling son. 'What a splendid fellow he is, Cornflower. I'll bet it was all his own idea too.'

⌒

As the morning sun rose higher, Redwall came to life. A team of young hedgehogs and squirrels sang lustily as they carried firewood, damp grass and flat rocks to the baking pit, which the moles were busy putting the final touches to.

'Dig'm sides noice'n square, Jarge. Gaffer, pat yon floor gudd an flattish loik.'

'Yurr, you'm 'old your counsel, Loamdog. Oi knows wot oi'm a-doin'.'

'Ho urr, be you serpint it'n deepwoise enuff?'

'Gurr, goo an arsk Friar to boil your 'ead awhoil, Rooter. May'ap ee'll cook summ sense into you'm.'

⌒

Friar Hugo paced several times around the fish and dabbed at with his dockleaf.

'Hmm, long time since I baked a carp. Brother Trugg, bring me bay leaves, dill, parsley and flaked chestnuts. Oh, and don't forget the hotroot pepper and cream, lots of cream.'

An otter lingered near the carp, licking her lips at the mention of the sauce ingredients.

'How's about some fresh little water shrimp for a garnish, Friar,' she suggested. 'That'd make prime vittles.'

The fat mouse shooed her off with his dockleaf. 'Be off with you, Winifred. I've counted every scale on that fish. Er, if you're going for water shrimp, I'll need at least two nets full for a decent garnish.'

∽

The bee folk had been extra productive and kind in this Summer of the Golden Plain, and honey was plentiful. It dripped off the symmetrical combs in shining sticky globules. Jess Squirrel and her son Sam were storing it in three flat butts, the clear, the set, and the open-comb type much favoured by squirrels. From the cellars came the slightly off-key sound of singing, a quavering treble from Basil Stag Hare, backed by the gruff bass harmony of Ambrose Spike.

'O if I feel sick or pale,
What makes my old eyes shine?
Some good October ale
And sweet blackcurrant wine.
I'd kill a dragon for half a flagon,
I'd wrestle a stoat to wet my throat,
I'd strangle a snake, all for the sake
Of lovely nutbrown beer. . . .
Nuhuhuhut broooowwwwwnnnnn beeeeheeeyer!'

Upstairs in the vegetable store, Mrs Lettie Bankvole was remonstrating with her young offspring Baby Rollo. He had learned the words after his own fashion and was singing uproariously in a deep rough gurgle,

'I strangle a snake an' wet his throat,
I wrestle a dragon an' steal his coat—'

'Baby Rollo! Stop that this instant. Cover your ears and help me with this salad.'

'I wallop a snake wiv a old rock cake—'

'Rollo! Go and play outside and stop listening to those dreadful songs. Strangling dragons and swigging beer – where will it all end?'

∽

Mattimeo was finding out that roses had sharp thorns. For the second time that day he sucked at his paw, nipping out the pointed rose thorn with his teeth. Tim Churchmouse had gone off shrimping with the otters, Tess stayed behind out of pity for the warrior's son.

'Here Matti, you stack those baskets on the cart for your mum. I'll arrange the roses for you. You've got them in a right old mess.'

Mattimeo winked gratefully at her. 'Thanks, Tess. I'm about as much use as a mole at flying, with all these flowers. I never thought it would be such hard work.'

'Then why did you volunteer for it?'

'I never volunteered,' he explained. 'Dad said I have to do it as part of my punishment for fighting with Vitch.'

Tess stamped her paw. 'Oh, that little rat. It's so unfair, it was he who provoked you into that fight. Look, there he is now, over by the tables, having a sly snigger at you.'

Mattimeo saw Vitch, leaning idly on a table. He sneered and pulled tongues in the young mouse's direction.

Mattimeo felt his temper rising. 'I'll give him something to stick his tongue out at in a moment,' he muttered under his breath. 'I'll throttle him so hard it'll stick out permanently!'

Tess felt sorry for her friend. 'Pay no attention to him, Matti. He's only trying to get you into more trouble.'

It was difficult for Mattimeo to ignore Vitch. Now the rat was wiggling a paw to his snout end at his enemy.

The young mouse straightened his back from the pile of baskets. 'Right, that's it! I've taken all I can stand of his insults.'

Quickly Tess dodged past Mattimeo and ran towards Vitch, who was still grimacing impudently. Angrily the young churchmouse picked up the first thing that came to her paw. It was a pliant rose stem. She ran toward Vitch, calling out urgently, 'Look out, Vitch, there's a great big wasp on your tail. Stay still, I'll get it!'

Startled by Tess's warning cry, Vitch obeyed instantly, turning and bending slightly so she could deal with the offending insect. There was no sign of a wasp behind Vitch.

Tess swung the rose stem, surprised at her own temper but unable to stop the swishing descent of the whippy branch. It thwacked down hard across Vitch's bottom with stinging speed.

Swish, crack!

'Yeeehoooooowowow!' The rat straightened like a ramrod. Leaping high in the air, he rubbed furiously with both paws at the agonizing sting.

Cornflower came hurrying over. 'Oh dear, the poor creature. What happened, Tess?'

The young churchmouse looked the picture of innocence, though she felt far from it. Blushing deeply she stammered an excuse.

'Oh golly. Vitch had a wasp on his bottom, but I couldn't brush it off in time. I think he's been stung.'

Vitch was thrashing about on the grass, tears squeezing out on to his cheeks as he rubbed furiously at his tender rump.

Cornflower was genuinely concerned. 'Oh, you poor thing. Don't rub it, you'll make it worse. Go to Sister May at the infirmary and she'll put some herb ointment on it for you. Tess, show him where it is, please.'

Scrambling up, Vitch avoided Tess's paw and dashed off, sobbing.

Tess turned to Mattimeo. 'Aaahhh, poor Vitch. It must be very uncomfortable,' she said, her voice dripping sympathy.

Mattimeo tried hard to keep a straight face. 'Indeed it must. It's a terrible thing to be stung on the bottom by a churchmouse, er, wasp, I mean.'

Cornflower put her paws about them both. 'Yes of course. Now you two run off and play. There may be other wasps about and I don't want either of you stung.'

'Come on, Matti, let's go water-shrimping with Tim and the otters,' Tess suggested.

'Great, I'll race you over there. One, two, three. Go!'

Cornflower shaded her eyes with a paw as she watched them run.

'What a lively young pair,' she said aloud.

Mrs Churchmouse arrived, carrying a pansy and kingcup bouquet. 'Yes, but you watch your Matti. He'll let her win, he's very fond of my little Tess.'

'Bless them, that's the way it should be,' Cornflower nodded, smiling.

7

It was late afternoon on the common land at the back of
Saint Ninian's. Slager had marshalled his band of slavers.
Threeclaws the weasel and Bageye the stoat stayed
inside the ruined church, together with the wretched
little group of slaves, who had been manacled to a
running chain. They were to await the return of Slagar
and the others that night.

Now the sly one reviewed his force. They were
dressed as a band of travelling performers. None looked
evil, Slagar had seen to that. Every ferret, stoat or weasel
had a silly grin painted on its face with berry stain and
plant dyes, and all wore various types of baggy comical
costume. The fox swept up and down the line, adjusting
a ruffle here, affixing a false red nose there.

Dressed as the Lord of Mountebanks, Slagar the Cruel
looked neither comical nor amusing. There was a
mysterious air about him, hooded and caped in swirling
patterned silk which showed the black lining of the
moon and stars motif at every turn.

'Right, listen carefully. Throw down any weapons you
are carrying. Right now!' His voice was a warning growl,
flatly dangerous.

There was an uneasy shuffling. The slavers were
apprehensive of entering the Abbey without weapons.

Slagar paced the ranks once more.

'Last chance. When I say throw down your weapons, I mean it. Next time I walk around I will search you, and anyone carrying a weapon – anyone, I don't care who – I'll kill that creature with his own armoury. I'll gut him, right here in front of you all. Now, throw down your weapons!'

There was a clatter. Knives, hooks, swords, strangling nooses, daggers and axes fell to the ground like a sudden shower of April rain.

Slagar kicked at a saw-edged spike. 'Wartclaw, gather 'em and sling 'em into the church until we get back. The rest of you, form up around the cart, ten in front pulling, the rest at the sides and back shoving. We'll take the path nice and easy now, travel at a steady pace. That'll bring us there in the early evening.'

∽

As they trundled along the path, the Sly One said to his minions, 'Leave all the talking to me. I know these creatures and I can handle them. Nobody talks, is that clear? I don't want any loose-tongued addlebrain blowing the gaff by mistake. If anyone speaks to you then pull a silly face, smile and turn a cartwheel. Act the goat. You're supposed to be a travelling entertainment, so look amusing. If they ask us to share their food, which they probably will, then mind your manners and don't go piggin' it down. Take a slice or a portion of whatever and pass the bowl to your neighbour. If there's ladies present, then be polite and offer them the food first, before you start wolfin' it down your famine-fed gobs. Be friendly with the little ones and keep your eyes out for any likely looking youngsters, straight-limbed, sturdy. Don't for the claws' sake recognize Vitch. You've never set eyes on him before. Right, any questions?'

Fleaback held up a paw. 'Er, how'll we know when the moment is right, Chief?'

'I'll tell you, dunderhead.'

49

Halftail was a little puzzled. 'But how will you know, Slagar?'

The sly one looked at him pityingly. 'Because they'll be asleep, nitbrain.'

'How will you know that they're all going to go asleep together at the same time?' Halftail persisted.

Slagar patted his belt pouch. 'Don't worry, I'll see to that. Oh, and after we've put on our performance, don't drink anything, whatever you do. When you are sitting at the table you can drink what you like, but not once you've left the table to perform.'

'Duh huh huh hu!' Skinpaw laughed oafishly. 'Yer goin' to drug 'em, aren't you, Chief?'

Slagar looked down from his perch on the cart. 'I'll drug you if you don't shuttup, turniphead.'

Halftail piped up again. 'But if we drug 'em all, what's to stop us taking over this Redwall place ourselves?'

The sly one nodded. 'I was wondering when somebody was going to ask me that one. Well, I'll tell you. I think the place is bad luck. Others have tried and failed, and I mean real warriors, not like you dithering lot. No, all I want is slaves and revenge. A mere pawful of rabble could never hold a place like that. You'll know what I mean when you see the big badger, or the otters. They really know how to fight. They're not afraid of death if their precious Abbey is threatened.'

'And we're going in there unarmed?' Halftail's voice sounded shaky.

'Of course we are, halfwit,' the fox said sarcastically. 'You can bet they'll search us, and we wouldn't last a second if they found arms on us. That Matthias the Warrior would go at us like a thunderbolt.'

'Matthias the Warrior? Is that the badger?' Halftail asked.

'No, he's a mouse.'

'Haha, a mouse,' Skinpaw sneered.

'Yes, a mouse. But you won't laugh when you see him. That one's a born warrior. He has a sword too, and I think it's magic.'

'A magic sword! Hoho, I might just borrow that for meself,' Halftail howled.

'Stop the cart!' Slagar commanded.

Immediately the cart ground to a halt. The silken mask puffed in and out furiously with savage temper.

'Don't dare touch that sword. Its magic is only for the Redwall mice, there's probably a spell on it. It would be the death of us. Stick to the slaving, do you hear me? It'll be bad enough stealing his son, but if you follow my plan we'll get away with it.'

There was an ominous silence. Dust rose off the path where the cart had stopped. The slavers looked doubtfully at one another, the unspoken question hanging like a rock in their mouths.

Steal the son of such a warrior, so that was Slagar's revenge. A fearsome warrior with a magic sword, strong enough to protect a whole abbey.

'Who told you to stop? Come on, stir your stumps and get this cart moving,' Slagar told them.

They pushed and pulled with mixed emotions.

'Do as you're told and I'll make you rich,' Slagar egged them on with his sly tongue. 'You all know me, Slagar the Cruel, the sly one. Nowhere is there a cleverer slaver than me. I am the Lord of double-dealing, and my plan will easily confound an abbeyful of honest woodlanders. There's not a stoat, weasel, rat, ferret or fox among them; they're too noble for their own good. They'll never find us. I will have my revenge on Redwall and you will all be rich, when we go to sell them where none can follow.'

Scringe the ferret asked the question, dreading the answer as the words tumbled out.

'Where'll we sell the slaves, Chief?' He swallowed hard and wished he had not spoken.

'In the Kingdom of Malkariss!!!'
A moan of despair arose from the slaving band.
Slagar was talking of the realm of nightmare.

8

Nadaz, the purple-robed Voice of the Host, led a party of black-robed rats up from the depths of the underground construction. The causeway steps wound their way around the sides of the abyss, from the green misted deeps to the broad torchlit ledge. The blackrobes halted, and Nadaz came forward until he stood before the statue of Malkariss. Sometime in the distant past it had been carved from a column of limestone which stood near the brink of the ledge. The thick column was the result of stalagmite meeting stalactite, and it reared from the ledge to connect with the high arched cavern ceiling. It was carved into a monstrous effigy of a white polecat with teeth of rock crystal and eyes of the darkest black jet. The torchlights from a large wheel-shaped chandelier illuminated the terrifying idol. Nadaz bowed his head and began chanting,

'Malkariss, Ruler of the pit,
Lord of the deep and dark,
I am Nadaz, the Voice of the Host
To which your servants hark.
Hear me, O Ruler of eternal night,
Whose eyes see all we do,
King of the void beneath the earth,
we bring our pleas to you.'

'Speak, Nadaz. Tell me that my Kingdom is ready.'
Malkariss's voice was a laboured hiss which echoed
around the rocks as it emanated from between the unmoving crystalline teeth of the statue.

The purple-robed rat stretched his claws in suppli-
cation. 'Lord Malkariss, the rocks will not haul themselves, nor will they be cut into blocks to be laid one on
another. Four more slaves have died of late. We need
more workers, strong young woodland creatures who
can labour for many seasons until they finally drop.'

Nadaz stood awaiting his master's answer, not daring
to look up at the awful glittering jet eyes.

'Are there no more new captives lying in my cells?'

'Lord, the cells have stood empty for a long time now.'

'What of the longtails at the river, have none passed
this way?'

'None, Lord, who dares to climb the high plateau and
risk the pine forest.'

'Hmmmm. Then you must carry on with what you
have and work them harder. Get word to Stonefleck. Tell
him to watch for the masked fox. He has been gone two
seasons now.'

There was a prolonged silence. The torchlights
flickered and winked from the flecks of mica and crystal
which studded the cavern walls as the blackrobes stood
impassively at the head of the steps, waiting upon the
Voice of the Host. Finally Nadaz bowed.

'Malkariss, I hear and obey!'

Turning, he swept though the ranks of blackrobes,
leading them back down the causeway steps. They were
soon lost in the green mist that arose from the depths.
From below, there came the sound of chiselling and
hammering, the scraping of great stones being dragged
and the crack of whips, intermingled with the weak
anguished cries of young woodland slaves imprisoned
beneath the earth into a life of forced labour.

The statue of the immense white polecat stood alone in
the torchlight. A sigh emanated from the mouth.

'Aaaaahhhhh, my Kingdom!'

9

At Redwall, sporting events for the youngsters had been going on since early afternoon. Matthias woke refreshed. He sat on the west wall steps with John Churchmouse, Abbot Mordalfus, Basil Stag Hare and old Ambrose Spike. They drank cider and watched the antics of a young mole trying to shin up a greased pole to retrieve the bag of crystallized fruits from its top. The little fellow was over halfway up, further than any had got, and the watchers on the steps yelled encouragement:

'Dig your claws in, Gilly. You'll make it!'

'Take it easy, old lad. A bit at a time, that's the way!'

'Stay still! Stay still! Oh he's slipping!'

Gilly slid slowly earthward, his face a picture of longing.

'Gurr, sloidy owd greasepole, ee be loik tryin' t' rassle wi' a damp frog. O shame on oi, ee carndy's still thurr.'

They applauded loudly. 'Good try young un, well done!'

Constance the badger came ambling over towards them. As she passed near to the greased pole, young Sam the Squirrel moved like lightning. He dashed a short way, bounded on to Constance's back, sprang up on her head and gave a mighty leap. It carried him over the top

55

of the greased pole. He snatched the candied fruit bag as he went, without a backward look.

'I say, was that fair?' Constance blinked owlishly.

Gilly and Sam sat laughing on the grass, sharing the fruits between them. The young mole patted Sam with a greasy paw as he stuffed a sugar plum in his mouth.

'Hurr hurr, bain't nuthin' in ee rules agin it, no zurr.'

'Look out, gangway, here come the runners!'

On the second lap of the Abbey grounds, the runners came by, Tess Churchmouse in front by a whisker and a tail. They sped by, jockeying frantically to be among the front runners on the last lap.

John Churchmouse puffed at his pipe between chuckles. 'She's a one for the running, my young Tess is.'

Mattimeo came dashing across, wearing a coronet of dripping duckweed on his head.

'Look what the otters gave me, I won, I won!' he shouted.

Streamsleek, a powerful young otter, followed in Mattimeo's wake, along with a group of young creatures. The otter slouched down on the steps, shaking water from his coat.

'Crimp me sails, but he did that, Matthias. Three circuits of the pool on a log. I had me course well charted to keep up with him.'

The warrior mouse handed Streamsleek the cider flagon and ruffled his son's damp back.

'Well done, Matti. You'd better let that duckweed tiara dry out a bit before you wear it, though.'

'Balderdash, spoils of war, wot?' Basil Stag Hare said through a mouthful of summer vegetable pastie. 'You wear it, young feller me bucko, 'twas honourably won.'

Tim Churchmouse came round from the south side of the Abbey, carrying baby Rollo Bankvole on his back.

'Look, everybody, this ruffian has just beaten me to first place in the sack race.'

They laughed aloud as baby Rollo flew a small paper

kite on a string that he had been given as a prize by Cornflower. Basil Stag Hare took the infant upon his knee. He gave him a drink from his cider beaker and a bite of his pastie.

'Right, Rollo you young rip. Let's hear you sing for old Uncle Baz, wot?'

Rollo willingly obliged, piping up in his gruff baby voice,

'Fight a flagon an' drink a dragon,
Gizzard a lizard an' split his blizzard,
Ride a spider for good ol' cider,
Gooooood oooooold ciderrrrrrrr!'

Suddenly Basil deposited the infant on the steps and shot up to the west ramparts. Mrs Lettie Bankvole was seen bustling across from the gatehouse doorway, where she had been folding napkins for the table.

'Ooh, you villainous lop-eared troublemaker, just let me get my paws on you and I'll make you sing a different tune.' Basil stood on a battlement peak, trying to reason with the furious mother of Rollo.

'But madam, I can assure you the little chap composes his own verses. Jolly good too, if you ask me. Top hole.'

'How dare you! I'd take a switch to you if I were your mother.'

'Fur forbid, ma'am. If you were my mater I'd chuck meself off the jolly old battlements and save you the trouble.'

Mrs Lettie Bankvole straightened her pinafore frostily. 'And don't you sit there grinning, Ambrose Spike, you're as much to blame as that excuse for a rabbit up there. Come here, baby Rollo, this instant!'

The outraged mother swept her offspring up and hurried away, chiding him as she went.

'Now don't ever let me hear you singing that dreadful song again. Say you're sorry for upsetting Mama.'

Baby Rollo thought about this for a moment, then broke out into song lustily.

'I'd roll a mole an' squeeze a sparrow,
Or shoot a rat wiv a big sharp arrow,
For good ol' bla-ha-ha-hack currant wiiiiiiine!'

Basil descended the stairs, muttering to himself, 'Inventive little wretch, must remember that verse, what was it? Strangle a mole with a great big marrow? Talented young blighter, wish we'd had him in the old fifty-seventh foot fighters' mess.'

                                                    *

As the bells tolled out, a chorus of mice could be heard singing around the grounds.

'To table, to table and eat what you may,
Come brothers, come sisters, come all.
Be happy, be joyful, upon our feast day,
Eight seasons of peace in Redwall.
So sing from dusk to dawn
And let the Abbey bells ring.
The sun will bring the morn,
And still we will merrily sing.'

The sweet sounds floated out, fading on the warm evening air, as every woodlander and Redwall creature hastened to take their place at table for the long-awaited feast.

Such festivity there never was!

                                                    *

Eight long trestle tables had been laid in a sprawling octagon, covered in the finest white linen, overlaid with pastel-hued mats of woven rushes. Intricate flower arrangements trailed night-scented stock, roses, pansies, kingcups, jasmine, lupins and ferns at the junction of each table. Places were set out and named in neatly printed small scrolls, each of which doubled as a napkin. Bowls of hot scented flower waters steamed fragrantly, awaiting the advent of sticky paws. There was no top table or concession to rank, and the humblest sat alongside the greatest, squirrels rubbed paws with mice, otters rubbed tails with voles, and moles tried not to rub shoulders with hedgehogs. Everything was perfect, except for the food. . . .

That was beyond mere words.

Salads of twelve different types, ranging from beetroot to radish, right through many varieties of lettuce and including fennel, dandelion, tomato, young onion, carrot, leek, corn – every sort of vegetable imaginable, cut, shredded, diced or whole. These were backed up with the cheeses, arranged in wedge patterns of red, yellow and white, studded with nuts, herbs and apple. Loaves were everywhere, small brown cobs with seeds on top, long white batons with glazed crusts, early harvest loaves shaped like cornstooks, teabread, nutbread, spicebread and soft flowerbread for infants. The drinks were set out in pitchers and ewers, some in open bowls with floating mint leaves, October ale, fresh milk, blackcurrant wine, strawberry cordial, nutbrown beer, raspberry fizz, elderberry wine, damson juice, herb tea and cold cider.

Then there were the cakes, tarts, jellies and sweets. Raspberry muffins, blueberry scones, redcurrant jelly, Abbot's cake, fruitcake, iced cake, shortbread biscuits, almond wafers, fresh cream, sweet cream, whipped cream, pouring cream, honeyed cream, custardy cream, Mrs Churchmouse's bell tower pudding, Mrs Bankvole's six-layer trifle, Cornflower's gatehouse gateau, Sister Rose's sweetmeadow custard with honeyglazed pears, Brother Rufus's wildgrape woodland pie with quince and hazelnut sauce.

To name but a few. . . .

The rule was to start with what you liked and finish when you felt like. Nothing was stinted and everyone was to make sure that their neighbours either side of them enjoyed everything.

'Hi, Tess, have some hot candied chestnuts.'

'Thank you, Matt. Here, try some of this almond wafer topped with pink cream. I've just invented it and it's lovely.'

59

'Yurr, pass oi that troifle, oi dearly do luv troifle. Hurr, coom on, Abbot zurr, you'm b'aint ayten 'ardly a boit. Let oi 'elp you t' summ o' thiz yurr salad 'n'bread'n'-cheese'n bell tower pudden.'

'Oh er, all together? Thank you, Foremole, most kind. Have you tried my Redcurrantwall Abbot Alf cake?'

'Strike me sails, Mordalfus, that's a nice long name for a good-sized cake.' Winifred commented. 'Ho, it tastes 'andsome. Pass us the cider, matey.'

'My, my, Basil, you're not saying much.'

'*Mmmfff scrumff grumphhh.* Action, laddie buck, that's the ticket. *Grmffff, munchmunch, slurrrp!*'

'Try some of my woodland pie, Matthias. By the fur, is that Basil behind the huge plateful over there?'

'Thank you, Brother Rufus. A little more nutbrown beer for you? Haha, so it is. Every time his ears show over the top of that pile of food he shoves more on it. Oh dear, I'm sure he'll explode before the evening's out. Hi, Basil, steady on old lad.'

'*Grmmmfff, munch.* Beg pardon, old mouse, can't hear you. Must be me old war wound, *snchhh, gulp!* Oh no, it's a stick of celery in me ear. How'd that get there, *chompchomp, grumphhh!*'

The Abbot was upstanding now. He beat upon the table with a wooden ladle.

'Silence, please. Give order and make way for Friar Hugo and the fish.'

The carp was on a low wide trolley. Hugo would allow none to help. Proudly he pulled and tugged until he drew it up to the table. Fanning himself with the tail-held dockleaf, he regained his breath.

'Abbot, the fish prayer, if you please.'

The eating stopped. All sat in reverent silence as Mordalfus spread his paws over the carp and intoned:

'Fur and whisker, tooth and claw,
All who enter by our door.
Nuts and herbs, leaves and fruits,

Berries, tubers, plants and roots,
Silver fish whose life we take
Only for a meal to make.'

There was a loud and heartfelt 'Amen' from all.

The Abbot gave the proceedings over to Hugo, and the fat little Friar cleared his throat.

'Ahem, my friends, this year I have created for you a dish known as *Carp Capitale*. You will observe that I marinated my fish in a mixture of cider and dandelion extract. It has been grilled on a turning spit, skinned and laid in a slow-cooking mixture of cream and mushrooms with hotroot pepper, then garnished with flaked almond, mint leaves and chopped greens.'

'Absolutely spiffin'. I say, Hugo, you old pan-walloper, d'you need a good steady-pawed fellow to help you t' serve the old trout, wot wot?'

Friar Hugo never blinked an eyelid, but there were titters and smothered giggles from every corner at Basil's offer. Hugo addressed the Abbot:

'Lord Abbot, before I serve you the first portion to taste, can I suggest jugged hare for our next banquet?'

Basil's ears stood straight up with indignation. 'I say, steady in the ranks there. I wouldn't be able to have any, doncha know.'

Amid gales of unrestrained laughter, Abbot Mordalfus dug his fork into the delicious dish. A whisker's-breadth away from his lips he stopped the loaded fork and said, 'Friar Hugo, my most old and valued chef, I pronounce this dish totally excellent merely by the sight and aroma, knowing that when I actually taste it I will be lost for words.'

A cheer went up at the Abbot's gallant pronouncement. Hugo fanned himself furiously with pleasure at the compliment.

Basil Stag Hare actually ate four portions, claiming that he had an otter ancestor somewhere in his family tree.

Then the toasting started, led by Ambrose Spike. 'I

would like to toast all Redwall Abbots past, and in particular good old Mordalfus, our present Abbot.'

'Yurr yurr, gudd owd M'dalfuzz.'

'I would like to toast Matthias the Warrior, our champion,' called out Brother Rufus.

'Good egg, I'll second that, old bean.'

'I would like to toast our young ones, the hope of future seasons to come.'

'Hear, hear, Cornflower. Well toasted.'

'Ahem, as a retired regimental buffer, I'd like to toast anything on toast, cheese, mushrooms, what have you. . . .'

'Oh, all right, Basil. Here's to tomatoes on toast.'

'I toast Mr Hare and Mr Spike.'

'Sit down, baby Rollo, and drink your milk.'

'Here's to the otters and the squirrels.'

'Bravo, here's to the sparrows and the moles.'

'To Redwall Abbey.'

'To Mossflower Woods.'

The toasts flew fast and thick. Laughter, song, good food, sufficient drink and friendly company were making it a feast to remember.

Then Slagar the Cruel knocked upon the door of Redwall Abbey.

10

Slagar turned to the group at the cart. They had been watching him banging fruitlessly upon the main gate.

'They'll never hear you, Chief,' Wartclaw ventured. 'We'll have to think of some other way to distract them.'

Slagar's paw was numb from hitting the woodwork. 'We? You mean me, don't you? Here, Skinpaw, sing that song. Halftail, get that little drum from the cart and beat it. Scringe, there's a flute in the cart. See if you can get a tune out of it.'

Skinpaw was the only one of the slavers who had actually been in a travelling show. Filling his lungs, he began singing the song of strolling performers, in a cracked voice.

'Lalalalalalala, we travel from afar,
Derrydown dill, over vale and hill.
We camp beneath the stars.
Lalalalalalala, good fortune to you, sir.
The strolling players bring to you
Magic from everywhere. . . .'

Skinpaw shrugged at Slagar. 'Chief, that's all I know, I've forgotten the rest.'

The sly one swirled his cloak impatiently. 'Then sing it over and over again. You two, try to pick up the tune on the flute and drum,. The rest of you, tumble about in the road and join Skinpaw on the "Lalala" bits.'

Slagar kept his eye against a joint that was slightly open in the solid gate timbers.

The entire troupe went through the routine several times. Slagar waved his paw encouragingly at them.

'Keep it up, louder, louder! I can see they've heard us, they're coming across the grounds. Keep it up, keep going.'

The hooded fox leapt aboard the cart. Crouching, he covered himself with a pile of old coloured wagon sheeting.

∽

There was a scraping of drawbars and bolts, and the door opened partially as Matthias came out on to the path, followed by Constance the badger and Ambrose Spike. They stood awhile, watching the performers, then Matthias called out. 'Hey there. What can we do for you?'

'Send 'em on their way, scruffy bunch of ragbags,' Ambrose Spike snorted.

'Ambrose, don't be so ill mannered!' Constance nudged him sharply. 'We can at least be civil to travellers. Leave the talking to Matthias and myself.'

Slagar bounded up in a whirl of coloured cloth. Leaping over the edge of the cart, he landed on the path, twirling his cape this way and that.

'Happy Midsummer Eve to you, my lords,' he said, doing his level best to keep his grating voice light and cheerful. 'You see before you a band of strolling entertainers, foolish fellows and peace-loving buffoons. We travel the roads merely to bring you songs, stories, tumbling and leaping, comical antics to amuse you and your families. Where do we come from? No creature knows, except I, Stellar Lunaris, master of the moon and stars.'

The fox whirled round and round, showing the lining of his cape, the silk shimmering and twinkling in the hot summer twilight on the dusty roadway.

Constance relaxed slightly. Only a band of travelling players. Her keen old eyes checked the ditch that ran west of the path for signs of others hidden there. It was clear.

Before he could be stopped, Ambrose Spike called out, 'And what will it cost us, this magical entertainment?'

Slagar stopped the cloak revolving and spread his paws. 'A crust from your grand table, maybe a drink of cool water and the safety of your Abbey walls so that my friends and I can sleep without fear through the night. Oh, do not worry, good creatures. We will sleep upon the grass out here if you fear us.'

Matthias the Warrior of Redwall stepped forward, rubbing his paw across the red pommel stone of the wondrous sword he carried sheathed at his side.

'We fear no creature. Redwall buried its foes many seasons back. Stay here a moment, I would talk with my friends.'

The trio drew back into the gateway, where groups of curious revellers had left the table and were peering round the gates. 'Well, what d'you think, Warrior?' Constance asked in a low voice. 'They look harmless enough to me, even though they are led by a fox.'

Matthias pursed his lips. 'Hmm, the rest are weasels, stoats and ferrets. Nothing that we can't cope with. They'd be outnumbered at least fifteen to one inside Redwall, and they don't seem to have any hidden army waiting to spring out in ambush on us. I think they look ragged but harmless enough.'

Behind them the young ones were eagerly craning their necks, calling out excitedly. 'Hurray! Clowns and tumblers. Oh, can we see them Constance?'

'Look, there's a magic one. Ooh, see his cloak!'

Vitch was leading the youngest in a chant. 'We want to see, we want the show. . .!'

Basil Stag Hare pushed his way though to Matthias. He was chuckling indulgently and waving his ears for silence.

65

'Steady on, chaps, haw haw! A jolly old concert party, wot? Don't be an old stick in the mud, Constance. Let the blighters in, as long as they don't pull rabbits out of hats.'

Constance shook her big striped head from side to side doubtfully. The chanting broke out even louder. Finally she winked at Matthias and nodded to the hooded fox.

'Oh all right! Come on then, you youngsters, move aside and let me open the gates, otherwise these tumblers won't be able to get in.'

The young ones gave a great cheer.

༄

Slagar was impressed with the long tunnel of arched sandstone. It denoted the massive thickness of the Abbey walls. The travelling troupe looked around at the great Abbey of Redwall standing in its own grounds, the magnificent alfresco feast lit by the flames from the baking pit. This was a place of riches and plenty.

They were patted down by Abbey dwellers searching for arms. Slagar shook his head sadly, 'Alas, these are untrusting times we live in.'

Abbot Mordalfus bowed courteously. 'Merely a precaution, friend. The feast is far from over yet. Kindly come and sit with us at table. There is plenty for all.'

The silken hood quivered as Slagar wiped away an imaginary tear.

'Such hospitality and kindness, thank you, sir. My friends and I will repay you by putting on an extra special performance for you and your good creatures.'

As they moved over to the table, nobody noticed Vitch slip a small scroll to Slagar. The sly one secreted it beneath his voluminous cape.

༄

Wartclaw crept up behind Skinpaw with a jug of water poised to throw at him. A ferret named Deadnose who stood facing Skinpaw was juggling three balls, unaware that Wartclaw was about to drench Skinpaw with the water.

The youngsters squirmed with glee as they shouted out, 'Look out, he's behind you!'

'Who, what did you say?' Skinpaw wrinkled his false red nose and grinned a silly grin.

'Ooooh, look out, he's behind you!'

Deadnose dropped one of the balls he was juggling. Skinpaw bent to pick it up at the exact moment that Wartclaw flung the water from the jug at him. The youngsters roared with laughter as Deadnose was drenched instead of Skinpaw.

Scringe darted in with a large floppy wooden clapper. He swung it and smacked Wartclaw across the bottom with a loud comic slap. Wartclaw whooped with surprise, dropped the jug and stepped in it by accident, getting his paw stuck inside. They ran off with Wartclaw hop-skipping, *clumpetty thump*, the jug fixed on his paw, while Scringe followed up, whacking his bottom with the clapper.

All the inhabitants of Redwall laughed merrily. Abbot Mordalfus held his sides as he chuckled to Basil, 'Ohohoho, I knew that juggler would get drenched, hahaha. Oh, look, the red-nosed fellow is eating one of the juggling balls, hee hee hee. It was an apple all the time, ohahaha!'

'Hawhawhaw. Silly old blighter. I say, the weasel chappie's trying to eat the other juggling balls. Oooh-oohoo, they're real wooden ones! Spit 'em out, old lad, y'll break your teeth.'

Slagar was prancing about the tabletops, giving out paper butterflies to the young ones, they flew just like real butterflies. Nobody noticed that every time he passed a jug, flagon or bowl a little powder was dropped into the drink.

Skirting the back of the gathering, Slagar stood behind the flames of the baking pit and threw a pawful of powder into the fire. It caused a whoosh of green flame to shoot upward. Leaping across the pit, the sly one seemed to materialize out of the middle of the emerald-coloured flames.

'Stellar Lunaris, Lunar Stellaris! I am the Lord of Mountebanks. Is there one among you named Ambrose Spike?'

'Aye, that's me over here. But how did you know my name?'

'The Lord of moon and stars knows all, Ambrose Spike. You are the keeper of the cellars, and your October ale next season will be even better than before.'

'Well I'm blowed, the jolly old firejumper knows about you, Spike me lad.'

Slagar whirled round. 'Is that Basil Stag Hare I hear speaking, famed scout and retired foot fighter?'

'Aye, and famous glutton and singer of dreadful songs.'

The sly one cocked an ear. 'Hark! Is that the voice of Mrs Lettie Bankvole, mother of baby Rollo?'

Mrs Bankvole was flabbergasted. 'Oh haha, yes, that's me. But how did you know, Mr Stellaris?'

'Gather round, gather round, good creatures of Redwall Abbey. I will tell you of secrets known only to the Lord of Mountebanks. But first you must drink a toast to the two who caught the big carp, your Abbot and your Warrior, two of the noblest, most brave creatures that ever lived.'

Fleaback, Skinpaw, Wartclaw, Scringe and the rest dashed around the tables, chuckling heartily and tickling little ones behind the ears while filling up every beaker and bowl.

Foremole stood up on a bench. 'Yurr's to Mattwise ee Wurrier, an' yurr's to Habbot 'Dalfuzz. Gudd 'elth, gennelbeasts.'

Beakers and bowls clinked together as the toast was drunk.

Slagar threw another pawful of dust into the fire. This time it rose up golden and smoking in a column as he called out in an eerie voice:

'Stellar Lunaris Fortuna Mandala, hark to me, all creatures.'

68

Mattimeo was fascinated by the magic fox. He put his cider down and watched with rapt attention. Now the fox had taken off his flowing silken cloak. He held it up and swirled it in front of him, slowly at first then getting faster and faster, chanting as he did:

'See the stars, see the moon,
Penned around by blackest night.
See the diamonds red and purple,
Silk and fire and blood and light.
See them turning, ever turning,
Like a great mandala wheel,
Spinning as the fire is burning.
What is false and what is real. . .?'

From somewhere near, Mattimeo could hear Mrs Churchmouse gently snoring. He tried to fix his eyes on the swirling cloak as it turned from diamond patterns to star-studded night skies. The fox's voice droned on and on, until finally Mattimeo could no longer keep his leaden eyelids from drooping.

He fell asleep across the table full of good food, well entertained and completely happy.

11

The day dawned humid and grey. Soon huge dark cloud masses bunched in a lowering sky, occasionally cut through by forked lightning flashes over to the west. Thunder rumbled dully from the far horizons of the Golden Plain, then drops of rain, each one as big as a beechnut, began falling.

Constance the badger was wakened by the wetness, combined with the scream of distress from baby Rollo.

'Mama!'

All around the badger, Redwall creatures were wakening, groaning and stumbling about in the heavy downpour.

Matthias held his throbbing head with one paw as he shook Constance. 'Quickly, let's get them all in out of the rain. Was that somebody shouting a moment ago?'

'Mama, Mama, wake up!'

Constance came fully awake as thunder boomed out overhead and the scene was lit by a branch of forked lightning.

'It's baby Rollo over by the north wallgate!'

Hurrying through the battering thunderstorm, Constance and Matthias dashed to where the little bankvole sat crying by the small gate low in the sandstone wall. He was shaking the still form of Mrs Lettie Bankvole.

'Mama, oh Mama, please wake up, I'm getting wet!'

The warrior mouse's head began to clear with the rain. 'Cornflower, over here! Take this little one inside. We must find out what's been going on here.'

Cornflower scurried off, carrying baby Rollo in her paws as she shielded him from the wet with her body.

'There, there, little Rollo, you come with me. Matthias and Constance will see to your mama.'

Basil Stag Hare dashed to join them, a skinny bedraggled figure in the rain. 'Oh, me poor old head. Hello, what's up, you two?'

Constance sat by the pitiful bundle on the grass, wiping rainwater from her eyes. 'She's dead! Matthias, who could have done this?'

Matthias had his forehead flat against the wall. Rain mingled with the tears that filled his eyes.

'Who else but that rotten fox and his venomous gang. I was taken in, fooled! Oh, the filthy cowards! How could they murder a helpless creature like Mrs Bankvole?'

From behind the open walldoor there came a faint moan. Matthias straightened up quickly and rushed towards the door as it swung back. John Churchmouse staggered out from behind the door, blood flowing from his temple where an ugly cut ran a jagged line from ear to ear. Matthias caught him, holding him up against the wall in the pouring rain.

'John, are you all right? What happened?'

The churchmouse wiped rainwater and blood from his eyes. He was obviously in deep shock, reliving the horrific events that he had witnessed.

'Stop . . . stop them . . . Get back, Mrs Bankvole. . . . No, no! Come on, Hugo. . . . Got to stop them. . . . Blood . . . can't see. . . . Where's Hugo, where's Hugo. . . ?'

He collapsed senseless against Matthias.

Constance stepped in, sweeping the unconscious churchmouse up with a single paw. 'I'll get John inside.

71

Winifred, cover Mrs Bankvole with a tablecloth for the moment. Matthias, Basil, see if you can find Friar Hugo!'

The big badger hurried off through the curtain of rain with her burden.

∽

The warrior mouse and the hare searched frantically around the grounds in the increasing downpour.

'Friar Hugo, where are you?'

'Hugo, come on, old lad. Call out if you can hear us!'

Winifred the otter bumped into Matthias as he rounded the bell tower. 'No sign of Hugo?' she asked.

'None at all, Winifred. He must have followed them out of the grounds. Hi, Basil! Come on, let's search the woodland outside the gate.'

The rain made loud splattering noises as it burst upon the tree canopy. Visibility was bad with rising mist in the woods.

Matthias searched in the loam, beneath bushes, behind trees and among ferns. Nearby he could hear Basil muttering through the deluge, 'Come on, Hugo, you old pan-walloper, show y'self. I promise I'll never raid your kitchens again, cross m' heart and hope to starve.'

Winifred the otter shook water from her sleek coat as she bobbed up and down, hoping to catch a glimpse of Hugo in the distance. She checked with Matthias.

'I don't think a fat little mouse like Hugo could have travelled further than this. Perhaps we'd better make our way back to the Abbey and search the grounds more thoroughly,' she suggested.

Suddenly Matthias went rigid. 'Listen, can you hear something, Winifred?'

A muffled noise came to them through the rain. The otter pointed. 'Over there. Quick!'

They crashed though the undergrowth to the place where the sound came from.

∽

It was Basil Stag Hare. He was crouching on the wet ground, hugging something to him and sobbing brokenly.

Matthias felt a huge lump like a lead weight in his chest as he knelt beside the hare. Winifred turned away, unable to look. The fat little Redwall cook lay limp and dead, unaware of the rain that beat down upon the favourite dockleaf his tail still held in its curl. Tears coursed openly down Basil's cheeks as he hugged the still form.

'Hugo old lad, what did they do to you?'

Winifred knelt with her friends. Silently she began brushing the loam and soil from the sodden habit and once spotless white apron of the beloved little Friar, then without warning she broke down and began weeping like a baby.

'He never did harm to a living creature. Why this. . . . Why?'

Basil stood slowly, his legs shaking as he held Hugo in his paws. 'Permission to carry my old friend back to his Abbey?'

Matthias remained kneeling on the ground, his fur saturated by the ceaseless rain.

'Permission granted, Basil. Winifred, will you tell them I'll be a little late back to Great Hall.' The Warrior's voice trembled as he spoke.

As Matthias watched his friends depart, he picked up the dockleaf that had fallen from Friar Hugo's lifeless tail and pressed it to his lips in silent remembrance of his friend.

∽

Inside the Great Hall of the Abbey a large brazier had been set up and lit. Steam rose from the fur of all the creatures as they rubbed themselves off on rough towels. Sister May from the infirmary moved among them, giving out doses of herbal medicine. Many sat on the stone floor, clutching their heads tightly to relieve splitting headaches. Matthias strode in, followed by Basil Stag Hare. He clattered his swordblade against a sandstone column to gain attention.

'Abbot, Constance, Winifred, Jess Squirrel, Warbeak

73

Sparra, Foremole and you, Basil, follow me down to Cavern Hole. The rest of you, stay inside, keep dry and warm, and look after those who are not well.'

A semblance of order was restored in Great Hall. Hot soup was being made in the kitchen, warm blankets were distributed by Brother Rufus and Sister Agnes, Sister May and Mrs Churchmouse tended John Churchmouse in the infirmary, while Cornflower took charge of baby Rollo.

$\backsim$

Down the steps in Cavern Hole, Matthias sat at the big table with the others. He looked around.

'Well, did any creature see what went on last night, can anyone shed any light on this terrible thing? I want straight answers, no guesses, please.'

There was silence, then the Abbot said, 'We will have to wait until John Churchmouse is recovered sufficiently to talk. The only other two witnesses to what went on are no longer with us.'

There was a stunned silence as the enormity of events sat like a heavy stone upon the little group.

Jess Squirrel stood up slowly. 'I'll go to the infirmary and see how Mr Churchmouse is faring.'

Basil livened up. 'That's the ticket, Jess. Action, that's what we need. Now, where do we start.'

The Abbot folded his paws into his wide sleeves. 'At the beginning, Basil. I think we all know who did this shocking thing.'

'Harr, boi 'okey we do, zurr,' Foremole growled. ''twas they rascally durtbags, foxes an' the loik, they'm magicked us t' sleepen.'

'Magicked my auntie's tail,' Winifred the otter snorted. 'That was a powerful sleeping draught. We should've known not to trust a fox, should never have let 'em in.'

Matthias banged the tabletop hard. 'Enough! No accusations or blame-laying, please. Now, you say that we were drugged by a sleeping draught, well, that makes sense. I remember the fox asking us to drink a toast. He could have slipped herbs or powders into the drinks any time at all while we were watching the entertainment.'

Ambrose Spike had walked in. His stickles rose stiffly. 'Aye, that's what he did, the scummy toad. Then he started twirlin' that cloak thing of his round and round. I couldn't keep me old eyes open.'

There were murmurs of agreement.

'Me too, it's the last thing I remember.'

'Aye, we were mesmerized, I tell you.'

'Lunar Stellaris my back paw, colossal cheek more like it, wot?'

Foremole's ground logic took over. 'Hurr, but wot worr ee arfter?'

'That's the question.' Matthias sighed heavily. 'We don't keep treasure or precious things that could be looted. There's only the sword and our great tapestry. I have the sword and I know our tapestry still hangs in Great Hall, I've seen it with my own eyes this very morning. So what was he after?'

Warbeak the Sparra Queen shook a wing. 'They um worms, must come from the northlands. All bad in north. They go back that way, open little wormgate in north wall.'

Basil seconded Warbeak. 'D' y' know, I believe you're right, old thing. When the bally rain stops chuckin' down I'll try and track 'em. Huh, 'fraid there won't be much to track after this downpour, though.'

'I think the Brothers and Sisters should take stock of everything, just in case there is something missing,' the Abbot suggested. 'Foremole, would you get a burial detail of your moles to dig two graves next to each other? Basil, perhaps you could see what you can find around that small north wallgate. The rest of you, when the rain stops, please help to bring the tables and stuff back in. We'd best get the Abbey back to normal running as soon as possible.'

75

Matthias stood up resolutely. 'Right, that's it then. I think I'll take a walk up to the infirmary and see how John is.'

～

Sister May and Mrs Churchmouse cautioned Matthias to be silent as he entered the sick bay. John Churchmouse lay pale and still but breathing evenly.

'How is he?' Matthias whispered.

Mrs Churchmouse smiled. 'Alive and recovering, thank you, Matthias.'

John opened his eyes slowly and looked around. Matthias pressed his head back to the pillow as he tried to rise. 'Take it easy, old friend, just lie there. But if you feel like talking, perhaps you could tell us what you remember of last night. Nobody knows what went on at the feast.'

Tears beaded in John's eyes. 'Friar Hugo and I had full cups already, so we didn't let them pour us more ale. Poor Mrs Bankvole was too busy looking after her baby to join in the toast. Matthias, there's no doubt about it, you were all drugged, even then Hugo and I were half hypnotized by that fox with the cape. When we saw what was going on we ran after them and tried to stop it, all three of us, the Friar, Mrs Bankvole and myself.'

'But what did go on, what were they after, John?' Matthias had an awful feeling in the pit of his stomach as he asked the question.

The churchmouse broke down sobbing. 'Our young ones, Matthias. They took my Tim and Tess, Sam Squirrel, Cynthia Bankvole and your Mattimeo!'

An icy claw gripped Matthias's heart. The words echoed from the doorway where Cornflower stood with baby Rollo.

'Mattimeo gone!'

'My Tim and Tess! Oh, say it's not true!' Mrs Churchmouse's voice was equally tinged with disbelief.

Baby Rollo was hidden by the aprons of Cornflower

and Mrs Churchmouse as they hugged each other and wept. John raised his head.

'Little Cynthia Vole and Sam Squirrel too, they took them all,' he said sadly.

Sister May began bathing John's wound. She dabbed away the tears that fell upon his brow.

'Poor Jess, whatever will we tell her? Dearie me, little Cynthia is an orphan. Bless the mite, what will become of her? What a cruel and heartless thing to do. Those wicked beasts, stealing our young ones away. What badness!'

Matthias put his paw about Cornflower's shaking shoulders. He was numbed. Thoughts of his son raced through his mind; the stern lecture he had given him, the double tasks. Now he was gone. It was as if half of his heart had gone too. He loved Mattimeo, who would do little things that reminded him so much of himself and Cornflower. Poor Cornflower. Even now she was trying to be brave, comforting Mrs Churchmouse.

Matthias held her tighter. 'Don't worry, Cornflower, I'll bring our son back. I'll bring them all back. Nothing can stop me doing that. He'll be back in his own bed in the gatehouse cottage soon, you'll see.'

Mrs Churchmouse went to tend John and Sister May slipped off to break the sad news to Jess Squirrel. Cornflower took Rollo over to the infirmary window. She stared out at the rain.

'I won't be going back to our gatehouse until Mattimeo is back,' she declared. 'I'll stay at the Abbey and mind Rollo.'

Matthias nodded silently as Cornflower dried her eyes and sighed, 'Oh Mattimeo, I hope no harm comes to you, my son. Poor Mattimeo.'

Baby Rollo spread his paws wide, his face as sad as Cornflower's. 'Pore 'timeo gone'd. Aaaahhhhh!'

Matthias joined them at the window, staring out into the rain. Sorrow and pain mingled with the cold lights of rage and vengeance in his eyes.

77

12

Mattimeo did not know at first whether he was awake or dreaming. The tip of his ear itched irritatingly, but it was as if there were leaden weights on his limbs. He could only raise his paw halfway, then the other paw would start to come upward as if pulled like a puppet on a string. From faraway he heard unpleasant sniggering and a loud swishing noise.

Crack!

The young mouse arched his back in agony as a searing pain lanced across him. His eyes opened with shock. He saw Vitch swinging a long thin willow cane. The second blow caught him low across the flanks. Stung by pain and rage, Mattimeo tried to leap up and teach the little rat a good lesson, but he stumbled, falling backwards with manacles clanking around him.

He was chained!

Vitch laughed nastily and raised the whipping cane slowly. 'Come on, spoilt baby, little Abbey pet, what are you going to do now, eh?'

Again and again the cane rose and fell, striking the young prisoner indiscriminately. In his excitement Vitch was jumping about as he wielded the thin willow.

'Haha, there's no silly badger to stop me now, is there? I won't have to scrub floors and clean saucepans now.

Take that and that and th—'

He danced in too close. Under the stinging rain of blows, Mattimeo saw Vitch's paw step within his reach. Crossing both paws tightly, the young mouse tugged hard, bringing the little rat crashing down. Mattimeo bit, butted and belaboured away at his tormentor with the slack of the chain.

'Help, help! Murder! He's killing me!' Vitch screamed in panic.

Threeclaws the weasel hauled them roughly apart. He kicked Mattimeo down and flung Vitch against the far wall.

'Hell's teeth! Stop screeechin' and shoutin', will you? What's going on here?'

Vitch was quivering with indignation. 'You stop shoving me about, Threeclaws. Slagar said I could take my revenge on that one when we had him chained up.'

The weasel looked at him disgustedly. 'Huh, you weren't makin' a very good job of it, were you? From what I saw, this mouse was givin' you a good hidin'.'

Vitch dashed forward swinging the cane. 'I'll teach him a lesson he won't forget this time!'

Threeclaws caught the cane and pulled it from Vitch's grasp, then grabbed the struggling rat firmly by the neckfur.

'No you won't, snotnose. I'm in charge while Slagar's not here. There's to be no noise, see. We don't want any creature who's out searching to hear anything. Now you just behave yourself, or I'll lay this cane across your back, rat.'

Vitch slumped against the windowsill, snivelling, but he obeyed the weasel's order.

∽

Mattimeo looked about. There were others chained up around the walls: mice, squirrels, hedgehogs, all of them young creatures. He saw Tim and Tess and Sam Squirrel chained against the far wall. Fetters clanking, he waved to them.

'Sam, Tim, Tess, how did we get here?' he asked.

'Silence there!'

Halftail the stoat shouted, and pointed a dagger warningly at Mattimeo. 'Shuttup, mouse. You've been told once. Save your breath, you're going to need it for marching.'

When Halftail moved out of earshot, a young badger chained next to Mattimeo whispered, 'That's Halftail. Watch him, he's a cruel one. My name is Auma from the west plains. What's yours?'

'Mattimeo, son of Matthias the Redwall Warrior.'

'Oh, so you're the one that Slagar was after.'

'Slagar?'

'Yes, the sly one, the hooded fox,' Auma explained. 'This lot are a band of slave traders. Though where they're taking us I don't know.'

'Ooh, where am I? Take these chains off me. Boo-hoohoo, I want to go home, boohoohoo!'

It was Cynthia Bankvole. She had just awakened, chained to the other side of Auma.

Threeclaws came hurrying over. He thrust his villain-ous face right up against Cynthia's tearful whiskers.

'One more peep out of you, missie, and I'll really give you something to cry about. Now cut out the whimper-ing.'

Cynthia was struck dumb with terror.

∽

Slagar came bounding in through the broken south window, the silken hood plastered wetly against his muzzle. He shook himself vigorously, showering rain-water about him.

'By the claw, it's bouncing down in torrents out there. Still, all the better for us. If we get going fast then there'll be no tracks to cover. They won't know which direction we've taken. On the other side of the leaf, that lot at Redwall will have been wakened by this downpour, so we can't afford to hang around. The false trail to the north should keep them busy for a while. Deadnose and

Fengal have taken the cart up that way, then they'll circle around and meet us in the forest south of here.'

Bageye lounged in a pew. 'What if they don't, Chief? Suppose they miss us? That wood out there is a big place, y'know.'

The face beneath the hood seemed to grin. 'Well, hard luck on them. It'll mean bigger shares for all of us.'

Bageye had to think about it for a moment, then he gave a slow smile.

'Oh aye, huh huh, so it will.'

∽

A long running chain was brought out, and the prisoners were made to stand as it was run through their manacled front paws and locked at either end. Mattimeo found himself standing between Auma and Tess, Tim and Sam were behind them. Slagar paced the line, checking links and shoving the captives into place. Satisfied that everything was in order, he pulled forth a strange-looking weapon and began twirling it about. It was a short wooden handle, from which ran three braided leather thongs, and at the end of each thong hung a round metal ball. They whirled and clacked sharply as he manoeuvred them expertly.

'I am Slagar the Cruel. You are my slaves now.' The silk sucked against his face as he spoke. 'When I say walk, you walk. If I say run, you run. If I decide you may live, then you will live. If I take it into my head that you may not live, then I will see to it that you die. If ever you should get the chance to escape or make a run for it, my little toy here will bring you back.'

The fox swung the weapon and hurled it. Flailing viciously, it wrapped itself around an oak upright at the end of some pews. The three metal balls slammed hard into the timber, snapping it off like a dead twig.

As Fleaback retrieved the weapon, Slagar shrugged carelessly at the captives.

'If you had any back legs left at all after my little toy hit you, I'd have to dump you in the nearest ditch because a

81

slave that is crippled for life isn't much use to anyone.'

Mattimeo swallowed hard. The cruel one clearly meant every word he said.

Slagar turned to his aides. 'Threeclaws, Halftail, we strike south. Keep 'em moving fast. I want a day and a night's forced march to put as much distance as we can between us and Redwall. Wartclaw, Tornear, bring up the rear. If it stops raining then cover our trail. Use your canes if they start hanging back or turning the water-works on. Right, quick march!'

The door was pushed aside as the straggling column made its way out into the torrents of rain that shook the leaves of every tree in Mossflower Woods.

13

It was early evening and the rain hammered down relentlessly. Abbot Mordalfus stood with Sister Agnes on the site of the feast. The roasting pit was a mass of soggy black embers. Mordalfus threw a scrap of parchment into it.

'This was how the fox knew all about us,' he explained. 'It was Little Vitch who wrote all the information about us. We gave him a home and he was a spy in our midst. John Churchmouse saw him running with those ruffians when they fled.'

Sister Agnes's whiskers shook with indignation. 'The little hooligan! To think that we took him in, sheltered and fed him, and that's how he repaid us, by spying and noting it all down for the fox. Young Mattimeo should have give him a bit more of what he gave him in the orchard, Father Abbot, that's what I say.'

'I agree with you, Sister,' the old mouse sighed. 'Sometimes violence can be fair when it is used as a chastisement against badness. Is that Brother Sedge waving to us from the Abbey? Come, sister, there may be some news for us.'

As they walked over to Great Hall the Matthias and Methusaleh bells rang out. They were out of sequence and not tolled with their usual vigour. Agnes pointed to the bell tower.

'That will be Cornflower, teaching baby Rollo to make our bells speak. How good of her, she's keeping little Rollo's mind off his mother. He still doesn't know she's dead.'

Sister Agnes wiped a tear away with her habit sleeve.

～

In Great Hall Matthias was drying himself off, in company with Basil Stag Hare, Warbeak and several of her sparrow scouts.

The Abbot shook a stern paw at them. 'Where did you go off to without as much as a word to me?'

Matthias tossed the towel aside wearily. 'We've been up the north road. Warbeak and her sparrows flew ahead of us. But the rain was too heavy, so there are no tracks.'

Basil blew droplets of rain from his whiskers. 'Tchah! Bally old rain. They've either travelled up that road a lot faster than we thought they could, or else cut off east into the woodlands or west out on to the plains. Couldn't make out a confounded thing with the old skyjuice pouring down like that.'

Warbeak fluttered her wings irritably. 'They worms, no can travel faster'n us with cart to pull. We catchem, you see.'

Abbot Mordalfus gathered up the wet towels. 'So, they could have travelled anywhere in three directions from the road. One thing is certain, no creature can track them in this rain, so what can we do?'

Thunder rumbled outside, a vivid lightning flash streaked across the windows of Great Hall. Basil twitched his ears miserably.

'No signs of this little lot lettin' up, old sport,' he said to Matthias. 'We're really at sixes and sevens, laddie. Can't sit around and twiddle our paws and can't get out and track 'em.'

Matthias wiped his sword dry, gritting his teeth angrily. 'Track them or not, we can't let them get away with our young ones.'

The Abbot folded both paws into his wide habit sleeves. 'We'll bury our dead and think hard while we're doing it.'

❧

Ambrose Spike and Cornflower kept baby Rollo at their side as they tolled the bells that evening. The sky was leaden purple-grey, and rain poured ceaselessly as the procession of Redwallers marched solemnly to the burying place. Dressed in his ceremonial robe, the Abbot stood over the twin graves, at the foot of which two weeping willow saplings had been transplanted.

Tearfully the woodlanders passed in single file, each leaving a small memento to their fallen friends, a young mousemother and a fat little Friar. Some brought flowers, others carried offerings of fruit and nuts, or a treasured object they thought might please, a paw-worked purse, a carved wooden ladle, a dockleaf made from green felt.

Matthias stood alongside Mordalfus, dressed in his full armour, bearing the sword. Together the warrior and the patriarch intoned the prayer for those who would rest for ever in the Abbey grounds.

'Suns that set as seasons turn,
Flowers grow and wither yet.
Who can say what flame may burn,
Friends that we have known and met.
Look into the young ones' eyes,
See the winter turn to spring,
Across the quiet eternal lake,
Ripples spreading in a ring.'

The rain continued unabated as they filed back to the Abbey, leaving Foremole and his crew to replace the earth gently over their fallen companions.

❧

Supper was served in Cavern Hole. Many had no appetite for food, Matthias least of all, yet he forced himself to eat his fill. So did Cornflower, as she fought back tears for her son and tried gallantly to cope with baby Rollo.

'Eat up, come on, all of you!' the warrior mouse urged his companions in a tight voice. 'There's nothing to be done except eat and store energy. Night has fallen and soon we must rest. But first thing tomorrow I will choose a rescue party. Rain or no rain, we strike north again. I will make that masked fox wish that he had never arrived at our gates, and we will bring our young ones back home to Redwall where they belong.'

∽

Rain slashed down through the bushes and trees, drenching slaves and slavers alike. Tess Churchmouse stumbled against Mattimeo and fell heavily into the churned-up mud, causing the line of chained prisoners to come to a bumping, clanking halt.

Halftail scurried up, swinging his cane. 'Gerrup! Up on your paws, you little backslider.'

Mattimeo threw himself forward, catching the stinging blow that was aimed at Tess. Auma lent a paw to help the churchmouse.

'Up you come, quick, back into line and keep going. It's the only way to stay out of trouble,' the badger advised her.

Between them, Mattimeo and Auma hauled Tess upright and shunted her forward.

'Thanks for your help, friend,' Mattimeo said.

The young badger shook rain from her striped muzzle. 'Listen, I'll give you a tip to pass on to the others. Don't let the running line drag. Hold it in your paws like this, not too tight, and give yourself enough slack to move easily. That way you won't be tripping up so often.'

Mattimeo gratefully passed the information to his friends. It worked well. However, Mattimeo was growing impatient with Cynthia Bankvole. She was constantly weeping, stumbling and dragging at the fetters. 'Why am I being kept prisoner and made to march through the rain and the wet like this?' she wailed piteously. 'I've

86

never harmed any creature. Look, my habit's all muddy and soggy. Oh, why don't they let us sleep? I'm so tired!'

Mattimeo could stand it no longer. 'Oh, stop snivelling and whingeing, Cynthia!' he snarled angrily. 'You've done nothing but moan and cry since you woke today.'

Tess Churchmouse interrupted his ill-tempered tirade. 'Mattimeo, don't speak to Cynthia that way! I'm sure your father wouldn't talk to another creature like that.'

Mattimeo tugged the chain rebelliously. 'Well, how am I supposed to talk to her? She's nothing but a whining nuisance. And another thing, why have I got to be like my father all the time?'

'Because you are the son of the Redwall Warrior, weak ones may look to you for defence and protection,' Tess replied in a level tone. 'Cynthia isn't as strong as you and she doesn't realize the danger we're in. No one has ever treated her in this cruel way before, and to add insult to injury, you start snapping and shouting at her. I know she's only a silly little vole, but that doesn't entitle you to be nasty to her.'

Mattimeo was dumbfounded. Tess was right, of course, but she had no reason to start shaming him within hearing of the others. He was about to start a justifying argument when Vitch strolled up, swinging his cane with a malicious grin on his face.

'Come on, you dozy Redwall lot, keep marching. Be strong like Mattimeo. After all, he's the one you can thank for all this. Slagar wouldn't have chanced within a mile of your precious abbey if he hadn't wanted to steal the famous warrior's son. Ha, just think, you'd all be sleeping safe and dry tonight in your dormitories if it weren't for Matt the brat.'

Tim Churchmouse ducked under a whippy aspen branch. He caught hold of it, swung it forward and let it go suddenly. It swiped Vitch across the chest, sending him sprawling in the wet grass.

The undersized rat sprang up. 'Think you're clever

don't you?' he said, his voice dripping hatred. 'Let me tell you something to cheer you up. Me and Slagar took care of the stupid fat Friar, Mrs Bankvole too, and that dozy father of yours. Haha, we did them good and proper, killed 'em. You won't be seeing them any more.'

Ignoring his chains, Tim sprang forward, dragging the others with him. He was on top of Vitch, biting through his ear before any creature could stop him.

'You filthy lying little ratscum, I'll kill you!' Tim shouted.

Slagar, Halftail and some others came bounding through the rainy curtain and flung themselves into the fray, laying about viciously with their canes, trying hard to pull the furious Tim off Vitch. Mattimeo, Sam, Tess and Auma hurled themselves into the melee, kicking and scratching madly. Even Cynthia Vole managed to get a few nips in.

It did not last long. Finally overcome by slavers, the captives were beaten back into line. Slagar blew mud and stormwater through the mouth aperture of his silk mask as he prodded the cane hard against Mattimeo's chest.

'You started this. You're the troublemaker. Well, I'll teach you a lesson you won't forget before you're much older.'

Vitch lay in the mud, holding his ear to staunch the flow of blood. He pointed at Tim.

'It was that one, he tried to bite me ear off, I was only walking along mindin' my own busi–'

The masked fox struck the rat's outstretched paw with his cane. 'I've told you once before, ratface. Now stop slobbering down there and get up on your paws, or you'll find yourself chained in line with these others.'

∽

For long, weary hours the slave line staggered and stumbled through the rain-battered forest. Mattimeo and his friends took turns napping as they marched, each keeping the other moving straight as they snatched a small respite. Brambles tore and tugged at their saturated habits, which clung tightly about them, making an extra burden to carry. Chain manacles rubbed and wore, cutting through fur to sore and chafed limbs. Paws that had been accustomed to soft Abbey sward soon became raw and pierced by thorns, stung by nettles. Caked with mud and drenched in rain, they staggered onward. No one was allowed to walk. The slavers drove them hard and fast, dogtrotting through woodlands and speeding up when passing through open clearings. Slagar was anxious to get as far from Redwall as possible while the rain kept covering their trail.

Dawn broke over the column. Sullen grey-black skies rumbled thunder, occasionally flashing forked lightning and keeping up the remorseless deluge of rain. Slagar shielded his eyes as he looked upward. Truth to tell, he was as weary as his slaves or slavers, having to lead, run up and down the length of the line all night and keep a constant vigil against trouble breaking out. He signalled to Wedgeback.

'We'll rest for a while. String 'em out between that beech and the big oak yonder. Keep them under that low fringe of shrub growing between the trees. Better feed 'em first.'

The captives were thrown an assortment of edible roots and plants. Water was everywhere, so there was no need to dish it out. After the lines were wound around the two broad treetrunks the captives were allowed to slump down. Half sheltered from the driving rain, they lay exhausted beneath the low bushes.

Mattimeo was jerked roughly out of his slumber as the chains were loosened.

'Come on, mouse, on yer paws. The Chief wants a word with you.'

The young mouse allowed himself to be dragged, half awake and pawsore, by Wedgeback and Threeclaws.

Slagar sat awaiting him in a makeshift den at the base of a big spruce.

'Come in, Mattimeo. You two, get about your business. I have something to tell our little friend which only concerns him and me.'

Wedgeback and Threeclaws departed. Slagar leaned back, the silken hood quivering and twitching as he watched his captive through the twin eyeslits. 'Come and sit here, Mattimeo,' he said, his voice sounding almost friendly. 'Try to keep your eyes and ears open. I don't want you dropping off to sleep just yet. I'm going to tell you a little true story, so pay attention.'

⌒

The dusty path outside Redwall Abbey had been churned into mud by constant rain. Gloomy puddles and stretches of water lay in the depressions of the road. Matthias pulled his hood up over his ears and signalled to the party waiting at the threshold of the main gate in the watery dawn light.

'We march north!'

Overhead, the Sparra patrols took off into the driving rain. Matthias, Jess Squirrel and Mrs Churchmouse headed the march. Mr Churchmouse was still too unsteady on his paws to be in the vanguard with the others who had lost young ones to the fox.

Basil Stag Hare joined them, still nibbling breakfast from a haversack tied about his narrow chest.

'Reminds me of the great rains ten seasons ago, or was it eleven? Filthy stuff, rain. Isn't much fun to drink, either. Sooner have October ale any day.'

Matthias could not resist a smile, despite the seriousness of the mission. 'Stop chunnering, you great old feedbag, and get tracking for signs.'

'What, er, righto sir. No sooner a word than a sniff, quick's the word sharp's the action, eyes front and all that.'

Progress was painfully slow. The ditch to the west and the flatland one side of the path had to be searched, the path itself and the woodland fringe on the opposite side were carefully scrutinized. Whether it was the continuous rain or the oppressive sky Matthias could not tell, but an air of hopelessness seemed to pervade the search.

$\backsim$

At mid-morning they left the path to shelter beneath some trees on the woodland side, squatting to share bread and cheese, passing a canteen of blackberry cordial from one to another. The atmosphere was decidedly suppressed as they crouched gazing out at the western plain, the horizon lost in a veil of rainwater, listening to the ceaseless pitter patter of raindrops on woodland leaves. Each creature had his or her own feelings of sorrow, grief, loss, regret, or just puzzlement as to why this sudden misfortune had been visited upon their peaceful Redwall home.

As always, Basil was first to shake things up. The gangling hare bobbed back upon the rainy road once more.

'Wallopin' weasels,' he called. 'What's all this? Layin' about under the trees like a load of saturated stoats, fillin' your faces like a pile of moonstruck moles, squattin' there with your great jaws flappin' like frogs at a flychasin'. Come on, let's be havin' you! Form up here, chins in, chests out, shoulders straight, paws at the correct angle to the fur of the hindlegs. Last one in line's on a fizzer. Jump to attention like this!'

Basil leapt high into the air, landing squarely on splayed hindpaws. No sooner had he hit the path with a squelch than he shot into the air again with his face squinched tight in pain.

'Yowchaballyhoop!'

Quickly Matthias was at his side. 'Basil, what is it, are you hurt?'

The hare held up a hindpaw. 'Hurt? I'm bally well near speared to death, old lad. Take a gander at me flippin' paw, will you? I've been skewered by a treetrunk.'

Matthias inspected Basil's hindpaw. 'Hmm, it's a large splinter, quite deep too.'

'Ha, splinter?' The retired regimental hare puffed his cheeks out indignantly. 'Splinter, y'say. My life, if that's not an enemy spear or at least a rusty dagger stuck in there m' name's not Stag Hare, sir!'

Matthias tried to keep a straight face. 'Righto, Basil, hop over on to the grass under the trees here. Jess, lend a paw, will you? You're good at getting splinters, er, treetrunks out. The rest of you, carry on north up the path. We'll catch up with you as soon as we've dealt with our wounded warrior here.'

Mrs Churchmouse hefted a copper ladle she had brought along to deal with the slavers. 'Right, form up and follow me. Search both sides of the road and the path as well. See you three later.'

Basil shook his head in admiration. 'That's the good old style. You give 'em mud and vinegar, marm, just like my old mum used to give me. Yowch! Whatcha doin', Jess? Tryin' to hack me old paw off?'

'Keep quiet, you big baby,' the squirrel snorted. 'Matthias, hold him still while I dig this splinter out. Hold steady now, I think I've got the end of it.'

'Ahoo ahah! Easy there, old tree-walloper. Oohooh!'

'Tree-walloper! I'll give you tree-walloper, you flop-eared foodbin. Be still, here it comes. Aha, gotcha!' Jess drew forth a long sharp wood splinter. 'Now suck your pad and spit out awhile, then I'll tie a few dockleaves round it. What d'you make of this, Matthias?'

Matthias peered closely at the splinter. 'Blue paint, it's got blue paint on it. I'll bet a bushel of acorns to a cask of ale it's from that cart.'

'See the trouble and pain I go to findin' clues for you buffers,' Basil sniffed nobly. 'I say, chaps, is that a piece of torn cloth on that bush behind you?'

Jess bounded over and retrieved the scrap of material. 'Indeed it is. Red and yellow, just like that covering the fox ducked under as we came out of the Abbey gate.'

They investigated, searching deeper into the woodland.

'Here's a broken branch. Rain never did that.'

'Some bark's been scuffed from this willow here.'

'Look, axle grease on the long grass!'

Matthias straightened up. 'That's it. They did pass this way, cutting off the road and striking east through the forest. If we hurry we may catch them up before night. They can't travel fast in woodland pulling a cart.'

'But what about the others?'

'Can't spare the time to fetch 'em, I'm 'fraid. Besides, they'd wander all over the show and hold us up.'

'You're right, Basil, we can deal with the fox and his band if we take them by surprise. Let's leave a message at the roadside for Mrs Churchmouse and the others in case they come back looking for us. Here, I'll write on this haversack with some charcoal and we'll stand it on a stick by the side of the path.'

'Capital wheeze, laddie buck. Right, forward the buffs and don't worry about B. Stag Hare esquire. It takes more than a splinter to keep a good scout down, y'know.'

A short while later, the trio had struck off east into the wet woodlands of Mossflower.

14

Mattimeo sat in frightened silence as Slagar undid the drawstring of his silk-patterned harlequin headcover.

'Watch, little one. Before I begin my story you must see this!' With a flick of his paw the fox whipped off the hood.

The young mouse swallowed hard. It was the most horrifying sight he had ever witnessed. Slagar's head was that of a normal fox, on the left side. His right side was hideous! Only the eye was alive and unwinking in the dead half of the sly one's face, the rest was scabrous furless flesh, with the side of the mouth twisted upward into a fiendish grin. Greenish gums and yellowed teeth hung out of the frozen jaw, and the skin beneath showed a mottled black and purple, hanging in folds, loose and lifeless.

Mattimeo was revolted, but he could not tear his eyes away from the awful sight. Slagar laughed, a short breathless cackle which trickled damply from the dreadful mouth.

'Look at me. Aren't I the pretty one?'

Mattimeo's stomach heaved queasily. 'H-h-how did that happen?' he gasped.

Slagar hid the injured side of his face by holding the silken hood to it. 'A long long time ago, or that's what it seems like. Anyhow, it was before you were born. I was a wandering healer fox. Me and my mother Sela the Vixen knew many secrets of healing arts and the herbs, nostrums, potions and remedies of the forest. Eight seasons ago your Redwall creatures fought a great war with the rats from the north. It was woodlanders who betrayed my mother to the rats. They speared her and she was left to die in a ditch. I was wounded and captured by those at Redwall. They held me prisoner in a room called the infirmary. Oh, they said it was only until I got well, but I knew better. A prisoner is a prisoner, no matter what they call the place where they keep him from his freedom and deny him liberty. So one afternoon, while your father's precious creatures were about their business, I escaped!

'Haha, no creature can keep me locked up for long,' he continued. 'As payment for my troubles I took some baubles from Redwall with me, silly little things, bits and pieces. As I ran from the Abbey I was stopped by some silly old mouse, some buffer called Methuselah, so I killed him. It was no great fight; his head cracked the wall and that was that. I was forced to flee for my life, with that great badger and a horde of woodlanders behind me. Deep into Mossflower I ran. I knew it well in those days. There was a hiding place, a small cave beneath the stump of a tree, and I hid there. If I had not been forced into hiding I would have escaped unharmed. Anyhow, there I was, hiding while half of the stupid Redwall creatures crashed around Mossflower trying to find me. I did not know that there was another creature in the darkness of that little cave with me, but there was. It was a serpent, a huge adder. I must have touched it in the darkness because it struck and sank its fangs in me, right here.'

Slagar pointed to his disfigured face, just under the jaw. 'Any other creature would have been instantly slain,' he boasted. 'Not me, though. I must have lost consciousness, because when I awoke it had dragged me through the forest to its lair. I was in burning agony, deep paralysing pain. Somewhere near me I could hear the snake sleeping. Silently I dragged myself away from that terrible snake's lair and out of that place of death. I hid out in Mossflower for two seasons. All the autumn and winter I lay in a den, treating myself with every herb, root, cure, poultice, medicine and nostrum I knew. Sometimes the pain was so great that I thought I must surely die, but I kept myself alive with secret remedies known only to healer foxes. Magic passed on to me by my mother, combined with the thought that one day I would grow well and strong enough to take my revenge upon Redwall, kept me alive better than herbs. I stayed alive to wreak vengeance upon those who had caused this injury to me, to make them weep bitter tears for my pain.'

With a quick movement Slagar donned his hood and fastened the drawstring.

'You lie!' Mattimeo protested. 'The creatures of Redwall would never hold or imprison an innocent creature who had harmed nobody. Our infirmary is for the sick, not for captives. You have not mentioned my father. What harm has he ever done to you?'

The sly one leapt up, kicking Mattimeo hard.

'Silence! Who are you to dare talk to me? I am Slagar the Cruel. My revenge is against all Redwall, and your father is the very symbol of all it stands for. He will learn the meaning of pain. Not a bodily pain as I have suffered, no, this will be a far more worrying agony, the loss of his one and only son. Halftail! Take this slave back and chain him with the others.'

As Mattimeo was led away Slagar called after him, 'Tell your friend the squirrel that you have talked with the Son of Sela.'

∽

The young mouse's friends had not slept. They lay half in and half out of the pelting rain, miserably wondering where Mattimeo had been taken. Suddenly Auma

nudged Tim, pointing to the two figures that materialized out of the downpour. They breathed a sigh of relief,
seeing it was Mattimeo with one of the guards.

Halftail pushed them aside roughly as he linked the
young mouse back on to the running chain. 'Move over,
you lot. Make space here, your little pal's back.'

They wriggled back, as far under the bushes as they
could. It was a bit drier there. Tim, Tess, Auma and Sam
listened intently as Mattimeo related Slagar's story.
When he had finished, Sam gave them the real version of
what had happened.

'I remember what took place. Tim and Tess wouldn't,
they were only tiny infants, and you weren't even born
then, but I was a season and a half old. Though I couldn't
talk much, I could see and hear well enough. If that fox is
the son of Sela, then his name is Chickenhound, or at
least it was then. He and his mother were traitors. Posing
as healers, they acted as spies for the rats, but they tried
selling information to both sides. Like all traitors, they
were discovered. The rats speared him and his mother
and left them in a ditch. Sela died, but Chickenhound
was only wounded. He dragged himself to Redwall, so
we took him in and cared for him. He repaid our
hospitality by stealing a sackful of the Brothers' and
Sisters' possessions and murdering old Methusaleh, our
recorder. Chickenhound ran away and was never heard
of again, until now.'

Mattimeo lay back in the damp grass. 'What a pity that
the snake didn't finish him off. He's still a sly fox, but
completely insane. The snake poison and his desire for
revenge have twisted his mind until he actually believes
his own story and really thinks he is in the right.'

Threeclaws poked his ugly head under the bushes at
them. 'Hoi! Get to sleep in there and no talking, or I'll lay
a cane across your backs!'

Tiny streams leapt and gurgled, rivers overran their
banks, the rain poured relentlessly down on Mossflower

Woods, rattling off the leaves, slopping in the under-growth, spattering summer flowers until they bent their heads under the weight of water. Beneath the shrubbery between the oak and the beech trees, the young prisoners chained on the slave line slept fitfully, knowing that in a short time they would be brutally roused and forced to march again.

∽

Mid-afternoon found Matthias, Basil and Jess still striking east into Mossflower. They were constantly finding evidence that the cart had travelled in this direction, such as crushed leaves, broken branches and bruised bark, but Mathias noticed that Basil did not look too pleased with the situation.

'What's the matter, Basil? We're on the right trail, aren't we?'

The lanky hare pawed rainwater out of his left ear, shaking his head. 'Oh, we're on some sort of trail, old mousemate, but there's quite a few things I'm not happy about, doncha know. One is this infernal rain. I was built for dry sunny flatlands, not great soppin' forests. Then there's this cart. There's supposed to be a band of slavers with at least three captives, though I'd say a bunch more if they'd been out robbin' young uns. Doesn't it strike you as peculiar that there are very few pawtracks about? We've only seen the odd one, or maybe two at the most. Now, they can't all travel in the cart, 'cos there's nothin' to pull it, except themselves. Got me? And if they were pullin' it an' walkin' alongside it, there'd be a lot more tracks of pawprints, mud churned up and so on.'

Matthias agreed with Basil's shrewd observations. 'You're right of course. That suggests two things: either we're walking into a trap, or it's just a ruse to lure us away from the real trail that the fox and his band have taken.'

Just then Jess Squirrel tumbled down from a sycamore. She was holding a paw to her mouth for silence.

'Ssshh! I was climbing a few trees to get my bearings and guess what? I've spotted the cart up ahead.'

'Where?' Matthias asked.

'About half a short march away on the bank of a stream. There doesn't seem to be anybeast with it, though. No sign of our young uns.'

Matthias drew his sword. 'Let's go carefully. They may be somewhere about, so keep low. Jess, you lead the way.'

∽

Silently as rain mist the three slid through the trees and bushes, their senses alert, ready to spring into action at the turn of a leaf. Matthias grasped the great sword of Redwall tight in both paws. Holding it upright, he peered across its double-edged blade, hoping fervently for a single glimpse of Slagar the masked fox.

Crouching low, they skirted a small grove of evergreens, the falling rain covering any slight pawnoise that was made. Jess quietly blew raindrops from her whiskers as she beckoned them to stop.

'See, over there, to the left of the rowan tree.'

Sure enough, there stood the cart, its gaily painted wheels and sideboards spattered with mud and scratched by branches. Over the top they could see the coloured canvas lying heaped upon the cart bed.

'Waitin' orders, sah. What do we do now, old scout?' Basil murmured.

Matthias weighed up the situation. 'Well, we've got it covered from this side, and the stream's at its back. Let's just lie here a moment and keep our eyes open for any signs of life.'

'Signs of life? Say no more, old warrior chops. That bally canvas on the old cart is movin'.'

There was a muted growling noise from the cart bed as the canvas twitched and bulged. Matthias issued orders.

'Jess, you take the right, Basil, the left. I'll go in front and centre. Careful now, if it is anything dangerous then be sure to give me room for a good swordstroke. Come on.'

The warrior mouse gave Basil and Jess a moment to

slip off and take up their positions, then he stood upright and walked silently to the cart, sword held at the ready.

Basil and Jess arrived at opposite ends of the cart at the same time as Matthias arrived in front of it. Taking up a stance with the deadly blade held ready for a thrust and slash, the warrior mouse nodded to his companions.

Simultaneously Basil and Jess grabbed opposite ends of the canvas and swept it off with one sudden heave. Matthias bounded on to the cart with a mighty leap, swinging the sword and roaring.

'*Redwaaaallll!*'

At the last moment Matthias swung the sword away. It struck the iron seatbar, sending sparks showering as a fat little otter lay in the cart with his bottom in the air and his head covered by both paws.

'Strike me rudder I didn't steal your rotten old cart I only wanted to play on it shiver me masts I ain't messed it up or broke nothin' on me affydavet I 'aven't,' he shouted in a continuous babble.

Having said his piece, the otter bounded over the side of the cart towards the river, but Jess leapt with him and caught him by the scruff of his neck. The sword had sprung from Mattias's smarting paws upon impact with the metal, and stood quivering in the earth a hair's-breadth away from Basil's injured paw.

Matthias jammed his paws into his mouth. Sucking furiously, he did a small dance as vibrating pain lanced through them.

Jess shook the fat little otter soundly. 'Be still, you little wretch, or I'll run you up a tall oak and drop you off the top!'

Basil sniffed disdainfully, stepped around the sword and confronted the captive. 'A little water pirate, eh? Right, laddie, name, rank and number. Quick as y'like now and no fibs, what're you doin' in that cart? Where's your slaver band got to? What've you done with our young uns? Speak up, you blinkin' rapscallion!'

The small otter reached behind him and tickled Jess

suddenly. She let go of him with a whoop. He looked at Matthias and nodded towards Basil.

'Stow me oars, 'e's a funny rabbit, that'n. Talks nice, though.'

Matthias and Jess burst out laughing at the creature's impudence.

Basil stalked off towards the stream, muttering to himself in a huff, 'Funny rabbit, indeed. No manners at all these water-wallopers. Shouldn't be surprised if his mother's tattooed and chews shrimp a lot.'

Matthias sat down in a dry spot under the cart and beckoned to the otter.

'C'mere, young un. Come and talk to me. I've got a son about your age. Come on, you've no need to be frightened.'

The little fat otter laughed. He flung himself under the cart and kicked at the axles and wheel spokes.

'Heehee, this is better'n playin' on top of the cart,' he giggled. 'My name's Cheek. What's yours?'

'Matthias of Redwall. What are you doing here, Cheek?'

'Oh, just playin' and sportin'. I like playin' and sportin'. D'you?'

'I did when I was your age. Tell me, were there any other creatures with this cart when you first saw it?'

'Stow me oars, I'll say there was. Two wicked old weasels, they called theyselves Deadnose an' Fengal. I stowed meself in the bushes an' watched 'em, so I did.'

Basil and Jess came to join Matthias when they heard this. Cheek looked from the squirrel to the hare. 'What's your names, you two?' he asked.

'Cheek's the right name for you, me laddo,' Basil snorted. 'You tell us what those two weasels were saying.'

Cheek giggled again. 'Heehee, tell you nothin' 'til you tell me your names.'

Matthias nudged Basil. 'Tell him your name and let him get on with his information.'

101

'What? Oh, righto. Allow me to introduce meself, young Cheek. I'm Basil Stag Hare, veteran scout and retired foot fighter, doncha know.'

Cheek giggled yet again. He was an inveterate giggler.

'Barrel Stick Chair? Silly name. Who's the mouse with the brush on her tail?'

Basil went a peculiar shade of red around his ears and cheeks. He was about to give Cheek a piece of his mind when Jess interrupted.

'My name is Jess Squirrel. How do you do?'

Cheek rattled a twig around the wheelspokes. 'I'm fine, Jeff. How are you?'

Jess was about to grab the young otter and teach him some manners when Matthias gave her a wink and signalled his haversack.

'Mmmm, I'm about ready for a late lunch, what d'you say to a vegetable pastie and a drop of cider, Jess?'

Jess opened her pack. 'I think I'll have a bilberry muffin and some cheese.'

Basil undid his haversack. 'Er, lessee, I fancy a few slices of nutbread and some candied chestnuts. Yes, that should be just the ticket.'

They pulled out the food and began eating with much munching, slurping and satisfied sighs. Cheek reached for a candied chestnut, but Basil slapped his paw.

'I'm 'ungry,' the little otter said, giving them what he thought was a pitiful look.

Basil licked crumbs from his whiskers. 'So you're 'ungry, eh? That's funny, I thought you were Cheek.'

Cheek attempted a half-giggle. 'H'hee, no, I mean I want food.'

Matthias nibbled the end of his pastie. 'Ah good, we're acting sensible at last. Right, information first, food later.'

Cheek eyed the food longingly. 'Well, them two weasels I was tellin' you of, they said to each other: "Let's dump the cart here and get back to the others." That was Fengal, of course. Then Deadnose, he says:

102

"Right, mate, I'm sick of trailin' this old thing around the forest in the rain. If we dump it here and now we can be back with Slagar and the rest by tomorrow night." Then they just leaves it 'ere an' off they goes. An' that's all I 'eard, so where's me vittles?'

Jess covered the food with her haversack. 'Not so fast. Which way did they go and how long ago was that?'

Cheek waved his right paw. 'Straight that way, must 'ave been about mid-mornin' or so.'

Basil stopped him as he made for the food again. 'Just two more things, you little blot. What's my name and what is that good lady squirrel called?'

Cheek looked seriously hungry. 'You're Basil Stag Hare and that squirrel's called Jess.'

'Aye, and don't you forget it, young rip. Come on, tuck in.'

Cheek went at the food like a savage wolfpack. What he couldn't swallow he packed into his cheeks like a hamster, and what he couldn't pack into his cheeks he tried to grab with his paws. Chuckling, Basil rolled him from under the wagon.

'I'd sooner keep you a day than a season, Cheek. Go on, be off with you now, back to your mum and dad.'

Cheek swallowed enough to allow himself to speak. 'Mums'n'dads? Cheek doesn't 'ave mums'n'dads. I want to go with you.'

Matthias shook his head. 'I'm afraid it's a long and dangerous journey. You might get hurt.'

Cheek giggled and rolled under the wagon again. 'Cheek doesn't get 'urt. Take me with you if I give you some more information, good information, somethin' that only Cheek knows at the moment,' he begged.

They looked at one another. Basil and Jess nodded. Matthias thought for a moment, then he too nodded.

'Go on then, Cheek. Give us your good information and maybe we'll let you come with us,' the warrior mouse agreed.

Cheek sprang from underneath the cart and spread his

paws wide. 'It's stopped rainin'. 'ow's that for good information?'

Basil clapped his paws together. 'Absolutely top-hole, Cheek old lad. Top marks for ingenuity. Matthias, I think we need a brainy feller like this if we're to get anywhere. What d'you say?'

The warrior mouse picked up his sword. 'Aye, top marks for sheer cheek. Well, come on then, sir, seeing as you've no mum or dad, but behave yourself.'

∽

The sky had ceased its weeping over Mossflower. Grey clouds started rolling back to reveal a powder-blue vault above, and warmth began seeping through to dry the woodlands as the sun continued its journey into summer. White feathery steam rose in banks off trees, grass, flowers and shrubs as the four companions stepped out on the track the two weasels had taken.

∽

Toward evening, Mrs Churchmouse led the members of the original search party back through the main gates of Redwall Abbey. She made her report to Constance and the Abbot, showing them the empty food bag they had found on the road.

'We travelled north until midday, then we turned back for Matthias, Basil and Jess, wondering what had become of them. When we reached the spot we had rested at in the morning we found this.'

Abbot Mordalfus turned the bag over and read the wording that had been written in charcoal. *'East thro' woods, signs of cart. B. S. Hare.'*

Constance inspected the bag. 'Good, they've found tracks. If ever there were three who could follow a trail, fight an enemy and bring the young ones back, it's Matthias, Basil and Jess.'

Mrs Churchmouse's lip quivered. 'Oh, I do wish I could have gone with them, just to see my Tim and Tess again.'

Constance patted her paw. 'There, there. Don't upset

yourself. We all would have liked to have gone with them, though you had more right than most. Those three won't rest until the young ones are safe, you'll see. Why, one day pretty soon now I wouldn't be at all surprised to hear banging on the gate and find Matthias, Basil and Jess standing there with the young ones looking hungry as hawks and ready for supper. Why don't you go and see how baby Rollo is? He's been asking after you, and Cornflower will have a nice bowl of mint tea waiting for you. Look in on Mr Churchmouse too. You'll find he's a lot better.'

Mrs Churchmouse sniffled a bit then smiled. 'Thank you, Constance, you are so kind and thoughtful. My my, just look at all the mud and wet on these clothes. I'd better go and put some nice clean dry ones on.'

When Mrs Churchmouse had departed, Constance turned to the Abbot.

'Gone east, eh,' she mused. 'Seems funny, taking the north road and then turning east. Why didn't they just leave through the east gate and go direct through Mossflower? It would have got them to where they were going a lot quicker if they really were travelling east.'

The Abbot sat forward in his chair. 'Exactly! If they really were travelling east. I don't like it, Constance. Foxes were ever the sly ones. Who can tell what goes on in the mind of a thief and a trickster. I am not at all happy about this whole affair, though I've no doubt that Matthias, Basil and Jess will sort it out and win through eventually. But suppose they are following a false trail?'

'What could we do about it?' The big badger shrugged. 'We are in Redwall, they are out there, somewhere. Goodness knows where; Mossflower is a big country.'

The Abbot touched a paw to the side of his head. 'They are the doers, we are the thinkers. Do not forget, this Abbey was built by doers, but it took thinkers to conceive the plans.'

'I agree, Father Abbot, but how do we go about helping them by thinking?'

The Abbot rose from his chair and picked up a lantern. 'Sleep, my old friend. Dreams are a good starting place. Dream and think, of Redwall, of Matthias and our friends, of the young ones taken captive and of the evil ones who hold them in bondage. Come and see me in the morning. We will breakfast together and tell each other what we dreamed and thought.'

Constance smiled. The old Abbot made it all sound so simple, but the best answers were the simplest, when all was said and done.

The evening sun sank slowly in the west as the bells tolled out over Redwall, heralding the calm after the storm.

15

With the passing of the rains, hot sunlight lanced through the upper foliage, and white steam tendrils curled and wraithed, climbing between the golden sunshafts to escape on the warm thermals. Mattimeo grunted with exertion as he pulled his paws from a morass of earth and leaves which the dragging limbs of the column were laboriously pounding into thick mud. Chained paws, warm soggy habits and the driving canes of the slavers gave little relief to the caravan of young animals. The running chain snagged between branches, got caught around bushes and tripped them when they least expected it. Sam caught a quick drink of water trickling from the broad stems of wild rhubarb, and he managed to grab a pawful of cloudberries as he passed, signalling to the others where they grew so they could follow his example. Auma munched the pitiful repast as she conversed with Tim in low tones.

'I've lost all sense of direction. All I know now is whether it's night or day,' she remarked.

Tim trudged stolidly on. 'We're travelling south. Where to, I don't know. I've been watching the signs my parents taught me to look for if ever I got lost in the woodlands; moss on trees, the position of the sun, even the earth down this way is different, more stones in the soil. You can take my word for it, Auma. South it is.'

Mattimeo joined in the conversation. 'I know we're tired and worn out, but pass the word along. Keep alert for the chance to escape, Slagar and his band must be as weary as we are.'

Tim shrugged. 'How are we supposed to escape, chained together like this?'

Cynthia Bankvole listened to them talking and began to get very upset. 'Please, don't escape and leave me here, I couldn't bear it.'

Mattimeo ground his teeth together. 'Don't worry, Cynthia. If we escape we'll take you with us.'

'Oh, no, leave me here,' Cynthia begged. 'Slagar would catch me and beat me and break my legs and leave me to die in a ditch, I'd be too afraid to escape.'

Mattimeo was about the ask Cynthia just what it was she really wanted, when he checked himself.

'Hush now, Cynthia,' Tess soothed her. 'Don't you fret, we won't make you do anything you don't wish to do. Listen, there's probably a whole army from Redwall out searching for us. Who knows, they might not be far behind us.'

Auma became excited. 'Of course! Mattimeo's father is a great warrior. I'll bet he's gathered all his fighting friends together and is hot on our trail. I know my father will be searching, though he's a plains badger and I'm not too sure whether he knows his way about in woodland.'

Mattimeo shook his head reprovingly at Tess. 'Who's being unkind now, eh, Tess? Don't you realize we've had a couple of days' heavy rain? Not even Basil Stag Hare could follow our trail through that, and we're well clear of the Redwall area now. Another thing, I'd like to bet that Slagar has laid some sort of false track to put them off the scent. You're only raising vain hopes by talking of things like that.'

'Well any hope's better than none!' Tess sniffed.

A stoat called Badrag strode past them, waving his cane.

'Come on, come on, less gabbin' and more marchin', you lot. The faster you march the quicker you'll get to rest. Move yourselves now, step lively.'

He carried on up the line, urging others on. When he was out of earshot Sam spoke up.

'I think Mattimeo is right. We should be trying to help ourselves and not waiting for others. I know there'll be a big search party out from Redwall, but it'd take a miracle to find us in this deep woodland after all that rain. The only thing I'd say is do the sensible thing, don't try any silly moves, and if any creature sees the chance of an escape, let us know so that we can organize it properly. Cynthia was right when she said what Slagar would do to anybody he caught trying to escape.'

Vitch darted through the bushes. He caught Sam a glancing blow, which was partly softened by the young squirrel's bushy tail.

'You talk too much, squirrel. Talking's not allowed between slaves. Another word out of you and I'll whack you proper!'

Sam's eyes narrowed and he growled dangerously at Vitch. The undersized rat swung the willow cane at him. With a lightning-fast move, Sam snatched the willow withe and snapped it. He flung the broken cane at Vitch, his teeth showing white and sharp.

'One day I'm going to get free of these chains, rat,' Sam vowed. 'When I do, all the canes in the forest won't stop me getting you!'

'That's if I don't get him first!' Mattimeo interrupted.

Vitch's nerve failed him. He dashed off up the line.

'Yah, you won't get loose where you're going!' he called back.

The rat ran straight into Slagar. The fox cuffed him soundly and threw him to the ground.

'Stow the noise, addlebrains! The rest of you, get the prisoners between those two big firs over there and secure the line chain. Threeclaws, come with me. I saw something interesting a while back. Wartclaw, you and

109

Badrag are in charge. Feed that lot and keep 'em quiet. Be ready to travel the moment I return. Got that?'

'Aye, aye, Chief.'

⁓

The captives found good dry grass to lie upon. It was nearing sunset now, and songbirds were shrilling their last plaintive tunes before nightfall. Cynthia Bankvole found some dried moss, which they stuffed between the manacles and their limbs. It was comforting and soothing. Tim shared some wild fennel and green acorns he had gathered on the day's march.

Auma lay with her chin on her paws, staring into the forest ahead of them. She was very tired and thinking of nothing in particular when she found herself staring into the eyes of a large frilled newt. The creature winked at her with his flat moist eyes.

'Little stripedog all chained up. Sillybeast, why d'you lettem do that to yer?' he asked.

'We've been captured by Slagar and his band. Who are you?' Auma whispered urgently as she called the others with a wave of her paw.

Mattimeo prodded Cynthia. 'Keep an eye on the guards. Let's see what this fellow has to say.'

The newt crawled a little closer, lying low to keep his bright red underbelly from showing.

'Name's Scurl Droptail. Too clever to lettem chain me up. See 'em pass here before, fox an' weaselfellers.'

'Scurl, can you help us?' Mattimeo tried hard to keep his voice calm.

The newt blinked and wobbled his crest. 'Why'll Scurl help you sillybeasts? Not lendin' yer my keys.'

'He's got keys!' Tess murmured to Mattimeo so Scurl could not hear. 'We must try to borrow them.'

Mattimeo licked dry lips, then spoke earnestly to the newt.

'Scurl, you must realize our position. We're in danger, we might never see our homes again. You must lend us your keys. I promise we won't keep them. We only want to borrow them for a moment.'

The newt closed his eyes and shot his tongue in and out as if he were in deep thought. Then one eye opened.

'Wotchergot? Cummon, wotchergot, 'ey? It'll cost you, oh yes, cost you. Scurl's keys don't borrow fer nothin' no, no.'

Sam nodded. 'That's fair enough, Scurl. Wait there a moment, will you.'

They huddled together, whispering.

'What do we use to bargain? I've got nothing,' Mattimeo said.

Auma produced some pressed blue flowers. 'They're mountain flowers. My father used to find them for me. They might not be worth anything, but they're pretty. Bet he's never seen mountain flowers.'

Tim spat something out and dried it on his habit sleeve. 'My lucky green stone, though it's not brought me much luck. I'm always sucking it. Look, it's quite flat.'

Mattimeo looked from one to another. 'Anything else?'

Tess took an object on a thong from about her neck. 'This is my seasonday gift from Mum. It's a carved beechnut shaped like a bell.'

Sam reluctantly undid something that was hidden by the long brush of his tail. He tossed it in with the pitiful collection. 'Mum's champion climber tailbracelet. It's made from baked clay and reedgrass, painted three different colours too. I borrowed it to wear for the feast that night.'

Mattimeo unfastened his soft white habit girdle. 'Suppose I'd better throw this in too. Dad said it belonged to old Abbot Mortimer before my time. It's a nice one.'

'Let me do this,' Tess offered. She gathered the objects up and signalled to the newt.

Cynthia Bankvole hissed a warning, remaining frozen in her upright position on watch. Immediately the newt dropped out of sight and the companions lay flat as if asleep.

Wartclaw strode over. He tickled Cynthia under her chin with his cane.

'Not sleepy, eh, missie?'

'Er, no sir,' Cynthia gulped. 'I can't seem to get any sleep.'

'Well, you ought to take lessons from your little pals yonder. Look, they're snoozin' like a pile of bees trying to last out the winter.'

Cynthia was too petrified even to look. She sat staring at Wartclaw with the cane pressing painfully into her throat. Wartclaw gave the cane a hard shove, sending Cynthia flat on her back, both chained paws clutching her neck.

'Get to sleep before I tuck you in with this cane, vole, and don't let me catch you napping when we start to march again,' Wartclaw's voice hissed close to her ear.

He strode off, chuckling to himself and shaking his head. 'Must've had a featherbed life in that Redwall place before we got our claws on 'em. . . . Huh, can't sleep, sir!'

Cynthia sat up partially. 'He's gone now. Oh, do hurry up!' she said, her voice trembling.

Scurl scampered swiftly up and seized the things.

'Hmm, notmuch, notmuch. Funny bell, though. Nice ring, soft white rope, nice on Scurl.' He held the white habit girdle against his red underside.

Tess gave a look of mock admiration. 'Oh, that does look nice on you. Now put the bracelet on your tail. No, like this. Let me see . . . oh yes, hang my beechnut bell around your neck. Very handsome. Tuck the blue flowers in the thong up by your frill. There! You can carry the green stone.'

Auma placed a paw upon Scurl's back. 'Just a moment, where's the keys?'

The newt gave her a scornful glance. 'Don't carryem. Huh, wouldn't carryem, gotter gofor em.'

Auma kept her paw firmly on Scurl. 'How do I know you'll come back?'

Scurl stood upright, his eyes wide and a dignified expression upon his face. 'Stripedog, you be no woodlander, right?'

Auma nodded glumly. 'No, I'm from the western plain. I'm a flatland badger.'

'I be woodlander, tellem 'bout woodlander rule, mouse.' Scurl smiled disarmingly.

Tess turned to Auma. 'He's right, we have a woodland code. All honest and true woodlanders are pledged to help each other and never to harm a living creature.'

Scurl removed Auma's paw and patted it in a friendly way. 'You see, stripedog.'

Before anyone could lay another paw on him, Scurl was away like a streak. He dashed back into the long grass, far from where the chained-up captives could reach him. They could see the red flash of his underside as he danced and pranced about.

'Sillybeast, sillybeast, trusting me.
Made you think I had a key.
Stupid you, clever me,
Scurl has pretty gifts for free.'

Angrily Auma tore up a huge sod of earth and flung it with all her strength.

Clumph!

It struck Scurl, knocking him flat. The crested newt lay for a moment then pulled himself up, spitting out gritty black earth and rubbing soil from his eyes.

'Might have adda key, might have letcher free, but you'll never know now, willyer.'

He scampered off into the night forest.

'What's all the shouting about here?'

Slagar and Threeclaws stood over the captives. Between them they had a small hedgehog. Threeclaws stooped to manacle the hedgehog to the running chain.

'I said, what's all the noise about?' Slagar repeated.

Tim grunted wearily. 'Oh, nothing really. That great

lump of a badger was rolling over in her sleep and pulling me about on the chain.'

Slagar kicked at Auma. 'Well, you won't have to worry about sleeping right now, we're marching again.'

A groan arose from the prisoners. Threeclaws ignored it, and glanced across his shoulder into the woodlands.

'Come on, let's get moving. We can be well away from this place by morning,' he said.

Slagar called Vitch. 'You and Browntooth stop at the rear and cover the tracks. I don't want that hedgehog's family knowing which way we've gone.'

∽

Sleepily they ploughed onward through the night-time woodland. A crescent moon above winked at them through the softly swaying treetops. Mattimeo caught a glance of Tess. She was brushing away a tear.

'Tess, what's the matter?'

The little churchmouse sniffed and dried her eyes.

'Oh, it's nothing. Only that seasonday present was the last thing I had to remind me of Mum and Dad and Redwall. Do you think we'll ever see them again, Matti?'

Mattimeo suddenly felt grown up and responsible. 'Of course we will, Tess. Take my word for it, I promise you.'

'Thank you, Mattimeo.' Tess managed a small smile. 'The word of the Redwall Warrior's son is good enough for me.'

'Stop that talking down there and get in line. Keep moving, d'you hear!'

The little hedgehog nudged Auma. 'Where are they taking us? Do they always shout like that?'

'Hmm,' the badger yawned. 'They're always shouting about one thing or another, though where they're taking us, well, your guess is as good as mine. I'm Auma. What's your name?'

'Jube.'

'That's a good name.'

'Glad you like it. I don't. It's short for Jubilation. I'm the only male in a family of ten females. You should see

114

my sisters, great big bullies they are. When I was born Mum said to Dad: "It's not a female. What'll we call him?" My old dad was so pleased he shouted: "O Jubilation!" But you can call me Jube. I'd dearly hate to be this Slagar fox when my family catches up with him and these rascals.'

For the first time in a long while the friends found themselves chuckling at the young hedgehog. He seemed quite unconcerned that he had been made captive, looking on it as only a temporary measure until his family caught up with the slavers.

Mattimeo dearly wished he could share Jube's optimism.

16

Cheek the young otter was never still. He kept bounding ahead of Jess, Matthias and Basil and running back to chide them.

'Come on, it'll be the middle of next season before we get anywhere, the way you plod along.'

Basil sniffed and shot a frosty glare at Cheek. 'Out of m'way, scallawag. We're following a trail and you're jumping over the pawprints. See, Matthias, here and here. I'd stake me reputation there's two of 'em. Weasels, prob'ly.'

Cheek wrinkled his whiskers impudently. 'Oh, for goodness sake! I know that, I've found their weapons up ahead.'

Jess grabbed Cheek by the paw. 'Where? Why didn't you tell us?'

'Huh, 'cos you never asked me, that's why. You're always too busy tellin' me off. "Don't run, come here, go there. . . ."'

Jess released the young otter. 'Right, show us.'

They ran behind Cheek as he bounded and scampered between the trees in the early morning sunlight. Suddenly he stopped and pointed.

Matthias was hurrying forward when Basil pulled him back as his paws began sinking.

'Steady on, old chum, it's a bally swamp. Now then, young feller m'laddo, see the danger of dashing ahead?'

The Warrior hopped to the firm ground, aided by Basil. 'Wait, I'll cut a long branch and we'll fish those weapons back.'

It was the work of a moment for Matthias to lop off a long larch branch. Jess held tight to Cheek as the young otter fished the weapons on to solid earth. They stood looking at the shattered spear and the curved sword which had been snapped clean through the centre of its blade. Basil gave a low whistle of amazement as he turned the ruined weapons over with his paw.

'Blow me down, what sort of creature has the strength to do this?' he wondered.

Matthias tossed the larch branch like a spear. It hit the bogland and disappeared like a stone in water.

'Well, whoever it was, there were two weasels who were so terrified that they ran the wrong way.'

'Yukk!' Cheek shuddered. 'What a horrible way to die, swallowed up by a swamp.'

'Aye,' Basil Stag Hare nodded grimly. 'Though 'twas all the villains deserved. Hmm, doesn't help us much, though. If we'd got to those two stinkers first we might have found out exactly where they were heading for. Now the bally old trail's completely cold.'

Matthias silenced his companions with a wave of his paw. 'Ssshhh! Don't say anything, just listen. What can you hear?'

Basil's ears twitched this way then that. He faced south with his whiskers aquiver. 'Battle, fighting, some sort of old barney goin' on over that way, I think.'

The warrior mouse unloosed the great battle blade from its back sheath.

'Cheek, stay behind. Jess and Basil, come on, let's take a look!'

∽

Throughout the night Abbot Mordalfus had tossed and turned on his simple bed in the dormitories above Great

Hall. Sleep had eluded the old mouse. With the arrival of dawn's first light he rose and crept quietly between the sleeping ranks of woodlanders. Ambrose Spike snored gently, pausing to snuffle and mutter in his dreams as the Abbot stole past him and carefully lifted the door-latch.

The rising sun flooded through the high east windows, sending a cascade of golden light to wash the west side of Great Hall, turning the old red stone to a dusty rose pink. Mordalfus stood facing the wall, allowing the warmth to caress his back. Through half-closed sleepy-weary eyes, he looked upon the figure of Martin the Warrior at the centre of the huge tapestry, bold and fearless. Swaying slightly on his paws, the Abbot spoke quietly to Redwall's first warrior.

'It's not easy for the body to sleep when the mind is working all night. The hours pass like seasons. Tell me, my friend who never grows old, where are the answers to be found? It is a peaceful and glorious morning in the Summer of the Golden Plain. Who would think that evil is abroad on a day like this? Redwall is safe, yet it is in great danger if the future of its young ones is threatened. Help me to help Matthias. Which way will he go? What paths must he travel? Where is the hooded fox and his band bound for? I am the Abbot, but at heart I am only Brother Alf the pond-keeper. At times like this the burden of our Abbey and its creatures is too much for my old back to bear.'

Mordalfus groaned slightly as he sat down upon the floor, an ancient mouse in his nightshirt. The rays of the warm sun caused his eyes to droop lower as he strove to concentrate upon the picture of Martin the Warrior. Gradually the likeness began to waver and sway in front of Mordalfus. Was it Martin he was gazing at? Or was it Matthias? Though it looked a lot like young Mattimeo. Strange, the tricks that two tired old eyes can play on their owner. His head drooped lower. Now he had no need to look up at the tapestry, for Martin was right in

118

front of him. From far away, as though it were through the mists of summers long dead and gone, the Warrior's voice came softly across the roof of time:

'Seek the Founder in the stones where the little folk go.'

❧

'Father Abbot, I'm surprised at you, sleepwalkin' in your nightshirt!'

'Eh, what, who?' Mordalfus came awake to find Constance the badger shaking him.

'Better not let Sister May catch you dressed like that, or she'll dose you with herbs against the cold. Come on, old feller, up on your paws now.'

The Abbot rubbed his eyes with shaky paws as he allowed Constance to stand him upright. 'Constance, oh, it's you! Ooh, I'm stiff. Couldn't sleep a wink all night, so I wandered down here at dawn to have a word with Martin.'

The badger chuckled as she escorted the Abbot to breakfast at Cavern Hole. 'Yes, I often have a word or two with our Warrior myself, though he never says anything to me. Still, it's a comfort sometimes to think that he's probably listening.'

The Abbot halted. After cleaning his tiny spectacles on his sleeve he donned them, looking over the tops at the badger.

'Ah, but he spoke to me, just before you woke me.'

Constance felt a cold prickle along the back of her neckfur. 'Indeed, and what did he have to say to you?'

'Seek the Founder in the stones where the little folk go.'

'Was that all?'

'Every single word.'

'I wonder what Martin meant by that,' Constance mused.

'So do I, friend. Let's have breakfast and think about it.'

Ambrose Spike and Brother Rufus had prepared the breakfast. The Abbot and Constance took their place at the large table with other Redwallers. Gossip flowed freely as bowls were passed to and fro, butter, oatcakes, fresh fruit, cinnamon toast, honey and pitchers of fresh cold milk. In the bell tower, baby Rollo and John Churchmouse had begun tolling the twin bells. Cornflower passed toast to Mrs Churchmouse.

'Your John is a far better teacher than you or I. Listen, baby Rollo's actually pealing in time with him,' she remarked.

Mrs Churchmouse toyed with the toast and honey. 'It'll take them some time to be as good at it as my Tim'n'Tess, though. Poor mites, I do hope that fox isn't making them suffer.' A tear fell into the bowl of milk alongside the little mousemother.

Cornflower put a brave face on. 'What, those two rascals! If I know anything, they'll have him run ragged. The things they get up to with my Matti and Sam Squirrel!'

'Seek the Founder in the stones where the little folk go.'

Silence fell upon the table. Ambrose Spike turned to the Abbot. 'Funny thing to say. What does it mean?'

Constance shrugged. 'We don't know. Martin the Warrior spoke to the Abbot a short while ago, and that's all he said: "Seek the Founder in the stones where the little folk go."'

Mordalfus stood up. 'I'm going to get dressed. See if any of you can make head or tail of it. It may be a message to help us find our young ones.'

Winifred the otter shook her head. 'But Matthias, Basil and Jess are out looking for them. They must be far away by now. Supposing we did find any clues, how would we let them know, when we don't even know where they are?'

Constance wagged a toast crust thoughtfully. 'Good question. I've had an idea. The rain has cleared now and the weather is good, so why don't we send Warbeak and the Sparra warriors out? There are enough of them, and if they fly off in different directions following the general path Matthias took, surely they must find them sooner or later.'

Cornflower poured milk for herself. 'Sooner I hope.'

Mrs Churchmouse got up busily from the table. A look of resolution had replaced the sadness upon her face. 'Well, at least we can be doing something instead of sitting around moping and leaving it all to Matthias, Basil and Jess. Everybody search, hunt, seek, high and low. Try and find something out about Martin's words. What were they?'

'Seek the Founder in the stones where the little folk go,' Constance repeated.

∽

A short time later, Cavern Hole lay deserted. Paws sounded upon stairs, doors slammed, walls were tapped, and all round Redwall Abbey voices echoed:

'Seek the Founder in the stones where the little folk go.'

17

Though the captives were hurried along, the going became easier. Thick forest gave way to grassy clearings, and rocks were much in evidence now, with here and there a large stony hill rearing out of the woodlands. As they marched, Mattimeo and his friends were able to gather fair quantities of cloudberry and pennycress, supplemented with hard pears and crab apples. Slagar was becoming more cautious, forever watching ahead and detailing guards to cover their tracks from the rear.

Vitch caught up with Threeclaws. 'What's the fox watchin' out for, more slaves?'

The weasel curled his lip at the undersized rat. 'What he's lookin' out for is his own business and none of yours, noseywhiskers. You just keep your eyes on those prisoners.'

'Ha, you're only sayin' that 'cos you don't know yourself,' Vitch sneered. 'Bet you don't even know where we're going.'

Slagar had heard Vitch. He stood still until the unsuspecting rat caught up with him. Then the sly one stepped on the rat's tail, stopping him short.

'So, you want to know where we're going, eh, Vitch?'

The rat gulped and shrugged nervously. 'Er, no, not really.'

The silken mask sucked into a hideous grin. 'Then that's good, Vitch, good. Because it's no use asking this thick shower of tramps and scavengers. They don't know. Only one creature knows where we're going, me. When we get these slaves to their destination, you'll either end up very rich . . . or very dead, if you keep asking about things that don't concern you.'

Slagar strode off, leaving Vitch dumbfounded but thankful that he had only received a verbal reprimand for his curiosity.

'Did you hear that?' Mattimeo whispered to Jube. 'Have you any idea where we're going?'

The young hedgehog nodded. 'South. That's the way that slave caravans always go. My dad an' mum said it's evil in the south. We never go there.'

∽

Shortly before noon they were in sight of two hills. Slagar called Threeclaws and Halftail.

'We'll camp in the canyon between those two hills. Take the slaves up to the south end of it, there's flat rocks with a river running through the middle. Stake them out there awhile, feed 'em and let 'em sleep. I'll stay up this end of the gorge with Bageye, Skinpaw and Scringe, on top of that hill to the left. I want to see if we're being followed. If I signal you, then move this lot south, quick as you can. We'll catch up with you later.'

Two stoats called Badrag and Browntooth walked alongside Mattimeo and the others. Sam and Auma began secretly baiting them. The squirrel and the young badger yawned loudly and stretched.

'Whooooyaawhhh! I'm almost asleep on my paws, Auma. What about you?'

'Whuuuyyaaaah! Never mind us, Sam, what about these poor guards? They've had their tails run off, marching and looking after us.'

'You're right there badger.' Badrag rubbed his eyes and yawned. 'Havin' to break camp and march in the middle of the night, keepin' you lot goin', takin' orders off Slagar. . . .'

Sam nodded sympathetically. 'Aye, not much of a life, is it.'

Browntooth stubbed his paw on a rock. 'Ouch! when are we goin' to stop and get a decent sleep an' something to eat, that's what I'd like to know.'

'It's a shame,' Auma clucked understandingly, 'that's what it is. Look, why don't I mind that big clumsy spear? You sit down on that rock and rest for a while. Sam, you'll mind Browntooth's old rusty sword for him, won't you?'

Sam smiled at Browntooth. 'Of course. Anything for a friend. You slip me your sword and go and get yourself a little rest with Badrag.'

The two stoats were nearly taken in until Slagar's voice called harshly from the head of the column, 'Badrag, Browntooth! Stop yammering and get those prisoners moving. Come on, liven yourselves up!'

Badrag spat on his paws and rubbed them into his eyes as he quickened the pace. 'Think you're clever, don't you, tryin' to get us in trouble with the Chief.' Browntooth snarled at Sam and Auma. 'Move along there. Come on, get those paws trottin', you slackers!'

∽

Matthias was first at the scene of the battle, with Jess close behind him. Twelve hedgehogs were attacking a badger, nipping and bulling from all sides with claw, tooth and spike. The badger was a huge male, even bigger than Constance. He carried a large double-headed battleaxe, but he was only using the long wooden-poled handle to ward off his attackers. Time and again they would charge, hurling themselves at the big badger with savage grunting noises, but still he did not use the battleaxe blade. Squealing hedgehogs were tossed high into the bushes by long powerful sweeps of the handle, and now and again he would lash out with his paw, causing them to ball up and roll away. Regardless of the size and obvious danger of the badger, the hedgehogs continued to fight him aggressively. They were strong fighters. One of them, an old male, would call out at intervals,

'You great stripy varmint, give us back our Jubilation or we'll spike you dead, so we will!'

The badger's patience was wearing thin, but his great strength was unabated as he bared his teeth and yelled back, 'What in thunder's a jubilation? You're all mad. Get back or I'll use this axe properly, on my oath as a warrior I will!'

Matthias, Jess, Basil and Cheek stood on the outskirts of the fight, completely ignored. The warrior mouse turned to Basil. 'There seems to be something wrong here. Woodlanders don't usually fight each other this way. Maybe they know something about which way the fox has gone. I'm going in to break it up.'

'Keep out of the way young feller,' Basil told Cheek. 'Right, Matthias me old scout, lead on.'

Matthias, Jess and Basil leapt into the fray, placing themselves around the badger. The warrior mouse brandished his sword and roared out. 'A Redwall, a Redwall!'

Basil's voice joined Matthias's. 'Blood'n'vinegar, mud'n'fur, up and at 'em!'

Jess's voice joined them both. 'Treetops and timber. Redwallllll!'

Immediately the fighting ceased. The big badger and the twelve hedgehogs looked in surprise at the newcomers. Basil Stag Hare took charge.

'Steady in the ranks thah, chaps! Right, listen out now, all fightin' an' skirmishin' to cease forthwith. Otherwise this blighter here'll chop you into bits with the great sword of Redwall. Now, what's all the jolly old tiz-woz about, eh?'

The badger added his voice to those of the hedgehogs as they all began talking at once.

'He stole our Jubilation!'

'Rubbish, I've never even seen a jubilation!'

'Yew great stripy ol' liar!'

'Liar yourself!'

'Don't you call her a liar or I'll break that there 'atchet over your skull, so I will!'

'I'd like to see you try it, spikebottom!'

'Ooh! D'you 'ear wot 'e called me, Dad?'

'Never mind wot 'e called yew, sticks'n'stones won't break our bones. You just give us back our Jub'lation, badger.'

Matthias struck the steel axehead with his sword blade. The sound rang out like a bell, restoring silence again. The warrior mouse pointed at the badger with his sword.

'One at a time, you first.'

The badger leaned upon his axe haft, his powerful chest heaving. 'My name is Orlando the Axe. I come from the western plain. My daughter Auma was taken by Slagar and his slavers, and I was searching for her when all these mad hedgehogs attacked me without any reason.'

The old male hedgehog began dancing excitedly. 'Harr, so that's it! Slagar an' his varmints, I might've knowed it. He's the one as stole our little Jubilation.'

Matthias pointed the sword at the hedgehog. 'Who are you and what is jubilation?'

The hedgehog waddled forward. He was the most untidy creature, with leaves, flowers, roots and creepers stuck to all his spines.

'I'll tell y'who I am, young feller,' he said. 'I'm Jabez Stump. This here's my wife Rosyqueen and these are my ten daughters. I've got a son too, splendid liddle 'og, name of Jubilation, at least I did have a son till that thievin' fox passed this ways.'

Matthias bowed. 'I too had a fine young son stolen from me by Slagar. I am Matthias the Warrior of Redwall Abbey. Allow me to introduce my friends. This is Jess Squirrel, champion climber and tree jumper. Her son Sam was also taken by Slagar, along with three others from our Abbey, two churchmice and a little volemaid. That young otter is Cheek, both by name and by nature. And last but not least, Basil Stag Hare, retired regimental scout and foot fighter.'

Basil made an elegant leg. 'At y'service, sah! Well, well, it seems that we all have a reason to catch up with that foul blot Slagar. I suggest we join forces. Actually, we lost the slavers' trail, and we'd be terribly glad of any help you could give us, wot?'

The badger hefted his huge axe. 'A sound proposition. I need help more than anybeast. I'm hopelessly lost in these woods, and it was only by chance that I came this far. Bear in mind, though, I'll be extremely useful when we catch up with these slavers.' Orlando accentuated this last remark by testing his axe blades on the side of his paw.

Jabez Stump and his brood drew to one side and had a whispered debate, then the hedgehog returned and offered his paw.

'So be it, we search together.'

Matthias, Basil, Jess and Orlando linked paws with Jabez. 'Together!'

Rosyqueen pointed the direction. 'South, that's the way the slavers always travel, though no one knows what lies beyond the great Southern Plateau. But afore you travel you must eat with us.'

⁓

The Stump family lived in a great hollow beech tree that had fallen on its side. They were not very strong on table manners. Immediately the food was set out, the ten husky daughters threw themselves upon it and had to be beaten off by their father to make room for the guests. Matthias and his friends thanked them politely and carried their portions of woodland stew, acornbread and cider outside because of the lack of room in the hollow log. They sat on a grassy sward, eating and watching the incredible scene inside. Rosyqueen hit out indiscriminately with a heavy wooden ladle as the ten daughters fought, bit, licked the stewpot, stole bread from each other and generally created uproar in the limited space.

'Bless their 'earts,' Jabez Stump laughed. 'They's all fine big maids wi' 'ealthy appetites. You should see my liddle Jube, though. He can outspike the lot o'them when 'e's at 'ome, hoho! It's a lifetime's work keepin' this lot fed, it is that.'

By now the hedgehogs had finished the food and were starting to eat the soft wooden casing that formed the walls inside the log. Rosyqueen belaboured them furiously until they spilled out on to the sward, tumbling and fighting for leftovers, so much so that Matthias and his friends were hard put to finish their meal in peace.

Jabez Stump tossed his soup bowl to one of them to lick as he stood up dusting his paws. 'Right then, we about ready to start trackin'?'

$\backsim$

They set off south, with Rosyqueen and the ten daughters waving a cheerful goodbye.

'You find them liddle uns now, d'you 'ear?'

'Aye, and bring us back some weasels to bully.'

'If we ain't 'ere when you returns it'll be 'cos we've etten the log an' gone a-searchin' for another. Goodbye!'

As Jabez was making his goodbyes, Basil Stag Hare whispered to Matthias and Orlando, 'Some blighter's watching us from those bushes to the right.'

Orlando moved casually in the direction of the bushes. 'Leave this one to me.'

But before the badger could move any further, Jess Squirrel was past him like a reddish streak. She flew into the bushes with a mighty leap and engaged the watcher. The foliage shook and trembled as the bushes thrashed noisily with the vigour of Jess's attack, and there were panicked cries from the shrubbery.

'Lemmego, lemmego! Ow ouch! Eek gurgh! You're hurting me!'

Jess emerged from the bushes, dragging Scurl the great frilled newt by his comb. 'Oho, don't you worry, sloppyskin, I'll hurt you! I'll tear you in pieces and feed you to the Stump family if you don't tell me where you got my champion climber's tailring from.'

She threw Scurl roughly to the ground. Completely

surrounded, the cheating reptile stared wide-eyed at Orlando, Jabez, Basil and Matthias. Using all his agility, he tried to make a swift escape, but the sword that buried itself in the ground at his nosetip and the immense war axe that thudded to earth a fraction from his tail warned him in no uncertain way that these creatures were warriors, not young woodland captives, and they meant business.

Scurl swallowed hard. 'I can 'splain. I'll tell you everything!'

Matthias flicked the swordpoint against the frightened newt's pulsating throat.

'That's my son's habit cord you're wearing. I think you had better tell us everything. Now!'

18

Baby Rollo was singing again.

'Seeker Flounder inner stones, oho,
I know where da lickle folks go.'

Cornflower was searching along the ramparts of the
eastern wall. The old redstone was warmed by the sun
and shaded by the quiet green heights of Mossflower.
She looked around distractedly.

'Baby Rollo, hush! We won't find anything with you
singing aloud like that, it's very distracting.'

Rollo gave her a winsome smile. He held a paw to his
chubby face. 'Ssshhhh, 'stracting!' he echoed.

Cornflower could not help laughing at the infant vole.
'Go on with you, you rascal. Why don't you pop down
and see Mr Spike in the cellars and lend him a paw? He'll
probably give you a drink of nice cold strawberry
cordial.'

Rollo sang lustily as he made his way down the
wallsteps.

'Seeker Flounder inner stones,
I catch a rat an' break his bones,
Give Mr Spike a good hard strike,
For good ol' strawhawhaw beherreeee corjulllllll!'

130

He tottered momentarily on the bottom step but was caught firmly by Winifred the otter, who happened to be passing by in the nick of time.

'Gotcha, you villain. Oof! You're a great lump of a baby bankvole. Hi, Cornflower. No luck? I think we're all in the same boat. Come down off there. It's getting too hot to be searching now. Let's go and have lunch. They've put out a picnic spread on the grass.'

∽

As Cornflower and Winifred sat with their backs against the Abbey wall, they were joined by Foremole.

'Yurr, missis, oil just see'd li'l Rollyo agoin' off down't cellars, hurr hurr. Ambrose'll be a-nappen. Due for a rude awaken, oi shouldn't wunner.'

The meal was simple; fresh summer salad, cold cider, and gooseberry crumble with nutmeg cream. Foremole munched thoughtfully, wrinkling his snout and blinking his eyes a lot.

'Hurr, gotten uz proper flummoxed, 'as yon puzzle. Nor a one yet a cummen up wi' no clues.'

Cornflower passed him the cider. 'It's difficult, I agree, but we must find the solution soon if we are to help Matthias. It's hard to know where to begin. "*Seek the Founder in the stones where the little folk go.*" Do we begin by seeking out the stones, the Founder, or the little folk, or all three?'

Baby Rollo came running towards them with a small canteen of strawberry cordial tied about his fat waist. Winifred laughed. 'Look out, here's the terror back again. I'll bet Mr Spike gave him what he wanted just to be rid of him while he takes his nap.'

They carried on eating and discussing the riddle. Baby Rollo sat between Cornflower and Foremole, continually butting in and trying to show them something he had in his paws. Winifred patted the baby vole's head.

'Yes, yes, very nice, Rollo. But please don't interrupt. Can't you see we're talking?'

Rollo would not be put off. He cut a comical figure,

muttering away as he wriggled his paws this way and that as if trying to hold on to something.

'Cornflow', lookit see, lookit,' he persisted.

Cornflower fed him on a piece of gooseberry crumble and wiped his face on the corner of her apron. 'Drink up your cordial like a good little vole now, Rollo. Please don't speak with your mouth full. Remember your manners. Oh dear, what is he so excited about?'

Rollo opened his paws wide, gurgling at the insect that ran backwards and forwards across them. 'Lookit, li'l folkses!'

All three stared in amazement. The infant was showing them something they had not thought of so far.

'It's an ant!'

'Of course, the little folk. That's what Methusaleh and old Abbot Mortimer always called ants: the little folk.'

'Yurr, clever li'l Rollyo, guddbeast, young zurr!'

'Tell us where you found him.'

Rollo pointed a paw with the ant still roaming across it. 'Mista Spike's cellar.'

⁓

Across the lawn they hurried, into Great Hall, down the stairs to Cavern Hole, through the small corridor at the far side and down the sloping ramp into the wine cellars. Ambrose Spike lay snoring gently, an empty jug beside him. At a nod from Foremole they tiptoed past the slumbering hedgehog and followed baby Rollo through the dim cellar. He led them to a tun barrel of preserved damsons, a huge old oaken affair which had stood there longer than any creature cared to remember. There was a crack between the staves where the withe had perished, causing a slight leak. Rollo pointed to the floor where a tiny pool of the dark sticky juice was congealing. Ants busily collected the sweet residue, trooping in a continuous column.

'Lookit, see, li'l folkses.'

Cornflower clapped her paws in delight. 'Good vole, Rollo. Come on, let's follow them and see where they go.'

The procession of ants marched busily along, hugging the wall, deeper into the cellars, where they took a right turn, following an old passage.

'Wait a moment,' Winifred said. 'I'll go and get a torch. It's very dark in here.'

They paused, watching the line of ants industriously plodding along, with other ants passing them on their way back to the juice. Winifred returned, and the light from the blazing faggot torch she held aloft helped greatly.

They continued down the old passage, which twisted and turned, dry, dark and musty. The light revealed a heavy wooden door barring the way. The ants, however, marched straight on, under the space at the bottom of the door. Between them they tugged on the tarnished brass ring handle. The door opened slowly, its iron hinges creaking rustily. This frightened the ants. They dispersed, breaking the continuous trail.

'Be still and quiet now, give the little folk time to settle,' Cornflower advised.

They waited until the ants had forgotten the intrusion upon their line and continued progress.

They were in a small cavelike room, full of forgotten barrels, tools and old benches. The ants wove a tortuous path, around crumbling and broken casks, firkins and butts, across the room to another passage which was little more than an unpaved tunnel. With baby Rollo still leading, they crouched and followed. The going began to get steep.

'This looks like some kind of disused working, maybe a mistake in the digging plans of the foundations that was left abandoned,' Cornflower remarked.

'Burr, could be, missus,' Foremole called from the rear. 'Oi b'aint been yurr afore. We'm a-goen uphill by moi reckernen. Oi spect they arnts knows where they be bound, tho.'

Sometimes old roots got in their way. With often a boulder they had to climb over, their heads scraping the earthy roof above, both Cornflower and Winifred began to wish for the sunny warmth of the afternoon above ground. Rollo was too excited to think of other things. He followed the line of ants eagerly. Foremole, who was used to the dark underground places, followed stolidly in the rear. They finally emerged into what was neither a room, passage or cave, it was a low, dim area supported by stone columns with a wall blocking the way at the far end. The torchlight showed the ants were climbing in between the mortared spaces of the lower courses, until three layers up they disappeared into a crack between two of the heavy redstone blocks.

Winifred went to the place and held the torch up. 'Well, that's where they're going, but I'm afraid we'd have to be the same size as an ant to follow. Hello, what's this . . . Look!'

Rollo and Cornflower rubbed dust and dry earth away from the surface of a sandstone block until lettering was revealed.

'Aha! It's the very foundation stone of Redwall Abbey. Let's see what it says,' Constance exclaimed. She urged Winifred to hold the light closer as she read aloud:

> 'Upon this stone rest all our hopes and efforts. Let Redwall Abbey stand for ever as a home for the peaceful and a haven for woodlanders. In the Spring of the Late Snowdrops this stone was laid in its place by our Champion, Martin the Warrior, and our Founder, Abbess Germaine. May our winters be short, the springtimes green, our summers long and the autumns fruitful.'

They stood in silence after Cornflower had read the beautiful inscription, the history and tradition of Redwall laying its kindly paw on each of them.

Foremole broke the silence with his mole logic. 'Aroight, you uns bide yurr awhoil, oi'll goo an' fetch ee diggen teams. This be a job fer mole skills.'

When he had gone, they sat gazing at the stone in the dwindling torchlight. It was Winifred who voiced their thoughts.

'What'll we find behind the wall, I wonder?'

⁓

The late afternoon sun shimmered and danced on the broad waters of a deep-flowing stream that ran through the rock-shelved floor of the canyon between two hills. Gratefully the chained captives drank their fill before lying down to rest on the sunbaked stone. Wedgeback the stoat sat nearby. He glared at them, pointing menacingly with his cane.

'Right, you lot, heads down, get a bit of sleep while you can. And just let me hear one move or murmur from any of you, by the fang! I'll have your tails for tea.'

As the stoat moved off, he slipped on a wet patch of rock. Jumping up quickly, he wagged the cane again. 'Remember what I said; eyes closed, lie still, and no chain-clanking, or you're for it!'

Most of the other prisoners stretched out so they could be alone, but Mattimeo and his friends huddled close together. The young mouse lay with his head against Sam's tail, and as they rested they whispered quietly among themselves.

'Wonder if old Ambrose Spike's down in his cellar having a snooze among the barrels.'

'Aye, d'you remember that day we sneaked down there and drank the strawberry cordial out of his barrels with hollow reeds?'

'Do I! Haha, good old Spike. Wish I had a beaker of that cordial right now.'

'Hmm, or a big apple and cinnamon pie with fresh cream poured over it, or maybe just some good fresh bread and cheese.'

Auma gave the chain a slight tug. 'Oh, go to sleep, you lot, you're making me hungry. Right now I wish I had a bowl of my father's mountain foothill stew, full of leaks and potatoes with gravy and carrots and onions and—'

'Huh, we're making you hungry? I thought your father was a warrior. They aren't usually good at cooking.'

135

'No, but my father Orlando is, though he told me never to tell any creature in case they thought he was getting soft, but he always cooked wonderful things for me to eat. S'pose it was 'cos I never had a mother. Or at least I can't remember her.'

There was silence as the young captives thought of their own parents. Mattimeo began to wish that he had never caused his father and mother any trouble. He looked down at his chains and resolved that if ever he got free and returned to Redwall he would be a good son.

'Matti, are you asleep?' Tess's urgent whisper broke into his thoughts.

'No, Tess. What is it?'

'I'll tell you but you must keep calm. When Wedgeback slipped and fell, he lost his little dagger. You know, the one he always carries tucked in the back of his belt. I've got it.'

Mattimeo tried to remain still, but his senses were alert. 'Great! Well done, Tess. Do you think we can use it to open the locks of our chains?'

'Ssshh, not so loud. I'm sure of it. I've just opened mine. It's only a simple twirl lock and the dagger point works perfectly. Stay still, I'll get it to you.'

Tim and the others had heard Tess.

'Good old Tess, this is the chance we've been waiting for!'

'We'll have to leave it for a bit. I can see the slavers lying down in the mouth of a cave over there. Wait for a while, until they're asleep.'

Mattimeo felt Tess sliding the dagger slowly under his outstretched paw. He slipped it up his habit sleeve. Yawning loudly, he turned over and huddled up so he could inspect the weapon. It was a small double-edged blade that ran to a sharp point. Mattimeo inserted it into the keyhole of his paw manacles and twisted a few times. The simple mechanism gave a small click and opened, and he had one paw free. It was only the work of a moment to open the other. He raised his head carefully

136

and looked over towards the guards, but they were not yet fully asleep.

'Auma, can you and Jube keep an eye on those guards and let me know when you think they're well asleep? Tim, I'm going to pass you the dagger. Work quietly, try not to rattle the chains.'

'Mattimeo, it's all very well getting our chains unfastened, but there are seven of us, where will we go?' Tess worried. 'Besides, I can't see seven escaping from here without some noise.'

Mattimeo unfolded his plan. 'Listen, all of you. There's only one way we can go, and it's the best way: straight into the river. We can slide off the bank one by one. There must be an overhang, if these rocks are anything to go by. We hide underneath an overhang, maybe upriver, going south. Slagar will think we have tried to go in the other direction, towards home. Besides, we can't be tracked if we stay in the water. We must find somewhere to hide under the bank and stay there. When all the fuss dies down, they'll have to continue to where they're going. When they're gone, then we can come out and make our way back to Redwall. Agreed?'

So it was agreed. The escape plan was to be carried out.

∽

With Matthias's sword point at his throat and Orlando's axe resting delicately upon his tail, Scurl told the best story that his agile mind could think up.

'They be woodlanders. Scurl tried to helpem. Please be easy with your longblade, warrior mouse. I see Slagar and his villains with slaves, so I say to me, I must helpem, helpem. But no good, weasels drive me off, stoats, ferrets chase Scurl. I could not help woodlanders.'

Matthias relaxed the sword point a fraction. 'Where did you get all these things: robe rope, seasonday gift, tail bracelet, blue flowers? The creatures that gave them to you, three mice, a squirrel and a young badger, are they all alive?'

137

Scurl nodded vigorously. 'Oyes oyes, woodlanders all alive. I throw food to them when Slagar not watching. They give me these and say; "Tell others to follow us."'

Orlando watched the crested newt. He did not like or trust the creature.

'Think carefully lizard,' the big badger said in a low, dangerous tone, 'because if I think that you are lying, then you have seen your last sunset. Which way did they go?'

Scurl swallowed hard.

'S-south . . . Straight south.' His voice was little more than a nervous whisper as he pointed the direction.

Orlando and Matthias looked to Jabez Stump. The hedgehog nodded.

'He speaks truth,' he confirmed.

Jess Squirrel gathered up the possessions that her son and his friends had parted with, and stuffed them into her backpack. 'I'll keep hold of these. If you've been telling the truth, you can have them back when we return this way. If you haven't, then we'll find you anyway and make you wish you'd never been born.'

With Basil and Cheek in the lead, they strode off south through the woodlands, leaving behind them Scurl the frilled newt, who without a moment's hesitation started running north, hoping that the grim-faced searchers would never again cross his path.

⌒

Towards evening, the shadows began lengthening. Above the treetops, Orlando spotted twin hills.

'Tracks heading straight there, old lad,' Basil said, reading his thoughts. 'Betcher the jolly old young uns are somewhere up there right now, wot?'

Cheek had begun to adopt Basil's mannerisms. He struck a pose and tried hard to waggle his ears. 'Oh, wot, wot. Definitely, old feller. Let's jolly well follow the jolly, jolly old rascals, wot, wot?'

A hefty cuff from Orlando's blunt paw sent the impudent young otter head over tail. 'Mind your manners, waterdog. Don't make fun of your elders and betters.'

Silently and with great care they approached the twin hills that reared from the forest floor in the failing light, Matthias and Orlando with weapons drawn in the lead, Cheek rubbing his head as he followed up the rear with Basil.

∽

Slagar's keen eye had picked them out. He lay on the summit of the hill, watching their progress, a cunning idea forming itself in his fertile mind.

Bageye, Skinpaw and Scringe watched the masked fox. They too had seen the searchers and were anxiously wondering what their leader would do about the warlike warriors who were getting closer by the moment. Slagar turned to them, his good eye glinting evilly from the mask as it sucked in and out with his excited panting.

'Right, here's the plan. Listen carefully now, I want no mistakes. Scringe, run down and tell Threeclaws and Halftail to march the prisoners into that cave at the foot of this hill. Make sure they leave plenty of tracks. Then march them straight out again, cover the tracks coming out and head them south at full speed. Bageye, Skinpaw, you come with me. We'll move further along this hilltop until we're above the cave. There's plenty of boulders and rocks lying about. We'll make a great heap on top of here, right above the cave.'

Bageye and Skinpaw looked quizzically at Slagar, but they knew better than to ask questions, even if they did not understand. Slagar the Cruel gave orders to be obeyed, not questioned.

Slagar led them along the crest of the hill, giggling wickedly to himself. Tonight he would have all the fish in one net and his revenge would be complete. They would die slowly, oh so slowly!

19

Late evening shades turned the stones of Redwall Abbey to a dull crimson, the last rays of the sun sending slender slivers of ruby and gold from behind a purple-blue cloudbank. Beneath the ground, Constance sat holding baby Rollo as they watched the Foremole and his team working expertly to remove the great foundation stone. They had bars, wedges and timber props, besides chisels and hauling ropes. The mole leader gave directions as he scuttled here and there surveying the job.

'You'm a-finisht chisellen thurr, Rooter?'

'Aye, that'll do et, zurr.'

'Jarge, set they wedgin's in. Gaffer'n oi'll sloid these yurr greasy planks under. You'n Rooter set they ropes'n'ooks in't stone. Stay a-clear, missis, an' moind yon hinfant.'

A large solid implement which the moles called a 'gurtpaw' had been set up. It was a strange affair resembling a sideways block and tackle. The busy mole workbeasts attached the ropes to a big round treetrunk bobbin and began cranking a long stout beech handle. Baby Rollo gazed wide-eyed. He whispered to Winifred the otter. 'What they doin'?'

'Hush now, little un, and watch. See, the slack's bein' taken up on those ropes the more they work that handle.'

Gradually the ropes tightened and began to creak and strain. The massive stone block moved a fraction, and its base was now resting on three flat well-greased sycamore planks. The moles began shouting in an even chant:

'Yurr she coom!
Hurr she doo!
Yurr she coom!
'eave, mole crew!'

The Founder's stone began sliding out of the place where it had been set long ages ago. It moved at an angle, leaving Foremole room to scurry in and jam two upright sections of green pine as props.

'Look Rollo, see, the big stone is moving!' Cornflower was almost dancing with excitement.

Ants dashed this way and that, stone ground against stone, rope hawsers creaked and groaned as the mole crew chanted their rock-moving song, with Baby Rollo's gruff little voice singing in time with them. More props were brought up as the stone block slid ponderously forward, leaving a large square hole in the wall.

'Cease'n'alt, moles, the job be dun!' Foremole's announcement set his crew to leaning and panting against the gurtpaw, their tongues lolling out as they passed a canteen of cider from one to another. The mole leader stood to one side and bowed low.

'Thurr it be, gennelbeasts, take they torcher an' 'ave a gudd viewen insoides.'

Smiling happily, Winifred and Cornflower congratulated the moles. 'Well done, Foremole. Thank you, team, you did work hard. We could never have moved such a stone without you.'

If a mole could have blushed, it would have been the Foremole. He and his crew stood about, awkwardly kicking the loose earth with their blunt digging paws.

'Hurr, bless ee, marm, it wurr a nuthin', glad to be o' survice.'

With Cornflower in the lead, they made their way

through the hole. The torch was guttering low. Winifred bade them stand still. Moving around the walls the otter found dried brushwood torches in rusting metal sconces. She touched each one with her own torch as she passed, and she soon had the whole place illuminated.

∽

It was a large square rock chamber with an earthen floor. In one corner there was a massive anthill reaching halfway up the wall. They skirted it, taking care not to disturb the little folk. Cornflower's breath caught in her throat at the sight that confronted them. It was a beautiful redstone statue of a wise old mouse, sitting on a simple chair of wrought stone, one paw upraised, the other holding open a stone book which lay in her lap.

Winifred gazed at the kindly old face. It had a wrinkly smile, small square spectacles perched on the end of its nose and drooping whiskers which gave it a homely look. 'By the fur! She seems to be watchin' us. I wonder who she was?'

Cornflower instinctively knew. 'That's old Abbess Germaine, the designer of Redwall. I'm sure of it. She looks so peaceful and gentle sitting there.'

Foremole brushed dusty earth from the base of the statue. 'Lookit yurr!' he called.

In the flickering torchlights, Cornflower stooped to read the inscription carved on the base plinth:

'Germaine, first Abbess of Redwall. I came from home to find a home. The seasons were good to me. Here I will rest with the little folk.'

Winifred nodded in admiration. 'That's how it should be. She looks a nice old cove, sittin' there with her specs an' her book.'

Foremole mounted the base and ran heavy expert paws over the statue. 'Creatur' oo carven this'n were a maister, mark moi word. It be a gurt piece o' work, hurr.'

'Yes indeed,' Cornflower agreed. 'Look, there's even a

little stone ant crawling up the pages of the book. But what are we supposed to be looking for?'

Winifred shrugged. 'Blowed if I know. Seems we've gone to a lot of trouble just to find a wonderfully carved statue. Very nice, but not much help.'

They began searching the chamber carefully from earthen floor to stone ceiling, checking each stone in the walls without success.

'Ho hummm!' Cornflower yawned. 'I think we'd better leave it for tonight and come here again tomorrow. It must be late night now. Come on, baby Rollo, or we'll miss supper. Come down here, you little terror.'

The infant bankvole had climbed up on the statue. He was sitting on the knee of the Abbess, alongside the stone book she held in her lap. Winifred went after him. He tried to wriggle away, but she caught him and lifted him off the statue's lap. As she did, Rollo grabbed at the replica of the tiny stone ant crawling upon the open pages of the book. Much to Winifred's annoyance, it came away in his paw.

'Naughty Rollo! Ooh, you little scallawag, you've broken the lovely statue.'

Rollo held the stone ant up to show Winifred that he had not broken it. There was a copper pin beneath it which had been holding it in place upon a small hole drilled in the stone pages. 'Not broke, Win, look.'

'Moind ee, missis!' The team mole Gaffer pawed Cornflower swiftly to one side and threw himself flat at the foot of the statue. When baby Rollo had picked up the stone ant on the copper pin, something happened to the book which lay sloping downward from the lap of the Abbess Germaine.

The pages of the book, which looked for all the world like a solid slab cunningly carved to represent a block of pages, slipped. A thin section slid out from the block and fell towards the floor. Luckily, Gaffer had noticed it beginning to move, and the fragile tablet of stone landed on his soft furred back as he lay beneath the statue.

Fortunately it was not damaged. Patting him gratefully on the head, Cornflower reverently picked up the delicate tablet in both paws.

'Well saved, Gaffer! This is what we were looking for. Who would have thought it. A stone page from a stone book, covered in writing too!'

20

Auma lifted her head slightly and nodded to Mattimeo. 'It's now. They've all dozed off. We must go, now!'

The dagger had been passed from paw to paw, and one by one the captive companions had freed themselves from the manacles. They looked towards Mattimeo, waiting upon his lead.

Willing himself to move carefully, the young mouse gripped the dagger blade between his teeth and summoned up all his courage. Rising slowly to a crouch, he edged forward along the sunwarmed stone of the riverbank, keeping a wary eye upon the sleeping slavers. Bit by agonizing bit, he crept along until he reached the water. Now he had to be extra careful not to make a splash that would waken their captors. Lowering himself gently into the smooth-flowing waters, Mattimeo caught his breath sharply as his body dipped deep below the warm surface into the cold undercurrent. Holding the rock ledge to keep from being swept away downstream, he nodded towards Sam.

The young squirrel stood boldly upright and moved straight into the water with a quiet confidence. He waved a paw at Cynthia Bankvole, who shuddered and huddled down against the rock whining. 'I can't do it, we'll be caught and they'll beat us. I'm scared!'

Mattimeo gritted his teeth against the dagger with impatience as he snarled against the blade. 'Move, Cynthia, move! Come on, you're holding the rest back!'

Auma gave her a gentle shove, murmuring quietly. 'Hurry now, there's a good little vole. You'll never see home again if you act frightened.'

The mention of home set Cynthia's trembling paws in motion. She stood hurriedly, dashed forward, tripped on some loose manacles and fell headlong into the water with a splash. Mattimeo and Sam grabbed her, stifling her mouth with their paws to stop her screaming out in panic. The escapers froze.

Vitch's eyelids flickered and a weasel lying by him grumbled in his sleep as he turned over. Auma let out a low sigh of relief. The peace had not been disturbed, the slavers slept on.

Tim and Jube went next, followed by Tess and Auma. The remaining slaves on the bank lay chained and asleep. None of them would have had the courage or nerve to attempt escaping; they had been captives far longer than Mattimeo and his friends, and they had seen Slagar deal with captured runners. It was not a pretty sight.

Mattimeo glanced up at the darkening sky gratefully. The twilight would aid them, and it would soon be night. Holding paws and staying close to the bank, the friends pushed their way upstream to the south. It was heavy going. The surface of the river was deceptively calm, belying the cold, tugging undercurrent. Wet habits weighted down by water soon made it even harder for the Redwallers, and they were grateful when Mattimeo pointed to an overhanging rock ledge. He pressed forward, moving slower because of the depth, and behind him he could hear his friends breathing hard through their nostrils as they followed in his wake.

The rocky overhang was an ideal hiding place. They chose a spot where silverweed and purple loosestrife bloomed thick, drooping over the soil-topped rock ledge to mingle with arrowhead growing from the shallows. It provided a perfect curtain. Crouching low at the rear of the underhang, they nodded silent congratulations to each other.

∽

Back along the bank, all hell suddenly broke loose with the return of Scringe.

'Come on, you lazy lot, up on your paws. Slagar says you've got to— Hey! Look at these loose chains! Halftail, Threeclaws, raise the alarm! There's been an escape!'

'Escape! Escape! The prisoners have escaped. Search every nook and cranny, they can't have gone far. Escape! Escape!'

Browntooth ran slapbang into Threeclaws. The weasel held the tender end of his smarting nose as he glared at the stoat, who sat on the ground rubbing his head. 'On your paws, clumsyclod. Get searching, hurry!'

'Oh, er, righto. Which prisoners are we searching for?'

Scringe had been checking the slave lines. He grinned wickedly. 'That Redwall lot, the female badger and the young hedgehog. Hoho, I wouldn't like to be in your fur when Slagar gets back.'

'Oh no, not the Redwallers.' Halftail groaned. 'Slagar'll have our guts for garters if that lot have gone missing, 'specially you, matey. You're supposed to be in charge.'

Threeclaws held his throbbing nose indignantly. 'Who, me? Not the way I heard it, bucko. You're the one who always wants to be boss when he's away.'

Vitch ran about waving his paws. 'Oh, stop arguing, you blockheads. Let's find them, or he'll flay the lot of us alive.'

Scringe stuck out his paw and tripped Vitch neatly. 'Watch who you're calling blockhead, dribblenose. I can see I'll have to take charge here after the mess you lot have made. Wedgeback, Badrag, go back the way we came. No need to go further than that big hill. Slagar would have spotted them if they'd got that far. Halftail,

147

Damper, search up ahead. The rest of you look around here, under rocks, behind bushes, anywhere they might be hiding. Vitch, Browntooth, into the water and search that river!'

Vitch stood his ground defiantly. 'Huh, who are you to be giving orders? I'm not going into any rotten old river. Who can tell how deep it is? Besides, it's nearly dark and there might be a pike in there or something. Ouch!'

Threeclaws stood brandishing the willow cane he had laid across Vitch's back. 'Do as he says. Get in that river, snivelwhiskers, and you, Browntooth, or I'll tie you in a sack with rocks and toss you in there myself.'

With a fine show of moody bad temper, Vitch began lowering himself gingerly into the water, followed by a resigned Browntooth.

'Yah! I suppose we'll have to do it if the rest of you are too scared to get your paws wet.' The undersized rat muttered aloud.

Scringe grabbed a passing weasel. 'Scared? Who's scared? Me and Skinpaw will search downstream, you and Browntooth look upstream, and we'll show you just who's scared, won't we mate?'

Skinpaw looked decidedly unhappy but tried to put a bold face on. 'Ha, we certainly will . . . You go first, Scringey.'

∽

Underneath the rock ledge upstream, Tim Churchmouse heard every word. He turned to Mattimeo. 'What are we going to do, they're searching the river?'

Tess plucked a hollow reed and bit the end off it. 'Look, remember these, remember we lay under the Abbey pond breathing through reeds like this last summer when Constance was looking for us?'

Mattimeo pulled a reed and bit the end. 'Oh yes, wasn't that the time you cut up one of Friar Hugo's best tablecloths to make a tent?'

Sam Squirrel blew through a reed to test it. 'If I remember rightly, that was you, Matti. No time to argue, though. Let's give it a try.'

Holding on to each other and the rocks on the riverbed, they submerged, closing their nostrils and using their mouths to breathe through the hollow reeds. It worked perfectly.

∽

Vitch clung tightly to Browntooth in the centre of the river as they waded neck-high against the flowing current. It was cold and deep. Browntooth shook the rat away from him.

'Gerroff! What are you tryin' to do, drown me? Go and search that side of the bank, I'll take a look at the other side. They couldn't hide in the middle of a river. Look, let go, will you, or we'll both be swept away.'

'Huh, you're not soft, are you, baggybelly? This side is full of overgrown ledges, and your side is nice smooth bank. Well, you can nibble your claws, fattie. I'm not going, so there!'

Browntooth forded his way toward the smooth bank. 'Do what you like, runt. When Slagar gets back I'll tell him that you wouldn't search the river properly, and we'll see what he has to say about that.'

'Snitch, telltale, gabbygob!' Vitch waded over towards the ledge, calling back insults.

∽

Mattimeo could dimly make out the rat's paws through the debris Vitch was churning up from the riverbed as he waded. The young mouse held his breath as the paws came slowly closer. Another few steps and he would tread on Auma's back. The badger huddled with the water waving through her coat, unaware of the impending danger as her eyes were shut tight. Mattimeo made a sudden decision. It was risky, but worth a try.

He struck out swiftly at the rat's paw with the small dagger.

∽

Yowchooch, glubglub. Help!' Vitch thrashed about in the water, losing his balance as he tried to clutch his injured paw. Swallowing water, he floundered about for a

149

moment. Then, galvanized by pure terror, he grabbed the overhanging plants and scrambling furiously hauled himself over the rock ledge up on to the bank.

'Aargghh! Browntooth, don't go near that ledge, mate. There's a big pike under there. Look, it bit me. Owowowow!' Vitch rocked back and forth, trying to staunch the flow of blood by stuffing the injured paw into his mouth.

Browntooth waded hastily across. Avoiding the ledge, he found a part of the bank where he could easily get out of the river.

'Well, they won't be under there, or anywhere up this end, if there's pike in the water. Are you sure it was a pike, mate? Maybe it was one of those giant eels with poison teeth. I shouldn't suck it, if I were you.'

Vitch spat out hurriedly and rubbed his mouth hard, forgetting the stabbed paw in his panic. 'Splurr! Yurgh! What'll I do, supposing that I've swallowed some?'

Browntooth lay flat on the rocky ledge, trying to peer over and get a glimpse of the monster. 'Oh, you'll soon know, if you turn purple and green and start swellin' up. That'll put a stop to your impudence, eh?'

༄

Beneath the ledge, Auma could take it no more. The air from the straw was not enough for her, and she broke the surface, blowing hard and sucking in breath.

'Whooaar!'

༄

Browntooth leapt backwards. Regaining his paws, he trotted off to join the rat.

'Cor, did you hear that, Vitchey? You're lucky you weren't eaten alive. It sounded like one of those giant things they talk about that lives in the bluesea place. Hoho, I'm not stopping round here.'

༄

Mattimeo and the others broke the surface beneath the ledge. Gulping air gratefully, they listened to the cries of the rat and the stoat receding down the bank.

'Maybe I won't turn purple and green, maybe it was just a sharp rock.'

'Are you kiddin', bucko? I never heard a rock sound like that.'

'Then it must have been a pike. They don't have poison teeth, do they?'

'I wouldn't know, I've never been bitten by one. How d'you feel?'

'I feel all right, 'cept for my paw. Ooh, it really stings and it won't stop bleedin'. Look.'

Cold and numb as they were, the comrades beneath the ledge tried to stifle suppressed giggles.

∽

Scringe had the remaining captives chained and ready to march. He shrugged in resignation.

'Well, if they can't be found, then they can't. So much the worse for us when the boss finds out. Right, let's march them into that cave over there, then out again and continue south. Wedgeback and Badrag, you cover the tracks coming out, but leave the ones going in.'

'Hmph! Sounds a bit silly, what've we go to do that for?' Badrag grumbled.

'Because that's what Slagar ordered, numbskull. Now get moving.'

∽

Darkness had fallen when Matthias and his search party reached the foothills of the gorge. Orlando looked about in the still night, brandishing his axe.

'I don't like it, Matthias,' the badger remarked.

'Neither do I, friend, but we've got to take the chance. We can't afford to wait until dawn. They may know we're following and have pushed on ahead.'

Basil Stag Hare pulled Cheek back as he tried to bound forward. 'I agree with you, old scout. Got to take the chance, wot? Faint heart never found fair young uns.'

'Then we'd best stick t'gether in case of a trap,' Jabez Stump cautioned.

Jess Squirrel chattered her teeth angrily. 'Trap! I'll give them trap if I lay paws on the filthy scum.'

151

Matthias silenced them with a wave of his sword. 'Keep your voices down, sound echoes in a place like this. We'll push forward fast and see if we can't spring our own ambush, but Jabez is right, stay together.'

A half-moon threw its pale light down into the hilly canyon, making eerie shadows as it played with the breeze stirring the stunted trees that grew amid the rocky foothills. Matthias marched silently in the lead, the fur at the back of his neck rising stiffly with the feeling of hidden danger. Orlando dropped to the rear and walked with a sideways shuffle, checking behind them as he gripped his huge war axe low on its haft, ready to swing like a deadly scythe at any back stabbers.

∽

Perched high on the tor of the hill beside a large mound of rocky rubble, Slagar whispered to Bageye, 'Where are they now? Can you see them?'

The stoat nodded. 'I can make out the shape of their group. They've entered the canyon now, see, by those juniper bushes, and they're heading this way.'

The Cruel One pulled the eyeslit of the silken hood wide around his eye. 'Ah yes, that's our little friends, all right. Now keep perfectly still and have those poles ready to paw. When I give the order, follow my lead.'

Skinpaw crouched behind Slagar with his paw resting on the long pole that was lodged beneath the rocky pile.

Without looking back Slagar hissed. 'Get your scurvy paw off that pole, you idiot. I don't want even a speck of dust to fall and betray our position.'

The weasel withdrew his paw swiftly.

∽

Down in the canyon, Cheek made a bound forward. Jess grabbed him by the tail. 'Where are you off to, little waterdog?'

'It's a river. See the moonlight glinting off it? Lemme go.'

Basil wagged an admonitory ear at the garrulous otter. 'Steady in the ranks there, young Cheek. This is no time

152

to go swimmin'. Where d'you think you are, at an otters' divin' gala?'

Jabez cast around by the river's edge. 'They camped here, for sure. See, some of the damp pawmarks are still visible. Now, let's see where they'd be movin' from here.' The untidy hedgehog rummaged about, snuffling and grunting quietly. 'There! Yonder cave is the perfect place to stay the night.'

Matthias peered at the dark cave entrance silhouetted against the lighter hillside scree in the thin moonlight.

'You're right, Jabez. The good thing about it is it looks as if there's only one way in or out. We'll get as close as we can, then rush it. Be careful how you strike in there, we don't want to injure any young ones. Cheek, you could come in useful there. Do you think you could get the captives out of the cave, away from the battle?'

The otter withdrew his tail from Jess's paw and gave a salute. 'Of course, I promise you they'll be safe, Matthias.'

Basil nudged Orlando. 'Very good, top-hole, wot? Our Cheek shaped up like a proper warrior to that. I knew in me heart there was somethin' good about that young rip. I was right, give him somethin' positive t'do an' he turns up trumps. Mentioned in dispatches, Cheek, m'laddo!'

Orlando turned to Matthias, his eyes beginning to glint red. 'The masked fox is mine, warrior.'

'Only if you find him first, friend.'

'Agreed. What are we waiting for?'

'Not a thing. Let's go!'

The great sword of Redwall and the battleaxe of the Western Plain swung aloft like twin cold fires in the moongleam.

'Redwaaaaaallllll!'

'Eulaliaaaaa!'

'Mossflowerrrrrr, give 'em blood'n'vinegar!'

Three things happened at once.

The searchers' war party thundered into the cave, swinging and yelling.

Seven fugitive heads popped up out of the water at the sounds of their parents and friends.

Three pairs of enemy paws heaved the poles upwards, sending a landslide of earth, rock, scree and soil hurtling downwards over the mouth of the cave.

21

Beeswax candles glimmered late in Cavern hole.

Cornflower, Winifred, Foremole and baby Rollo sat at table with the Abbot and Constance. The slim stone tablet lay on a folded towel to prevent any damage.

Over a supper of mushroom soup, apple and celery slice, hazelnut bread and hotspice herb beverage, Cornflower had related the strange tale, not forgetting the part baby Rollo had played.

Abbot Mordalfus shook his head in wonderment. 'Marvellous! You found the tomb of our Founder, Abbess Germaine, thanks to baby Rollo. Sometimes the gift of an inquisitive nature to the young can be greater than that of the wisdom which comes of age. I trust you put the stone back when you left.'

Foremole tugged his snout respectfully. 'Hurr, 'deed oi did zurr, she'm all shut in again naow.'

'Pity, I'd have loved to see it, just once,' Mordalfus sighed.

Constance indicated the tablet with an impatient paw. 'Please, can we get on with this? What does the writing say on the stone?'

Winifred threw up her paws in despair. 'It says nothing, blow me sails! There's only a lot of funny scratches on it.'

155

The Abbot studied the strange marks, focusing through the small square spectacles perched on the end of his nose. 'Wonderful! Amazing! A perfect example of ancient Loamscript.'

Constance scratched her headstripes. 'Loamscript, what in the name of fur and feathers is Loamscript?'

'Tut, tut, Constance,' Mordalfus said, without taking his eyes from the stone tablet. 'I see you have forgotten all the history lessons you learned as a young one. Who was your teacher and what were you told about the beginning of Redwall history?'

Constance frowned. She drummed paws on the table-top and looked at the ceiling for inspiration. It was not too long in coming. 'Er, er, it was Sister Garnet. No, it was Methusaleh. Ah yes, good old Brother Methusaleh. Haha, he used to look at me over the top of his glasses just the way you do, Abbot. I remember he often tweaked my whiskers if I dozed off on a sunny afternoon at lessons in the orchard. Ah, but that was more seasons ago than I care to remember.'

The Abbot smiled fondly at Constance. 'Then let me refresh your memory, you dozy badger. Redwall Abbey was founded after the war of the wildcats by Martin the Warrior, who came from the northlands, and Abbess Germaine, who travelled with a band of woodland mice from a place called Loamhedge. Apparently they were driven from there by some sort of plague. Old Methusaleh had a book written by one of Germaine's followers in Loamscript. Now, as I remember there was only one other creature who was clever enough to learn Loamscript from Methusaleh. A little churchmouse named John. . . .'

Cornflower sprang up. 'What? You mean our John Churchmouse, our recorder?'

The Abbot folded his spectacles away into his wide sleeve, chuckling. 'The very same! Cornflower, do you think you could go and rouse him?'

Winifred picked up the snoring form of baby Rollo

from his chair. 'I'll come with you,' the otter volunteered. 'It's time this bundle o' mischief was tucked away for the night.'

They hurried off to the dormitories.

⌒

John Churchmouse came down with Cornflower and Winifred. He nodded almost apologetically to those around the table.

'Couldn't sleep, y'see. I don't sleep much these nights, thinking of my Tess and Tim and wondering if Matthias and the others have found them yet.'

Mordalfus slid the tablet across to him. 'Sit down, John. Here's something that may help to bring your young ones back. It's written in Loamscript. Can you read it?'

John stroked his whiskers. 'Well, it's a long time since I read any Loamscript. Many, many seasons ago. Haha, that was when Methusaleh used to tell me about this sleepy young badger in his class, what was her name now. . . ?'

Constance tapped the table with a blunt paw. 'Never mind, prize scholar. Get on with it.'

John winked at Cornflower. 'Righto, I'll give it a try. Could I borrow your glasses, please, Father Abbot? I left mine by the bedside.'

With the Abbot's spectacles perched upon his nose, the churchmouse picked up the stone tablet, and moved a candle nearer to help him. His lips moved silently and he stroked his whiskers a lot. Sometimes shaking his head or nodding it knowingly, he traced the strange-shaped writing. Finally he placed the tablet down on the table. Cupping his chin in his paws, he stared dreamily off into space.

Five voices enquired aloud with impatience, 'Well?'

'Oh, ah, yes. Sorry, funny how it all comes back to you, isn't it? D'you know, when I first looked at the stone it didn't mean a thing to me, it might well have been written in butterflyese. Then suddenly it was clear as a stream in spring.'

157

The Abbot leaned forward until his nose was near touching that of the churchmouse. 'John, you can be a singularly annoying creature at times. Would you please read us the translation. Now!'

Immediately, John adjusted the glasses, coughed and began reading.

'Through the seasons, here I lie,
'neath this Redwall that we made.
Solve the mystery, you must try,
Graven deep it will not fade.
Somewhere twixt our earth and sky,
Birds and gentle breezes roam.
There a key you might espy,
To that place I once called home.
Take this graven page and seek
What my words in stone could mean.
What can't fly, yet has a beak,
Mixed up letters evergreen.
Two Bees, two Ohs
One Sea, one tap,
And weary without A.
Leave me now to my long rest,
Good fortune on your way.'

Around the table they sat in silence, awed at the beauty and mystery of the ancient verse, until Cornflower shifted her chair noisily and destroyed the mood.

'Thank you, Mr Churchmouse. Very pretty, I'm sure, but what does it all mean?'

Constance rubbed her weary eyes. 'It means we've got a long complicated riddle to solve. Not tonight, though. I'm all for sleeping at this late hour.'

John Churchmouse returned the Abbot's spectacles. 'I'll second that. It's all very exciting, but I think we'd best sleep on it. Tomorrow morning will bring clear minds with a fresh approach.'

The Abbot rose slowly, stretching and yawning.

'Tomorrow morning, then, out in the orchard where there's sun and shade. Goodnight all.'

∞

After they had gone, Cornflower remained sitting at the table with the stone tablet in front of her. Carefully she turned it this way and that, studying the curious Loamscript, tracing it carefully with her paw. Some secret instinct deep inside her said that there was more to the thin stone slab than John had discovered in the writing.

But what?

22

A massive slide of earth, soil, shale and scree mixed with huge boulders that had torn away a section of the hillside from top to bottom lay squarely across the cave entrance, trapping Matthias and his friends tight inside the cavern.

∽

On top of the hill, Slagar and his cohorts were surprised and shaken by the scale of the landslide they had caused. Clouds of choking dust arose in the silvery moonlight around them. Bageye and Skinpaw buried their faces against the earth, scared to move. The masked fox lifted the bottom of the hood and spat gritty dust. He was about to howl his triumph at the night sky when Mattimeo and the escaped captives heaved themselves from the water and dashed towards the mound of debris with shouts of dismay.

Slagar grabbed Bageye and Skinpaw by their tails and dragged them swiftly back, down the opposite side of the hill.

'Ow! Ouch! Leggo, Chief!'

'Arrgh! Yer pullin' me tail off!'

The Cruel One cuffed them soundly about the ears. 'Silence, idiots! Where did they come from?'

'Where did who come from?'

'Mattimeo and his lot. They're down there now, trying

to unblock the cave entrance.'

'I never saw 'em, Chief.'

'You wouldn't, muckbrain. You and your crony were too busy kissing the ground.'

'They must've escaped. We'll go down there and round them up, eh, Chief.'

'Blockhead, there's not enough of us to capture 'em all. They'd scatter away like a shot. How could three of us catch seven of them, idiot! Listen, I'll stay here and keep an eye on them, you two get running and catch up with the others. Tell Threeclaws and Halftail to chain the prisoners up and stay with 'em, then bring the rest back here. Do it quietly, and we'll surround our little friends down there so none of them will escape a second time.'

'Righto, but what if they manage to dig their friends out of that cave while we're away?'

'Don't talk rubbish,' Slagar sniggered. 'Nothing on earth could move that lot. It isn't a cave any more, it's a grave. Now get going and bring the rest back here quickly. When you get back, lie low, stay silent, and wait until I give the signal.'

Bageye and Skinpaw trotted off into the moonlit forest.

Slagar ripped off his patterned silk headmask and breathed deep, his mutilated face twisting into an insane smile as he listened to the young ones on the other side of the hill trying desperately to reach their parents and friends through an impenetrable mass of earth and rock.

∽

Inside the cave the dust had settled. Matthias felt about in the inky blackness until he found his sword. All around him there was spluttering, coughing and confusion. The warrior mouse wiped dusty earth from his mouth and called out, 'Is everybeast all right?'

'Alright? Steady on, old sport. A feller can hardly be all right when he's buried up to his middle in rocks and whatnot.'

The warrior mouse groped about slowly in the dense

161

gloom. 'Stay where you are, Basil. Don't move. We'll get you free. Now, are the rest of you safe and unharmed?'

'I'd be all right if this hedgehog didn't keep a bumpin' into me—'

Cheek the otter's grumbling was cut short by Orlando's rumbling growl. 'Then stay still and stop bobbing about. You've run into me twice. Here, whose bushy tail is this?'

'Mmmmm, ooohhh! What hit me?'

Matthias moved to where the voice came from. 'Jess, are you all right?'

'I think so. A great slab of something got me from behind. No damage done, though. It just knocked me flat for a moment or two. What happened?'

'Kaaachoo!' Jabez Stump sneezed. 'I don't think this hillside would stand still for ages then suddenly decide to slide one night for no good reason. Seems to me as if we've been lured into here and trapped.'

Matthias and Orlando had crawled over to where Basil lay buried and were trying to dig him out. The old hare bore up bravely, helping them where he could.

'I think you're right, Stump old lad. Ha, here's a pretty thing, a bunch of seasoned campaigners caught like shrimp in a barrel, wot? I'll bet a salad to a soupbowl it was old slyboots, the masked thingummy, what d'you say, Matthias?'

'I say keep still, Basil. Orlando, can you put your back to this rock and push it away from him? One of you grab his paws and start pulling while I dig the loose stuff away.'

Cheek sprang forward and tugged Basil's paws with gusto. 'Heave ho, old Sir Hare. Out you come, now.'

'Yaggh! Beastly young blighter, you're standin' on me ear!'

Orlando put his strong back against the rock that was trapping Basil. He gave a mighty grunt as he threw his weight against it. 'Grrumph! That's it. Hurry now, I can't hold this much longer.'

Jabez and Jess helped Cheek. As Matthias dug furiously, they gave a good long heave. Basil popped out like a cork. The big badger let the rock go. There was another cloud of dust and a rattling of pebbles as the heap of hillside rubble settled.

Basil stamped his paws experimentally. 'Bit stiff an' all that. Still workin' hunky dory, though. Well, what a load of old ninnies we are, eh, lettin' ourselves get bamboozled like that.'

'Let's not start blaming ourselves,' Matthias cut in sharply. 'What we did seemed a good idea at the time. The thing now is, how do we get out of this fix? Has any creature got flint or tinder to make light?'

Jess squirrel wiped a paw across her brow. 'Not a very good idea, Matthias. Haven't you noticed it's getting quite warm in here? That means we're using up the air. If we start making fire we'll use it up double quick and suffocate.'

Orlando slumped back against the cave wall. 'You're right, Jess. Those slavers meant this to be our tomb and they've done a good job of it, worse luck. Give me a moment or two to rest, then I'll see if there's any possibility of digging our way out, or at least making a small hole so that fresh air can come in.'

'It's this dark I can't stand, not bein' able to see anything, all hot an' covered in dusty muck with a whole hillside on top of us. I can't even see me paw in front of my eyes!' Cheek's voice sounded close to panic.

Basil patted him firmly. 'Now then, young otter m'lad, chin up. There's nothin' to get in a funk over. When I was with the border patrol we were in lots of tighter places than this one, wot? Never say die, Cheek. Ha! I'll betcha we'll be out of here before the night's over. Don't worry young waterdog, you'll be wallopin' about in the river by tomorrow night.'

Cheek sat close to Basil and waited while Jess and Orlando took first shift to dig a way out of the landslide.

Around the friends the air seemed to grow darker and heavier as they lay trapped in the bowels of the hill.

∽

On the outside, Mattimeo scrabbled furiously at the loose shale and earth, alongside Auma. The others dodged around the heap, trying to find a likely spot to dig. Auma grunted and strained as she tried to dislodge a huge boulder.

'It was my father, Orlando the Axe,' she told Mattimeo. 'I'd know his battle cry anywhere. Oh, please let him be all right.'

Mattimeo stopped digging for a moment as he watched the loose earth slide swiftly in to take the place of the boulder Auma was moving.

'I saw my father, and heard him too. Even in the night, I think I recognized Jess and Basil. There were a few others too, but it was all over too fast to see who they were. Bah! We're getting nowhere like this. Look, every time you dig out a bit, the earth slides in and fills the gap again.'

Cynthia Bankvole sat down and let the loose earth run through her paws. 'It's no use, what can we do against all this? It would take ten teams of moles a full season to move all this earth, and some of these boulders look as big as a cottage.'

Sam Squirrel shouldered her roughly aside. 'Doesn't matter. My mum's in there, so we've got to keep trying. Come on, Cynthia, up on your paws and get digging.'

'Jube, look about for a big branch or something I can use as a lever against these rocks,' Auma called out. 'How are you doing, Matti?'

Mattimeo straightened up. 'Not very well. I suggest we all dig in the one spot.'

Tess came hurrying over. 'Look, I've found some flat slatey pieces. They'll do to dig with.'

∽

Dawn's first light glimmered in the east, a soft rosy glow dispersing the night from the deep greenery of Moss-

164

flower Woods. The sun rose steadily, drying the dew from leaf and flower as the young woodlanders dug wearily in the shifting mass of debris.

Slagar lay on top of the gorge, watching them as he murmured, 'Keep digging, my little slaves. Tire yourselves out so that you won't run and dodge. I can see my slavers threading their way through the forest yonder. They'll soon be here. Dig away, you young fools. You'll never see your friends or parents again.'

23

In the summer peace of the beautiful old Redwall Abbey orchard, a group of creatures sat taking alfresco breakfast among the fruit trees. Abbot Mordalfus presided.

'Let us put our minds together, friends. If we wish to help Matthias and our young ones, we must solve the riddle of this poem.' The Abbot tapped the stone tablet. 'Where does the poetry end and the clues begin?'

John Churchmouse put down his bowl of mint tea and placed his paw in a very certain manner between two lines of verse.

'Right there, I'm sure of it. Listen:

"Through the seasons here I lie,
'neath this Redwall that we made.
solve the mystery, you must try. . . ."'

John tapped his paw down decisively. 'There, right there. I couldn't sleep for thinking about it. Here's where the real clues begin:

"Graven deep it will not fade.
Somewhere twixt our earth and sky,
Birds and gentle breezes roam.
There's a key you might espy,
To that place I once called home."'

166

The Abbot toyed with a slice of apple. 'I think you're right, John. In fact, part of the answer leapt out at me as you recited those words. It was the line that went: *"To that place I once called home."* Right, if this was written by old Abbess Germaine, then the place that she called home before she built Redwall was Loamhedge. However, that was all so far away and long ago in our history that the location of Loamhedge has been forgotten long before my time and that of many Abbots and Abbesses before me.'

John nodded agreement. 'Of course, old Loamhedge. That must be the place where the fox is taking our young ones, there or somewhere in the Loamhedge area. I can recall asking Brother Methusaleh where Loamhedge was, but even he didn't know. How are we supposed to find it?'

Cornflower pointed at the stone tablet. 'Obviously the answer is in the rhyme, because it says: *"Take this graven page and seek. What my words in stone could mean."* Surely that's a start.'

'Burr, 'scuse me marm, oi thinks it be afore that, even: *"Somewhere twixt our earth'n'sky, burds an' gentle breezes roam."* Whurrs that?'

'That's where we might espy the key, accordin' to that there,' Ambrose Spike chuckled. 'Best look about for a key floatin' round in midair. Silly, I calls it.'

John looked severely over the top of his glasses. 'Silly it may sound, but it's a serious business, Spike.'

'No need to get huffy, dear,' Mrs Churchmouse interrupted hastily. 'Let's all look up and see what we discover between earth and sky.'

Winifred Otter summed it up in a word, 'Treetops.'

They sat looking at the treetops. Mrs Churchmouse was just beginning to regret her foolish idea when Cornflower said, 'The top of our Abbey, maybe?'

A slow smile spread across the Abbot's face. 'Very clever, Cornflower. What better place for our Founder to leave a clue than at the top of the very building she designed. So, I'm looking up at our Abbey. Tell me, somebeast, what am I looking for?'

The answers came back.

'Something graven deep?'

'Words in stone?'

'Something that can't fly but has a beak?'

'How about mixed-up letters evergreen?'

'Two Bees and two Ohs?'

'What does an Oh look like?'

'Well, I know what two bees would look like.'

John Churchmouse banged his beaker upon a wooden platter. 'Quiet! Quiet, please! All this shouting is getting us nowhere. Cornflower, will you kindly stop baby Rollo playing with that stone tablet!'

Cornflower sat upon the grass with Rollo, who was running his paws over the slim stone.

Mrs Churchmouse tried to pacify her husband. 'Don't shout, dear. I'm sure Rollo won't harm it.'

Cornflower was shaking with silent laughter. John was not amused. 'I'm sorry, but I fail to see what's so funny about it, Cornflower.'

'I'm not laughing at you, John, I'm laughing at baby Rollo. Here we are puzzling our brains out and Rollo has found the answer again.'

'Where?'

'Right here on this stone,' Cornflower explained. 'Come and look. I didn't notice it until I watched Rollo passing his paws over the writing. Watch him, you'll see he stops his paw every time he finds a letter in green.'

The Abbot hurried over to watch Rollo. 'By the fur, you're right, Cornflower. Good baby, Rollo. *Mixed up letters evergreen*. Come on, little one, show me. Your eyes are better than mine. John, get that charcoal and parchment. Take the letters down as I call them out to you.'

Obligingly Rollo began dabbing at various letters with his chubby little paw. Mordalfus relayed them to John Churchmouse. 'First one letter B, second one letter B.'

Ambrose Spike scratched his snout. 'Will somebeast

tell me what in the name of acorns is going on here? Two green bees, letters graven in stone, I always thought bees were yellow and brown.'

The Abbot looked skyward patiently. 'Come here, Ambrose, let me show you. Look at the poem. Can you see that certain letters have been filled in with green vegetable dye? Right. I've just given John the first two, they are letter Bs not actual bees. See, here are more green letters.'

It was still all a bit above Ambrose. He stared at the letters, shook his head and trundled off. 'Huh, I've got work to attend to in the cellar. I can't hang about playin' word games. You can't drink stone messages, but good October ale, that's a different matter. You lot'd look sick without my casks of berry wine, mark my words!'

John Churchmouse glared over the top of his glasses at the retreating cellar keeper.

'Now, where were we? Two letter Bs. What's next Abbot?'

'Two letter Os, John. Wait, I think Rollo has found more. Yes, there's a letter C. Well done, young un. Any more?'

Baby Rollo was enjoying himself. He waved his paw dramatically, stabbing it down as the Abbot called out the letters he indicated. 'Take these down, John. T, A, P, W, E, R, and a letter Y. There I've translated the old letters pretty well. Is that the lot, Rollo?'

The infant waved to them and pursued Ambrose to the wine cellar.

'Aye, that's it,' Cornflower chuckled. 'What have we got, John?'

'B, B, O, O, C, T, A, P, W, E, R, Y. Twelve letters in all, though they're fairly well jumbled. I can't make head nor tail of it. Why couldn't Abbess Germaine have written what she meant clearly?'

The Abbot stood up and stretched. 'Because then it would not have been a secret. Those letters are the key. Once we get them in the right order, we'll know what the next move is to be.'

In the darkness of the cave, Orlando choked and coughed as he sought wearily about until his paw touched Matthias.

'Listen, friend,' Orlando said, keeping his voice low so that the others would not hear, 'I don't know how much rubble has fallen across this cave mouth, but I think we both know it's far too much for us to move. We're becoming weaker, Matthias. The air is running out in here. I keep feeling dizzy and wanting to lie down to sleep.'

Matthias clasped the big badger's paw. 'Same here, Orlando. But don't let the others know. Young Cheek will only panic and Basil will start jumping about trying to think up schemes to get us out. I know it's hard, but we'll just have to sit here and try not to fall asleep.'

'Do you think there's anybeast outside?'

'The only ones I can think of are Slagar and his gang. We'd be in no condition to fight them, even supposing we could get out.'

'I wish we had a strong mole with us.'

'Aye, and if wishes were fishes there'd be no room in the river for water.'

'I'm sorry, Matthias. I was only thinking aloud.'

'Pay no heed to me, Orlando. It's this terrible darkness, the heat and the lack of air—'

'And this confounded dust in me ears, laddie buck!'

'Basil! You were listening to us.'

'Say no more, old lad, say no more. Backs to the wall and all that, I say, I don't suppose anyone's got a bite to eat stowed on 'em?'

Even young Cheek managed a faint laugh. 'Trust you to think of food at a time like this, mate.'

'Sorry, Basil, we left the supplies outside so they wouldn't hamper us in the ambush,' Jess Squirrel called from the far side of the cave.

Jabez Stump yawned. 'Some ambush, eh? We've got ourselves rightly scuttled, you mark my spikes. Best thing is to sit quiet, think hard and breathe light.'

A gloomy silence fell as they acted on the hedgehog's good advice.

∽

Mattimeo dug and scrabbled wildly at the huge ever moving landslide. The sun was reaching its zenith and the digging was becoming more heated and futile. Grunting with exertion, he straightened up and passed a paw across his brow as a pile of loose earth rattled around his ears. Mattimeo's quick temper snapped. He seized a pawful of pebbles and flung them at Tim, who was digging higher up the pile.

'By the fur! Can't you stop loading muck down on top of me every chance you get?' Mattimeo grumbled.

Tim straightened up. 'Sorry.'

'Sorry's not good enough,' Mattimeo snorted. 'Just watch where you're chucking that stuff, will you!'

Tess passed Mattimeo a broad leaf containing water she had scooped from the stream. 'Here, drink this and cool down. We'll get nowhere yelling at each other.'

Mattimeo dashed the leaf from her paw, his face livid with anger. 'It's all right for you to talk, your father isn't buried in there, is he? Where in the name of the claw has that hedgehog got to? It's going to take him half a season to find a branch so we can lever these rocks out—'

'Over here, little hero. We've got your friends over here!'

Bageye and Skinpaw had Jube and Cynthia tied by their necks on a rope.

Still flushed with temper, Mattimeo grabbed a chunk of rock. 'Come on Auma, Sam, let's charge them!'

They had reached the lower edge of the rubble when Slagar's voice rang out mockingly behind them, 'My, my, aren't we the bold ones? Go ahead, try it.'

Mattimeo whirled about to face Slagar and half a dozen others who had circled round to join him. They were all heavily armed. The young mouse, still driven by rage, hurled a rock. Slagar dodged it easily and drew out his fearsome weapon. The three leather thongs whirred as

171

he swung them in a circle, the metal balls at the ends of the thongs clacking together viciously. The masked fox pointed at Tess Churchmouse.

'Drop that rock, mouse. Any of you runaways make a move and I'll smash little missie's skull to a pulp. I never miss.'

Tess closed her eyes tight and clasped her paws together. 'Run Mattimeo! Run for your life back to Redwall. Bring help!'

'Go on, do as she says,' Slagar sniggered with glee. 'After I've killed her, I'll kill you. To slay the Warrior of Redwall and his son in such a short time would make my revenge complete.'

The rock fell from Mattimeo's open paw. Hot tears sprang to his eyes as he hung his head in defeat.

They were roughly herded together by Bageye and Skinpaw. The rope was looped about the neck of each of the friends as Bageye bound their paws in front with thongs.

Slagar nodded towards the south woodland fringe. 'Right, let's go. Oh, you can take your time now, there's nobody following us any more. Hahahaha!'

Auma made a strangled noise, halfway between a growl and a sob. Dragging the captives with her, she fell back upon the huge mound of rubble and began digging furiously. It took all the slavers to drag her off.

Beating with canes and rope ends, they bludgeoned the little group off along the south trail through the summer woodlands.

Realization of what had taken place hit Sam Squirrel like a bolt, and tears trickled from his eyes. They all cried.

All except Mattimeo. His eyes were dry. Jaws clenched tight, he strode upright, ignoring all about him but Slagar. Never once did his gaze leave the figure of the masked fox.

Slagar dropped back a pace to talk to Skinpaw.

'How far off are the others?' he asked.

'Within two marches of the great cliffs. I've told them to wait at the foothills until we arrive, Chief.'

'Good. It shouldn't be too difficult to catch them up. What are you staring at, mouse?'

'You should have killed me back at the canyon.' Mattimeo's voice was flat and contemptuous.

Slagar eyed the bold young mouse and shook his head. 'I've killed your father. His sword is buried with him. That's enough for one day's work. You, I will let live to suffer.'

Mattimeo stopped marching. His friends stopped also. The young mouse's eyes were hard with scorn.

'Then you're not only a cowardly murdering scum, you're a fool. Because from now on I live with one purpose only: to kill you.'

Slagar was taken aback by the determination and loathing that emanated from Mattimeo. He glared savagely at him, trying to frighten the young mouse into submission. Mattimeo glared back, completely unafraid. He was a different mouse altogether.

Snatching the willow cane from Skinpaw, the Cruel One struck out, lashing Mattimeo several times. The cane snapped. Slagar stood shaking, breathing hard through the silken mask.

Mattimeo curled his lip defiantly. He had not even felt the blows. 'Get yourself another cane and try harder, half-face!'

'Skinpaw, Bageye! Keep this one marching up front with you. Move!'

Mattimeo was dragged off to the front of the column. Slagar marched behind, visibly shaken, glad that he could not feel the young mouse's eyes boring into him from behind.

24

Afternoon tea in Cavern Hole was served amid a great buzz of excitement. Copies of the twelve letters discovered by baby Rollo had been distributed, and there was a prize of a pink iced woodland plum and spice cake baked by the Abbot himself. John Churchmouse was strongly fancied to win it, though Abbot Mordalfus was having a serious try. Being the proud maker of such a cake, he wanted to keep it and admire it awhile. Baking was the Father Abbot's latest accomplishment. Ever since the making of his Redcurrantwall Abbot Alf Cake, he had been longing to try his paw at cake-making again. The moles formed a joint crew, and they sat scratching their velvety heads as they gazed at the twelve letters.

B B O O C T A P W E R Y.

'Burr, all oopside backwards, if'n you arsken oi.'

'Hurr, quit talken an' get thinkin, Jarge, or you'll never win yon pinkice cake.'

Cornflower had joined up with baby Rollo and Mrs Churchmouse. Winifred, Brother Sedge and Ambrose Spike sat together. In various corners of the room small groups kept hard at it, trying to solve the mystery of the twelve letters. Every once in a while some creature would approach the Abbot with a possible solution. Mordalfus in his position as judge looked each one over

174

with a discerning eye. 'Hmm, *Baby power to be*. Sorry, Sister May. As you see, there's only two letter Bs in the puzzle and you've used three. Next. Ah, Winifred, let's see your entry. *Coop Water Byb*? What in the name of acorns is that supposed to mean? No, I can't accept that one. Ah, John, well now we'll see who has won my beautiful cake.'

John Churchmouse peered expectantly over the top of his glasses as the Abbot read out his solution.

'*Cot Abbey prow*. Strange words, John. Have you any reason for your answer?'

John polished his glasses, looking slightly sheepish. 'Not really, Abbot. I tried several combinations, but this looked the most likely.'

Mordalfus put John's entry to one side. 'Well, who knows? We'll keep it as a possibility. Thank you, John.'

'Thank you, Abbot. Er, have *you* tried to solve it yet?'

'No, I think it only fair that I stay as judge. However, if it isn't solved tonight then you can be judge tomorrow and I'll have a try then.'

'We gorrit! We gorrit!' Baby Rollo ran forward, waving a parchment. He stumbled, fell, scrambled up and placed the crumpled entry in the Abbot's lap.

The kindly old mouse's eyes twinkled as he lifted Rollo on to the arm of his chair. 'You're a clever fellow, Rollo. Did you solve this all by yourself?'

Cornflower and Mrs Churchmouse winked at the Abbot. 'Of course he did. We couldn't have done without him.'

Mordalfus nodded wisely. 'Well, let's see what you've got. *Abbey top crow*. Ha, now this really looks like something we can investigate. *Abbey top crow*, eh? Good. Well done, baby Rollo, not to mention your two helpers, of course. I think the cake goes to the three of you.'

Cornflower, Mrs Churchmouse and Rollo went into whispered conference, finally emerging with the decision that everyone be given a small slice, much to the delight of all.

After tea, the Abbey dwellers gathered on the sward in front of Redwall. Shading their eyes, they gazed up to the high roof. Queen Warbeak and her Sparra warriors were circling the spires, turrets and crenellations at the Abbot's request. There was not long to wait. Shortly Warbeak came zooming down at great speed and perched on a windowsill to make her report.

'Round top of roof, fourbirds, fourbirds,' she told them.

The Abbot could hardly suppress his excitement. 'What sort of birds? How high? Where?'

The Sparra Queen closed her eyes, remembering the locations and types of bird. 'Backa roof, hawkbird. This side, gooseflier. Other side, owlbird. That side, crowbird. All wormbird stone, you see.'

Cornflower took a few paces back and pointed upwards. 'I can see a wild goose carved this side. I can just make it out. Look, it leans outwards with its wings spread. Funny, I've never noticed it before.'

The Abbot settled his paws into his wide sleeves. 'There are a great many things about Redwall that we do not know. It is an ancient and mysterious place. The longer I live here the more I see how everything our ancestors built into it has a story or a reason. It is all part of the Mossflower tradition and history. The goose is facing west towards the sunset and the great sea. That is the way they travel each late season. I think the hawk must face north. It is a warlike bird, and the northlands were always troubled by war. The owl, I guess, will face east to the dense forest and the rising sun. That only leaves one way for the crow to face.'

The party walked round to the remaining side of the Abbey. John Churchmouse adjusted his glasses and pointed.

'South, the crow points south! What can't fly, yet has a beak? The crow made of stone, of course. We've found it! If only Jess or Sam Squirrel were here, they could climb up and investigate it.'

Queen Warbeak puffed out her feathers. 'Why squirrel climb? Sparra fly, me 'vestigate um crow stone.'

The Sparra Queen was off like an arrow. From below, she looked like a small black speck as she hovered around the crow statue, which protruded from the high eaves. Warbeak did not stay long. She fluttered about, then winged down, landing with a sprightly hop on the gravelled path.

'Much wormsign, go this way, go that way, up, down, round, round.'

'Just as I thought,' John Churchmouse groaned. 'There's writing on the statue, but sparrows cannot read at all.'

Mardalfus nudged him. 'Hush, John. We don't want to offend Queen Warbeak. She's doing all she can to help. We'll just have to think of a way to get a copy of that writing down here.'

Warbeak watched them talking. She knew what they were discussing. Cocking her head to one side, she winked her fierce bright eye. 'How you do that. Sparra no can carry um mouse, too wormfat, too big. Sparra no read um wormsign like old mouse Abbot do with book. Plenty problem.'

The Abbot stroked his whiskers thoughtfully. 'Indeed it is, Queen Warbeak, but we must help Matthias.'

'Teach those birds to do a rubbin'.' Ambrose Spike stepped forward with parchment and charcoal sticks. 'I've often done it meself on some of the old barrel carvin's in the wine cellar. Pretty patterns they got carved on 'em.'

Cornflower clapped her paws together. 'Of course, that's the answer. I'm sure Queen Warbeak could rub over a parchment with charcoal if her Sparras held that parchment flat upon the writing. Here, give me a moment or two with Warbeak. I'm sure I can teach her.'

∽

With no sense of night or day, it was impossible to tell how long they had been trapped inside the cave. The air had become thicker, more rancid and hotter. Matthias felt his head throbbing with pain. He tried to stop his leaden eyelids closing in sleep and all around him he could hear the shallow, ragged breathing of the others. He had tried talking to them several times, but it was little use, they were all in a deep sleep approaching a state of coma. Gripping the handle of his marvellous sword tightly, he tried to concentrate on a way out. There was little hope. They were entombed in a cavern of virtually solid rock with a massive slide of earth and stone sealing the entrance.

The warrior mouse could stay awake no longer. He leaned back against the gently heaving bulk of Orlando and let his resolve drift. At first it was quite a peaceful feeling, save for the lack of air, which made breathing difficult and painful, but gradually his senses began to numb and he breathed shallowly in short pauses. As blackness enveloped him, the warrior mouse began dreaming.

He was in the Great Hall of his beloved Redwall Abbey. Sunlight streamed through the high windows in a coloured cascade, filtering through the stained glass, weaving patterns on the cool stone walls. Matthias was walking towards the long tapestry. He knew where he was going: to see Martin the Warrior. Yes, there he was, the great Founder Warrior and Champion of Redwall, standing proud in the centre of his tapestry. Matthias was not at all surprised when Martin stepped out of the woven cloth and confronted him. He went forward to shake paws with Martin, but the figure backed away. His face was scowling and he picked something up from the floor. It was Orlando's huge battleaxe!

Matthias was shocked. Martin advanced upon him and prodded the axehead into his side. It nipped him painfully.

'Ouch! Martin, it's me, Matthias. Why are you attacking me?'

Martin jabbed Matthias in the side again, this time calling out in a loud accusing voice, 'Why do you sleep, Warrior? You must save your son and his friends.'

Matthias tried to reach his sword to defend himself as Martin thrust at him again, but his paws felt lifeless. They hung limp by his sides. He winced with pain as the great axe seared his side again. 'A warrior who sleeps in time of danger is no warrior but a coward!'

'Ouch, stoppit!'

∽

Matthias awoke to find he had somehow rolled off Orlando and was lying on the head of the axe. Each time he moved, it dug painfully into his side. Sitting upright, he rubbed the spot, realizing it had all been a fevered dream. But it was also help and a warning from his fellow warrior spirit.

Forcing himself upright, he held the axe by the twin blades, and by staggering about in the dark he located the blocked entrance. With agonizing slowness he pulled himself as high as he could up the sloping hill of debris until he was at its topmost point. Breathing hard, sweat starting out all over beneath his habit, Matthias began probing the rubble heap with the long axe handle. Pushing and shoving laboriously, he felt the long axe haft sink into the hill. Sometimes it struck a rock, but with a bit of manoeuvring he thrust it past the obstacle. Almost the full length of the haft was buried in the pile. With a final effort he gave one last painful shove, and fell forward as the haft buried itself entirely. Slowly, wearily, he started waggling the shaft by pushing the twin blades from side to side, then very carefully he began withdrawing the axe from the hole he had made, with painstaking care sliding the axe back until it came all the way out.

Matthias knelt paw-deep in the rubble, hardly daring to draw breath.

Like the first kiss of sun upon ice in spring, he felt it on his whiskers. . . .

179

Fresh air!

Tears of gratitude flowed freely through the dust upon the Warrior's face. Cool, clean, fresh air and a shaft of daylight poured in.

'Thank you, Martin. Thank you for our lives, my long-dead warrior friend.'

∽

Scrambling down off the heap, Matthias located Basil. Rubbing the hare's limbs and tugging at his ears, he pummelled and massaged as best he could. It took quite a while before there was any response, then Basil soon proved he was his old self.

'Owch ooch! Steady on, laddie. Tchah! Why'd you wake me, I was halfway through a leek and lettuce pastie and just gettin' ready to demolish a summer salad as big as a house. Huh, could've done it too if you hadn't come along. I say, my old head's burstin'. It must've bin that cask of elderberry wine me and old Spike drank together. Haha, I got more than him, though. Bigger swallow, y'see.'

Matthias ruffled Basil's ears gratefully. 'Come on, up on your paws, you old glutton. See to young Cheek, while I'll deal with Jess. It'll take three of us to bring Orlando round. I hope he hasn't stopped breathing altogether.'

It took them a considerable while to wake the others. Fortunately they were all still alive, though Orlando gave them a few anxious moments, and heads still ached. However, they were uplifted and heartened by the small flow of fresh air and the shaft of daylight that penetrated their tomb. Finally Orlando sat up, nursing his head.

'Ooh! I've got a headache big enough for ten badgers. I never knew fresh air could taste so good, though. It's like drinking from a cold mountain stream in midsummer.'

'Steady on, old chap. Don't start talkin' about cold drinks, it's more than a body can stand, doncha know. Why, I remember the best drink I ever ha—MMMMFFF!'

Jess had stifled Basil's reminiscences with her thick

furred tail. She held up a paw for silence. 'Ssshhh listen!'

In the sudden stillness they could faintly hear noises from outside.

Cheek danced up and down. 'There's some creatures out there, I'm sure of it!'

They listened intently. Sure enough, faint sounds filtered in with the air and light through the hole.

Jabez Stump voiced his feelings: 'Could be friends, or mayhap they could be enemies.'

Orlando stood in the shaft of light. 'Who cares, as long as we get out of here. Friend or foe, we can sort out later.'

Matthias picked up his sword decisively. 'Orlando is right, we must get out of here. Now, we must take a chance. It's a double risk because we may destroy our air supply. Are you with me?'

There was an immediate call of agreement.

Taking Orlando's axe, Matthias tied his swordbelt to the end of the handle, then he gave it to Basil. 'Here, you've got the longest limbs, old fellow. Push that through the hole and waggle it about to attract attention.'

Taking the battleaxe, Basil shinned up the rubble and pushed the improvised pennant into the hole. Darkness fell as the light was blocked out. Cheek whimpered a bit then fell silent. All that could be heard was Basil grunting with exertion as he strove to gain attention, waving the handle to and fro by means of twisting the twin axeheads round and round.

'Anything happening yet, Basil?' Jess Squirrel called out hopefully.

'Can't tell yet, Jess. . . . Wait, I think someone has hold of the other end. Yes! They're pushing the axe back. Oof! Steady on. Think I'd better pull the handle back in so we can parley through the jolly old hole with thingummybobbins, whoever they are.'

Matthias scrambled up beside Basil. Luckily the hole was still open, even slightly wider when the axe handle was withdrawn.

Matthias put his mouth close to the hole and shouted,

'Hello out there. We're trapped. Can you help us out?'

They waited.

From outside came the faint sound of many voices. They seemed to be squabbling and arguing. One voice came clearly to them down the narrow aperture. It was gruff and commanding.

'Who are you? State your name and tell us if you are of the Guosim?'

Matthias leaned back and gave a sigh of relief. 'The Guosim! Thank goodness, they're friends.'

Orlando climbed up the rubble beside Matthias and Basil. 'Guosim, who in the name of stripes are they?'

'Careful what you say,' Matthias cautioned the big badger. 'Leave the talking to me. Guosim are the Guerilla Union of Shrews in Mossflower. They can be very touchy and argumentative, and everything they do is governed by their own union rules and laws. Keep quiet now and let me be spokesbeast.'

'If you are the Guosim, then let me talk to your Log-a-Log,' Matthias called down the hole.

Several voices came back at him.

'Who are you?'

'How do you know we have a Log-a-Log?'

'Are you a friend or foe?'

There was a scrabbling noise and more sounds of dispute. This time the voice that came through was strong and louder than the rest.

'Out of my way! Give me room. Stand back, I say! Hello down there. I am the Log-a-Log. What do you want of me?'

Even in the urgency of the situation Matthias could not help smiling as he answered. 'Log-a-Log, you old bossywhiskers, it's me, Matthias of Redwall!'

The reply was a gruff chuckle. 'Well, crumble my cake! Matthias, you old swordswinger, I should have known that Redwall accent. Ha, you're in a pretty pickle, no mistake. Don't worry, friend, I'll soon have you out of there, but first I've got to settle a small dispute out here.

Some of these shrews seem to think they know more about Guosim rules than their Log-a-Log. Leave it to me, I'll soon straighten them out. Meanwhile, you just sit tight. We'll need digging tools and rocks and timber for shoring. This rubbish keeps sliding and moving. It'll be a tricky task, but don't worry, I'll have supper ready for you when we haul you out of there. How many are you?'

'Six altogether, Log-a-Log, a hedgehog, a badger, a young otter, Jess Squirrel and Basil Stag Hare.'

'What? That old scoffin' windbag. I'm sorry I mentioned supper.'

Basil's ears stood up indignantly. 'I say, steady on, you scurvy little log-floater. Scoffin' windbag indeed!'

Jess Squirrel stifled a giggle. 'I'd say he wasn't far wrong there, eh Matthias?'

It was late afternoon when the shrew digging party broke through. The friends had sat in darkness most of the day, listening to digging and shoring interspersed with orders and arguments. Suddenly they were showered with rubble as a small head broke through framed by light.

'Flugg, stop bickerin' and pass me that branch. There! That ought to do it. Hello, cave dwellers. I'm Gurn, the best digger the Guosim have got. Some say my grandad was a mole.'

Orlando thrust forward a huge paw and patted the shrew. 'Well, Gurn, I can't tell you how glad we are to see you. I'm Orlando the Axe.'

'Hmm, big feller, aren't you? I hope this tunnel's wide enough to take you. You'd better go last, Orlando. Smallest first.'

It was a painstaking and bruising operation, as one by one the friends were attached to a rope and forcibly pulled through by scores of shrews. Orlando waited until last. The tunnel caved in behind him as he was hauled and tugged along the makeshift rescue shaft.

In the early evening sunlight, Matthias and his friends laughed and splashed in the shallows of the river as they bathed away the dust and dirt of their imprisonment. Sunlight, clean air, fresh water and the sight of green growing things combined to make them realize how lucky they were to be alive. Even Jabez Stump chuckled happily as he splashed water into the air.

'Hohoho, if'n my old family could see me now. It's many a long season since this beast risked a bath, I can tell you.'

∽

Later that evening they sat around a shrew campfire, eating oatbread baked on flat rocks and drinking fresh river water with herbs crushed into it. Matthias told Log-a-Log all that had taken place from the night of the feast celebrating the Summer of the Golden Plain, up to the incident of the cave.

The shrew leader shook with rage. 'Slavers! The slime of Mossflower, treacherous murdering rogues. Our Guosim scouts have heard reports in Mossflower since the end of spring about that masked fox and his dirty crew. I'm with you and your friends, Matthias. We'll track 'em and put an end to their evil trade. Taking young ones from their homes and families. I tell you it makes my blood boil just to think of it.'

Basil had been munching his oatbread and gazing around the shrew camp. ''scuse me, old Log-a-thing, I know it's not unusual for you shrew fellers to argue a bit, but by and large you usually stick together. So tell me, what are that small group over there sittin' on their own around a separate fire for?' the old campaigner wondered.

Log-a-Log sniffed and threw a dead root on the fire. 'Oh, that lot. They're trouble, Basil, particularly that young feller Skan. He's been challenging my leadership lately. It'll all come to a head tonight when I announce our new plans. When it does, I'd be grateful if you could keep your friends out of it, Matthias. No offence, but this is Guosim business.'

Matthias nodded. 'As you wish, Log-a-Log. Anyhow, I've no desire to be caught in the middle of a shrew argument. I've seen 'em before. But please don't let us be the cause of your trouble. You freed us from the cave and we are thankful for that. We can carry on our hunt alone, old friend.'

The Guosim leader's eyes were bright and fierce. 'Matthias, we are going with you, and that is final. Mossflower needs to be kept free of evil if woodland families are to live in peace. It is no less than our duty to help. As for the coming trouble, you leave that to me.' Log-a-Log took out a round black stone from his sling pouch and stood up. A smile hovered about his face momentarily. 'Besides, life's not much fun to a shrew without trouble.'

∽

The slavers caught up with the main party two hours after nightfall. Mattimeo and his friends found themselves locked and manacled back on to the slave line. They slumped down wearily, tired and sore and hungry.

'None for you escapers,' little Vitch sniggered evilly as he fed the other slaves. 'Slagar said so. A taste of real hunger'll make you a bit more obedient. Slagar says that when he's got a bit more time he's going to deal with each of you personally, especially you, little Redwall pet. Heeheehee.'

Mattimeo bared his teeth and went into a crouch. Vitch hurriedly backed off and left them alone.

They looked around, trying to take stock of their surroundings in the dark of night. One thing was obvious: they were camped in the foothills of an immense cliff range. The huge high plateau reared up behind them, blocking out the night-time sky. Sam craned his neck backwards as he gazed up.

'I wonder how we're supposed to get up there?'

Jube lay back, closing his eyes. 'We'll find out tomorrow, on an empty stomach too.'

They lay down to sleep, but Mattimeo sat up, staring

in the direction of Slagar. Tess watched him. He was different, older, tougher and something else she could not quite put her paw on.

'Mattimeo, what is it?' she asked. 'You've changed since we were recaptured.'

The young mouse patted Tess's paw. 'It's nothing, Tess. Go to sleep. I'm sorry I got angry at Tim today. In fact, I'm sorry for a lot of things. Perhaps you were right when you said that I should be more like my father. Maybe it's a bit too late now, but I'm certainly going to try. From now on Redwall must live on through Martin, my father and me. I was born the son of the Redwall Warrior, sword or no sword, and that is what I intend to be, to myself, and most of all to you and to my friends.'

It was then that Tess Churchmouse realized Mattimeo was no longer the wild and wayward young mischief-maker he had always been. Sitting next to her was a mouse who looked like Martin and Matthias. Despite the fact that they were captives in a strange place, she felt suddenly safe and protected in his presence.

The young one had become a warrior!

25

Cornflower, Abbot Mordalfus, Foremole and Queen Warbeak were in the gatehouse cottage. It had long gone midnight, but they sat around on the hearthrug with the parchment before them. It was covered by the markings of the charcoal stone-rubbing taken from the stone crow high on the south wall of the Abbey.

The Sparra Queen preened herself proudly. 'Verree good, eh? Sparra no missee thing, get all um wormsign.'

'Hurr Hurr, that you'm 'ave, clever ol' burdbag,' Foremole congratulated her.

The Father Abbot folded back his sleeves. 'Thank you, Queen Warbeak. Well, let us see what we have here. A map, by the look of it, and a poem to translate. I can do that. Watching John brought it all back to me.'

They scanned the parchment.

> 'Those who wish to challenge fate,
> To a jumbled shout walk straight.
> Sunset fires in dexteree,
> Find where Loamhedge used to be.
> At the high place near the skies,
> Look for other watchful eyes.
> Sleep not 'neath the darkpine trees,
> Be on guard, take not your ease,

Voyage when the daylight dims,
Danger in the water swims.
Make no noise with spear or sword,
Lest you wake the longtail horde.
Shades of creatures who have died,
Bones of warriors who tried.
Shrink not from the barren land,
Look below from where you stand,
This is where a stone may fall and make no sound at all.
Those who cross and live to tell,
See the badger and the bell,
Face the lord who points the way
After noon on summer's day.
Death will open up its grave.
Who goes there. . .? None but the brave.'

The Abbot nodded wisely. 'It's a lot clearer now. This is a crude map and a poem that tells a bit more than the last one. In fact, it's a key to the rhyme that was found beneath the Abbey.'

Cornflower was puzzled. 'How so, Father Abbot?'

The old mouse tapped his paw upon the design in the bottom corner. 'There. "Thorn", "shout". That's only north and south mixed up. . . . A jumbled shout, as in: *walk straight to a jumbled shout.'*

Cornflower smiled as recognition dawned. 'Of course, it means go due south.'

Foremole wrinkled his nose. 'Whoi didden oi think o' that? If you'm a-walken south then sun must be a-setten in dexteree.'

'Where is dexteree?' It was the Abbot's turn to look puzzled.

Foremole chuckled and pointed at the Abbot's left eye. 'That'n thurr be sinistree.' Moving his paw, he pointed at the Abbot's right eye. 'An' that'n be yurr dexteree.'

The Abbot smiled and scratched his head. 'Foolish of me. Sinister and dexter, left and right. In the old language of Loamhedge, sinistree is left eye, dexteree

188

right eye. So you must be travelling south with the sun setting in your right eye. Thank you, Foremole.'

'Moi pleasure, Abbot zurr.'

'So one thing is apparent,' Cornflower interrupted, 'keep travelling south, straight south, no matter what. I hope Matthias is doing that, wherever he, Jess and Basil are now. Oh, Father Abbot, if only we could get this information, this map and poem to them right now. They mean very little to us sitting here in Redwall, but to my Matthias, why, he might be able to see the very places the map and poem tell of.'

'Indeed,' the Abbot shrugged sadly. 'Not only that, but it tells the exact route and even clues to the dangers they will encounter: the woodland trees, the water, when to cross it, the longtails, the place where stones fall and make no sound – it's all here – badgers' heads, bells, Lord of Mossflower. Cornflower, you are right, it's about as much use to us as a snowfall in summer, but to them. . . .'

'Then you make copee. All Sparra fly, all Sparra, much long, fly plenty, find um my friend Matthias with old longears and treejumper. We find um, you see.'

Cornflower was taken aback. 'Queen Warbeak, I don't know, but how. . . ?'

The Sparra Queen hopped on to the mantelpiece and cocked her head to one side jauntily. 'No worry. Warbeak Queen, Sparra warriors do what me say. Matthias, Redwall, all good to Warbeak and Sparra folk. We do um this for you, for you.'

'Splendid!' For a mouse of his many seasons, the Abbot did a surprisingly agile leap up on to his paws. 'I will rouse Brother Sedge, Sister Agnes, Brother Rufus, Sister May. Together with myself and John Churchmouse, they should be able to copy the map and the poem several times over before first light. I take it you will want to leave at dawn, Queen Warbeak?'

The sparrow bowed gravely. 'First wormlight, old-mouse Abbot, all Sparra fly south.'

189

Outside the gatehouse window, other ears were listening. A large magpie clacked his beak together in satisfaction and took off for the woodlands beyond the Abbey's north wall.

BOOK TWO

General Ironbeak

26

Matthias and his friends watched in silence as Log-a-Log held up the black stone in one paw and addressed the shrews seated on the river bank in the quiet summer's evening.

'Members of the Guosim, you have heard the tale Matthias of Redwall and his friends related to us. There is evil abroad in Mossflower; this we already knew. Slavers, the masked fox and his band, have captured young creatures. Even now they are marching them south.'

'So, what has this got to do with us?' the shrew named Skan interrupted.

Log-a-Log turned on the insolent one. 'Silence, Skan! Do not show your bad manners by calling out while I hold the stone at a council meeting. If you wish to say anything, then wait until I have finished and it is your turn to hold the stone. This is the rule of the Guosim.'

Skan sniggered and muttered something to his cronies. Standing boldly, he faced Log-a-Log.

'It's a stupid rule, like all your silly Guosim customs. I am a free shrew and I'll talk when I feel like it.'

Immediately a hubbub and argument broke out on both sides.

Orlando pawed his axe, he made to rise, but Matthias

warned him, 'Sit still friend. Leave this to Log-a-Log.'

The shrew leader restored order by raising his voice above the rest.

'Logalogalogalog! Listen to me, shrews. The creatures of Redwall have always been our good friends. If we were hungry, if we were hurt, if we were sick, the Brothers and Sisters of the Abbey would help us without question. It is our duty to help them now. I say we go with Matthias and his companions. We will fight the slavers and rescue the young ones. Are you with me?'

There was a loud shout of agreement from the main body, but Skan and his followers stood to one side, silent and sneering. Log-a-Log walked stiff-legged to where Skan stood. The shrew leader thrust his face close to the young usurper, his hackles bristling dangerously.

'And you, Skan, are you for the Guosim or against it?'

'Guosim, huh!' Skan said scornfully, though he avoided Log-a-Log's eyes. 'A pile of old fuddy-duddies making outdated rules and regulations, why should me and my friends get ourselves slain or injured sorting out the troubles of others. I say we mind our own business.'

Log-a-Log smiled coldly. 'So, it has come to this. You have been pushing and prodding me for quite a while now, Skan. Perhaps you would like to be the new Log-a-Log of the Guosim? Well, now is your chance. Let's see if you fight as bravely as you talk. Come on, Skan, knock this council stone from an old fuddy-duddy's paw.'

The shrew leader stood in front of the young rebel, holding out the stone for all to see. He looked relaxed, though his whole body was tensed like a steel spring. Skan stood half a head taller than Log-a-Log. For a moment it looked as if he were about to do something, then he saw the light of battle in the shrew leader's eyes and his nerve failed him. He turned away.

'Yah, who wants to be bothered with the Guosim? I'm away to roam free and do as I like. Come on, shrews.'

Skan and his group of followers marched off into the fading light.

There was an audible sigh of relief throughout the shrew camp. The main body, who were with Log-a-Log, sat back and relaxed amid a general chatter of conversation.

Orlando nudged Matthias. 'He's not short of courage, your friend Log-a-Log. That Skan was bigger and heavier than him by far. Do you think he could have beaten him?'

Matthias smiled knowingly. 'Log-a-Log may be small, but he's the fiercest shrew warrior I've ever seen, though he's no bully like Skan. The rest of the Guosim know this. Log-a-Log is a good leader, he's as wise as he is brave.'

Log-a-Log came and sat with them. He clapped Matthias on the back. 'Sorry about that, old Redwaller, though it's none of your fault. Skan and his pals have been niggling at me all season, and it had to come to a head sooner or later. Ah well, at first light tomorrow we'll follow the fox. He's travelling south; my scouts have cut his track several times over the past few days.'

～

Slagar rose silently while the rest slept. He made his way quietly through the camp and across the foothills until he was at the base of the gigantic cliffs which stretched away in both directions as far as the eye could see. Drawing out his leather-thonged weapon, he twirled it until the metal balls clacked together loudly in the still night air. There was an answering rap from the top of the plateau, as if two rocks had been banged sharply together.

Slagar the Cruel smiled beneath his silken mask. He looked up and saw the two rope ladders uncoiling themselves as they fell from the heights. Giving each of them a tug to make sure they were secure, the fox stole off back to the camp and his slave line.

The peace of a warm summer night lay over Mossflower. It was a peace that would not last.

27

General Ironbeak perched in a great cedar which stood near the northern woodland fringe close to Redwall in Mossflower country. On the bough beside him, the crow Mangiz watched golden dawn light flooding from the east. On a lower branch, three magpie brothers, Quickbill, Brightback and Diptail, awaited the raven General's orders. In the trees to either side of them a small army of rooks were gathered, basking in the mild summer weather; it was a welcome change for all.

The birds respected Ironbeak as a shrewd commander. He had given them victories and kept their bellies full, and he was the most feared fighting bird in all the far cold northland. General Ironbeak had led his fighters from the bleak places of the north to this new territory, and they marvelled at the warm weather, the vast green forest with its cool shade, plentiful water and easy foraging. They sat in the lower terraces of the foliage, content in their new surroundings, but ready to fly at Ironbeak's bidding.

The raven General relied upon the word of his seer, the crow Mangiz. He seldom arrived at any decision without first consulting him. Today was different. During the night, Quickbill the magpie had made his report, apprising the General of the latest news from

Redwall. Now Ironbeak and Mangiz perched side by side, their eyes half closed, not looking at each other as they talked.

'*Arrah!* It is as I said, my General. The great redstone house is only a smallflight from us. You heard Quickbill, soon the sparrows will be gone and there will be none to give warning against us.'

The raven blinked as sunlight caught the corner of his eye. 'My good right wing, Mangiz, it is as you foretold. Truly the redstone house is a wonderful place. Tell me more of it.'

The impassive crow ruffled his neck down into dark breast feathers. 'The sparrows fly south, my visions told me this. Where they go I do not know. *Grakk!* That need not concern us. The roofspaces will be unguarded, and we can take care of any old ones or nestlings that are left. Below on the ground there are many earthcrawlers, a great stripe-dog, hedgepig, waterhound and mice wearing robes. There are no warriors or fighters to do battle with.'

Ironbeak came alert as the distant sounds of the Matthias and Methusaleh bells tolled out a new day in the Summer of the Golden Plain.

'Listen, Mangiz, the bells are welcoming us. It is a great thing to have a redstone house with bells. *Arrak!* The only time before this that I heard a bell was upon the northland's great waters. It was on a ship that sank in a great storm. I never knew that houses had bells. What else does your vision tell you about the redstone?'

The seer crow shut his eyes tight. 'The place has big lands enclosed by a wall. Enough food grows there to feed the whole northland, and there is a pool with fishes in it. Take my word, it is a place of plenty.'

Ironbeak's bright eyes shone. '*Yagga!* Well told, my Mangiz. You are seldom wrong. Quickbill, take your brothers and watch the redstone house. Do not be seen. When the sparrows are gone, report back here. Grub-claw, Ragwing, take sentry duty. The rest of you keep low and hidden. Rest awhile, my fighters.'

The three magpies dipped their tails in salute before winging off through the trees. Amid a ruffling of feathers and scratching of talons, the others settled down to enjoy a rest in the warm summer morning. Ironbeak shuffled restlessly along the maple bough. He was clearly impatient.

'We have travelled far together, my General,' Mangiz said soothingly. 'Wait now, the great redstone house will soon be yours. You will conquer it from the top downwards. Walls were built only for earthcrawlers. We will arrive like silent arrows from the sky. Patience, Ironbeak.'

The raven leader settled down, reassured. 'This is a good land to be in, Mangiz. It is not cold like those northlands, and the redstone house will be mine. It was your visions that first saw it; if you say the signs say wait, then we wait.'

～

Cornflower and Mrs Churchmouse stood on the south ramparts, keeping tight hold of baby Rollo as he waved and shouted. The bells pealed merrily while the Sparra folk of Queen Warbeak flew south across the woodlands in the cloudless blue morning. Constance and the Abbot cheered as lustily as any at the brave sight. The Sparra Queen circled the Abbey once, then dipping her wings she dropped like a stone, taking up a zinging flight as she brushed by the creatures on the battlements.

'We find um, you see, we find um!' she called.

Warbeak flew high, shooting like a speeding arrow into the vanguard of the feathered squadron. Soon they became dark specks which rapidly disappeared into the distance over Mossflower.

John Churchmouse flexed both his paws and massaged the back of his neck wearily as he descended the wallsteps with Brother Sedge.

'Whew! Well, thank goodness that's over. Maybe we can catch up on a little sleep now, eh, Sedge?'

Brother Sedge grubbed charcoal-stained paws into his

red-rimmed eyes. 'Aye, it's straight up to the dormitory for me, John. It certainly takes it out of you, sitting up all night drawing maps and writing poems. I just hope that one of those birds finds Matthias and the others. I'd hate to think that we worked in vain.'

John stretched wearily. 'Ho hum! Well, there's at least twelve copies and they're all carried by trusty Sparra scouts. If they can't find them nobeast can. I wonder what's for breakfast?'

'Breakfast indeed, John Churchmouse,' Mrs Churchmouse tutted airily as she passed by. 'You've done nothing but eat all night. Still, I suppose you could find room for some nutbread, blackcurrant cordial and elderberry pancakes before you sleep the day away.'

John leaned wearily against the Abbey wall. 'Hmm, s'pose so, dear. I'll be in soon. Tell that baby Rollo to save a pancake or two for me. Basil certainly taught him how to deal with the rations, the little nosebag.' He wiped his grimy paws on his habit and blinked owlishly. ''s funny, I could swear I saw a magpie above the west wall just then, did you see anything, Sedge?'

Brother Sedge stifled a yawn. 'Oh come on, John, let's get breakfast. You're seeing things. There hasn't been a magpie ever recorded in this neck of the woods.'

The morning wore on with the gentle pace of Redwall life. Three magpies winged their way low and slow to the maple at the north fringe.

∽

That same morning saw Matthias and his friends marching shoulder to shoulder with Log-a-Log and the shrew army, south through the trees, upon the trail of Slagar. Orlando stopped in a clearing and pointed ahead with his axe.

'Is that a cloudbank on the horizon, or some sort of landrise?'

They halted and gazed in the direction he was pointing.

Matthias shook his head. 'Could be anything. What d'you think, Log-a-Log?'

The shrew leader shaded his eyes. 'That must be the Great South Cliffs. I've heard of them, but the Guosim have never wandered that far south before. Well, let's press on and see for ourselves. I reckon we should make them by late evening if we march at the double.'

A short meal break was taken for shrew oatcakes and water. Keeping the cliffs ahead as a bearing, the searchers set out at a fast double pawstep.

∽

Slagar had split his band in two, half in front and half behind the slave line as they began the ascent of the rope ladders hanging down from the top of the plateau. The masked fox snapped out instructions.

'Listen you lot, keep your paws tight on those rungs. Don't look up or down. It's a good drop, even from halfway up these ladders. You wouldn't live through it, so if you want to reach the top in one piece then keep your wits about you. Threeclaws, you go first to show 'em. When you reach the top make sure the prisoners are well staked down until I get there. Stonefleck's waiting up there. Do as he says. Right, get going!'

∽

Mattimeo climbed stolidly, trying hard to keep some slack in the running line to make it easier for Tess and Cynthia, who were on the rungs below him. Auma climbed steadily. She was above Mattimeo. Young Jube would slip now and then, accidently kicking the badger on her head, but she toiled upwards without complaint. Tim was above Jube and Sam was the top climber, being the more experienced. He chanced a look below when they were over halfway up. The drop was dizzying, even for a squirrel. The other slaves were way below, treading nervously on each separate rung as they were chivvied along by the slavers.

'Come on, dozypaws, or you'll feel my cane.'
'Up, you stupid creature, don't look down.'
'Hey you, get a move on up there.'
'Ow! You great lump, you're treading on my paws.'

It was mid-afternoon by the time they reached the giddy heights on top of the cliffs. At first no creature noticed the big rat who sat watching them from a rocky outcrop. It was only when he moved towards them that they could distinguish him. Stonefleck was grey and dirty white with black markings. He could lie still anywhere and be taken for a rock, a ground shadow or part of the scenery. He was large for a rat and not given overmuch to talking, and he carried a heavy bow and a well-laden quiver of arrows. Threeclaws was taken aback. Stonefleck seemed to materialize out of the rocks.

'Where's the masked one?' The rat's voice was flat and toneless.

'He'll be here soon. Are you Stonefleck?'

The rat did not reply. He seated himself at the cliff's edge and awaited the arrival of Slagar, looking for all the world like a boulder perched on the brink of the plateau.

∽

The slave lines were staked to the ground by pegs. Mattimeo and the other captives sat regaining their breath after the long climb, which had been made doubly difficult because of manacles and running line. The slavers surrounded them, panting hard from their exertions. Over the cliff edge, Mossflower sprawled away into the sunlit distances. Tess stared out hopefully. Somewhere out there was their beloved Redwall Abbey, though it was too far away to see. The little churchmouse comforted herself with the thought that her mother and father, if they were alive, would probably be going in to afternoon tea in Cavern Hole. She brushed a tear of homesickness from her eye and sniffed.

∽

Slagar was last up. He nodded to Stonefleck.

'Is this all you brought?' the rat asked, indicating the captives.

The silk mask pulled in and out against the Cruel One's face as he breathed heavily. 'It's enough, rat. They're all young, strong and healthy. If you wanted more, you should have tried climbing down from here and catching them yourself. I'll speak to you later. First I've got business to attend to. Wedgeback, get yourself over here!'

'Who, me?' The stoat pulled a paw at himself.

'Who d'you think, numb brain, the weasel behind you? Come here.' Slagar's voice was tight and dangerous.

Nervously Wedgeback looked round at his companions. They seemed to be intent on minding their own business; nobeast wanted to see what was about to happen. Falteringly the stoat made his way over to the cliff edge where Slagar stood waiting. The masked fox seized a pawful of Wedgeback's soft belly. Digging his claws painfully deep, he pulled the frightened stoat forward until he was breathing down the terrified creature's nostrils. A slight breeze rippled the silken hood mask. Slagar had never looked more scary. The stoat gulped aloud, his face a fraction from the slitted eyes. Slagar was actually smiling.

'Wedgeback, old friend, let me tell you something. When I leave you in charge of the prisoners, it means that you have to guard them carefully and let none escape.'

'B-but S-Slagar, I. . . .'

'Hush, ssshhh!' The Cruel One's voice was deceptively soothing. 'Don't interrupt, it's bad manners. You've got a lot to learn, Wedgeback. Pity you won't have time, though. Where was I? Oh, yes. You know the trouble we went through to get those creatures from Redwall Abbey, yet the moment my back was turned you let them escape, didn't you?'

The stoat was almost incoherent with fear. Slagar's claws were piercing his belly and he felt totally helpless. 'I didn't know they were g-goin' to 'scape, honest.'

Slagar began slowly turning Wedgeback so that the stoat had his back to the cliff edge. He was teetering on the brink.

'But they did escape. No thanks to you, I caught them

again. There's no room in my band for blunderers, Wedgeback. You'll have to go.'

Wedgeback's eyes rolled wildly. 'I'll go, Slagar. I promise I'll never come back again. Please don't hurt me, just let me go.'

'As you wish my friend. Goodbye!'

Slagar let go of the stoat, at the same time giving him a slight push. The luckless Wedgeback vanished over the edge of the heights with a scream of despair.

∽

Dumbstruck at the horror of the callous killing he had just witnessed, Mattimeo shuddered. Turning his head aside, he clasped Tess and Cynthia, who buried their faces in his robe.

∽

Slagar peered over the cliff edge at the broken carcass on the rocks below. Stonefleck joined him, his face still impassive as he pointed to a small group making their way through the foothills.

'Look, fox, shrews. Do you know them?'

Slagar peered hard at the group. They were just arriving at the rope ladders. Momentarily they recoiled with horror at the sight of Wedgeback's corpse. Cupping his paws round his muzzle, Slagar called down to them. 'Who are you and what do you want?'

The answer came floating faintly up on the warm afternoon air. 'I am Skan and these are my followers. I have information for Slagar.'

'I am Slagar,' the fox called back down. 'Bring your friends up here, Skan. Use the rope ladders.'

While the shrews made their way up the cliff face, Slagar held a silent conference with his band. They nodded at his plan. The masked fox laughed quietly.

∽

Skan and his followers were panting with exertion as they pulled themselves on to the plateau. At a signal from Slagar, the slavers pulled the rope ladders up.

While his followers sat about on the clifftop regaining their breath, Skan spoke to Slagar.

'Whew! What a time we've had. We ran all the way, following your trail through the woods. We haven't stopped or eaten a thing today. Listen, there's a whole army coming after you: Log-a-Log and his shrews. They rescued Matthias and those others from the cave, dug 'em out. . . .'

Slagar was surprised. 'What? You mean to tell me those Redwall creatures are still alive?'

Skan wiped sweat from his brow. 'Phew! Oh yes, very much so. In fact, they've joined up with the Guosim, that's the shrews you know, and together they've vowed to track you and your band down and slay the lot of you.'

The fox stroked his silken mask pensively. 'Hmmm, well, that's nothing new. There's lots of creatures would like to slay me. By the teeth of hell! I thought I'd buried those Redwallers for good. But why should you dash all the way here to tell me this?'

'Because I want my revenge on Log-a-Log and his stupid Guosim, and you can help me.'

'Oh, I see,' Slager nodded. 'You and your friends have broken away from the shrews due to some sort of bad blood, is that it?'

Skan narrowed his eyes. 'Something like that, but that's my worry, not yours. The thing is now for us to join together and defeat them. Together we can be a strong force.'

Slagar helped Skan up and put a friendly paw about his shoulders.

'What a good idea, Skan. However, I have no need to fight with anybeast following us. See, the ladders have been pulled up. There's no way we can be attacked, we're completely safe up here.'

Skan looked angry and puzzled. 'But what about me and my followers?'

Slagar chuckled. 'Well, you can climb down and fight them yourself if you wish, or you can stay up here with us.'

The shrew was crestfallen. 'I thought you'd want to fight them and be rid of them. I suppose we'll have to stay here and join up with your band. We're too few to face them alone.'

Slagar signalled to his crew and they began forming a semicircle around the shrews, who were standing with their backs to the cliff edge. The slavers were heavily armed. 'Right, it's a deal then, Skan,' Slagar said. 'We'll let you join up with us. Not with my band, of course, but with my slave line.'

The fox suddenly grasped Skan in a headlock, relieving him of his short sword, which he held at the shrew's neck. 'Surrender your weapons, or he dies and you lot go over the edge!'

'You traitor, you scum! We came here to warn you,' Skan spluttered.

'So you did,' Slagar laughed scornfully. 'You were prepared to sell your own kind out. Let me tell you, Skan, when it comes to double-dealing, there's nobeast better at it than Slagar the Cruel. Chain 'em up!'

Weeping with frustration, the shrews were disarmed and chained to the slave line.

∽

Reaching across, Auma pinned Skan to the ground with a hefty paw at his throat.

'Give me the right answers, turncoat, or you're dead. My father is Orlando the Axe, that mouse's father is Matthias of Redwall, the squirrel has a mother named Jess and the young hedgehog there, his father's name is Jabez. Are they alive and well?'

Skan gurgled and spluttered until Auma released him.

'Yes, yes, they're alive, and an old hare named Basil and a young otter too, though I didn't get his name.'

Mattimeo and his friends laughed with delight and relief. Auma gave Skan a mighty pat on the head that completely stunned him.

'Haha, they're alive. Oh, I do feel better now!'

28

The evening bells tolled out across the countryside at Redwall. It was a windless summer twilight; not a leaf stirred on branch or bough, the earth and grass were still warm from the hot afternoon. The Abbey dwellers ceased their daily tasks and went indoors for the evening meal. Mole cooks had baked a traditional tater'n'turnip-'n'beetroot deeper'n'ever pie, there was fresh fruit and cream, mint wafers and cider. A garland of yellow flowers graced the table centre in honour of the season.

None of them knew that murder had been done that day.

∽

When the sun was at its zenith, General Ironbeak and his raiders had flown up as high as they could, hovering on the high thermals far above Redwall, then they quietly plummeted down. Four by four they came, each bird entering under the high eaves from a different point. The General led the secret attack, swiftly and silently dealing death to the few old sparrows and late nestlings who were unable to fly. The dreadful deed was accomplished with quiet efficiency; Ironbeak and his birds were seasoned warriors.

∽

Mangiz perched in the crossbeams next to his General

while the rooks searched through the pitifully empty sparrow nests. One cackled harshly. Ironbeak swooped down and felled him with a savage peck.

'Silence! The great redstone house is not yet ours. I do not want those creatures below to know we are here. Quickbill and his brothers will bring in food soon, when night falls. Until then you must all be still and make no noise.'

He flew back to perch with Mangiz, but the crow seemed somewhat disturbed. Ironbeak noticed his seer was not his usual self.

'What is it, my Mangiz? Are you having more visions?' he asked.

'No, the strange thing is that my vision is clouded. The eye within my mind has been blurred since we came here today. Whatever I try to see becomes difficult. It is an earthcrawler, a mouse dressed strangely; he carries a sword and seems to bar all my visions.'

Ironbeak closed his eyes. 'Do not worry, Mangiz. Maybe it is a good omen.'

Mangiz clacked his beak doubtfully. 'We will see, my General.'

∽

'Come on. Oops a daisy! Up the stairs to bed with you, little Rollo.'

Mrs Churchmouse chased after baby Rollo, but he ducked beneath the table and began singing.

'I wrestle a fish upon a dish,
Cut off his 'ead while he's in bed,
an' take a rat an' make him dead,
for gooooooood ooooooold cideeeeeeeerrrrrrr!'

Sister May and Cornflower helped Mrs Churchmouse. They scrambled under the table and chased Rollo out into her waiting paws.

'Gotcha, you little monster. Now off to bed with you.'

'No no, dowannago! Dowannagorrabed!'

'Please, Rollo, be a good fellow. Tell you what, if I

come up with Cornflower and Sister May and we sing songs, then will you go?'

Rollo chuckled until his little fat body shook. 'Yep, yep. Singa singa song f' Rollo.'

∽

The three mouse ladies took the infant bankvole up to the dormitory on the floor above Great Hall, where he was dutifully put into a cot.

After several songs, Cornflower held a paw to her lips. 'Ssshhh, he's sleep. Come on, quietly now.'

Rollo opened one eye. He watched them tip-paw out. As soon as the door was closed, he pulled his nightshirt above his paws and scrambled out of the cot.

Halfway down the stairs, Sister May heard the dormitory door slam. 'Mercy me, the little rogue has escaped. Quickly!'

They bounded back up the spiral staircase, reaching the landing in time to see Rollo climb another curving flight of stairs.

Cornflower stamped her paw down hard. 'Back to bed, baby Rollo, this instant!'

Rollo turned and giggled, then he waved to them. Mrs Churchmouse heard a slight noise on the stairs above Rollo, and was about to call out to him. Suddenly a large raven poked its villainous black head round the spiral and seized Rollo by the nightshirt in its wicked beak.

The little bankvole screamed aloud as he was dragged backwards up the stairs.

∽

Darkness had fallen when Matthias and his new-found army reached the foothills. They were forced to camp there for the night until morning light revealed their position. Shrew fires glimmered, and the chatter and noise of the argumentative little beasts made Matthias wish Log-a-Log had never offered the help of the Guosim. The warrior mouse sat alone on the brow of a small rise, then he was joined by Orlando and Jabez Stump.

The hedgehog nodded towards the cliffs rearing high overhead. 'Puzzles me as to 'ow any creature 'ceptin' a bird could get to the top of there. You're sure they went this way?'

Basil Stag Hare sauntered up out of the darkness. 'Sure? You could bet your summer spikes on it, old lad. They've scaled the bally heights all right, though how they did it beats me. One clue though, I've just stumbled over the carcass of one of those stoat fellers. Either he thought he could fly or he missed his paw hold. Ugh! Nearly put me off m'supper, it did.'

'It must have been pretty grim to banish thoughts of food from your mind, Basil,' Matthias chuckled. 'The question is, how do we get up there tomorrow?'

Orlando tested his axe blade against his paw. 'And when we do get up there, d'you think they'll have laid some sort of trap? Maybe the fox is waiting until we're halfway up to start hurling rocks and boulders down on us.'

'That's a chance we'll have to take,' Matthias shrugged, 'though I don't think Slagar knows we're alive. He'll probably press on to get his captives to their destination, wherever that is.'

The old hare squatted down beside Matthias. 'I picked up the tracks of that young shrew Skan and his cronies this afternoon. They were making for this point well ahead of us. I think the bally old fox knows we're still alive and kickin', one way or another.'

The warrior mouse unbuckled his sword and lay down in the grass.

'We'll know tomorrow. Rest now.'

∽

Mattimeo and his companions on the slave line were being driven hard and fast. Evidently there was to be little rest that night. Slagar and Stonefleck led the column. Before they set out, the masked fox had addressed them:

'Tonight you must move swiftly and silently. I tell you

this because there is no other way. Stonefleck here will guide us, he knows the paths to take. When we reach the forest, there is danger, so be silent, travel fast, and you will come out unharmed. Now get moving!'

It was difficult going. They were forced into a stumbling dogtrot; the chain manacles and the heavy slave line were a great handicap for the prisoners. Surprisingly, the slavers helped them all they could. Sam was baffled.

'Matti, Tess, why haven't they got the canes swinging? Usually we get beaten and bullied, but all of a sudden they're being almost nice to us.'

Auma caught Tim as he stumbled. 'They're not shouting and yelling at us either. I'd say they look pretty frightened themselves.'

'There's a forest up ahead,' Jube called back to them in a loud voice. 'D'you suppose that has something to do with it?'

'Please, don't shout or you'll get us all killed!' Drynose the weasel guard had an almost pleading whine to his voice.

∽

The forest, when they reached it, looked eerie and forlorn in the dim light. Old gnarled trees spread their knotted branches wide and low, there was little grass on the floor, and no flowers were to be seen anywhere. Mattimeo saw the withered and bleached skeleton of a rat dangling from a bough halfway up a tree, and there were other bones too, scattered here and there throughout the branches. The young mouse decided to keep quiet about them; no sense in panicking his friends, chained up as they were.

'I've noticed those bones too,' Auma whispered in his ear. 'We'd best keep quiet. If anybeast gets attacked it'll probably be us, who have no chance of making a run for it.'

Bending low to avoid hanging branches, they pushed onward as fast as possible, following Slagar and Stonefleck. Occasionally Mattimeo could hear guttural noises up in the trees, and now it seemed that everyone had spotted grisly remains hanging in the boughs, though no creature made mention of it.

Tess Churchmouse shuddered. She had never been in such a sinister place. Catching up with Mattimeo, she grasped the back of his robe and clutched it tight. The young mouse patted her paw in the darkness.

'Don't be frightened, Tess,' he whispered. 'We'll make it. There's nothing to be afraid of. Hold tight and look straight ahead.'

Tess was comforted by his quiet confidence.

Marching half the night, pawsore and exhausted, they carried on, driven by fear of the unknown. Stonefleck nudged Slagar. He pointed ahead to a break in the trees. The forest was thinning.

At that very moment, Browntooth the stoat, who was marching on the left flank of the slave line, received a sharp jab in the eye from an overhanging branch which Halftail had brushed to one side. The springy branch swished back into place just as the unfortunate stoat drew level with it. The spell of silence was broken by his screams.

'Arrrgh! Owow! Me eye, me eye!'

Slagar broke into a fast sprint, shouting as he went, 'Run for it, follow me, to the shore, to the shore!'

The slavers dashed off, leaving the captives to fend for themselves. They ran, tripping and stumbling, scrambling over their fallen comrades in an effort to get out of the woods.

'Pick up the rope, keep in line, run as fast as you can,' Mattimeo shouted to the slave line. 'Help the others, if one of us falls we're all done for!'

They went pell-mell, pulling their stumbling comrades up with the line as they ran, and the back runners were virtually dragged along. Suddenly the air was full of harsh cries, and a number of dark shapes descended upon them. It was a fierce onslaught on slaves and slavers alike. The screams of the injured echoed round in the forest. Auma felt sharp claws strike back at her back. She bared her teeth, snapping at the thing that was attacking her.

'Help, help! Eeee!'

Caught by several of the strange attackers, Skan the shrew began to rise into the air. He screamed and kicked for dear life. Tim and Mattimeo felt the slaveline straining and dragging them back as Skan was pulled upwards. Auma turned and grasped the rope in her teeth. Aided by Tim and Mattimeo, she tugged sharply. Skan fell to earth with a bump, but even this quick action had not saved him.

～

Rushing from the forest, they found themselves on the broad shores of a wide river, it glimmered and waved in the starlight. Slagar stood by a broad trench covered with boughs urging them on.

'Come on, in here, hurry!'

Gratefully they threw themselves under its protection. Most of the slavers had already arrived, and they sat shivering and breathless. Slagar was the last to enter. 'Scringe, Vitch, cover each end of this trench,' he ordered. 'Keep yourselves awake, and keep an eye on those woods. Threeclaws, did all the slaves make it?'

'All except Skan the shrew. He's had it, Chief.'

'Then unchain him and sling his worthless hide out. What about you lot, are you all right? Anybeast missing, Halftail?'

'Two of ours, Chief; Browntooth and Badrag. I saw 'em go meself. It was 'orrible, screamin' an' kickin' they were. By the claw! What are those things that attacked us?'

Stonefleck squatted impassively. 'The painted ones,' he said, his voice flat and matter of fact.

Slagar moved aside as two slavers carried the dead Skan out. 'Look at that, a good slave lost to those devils out there. It's just as well Browntooth got taken. I'd gut him myself if he was here, screaming and yelling like that.'

Auma rubbed a paw across her bleeding back. 'Painted ones, I've never heard of them before.'

'Quiet back there!'

Slagar paced the slave line. 'You lot can have a long rest. It's too late to cross the river now, we'll have to wait until tomorrow night. Right, Stonefleck?'

The rat strung his bow. Selecting an arrow from his quiver, he poked it through a gap in the boughs which covered the trench and fired straight up into the night sky. The arrow gave a shrieking whistle as it sped upward.

There was a moment's silence, then an answering whistle from an arrow fired on the other side of the river. Stonefleck unstrung his bow.

'Tommorrow night, Slagar, my rats will be waiting.'

29

Baby Rollo screamed. The raven had him tight by the nightshirt, and he wailed in terror as the big bird tugged and pulled, shaking its head fiercely from side to side.

Cornflower and Mrs Churchmouse momentarily froze with horror at the awful sight.

But not little Sister May. She went immediately into action. Rushing to the stairs, she sprang up and grabbed baby Rollo, at the same time sinking her teeth into the raven's foot, which she bit clear through to the bone.

The bird promptly let go of his prize. He gave a loud, agonized squawk and fell flat upon the stairs. Rollo yowled, Sister May screamed, and they both tumbled down the spiral staircase. Cornflower and Mrs Churchmouse dived in. Clutching Sister May and little Rollo, they hurried downstairs towards Cavern Hole, all four shouting aloud:

'Help! Help! Strangers in the Abbey! Help!'

Like a great grey furred juggernaut, Constance came bounding out of Cavern Hole, closely followed by Winifred the otter, John Churchmouse and Foremole.

Between them, the three mice gasped out the story of what had happened. Rollo had got over the fright quickly. He kept pointing a chubby paw over his back to show them all the tear in his nightshirt where the big bird had seized it.

Constance wasted no time. She got the little group safely back to Cavern Hole and issued emergency orders.

'Brother Trugg, sound the alarm bells. Winifred, Ambrose, Foremole, Brother Sedge, gather staves and light some torches. We must find out more about this strange bird. Cornflower, tell the Abbot where we have gone. The rest of you, stay down here. Don't go wandering off alone.'

∽

Torches shone on the darkened spiral stairway as Constance led the party. They had searched the dormitories, the sick bay and all the first-floor passages, and were now on the second-floor staircase which led to the gallery overlooking Great Hall. Foremole went snuffling along to an old side staircase, a straight flight which ran up to the disused chambers on the east wing of the third floor. He held up a paw and called out, 'Yurr, over yurr. Lookit oi found.'

A faint trace of bloodspecks spattered the bottom steps. Constance held up a torch to investigate.

The shadows leapt back to reveal a large raven standing on the top stair, together with a crow and six rooks. Boldly the badger climbed the stairs until she stood one step below the intruders.

'Who are you and what are you doing in our Abbey?' Constance demanded, never one to mince words.

The crow strutted forward imperiously. 'I am Mangiz the Seer, General Ironbeak's strong right wing. Bow your head and show proper respect when you speak to me, stripedog.'

Constance promptly batted Mangiz beak over tailfeathers in one mighty sweep of her powerful forepaw, then with a roar she charged in among the rooks.

Ironbeak and his fighters retaliated instantly. They were on Constance, pecking, scratching and tearing.

Winifred and Ambrose ran to her rescue. Belabouring furiously, they whacked away at anything feathered with their stout staves.

The fight did not last long. Ironbeak and his fighters were driven back by the fast onslaught of the Redwallers. They retreated to a boxroom, slamming the door and locking it from the inside.

Constance shook blood from her muzzle as she banged on the door. 'You in there, Ironbeak or whatever you call yourself, get out of this Abbey and take your birds with you. We do not allow trespassers at Redwall.'

The reply was instant and bold. '*Yaggah*! I am General Ironbeak, greatest fighter in all the northlands. This is my redstone house, and I will slay you all if you do not leave.'

The Abbot came hurrying up, accompanied by Brother Dan and Sister Agnes. He motioned Constance to be silent. Though the badger was obviously fuming with temper she bowed to the Abbot's wish.

The old mouse rapped lightly on the door. 'Hello in there. I am Mordalfus, Abbot of Redwall. I'm sorry if there's been a misunderstanding. We mean you no harm, we are a friendly order of creatures. If you wish to stay the night then you may. We have food and treatment for any creature who is sick or injured. Hello, can you hear me?'

This time it was Mangiz the crow who replied. 'General Ironbeak's word is the law. This place is his now. We are in your roof spaces, and there are many of us, all seasoned warriors from the north. There were some sparrows when we arrived, but they have all been slain. You too will be slain if you do not leave the redstone house.'

The Abbot shook his head sadly as Constance pulled him gently away. Foremole struck the door with his staff. 'Yurr, burdbags, Redwall be ours. Better wurriers than you'm 'as troid to take it offen us an' failed mizzuble, so they 'ave.'

There was no sound from the other side of the door.

Winifred shouldered her stave. 'Sounds as if they've gone. We'd best get back to Cavern Hole and decide what we are going to do.'

∽

There was a loud hubbub and clamour in Cavern Hole, and sleep was forgotten. Sister May was the heroine of the hour after Cornflower and Mrs Churchmouse told how she attacked the big bird single-pawed to rescue Rollo.

Sister May was a simple and modest mouse. 'Well, mercy me, I may be only the infirmary Sister, but I couldn't let that great bully harm our Rollo,' she told them. 'Poor little mite, he was frightened clear out of his wits, and so was I. Do you know, I'm still not sure it was me who attacked that bird.'

There was general laughter and a rousing cheer for Sister May.

Foremole and Constance were whispering together in a corner when the Abbot banged a wooden bowl upon the tabletop.

'Quiet. Quiet, please! Well, eight seasons of peace since the Great War and now one summer strewn with trouble. First the fox and his band, now this!'

Several voices called out.

'If only Matthias were here!'

'Yes, he'd know what to do!'

'Matthias, Basil and Jess would soon sort those birds out!'

Whump!

Constance's heavy paw shook the table. 'Silence, listen to your Abbot!' she ordered.

Foremole raised a paw. ''scuse oi, me an moi moles got wurk t'do. May us be 'scused, zurr?'

The Abbot looked over the top of his spectacles. 'Certainly, Foremole. Now, the rest of you listen to me. Wherever Matthias is now, or Jess Squirrel, or Basil, I'm sure they would wish us to get on with this problem and help ourselves.'

There was a murmur of agreement.

Abbot Mordalfus continued his address:

'Thank you. I must say a word regarding Sister May. What she did tonight was very brave—'

'Aye 'twas that,' Ambrose Spike piped up. 'Maybe she's after our Warrior's job instead of mindin' that old infirmary.'

Sister May blushed to her whiskertips. 'Oh, what a naughty thing to say, Mr Spike!'

When order was restored, the Abbot continued:

'Perhaps Ambrose is right, maybe we do need a Warrior in a situation like this. Can anyone suggest a suitable candidate?'

The call was unanimous:

'Constance, Constance!'

The badger stood up. 'First, I suggest you all bed down here for the night. It doesn't look too safe up in the dormitories at the moment. If you must leave Cavern Hole, let Winifred or Ambrose know. Do not wander about alone, especially out in the open. I will sleep on the steps between here and Great Hall tonight. Tomorrow we'll decide what to do about the raven and his crew.'

There was a great bustle of activity. Some of the infants thought it great fun to be sleeping in Cavern Hole and they made blanket tents from the edge of the table to the floor.

Constance sat on the steps with the Abbot and Ambrose.

'What do you make of all this, Constance?'

'I'm at a bit of a loss to say, Abbot. They must have been watching the Abbey, because they wouldn't have found it so easy to occupy the roofspaces with Queen Warbeak and all her warriors at home.'

'Aye, now it's up to us to make 'em see the error of their ways and send 'em packin', gurt cheeky birds.'

In the roofspace, General Ironbeak held a conference with Mangiz.

218

'*Krah*! The big stripedog is dangerous, Ironbeak.'

'The hedgepig and the waterhound too. We underestimated these earthcrawlers, Mangiz. They will have to be taught a lesson.'

'Aye, tomorrow will be their dying day,' vowed the crow. 'Oh, you are bleeding, my General.'

Ironbeak was glad he had been alone when Sister May attacked him. It would not do for his fighters to see their leader vanquished by a small female mouse. He shook blood from his talon.

'*Yaah*! It is nothing, a scratch. As you say, my Mangiz, tomorrow will be the dying day of these earthcrawlers. Post sentries at the eaves, and watch for Quickbill and his brothers bringing in supplies.'

Dawn was long past at the foot of the high cliffs. Matthias and the searchers had reached the cliffs after dark, and ever since daybreak they ranged far and wide. Everywhere they were faced with sheer inward curving expanses; nowhere was there a way up to the plateau. It was just before mid-morning when Matthias sat on a small mound with Basil and Cheek. The old hare shook his ears mournfully.

'Bollywoggled. That's what we are, old lad, flummicated! Blow me, there's no way to the top of that cliff unless we sprout wings.'

'We need a big ladder. That'd be better than wings,' Cheek sniggered impudently and ducked Basil's paw.

Jabez Stump marched up with a huge brown owl waddling behind him. 'Matthias, meet Sir 'Arry the Muse.'

The owl bowed gravely and blinked his enormous eyes.

Matthias bowed courteously in return. 'Good morning, Sir Harry. I am called Matthias, Warrior of Redwall, this young otter is Cheek, by name and nature. Last but not least, allow me to present Basil Stag Hare, retired scout and foot fighter.'

Basil made an elegant leg. 'Ah y'service, sah. But why are you called the Muse?'

The owl struck an artistic stance.

'Why, pray, do you suppose?
I'm master of poetry and prose,
No equal have I in field or wood,
No creature a smidgeon, a fraction as good.
And if you need a poet, why, here's one to choose,
This Owl. . . . Sir Harry the Muse.'

'Oh bravo! Bravo sir, well said!' Basil applauded him loudly.

Matthias leaned on his sword. 'Well said indeed. Unfortunately, we are not looking for a poet at the moment, Sir Harry.'

The owl blinked in a dignified manner.

'Then tell me what you need.
Someone to perform a deed?
A mummer perhaps, or a singer of songs?
A champion, a righter of wrongs?
A companion, maybe, to stand at your side?
For my talents are varied and wide.'

'We're looking for some creature who's too modest for words, haha.' Cheek anticipated Basil's paw this time, and dodged to one side.

Matthias nodded towards the clifftop. 'We need someone who can get us up there.'

Sir Harry preened his feathers, averting his eyes from Matthias. 'Cake, have you any cake?'

'You didn't talk in rhyme then. Why?' Matthias smiled.

'Because this is business. Verse is for conversation and pleasantry. Business is business, straight speaking.'

Matthias spread his paws, opening his eyes wide in imitation of the owl.

Business for goodness sake,
Perhaps we can find some cake.
Maybe my friend we will bring to you
A shrewcake baked by a shrew.'

At first Sir Harry looked undecided, then he stamped his talons and clacked his hooked beak in approval.

'Not bad, not bad at all.
At least it made me smile.
For a Warrior, I'd say quite good,
You have a certain style.'

Matthias sheathed his sword. 'Wait here, sir. I'll be back in a short while, then we can talk business.'

The warrior mouse set off in search of Log-a-Log and his shrews.

∽

Basil cleared his throat noisily and faced Sir Harry.

'I beg you listen to me,
I'm a fellow spirit, you see.
I was once considered a champion poet.
I just thought you'd like to know it. . . .'

Cheek tittered and avoided Basil's paw in the same instant.

Sir Harry turned his back and delivered a cutting line:

'I beg, I implore you, sir,
Stick to being a hare!'

Basil twiddled his ears huffily. 'Hmph! Some chaps wouldn't know a rhyme if you chopped it up and served it with custard in a bowl. Stick to being a hare, huh!'

∽

Matthias reappeared with Log-a-Log. The shrew leader was carrying a flat white cake, its sides oozed honey, and dark specks at its middle were definitely some kind of dried fruit baked into it. He presented it to Sir Harry.

The owl looked it over dubiously. He pecked at the

cake, made small noises of approval, then gobbled it up greedily. Crumbs of shrewcake still clung to his beak as he nodded in satisfaction.

'Excellent! Didn't look like much but it tasted wonderful. How many more of these have you got?'

Matthias shrugged. 'As many as it takes. The Guosim are good cooks. All they need is a small fire, a thin slab of rock and their own ingredients. But first I want to know more about that plateau. Is there a way up?'

'Of course there is,' Sir Harry snorted, spraying crumbs over Cheek. 'Nothing moves around here that I don't know about. I watched the fox and his band taking a slave line up there yesterday. There are rope ladders on the top. They pulled them up so you couldn't follow. How many shrewcakes in a batch?'

'Eighteen,' Log-a-Log told him.

'That many? Good! I'll fly up and drop the ladders down, but don't ask me to do any more. I stay well clear of the toplands normally. It's a strange world, too much death.'

Sir Harry did a short ungainly run and took off into graceful flight. He circled and wheeled, then flew up to the clifftop.

∽

Log-a-Log called the shrews together, issuing orders to the two on cooking duty. Basil and Matthias marshalled the rest into lines ready for the ascent.

Jess squirrel watched the top anxiously. 'Look out, stand back, here come the rope ladders,' she reported.

Bumping and unfurling their way down the cliff face, the twin ladders unravelled, stopping just short of the place where Cheek stood.

Jess sprang on to one, scuttling up with all the agility of a champion climber, calling out as she went. 'Wait there, I'll go to the top and make sure all is secure.'

Sir Harry came winging down. He stood counting the shrewcakes as the cooks laid them on the grass to cool. Satisfied the total was correct, he turned to Matthias.

'Our business is concluded,
You've paid me what I'm due.
The journey ahead is perilous,
Good fortune go with you.'

Jess waved all clear from the top. Matthias and Log-a-Log mounted the rope ladders and began to climb.

'Good luck and good eating to you, Sir Harry,' the warrior mouse called back. 'I hope we meet again.' The poetic owl bit into a shrewcake. He burned his tongue on the hot liquid honey but carried on eating and muttering,

'Those that venture upward,
Are only the brave and insane.
Though I hate to predict,
From the path that you've picked,
I doubt that we'll meet again.'

Matthias was too far up the rope ladder to hear. He was intent on reaching the plateau, regardless of what lay in store.

30

Foremole and his crew erected a barrier across the corridor next to the first-floor dormitory. The industrious creatures had brought lots of special mole equipment with them, and they began laying a surprise for any intruders who ventured down the spiral staircase towards the barricade. Foremole smiled and chuckled as he supervised.

'Yurr, Jarge, lay it on good'n'eavy across yon stairs. Rooter, you'm sprinkle aplenty stonedust o'er the top. Hurr, slap 'er on, Gaffer, doant be stingy with it. Ho arr, oi'd dearly loik to see anybeast put paw or claw atop o' that liddle lot.'

Shaking with glee, the moles stood back to admire their work. The bottom six steps had been liberally smeared and coated with a thick layer of Blackmole Tunnel Grease and Rockslide Burgoo mixture, a combination which often proved invaluable to tunnelling moles when they encountered immovable stones. Over the top of this was sprinkled a fine layer of sandstone dust. To the casual eye it looked exactly like a normal sandstone stair. Fine blackened tripwires had been stretched across the stairwell on the seventh and eighth steps. Immediately in front of the barrier, facing the stairs, two green saplings were fixed in wall torch brackets, bent back and held by a restraining rope, between them was tied an old blanket loaded with a mixture of stones, soil and a special vegetable compound, mainly stinkwort and wild garlic pounded together with dogs mercury plant.

Foremole covered his nose as he patted the huge catapult gently. 'Ahurr hurr, we'm woant 'ave to lissen for 'em after this!'

Rooter wiped tears of merriment from his eyes. 'Boi 'okey we woant, ee'll smell 'em a gudd day's march off, hurr hurr.'

⌁

Outside on the grass in front of the Abbey, Constance was covering for the mole activities with a decoy. Any creature who could twirl a sling or fire an arrow was brought out to help.

Ironbeak and Mangiz had come out on to the bell tower roof with some rooks. They basked in the warm morning sun, watching the pathetic attempts of the fighting squads below.

Ambrose Spike marched up and down in fine military fashion with baby Rollo in tow twirling a tiny sling.

'Right, troops, here's the drill. I want to see how many decent archers and slingthrowers we can raise. . . .'

Baby Rollo echoed the last words of each phrase. 'Flingthrowers 'e can raise. . . .'

'Now, when I give the command, fire and sling away at the bell tower. But mind, keep an eye on those missiles. What goes up must come down.'

'Go up mus' come down.'

'Be careful you don't get a stone on your head or an arrow in your paw!'

'Narrow in y'paw!'

'Just a moment, Sister May. Point that arrow the other way, please, marm, otherwise you'll end up shooting yourself in the nose.'

'Shooten inner noses!'

Ambrose raised his paw. 'Redwall defence volunteers. Ready, aim . . . fire!'

Most of the stones and arrows did not go even a quarter of the way up the belltower. They fell short, clattering off the solid masonry of Redwall Abbey.

∽

General Ironbeak was amused at the puny efforts of the creatures below. He sat enjoying the spectacle while his birds danced jibingly upon the roof, cawing and cackling insultingly.

'*Yakka*. Hey, earthcrawlers, we're up here!'

'*Cawhawhaw*! What a bunch of ninnies.'

'Look at that old mouse, he's slung himself on his back!'

'*Cahaha*! Please shoot me. Look, I'm standing with my wings spread to make an easy target.'

'*Rakkachak*! See that baby mouse, he tossed a rock up and it came down right between his ears!'

Ironbeak paced the stone guttering, hopping neatly on to a gargoyle spout.

'Fools! Why do they waste their energy like this, Mangiz?'

'Who knows, my General. Maybe it is anger at the death of the sparrows which drives them to do this.'

'Ha, idiots! Some too young, others too old, none trained in the way of the warrior.'

'True, Ironbeak. There is only the big stripedog who is dangerous. How can they hope to defeat us like this?'

'*Kaah*! You worry too much Mangiz. Let them waste their energy. It is a fine summer day and the sun will grow hotter. We will stay here and let them try to redouble their efforts. When they are tired out, we will strike. I have a plan. Listen, my fighters. When you see me spread my wings, then dive as fast as you can and go in pairs. Kill if you must, but try to pick one or two up. I want to see what they do if we are holding hostages. Maybe then they will see it is no use trying to defy General Iron—'

Bong! Boom! Clang! Bonggggg!

The Matthias and Methusaleh bells directly beneath

226

the bell tower roof tolled out vigorously. The noise was deafening to Ironbeak and his birds, separated from the bells by only a single layer of slates. Taken completely off guard, they flapped off in all directions, cawing loudly.

Below in the belfry, Cornflower and Mrs Churchmouse heaved and tugged furiously on the bellropes, their paws leaving the floor at each recoil.

Bongdingboomclangbangbong!!!

Ironbeak was last to leave the roof. He tried calling to his warriors, but his voice was lost in the clanging melee. With his head resounding to the metallic cacophony through to his very beaktip, the raven flapped off heavily into the air.

John Churchmouse clapped Ambrose upon the back.

'That'll teach' em to laugh at our army, eh, my old Spike!'

Constance opened the Abbey door. 'Come on inside, I'm closing the door now. I hope we gave Foremole and his crew time to set their surprise up.'

With his head still ringing from the bells, Ironbeak flew under the eaves to the roofspace in a black rage.

'Mangiz, take four with you and see if you can pick up any lone stragglers outside. The rest of you follow me. Get that roof trapdoor open quickly. We'll fly inside to the upper gallery and beat them to the stairs.'

'Beat what chairs, Chief?'

The crow had not recovered his hearing properly. Ironbeak buffeted him flat with a hefty wing blow.

'I said "beat them to the stairs", antbrain. Now get that trapdoor up and follow me.'

Half way across Great Hall, Abbot Mordalfus bumped into Constance. The badger glanced up.

'Dust!' she exclaimed. 'They're opening up the ceiling

trapdoor. Quick, clear the Hall. Let's get upstairs. By the way, Abbot, well done with the bells.'

As they pounded up the stairs, the Abbot called to Constance. 'I thought the bells were your idea. I knew nothing of it until I heard them ringing.'

'Well, whoever it was, they struck just the right note, hahaha.'

Both parties reached the barricade area at virtually the same time. The Redwallers stopped behind the barricade. Ironbeak could not fly on the spiral stairwell, so he came hop-skipping round the stairs in front of his fighters and hit the first tripwire.

Unable to stop himself and being jostled from behind, he injured his dignity and his bottom by trying to pull back and slipping heavily upon the grease. It was utter confusion, feathers, beaks, claws and wings massed in an insane jumble as the warrior birds tried to stay upright on the curving stairway. They slithered and bumped, slid and collided, slipped and cracked wings, talons and heads together. Black slimy grease pounded into a gritty porridge with the stonedust was everywhere. Each time a bird tried to regain its balance the situation worsened.

'*Yggah*, leggo, you're pulling me over!'

'Gerroff, you're all slimy . . . whoops!'

'*Yakkarr*! You're breakin' me wing!'

'Get your greasy claws off me. Take that!'

'Yugg, muy beaksh fulluv greash!'

On the other side of the barrier, the Redwallers danced with glee. They imitated the scorn the birds had heaped on them from the bell tower roof.

'Cawhawhaw, what a bunch of ninnies!'

'What's the matter, can't you stand on your own two legs!'

'I'll say he can't, his pal's standing on them for him. Ha ha!'

'Ho ho! Come and get us, we're over here, it's not far to walk.'

'Yurr, 'ello, greasybeak, 'ow do you loik a taste o' molegrease?' Foremole waved a sharp knife aloft. 'Geddown flat naow, gennelbeasts, yurr she goo's!'

He severed the catapult rope with a single slash.

∽

Chaos was added to confusion.

The huge slingload shot forward, flattening birds who were trying to stand. Rocks, soil and rotting vegetable matter pounded in a torrent upon the floundering birds. The evil smelling compound enveloped them.

Completely defeated, the birds slithered messily up the stairwell. Ironbeak tried to spit the evil concoction out as he thudded and bumped his way up, sometimes slipping back a stair, often falling heavily against the walls. All around him his warriors suffered the same predicament. Floundering, cursing and skidding, they beat an ignominious retreat, with the laughter of the Redwallers ringing in their heads.

'Hahaha, wash that little lot off.'

'Hope you've got a birdbath up there, hohoho!'

'Heeheehee, I suspect foul play!'

Ironbeak supported himself against the wall.

'*Yagga*! You've signed your death warrants,' he threatened. 'The moment you set paw outside, we'll be waiting on the rooftops. You will be slain without mercy.'

'Yah, go and boil your beak, General Pongo!'

∽

It was a long hot day in the crowded trench. The sun's rays baked through the covering of boughs as slaves and slavers alike tossed and turned in the cramped conditions. Only Stonefleck sat calm and motionless. Slagar wiped his paw round under the silken face mask.

'If it gets any hotter, we'll roast. Maybe we should have tried to cross the river before dawn, eh, rat?'

'You would have been caught out on the open water in daylight. That means death.'

Slagar scratched moodily in the sandy soil. 'Your mob had better be ready as soon as the sun sets.'

Stonefleck's expression did not change. 'They will be.'

～

Mattimeo moved restlessly in his sleep. Dreams of the dark forest they had left echoed through his mind.

～

Matthias and his friends ate as they marched across the plateau with the shrews. Log-a-Log pointed out the slavers' tracks.

'Nice and clear, still travelling due south.'

Orlando's face was grim. 'Aye, the fox didn't suppose we'd be following him.'

Basil shaded his eyes. 'I say, that looks like a gloomy old forest we're heading towards. Any more shrewcake left?'

Jess absentmindedly passed him one. 'It's a pine wood. I don't like the look of it.'

'Nor do I,' Jabez Stump agreed. 'Just a feelin' in my spikes, I s'pose, but it looks as if it's sittin' there a-waitin' for us.'

Cheek laughed nervously. 'Ha ha, old doom'n'gloom. Funny, I haven't got a feelin' in my spikes. Maybe 'cos I don't have any.'

Basil slapped him heartily on the back. 'That's the spirit, Cheek m'boy. Chin in, chest out, good straight back and a stiff upper lip, wot. Look out, pine trees, here we come!' The woods looked deceptively close. Even though they stepped out briskly, it was past noon when the party arrived at the beginning of the pine fringe.

Log-a-Log called for cooks to make a meal. 'We'll eat and rest awhile here, because we won't be stopping once we get among those trees; we'll do a straight march through until we're clear of them. Is that all right with you, Matthias?'

'Good idea, Log-a-Log. A rest and some food will set us up nicely and we'll be fresh for the march.'

～

A short while later they formed up into close marching order. Weapons at the ready, they set off into the trees

230

with Log-a-Log and Matthias up front, while Orlando and Basil guarded the rear. The first thing that struck them was the absence of daylight filtering through the thick foliage of the close-growing pines, then the complete, awesome silence of the place.

'No use trying to look for tracks among these thick pine needles on the ground. And that strong scent from the trees blocks out everything.' Log-a-Log's voice was muted and hollow.

'Yaggh! Look, up there!'

Log-a-Log grabbed the wide-eyed shrew who had called out.

'What are you shouting about?'

'Skeletons, bones. Can't you see them hanging in the trees? It's a warning. We'd better go back!'

Orlando came rushing forward. 'Bones are bones, shrew. Nobeast is turning back. They can't bite you, see.'

The badger whirled his axe and crashed it with stunning force deep into a tree trunk. The reverberation of the mighty blow caused bones to come clattering down to earth. Orlando tugged his warblade free.

'Dead bones never harmed anybeast. Now get marching.'

Suddenly a series of ear-splitting screams pierced the stillness and the trees about them began shaking as if moved by a mighty wind. Several shrews fell, cut down by sharp wooden lances. Matthias dodged to one side as a lance buried itself in the ground by him.

'Help! Heeeeelp!' Cheek gave a strangled cry and began rising swiftly into the trees, hauled up on a thin braided noose looped expertly around his body.

Log-a-Log acted swiftly. He fitted a stone to his sling. Whirling it, he loosed it among the lower branches. A small thin creature painted all over with green and black vegetable dyes fell senseless to the earth. The trees were alive with hundreds of others, chattering and screaming, swinging nooses and jabbing downward with sharp wooden lances. Basil plucked up a fallen spear and hurled it back.

Matthias crouched, drawing his sword, as Jess squirrel bounded up. 'Jess, they're some kind of treeclimbers. Can't you do anything?'

'The little savages, they don't seem to have any language, just screaming and growling. There's hundreds of 'em, Matthias, and they mean to kill us.'

The warrior mouse swung his blade at one of the painted ones who had ventured too low.

'Worst thing we could do is to make a run for it. Besides, they've got Cheek. The shrews are holding them off with slingstones, but that won't last.'

Orlando thundered past them, roaring. He struck trees left and right with his axe, jarring the savage beasts out of the branches. Shrew daggers made short work of them, but for every painted one that fell it seemed there were ten to take its place. The air rang with the snapping of branches and the screams of the painted horde. Above it all, Cheek could be heard sobbing loudly, 'Help! Save me, Basil. Don't leave me. Heeeelp!'

The old hare was leaping and kicking out with his long dangerous limbs. Anybeast that got too close was knocked out instantly.

'Chin up, Cheek old lad, I'm doin' me best!' he called encouragingly.

Amid the rain of javelins that hissed down and the stones that whizzed up into the pines, Jess Squirrel's teeth began to chatter madly. Her eyes grew red with battle light and she was far bigger than any of the strange attackers.

'Savages! Cannibals, tree freaks!' she shouted. 'Here, Matthias, there's only one way to settle this. I think I've spotted their leader, that little brute over there. Look at him screaming and dancing away like a mad thing. He's sending another lot in against us. I'm sure, that's the chief. Lend me your sword; there's only one thing this crazy tribe will understand.'

Grabbing the sword, Jess swung skilfully aloft. She was like a dusty red streak of lightning. Any foebeast standing in her way was hacked aside. The painted leader saw her coming. He screamed at the others and pointed to Jess, but she bulled her way through, scattering the painted attackers like ninepins. The leader hesitated a second to see if she had been brought down. That second's wait cost him dear.

As he launched himself off the bough, Jess landed next to him. She seized him by the tail and hauled him roughly back. Grasping him by the ears, Jess gave a strong heave and held him kicking and dangling. Then she swung the sword in a glittering arc, shouting, 'Redwall! Redwall!'

The savage chief, held fast by the ears with the great sword flashing in front of his eyes, gave one loud piercing squeal.

Immediately all activity halted.

The small green and black painted beasts crowded the branches and packed the boughs, uncertain of what to do. One or two of the bolder ones began edging forward, until Jess swung the sword as if to strike. The captive leader gave a series of angry screams, so they fell back and remained still.

Basil paced up and down, using a broken lance as a swagger stick. 'Quick thinkin', Jess. That stopped the little devils. Y'deserve a mention in despatches for that, wot?'

Jess glared about her fiercely. 'It wouldn't do any good mentioning anything to this horde of hooligans. They don't have any recognizable language, screams and squeals are their only way of communication. How do we get out of this? It's like having a serpent by the tail.'

Basil turned to Matthias. 'She's right, y'know. We're caught in a bloomin' old standoff. The moment she lets that chap go we'll have the whole silly tribe down on our heads.'

Matthias had been thinking furiously. He whispered

to Log-a-Log before shouting up to Jess, 'See if you can make them understand that we want to trade their leader for Cheek. Leave the rest to me. I've got an idea and with a bit of luck it might work.'

Jess went into a series of mimes. She pointed at Cheek, then pointed to the ground. Holding the leader at paw's length, she let the sword hang loose by her side. The performance was repeated several times before the leader realized what she meant. Screeching and growling, he pointed at Cheek, then to himself.

'When they're both free, what then?' Orlando whispered to Matthias. 'We've broken the standoff but they won't let us walk unharmed through their territory.'

There was a clicking, scratching sound from the shrews surrounding Log-a-Log. Matthias watched anxiously until Log-a-Log winked at him. All was ready. Matthias took a deep breath.

'Stay close together when we have to move. Try not to turn your backs on the painted tribe. Right, Jess, let their chief free. They're releasing Cheek.'

The young otter scrambled free of the rope and made a hasty decent. Bumping and tripping, he half fell, half climbed, out of the tree.

Jess gave the leader a slight push and vaulted neatly down, returning the sword to Matthias.

There was a pause as the maddened creatures bunched to attack.

'Logalogalogalog!'

The shrew leader leapt forward with a blazing pinewood torch in either paw, grinning and showing his teeth. He made as if to touch the heavy pines that oozed resin all round him.

For the first time, the painted ones showed fear. They chattered and screeched wildly, bounding high into the trees at the sight of fire. Log-a-Log shook the torches in their direction.

'Haha! Desperate measures call for desperate

234

remedies, my friends,' he called. 'You're frightened of the flames, aren't you? One move, and I'll burn your forest and you with it.'

Matthias, Orlando and Basil started the column marching south.

'Come on Log-a-Log,' Matthias urged. 'I think they understand what we mean. Jabez, Cheek, get those extra torches from the Guosim and stay close to Log-a-Log. Don't let the fire go out.'

∽

Backing and shuffling, they made their way southeast through the dark pinewoods, grateful for the light of the torches. Progress was slow. Matthias could not see the painted ones but he knew they were in the trees above, following every step of the way.

Night had fallen by the time they had made their way out of the pines, to the shores of a great river. There was plenty of wood about at the forest edge, so Log-a-Log and his shrews made a huge bonfire, laying in a good supply of wood to last until dawn. The strange tribe of painted ones had retreated back into their pine forest, but Matthias took no chances. Sentries were posted. A meal was prepared, then they sat about on the bank, discussing the day's events, while deciding how to cross the river next day.

∽

Further south down the river, Mattimeo and his friends sat at the centre of a huge log raft surrounded by slavers. Two thick ropes connected the ferry to the far shore.

Slagar watched them rise and dip in the waters. 'Your rats pull strong and well, Stonefleck. We will soon be across.'

The deadpan expression did not leave Stonefleck's face.

'I have more fighters at my command than leaves on the trees, fox. Look behind you, on the shore over there. Your pursuers have made it through the pinewoods. They must be brave and resourceful. We will see just how brave on the morrow. My army could do with a bit of fun.'

Slagar gazed into the darkened waters. 'That's if they make it across the river!'

～

The confines of Cavern Hole became oppressive to John Churchmouse, although his wife actually enjoyed the close community, chatting with Cornflower and looking after baby Rollo. They were probably getting ready to rise and prepare breakfast with the Brothers and Sisters. John slipped out quietly, his recording books and pens in a satchel over his shoulder. He slid past Constance, who was sleeping on the stairs, crossed Great Hall and installed himself on a corner window ledge. It was a peaceful little niche where he often sat to write and morning sunlight flooded in, warming his face.

John opened his recording book as he gazed out at a corner of the orchard, watching three magpies flap off heavily until they were out of his vision.

By the fur! Those cheeky birds had a nerve. Occupying the Abbey roofspaces, and now filching supplies from the very orchard that the Redwallers tended so lovingly.

The mood for writing left John. He closed the book and climbed down from the sill. Help would be needed in the kitchens.

～

There was a disturbance at the top of the stairs between Great Hall and Cavern Hole. John broke into a run, the satchel bumping at his side. The crow they called Mangiz bowled him flat as he flapped off into the air towards the upper galleries.

Constance blundered into John and tripped. She sat up, shaking her paw at the bird.

'Scum, kidnapper, you filthy brute!' she shouted.

John stood up, dusting his habit off. 'What's happened, Constance? What is the matter?'

'Bad news, I'm afraid, John. You'd better come down into Cavern Hole. This concerns you.'

236

The Churchmouse followed the badger anxiously.

～

The creatures who were up and about gathered round Constance as she flung three scraps of material down upon the table.

'Look at this!'

The Abbot picked them up. 'Scraps of material. What are they?'

Constance ground her teeth together angrily. 'Pieces of Cornflower and Mrs Churchmouse's aprons and a fragment of baby Rollo's little habit. They've been captured by the birds.'

Abbot Mordalfus shook his head in disbelief. 'Impossible. Surely they were here last night, weren't they? Did anybeast see them?'

Foremole shrugged. 'May'ap, but maybe not. Oi niver thought of a-looken for 'em.'

John Churchmouse dashed his satchel to the floor. 'My wife, captured by those filthy birds. Where have they got her?'

He made a dash for the stairs and was stopped by Winifred and Ambrose. The churchmouse struggled furiously.

'Let me go, there's no telling what those murdering savages will do to her!'

'John Churchmouse, be still!' ordered Mordalfus. 'Come and sit by this table, sir. Come on, do as I say. You aren't doing anybeast a bit of good behaving like this. Let us hear what Constance has to say.'

John looked up in suprise. It was seldom that the Abbot spoke harshly to any creature. The fight went out of him and he allowed Ambrose to lead him to a chair.

Mordalfus turned to the badger. 'Constance, tell us all you know of this incident, please.'

'Father Abbot, there's not a lot to tell, I'm afraid. Yesterday Cornflower and Mrs Churchmouse were in the bell tower. Rollo must have joined them later. Well, when I called all the creatures in and shut the Abbey door

I must've locked them out. They probably didn't hear me calling. There's no entrance to the Abbey from the bell tower, so they must have tried later to cross the grounds. Those birds caught them in the open. The crow said that they took them to the roofspaces. General Ironbeak wants to see us outside at noon.'

∽

Sitting in a corner of the dimly lit roofspace, Cornflower and Mrs Churchmouse tried to make themselves as unobtrusive as possible, keeping baby Rollo quiet and still. General Ironbeak and his birds had returned from their dust bath on the path outside Redwall. It had done little good, and in the end they had resorted to wallowing in the brackish ditchwater to rid themselves of the sludge which clung to their feathers. It was not a great improvement; the stench still clung to them.

Ironbeak glared ferociously at his captives. '*Yagga!* You and your friends will pay dearly for this insult.'

Cornflower covered baby Rollo with her torn apron. 'You great bully, you deserve all you got!'

Mangiz had not been caught by the trap on the stairway, and he stayed slightly apart from his General, turning his beak to avoid the unpleasant odour.

'*Kraah!* Silence, mouse! At noon you will get all you deserve. You should be pleading with the mighty Ironbeak to spare your miserable lives.'

Mrs Churchmouse eyed the crow with distaste. 'We would never grovel to ruffians like you. Slay us if you want, but you will never conquer Redwall Abbey.'

'Brave words are like empty eggshells. You will beg when the times comes,' Mangiz predicted.

Rollo peered out from under the apron.

'Gen'ral Pongo!' he said, making a face.

'Silence! Keep that small one quiet or we will kill him now.'

'Oh, shut your beak, you coward!' Cornflower called out indignantly. 'Killing infants is probably about all you scavengers are good for.'

Mangiz was about to reply when Ironbeak silenced him.

'Mangiz, enough. We do not argue with mousewives.'

Mrs Churchmouse rummaged in her apron pocket and found some dried fruit she has been using in the kitchens. She gave it to baby Rollo and sat with her paw about him.

'I wish your Matthias were back, he'd know what to do,' she whispered.

'He certainly would, but don't worry, your John and Constance and the Abbot will see we come to no harm. It's Rollo I'm concerned about. They can do what they like with me, as long as they don't harm a hair on that baby's head.'

Mrs Churchmouse stroked Rollo's tiny ears. 'Yes, bless him. D'you remember when your Mattimeo was this size? My Tim and Tess weren't much older, and they were a trio of rascals, I can tell you.'

Cornflower smiled. 'Aye, but we had happy times with them. I hope, wherever they are now, that they're safe and well.'

'They'll all come marching back up that road one fine day, I know it. Then the enemies of our Abbey will rue the day they were born.'

31

Stonefleck's army was indeed a large one. Mattimeo had never seen so many rats. They swarmed through the bushes, trees and hillocks of the far shore, efficient and silent. Every rat carried a bow and arrows, and they gathered in groups, each under a leader who took his orders from Stonefleck the commander. The captives were secured among the trees, but Mattimeo could still see the river. He sat with Tim and Auma, listening to Stonefleck and Slagar conversing.

'Let us see if your pursuers can make it across the river, Slagar. They are a determined band, but they have not met my longtail army yet. All they have had to contend with is a few slavers.'

'I have a slave line to worry about,' the Cruel One sniffed. 'Open warfare is not my business. Besides, you have a mighty army.'

'Aye, and every one of them an expert archer. I could deal with those woodlanders using only a quarter of my force.'

'Huh, then why don't you?' Slagar challenged him.

'Because I never leave anything to chance. Are you going to stay and watch, just to make sure your enemies get slain?'

'No, I will carry on south. If your army is as good as

you boast, I should have no need to worry about being followed. Threeclaws! Form them up into line, we've got a full day's march ahead.'

◇

Mattimeo and his companions were jostled and prodded by Vitch. 'Say goodbye to your father and his friends, Mattimeo, they will be dead creatures before this day is through,' the rat taunted him.

The young mouse did not allow himself to be baited by Vitch, even though his heart sank at the thought of his father and the rest being caught out on the open water by the huge rat army that lay in wait on the shore of the river. He took a deep breath and smiled carelessly at the undersized rat.

'Your master Slagar could not kill my father, neither will Stonefleck and his vermin. The warrior of Redwall has proved himself before now against rat armies, and he will live to free us. When that day comes, you and I have a score to settle. I'll be looking for you, Vitch.'

As they were herded away through the trees, Mattimeo allowed himself one last backward glance at the far shore beyond the river shimmering in the morning sunlight. Though he could not see his father, he murmured under his breath, 'Martin keep him safe!'

◇

The sounds of axe and sword had been ringing through the pine fringe since dawn. Many of the trees at the edge had not been able to take proper root in the loose sandy soil of the banks, and some were only half grown. Orlando swung his mighty axe with long, powerful strokes, often felling a tree so that it took one of its weaker neighbours down with it. Matthias had cast his habit aside. He slashed and hacked at the branches of each felled tree, trimming it so that Cheek, Basil, Jess and Jabez could roll it down to where Log-a-Log was in charge of raft construction.

'Flugg, bring those ropes over here,' Log-a-Log ordered. 'Gurn, soak that moss well and mix it with soil; I

241

want good caulking that won't leak. Garr, I need that trunk over here. You others, help him.'

There was little the Guosim leader did not know about water-craft. Log-a-Log was a ferry shrew, the son of ferry shrews. He watched the flow of the river, pointing out his course to Basil.

'We'll take a wide sweep upriver, then I'll bring about in midwater and land us on the other shore somewhere about there, see? That way we'll be going due south again.'

Basil dipped one ear. 'Aye, aye, Cap'n, as you say. Bear in mind, old feller, that I wasn't cut out for a nautical career. I'll have to have a substantial meal first. No use bein' watersick on an empty tummy, wot?'

It was early noontide before the raft lay completed in the shallows. Log-a-Log folded his paws and shook his head.

'Bit rough, Matthias. Best I could do at short notice.'

Matthias passed him apples and shrewcake. 'She's a stout raft, Log-a-Log. I couldn't ask for better. I know you'll use all your skills to get us safely across. What are you so worried about, young Cheek?'

The otter stroked his dry nose. 'It's er, well, er, d'you see. . . . Well, it's the water, Matthias. I've always been a bit frightened of it. Oh, the odd stream and woodland pool aren't too bad, but look at the size of that old river. I never saw anything so big and fast-flowing in Moss-flower.'

Basil flung an apple core into the river. 'Haw haw! Well I've heard everythin' now, a bally otter who's frightened of rivers. Curl my whiskers, that's a good un.'

'Now, now, Basil,' Jess chided the scoffing hare, 'you're not too fond of the water yourself. It's bad form to make fun of another creature who feels the same.'

Basil relented and flung a paw around Cheek. 'Righto, point taken, Jess. Here, young otter m'lad, what say you and I stay together in the middle of the raft? We can hang on to each other and get into a fine old blue funk together, eh?'

Jabez Stump trundled aboard the raft. 'Ah well, we can't hang about here all day. There's a river to cross. You comin' aboard, Warrior?'

Matthias sheathed his sword and leapt on to the floating logs. 'Keep your heads down when we reach the other side. No telling what's waiting over there,' he warned.

Log-a-Log grasped the forked branch which served as a tiller. 'All aboard! Cast off on shore, poles ready riverward, bring her round. Steady as she goes, we're under way!'

∽

The raft bobbed and swayed out into the current. Blue waters reflecting the skies above rushed and danced to white foamy peaks spraying into the breeze.

The eyes of Stonefleck's rat army watched eagerly from the far bank as the little craft started its journey towards them.

∽

General Ironbeak landed skilfully on the path in front of the main Abbey door. He tucked his wings away neatly, parading up and down with a swaggering gait.

The door swung open, and Constance and the Abbot stepped outside, followed by John Churchmouse. The Abbot nodded civilly.

'Good afternoon. Do you wish to go inside?'

Ironbeak cocked his head on one side, eyeing them boldly. '*Yaggar*! What I have to say can be said out here, earthcrawlers. I hold the upper claw today. Maybe if you had killed my fighters and me on the stairs yesterday, instead of playing your silly little games, you would have been the victors. It is too late now; we meet on my terms.'

Mordalfus tucked his paws into the wide habit sleeves. 'Then speak. What is it you want of us?'

'Complete surrender, old mouse!'

'I am sorry but that is impossible,' the Abbot replied.

'Nothing is impossible if you hold dear the lives of your creatures.'

'We have lost Brothers and Sisters before now.'

'Aye, but that would have been without choice,' the General pointed out. 'Step forward a bit and look up to the rooftop of this redstone house.'

The three friends walked out on to the path. Shading their eyes, they looked up.

Ironbeak gave a harsh cry and waved one wing.

The three captives were forced to the roof edge, where they could be seen. John Churchmouse groaned aloud. Constance stood close to him and whispered, 'Courage, John. We'll get them back for you. Trust your Abbot, let him do the talking.'

The tiny figures high above swayed in the breeze, skirts billowing out as they kept hold of baby Rollo, who was waving cheerily.

'*Karra*! High, isn't it.' General Ironbeak preened his wing feathers as he spoke. 'Oh, not to a bird, but to an earthcrawler it is as if your head were bumping the clouds. It's a long way down too, if you don't hit the sides or bounce off a few gutters. Who knows, you might even smash through one of those low roofs. Imagine all that happening to a baby mouse. There wouldn't be much left to tell the tale when hē hit the ground.'

John Churchmouse bit his lip until the blood trickled to his chin.

The Abbot disguised his true feelings and shrugged carelessly. 'Then as far as I am concerned you have our surrender, but not completely. Unfortunately, I am only the voice of one, and this Abbey belongs to us all, not just me. We must have a little time to consider your offer, then a vote will have to be taken.'

Ironbeak raked the path fiercely with his talons. 'I will have your complete surrender. Now!'

The Abbot sat upon the path. Plucking a blade of grass, he sucked it, shaking his head.

'I am very sorry, but it is not my decision. Throw the

captives from the roof if you must. All our creatures are not present, and it is not possible to give you a firm decision right now. We need time to discuss this and take a ballot.'

Ironbeak kicked gravel left and right, realizing that if the captives were slain his bargaining power was lost.

'You say you need time. How much time, earth-crawler?' he demanded.

'Oh, at least three sunsets.'

'That is too long. How do I know you are not planning something?'

The Abbot looked old and frail, and he smiled disarmingly. 'General, you give us too much credit. What could we do against you in the space of three sunsets? We are not warriors, we cannot fly like you birds, we are only earthcrawlers. Besides, you hold the captives. What better insurance of our good behaviour?'

The raven signalled Mangiz to have the captives taken into the roofspaces.

'Two sunsets, not three.' He clacked his beak decisively. 'Two sunsets and no longer!

Mordalfus stood up and bowed gravely. 'Thank you, Ironbeak. You shall have our answer two sunsets from now.'

32

The raft was proving successful. Though the water hammered it hard in midcurrent, it held together admirably. Log-a-Log was in his element, manoeuvring the tiller as he shouted out orders above the rush of the waters. The long poles they had used for punting were now useless as a means of propelling the craft, and they relied upon the steering skills of the shrew leader.

Matthias stood at the forward end scanning the other shore, Basil and Cheek hung on to each other for dear life, with Jess, Jabez and Orlando near to paw, surrounded by shrews who packed the floating deck to its edges. They were past the midriver point when Matthias made his way across to Log-a-Log.

'How is she handling?'

'Oh, fine, Matthias, fine,' Log-a-Log said airily. 'As you can see, we've sprung a small leak or two, but nothing to worry about. I'll make for that spot over there. It's a curving inlet and the water looks almost still, so it must be by-passed by the main centre current. Are you all right, not worried about anything?'

'Not exactly worried, just keeping my eyes, ears and wits about me,' Mathias admitted. 'That shore looks a bit too peaceful for my liking.'

'Ha, anything that looks peaceful is exactly to my liking.'

∽

Stonefleck stood with his back to a rock on the open bank, completely disguised by his strange coat. In his paws he held a bow with an arrow notched on its string. Coolly he watched the raft looming larger, knowing that his formidable army were waiting, bows at the ready for their leader to fire the first arrow.

∽

Basil relaxed his grip on Cheek. 'Ha, we're not bad sailors after all, young Cheek. Can't you feel the water gettin' smoother, not so much of that infernal bobbin' up and down like a duck's bottom?'

'That's as may be Basil, but I won't feel easy until me young paws are on dry land again,' the otter said nervously. 'Lookit that Log-a-Log shrew, he's enjoyin' it all. I bet he'll be sorry to leave this raft.'

'Stand ready with those poles,' Log-a-Log called to the shrews seated at the outboard edges. 'We'll be into still waters soon.'

A hissing volley of arrows speeding like flighted death cut down the six shrews who stood grasping the poles. They toppled lifeless into the water.

Immediately, the shore was alive with innumerable rats unleashing arrows one after another into the unprotected creatures on the flat raft deck.

Taken completely by surprise, there was only one course of action open to Matthias. Ducking and dodging flying shafts, he yelled, 'Overboard! Everybeast overboard. Stay on the river side of the raft. Keep low!'

There was a mass scramble, making the raft tilt perilously. Matthias, Log-a-Log and Jess unfastened their slings. All around them the shrews leapt into the water, clinging to the side of the raft furthest from the shore. The three friends launched slingstones at the attackers, but they did little good. Arrows still poured back at them like spring rain.

'Log-a-Log, Jess, get off the raft, hurry!' Matthias shouted urgently.

The squirrel and the shrew did not stop to argue, they abandoned the heeling raft and took to the water. Matthias went last.

～

Stonefleck looked at the sky. Twilight was arriving. He signalled a cease-fire.

'Wait, they're in the water now. Let's watch the sport before we open up again. But pick off any loose ones that you sight.'

The rat army packed to the water's edge, gazing at the bobbing raft an arrow's-length away.

～

Basil spat out a mouthful of river water as he clung to the side of the raft.

'Ambushed!' he said disgustedly. 'Where in the name of fur and claw did that mob spring from? They're no slouches with those bows, Orlando.'

'If I could reach them with my battleaxe, I'd show them I'm no slouch, the filthy assassins. Ouch, what was that?'

There were shouts and screams from the shrews.

'Ow! I've been bitten!'

'Ouch, ow! Me too!'

'Owooh! I'm bleeding!'

Matthias gritted his teeth. 'Silence. Be still. It's probably nothing.'

Jess changed places until she was by Matthias. 'Owch! It's like sitting on a beehive,' she complained. 'Cheek's got more sense. Look, he's still on the raft.'

A shrew who had been bitten tried hauling himself out of the water; he took an arrow between the eyes. Another shrew tried swimming away from the raft; two arrows sank him. The rats were sniping from the bank at anything that popped up or moved.

Cheek lay sprawled flat in the centre of the raft, ignoring Matthias.

'Come off that raft, Cheek. You'll be shot,' Matthias said sharply.

'No fear. Lie low and cling tight, that's what I'm going to do. I'm not going into that river.'

Basil sucked up water and spat it at the young otter.

'You little nuisance, come off that raft, sir. Off, I say!' he ordered.

Matthias felt tiny teeth bite his tail. He kicked out and was bitten again.

'Leave him, Basil. Let's think of some way out of this. The raft is drifting towards those rats. Duck! They're firing again.'

More volleys of arrows followed.

～

For the first time in a long while, Stonefleck allowed himself a tight smile of satisfaction. 'We've got them. They're sailing towards us. Keep up the arrows! Those who aren't eaten will be shot. I want no captives. We're not slavers; leave that to Slagar.'

～

Jabez Stump was being bitten on his unprotected paws.

'I can't stand much more of this,' the hedgehog winced. 'What's to be done?'

'Hold the raft tight,' Log-a-Log called out. 'Try backing water. We might just tow it off into the main current again and get washed away from this lot.'

They tried as hard as they could, and the raft backed off slightly.

'It's heavy going. Cheek, will you get off that raft. We're towing your weight down here,' Matthias said crossly.

Cheek lay flat, clinging tighter to the deck as arrows whizzed over him in flights.

'No! Go 'way, leave me alone.'

Orlando lost his temper. He took the battleaxe by its head and made a mighty sweep at Cheek with the long handle.

Darkness had practically fallen, and the young otter

did not see the axe handle coming. It struck him a blow and pushed him off into the water with a loud splash. 'Yah gerroff, you great stripedo—'

Splash!

Cheek could not deny his birthright; he was an otter through and through. As skilfully as any fish, he cut through the water surrounding the raft, appearing alongside Basil.

The hare looked at him suspiciously. 'You're chewing, young Master Cheek. Where are you hidin' the food?'

Cheek smacked his lips. 'Little fishes. The river's swarmin' with 'em, there must be millions. Taste lovely, though. I'd have got into the water sooner if I'd known I wasn't goin' to be afraid and all this food was here.'

With that, he disappeared beneath the surface and began filling his stomach with the finny delicacies. Cheek was biting back.

∽

On shore Stonefleck rapped out orders to one of his Captains. 'Light some flaming arrows. Shoot at the raft. Hurry, or they'll paddle it out of our reach. Tell the others to get the ferry going. See if we can get closer. The rest of you, keep firing.'

The rat Captain looked questioningly at Stonefleck. 'But surely they'll be eaten by the fishes?'

Stonefleck fired off an arrow before replying, 'It's the otter. I forgot about that one. He'll eat those fish like a pig at acorns.'

'But there's far too many fish for him to eat, Chief. The water's alive with 'em,' the Captain argued.

'Fool! Once those fish sense there's an otter in the water, they'll stay away from that area. Then those creatures will be able to paddle the raft out into the mainstream current. I want to finish it here tonight, not in the morning a night's march down the bank. Now get about your business.'

∽

Matthias heaved a sigh of relief. 'Whew! At least those fish aren't biting so much.'

Cheek popped up beside him. 'Yum, yum. You've got me to thank for that!'

Orlando ducked him back under with a big blunt paw.

'Stop gabbing and keep scoffing. You to thank indeed! You mean you've got my axe handle to thank. And don't think you won't taste it if you don't keep those fishes away, young otter.'

The night sky was cut by the light of a flaming arrow which shot through the dark to bury itself in the side of the raft.

Jess put it out by squirting a mouthful of water at it. 'Fire arrows, Matthias,' she remarked, 'Look, I can see by the light of their fire that they're launching a raft.'

Matthias redoubled his efforts.

'Hurry, everybeast, kick out as hard as you can.'

Cheek gripped a trailing rope in his teeth and swam strongly with it. The raft doubled its speed. Arrows zinged all around them as the rats leant over the rails of their own ferry raft.

'Keep down, keep pulling, keep paddling,' Orlando yelled. 'They're coming after us.'

As he shouted, a shrew next to him let go and floated away, transfixed by an arrow.

$\backsim$

Stonefleck was on the raft, firing arrow after arrow.

'Don't let them get away,' he exhorted his army. 'Get the poles. Come on, get pushing with those poles. Fire! Keep after them!'

With superior numbers and long poles, the rat ferry drew closer to the raft. Stonefleck waved to the shore.

'No more fire arrows,' he ordered. 'You might hit us. We've got them now!'

$\backsim$

Log-a-Log spat into the water.

'Did you hear that, Guosim. Kick now. Kick for your lives!'

The raft pulled away fractionally, but Stonefleck urged his rats to greater efforts with their long poles.

The two vessels were only separated by a thin margin of river. Stonefleck and a few chosen rats stood outside the rails of the ferry, preparing to jump from one craft to the other. The light of victory gleamed in Stonefleck's normally impassive eyes.

Matthias pulled himself up and saw what was happening.

'It looks as if they're going to board us,' he said gloomily.

Orlando heaved himself from the water and stood dripping on the deck of the raft, waving his battleaxe.

'Come on, rats, let's see what you've got inside your heads!' he taunted.

An arrow from the rat ferry struck Orlando in his paw. He pulled it out contemptuously. Snapping it easily, he flung it at Stonefleck.

'You'll have to do better than that to stop me, ratface!' he called.

Suddenly the raft sped off downriver on the rushing current. The rat ferry stopped stock-still, throwing Stonefleck and several others into the water.

Hurriedly, the rats dragged their leader and the others back aboard.

Stonefleck twanged his wet bowstring and spat water. 'Why didn't somebeast untie the ferry towropes? Pull us back to shore. We'll have to follow along the bank.'

A ragged cheer arose from the shrews' raft as the friends disappeared into the night on the rushing water.

∽

That evening, a group sat around the table in Cavern Hole discussing General Ironbeak's ultimatum. The reaction was angry and indignant.

'Who does he think he is? Redwall isn't conquered that easy.'

'We beat them once, we can do it again.'

'Aye, but this time Ironbeak has the hostages.'

'He'll kill them if we don't surrender.'

'Hurr, he'm a crafty owd burdbag, that'n.'

The Abbot rapped the table. 'Silence, please. We have no time to sit about arguing. What I need is some sensible suggestions. Let us review the position. The raven has the hostages, and no matter how we try to buy time or debate, he'll kill them eventually, make no mistake about that. I tried to bluff him today, possibly I succeeded, but it won't last. Listen, even if it meant the loss of just one life, I would have to surrender the Abbey. We cannot have three deaths on our heads; it is against all our principles.'

Winifred the Otter thumped the table with her tail. 'Play the villain at his own game, then. What's the name for it? Er, subterfuge, that's it. We'll use subterfuge.'

Every creature sat up bright and attentive. When there was no response to Winifred's suggestion, they slumped back.

'We'm gotter be a-thinken 'ard, rasslin' wi' uz brains,' Foremole urged.

More silence followed.

'Surely somebody must have a glimmer of a plan?' Winifred said sadly.

'Here comes supper. Let's think while we eat,' the Abbot suggested.

'Good idea,' Ambrose Spike agreed. 'Sometimes I thinks the brainbox and the stomach bag is joined up some'ow. Hoho, I say, they done us proud, acorn salad and spiced apple'n'damson pie—'

'Pie, that's it!'

They turned to stare at John Churchmouse.

'I was trying to remember the name of those black and white birds that are with Ironbeak. It's pie. Magpie!'

The Abbot put aside his platter. 'Go on, John, think hard. Have you got an idea?'

John scratched his whiskers in frustration. 'Oh, if only I could remember what it was. It's stuck right between the tips of my ears. Hmph! It's no good, I've forgotten now.'

Ambrose supped October ale noisily from a beaker.

'Pity, I thought you was goin' to come up with a plan to get your missus an' Cornflower an' that babby down off the roof.'

'The roof, the magpies, that's it!' John Churchmouse banged his paw down on the table, squelching a wedge of pie by mistake. 'Of course, I saw those three magpies only this morning, robbing our orchard and flying up to the eaves. Those birds are Ironbeak's supply line. He needs them to bring in food!'

'And if we could capture 'em, we could do a swap,' Winifred said through a mouthful of salad. 'Three magpies for three hostages. Good idea, John.'

'Burr aye, vittles be of more use to burdbags than 'ostages. Otherwise they'd be a-starved from 'unger,' Foremole added.

Constance rapped the table. 'Right, let's get a proper plan organized. What we propose is to capture the three magpies and exchange them for the hostages. No army can survive without supplies, and Ironbeak knows this. He wouldn't be able to keep his followers here if they were starving. This way we can save Redwall and get the hostages back. But how do we capture the magpies?'

The Abbot held up a paw. 'I used to be the Abbey fishermouse before I was Abbot. Could we not snare them with fishing nets? We've got lots of big nets.'

'Well said, Abbot, but magpies are not fishes. How would you snare them into nets?' Constance asked.

Ambrose Spike poked his snout out of the ale beaker. 'Find out where they get their food supplies and put down bait.'

'I think they get their supplies from our orchard,' John Churchmouse said, licking pie from his paw.

Little Sister May was highly indignant. 'I'm certain they do, Father Abbot! Only today I saw them from the infirmary window, those three dreadful birds, stealing from our orchard. Anything that falls ripe from a bush or tree, they carry off. It's theft, that's what it is.'

'Durty ol' burdbags, oi was a-wonderen whurr all they ripe strawb'rries was agoin'.'

'Exactly, Mr Foremole.' Sister May wagged a reproving paw. 'At one time it was only you and Mr Stag Hare who used to steal them, but those three birds, gracious me! You'd think we were growing strawberries just for their benefit. I watched them guzzle down a great load before carrying off as much as they could with them. Disgraceful!'

Foremole covered his eyes with a huge digging paw. 'Hurr hurr, Sister. Oi was only a-testin' they berries. It were mainly young Mattimeo an' that Tim'n'Tess wi' thurr squirrel pal as scoffed most o' them. Hurr hurr, young roguers!'

'You're right, Foremole,' John Churchmouse sniffed. 'I only wish they were still here to do it, I for one wouldn't grudge them the odd strawberry from the patch.'

There were murmurs of agreement from all.

Little Sister May blew her nose loudly. 'Well, talk like this isn't getting many dishes washed. I've got an idea. Suppose we gather the ripest strawberries and sprinkle them with some sort of knockout drops, then we could put them in one place in the orchard and lie in wait with the nets.'

'Sister May, I'm shocked and surprised at you!' Abbot Mordalfus shook his head in amazement. 'What a good idea. But I'm not sure we know enough about knockout drops. That's the sort of thing the masked fox used on us. You can look to villains for that sort of thing, but we are only simple Abbey dwellers.'

'Leave it to me Father Abbot,' little Sister May smiled sweetly. 'I have enough herbs, berries and roots in my infirmary cupboard to lay a horse out flat. Oh, it will be exciting. I've always wanted to try my paw at knockout dropping.'

Foremole tugged his snout in admiration. 'You'm a proper liddle fiend an' no mistake, marm. Oi'll escort you up to 'firmary to pick up your potions an' suchloik.'

Ambrose Spike crooked a paw at the Abbot. 'Follow

me, I've got your big nets stowed away in my cellars.'

Mobilized by fresh hope, the Abbey dwellers went about their tasks.

Up in the roofspaces Cornflower rocked the sleeping baby Rollo upon her lap as she and Mrs Churchmouse conversed in hushed tones.

'Look, bless him, he's snoring away like my Mattimeo used to when he was a baby,' she said, becoming sad. 'I don't think there's a moment of one day since Mattimeo's been gone when I haven't thought of him. First I worry, then I tell myself it'll be all right because Matthias will have probably found him, then I go back to worrying, then I tell myself he may have escaped. Oh, Mrs Churchmouse, if only they were all babies again like Rollo.'

'Aye, those were the best times. My Tim and Tess were a right pair of little scallywags, I can tell you. Mr Churchmouse and I never got a wink's sleep that first season they were born. All they wanted to do was play the whole night long. D'you suppose that the raven will really have us thrown from the roof?' asked Mrs Churchmouse apprehensively.

'He'll do what he has to, Mrs Churchmouse. I'm afraid of him, but I don't care what happens as long as that horrible bird doesn't get Redwall. That would be the end.'

The churchmouse stroked baby Rollo; he had stopped snoring and started sucking his paw.

'What hope is there for this poor little mite, no mummy and a prisoner too?' she wondered.

Cornflower sighed. The roofspace was dark and chilly with night draughts sweeping in under the eaves. All around them the black birds perched in the rafters, and it was difficult to tell whether they were awake or sleeping. She wondered where Matthias was and what he would be doing at this moment. Thinking of her husband, the Redwall Warrior, gave her courage again.

'Don't you fret, Mrs Churchmouse. Our friends in the

Abbey will have made plans to free us, you'll see. Let's try and get a bit of sleep. Here, we'll share my old shawl.'

Clouds scudded across the moon on their way across the night sky, while a million stars twinkled over the gently swaying forest.

33

Mattimeo was awakened by the sound of the night guards. Bageye and Skinpaw were on duty, and they walked past the sleeping captives conversing in low earnest tones. The young mouse could not hear what was said, though he strained his ears to catch any hint as to their eventual destination.

'Matti, are you awake?'

'Only just, Tess. Keep your voice down, the rest are still asleep.'

'Is anything the matter?' the churchmouse asked.

'Yes and no,' he replied. 'I was trying to hear what the guards were talking about. They've seemed very edgy since we left the forest and hills where Stonefleck and his rats live.'

'That's strange, I noticed the same thing last night, before we camped down here. They're all so silent and uneasy, even Slagar.'

Mattimeo raised his head, taking in the scene around him. The earth was flat, dry and dusty; no trees grew and there was little sign of any grass, shrubs or greenery. It was a dusty brown desolation stretching out before them.

'I tell you, Tess, I don't like it myself. This far south Mossflower country is very odd. Listen, you can't even

258

hear a single bird singing. What sort of land is it where even the birds cannot live?'

Young Jube the hedgehog stirred in his sleep, he whimpered and turned restlessly. Tess passed her paw gently over his headspikes, and he settled down into a quiet slumber.

'Poor little Jube,' she said sympathetically. 'He used to be so confident that his father would rescue him, and treated the whole thing as if he were only along with us for part of the journey. I'm worried about him, he's so thin and sad-looking these days.'

Mattimeo smiled at the churchmouse. 'You sounded just like your mum then, Tess, always fussing and worrying over some young one. You're right, though, Jube isn't his old self any more. In fact, none of us are, we're much thinner and older. I'm not surprised, after all we've been through since that night of the feast at Redwall.'

Tess looked at her habit. It was torn, dusty and stained.

'It all seems so long ago. I think we've grown up a lot since then. Ah, well, the main thing is that we're still together. We've made friends, too. Look at Auma; I couldn't imagine life without her and Jube any more.'

Slavers and captives alike began wakening. Mattimeo winked at Tess and smiled as cheerfully as he could.

'We'll come through it all, you wait and see,' he said comfortingly. 'Ho hum! Another nice sunny day for a walk, eh, Tess? I wonder where old Slagar is taking us today. Nut-gathering? Picknicking? What do you think?'

Tess stood up, looking a bit more like her old self. 'Oh, I think we'd better just stay with the rest and have a nice ramble,' she chuckled. 'What about you? Would you like to play follow my leader – or should I say, follow my Slagar? Come on, mouse, pick up your daisy chain and let's go.'

Bageye checked their manacles, muttering in a sullen voice, 'Huh, don't know what you two have got to laugh about.'

Orlando waded ashore towing the raft behind him. It had been a hard and dangerous night, fighting their way out of the main current back into the shallows. The crew had poled the raft into a small bay. Wet and weary, they stumbled on to dry land in the pale dawn light, shivering after their nightlong ordeal on the swift choppy river.

Basil slicked water from his long drooping ears. 'Whaaw! Here's one old soldier who won't complain when the sun starts getting hot. No chance of a bite o' breakfast, I suppose?'

Matthias dried his sword carefully on a tussock of grass. 'No chance at all, old soldier. Those rats will be dashing along the banks right now, hoping they'll catch up with us. We'd better move fast if we want to stay alive. Log-a-Log, you and Cheek tow the raft out a bit. The current will carry it away; no sense leaving it here as a marker where we came ashore. Jess, Jabez, would you take the rear and try to cover our tracks from the bank? Leave them as few clues as possible; it may buy us a bit of time.'

Jess Squirrel bounded up a nearby tree, took a quick look around and descended speedily.

'Matthias, we'd better hurry,' she urged. 'I could see movement in the bushes further up the bank. If we stay here much longer we're going to have company.'

'Right, Jess. Come on, everybody. Keep me in sight. I'm going to take a curving sweep into these trees, then with a bit of luck we'll circle south and miss the rats. Hurry now, let's get out of he—'

An arrow bedded in the ground. It stood quivering a fraction from Orlando, who kicked it into the river.

'That's the trouble with being my size, you make a good target. Let's run for it!'

∽

The rat advance scout fired a whistling arrow upwards to alert the main body. Stonefleck turned in its direction.

'They're trying to head south through the trees. Follow me, we'll cut them off.'

He set off at a tangent, cutting into the woodland to outflank Matthias.

Morning sunlight slanted into the trees as swarms of rats ran silently, keeping abreast of their leader. Stone-fleck halted on a sloping hillside and listened carefully: they were coming. Nodding to his followers, he dropped down behind an oak. The rats spread themselves among the other trees, notching arrows on to bowstrings. He could not have timed it better. The woodlanders came hurrying through the forest below, looking back over their shoulders to see if they were being pursued.

Stonefleck let fly a shaft at the mouse in the lead, hoping to catch him in the side of his neck. The mottled rat gave a grunt of disappointment as the arrow pinged harmlessly off the hilt of a big sword the mouse was carrying slung across his back and shoulders. A hail of arrows hit the main party below, shrews fell slain and wounded as the mouse in the lead shouted:

'Ambush! They're on our right flank. Follow me!'

They rushed for cover in the protection of the forest to their left. Stonefleck dashed down the hill after them.

'Charge!'

It was a lucky accident that Stonefleck tripped over a protruding tree root. The rats swarmed past him in a headlong attack, only to be met by Matthias and Orlando.

The two warriors had taken a temporary stand, allowing the rest of their party to get away. Armed only with bows and arrows, the rats could not fire in close combat. Orlando took the first two with a cleaving sideways chop of the huge war axe, while Matthias stepped swiftly from behind a tree and slew a rat who was dashing past. Turning quickly, he took another on the point of his sword. Orlando thundered into a group of the front runners. Wielding his axe, he scattered them like chaff, roaring aloud his battlecry:

'Eulaliaaaaa!'

'Redwallll!'

Matthias was at his side, the scything, whirling blade cutting a deadly pattern of cold steel amid the rats.

Stunned by the shock of the wild attack, the rat horde fell back. Stonefleck ran up, urging them forward.

'Rush them, there's only two. Come on!'

They regrouped and dashed in, yelling wildly, but the two warriors were gone!

∽

Matthias and Orlando ran panting into the main party a short distance ahead. The warrior mouse was angry.

'Why didn't you keep running? We would have caught up with you.'

Basil shook his head. 'We couldn't, not after we heard all the screams and shouts from back there. We were about to go back and help you.'

'You should have kept going,' Matthias repeated. 'No time to argue now, here they come again.'

Log-a-Log broke into a run, pointing ahead. 'Look, there's a clearing over that way. Let's get to the other side of it and hold them off with our slings.'

∽

Stonefleck and his horde were hot on the trail. They had covered half the clearing when a deep shrew voice called out:

'Sling!'

A rain of hard river pebbles struck the rats, felling several and driving the rest back. Stonefleck grouped his force at the other side of the clearing. They stood among the trees and returned fire with arrows. Screams and cries rang out as the battle raged back and forth, shafts going one way, stones flying the other. Basil took charge of the slingers, forming them into three ranks.

'First rank, sling and reload! Second rank, sling and reload! Third rank, sling and reload!' he ordered.

Matthias and his friends did as best as they could, dodging from tree to tree, picking off the odd rat with their slings.

Jess took a brief respite and dropped down by Matthias.

'I'm out of stones. Have you got many left?' she asked the warrior mouse.

'Hardly any. They're no match for arrows, Jess. Look, there's more rats arriving by the moment; we're outnumbered by at least ten to one.'

'At least. They only have to follow us and pick us off one by one, and we can't make a run for it now, their firepower is too heavy. I'd hate to die this far from Redwall, Matthias.'

'Me too, Jess, but they've got us pinned down now. It was a mistake to try and make a stand, but they'd have caught us if we'd kept running. I'll have to rack my brains and see if I can't come up with— What's that?'

'Sparra kill! Kill! Kill! Eeeeeeeeeee!'

Queen Warbeak and her Sparra fighters hurtled into the rats like a winged shower of small beaks and talons.

Jess leapt forward. 'Matthias, it's Warbeak and her Sparra folk. What are they doing here?'

'I don't know, but they'll be massacred if we don't help them. Basil, Log-a-Log! Come on. Chaaaaarge!'

$\backsim$

Quickbill and his two brothers Brightback and Diptail had found an easy source of supply for Ironbeak's fighters. Why forage in the woods when there was a beautiful orchard right in the grounds of the big redstone house?

With the Redwall inhabitants forced to stay indoors, the three magpies had grown bold. Now they did not even bother foraging by night. Each day they would fly down to the orchard and eat their fill before loading up with supplies to take to the roofspace. Quickbill was amazed at so much different fruit growing in one place; he had never encountered an orchard before.

'*Hakka*! The northlands were never like this, brothers; apples, pears, plums and the juicy red berries!'

The trio stood around the strawberries on the ground, unhurried, each seeking out a bigger strawberry than the one his brother was eating. They were behaving like naughty young ones raiding the orchard.

'*Chakka*! Look at this one, it is like two stuck together.'

'*Yaah*, but this berry is more red and shiny, see.'

'*Kacha*! I will eat them all as long as they are fat and juicy.'

The magpies' long tails dipped and jerked as they gobbled the strawberries with swift bobbing head movements. They carried on, comparing berries as they greedily ravaged the well-tended strawberry patch. Suddenly Brightback belched, then he staggered and fell awkwardly.

His two brothers cackled aloud at the sight.

'*Chahaha*! The red berries are making you too fat to stand, brother. We will load our bags and fly back up.'

Diptail pecked at a berry and missed. His beak struck the soil. Smiling foolishly, he flapped his wings and fell flat.

'*Yakko*! The red berries are magic. I cannot fly,' he giggled.

Quickbill yawned. He lay in the soil, flapping his wings against it with a silly grin on his face.

'*Coohoo*! Look at me, I'm flying.'

∽

Led by Constance, a group of Redwallers crept out from behind a buttress at the east corner of the Abbey. They were carrying nets.

'Easy now, let's bag all three at once.'

Quickbill was the strongest of the three. He saw the shadow of the net spreading over him, but he felt unable to do anything about it. Diptail was in a deep drugged sleep. Brightback tried to keep his eyes open, but they snapped shut. The net fell on them, trapping the three birds squarely at its centre. They lay stunned amid the remains of the knockout strawberries.

Little Sister May came out from behind the raspberry canes, wagging a paw at the sleeping thieves. 'It serves you right. I hope you wake with dreadful headaches!'

Constance and Winifred rolled the magpies tightly in the nets. 'They can't hear you, Sister,' Constance told her. 'Let's get them inside before we're spotted.'

Pushing and tugging, they lugged their feathered hostages inside.

The Abbot dusted off his paws. 'Well done, my friends. What do we do now, wait until the appointed time or open negotiations right away?'

Constance gave a huge grin. She was beginning to enjoy herself.

'Allow me, Father Abbot. Leave it to Ambrose and me. We'll go and inform Ironbeak that we have three chickens in the bag. The rest of you, take up your posts at the windows, and make sure there are plenty of arrows and spears showing.'

$\backsim$

Constance and Ambrose strolled out in leisurely fashion. The badger threw her head back and called up to the roof, 'Hey, you up there! Irontrousers, or whatever you call yourself. Get down here, I want a word with you.'

Ambrose sniggered into his paws. 'I wish Basil Stag Hare was here, he'd think of some good names to call that bird.'

There was a short silence, then Mangiz appeared at the eaves. The crow flapped down to a lower roof level.

'Are you ready to surrender so early, stripedog?' he asked.

'Go and boil your beak, featherbag!'

'Silence, earthcrawler. My General sent me to speak with you.'

Ambrose wrinkled his snout at Mangiz. 'Listen, maggotbrain, you just flap back to your Chief and tell him that we want to speak to the big fish and not the little worm. Hurry up now, don't stand there gawpin'!'

The seer crow was outraged. 'Mangiz does not forget an insult, hedgepig.'

Ambrose smiled cheekily. 'Good, then here's a few more for you to remember, you pot-bellied, cross-eyed, feather-bottomed excuse for a duck. Now be off with you before I really get goin'!'

When the crow had gone, Ambrose turned to Constance. 'What d'you think, stripedog, was I a bit too hard on him?'

Constance thought for a moment. 'No, no, on the whole I thought you did quite well, hedgepig.'

～

Ironbeak flew out with Mangiz and several of the rooks. They came down to the lowest roof. Constance did not mince her words.

'Hello there, Ironbum, or is it Tinbeak? I can never remember. Anyhow, about the three hostages you're holding, don't you think it's high time you let them go?'

Ironbeak suspected by the badger's tone that something was amiss, but he kept up a bold imperious front.

'If you have not come to surrender, they will die, earthcrawler.'

Ambrose wriggled his spikes. 'I knew you'd do no good talking politely to that bird.'

Constance stopped her teasing. Now that she had drawn the raven out, her tone became harsh and serious.

'Listen to me, Ironbeak. We are holding your three magpies prisoner. If you harm a single hair of those hostages, I will personally drown those birds in our Abbey pond. Is that clear?'

The birds on the roof cawed and cackled in consternation. Ironbeak silenced them with a wave of his wing.

'You have captured Quickbill and his brothers? I do not believe it.'

Constance moved to the Abbey door. 'Then I will show you the proof. We have cut your supply line; you will starve without the magpies.'

Constance went indoors. A moment later, she was dragging out the net with the three magpies inside.

'They say that seeing is believing, what do you say to that?' she called.

Ironbeak peered over the guttering. 'I say that it was very clever of you, stripedog. But it will do you no good, I will send others out to forage.'

'Oh, as I understand it, warriors are warriors, not

scavengers. Your fighters could not do the job, that's why you had magpies.'

'*Kaah*! Then we will become scavengers, we will take the food from that place you call orchard.'

Ambrose pointed to the windows. 'No you won't, we've got archers, sling-throwers and javelins stationed at the windows facing the orchard. It is not as far to shoot from there as it is from the ground to the rooftop. Send a few of those birds into the orchard now and you'll see what we mean.'

Whilst Ironbeak stood on the roof digesting this information, Ambrose pointed at the remains of the strawberries lying in the patch.

'Shoot!'

There was a twang and hiss from the windows. Four arrows and two javelins stood quivering among the strawberries.

Ironbeak swallowed hard. 'What do you want?'

Constance kept a heavy paw upon the net. 'You know what we want, an exchange of hostages.'

'What you ask is not possible.'

'Then your army will starve in the roofspaces,' she warned.

'We will kill your mice if you do not surrender,' Ironbeak countered.

'And we will kill your magpies. This net is weighted with stones. They will drown in the pond.'

'You are peaceful creatures. I know your ways, you could not do such a thing.'

Constance seized the net in her paws and then began dragging it to the Abbey pond.

'Your mistake,' she snarled savagely. 'They may be peaceable creatures; badgers are not. It will be a pleasure to rid Mossflower of this scum. I am done with talking!'

The big badger tumbled the net into the shallows.

Revived by the water, the three magpie brothers awoke, spluttering.

'*Yagga*! Save us, Ironbeak, save us. Help, we will drown trapped in this net. Ironbeak, General, save us!'

The birds on the roof danced anxiously around their leader, cawing and flapping. Mangiz whispered something to him. The raven General cocked his head towards the crow, his bright eye roving across the scene at the pond.

When Mangiz had finished, Ironbeak spoke in a level voice:

'Stop! Do not drown my magpie brethren. They have served me well. I will talk terms with you.'

A great cheer arose from the defenders at the window slits.

Constance gave a silent sigh of relief. 'Then you agree to our request, three in exchange for three?'

Ironbeak spread his wings. 'So be it! The exchange will take place here, in front of this redstone house when the evening bells toll at sunset.'

Ambrose exchanged glances with Constance.

'Let the hostages be freed here and now!' she proposed.

Ironbeak folded his wings and closed his eyes with finality. 'Do not stretch your luck, earthcrawlers. You have gained a victory. The exchange will take place as I say. Agreed?'

Constance hauled the net from the shallows. 'Agreed!'

When the birds had flown, Ambrose shook his head at Constance. 'It's some sort of trap, I can feel it in me spikes. That bird has somethin' in mind for us. Didn't you see him whispering with the crow? They were hatching a plan.'

The Abbot came out to greet them.

'I agree with Ambrose,' he said. 'They are obviously working out a trap. You did well. It was a good bluff, Constance.'

The big badger looked grim. 'It was no bluff, Father Abbot. I would drown a dozen like these in the net if our Abbey or our creatures were threatened. We will wait and see what they have planned for sunset.'

268

34

Queen Warbeak and her sparrows stood little chance against the rats. Many of them were shot in the air. But the Queen and her Sparra warriors were brave and reckless fighters, and they plunged in regardless of danger. Matthias and Orlando headed the charge across the clearings; the shrews drew their short swords and followed. Cheek, Jess and Jabez whirled slings loaded with stones as clubs, and Basil hurtled in with both long back legs kicking dangerously.

'Redwaaaall! Mossfloweeeer! Guosim! Logalogalog!'

The speed of the attack, combined with the sparrow assault, took the rats off guard. They fought tooth and claw, using arrows to stab with, but they were no match for the force that came at them, despite their superior numbers.

The shrews were fearsome warriors at close quarters, with their short swords. They fought in groups facing outwards. Circling and milling, they created a carousel of slaughter. Rats fell screaming and kicking everywhere. Cheek and Jabez stood back to back, thwacking away with their loaded slings. Sparra warriors fastened their claws into rats' heads and pecked madly at their faces. The rats were unused to being attacked in their own territory and they fought mainly a defensive action.

Many brought down shrews and sparrows. However, they were no match for Matthias and Orlando; the axe and the sword swathed into them at every turn. And rats flew high in the air from Basil's awesome kicks.

The battle raged back and forth. The woodlanders were still greatly outnumbered, though their weapons and fighting skills were superior. It might have gone one way or the other, when Log-a-Log turned the tide. He spied Stonefleck slinking away into the trees, and using his sword as a spear, he launched it at the rat Chieftain. His aim was true. Stonefleck fell, slain by the sword Log-a-Log had thrown.

When the rats saw their leader fall, the fight went out of them. Screaming and wailing, they scurried off into the trees.

∽

Matthias stood leaning on his sword, breathing heavily. Ignoring the cuts and bites he had taken, the warrior mouse extended his paw to the shrew leader.

'Well thrown, Log-a-Log!'

The shrews gave a loud cheer for their leader.

Matthias looked around. The slain littered the edge of the clearing like leaves in autumn.

'Where is my friend Queen Warbeak?' he asked.

His heart sank within him. A small group of Sparra warriors who had survived the battle were grouped about their fallen Queen. Matthias, Jess and Basil knelt by her side, tears streaming openly down their faces for the Sparra Queen lying there. Warbeak's eyes were dimmed in death, the breeze moved her feathers gently.

A sparrow passed Matthias a small scroll. 'We come alla way from Redwall,' he told the warrior mouse. 'Abbot say give you um this. Queen see you in trouble with ratworms. She say help um friend Matthias.'

∽

Jess lifted Warbeak lightly, and carried her up into a sycamore tree. Laying her on a broad bough, she covered the Sparra Queen with leaves in the time-honoured Sparra fashion.

Matthias sat at the foot of the sycamore, his head in both paws, grieving for Warbeak.

Basil came over and patted Matthias. 'There, there, old lad. I know it's a pity she had to die so far from Redwall, but she saved us by her courage.'

Matthias plucked at a blade of grass. 'Yes, the Queen loved Redwall. That was the bravest thing I've ever seen any creature do, Basil. She threw herself and her warriors at those rats, knowing they stood no chance. They flew in against arrows and attacked with only beak and claw.'

Orlando wiped his axe blade on the grass. 'I never knew your sparrow friend, Matthias, but she saved all our lives by her brave action. I've seen creatures ten times her size without a quarter of her boldness. What a warrior!'

Jess Squirrel looked up to the leafy shroud on the tree bough. 'Good old Warbeak, eh? Totally mad, of course. She'd rather die than miss a good fight. I'll bet wherever she is now that she's chuckling at us standing round blubbering like a load of Abbey babes who have to go to bed early, instead of getting on with our search for the fox.'

Matthias rose dry-eyed. He stuck his swordpoint into the ground.

'Aye, Jess, you're right. We've got some burying to do here, then we will leave this place. I never want to set eyes on it again. We must carry on south.'

∽

Later that day they halted in a quiet place, an ash grove, far from the clearing where the battle had taken place. Matthias took stock of the situation. The surviving sparrows would fly back to Redwall, taking with them the news that the warrior mouse and his friends were alive and well, still on the trail of the young captives. Log-a-Log and the remainder of the now depleted Guosim voted firmly to stay with the friends and see the mission through. They settled down to study the map and writings that had been sent from Redwall.

Matthias scanned the parchments carefully.

'By the fur, I wish we had met up with Warbeak before we did. Listen to this:

> "Those who wish to challenge fate,
> To a jumbled shout walk straight.
> Sunset fires in dexteree,
> Find where Loamhedge used to be.
> At the high place near the skies,
> Look for other watchful eyes.
> Sleep not 'neath the darkpine trees,
> Be on guard, take not your ease,
> Voyage when the daylight dims,
> Danger in the water swims.
> Make no noise with spear or sword,
> Lest you wake the longtail horde.
> Shades of creatures who have died,
> Bones of warriors who tried.
> Shrink not from the barren land,
> Look below from where you stand,
> This is where a stone may fall and make no sound at all.
> Those who cross and live to tell,
> See the badger and the bell,
> Face the lord who points the way
> After noon on summer's day.
> Death will open up its grave.
> Who goes there. . .? None but the brave."

'Look at this map, we've come through all these places. There are the cliffs, here is the pine forest, here the water with the bows of the rats on the far shore. This place here, hummocks and trees, this is where we are now. What do you think, Basil?'

'You're right, of course, old warrior. Hmm, sound advice too. It warns of the dangers in the woods, even gives the little fishes a mention. Ha, *"voyage when the daylight dims"*; maybe we would have stood a chance of giving those rats the slip if we'd crossed by night. Well,

well, a jolly old bit of prophecy here. Creatures certainly did die, and we've left the bones of warriors back there. But what's all this about shrinking from barren lands, eh? The only thing I ever shrunk from was lack of food, wot?'

Orlando checked the map. 'Jess, do you think you could climb a high tree and look over to the south?'

To an expert climber like Jess this was but the work of a moment. She was up a hornbeam in the twinkling of an eye.

'We're nearly out of the woodlands,' she called down from the topmost branches. 'I can see some sort of plain beyond. It looks very bare and dusty.'

Matthias nodded approval. 'Well at least we're on the right track, but we've no way of telling how far south we've travelled. I suppose we'll have to try and cross the barren land and look for some place where we can look below to where a stone may fall and make no sound at all. Does that make any sense to you, Orlando?'

The badger shook his head. 'It's all a mystery to me, but if it will help us to get our young ones back, I'm game to try. I know nothing of badgers' heads and bells and lords who point the way and death and graves, though.'

Matthias stood. 'Nor do I, friend, but I intend to find out. Log-a-Log, will your Guosim be ready to march at daybreak?'

'Ready as ever, Warrior. We'll soon see what other little surprises this strange southland has in store for us.'

35

The Abbey bells tolled their eventide watch over Redwall as the sun sank below the western plain.

Constance had taken no chances with the three magpies. They huddled miserably in a corner of Cavern Hole, each with its pinion feathers bound, legs hobbled and beak shut tightly with twine. Constance and the Abbot sat together in the opposite corner, listening earnestly to Ambrose Spike's report.

'There ain't been a move out of anybird, we watched the eaves all afternoon, Brother Trugg, Foremole and meself. Not a feather or a beak stirred.'

The Abbot scratched his chin. 'Strange, I was sure that Ironbeak would try to lay some sort of trap, either him or that sly crow. Odd, very odd.'

'Odd or not,' Constance shrugged, 'the sun's going down. We'd best get these three outside and exchange them for three decent creatures. Winifred, will you and Foremole see that archers and javelins fill the main doorways behind us? Keep them facing Ironbeak and his company in case of trouble.'

Foremole saluted dutifully. 'Doant ee wurry, marm, us'll give'm billyo if'n they moves a claw.'

General Ironbeak's hostages had been carefully flown

274

down a short time after sunset. The two mousemothers kept their eyes shut tight as they were borne through the air by six rooks. Baby Rollo, however, enjoyed the flight immensely, whooping and giggling as he tugged at the three birds that were carrying him. They landed safely in front of the Abbey pond, then surprisingly the carrier birds flew off, leaving the hostages guarded only by Ironbeak and Mangiz. To forestall any thoughts of escape, the two birds kept their fearsome beaks close to Rollo's head, knowing that neither Cornflower nor Mrs Churchmouse would attempt anything whilst the infant was threatened. Slowly they walked across to the main Abbey door.

Constance and Ambrose awaited them, standing to one side of the three magpies. The open Abbey doors were crowded with determined Redwallers armed to the teeth.

Ironbeak halted short of the door.

'Why are all your creatures armed and menacing us like this. I understood this was to be a friendly exchange?' His voice was harsh and commanding.

Foremole waved a large spear at the raven. 'Harr, doant make oi larff, you'm the vurmints wot been a-doin' all the tricksterin' an' attacken. Thus yurr's wot us calls porteckshun 'gainst crafty ol' burdbags.'

Mangiz pointed with his wing. 'Why are these birds bound like this? We have not tethered your creatures.'

Ambrose winked at the crow. 'Prob'ly 'cos mice don't have beaks and wings, puddenhead.'

'I will not stand here to be insulted by you hedgepig,' Mangiz fumed.

'Then stand somewhere else and I'll insult you there, featherbag!!'

'Ambrose, do not provoke them,' Constance interrupted. 'We are here to make a peaceful exchange of hostages, one for one. Cornflower, are you all right?'

'Yes thank you, Constance. As well as can be expected under the circumstances.'

Constance bowed stiffly to Ironbeak. 'Thank you, raven. As you can see, the magpies are unharmed, apart from being restrained, otherwise they have been well treated.'

Ironbeak cast his bright eyes on the doorway. 'You must think me a fool! I make no exchanges while we are faced with weapons. Tell your creatures to put down their arms.'

'Aha! I thought so,' Ambrose whispered to Constance. 'This is where the raven shows 'is feathers. The moment we drop our weapons, 'e'll spring 'is trap, whatever it is.'

Constance watched Ironbeak as she murmured back, 'I know what you mean, Ambrose, but what can we do? He has kept his word, even coming unarmed to meet us. We cannot face him with an army geared up to the teeth.'

'Hmm, I suppose you're right. Leave it to me.'

He turned to the Redwall contingent. 'Lay those weapons down and listen to me. If the raven or his pal try one false move, then grab the armoury up fast and make the pair of 'em into pincushions.'

Ironbeak had heard what went on and nodded. 'Do as you will. We have come here only to trade hostages, no tricks.'

Constance banged her paw down upon the path. 'Then let's get to it and stop fussing about or we'll be here to see dawn break.'

Ironbeak nodded to Mangiz, and the crow started the exchange.

'We release them at the same time, one for one. First the infant for Quickbill. Agreed?'

Constance untied the first magpie.

'Agreed!'

Rollo was aware of the gravity of the situation. He strode slowly across to Constance, crossing paths with Quickbill. On reaching his friends the little Bankvole began singing:

'Kick a magpie in the eye,
Shoot a crow wiv a great big bow. . . .'

Winifred swept him up and hurried indoors.

'Now the one called Cornflower for Brightback.'

'Agreed!'

The mouse and the magpie passed each other in silence. Tension mounted in the air now that there were only two left. As Cornflower embraced Constance, the harsh voice of Mangiz sounded:

'Last, the churchmouse for Diptail.'

'Agreed!'

The exchange took place without a hitch.

Both sides stood watching each other.

At a wave from Ironbeak, the magpie brothers and Mangiz flew off, then the raven General fixed his eyes on Constance.

'I will continue to attack you. It is my destiny that I should rule in the great redstone house.'

The badger gave him back stare for stare.

'Others have tried to conquer Redwall, warriors greater than you. We are still here, right is on our side, justice too. One day our warriors will return home, then you will be driven off or slain.'

Ironbeak was unmoved. '*Hakka*! We shall see. You are not as clever as you imagine, none of you. Did it not occur to you that my fighters were not with me to see the exchange take place?'

'Oh nuts'n'acorns,' Ambrose groaned. 'I knew the villain had somethin' hidden up 'is feathery sleeve.'

'While I was drawing out this business for as long as possible,' Ironbeak continued, 'my birds were in your orchards loading up many supplies. I kept you talking long enough for them to make several trips. Your sentries who should have been guarding the windows facing the orchard were watching me and Mangiz in case we tried something. Anyway, black birds cannot be seen flying by night. Also, I must tell you that we have moved down to your infirmary and dormitories. I am conquering this place from the top downwards. Now you are left only with the place called Cavern Hole. If you try to cross the floor of Great Hall after dawn tomorrow, we will be watching from the galleries, ready to attack you. We have all the supplies needed, and you will be held to a state of siege below the floor of this place. You and your friends might think yourselves clever, but you are not wise enough to outsmart General Ironbeak.'

The raven shot off into the night sky like a dark arrow.

∽

Constance shook her head wearily. 'He wouldn't have outsmarted Matthias.'

Cornflower patted Constance. 'You were wonderfully brave to get us free. We're not beaten yet, as long as we're alive and Redwall stands, there is hope,' she said reassuringly. 'We must defend the Abbey and keep it safe, especially for the day when Matthias returns with Mattimeo. Strange, isn't it, I keep thinking of my little Matti, even at the oddest times.'

Constance smiled fondly. 'That's because he's your son and you're his mother. Whenever I look at you I can tell you are thinking of him. Any creature would be glad of a mum like you, Cornflower. Here, what's this, tears?'

Cornflower sniffed and wiped her eyes. 'No. I'm just a little tired, I suppose. I hope Mattimeo is getting his proper sleep, wherever he is.'

∽

The trek across the great barren country started at daybreak. Canteens had been filled at the last woodland pool. Supplies were very low but the shrew cooks had done them proud. Log-a-log and his scouts had foraged the woodland fringe, and fennel, cloudberry and dandelion, together with some half-ripened hazelnuts, had been thrown into a large communal salad, with the addition of some dried fruit and the last of the cheese. Then a good meal had been eaten facing the flat expanse of sun-scorched earth.

Basil sniffed the dry air.

'Useless trying to scent anything around here. Still, the tracks are clear enough. I can see them from here, runnin' off in a straight line. They're a day and a night ahead of us, I reckon.'

He stood, stretching his long limbs, gazing out at the already shimmering horizon as it wavered and rippled with the fierce heat.

'Right lads, quick's the word an' sharp's the action, eh? Form up here and follow me. No lagging and sitting down on the bally old job. By the left . . . wait for it, Cheek . . . quick march!!'

The little column trekked off into the unknown expanses of the desert ahead of them, leaving behind the final fringes of Mossflower.

༄

Slagar had driven both captives and slavers hard. Marching by night and resting by day, they had crossed the wasteland. Footsore and weary, Mattimeo and his companions helped each other along. Their mouths were dry and parched from lack of water, the manacles rubbed and chafed. Tess caught Cynthia Bankvole as she stumbled for the umpteenth time.

'Up now. Stay on your paws, Cynthia. It's daylight, so they'll let us rest soon.'

The volemaid licked dusty lips with a dry tongue. 'I hope so, Tess. I can't stand much more of it, though I don't know which I'd prefer right now, a drink or a sleep.'

Auma lent her size and strength, supporting them both with a paw at their backs. 'Keep going. I can see something ahead, though I don't exactly know what it is. Can you see it, Sam?'

The young squirrel strained his eyes. 'Looks like some sort of a black shadow with bushes and trees on the other side of it. Whatever it is, it has to be better than this wasteland. I think they're planning to let us rest when we reach there. Keep going, it shouldn't be too long now.'

༄

Distances in the drylands were deceptive. It was gone

279

mid-morning when the slave line halted at the place which Auma and Sam had sighted. Cynthia Bankvole drew in a sharp breath and clapped a paw over her eyes, then sat down, dizzy with fright.

They had arrived at the brink of an abyss!

A huge rift in the earth opened before them. It was as if the world were splitting through its middle. Impenetrably black and endlessly deep, it stretched away in either direction as far as the eye could see. Though they were standing at its narrowest point, the distance across yawned many times the length of a tall beech tree. The captives stood wide-eyed in astonished silence at the awesome sight.

Across the gorge a swaying construction of rope and wood stretched. It was secured at either side by thick stakes driven deep into the earth, but the centre of the rough bridge dipped perilously into the chasm.

Jube buried his face against the dusty ground. 'Ooooh! I'd as soon die as try to cross that!'

A moan arose from the slave lines. Others felt the same as Jube, and even the stoats, weasels and ferrets who had come this far with Slagar began muttering among themselves.

The masked fox stood leaning against the stakes, watching them. He had come across this problem before and was ready for it.

'Frightened, eh? Legs turned to jelly, have they?' he taunted them.

'We never bargained for anything like this, Chief!' Threeclaws gulped.

Slagar strolled to where two weasels, Drynose and Damper, stood guard over the expedition's food and water. Pushing them to one side, he took the three large water canteens and carried them to the head of the bridge.

'What d'you mean "bargained"? You're not here to bargain, you are here to obey orders. You, Skinpaw, show them how it's done. A weasel like you isn't afraid of crossing a bridge.'

Skinpaw shook his head vigorously. 'Ask me to do anything, Slagar, anything. March, fight, climb mountains, cross rivers . . . but not that!'

The silken masked fluttered. The Cruel One seemed to be smiling beneath it. He turned to his slavers one by one.

'You, Halftail, or you, Vitch? How about you, Scringe? Or Bageye there? No?'

They remained silent, while Slagar spoke as if he were cajoling nervous young ones.

'Oh, come on now, it's only a little bridge across a gorge. Besides, do you see the bushes and trees on the other side? There's a lovely little pool there, full of nice cold water. Just think, you can drink all you like.'

Skinpaw eyed the canteens that Slagar held.

'We've got water, Chief,' he pointed out.

The fox swung the canteens out wide, letting go of them. He leaned over, watching them disappear into the abyss.

'Where? I don't see any water. Now, you spineless toads, listen to me. You have a choice: either you cross this bridge and drink water, or you stay on this side and die of thirst!'

Threeclaws was the first to go. He stepped gingerly out on to the swaying bridge, gripping the rope sides tightly. Carefully he tested each wooden slat before putting his weight on it.

When he was a short way out Slagar called, 'Fleaback, Scringe, pick that line up and start the prisoners going. Halftail, you go with them. The rest of you follow after they've crossed.'

Encouraged by Threeclaws' slow but sure passage, Fleaback and Scringe stepped on to the bridge, tugging the leadrope.

'Come on, you lot. Step lively, and no hanging back or stumbling,' Scringe chivvied them.

Mattimeo could not shut his ears to the sobbing of

Cynthia and Jube, who were in a state of frozen shock. He tore a strip from the hem of his habit and bit it into two pieces.

'Here, Tess, put these around their eyes. Cynthia, Jube, listen. Hold on to Tess and Auma, and keep going. You'll be all right.'

The trick worked. Groping awkwardly, the blind-folded creatures held tight to Tess and Auma, who, though they were both frightened of the swaying, sagging bridge, found that a lot of the fear was taken out of the crossing by attending to Cynthia and Jube.

Only Sam Squirrel was totally fearless about the bridge. At one point Tim had to remonstrate with him for making the structure wobble with his jaunty walk.

'Hey, go easy, Sam,' he called nervously. 'There's others on this bridge not as clever as you at crossing gorges.'

'Oops! Sorry, Tim. Never mind, we're nearly over now.'

Mattimeo tried not to glance down into the bottomless depths. He dearly wished he had his paws on firm ground again.

∽

The crossing was made without incident. Safely on the other side, everybeast breathed a huge sigh of relief. Slagar led them a short way into the bushes.

'There's the pool. Drink as much as you like. Three-claws, see they're fed and watered, then secure the line. Halftail, come with me.'

Slagar walked back to the edge of the gorge. While Halftail watched, he crossed back over the bridge. Then the masked fox got out flint and steel. It did not take long to get the dust-dry ropes burning. As soon as they were alight he bounded on to the bridge and crossed back with surprising speed and agility. Chuckling to himself, he watched the ropes burn through. The bridge swayed and collapsed with a clatter of wooden slats as it struck the wall of the chasm beneath them. Slagar took Halftail's dagger and sawed through the taut ropes which held the weight of the bridge. He leapt back as the whole structure slipped away with a creaking, groaning snap. They waited awhile, but there was complete silence from the depths of the abyss.

Slagar smiled. 'See, completely bottomless. Nobeast can follow us now!'

36

A full-scale council was in progress at Cavern Hole.
Winifred the Otter winced as Sister May applied
poultices and herbs to her deeply scratched back.

'Aaahh! Go easy, Sister, that's the only back I've got.
Ouch!'

Sister May went about her task, ignoring the protests.
'Hold still, you silly otter! You were told not to cross
Great Hall but you would not listen. Stop wriggling
while I attend to this scratch on your ear.'

'Ow! What are you trying to do, pull me lug off? That
ear's got to last me the rest of my life, you know!'

Constance pointed to Winifred. 'As you can all see,
she was injured merely trying to cross Great Hall. You
must stay down here. Ironbeak and his birds are waiting
in the galleries, and if one of us so much as shows a
whisker outside Cavern Hole he or she will be slain.
Winifred was lucky, she was swift enough to get away.
Under no circumstances must you try to leave here.
Besides, where would you go?'

'Well, I for one would go to my little gatehouse
cottage,' Cornflower answered. 'Or I might gather fresh
fruit and vegetables and water. It seems to me we're
letting this Ironbeak have it all his own way.'

There were shouts of agreement.

The Abbot called for order. 'Please! Our first concern is the safety of every creature here. We must stay where it is safe. There are plenty of stores. The cupboards and larders are well stocked, there is ample food in the kitchens and we have the entire stock of the wine cellar available. I have spoken to Brother Trugg and the only shortage will be fresh water. It must be used only for drinking. Bathing, washing and other uses are forbidden.'

There was a lusty cheer from Rollo and some other young ones camped beneath the table.

'I'm glad someone approves,' Constance smiled. 'Well, if that's all we'll just have to put up with the situation for a while.'

'Put up with the situation indeed!' John Churchmouse snorted indignantly.

Cornflower laughed aloud. 'Oh, John, you sounded just like my Matthias then.'

At the mention of the Warrior's name a silence fell.

'I do hope our young ones are safe,' Mrs Churchmouse fretted. 'When I think of my Tim and Tess and Sam Squirrel and Mattimeo and Cynthia, where they may be now, or what those villains may do to them. . . Oh, I do hope Matthias brings them back safe to us.'

She broke down in tears.

'There, there, m'dear,' John said, patting her gently. 'Don't you cry, they'll be all right.'

Baby Rollo began patting her skirt from underneath the table, clucking in an imitation of John Churchmouse. 'There, there, me dear. Don't oo cry, be all right.'

Every creature laughed, and even Mrs Churchmouse managed a smile through her tears.

Ambrose Spike lifted Rollo up on to the table. 'That's the stuff, old Rollo. You get all these wet blankets cheerful again. Right, what's next, you little ruffian, eh?'

The tiny bankvole wrinkled his nose, uttering a single word: 'Plans!'

The hedgehog shook his head in admiration. 'There

y'are, out of the mouths of baby beasts an' innocent creatures. Plans! That's what Matthias would have said if he were here, stiffen me spikes. He wouldn't want us mopin' an' cryin'.'

Cornflower stamped her paw down hard. 'You're right, Ambrose. Let's get our thinking caps on. That's if we ever want to walk freely around our own Abbey and pick our own fruit from our own orchard, or even just sit on the walls in peace and watch the sunrise over Redwall. I say; let's not be beaten by a flock of birds!'

Constance touched a paw to her snout. 'Ssshh! Let's do it quietly. You never know who may be listening.'

‿

While the badger was speaking, Winifred the Otter crept to the foot of the stairs that separated Cavern Hole from Great Hall, picking up a small turnip that Baby Rollo had been playing with. Tip-pawing halfway up the stairs, she paused a moment then flung the turnip as hard as she could.

Bonk!

There was a hollow noise of turnip striking beak, followed by a loud squawking caw.

Winifred nodded with satisfaction. 'Good shot! Let him go and tell old Irontrousers about that!'

‿

'If we are making plans, has any creature got a suggestion?' the Abbot asked, keeping his voice low.

'Ho urr, oi 'ave. If'n you can't cross Gurt 'all or goo out Abbey, whoi doant me'n moi moles tunnel out?'

There was no doubting Foremole's logic, as Constance was first to agree.

'Splendid idea. There's no telling what we could do if we could tunnel out without Ironbeak knowing. However, I was thinking of what he said last night. If he means to conquer Redwall, he must attack us down here sooner or later. It will become fairly obvious to him that we have lots of food to keep us going, so in the event of not being able to starve us out, he'll attack Cavern Hole. I think we should barricade the stairs to keep them out.'

There was unanimous agreement for the tunnel and the barricade, and the busy Redwallers set about their tasks with a will.

～

Out on the sunbaked wastelands, Matthias and his followers were slowed down from a brisk march to a shambling gait. Basil Stag Hare crossed his ears loosely over his head in an attempt to provide himself with some shade.

'Whew! D'you know, I'll never look a hot scone in the face again, knowin' it's come out of a jolly old oven as hot as this place.'

Cheek tenderly pawed his dry nose. 'Huh, quick march and follow me, lads. We should have travelled by night instead of listenin' to you, flopears.'

Basil brushed at his drooping whiskers. 'I'd give you a swift kick if I had the energy young feller.'

A broad black shadow fell across Matthias, but he carried on, enjoying the shade without thinking where it had come from.

'Get down!'

The warrior mouse was thrown flat as Jess tackled him from behind. As he hit the dust, Matthias felt a rushing breeze pass over him. He turned over and looked up.

Two great buzzards circled overhead, wheeling and soaring as they waited for a chance to catch any creature off guard.

Log-a-Log fitted a stone to his sling as he sighed wearily, 'Heat, thirst, desert, big birds. What next?'

The slings had little effect on the buzzards, as the great dark birds would see the stone coming and fly out of range with ease.

Orlando called a halt to the slinging. 'Stop, stop! You're only wasting energy. Let's ignore them. Well, not exactly ignore them, if you know what I mean, but keep an eye on them. Matthias, you take the front of the column, I'll take the rear. If they get too close we might get the chance of a sword or axe strike, and that'll put paid to them.'

As if sensing what was going on below, the two buzzards grouped and attacked the centre of the band. They dived so speedily no creature had a chance to do anything. There was a scream, and the two great hunting birds rose into the air with a wriggling shrew pinioned between them. From out of the blue they were joined by a third big bird, who soared down with wings outstretched.

'Look, there's three of them now.'

'That's no buzzard, it's attacking them!'

Butting into the buzzards like a battering ram, the strange bird drove them downwards, causing them to drop the shrew, who bumped to earth in a cloud of dust. Clawing and biting, the other bird, who was stockier and shorter than the buzzards, battered away with wing and talon, screeching loudly until it drove them off. Circling to make sure it had driven the predators away, the bird dived and landed next to Orlando.

It was Sir Harry the Muse.

'Pray accept my apologies, sir,
My conscience was bothering me,
So I had to take to the air.
And now I am back, as you see.'

Matthias ran to greet the poetic owl. 'Well timed, Sir Harry. Thank you for your help!'

The owl blinked at the sun.

'I'd sooner fly 'neath the moon.
I dread the hot afternoon,
The heat's infernal and owls are nocturnal.
I hope the sun sets soon.'

The shrew who had been caught by the buzzards was not badly injured. He opened his pouch and offered the owl half a shrewcake which he had been saving. Sir Harry accepted it gravely, bowed politely, then devoured it in a most undignified manner.

'Mmmff, 'sgood, scrumff, 'slovely!'

The poetic owl waddled along beside Matthias as the warrior mouse explained their position.

'I'm afraid we're very low on supplies. We could only manage to feed you with the same amount as we are rationed to. Don't tell me you really suffered from conscience pangs, Sir Harry. You must have another reason for flying all this way to be with us.'

'I'd call that a very smart guess.
In fact, you've called my bluff.
My reason, I must confess,
Is not for food and stuff.
I get tired of being alone,
Can I come along with you?
I've heard you talk of your home,
Could I live at Redwall too?'

'Humph! Pesky bird would scoff us out of the blinkin' Abbey!' Basil snorted huffily.

Matthias glared reprovingly at the hare. 'Basil! Courtesy and good manners cost us nothing.'

The old hare blinked grumpily and unfolded his ears. 'Oh well, in for an acorn, in for an oak. I s'pose it'd be all right for him to live at our Redwall. Huh, save me gettin' all the jolly blame any time a mouthful of food goes missin', wot?'

Sir Harry did a hop and a skip.

'I knew you'd see things my way.
It's settled then, it's done.
And if food goes missing I'll say,
"Blame me, sir, I'm the one."'

'Don't worry, I will, old chap,' Basil muttered under his breath.

Orlando reared up, shading his eyes with a big paw.

'Remember that long black line on the map, Matthias? Well, I think I can see it. We should make it sometime about sunset.'

Matthias pulled the map out. 'Hmm yes, a sort of broad black band. I wonder what it is?'

Basil was still muttering to himself, 'Huh, soon find out, I s'pose. If it's anythin' to eat, I'll bet that owl gets there first. Hmph, poetry indeed!'

⁓

Orlando's estimate was correct. It was just as the sun began dipping beyond the western horizon that they stood on the edge of the great gorge. They gazed awestruck at the massive fissure splitting the land asunder. Orlando and Matthias peered over the edge.

'By the fur and claw! Look at that!'

'How are we going to cross a gap that wide?'

Sir Harry sat back on his tail feathers.

'Tho' I'm the most poetic of birds,
Right now I'm lost for words!'

Log-a-Log whirled his sling and shot a stone down into the abyss. There was neither sound nor echo came back.

Orlando quoted the lines of the poem from memory:

'Shrink not from the barren land
Look below from where you stand,
This is where a stone may fall and make no sound at all.'

Jabez shook his head in wonderment.

'So this is what a broad black band on a map looks like.'

37

Half-eaten fruit, some of it rotten, lay scattered between the upturned beds, torn sheets and stained walls of the once neat dormitory, and a window had been broken so that the magpies and rooks could fly in and out at will. The fighters of General Ironbeak had smashed the small wooden lockers and tables. They lay about in the wreckage, some sleeping, others eating. Ironbeak had taken the infirmary and sickbay as his headquarters. Mangiz explored the cupboards, poking his beak into Sister May's collection of herbal remedies.

'*Yagga*! Why do these stupid earthcrawlers keep dead leaves and grasses? They are not good to eat, so what use are they?'

Ironbeak perched on Sister May's wooden stool. 'Who knows, Mangiz. That is nothing to do with our problem. I am certain that the earthcrawlers have plenty to eat and drink down in that place called Cavern Hole. The time is coming when we will have to think about an attack. We will go in there and drag them out.'

Mangiz stood on the medicine cupboard, shaking his head. 'That would be like using a boulder to crush an ant, my General. I am sure there must be a better answer to your problem.'

'Then tell me, Mangiz. You are my seer. Are the

pictures becoming clear in your mind again?'

'My vision is still clouded by the mouse that wears armour, but I am not relying on dreams and visions; soon now I will think of an idea.'

'*Kacha*! Then think quickly, Mangiz, or the summer will be gone. When the brown leaves blow and the wind becomes cold, I want those earthcrawlers to be only a memory as I rule in my great redstone house.'

∽

Foremole had wasted no time. He and his crew had tunnelled through from Cavern Hole to the grounds. They emerged by the west wall, poking their snouts out into the sunlight.

'Hurr hurr, you'm may's well try an' keep watter in a sieve as stop'n uz moles agoen whurr we do please.'

'Aye, Jarge, whyrr to naow?'

'Oi'm a-thinken us'd best tunnel to pool.'

'Burr, then to Miz Cornfl'er's liddle 'ouse by yon gate.'

'Doant ee forget a noice deep'n to orchard.'

Soon a veritable network of tunnels was under construction.

∽

Rollo was not too pleased. They had taken the big table for the barricade and now he had nowhere to camp. He soon cheered up when Ambrose Spike allowed him to help with the hammering and nailing of the barrier. Chairs and benches, cupboards and shelves, together with the large banqueting table, were placed across the bottom step of Cavern Hole. Ambrose and Winifred had given it a lot of thought. There were spaces to fire arrows through, slits for javelins and spears, plus a form that the defenders could stand upon to sling stones over the top at the enemy.

The Abbot and Sister May had done a thorough stocktaking of all food in the larders and drink in the wine cellar, and there was little danger of provision shortage.

Constance checked the weaponry. Besides the standard arms, there were lots of kitchen utensils that could double as fearsome implements of war. The badger brandished a copper-bottomed saucepan thoughtfully.

'What d'you think, Cornflower?'

'It would make quite a fetching war helmet for you, Constance.'

Brother Sedge snatched it from the badger. 'D'you want Mossflower vegetable stew with dumplings or not?' he asked crossly.

'Oh, sorry, I didn't know you were planning to use that saucepan.'

'Here, take this rolling pin. It'll make a useful club. And put that frying pan down, please. I'm cooking redcurrant pancakes with apple slices,' Brother Sedge told the badger indignantly.

'Oh, er, right! Is this pan all right to borrow?'

'Perfectly. Then I won't have to make any hazelnut cream sauce to pour over my pancakes.'

Constance put the pan down quickly. 'No hazelnut cream sauce, unthinkable! Brother Sedge, I've just had a splendid idea. Why don't you invite the birds down to lunch and feed them to death. Hahaha!'

Brother Sedge picked up a ladle aggressively. 'Are you insulting my cooking, badger?'

Cornflower shook with mirth. 'Oh dear no. I'm sure she meant the remark as a compliment. Come on, Constance, let's see if any of the gardening tools can be of use to us.'

They retreated chuckling as Brother Sedge sliced apples savagely.

⁓

Foremole reappeared through the tunnel entrance into Cavern Hole. He waved to the Abbot.

'Lookit yurr, 'dalfus zurr, fresh watter aplenty!'

Moles climbed out, bearing buckets of water on poles between them – proof that the tunnel to the pond had been completed.

The Abbot was well pleased. 'Thank you, Foremole.

Now we have all we need. Look, Mrs Churchmouse, fresh water, as much as we need.'

Mrs Churchmouse rolled her sleeves up busily. 'Wonderful! I think it's high time for somebeast to get a bath.'

Rollo gave a yelp of dismay and tried to crawl into the tunnel, but he met Gaffer who was climbing out.

'Urr you'm be, marm. You scrub that liddle feller noice an' clean naow.'

Baby Rollo was carried off protesting loudly, 'I wanna be a mole. Moles don't get baffed!'

Mangiz had been thinking very hard. 'My General, last time I was in the galleries of Great Hall I saw the mouse in armour. He was not a real live mouse, but a picture on a great cloth that is fastened to the wall. The earthcrawlers must value him highly.'

'What if they do, Mangiz? A piece of cloth is a piece of cloth. How can this help us?'

'Maybe they value him highly enough to defend him.'

'What is going on in your head, my Mangiz? Tell me.'

'I am thinking that we will not have to attack the earthcrawlers. If they saw us trying to take the big cloth with the picture of the mouse on, they would come out and attack us to save it.'

Ironbeak clacked his beak together sharply. '*Chakka*! We would catch them out in the open. This is a good plan. Mangiz, you are my strong right wing.'

The sun slanted through the windows of Redwall Abbey. It shone on the large tapestry in the peace and quiet of Great Hall.

BOOK THREE
Malkariss

38

The arrival of a cool summer morning did not make the gorge look any less wide.

Jabez Spike shook his head despairingly. 'Twould be simpler to float a stone across a river than to get all these creatures across that great dark pit.'

Breakfast was frugal and the water ration had run low. They ate and drank in silence. Basil Stag Hare looked longingly at the bushes and vegetation on the opposite side.

'I'll wager there's tender young plants and lots of water over there, wot?' he said wistfully.

Cheek gulped his water ration in a single swig. 'Wish you'd stop goin' on about food'n'water, Basil. Otters need water more than some old dried up twig of a hare, y'know.'

Orlando strolled moodily round the blackened stakes that had held the bridge. 'That fox! He really thought of everything, didn't he?'

Jess had a faraway look in her eyes. She stroked her tail thoughtfully before peering over the edge of the gorge.

'Hmm, chopped the bridge off completely at both sides, did he? Hmm. Matthias, do you think our owl friend could fly down into the ravine and cast his eye about for the remains of the bridge? I've got an idea.'

Matthias looked enquiringly at Sir Harry. The owl stretched his impressive wings.

'The work of a moment, dear sir,
To a useful fellow like me.
I'll chance a flight down there.
We'll see what we shall see.'

The sunlight shone through his outspread wings as he executed a graceful soaring motion. Diving swiftly, he was soon lost to view within the dark abyss.

Jess instructed Orlando on the next part of her plan.

'Lend me your battleaxe, big fellow. Oof! On second thoughts, you hold it. Now do as I tell you. Stand it upright against those stakes which held the bridge. Good! Log-a-Log, could you bring some rope?'

The shrew leader rummaged about until he found a small coil. 'Here's your rope, but there isn't enough to get us a fraction of the way across that gap.'

Jess uncoiled the rope. 'I have no intention of trying to cross with this piece, Orlando. Hold the axe still while I lash it to the stakes.'

Sir Harry reappeared over the edge.

'This is your lucky day.
I'll tell you what I found.
As I was winging my way
Far below the ground.
The bridge cast over the edge,
Complete with slats and all,
Hangs from a rocky shelf
Which juts from the canyon wall.'

Jess secured the axe bolt upright. 'Well done! I knew a long wiggly thing like a rope bridge couldn't fall far without getting caught on something. I don't want the slats; they're not part of my plan. Can you bring me one of the long ropes? Do you need a knife?'

Sir Harry blinked indignantly.

'What need of a blade have I?
No sword or knife do I seek.
I am monarch of the sky,
With fearsome talon and beak!'

With a hoot and a whoosh he shot back into the depths.

Jess shrugged apologetically. 'Hope I haven't offended him.'

∽

Slagar glanced around nervously. They were passing through pleasant brush country, mainly bushes and shrubs, with the odd tree dotted here and there. The whole area gave Mattimeo the impression that once long ago it had been gardened, cared for and cultivated. He walked in line with his friends, along what appeared to have been the path of a terrace. Flowers still grew in clumps, and rocks ran in a straight line, probably bedded there by some industrious creatures in the dim past.

Tess spoke into his ear from behind, the sudden sound causing Mattimeo to jump slightly.

'Why are there no birds singing?' she asked.

The young mouse was mystified. 'You're right, Tess. I couldn't say what made me uneasy about this place at first, but you've put your paw slap on it! There's no sound, no noise of grasshoppers, birds, the things you'd normally expect to hear on a bright summer's day. Even Slagar doesn't look too happy with this place.'

Tess clinked her chain manacles gently. The sound hung on the still air.

'It is beautiful though. I'd like to stop and sit here awhile. Do you know, it reminds me somehow of our Abbey. Look, there are ripe berry bushes over there, and daisies and roses too.'

Sam, who was in the front, stared ahead into the distance. 'I can see two tall rocks shaped like a badger's head and a big bell.'

'Silence back there, or you won't live to see nightfall. Pick those paws up and march faster!'

Vitch obeyed unconsciously, speeding up until he overtook his leader.

Slagar cuffed him bad-temperedly. 'Where d'you think you're running to? Get back and watch those prisoners, and keep from under my paws, rat.'

∽

Orlando looked doubtfully at the contraption Jess had set up. High over his head the thick bridge rope was fastened to his axe top. The rope ran out across the abyss, taking a steep downward slope until it reached the stakes on the far side, where Sir Harry had secured it close to ground level. The big badger scratched his muzzle.

'How's it supposed to work, Jess?' he asked dubiously.

'Quite simply. Matthias, would you go first and show him?'

The warrior mouse shinned swiftly up the stakes. Removing his belt, he swung it over the rope with one paw, catching the other end as it came down. He stood with his paws twined in the belt that hung either side of the bridge rope.

'Ready, Jess,' he called.

The squirrel climbed up and gave him a good push.

Whizzing across the gorge from the rope lashed around the axehead, Matthias sped on a straight downward course, lifting his tail clear as he hit the other side in a cloud of dust. He jumped to his paws, waving triumphantly. Log-a-Log and his shrews cheered aloud.

Jess turned to Orlando with a smile. 'That's how!'

'I'm not sure, Jess. I might be too big and heavy.'

'Then you can go next to last,' the squirrel said decisively.

'Who's going last?'

'Me, of course. You want your axe back, don't you? Right then. I'll untie the rope, lash your axe to my back and swing across. Don't worry, I'm a good treeflyer. I'll go straight down into the gorge on the end of the rope, stop myself against the opposite wall and climb up.'

300

Orlando wiped a dusty paw across his brow. 'I'm glad it's you and not me trying that. By the way, please take care not to lose my battleaxe down there.'

'Oh, stop fussing, you great lump, and help that shrew up on to the rope.'

∽

Jess's plan worked well and the operation went smoothly, though with one or two minor hitches. Sir Harry was kept busy flying to and fro to borrow belts for those who had none. When Orlando's turn came he persevered bravely. However, his size and weight caused the axe handle to bend and the rope to belly. The badger was stuck in the middle, hanging perilously over the abyss. He was moved by Matthias and his friends throwing their weight on and off the rope until it began to twang and vibrate, and Orlando moved slowly along it. At the edge, he had to be hauled over the brink by Basil, Cheek and several shrews. When it was her turn to go, last of all, Jess the champion squirrel of Redwall did the crossing in swashbuckling style. Untying the rope, she bound Orlando's axe to her back and leapt straight into the gorge, grasping the end of the bridge rope. Down she sped, suddenly snapping to a halt, then with practised skill she swung across and bounded up the rope, paw over paw.

'Here, Orlando,' she panted, 'hurry and get this clumping great hatchet off my back. I can't stand straight with the weight of it.'

'I'll leave you tied to it if you call it a hatchet again, squirrel.'

∽

The pool among the bushes was like a cool oasis. They washed the dust off, bathing and splashing in the clear water. All save Jabez Stump, who sat munching cow parsley.

'Tain't natural, bathin', otherwise we'd have all been born fishes,' the hedgehog objected.

The foragers found plenty of berries, fruit and plants,

even a crab apple tree laden with tiny golden crab apples. The friends lounged about, eating and dozing, almost reluctant to leave this haven of plenty.

Log-a-Log nibbled wild celery as he made his report to Matthias.

'The scouts have picked up the trail, going south as usual. It's easy to follow.'

Matthias nodded, studying the map and the poem. 'Aye, it looks like plain travelling. There's no obstacle ahead, unless you count these two rocks, the badger and the bell!'

39

'Constance, Abbot! Birds are trying to steal our tapestry!'

Brother Trugg tripped over his habit and fell as he dashed from the barricade where he had been standing sentry duty.

'Get slings, arrows and javelins. Pull the table aside quickly!'

The defenders rushed up the stairs into Great Hall.

Three magpies were struggling with the wall fastenings of the heavy tapestry. They ignored the charging animals, remaining intent on what they were about.

Before the Redwallers had a chance to marshal their forces and open fire, they were beset by birds. Rooks hurtled down from the galleries, pecking and clawing. General Ironbeak and Mangiz, leading a small force, dropped down behind them. Amid the confusion, Constance saw what was happening: Ironbeak was trying to cut off their path back to Cavern Hole. She whirled, dealing a rook a heavy blow that sent it spinning as it buried its claws into her neckfur.

'Back, back. Return to Cavern Hole, everybeast. Hurry!' she ordered.

Two rooks were trying to drag Sister May off by the back of her habit, but John Churchmouse thwacked them soundly with a javelin.

'Gaahh, scat! Come on, Sister, follow me!' he cried.

Calmly the little Sister shot off an arrow. 'Got him! Ha, he won't sit down for a season. Take that, you horrible bird! Oh, right. Come on, Mr Churchmouse, I'll protect you.'

Ambrose Spike took a run at a group of birds who were attacking Cornflower. Curling himself tight, he went spinning into them like a flying ball of needles, and they rose to the air, squawking.

Constance lashed about with a frying pan, the weapon making a loud bong every time she scored a hit.

'Get out of our Abbey, you scavengers!'

Bong!

'Look out behind you, Abbot!'

Bong!

Constance hurtled at Ironbeak and Mangiz. The sight of the large badger with teeth bared made them jump to one side. She growled and snarled like a wild beast, charging them recklessly so that they had to take to the air. The other birds followed their leaders' example.

Winifred the Otter saw the way clear to Cavern Hole.

'This way, everybeast!' she called.

$\backsim$

They clattered down the stairs and slammed the table back into position and not a moment too soon. Ironbeak saw his trap had been foiled and he chased several birds down the stairs.

'After them! They must not escape!'

Winifred and Constance were waiting.

'Now!'

Two javelins shot from the arrow slits in the barricade. One rook fell slain. Another took the javelin in his leg. Hopping and cawing, he followed his fellow fighters up the stairs in a hasty retreat, the javelin clattering and dragging from the limb it had pierced.

Ambrose Spike pushed a form up to the defences. 'Stand on this, you archers. See if you can fire across at those magpies.'

Several of the Brothers and Sisters took their place and began loosing shafts at the thieves. The arrows fell miserably short, though they did have the effect of deterring other attackers from coming down the stairs.

Constance slammed a heavy paw against the wall. 'The thieving, pilfering barbarians, how dare they steal our Warrior's tapestry!'

Foremole tugged at her fur. ''scusin' oi, marm. Whoi doant ee use our tunnels?'

'Tunnels? But how? What good would that do?'

'Hurr, you'm could come at um throo main door. They baint be aspecten that.'

'Of course. What a great idea!' Constance exclaimed. 'Half of you stay here with the Abbot, I'll take the rest through the tunnel to the nearest exit outside. If we're sharp enough we can launch a surprise attack on those magpies, seize the tapestry, and go out of the Abbey and straight down the tunnel back to here. Come on, Winifred, Ambrose, Cornflower; and, Foremole, would you come too with some of your moles?'

'Surpintly, marm. Uz'll give um boi okey, hurr that uz will!'

'I come, I come. Me too!'

'Nay, young maister Rollyo, you'n stay boi yurr an' shoot arrers.'

∽

Quickbill and his brothers were loosening the final fastenings, General Ironbeak and his fighters were on the floor of Great Hall, and they hid each side of the wall at the top of the stairs, waiting for another foray from Cavern Hole.

'Chakka! Block these stairs well next time, and we will have them out in the open. You, Grubclaw, and you, Ragwing, stay by me. Try to get the big stripedog in the eyes.'

Diptail and Brightback undid the last loop from its hook on the wall. The large tapestry slid down to the floor.

'Yaggah! We have it, brothers!'

'Redwaaaaall!'

Constance came thundering down upon them from the open doorway. Diptail lost his proud tailfeathers with one sweep of a blunt paw. Brightback and Quickbill shot into the air like startled flies. Cornflower, Ambrose and Winifred hurriedly rolled up the tapestry while Foremole and his crew stood whirling slings.

Mangiz spotted them. '*Kragga!* The earthcrawlers are over there, Ironbeak!'

The raven General sprang forward, followed by his rooks. Unwittingly they exposed their backs to the stairs. A hail of arrows and slingstones from the barricade behind them caught the birds unawares. Ironbeak dodged out of the line of fire, his eye smarting from a pebblestone.

'After them! This way, you wormheads, away from the stairs!'

They were halfway across Great Hall when the main door slammed and the tapestry rescue party were gone.

The fuming Ironbeak laid about with his hard yellow beak.

'Useless, stupid blunderers! Worthless, clumping idiots! Where are those chicken-hearted magpies? Quickbill, take those blockhead brothers of yours outside and see where the earthcrawlers have got to.'

∽

The Abbot smiled with pleasure and relief as the long roll of tapestry was fed out of the hole by the moles.

'You acted courageously, my friends. Martin is certainly back among us.'

Cornflower turned to Foremole. 'Is there a tunnel through to my gatehouse cottage?'

Foremole tugged his snout. 'Aye, missus. Oi dug it meself.'

'Splendid. Sister May, would you come with me tonight? We may as well make use of the tunnels. I have an idea. It may not defeat Ironbeak, but it will certainly give him and those birds something to think about.'

Baby Rollo rolled himself in the tapestry and giggled as Gaffer mole tickled him. John Churchmouse looked severely over the top of his glasses.

'Come out of there this instant, Rollo. What would Martin think?'

Mrs Churchmouse chuckled. 'He'd probably think it quite nice to have some company after hanging alone on the wall all that time.'

∽

General Ironbeak was in a fine fit of rage as he stalked up and down the sickbay and the infirmary. Mangiz and the three magpie brothers stood stock-still, waiting for his wrath to unleash itself upon them. They had failed to find any trace of the exits and entrances to the cunningly dug mole tunnels.

'*Kacha*! You slugbrained dolts, do you mean to tell me that you could not find a few creatures carrying the big cloth?'

Quickbill looked down at his claws. 'We searched, we looked everywhere, Ironbeak. There was not a sign of any creature.'

'Not a sign? You speak foolishness. They are earthcrawlers, not birds. They could not fly off into the blue. Where did they go?'

'The big stripedog charged us, General. We could not fight it. By the time you sent us outside, we could not find any trace of them. We did not expect them to come through the doorway like that. You were supposed to have them penned up in that place by the stairs.'

Ironbeak moved like lightning. He pulled Quickbill up against the wall and felled him with a sharp blow from his heavy beak.

'*Yaggah*! Don't tell me what I was supposed to be doing. You forget yourself, magpie. I am the leader. Mangiz, do your visions see anything? Does your mind's eye tell you where the earthcrawlers went?'

The crow shifted nervously. 'My visions are still clouded, Lord.'

The raven eyed him scornfully. '*Yach*! Not the mouse warrior again?'

'Ironbeak, I see what I see. The mouse wearing armour blocks my visions and hovers in my thoughts. I cannot explain it.'

'*Hakka*! Is this the Mangiz who served me in the northlands? I think this redstone house is making you like an old thrush. The mouse is only a picture upon a piece of cloth. We have seen this, we know it is true. I have not seen a mouse in armour striding around here, nor have you, yet you stand there dithering and flapping. "Lord, my visions are clouded. A mouse wearing armour hovers in my thoughts." *Kacha*! Get out of my sight. I will do my own thinking. You have failed me, Mangiz.'

As Mangiz turned to go, there was a scratching and chirping in the doorway. Ironbeak leapt forward.

'Sparrows! Get them!'

∽

The five sparrows who had been listening at the door flew off. Ironbeak and Mangiz were in hot pursuit of them as they rounded the stairwell and flew down towards Great Hall.

'Sparrows! Get them!' Mangiz echoed his leader's cry to the patrols in the galleries.

The sparrows fluttered and veered, not certain of where to go next. One of them was taken by the beaks and claws of three rooks. It stood no chance.

'Sparra, Sparra, down here!' the voice of Constance boomed up from Cavern Hole.

Like four arrows straight and true, the Sparra warriors shot down the stairs and over the top of the barricade, to land safely among their Redwall friends. A lively volley of slingstones discouraged any pursuit by Ironbeak's fighters.

∽

All the Abbey creatures gathered in Cavern Hole to hear the report of the four survivors who were all that was left of Queen Warbeak's brave little army. They told of the long days searching fruitlessly down false trails through the thicknesses of Mossflower country in the far south, of hawk attacks and uneasy nights spent in strange trees, of all their adventures, right to the time they found Matthias and his friends in dire peril. There followed a harrowing tale of the hard-won battle, culminating in the death of Queen Warbeak and nearly all her command. Many Redwallers wept unashamedly, for Warbeak and her warriors were great friends and true Redwallers.

There was heartfelt relief and the sadness gave way to cheers at the news that Matthias, Basil and Jess, together with old shrew comrades and some new companions, were alive and well, still hot on the trail of the evil one and his band who had kidnapped the young ones from the Abbey.

The Abbot ordered food to be brought for the weary sparrows, who had flown night and day to be back at Redwall, then he informed them of developments since they had left: the arrival of General Ironbeak and the slaying of the old Sparra folk and the nestlings by the ruthless invaders.

One of the sparrows related what they had heard outside the infirmary door.

Cornflower clapped her paws together. 'I knew it. I was right! Martin the Warrior *is* watching over us. Oh, I'm so glad I thought up a little plan earlier on. This makes it so much better, knowing that those villainous birds are uneasy about the warrior's spirit protecting our Abbey. Now I think my scheme will really work!'

'I think you should tell us what this plan is before you decide to go off doing things by yourself, young mouse,' the Abbot said firmly.

Cornflower explained.

∽

Mangiz perched in the galleries with Ironbeak. Both birds were watching the floor of Great Hall below.

'General, do you think those sparrows heard us talking?' Mangiz wondered.

'*Chagg*! Who cares about a few sparrows? You see, Mangiz, you are worrying about stupid things. It is as I said, you are becoming wary of your own wingshadow now. Leave me alone, since it is I who now has to do all the thinking. You must not bother me with talk of sparrows and armoured mice.'

'So be it, Lord.'

Mangiz flapped off to the dormitories in a sulk.

∽

Ambrose Spike and Brother Dan selected a long barrel stave and set about carving it with their woodworking tools. As he worked, the hedgehog muttered, 'A sword, like the great sword of Martin that Matthias carries. Wish I had it here as a model. Still, I can remember fairly well what it looks like.'

'I can recall the exact details of our Warrior's sword, fortunately,' Brother Dan sniffed.

Ambrose sniffed back at him. 'See that barrel of October ale yonder? I've got to remember to tap it before autumn. See those barrels of cider, I've got to remember to add honey to them in a day or so, or they'll go bitter. Now that big barrel of strawberry cordial, well, I've got to remember to strain it off into jugs for the evenin' meal tonight so that it'll be cold and clear. So you carry on recallin' what you like about the Warrior's sword, Dan. I've got enough to remember, thank you.'

∽

Evening was falling with a glorious red sunset as Cornflower and Sister May, accompanied by several moles, slipped from the tunnel exit into the gatehouse cottage. Barring the door, Foremole checked at the windows to make sure they had not been seen.

'Nary a sign o' burdbags, missus. We'm be safe enuff.'

Cornflower went into the bedroom and opened the chest where Matthias kept his warrior's garb.

'See, it's all here, Sister May, the armour and everything. All my Matthias took was his sword. He likes to travel light.'

Sister May helped Cornflower to unpack the helmet and greaves. Laying the burnished breastplate upon the bed, she eyed it doubtfully.

'Dearie me, it's all very heavy. Are you sure you'll manage to walk with it on?'

Cornflower shrugged. 'I won't know until I try, but I'm fairly strong. Give me a paw with this shoulderplate, will you.'

Shortly afterwards, she clanked out into the living room, fully armoured.

Foremole shook his head admiringly. 'Burr, you'm looken a soight a'right missus. Oi never see'd ought loik that. Strewth, but for your face oi'd say 'twas Marthen a-cummed back agin.'

Sister May emerged, carrying a piece of filmy gauze. 'Not to worry, Mr Foremole. I'll make a face mask, and in the dark she'll seem quite pale and ghostly. I must say, Cornflower, all that bulky armour makes you look quite large and impressive.'

Cornflower clanked about, gazing down at the gleaming metal.

'Let's hope it fools the birds tonight.'

40

Basil dodged about in the rays of the setting sun.

'I say, look you chaps, this must have been a herb garden. Aha, mint. Yumyum, I'm rather partial to a bit of fresh mint. Achoo! Bless me, there's thyme around here somewhere. It always makes me sneeze. Achoo! Ah, here 'tis, hmm, very tasty too. Achoo!'

The trackers were camped in the old cultivated garden land, shrew fires burned red against the twilight, and a delicious aroma permeated the air. Cheek took a taste from the end of a ladle. 'Gaw, marvellous. What is it?'

Log-a-Log chopped wild chicory with his sword and threw it in the pot. 'That's special. There's so much still growing round here that we have a wide choice. I'm calling it hunters' hotpot. There's only water to drink, but I'm making apple fritters in honey to follow.'

Jess Squirrel looked over towards the twin black silhouettes of the badger and bell rocks in the distance.

'What an amazing sight, Matthias. You'd think for all the world that those shapes were real.'

Matthias was busy with Jabez Stump and Sir Harry. They were studying the map and poem again.

'Well, that's the badger and the bell, but this next part sounds pretty desperate:

"Face the Lord who points the way
After noon on summer's day.
Death will open up its grave.
Who goes there. . .? None but the brave."'

They sat in silence around the fire, weighing the ominous words.

Sir Harry waddled across to sniff the aromas of the cooking pot, and returned heartened.

'Dread words do not alarm me
When food is on its way.
No parchment threat can harm me,
Lead on, lead on, I say.'

Basil gobbled a lettuce leaf. 'Well spoken, me old featherface. I feel exactly the same. I can face death after dinner any time; only thing bothers me is that I might miss tea and supper, wot?'
Robbed of his noble moment, the owl glared at Basil and stalked off.

Matthias tapped the map. 'This thing here bothers *me*. It's like two lines, one at an angle to the other, with sort of little splinters sticking off all along it.'

Log-a-Log banged the side of the pot with the ladle. 'Come on, come on, never mind death and doom and mysteries, this hotpot's ready. Form a line. No shoving in ahead, Basil. Get to the back, go on!'

Amid much jollity and laughter the shrews lined up with Matthias and his friends to be served. Basil was eagerly holding his bowl out for a portion of the hunters' hotpot when an eerie voice rang out:

'Doom! Dooooooooommmm!'

Log-a-Log paused, the ladle deep in the pot. 'What was that?'

Basil waggled his bowl. 'Don't know, old chap. Fill the bowl, please, there's a good fellah.'

Matthias and Orlando grabbed their weapons, but a call from Cheek reassured them:

'It's all right. An old rabbit's showed up over here.'

The newcomer was an ancient rabbit. He even had a wispy white beard. He staggered into the firelight, waving his paws and shouting in a wavery voice:

'Doom, death, destruction and darkness. Doom, I say. Doooom!'

Basil waggled his ears at the ancient one. 'I say, old chap, push off and let a bloke have his hotpot, will you.'

They gathered around the rabbit. Matthias bowed to him.

'I am Matthias the Warrior of Redwall and these are my friends. We mean you no harm. What is your name, sir, and what is this place called?'

The rabbit stared straight ahead. 'Doom. All about me is doom!'

'Oh, give your whiskers a rest, you old fogey,' Basil called out as he nudged Log-a-Log to use his ladle, 'or I'll never get served. Doom, doom, death'n'destruction! Can't you say anything that doesn't begin with a D?'

The old rabbit slumped down, his limbs trembling with age. Matthias placed his bowl of food in front of the rabbit and draped a sack about his shaking form. The creature ignored the food and continued his mutterings of death and doom. Cheek peered closely at the old rabbit.

'He's fuddled. Got a headful of black dust,' he remarked.

Basil gave the otter a stern glance. 'Mind your manners in front of your elders.'

Matthias turned the same stern glance upon Basil. 'Listen to the pot calling the kettle black. You don't seem to be setting Cheek much of an example.'

The warrior mouse squatted down in front of the old one, pointing to the tall rocks. 'Tell me, sir, what lies beyond those rocks?'

For the first time the rabbit appeared to hear the question. He looked towards the badger and the bell, shaking his head.

'Death and darkness, terror and evil!' he intoned, then fell silent and would say no more.

Orlando leaned upon his axe. 'It's no use, Matthias, the poor old fellow is frightened out of his wits. Leave him there with that sack and the food. Perhaps he might come round later and talk to us.'

Jess Squirrel shook her tail. 'I wonder what caused him to be like this. It must be something pretty awful to make a creature behave so. Look, Matthias, he's getting up.'

The old rabbit rose slowly. Walking towards Matthias, he stroked the sack that was draped about him as if it was some kind of comforting robe. Halting in front of the warrior mouse, the ancient one untied a woven grass binder from his paw. A piece of stone dangled from it. Without a word he pressed the object into Matthias's paws and wandered off into the night, clutching the sack about him like a cloak. Log-a-Log and Jabez intercepted him, but Matthias motioned them away.

'Let him go, poor creature. He seems to be very fond of that sack. Maybe he gave me this in exchange for it.'

Basil inspected the stone hanging from its grass bracelet. 'Funny lookin' doodah. What d'you suppose it is?'

'I've no idea. It looks like the model of a small stone mouse. Probably some kind of ornament that he wished to give us in exchange for our hospitality.'

The warrior mouse looped it about his sword belt and sat down to finish the evening meal with his friends.

∽

The half-moon gleamed fitfully down on the scene at the foot of the tall rocks. The summer night was warm, but eerie and silent. Jube whimpered in his sleep, and Tess stroked his head until he fell silent. Auma stared up at the strange gloomy rocks rising like twin sentinels in the darkness.

'I don't like it here,' she said, shuddering. 'All my life I lived by the mountains of the Western Plains. They were sunny and friendly; these are not.'

315

Tim reached out and touched the rock wall, which was still warm from the sun.

'They're only rocks like any others. It's just that nature shaped them differently,' he reassured her.

'Quiet there! Get those eyes shut and sleep, or you'll feel my cane.'

Threeclaws strolled by swinging his willow withe. He checked that they were still and silent before moving on to join Slagar.

The Sly One stood between the rocks, his silken mask making a splash of colour against their dark surface. He turned at Threeclaws' approach.

'All still?'

'Aye, they're quiet enough, Chief.'

'Good. We'll soon be rid of them.'

'Where is this place you're taking them, Slagar?'

'Are you questioning me, Threeclaws?' the fox asked sharply.

'No, Chief. I just can't help wondering when all this marching's going to stop and when it does, where we will be.'

'Don't worry, Threeclaws, I'll take care of you and the rest. I'm telling you this because I know I can trust you. Listen, mate, you've been the one I could always rely on. Some of those others, especially Halftail and that little Vitch, need watching. Pretty soon now I'll be gone for a day or two. I want you to do something for me: keep an eye on them. I'll leave you in charge.'

Threeclaws felt proud and pleased with himself. He had never heard the masked fox call anybeast 'mate'. He felt privileged, standing and talking to the leader as if they were both equals.

'Leave it to me, Chief. I'll watch them when you're away. Huh, Halftail and Vitch, a stoat and a rat, who'd trust them? You need a good loyal weasel like me.'

Slagar patted Threeclaws on the back.

'You took the words right out of my mouth, Three-claws,' he chuckled. 'You're the weasel for me. Listen, when all this is over I'll need a good fellow at my right paw to share a lot of power and riches. Is it a bargain?'

The weasel shook Slagar heartily by the paw. 'A bargain, Chief. Rely on me!'

'I do. Now go and keep a watch on that lot.'

Threeclaws saluted smartly and marched off with his head high.

'Fool!' Slagar sneered beneath the silken hood as he watched the weasel go.

∽

Halftail was slumbering against the bell rock when Slagar stirred him.

The stoat tried to give the impression that he was alert. 'Is that you Chief? I was just lying quiet here, watching the captives,' he pretended.

'Good, good. I've often noticed that you're the one who stays awake and keeps a check on things, Halftail.'

'You have? Oh, er, yes, well. Somebeast has to do it, I suppose.'

'I know I can depend on you. I often say to myself, it'll be all right for me to take a nap, Halftail's looking after things. Listen to me, my good friend. I'll have to take a short trip soon. I'll leave you in charge here, but don't say anything. I want you to watch Threeclaws carefully. He's been getting a bit big for his fur lately. I don't trust him.'

Halftail nodded wisely. 'Don't think I haven't noticed it too, Chief. Those weasels are all the same, I've never trusted them.'

'That's because you're like me, Halftail. You've got sense and you're a natural leader. You stick with me, friend, and I'll see that you're well rewarded. I'll take care of you.'

Halftail opened his eyes wide. 'You mean it, Slagar?'

'Of course I do. Faithful service should always be well rewarded. By the way, have you seen Vitch about?'

'Yes, he's over there by those bushes.'

'Right, I'll go and have a word with him. I may need to

317

take him with me for a day or two. Remember now, mouth shut, eyes open. I'm counting on you, Halftail.'

'You can trust me, Slagar.'

～

The Sly One sat down by Vitch beneath the bushes. The young rat drew back slightly, afraid of Slagar.

'Listen carefully, Vitch, I have something to tell you.'

'But Slagar, I haven't done anything wrong, I've been wa—'

'Quiet, Vitch. Keep your voice down. I know you've done nothing wrong, in fact you've been very good lately.'

'I have? Oh, I have. I've been keeping those Red-wallers on their paws, and the others too. I make them march as fast as they can go.'

'Yes, I know you do,' the masked fox said silkily. 'That's why I've got a surprise for you. Now very shortly I'll be leaving here and taking the slave line with me, but I must leave the others to wait here until I return. This is where you come in, Vitch. I want you to come with me to help with our captives. Meanwhile, tell Scringe and the rest to keep an eye on Threeclaws and Halftail. I think those two are plotting behind our backs, Vitch. They're not to be trusted.'

The little rat dropped his voice to a conspiratorial whisper. 'Threeclaws and Halftail, those two bullies, they're always pickin' on me. I thought they were up to something. You leave it to me, I'll tell Scringe and Skinpaw and the others to mark them well.'

'You do that. We don't want them stirring up trouble while we're away, now do we?'

'Right! The dirty traitors. Er, where are we going, Chief?'

'I can't say too much right now, Vitch, but I'll tell you this much. I need a good assistant to give orders for me. It's a job for somebeast like yourself, the chance to prove you can handle power.'

Vitch could not help rubbing his paws together with

excitement. 'I'm the one for the job, Slagar. I'll prove it to you.'

I know you will, Vitch. That's why I picked you.'

∽

Slagar crept away to resume his watch between the rocks, satisfied that he had laid his plans well. From the moonlit terraces below the badger and the bell, other eyes watched him through the warm summer night.

∽

Slagar stood quite still, not daring to move a muscle. From out of the surrounding darkness grey rats had come silently. He was now surrounded by them. There was a vast army of the creatures, each one robed in black and carrying a short stabbing spear with a broad leaf-shaped blade. There was not a single sound from any of them. As well as he could, the Cruel One took stock of the situation.

The rats encircled the camp. Eyes glimmered in the bushes, spearblades shone everywhere, around both the tall rocks and in the narrow defile between. They far outnumbered Stonefleck's horde, which guarded the riverbanks. The masked fox had encountered them before when he had passed this way. He remained unmoving, awaiting a sign.

The creatures in front of him parted as a purple-robed rat came towards Slagar. This one did not carry a spear; in his paw he held a white bone sceptre surmounted by a mouse skull.

The rat spoke no word.

'You have come for the slaves. I was waiting for you, Nadaz,' Slagar said, his voice sounding hollow in the silence.

The rat called Nadaz shook his sceptre. The skull rattled against its bone handle, and Slagar fell silent.

Nadaz pointed the sceptre at the fox then swept around to point it at the sleeping captives. Turning again, he pointed between the twin rocks, indicating the direction they would be taking.

Slagar nodded his understanding.

∽

Dark forms surrounded Mattimeo and those chained to the slave lines. The young mouse came half awake as he heard Tess give a muffled groan. Silent paws held his head still, and a pad of leaves holding the ashes of burned grass and herbs was pushed up against his mouth and nostrils. Mattimeo struggled, but the overpowering scent of the compress was too strong to fight against. Dark mists rolled in front of his eyes as his body slumped limply against the folds of a black robe.

The senseless forms of the captives were placed on large oblong shields. Eight rats bore each shield.

Vitch was awakened by a shake from Slagar.

'Ssshh, don't make a sound. Follow me and keep quiet. We're on our way,' the fox warned.

As Vitch rose, he accidentally stood on Damper's paw. The weasel awoke with a whimper. Seeing the captives being carried away, he jumped up.

'Slagar! Where are they . . . aargh!'

At a sign from Nadaz, one of the rats slew Damper with a swift thrust of his stabbing spear.

Vitch shook with terror as a bag was placed over his head. Slagar whispered to him as his own head and mask was enveloped, 'Don't panic, they won't kill us. Just go where they direct you.'

The silent army moved off south between the twin rocks with their unconscious captives and the two slavers.

The pale moon shone down on the body of Damper. He lay still in death, with his sleeping companions nearby unaware of what had taken place in the soft summer night.

41

The same moon that shone over Mossflower sent silver grey shafts of light through the windows of Great Hall. Two rooks perched in the upper galleries on sentry duty. Half awake and half dozing, they stared down at the scene below. Dark shadows softened the corners of the stones, with lighter areas where the moonlight shone in.

One rook shifted his claws uncomfortably. '*Graah*! It is better in the day when the sun shines warm and bright.'

His companion shook a wing to keep awake. 'You are right, Ragwing. I do not like this place in the darkness.'

'The earthcrawlers are all asleep down in that Cavern Hole place. Why do we have to stand about here all night? Nothing ever happens.'

'Do not let the General hear you say that. If he says stay here all night, then we obey.'

'Aye, you are right. When the darkness comes again two others will have to stay guard and we will sleep upon the soft beds of the earthcrawlers.'

'*Krakkah*! They are good beds. There was nothing like them in the northlands.'

'What is that, Grubclaw? Did you see something move down there?'

'*Graah*! It is only shadows.'

'No, over there. Look, the big door is open. See, something moves!'

Slowly emerging from a patch of deep shadow, a ghostly figure glided into a shaft of moonlight.

The two rook sentries stood thunderstruck.

It was a mouse in gleaming armour, the mouse from the big cloth!

The spectre turned to face them, but it had no face! There was just a grey misty area where the face should have been. Raising a fearsome-looking sword, it pointed directly at the fearbound birds and intoned in a deep booming voice:

'Death comes if you stay in Redwalllll!'

Before the echoes had finished rebounding around Great Hall, the panic-stricken birds had fled in terror, tumbling and bumping into each other in their haste to get away from the ghastly sight..

$\backsim$

Ironbeak was shocked into wakefulness by Grubclaw and Ragwing. The infirmary door banged open wide as they hurtled through, feathers flying in all directions.

'General, *Yaggah*! *Whoocaw*! A ghost, a ghost!'

'Death, it said. Death! *Kraggak*! Save us!'

Ironbeak struck out with both wings, belabouring the rooks. 'Silence, you thickheads! Mangiz, come with me. You two, quickly, show us where you saw this thing.'

The four birds hurried through to the sentry post in the galleries.

Ragwing pointed a quivering claw. He was shaking uncontrollably. 'Th-there-th-there-th-theretherethere!'

Ironbeak pushed him aside roughly. 'Fool, I see nothing.'

'We were here and all of a sudden there it was. Right there!' Grubclaw tried to explain.

Ironbeak stared down at the spot they were both pointing to. '*Kraak*! There isn't anything there! Right. You, Ragwing, tell me exactly what you saw, or I'll make you more frightened of me than any ghost you've ever seen. Now stop yammering and stammering and talk slowly!'

'Well, Chief, me and Grubclaw were standing right here on sentry. We weren't sleeping, oh no, we were wide awake. Then I says to him "What's that moving down there?" and he says to me, "It's only shadows." *Kraakh*! When we looked again, there was a mouse, just like the warrior mouse on the big cloth, except this one had no face. It waved a sword at us, a big long sword, and it said; "Death comes to you if you stay in Redwall." That ghost spoke in a voice like no mouse. It was like thunder over the northland mountains, it was like, like—'

Ironbeak waved his wing threateningly. 'Enough! I have heard enough. A ghost of a mouse, eh?'

Grubclaw could not help himself calling out, 'A m-mouse all in armour, Chief. With a big sword!'

Ironbeak zoomed over the galleries. Winging downwards, he landed on the floor.

'And this is where it stood. Well, do you see any ghost now, do you?' he asked, his voice echoing around Great Hall.

The two sentries shook their heads numbly.

Ironbeak called out, '*Kraggah!* Ghost! I am General Ironbeak, greatest fighter in all the northlands. Come, ghost, see if you can scare me!'

The raven stood boldly in the shaft of moonlight on the floor of Great Hall. Nothing happened.

'General, the big door is still open,' Mangiz called down to him.

Ironbeak stalked outside. He looked around, then came in again. Slamming the door after him, he flew up to the galleries.

'You see, nothing inside, nothing outside. No mouse in armour, ghost, call it what you will. Nothing!'

He turned upon the two sentries, waggling his murderous beak under their eyes, his voice heavy with menace. 'So, tell me again. What did you see?'

323

'Nothing,' they said in fearful unison.

'Then who opened the big door?' Mangiz asked.

Ironbeak's eyes glittered with rage, as he nodded to the sentries. 'Carry on guarding this place. Mangiz, we will go back to the room.'

∽

As the crow entered the infirmary, Ironbeak gave him a kick which sent him sprawling. Mangiz looked up in surprise. The General had struck other birds before, but never his seer. Ironbeak stood over him.

'This is all your doing, crow,' he said, his voice thick with anger. 'You and your clouded visions. *Kacha*! A ghost mouse wearing armour, those rooks were scared witless. Then when I go and prove to them there is no ghost, what does my strong right wing have to say?'

Ironbeak imitated Mangiz's voice mockingly: '"Then who opened the big door?"'

The crow cringed, trembling as the General continued:

'So, I show them there is no ghost and you start convincing them there is one. I am no ghost, Mangiz, and what I say is final. I will teach you not to open your beak at the wrong time.'

The crow screeched in anguish as the big raven's talons came down.

∽

Ambrose Spike placed a bowl of hot celery and cream soup before Cornflower as Sister May removed her helmet.

'Try some of this. It'll help keep your spirits up. Hohohoho!'

Constance held her sides, wiping tears of laughter from her eyes.

'Ohaha, oh dear! I must say you looked hauntingly beautiful in your armour tonight, Cornflower. Oh haha hee hee hee!'

Not intending a pun, Sister May remarked as she folded the gauze facemask, 'I'm glad it worked. It goes to show you what can happen from the ghost of an idea – oh dear!'

They fell about laughing.

'Did you see their faces when you pointed the sword at them?'

'Hahaha. They kept bumping into each other when they tried to fly off together.'

'That was thanks to Constance's ghost voice. It's enough to scare anybeast. Hohoho! Go on, Constance, do it again.'

The big badger cupped her paws around her mouth and called in a sepulchral voice: 'Leeeeaaave some of that soooooooup for meeeee!'

∽

Outside on the gallery sentry post, Ragwing shuddered on his perch.

'What was that? Did you hear it, Grubclaw?'

The other rook pecked his companion hard upon the bottom.

'*Yak*! Don't you start that again, you've got us into enough trouble for one night. Now go to sleep. That way you won't be able to see anything worth reporting with your dim imagination.'

42

There was dissension and mutiny in the camp of Slagar.
The slavers woke to find the slaves and their leader gone.
Worse followed when Drynose the weasel found the
lifeless body of his comrade Damper.

'The filthy murdering fox, he's stabbed my mate
Damper,' he cried out.

Halftail attempted to pacify him. 'Rubbish! Slagar
wouldn't kill one of his own.'

'Hah! Well, what about Hairbelly and Wedgeback? He
done 'em both in.'

'Drynose is right. You keep out of it, Threeclaws. I'll
bet you that lousy masked murderer has even killed little
Vitch. Look around. Can you see Vitch?'

'Vitch isn't dead,' Scringe butted in. 'Slagar's taken
him along somewhere.'

Halftail brandished a dagger at Scringe. 'Somewhere?
What d'you mean, somewhere? You've been spying and
listenin' to things that don't concern you, Scringe. I think
you're a dirty traitor.'

'Dirty traitor, eh? Listen who's talkin'. You're the
turncoat, bucko. Slagar told me to keep my eye on you.
And don't you start waving that dagger at me, snot-
whiskers. I've got a sword twice as big as that. Look!'

Halftail rushed Scringe as he tried to draw his sword.

Taken unawares, the ferret was easy prey to the stoat's dagger. He fell mortally wounded. Halftail turned upon the rest.

'That's what spies and traitors get. Anybeast want some? Come on!'

Threeclaws pulled out a vicious-looking hook. 'Hey, Halftail. You've got a lot to say for yourself. Who do you think you are, the Chief?'

'I am, as far as you're concerned, weasel, Slagar left me in charge when he told me he'd be gone for awhile.'

Threeclaws brandished the hook, nodding to Fleaback and Drynose, and all three advanced slowly upon Halftail. Threeclaws grinned wickedly.

'Slagar left *you* in charge? Whose paw do you think you're trying to pull? He would have left one of us weasels in charge, wouldn't he, mates.'

Halftail snatched the sword from the dead Scringe. He swished it at them and jabbed with his dagger.

'Get back, weasels, leave me alone or there'll be real trouble when Slagar returns.'

Threeclaws circled slowly, swinging the hook. 'You must have bread for brains if you think the fox is coming back, you idiot. Why do you think he took the slaves with him? He's got no intentions of coming back. Ha! No wonder they call him the Sly One.'

Drynose made a rush at Halftail. The stoat leapt to one side and spitted the weasel with his sword. He shouted an appeal to Bageye, the only other stoat in the group:

'Come on, Bageye. Slagar left me in charge, help me out, mate.'

Before Bageye could rise to his paws, Wartclaw and Snakespur, two other weasels, jumped on him. Their iron hooks flashed once. 'We've got this one, Threeclaws, go on, finish Halftail!'

Halftail fought like a mad creature, he wounded Skinpaw and was about to finish him when Snakespur struck him from behind with his hook. Halftail was dead before he hit the ground.

The survivors of the mutiny sat about licking their wounds and eating any provisions they could find. Out of the crew that had taken the young ones from Mossflower there were only five weasels remaining, Skinpaw, Fleaback, Threeclaws, Wartclaw and Snakespur. Undecided, they lounged about the camp. Threeclaws fancied himself as leader, but after the slaughter that had taken place he decided to stay in the background lest one of the others challenge him for supremacy. Besides, who knew? Slagar might come back, and then there would really be trouble.

As if reading Threeclaws' thoughts, Snakespur grumbled aloud, 'Deserted, that's what we've been mates, deserted. That scurvy fox has left us in the lurch and gone off to get the reward for the captives himself. What makes me so mad is that we've followed him like a pack of fools all this time. "Yes, Chief", "No, Chief". Huh! Now where are we? Half a season's journey into the middle of nowhere, with empty paws and empty bellies too, by the look of those slack ration bags.'

'But what about little Vitch,' Fleaback interrupted. 'I wonder what's happened to him?'

Snakespur slashed at the grass with his iron hook. 'Dead as a pickled frog, for all I care. What's one rat or more got to do with us? We're weasels, mate. Oho, I tell you, I'd like to have that fox's guts at the end of this hook right now.'

'Brave words from the scum of the earth!'

A large male badger had walked quietly into the camp. He stood testing the edge of a big double-headed battleaxe with his paw. The weasels leapt up, unsure of what to do against the huge warrior, without a leader to galvanize them into action.

Orlando gave a cold smile.

'Run or fight, eh, baby stealers?' His voice was deceptively calm. 'I know you haven't the courage to fight. There's only five of you and not a gang. Ah well, if you're not going to fight then you must run like the cowards you are. But even then you won't get far, because you're surrounded.'

Matthias and his friends stepped from the bushes and the rocks.

Wartclaw began trembling violently. 'It was Slagar. It was his idea. We don't even count. Look at the way he's deserted us.'

Matthias pointed at the bodies of the fallen. 'Tell me, weasel, what happened here?'

'It was the masked fox. He did it!'

'You lie! We lay hidden and watched it all. You murdered your own comrades. Listen to me. If you do not speak the truth then you will all join them. Is that clear?'

The weasels nodded vigorously.

Jess Squirrel faced Skinpaw. 'Where has Slagar taken the captives?'

'I know you're not going to believe me,' the weasel moaned in despair, 'but when we woke this morning he was gone. The prisoners too, and a rat named Vitch.'

Matthias drew his sword. The five weasels began pleading:

'It's true, it's true!'

'Please, sir, believe us!'

'See that dead weasel there? He's Damper. We found him slain when we woke. He must have tried to stop Slagar leaving.'

Log-a-Log drew Matthias aside and whispered, 'He's probably telling the truth. My scouts have discovered tracks. They've been well covered, but there were rats here. Matthias, I'm not just speaking about a group; this was a horde, a mighty army.'

The warrior mouse nodded. He turned to the five weasels.

'I believe you. Now try to remember, did any of you wake last night and see who was here?'

'No, sir, no.'

'We were asleep.'

'Slagar took the watch alone.'

Basil picked up a rope and made five loops in it.

'Right, c'mere, you wicked weasel types. Put these nooses around your dirty necks. Stop blubberin', we ain't goin' to string you up. Though it's all you richly deserve, wot? Wretches! Now, we'll let you march up front. Isn't that good of us? That way you'll get the benefit of any bally old traps that've been laid for us: poison arrows, swamps full of mad frogs, great eagles that rip your jolly old eyes out, an' suchlike. Cheer up, chaps, it'll be fun!'

Cheek found Threeclaws' willow cane and gave it to Basil. 'I say, a blinkin' flogger. Is this what you keep the slaves goin' with, sort of give them the odd whack. Like this, and this, and this! Whack! Swish! Thwack!'

Matthias stopped Basil. There was a sound from the bushes, and the old rabbit tottered out, still wrapped in his sack. He walked round the captured weasels, staring at them with rheumy eyes.

'Death, death, is this all he left? Last time the masked one came this way none of his band lived. Dead, all slain!'

Matthias tried questioning him further but he staggered off into the bushes, still moaning about death and doom.

Orlando watched the ancient one until he was lost to sight.

'Matthias, that one knows a lot more than we think. Did you hear him? He's seen Slagar passing through here once before. It must be an old game with the fox to pick out a band of vermin and promise them the sky, then when he gets near his destination he either dumps his helpers or slays 'em, one way or another. Then he's free to reap the rewards of his filthy trade all for himself.'

'Yes,' Matthias agreed, 'but what does he get out of it? What is his reward?'

Orlando shrugged. 'Maybe we'll find out when we catch up with him. One thing is clear; now that he's got rid of his band he must be near the end of the journey. Though where that is, your guess is as good as mine.'

Matthias stood between the two tall rocks. He drew out the parchment. 'I hope this will take some of the guesswork out of it, friend.'

He indicated the space between the badger and bell rocks. 'This is where we are now. Let me see, the poem says:

"See the badger and the bell,
Face the lord who points the way
After noon on summer's day.
Death will open up its grave.
Who goes there. . . ? None but the brave."

Jabez squatted beside the bell rock. 'Not long to go till afternoon. We'll rest here. Where's this lord who's supposed to be pointing the way?'

They gazed out at the country. It was mainly grassy hills dotted with scrub and groves of trees. In the late summer morning there was no indication of mystery, death or doom. It all looked fairly plain and harmless.

Orlando shook his head. 'Well, whoever the lord is, he's not come out to show us anything yet. I'd best give a shout. He may be taking a nap.'

The badger cupped his paws to his mouth and roared until the valley echoed:

'Hi there! Are you listening, Lord? This is Orlando of the Axe from the Western Plains. Come out and show us the way!'

The echoes died on the summer air.

'No, no, you're doin' it all the wrong way, old stripetop,' Basil chaffed Orlando. 'Here, let a chap with a touch of breedin' have a jolly try.'

Basil stood beyond the rocks. Throwing his head back, he yodelled out in a wobbly tenor.

'Hullo there! I say, Lord old fellah, it's Basil, one of the Mossflower Stag Hares, doncha know. Listen, why don't you toddle out an' point the way to me and my pals? Super wheeze, wot?'

The only sound that could be heard in reply was Orlando sniggering.

Matthias offered Basil a shrewcake, and he wandered off eating and chuntering to himself, 'Confounded bad form, you'd think the rotter'd have the manners to answer a chap!'

Jess was also muttering to herself. '"*Afternoon on summer's day*". What part of the afternoon: midday, high noon, middle of noon, late noon? How are we supposed to know. Silly rhyme, if you ask me. What d'you think, Matthias?'

'I think it means before the early evening, Jess. Look, the words are separate, it doesn't say "*afternoon*", it says "*after . . . noon*". Another thing, "*the lord who points the way*" doesn't have to be a living creature.'

Jess looked puzzled. 'How do you know that?'

'Easy. The badger and the bell are both rocks. We identified them by their shapes. So why can't the Lord who points the way be a rock?'

Cheek sidled up. 'Or even a tree.'

'Why do you say that?'

'Because I've just climbed up this badger rock a way and had a look around. The one thing that stands out like a landmark is a tree. It's sort of directly in line with the path between these two rocks, but we can't see it from where we stand down here.'

Jess Squirrel raced up the rock face of the badger peak like an arrow from a bow.

'It's there, Matthias,' she called down. 'I can see it. The biggest fir tree in the world. What a sight! It's colossal!'

∽

The early noonday sun beat down on the summit of badger rock. Matthias, Jess and Cheek stood atop the tall edifice, looking down at the tree in the distance. The warrior mouse grasped the rope Jess had rigged.

'Come on, let's get down from here and get moving. I

want to arrive at that tree before the sun goes down. I
know exactly what to do and what to look out for now!'

43

Mattimeo's eyes opened slowly. He felt sick and groggy, but above all frightened. Lifting his manacled paws, he rubbed his eyes. The last thing he remembered was being held whilst a hooded figure pressed something against his face. The overpowering sweet sickness of it still hung upon his breath. He had lost count of time. Though it was dark he felt he was in some sort of chamber, and outside it might be night or day; he had no way of knowing.

The creatures around him were groaning, moving restlessly as the effects of the soporific wore off. Then the familiar heavy paw of Auma touched his.

'Mattimeo, is that you? What happened? Where are we?' the badger asked worriedly.

'I don't know. It's too dark in here. Feels like a kind of stone room, like Ambrose Spike's wine cellar at Redwall.'

'I don't like it. It's cold, too. Are the rest of us all here?'

The others had awakened, and they dragged themselves over to the sound of Auma's voice. Though their presence was of small comfort, the young mouse could not shake off the dread aura surrounding him. A shrew whimpered in the darkness, then the jangle of keys outside warned them that some creature was about to enter.

A torch flared and they covered their eyes against the brightness of the light. Shadows danced about the stone walls as the torch-bearer entered. It was a rat in a long purple robe. His eyes glinted dully in the flames from the torch, and when he spoke his voice was flat in tone, but menacing and imperious.

'I am Nadaz, Voice of the Host,' he said. 'Do not move or dare to talk with me, or you will regret it. Nadaz commands the breath that comes from your mouth. I am the power of life and death over all of you. There is no light in here, nor is there food and water. You will be left in this place until I decide that you are fit to use your eyes again, to eat and to drink. Malkariss has spoken!'

The light was extinguished with the slam of the door and the turn of the key.

'Who is Malkariss?' Cynthia asked. Her voice sounded hollow and scared.

Tess grasped her paw in the darkness. 'I'm certain we'll find that out soon enough.'

∽

Slagar followed Nadaz. They passed through tunnels and rooms, with Vitch trailing nervously behind.

Some of the chambers and corridors they walked along had obviously been built a long time ago by master craftsbeasts; other were crude, hacked and gouged from the earth, with boulders, hard-packed soil and severed tree roots showing in the light of the torches which burnt in wall brackets throughout the strange place.

A long winding passage gave way to a broad rock ledge, and Vitch gazed around in awe. Crystal and mica deposits in the rocks reflected the torchlights of a huge wheel-shaped chandelier, and on the brink of the ledge stood a colossal statue hewn from white limestone. It was the standing figure of a monstrous white polecat, with teeth of crystal and glittering eyes of black jet. Beyond it the ledge dropped away to the depths of the earth. Around the walls winding down to the deeps was a narrow carved stairway which started from the left side of the ledge, losing itself in the misty green light below.

Nadaz beckoned Slagar and Vitch to stand on a groove in the rock some distance away from the statue. The purple-robed rat moved slowly with bended head until he stood close to the figure.

'Who comes near Malkariss?' a sibilant voice echoed from between the crystal teeth.

Nadaz answered, keeping his head bowed, 'It is Nadaz, Voice of the Host, O King of the deep, Lord of the abyss, Defier of the sun! The fox Slagar has returned, bringing many creatures young and strong to work in your realm beneath the earth.'

There was a pause, then the voice from the statue spoke again.

'Who is the other one?'

Nadaz went to Slagar, and a whispered conversation took place.

The purple-robed rat returned to his former position. 'He is a young rat named Vitch. The fox says that if it pleases you he is a gift, to serve in the ranks of the Host.'

'He is not born to the Host, our ways are not known to him.' The voice was curt and dismissing. 'A rat that comes from the place of woodlands is of no use to us. Chain him with the slaves!'

Two black-robed rats appeared out of the shadows. They seized Vitch and chained him, dragging him off as he screamed at Slagar, 'Save me! Don't let them do this to me! I was loyal to you, I served you well. Help me, Slagar!'

The masked fox did not even turn to look at Vitch. He stared at Nadaz and shrugged.

'I thought he might have been useful, being a rat like yourself.'

The voice cut short further conversation between Slagar and Nadaz: 'Keep the new slaves in darkness without food until I decide they are fit to work. Hunger and lack of light is a sound lesson for creatures that have known freedom in the woodlands. Ask the fox what he wants of me.'

Nadaz conferred with Slagar again.

'Malkariss, All-powerful One. Slagar says to remind you of your promise when he brought you the last slave workers: that you give all the land above ground to him, from the gorge to the south boundaries of your realm. He says he will serve your interests faithfully and be your voice above ground.'

'Tell the masked one to be patient awhile. Take him down below and show him the work that is being done to complete my underworld kingdom. I will watch him for a time, and when I have made up my mind that his voice above ground would serve me as well as yours does beneath the earth, then I will send for him.'

Slagar could hardly wait for Nadaz to walk back to him. He had heard the voice of Malkariss clearly.

'Listen, rat, tell your master that I've kept my side of the bargain. He promised me that land; now you go and tell him I have a right to the territory!'

Nadaz rattled the skull on his sceptre. The masked fox was suddenly surrounded by the black-robed rats with their short stabbing spears held ready. The Voice of the Host confronted Slagar.

'You don't tell me anything, fox. You have no rights here, and never dare to make demands upon Malkariss. Your audience is over. Come with me now. If the Lord of the abyss wants to reward you he will do it in due time. Until then, keep a rein on your tongue.'

Feeling far from satisfied, the masked fox was led away down the curving causeway steps by Nadaz and his servants.

∽

The diamond-patterned skullmask moved this way and that as Slagar descended into the green depths. The steps wound down into the earth until they reached the cave bottom, where the green light came from whatever fuel burned in the torches and braziers that dotted the vast and intricate workings.

The Sly One was impressed. Dwellings had been

337

hewn into the rock, streets and avenues stretched before him, some of them looked as if they were part of another building from another time. Groups of young woodlanders, painfully thin and covered in rockdust, worked beneath the whips of their cruel taskmasters, dragging boulders and cutting and dressing stones into square and oblong blocks. Slagar caught a glimpse of some huge unearthly-looking creature that he could not identify.

Nadaz urged him past a band of slaves mixing mortar and cement. Strangely shaped amphitheatres and high arched caverns gave way to a halflit passage, then the party halted in front of a wall. Carved upon it in relief was a weird and curious mural with the figure of Malkariss at its centre.

Nadaz turned to him. 'This is the limit of our workings. Go now, my blackrobes will take you to your chamber, and there you must wait until Lord Malkariss gives his decision. You are fortunate fox. Apart from the creatures I command, you are the only one who has set eyes upon the underground world.'

As the black-robed rats led Slagar away, he watched Nadaz from the corner of his slitted hood. The purple-robed rat touched the left paw of the carved polecat and the figure swung inwards. As Nadaz went through, Slagar managed to see a shaft of light on the other side before the carving was pushed back into place.

The Sly One made a mental note that this was a secret exit, then in silence he allowed himself to be led back up the causeway steps. Slagar neither liked nor trusted Malkariss and Nadaz, but he was confident that he could outthink them both. One day he would rule all of this land, above and below ground; at present he was content to wait. The delivery of the slaves had gained him entrance to this strange world. Malkariss would probably think he was an efficient servant, and promotion would follow. Slagar would bide his time, he was nobeast's servant; only one position interested the masked fox. Complete and utter ruler.

The afternoon had begun fading away in pink-tinged sunlight when Matthias and his friends arrived at the tree. It was a giant pine, standing alone.

Orlando stood and stretched to his full height against it. 'By the stripes! It's so big it makes me feel like a pebble against a mountain. I'll bet it'd take a lot of otters tail to tip to go round a trunk this size, eh, Cheek?'

The young otter patted the immense girth of the bole. 'I'll say it would. Have you ever seen one like this before, Jess?'

The squirrel shook her tail in admiration. 'Never. It's a wonderful sight. Pity it stands alone, because you can only climb up it or down, you couldn't leap to another tree. The nearest ones are over there. See? Where Matthias is heading. Hey, Warrior, where are you off to? I thought you wanted to see this tree.'

Matthias walked in a straight line with a measured pace, keeping his eyes to the ground.

'It's not the tree I wanted to see, only its shadow.'

Basil caught up with him. 'What d'you want with a bally shadow, old lad?'

Matthias kept walking deliberately. 'Remember the rhyme, "face the lord who points the way, after noon on summers day." Right, the tree is the lord who points the way, and it's gone noon, nearly evening. The shadows are at their longest now. Look at our shadows, they're much longer than we are. So, if the tree is the biggest thing around, it has the longest shadow. I have an idea that where this shadow ends we'll find what we're looking for.'

The rest of the searchers rushed to join him. Like creatures in some solemn procession, they walked along with heads bowed, following the path of the giant pine's shadow.

It ended upon a humped rock sticking from the heath a short way from a copse. They gathered around the rock.

'So, here it is.'

'Well, what now?'

Matthias banged upon it with his sword hilt. It sounded quite solid. Log-a-Log scratched it, Jess jumped upon it, Orlando tried to push it. In various ways they all tried to make the rock yield up its secret, to no avail. Basil lay flat on his back on top of it, staring up at the rapidly fading day.

'Don't think much of your idea, old chap. Bit of a damp squib, wot? A rock's a rock and that's all this one is.'

Matthias stubbed his paw against the stone. 'Ouch! Listen, I'm convinced that this is it, this is where the poem says that death will open up its grave.'

'Just as well we never found it,' Cheek gulped.

Basil leapt from the rock. 'Aha, but we might yet. I've remembered something too: our old eating game from the border scouts and foot fighters regiment. You see, we used to put out a great plate of food each, all heaped up as high as they'd go. Now, the one that threw the longest shadow won it all. Never took part meself, food's far too serious to gamble with. But on summer's day, that was different. I knew I'd win then, because you get the longest shadows of all on summer's day.'

Matthias was becoming impatient. 'Summer's day – what summer's day, Basil? Summer is full of days.'

'So 'tis,' Jabez Stump interrupted, 'but to us old woodlanders there's only one summer's day: right in the middle.'

Orlando nodded wisely. 'Aye, that's midsummer's day. My dad told me that.'

'Thank you!' Matthias sighed. 'But where does all that get us? We don't know how far the shadow would fall on midsummer's day.'

'No, we don't,' Jess agreed. 'However, we could make an educated guess. At least we can see the direction the shadow of the tree is going.'

They spread out in a straight line from the end of the pine shadow.

'Of course, the tree might have been even taller at the time the poem was written,' Jess called out. 'It's very old,

340

and it could have lost a bit off the top in a storm or something. I wonder where it was supposed to end?'

It was in the copse!

One of Log-a-Log's shrews was first to find it. He held up his paw. 'Over here, look!' he shouted excitedly.

A carved stone step screened by bushes was what they had searched for. A few sweeps of Orlando's axe cleared the surrounding bush, revealing similar steps, a whole flight of them ran out of sight down into the ground. Matthias traced the less worn edge of the first step carefully with his paw. He looked up at them with a stunned expression on his face.

'I know what this place is!'

Orlando peered at the lettering. 'Loamhed. What does it mean?'

Matthias sat upon the step, his paw at the spot where the word ended.

'The rest of it has been worn away. This was Loamhedge. The mice who founded Redwall with Martin the Warrior came from Loamhedge Abbey. They left because of the great sickness that brought death to many creatures. I can remember when I was a little mouse at my history lessons, Great Abbot Mortimer told me of the founders. Abbess Germaine brought the Brothers and Sisters from a place called Loamhedge Abbey, but where exactly it lay nobeast knew. Now we have found it.'

Matthias pushed away the overgrown grass from the side of the step, exposing a standing line of carved mice. The middle one was missing. He drew from his belt the talisman that the old rabbit had given him. It fitted neatly into the centre space.

'See, here's the missing one. That fuddled old rabbit knew where old Loamhedge once was, and he gave me this because it was the only thing of value he possessed. Maybe he too was a slave one time and managed to escape from here, who knows. Great Abbot Mortimer used to say that Loamhedge was a building that was nearly as large as Redwall Abbey.'

Orlando tapped the step with his axe handle. 'What's it doing down there? Are they the cellar steps?'

Jabez Stump looked about the copse. 'No, they couldn't be. If this Loamhedge place had been destroyed, the land would have been covered in debris and great buildin' stones. This must have happened at the dancin' of the cliffs.'

Orlando scratched his stripes. 'I'm completely baffled now. An Abbey called Loamhedge that was here but isn't now, and dancing of the cliffs. What's it all about?'

'We Stumps lived in South Mossflower by the cliffs longer than anybeast,' Jabez explained. 'My old grandpa used to tell me about the days of Josh Stump, his great-great-great-grandpa. They say one day long ago our family lived atop of that cliff, but it started a-shakin' an' tremblin' as if the whole cliffs were dancin'. When it stopped, old Josh Stump he said, "I won't live atop of no dancin' cliffs no more," and he took the family to live down in Mossflower Woods. Never a Stump went up 'em again, until I did to search for young Jube.'

Recognition dawned upon Matthias. 'Of course, it must have been an earthquake long ago. That was what caused the great gorge we crossed. Yes, and those gardens we passed through. No creature ever had gardens and orchards on such bumpy land. The earth had shifted! You see what happened? Loamhedge Abbey must have been swallowed up when the ground moved. These steps would be dormitory stairs or attic steps, and the whole building must have just dropped straight down into its own cellars. Maybe even further, with the great weight of it all.'

∽

Ironbeak was determined to confront the ghost. He gave the sentries a night off. Taking Mangiz with him, he stood at the sentry post in the galleries as the last crimson sunburst hit the windows of Redwall Abbey, bathing the floor in a glorious deep rose-coloured light. Mangiz watched it through swollen eyelids.

'Mayhap the mouse in armour will not walk until the middle of the night, my General,' he said wearily.

'*Yarrak*! Mayhap it does not walk at all, fool. Mayhap it does not exist. That is what I have brought you here to prove. Tired eyes of dozy rooks will see frogs fly or stones lay eggs. I am Ironbeak, I know better than to believe such things. So should you.'

Mangiz held his counsel, deciding discretion was the better part of valour.

⁓

The sparrow who had been watching them from a slit window made his report to Cornflower and Constance.

'Bird say you no come, black crow worm no so sure. Both wait above Great Hallplace, now.'

Baby Rollo was having imaginary adventures dressed in the helmet of the Warrior. He waved the sword frantically, singing aloud:

'Kill a bird wivout a word,
Hit a black rook wiv a heavy book,
Bang a crow an' make him go. . . .'

Cornflower relieved him of the wooden sword. 'Stop waving that thing about, Rollo. You'll put somebeast's eye out with it. So, the General is waiting for the ghost to walk again. Let him wait. When it gets dark enough he won't be disappointed. The spirit of Martin the Warrior will roam abroad.'

Constance gently polished the burnished breastplate. 'You must be careful. He won't be as easy to fool as those two last night. I think we need a more intricate plan this time.'

Cornflower laughed. 'Good, then let's sit here a good long while and think up a clever scheme. Don't forget, it was our turn on supper duty tonight, but we'll be excused because we're working for the Abbey war effort. John Churchmouse and Ambrose Spike will have to cook the supper.'

343

Constance stifled a giggle. 'Oh no! John and Ambrose, there'll be war in the kitchen when those two meet over the cooking pots. Right, down to business. Let's get our thinking caps on.'

The rooks of General Ironbeak were perched in the dormitory. They listened in awed silence as Grubclaw and Ragwing related their encounter with the Abbey ghost, especially as the two rooks were not above adding bits to make it a good story now that Ironbeak and Mangiz were not there.

'*Hakka*! It was dark out there last night. I could feel in my feathers that something was going to happen,' Ragclaw began.

'*Kraak*! Me too. It was darker and gloomier than the bottom of a northland well. So Ragwing and I stood sentry with beaks and claws at the ready for any funny business, didn't we, bird?' Grubclaw added.

'Aye, we did that. Then suddenly Grubclaw says to me, "Ragwing, can you see that shadow down there?"'

'How could you see a shadow if it was pitch-black?' a rook interrupted.

'Well, er, er. It was the moonlight coming in through the windows. Yes, that's right it was the moonlight, anyhow—'

The rook butted in again. '*Kaah*! What a load of old eggshells. It was dark as a northland well, but with moonlight shining through the windows.'

Grubclaw ruffled his feathers airily. '*Kragga*! Who is telling this, you or us? We know what we saw. But we can keep it to ourselves if you start making fun of us.'

The other rooks silenced the interrupter.

'We saw a shadow in the moonlight,' Ragwing continued. 'Well, at first we thought it was a shadow, but when we looked closer it was an earthcrawler.'

Grubclaw nodded solemnly. 'A ghost mouse, all in armour. It seemed to appear from nowhere. *Graak*! It was carrying a long sword and it had no face. It moved like a feather in the breeze. I think it was floating, don't you, Ragwing?'

'Yes, it definitely floated. And another thing, it carried the long sword as if it weighed nothing. It must have had great spirit strength. The cold lights burned from its eyes like fire in ice—'

'I thought you said it had no face. How could it have burning eyes?'

'*Yaggah*! Will you shut your beak and listen? It was, it was, er, the white moonlight shining on it, yes, it made the face that this ghost didn't have look like two burning eyes. *Haak*! We saw it, I swear on my egg and nest. Isn't that right, mate?'

'True, true. It seemed to know we were watching it, because it turned to face us. We perched there, ready to attack if the ghost mouse tried anything.'

'And did it? Try anything, I mean?'

'*Krakkah*! Did it! Well, it pointed with this great sharp sword and said; "Death to all who stay in the redhouse!"'

'Aye, that's the very words it said. But the voice! *Kaah*! It was like thunder over mountains, I wonder you lot didn't hear it.'

'We were sleeping. So, what did you do?'

'*Haak*! I'll tell you what we did, we shook our claws at it and said; "You come any closer, ghost, and you'll have us to deal with. Stop there while we go and bring General Ironbeak our Chief,"' Grubwing embroidered.

'Aye, we backed off, ready to give a good fight if it came floating up to the galleries. Ironbeak and Mangiz came out, Mangiz was shaking like a fledgling whose mother has left it,' Ragwing added.

'What did Ironbeak do?'

'*Kaah*, him! He flew about a bit and could not find the ghost, so he said he didn't believe us and flew off to get some sleep.'

'So where did the ghost mouse go to?'

'*Yakkah*! I don't know. To the place where other ghost mice go, I suppose.'

345

'You mean, there might be others?'

'*Kagg*! I'm not saying anything, but I wouldn't be surprised at all. The big door was open wide, Ironbeak couldn't deny that.'

The conversation carried on, getting more horrific with each imagined detail until some of Ironbeak's fighters decided that conquering the redstone house was not such a good idea.

'Did you see Mangiz today? He was badly knocked about.'

'*Yagg!* Do you think the ghosts had something to do with it?'

∽

Ambrose Spike threw a careless pawful of hotroot into the simmering watershrimp soup.

John Churchmouse glared at the hedgehog over the top of his steamed-up glasses. 'Ambrose, the recipe says half a spoon of hotroot. Why didn't you measure it?'

The old hedgehog bustled John to one side. 'Don't tell me how to make shrimp and hotroot soup. I learned my recipe from otters. A pawful, that's what you need. Let's see if that roseleaf and cowslip custard is ready.'

'Don't you dare touch my custard, you rough-pawed cellar keeper. It'll be ruined if you open that oven too soon. Come away.'

Ambrose could not get past John to open the oven. He snorted and began furiously kneading nuts into a batch of honeysuckle scones. John tugged his whiskers in despair.

'Honeysuckle scones have a delicate flavour all of their own. Sister Agnes's recipe calls for beechnuts, but you've put acorns and hazelnuts in. Where did those beechnuts I shelled go to?'

Ambrose wrinkled his snout and kneeded faster. 'Oh, those. I ate 'em. There was only a few. I'm very partial to a beechnut now and again.'

John clapped a paw to his brow. 'You didn't wash your paws. The whole batch will taste of hotroot!'

Ambrose grinned wickedly. 'So what? Ginger 'em up a bit. Give them more blackberry wine to drink and they won't notice the difference. Come on, quill-pusher, get those onions peeled.'

John flung down his oven cloth. 'Peel them yourself, barrel-minder!'

∽

Late that night a breeze sprang up. Clouds scudded across the moon, sending shifting patterns over the Abbey floor beneath Ironbeak and Mangiz. The Methusaleh and Matthias bells rang briefly, stopping abruptly to leave an eerie silence in their wake.

'How can the bells toll when we have the earth-crawlers trapped in that room below?' Mangiz murmured to Ironbeak.

'*Kagga*! Hold your beak,' Ironbeak silenced him. 'I don't know how they rang the bells and I don't care. It might be a diversion to stop us watching here. Keep your eyes on the floor below, over by the big door.'

They waited and watched.

So did the rooks from the dormitory, who had sneaked out on to the far corner of the galleries. Curiosity had overcome their General's command to stay in the dormitory. They had to see for themselves.

∽

The main Abbey door creaked on its hinges, slowly opening.

The raven and the crow held their breath as they watched it. A few dried leaves drifted in on the sighing breeze, pale moon patterns swayed on the worn stone floor, and the darkness in shadowy corners seemed to grow deeper.

The tomblike silence was broken by a voice like rolling thunder:

'Death waits in this place for those who stay!'

Mangiz felt the feathers on his back rise as if a cold paw had touched them.

The ghostly phantom appeared. It came in slowly by

347

the doorway, halted, looked up at Ironbeak and pointed with the sword.

'See, General, there it is, the armoured mouse!' Mangiz exclaimed.

Ironbeak buffeted the crow savagely. 'Shuttup, idiot. I'm going to deal with this once and for all!'

The raven went into a short run. He hurled himself over the galleries and sped towards the floor of Great Hall.

The apparition took one pace backward and vanished completely!

There was a cry of horror from the rooks. General Ironbeak skidded to a halt. Landing clumsily in his haste, he bowled over in a bundle of feathers. Swiftly regaining his balance, he dashed outside. It was mere seconds since the ghost had disappeared, but the grounds in front of the Abbey were completely deserted.

Ironbeak whirled about, baffled. He tore at the grass with his talons before rushing back inside. Hither and thither he darted about on the floorstones. Finally he halted, his powerful frame heaving with exertion. Looking upward he sought something to vent his rage upon. The rooks in the corner of the gallery! They cackled as they dashed to get back to the dormitory, but Ironbeak was swiftly among them, lashing out left and right, tearing with his claws, slamming with strong wings and hitting out with his vicious beak.

'*Yagga, krakkah*! Why did you not fly down and catch the thing? You were closer than I was. Get back to your perches, you swamp flies. Go on, out of my sight, you soft-beaked craven! You will forget what you saw here. It was only a trick of the moonlight. If I hear one bird speak of it I will break his wings!'

The rooks fled the scene, with Ironbeak chasing them. Mangiz slipped away quietly from the other end of the galleries, not wanting to face his General's rage. Great Hall lay quiet and still once more.

Behind the half-open door, Constance and Foremole folded the black cloth which they had used to make Cornflower vanish. The three Redwallers slid silently from the Great Hall, out into the tunnel and back to Cavern Hole, where supper was set out ready for them.

The Abbot took the sword from Cornflower as she unbuckled the armour. 'Well, how did it go?' he asked anxiously.

'Perfect, Father Abbot. I appeared, the birds were terrified, the raven flew at me. It was perfect.'

'Ironbeak flew at you? How did you escape?'

'Easily. Constance and Foremole tossed the black cloth over me, I dodged round the door and we all hid behind it. Ironbeak searched outside and inside, but he didn't look behind the door.'

Foremole wrinkled his nose. 'Yurr, these scones tastes loik 'otroot. Burr, gimme watter. There be enuff 'otroot in yon soops to set afire to you'm!'

Ambrose gave him a look of injured dignity. 'Try some of the roseleaf and cowslip custard.'

The Abbot prodded it gingerly. 'Oh, is that what it is? I thought it was a collapsed bird's nest.'

Ambrose sniffed and went off to the wine cellar with his snout in the air. 'Well, I enjoyed it. You lot don't deserve a good cook!'

∽

Night had fallen over the copse. Matthias and Orlando sat upon the step, putting an edge to axe and sword against the stone. Shrews filled their sling pouches, Basil ate his fill, and Cheek and Jess fashioned javelins, hardening their points over the campfire. Daggers, swords and knives were tested, bows made from strong green boughs, arrows tipped and hardened in the fire. It was but a few hours to dawn when all the preparations were completed. They lay down to take a brief rest.

Before they slept, Matthias, Jess, Orlando and Jabez stood above the stone step. They held paws foursquare and swore a solemn oath.

44

The fighting rooks of General Ironbeak were badly frightened. At first it had been exciting to perch and talk of the ghost, when none of them really believed there was one. But now they had seen it with their own eyes, a terrifying phantom that uttered dire warnings. Ironbeak himself could not harm it; the thing had vanished completely in a trice.

All through the night the sentry posts had been deserted while the rooks huddled together in the darkened dormitory, whispering of the awesome event. Grubclaw and Ragwing had been right, so had the wise Mangiz; the great redstone house was a bad place to be. The advent of a golden sunlit morning did little to change their minds.

That task was left to General Ironbeak, and he set about it with gusto. Sunrays flooded through the broken dormitory window, turning the raven leader's black wings an irridescent green, flecked with tinges of blue. He paced up and down with an aggressive rolling gait as he confronted his command.

'*Yaggah*! You cuckoo-brained bunch, can you not see it is all a trick the earthcrawlers are playing on us?'

The rooks shifted uneasily, inspecting their feathers or staring down at their claws. Some of them looked to

Mangiz, but the crow had distanced himself from the whole thing by perching upon a cupboard with his eyes closed.

Ironbeak carried on ranting. '*Kaah*! I flew down to attack this so-called ghost, and did it strike me dead, did it attack me, did it even stay to defend its Abbey? No, it hid away by some silly little trick. It fooled you all, but it did not fool Ironbeak, nor did it scare him. I am the greatest fighter in all the northlands. An earthcrawler mouse with bits of metal does not scare me. I will face it right now, or in the middle of a dark night. Mangiz, is what I say true?'

The seer crow opened one eye. He knew better than to argue with the raven leader.

'The mighty Ironbeak fears no living thing. He speaks true.'

∽

Baby Rollo was taking cooking lessons. Brother Dan and Gaffer were teaching him to make breakfast pancakes of chestnut flour and greensap milk, studded with dried damson pieces preserved in honey sugar. The infant bankvole was far more concerned with the tossing of the pancakes than the mixing of them. Brother Dan was up to his paws in the sticky mixture, and blobs of it clung to his ears and nosetip. Gaffer discovered he had a sweet tooth for preserved damson pieces. The mole sorted through the supply for the choicest bits and promptly ate them.

Winifred the Otter caught all three of them like guilty young ones as she entered the kitchen.

'What's the hold-up out here? There's a lot of hungry creatures waiting for breakfast out in the – Well, swish my tail! What in the good name of bulrushes is going on? Rollo, stop sticking those pancakes to the ceiling, this instant!'

Rollo was in the act of throwing a pancake from the pan at the ceiling. He stopped, and the pancake flopped neatly over his head, covering him to the neck. A pancake slowly detached itself from the ceiling and began to fall. Winifred grabbed a plate and ran to catch it.

'Brother Dan, stop playing round with that batter like a hedgehog in mud and help me.'

Winifred caught the falling pancake as Brother Dan took a plate in his sticky paws and went after another potential dropper. Gaffer began trying to remove the pancake from baby Rollo's head. The infant had eaten a hole in it to give himself some breathing space. Sensibly, Gaffer began eating from between Rollo's ears.

'Hurr, bain't gonna pull this'n offa you'm, Rollyo. Best scoff away both'n uz 'til it be gone. Hurr hurr!'

Cornflower appeared in the kitchen doorway. She tried to look very forbidding, while at the same time doing her best to stifle the laughter that was bubbling through at the comical scene.

'Shame on all four of you, hahaha, er, hmph! What on earth are you doing, heeheehee, ahem! Gaffer, will you stop trying to eat that infant's head and remove the pancake with some flou-flou-hahahahaoheehee! Flour!'

As she spoke, a pancake dropped from the ceiling squarely on to her nose and hung there like a tablecloth.

The five of them sat down upon the kitchen floor, laughing uproariously, holding their aching sides as tears rolled unchecked down their cheeks.

'Waaaahahahahohohoheeheehee! It's a good job we hadn't ordered porridge for breakfast.'

'Hoohoohurrhurrhurr! Nor soo – soo – hurr, hurr, soup, missus!'

∽

Far out upon the western plain, a great dark red bird crashed to earth among the dandelions and kingcups and lay among the yellow flowers like a red sandstone rock. The great bird's sides heaved and her neck pulsed as she greedily sucked in air. Her eyes dilated and contracted, fearsome orbs of tawny umber, flecked with turquoise and centred with gleaming black, as she scanned the blue sky above for predators.

One wing tucked neatly across her back, the other hanging limply at her side, she made a flapping run and gained the air. The red bird flew with a painful rolling motion, the injured wing flopping lower than the good one. Flight was becoming too difficult to sustain, so she came to earth again, this time in a rolling heap of feathers as she struck the plain floor, scattering buttercup petals in all directions.

The great bird rested momentarily, her huge curved beak gaping open, tongue hanging to one side. Doggedly struggling to her legs, she walked for a while, the injured wing trailing limply in the dust, her eyes fixed upon the building in the distance at the woodland edge. It was not so open there. Her beloved mountains were too far away, so she would try to make the building before sunset. There would be places where she could lie and rest, nooks and crannies where she could not be caught out. The open plains made her feel vulnerable; in flight she was a redoubtable hunter and fighter, but crippled like this she could only keep low and hope there were no flocks of other birds abroad that would relish the chance to attack an injured bird on the ground.

Flapping and hopping, scrambling and crawling, the great red bird made her way east towards the building which offered refuge.

∽

On the farflung south reaches of the plateau lands, dawn broke placidly over the copse. Matthias rose and picked up his sword.

'A good day to settle business, Orlando.'

The badger shouldered his axe. 'We travelled a long way to see this dawn, my friend. A good day.'

All around, shrews were girding themselves up for war; bows, arrows, slings, lances, even clubs were got ready. As Basil lugged the five weasel prisoners along on a makeshift lead, they wailed pitifully:

'No, no, please, don't make us go down there!'

'We'll be killed, we won't stand a chance!'

'We have no weapons, we'll be slain!'

Basil tugged the lead sharply. 'C'mon, step lively there, you wingeing weasels. You've lived like cowards; try to die like heroes. Hmph! Fat chance o' that, eh, laddie buck? Stop snivellin' and wipe your nose, you villainous vermin.'

They broke away from Basil's grasp and flung themselves in front of Matthias, grovelling shamelessly.

'Spare us please, sir, spare us!'

Sir Harry flapped down from an alder.

'There's nothing affects a craven
Like the thought of sudden death,
The idea he might not see the night
Or draw another breath.'

Orlando kicked a weasel in the rump as he stepped over the prostrate creatures.

'You know, Matthias, these scum aren't going to be a bit of good down there. They'll probably give the game away with all their sobbing and bawling. Shuttup, you snivelling snotnoses, or I'll finish you here and now!'

The weasels fell silent. Matthias leaned on his sword, stroking his whiskers.

'You've got a good point there, Orlando, but what do we do with them if we don't send them ahead of us on the stairs?'

Orlando hefted his battleaxe. 'Let me finish 'em off now, and save a lot of trouble.'

The weasels began moaning afresh. 'Stop that crying, d'you hear me, stoppit!' Matthias snorted impatiently. 'Right, here's what we'll do, Orlando. I couldn't let you kill them in cold blood, that isn't our way. We'll set them going southward. Sir Harry, would you accompany them on their way to make sure they keep going? Sorry about this, but there probably won't be a lot of space down there for you to fly about, and you'd get into trouble under the ground.'

Sir Harry shrugged.

'As you wish, as you wish, Matthias.
We each have a role to be filled.
I'll take these weasels south for a bit,
But the first one to cry gets killed!'

The owl picked the lead rope up in his beak and flapped off, with the five weasels stumbling and hurrying behind him.

Basil watched them go. 'Pity about old Harry. He looked a bit peeved to me. D'you think he's gone off in a huff, Matthias?'

The warrior mouse nodded. 'I've no doubt he has. Don't worry, he'll be back. Meanwhile, I'd like a last word with everybeast. Gather round and listen to what I have to say to you.'

∽

The small army squatted in the copse, while Matthias stood on the top stair of old Loamhedge and addressed them.

'First, I want to thank you all for your help and for coming this far with me. You have left your homes and territories far behind. Orlando, Jess, Jabez and myself have good reason to live or die today. You see, we have young ones to rescue. The rest of you, I cannot ask you to sacrifice your lives for our cause; they are not your young ones down there.'

Basil Stag Hare stood up. 'Beg pardon, old lad, but young Tim and Tess are down there. What'd my old chum John Churchmouse and his good lady wife say if I came back empty-pawed without their young uns? Coming with you? I'll say I am, bucko. You try and stop B. S. Hare esquire!'

Cheek stood by the hare. 'I'm with Basil. He's a grumpy ol' frump and I like him, so there!'

Basil and Cheek went to stand with Matthias. Log-a-Log drew his short sword.

'Shrews and Guosim are friends of Redwall. I never started a job that I didn't finish. I go with you.'

The whole of the Guosim moved as one with Log-a-Log to stand at Matthias's side.

Orlando raised his huge axe. His voice was tight with eagerness as he called: 'Come on, Warrior, what are we waiting for?'

∽

Mattimeo and the slaves had been taken from their darkened cell. Nadaz and several black-robed rats led them to the edge of the ledge where the statue stood. They were permitted to look over into the depths.

Through the greenish mist, Mattimeo could make out the thin bedraggled forms of scores of young creatures: squirrels, otters, hedgehogs, mice. They were hauling huge blocks of stone on towropes, and rats stood guard over them with whips and cudgels, urging them with heavy blows to greater efforts. Other young ones were lifting the stone blocks into position with pulleys and tackles, while yet other young woodlanders laid mortar and limestone cement in the gaps that were to receive the stones. Sometimes a young creature would cry out and fall over exhausted, only to be beaten by the rats until he or she got up, or lay permanently still.

Numbed by the horror of it, the new slaves were led before the statue and forced to bow their heads whilst Nadaz spoke to Malkariss.

'I am Nadaz, Voice of the Host. O Ruler of all below earth, these are your new servants. What do you require me to do with them?'

The hairs rose on Mattimeo's neck at the sound of the voice emanating from the crystal-toothed statue's mouth.

'They have looked upon my kingdom. Soon they will have the honour of building it for me,' it proclaimed.

From his bowed position, Mattimeo glanced along the line. He saw Vitch chained and held by two rats. The young mouse nudged Tess.

'Look who's there, our little slave-driver being re-warded for his services. I hope they chain me next to him for a while down there.'

357

Tess stamped her paw hard against the ledge, her eyes blazing. 'They can chain me next to who they like, but I'm not building any filthy underground kingdom for a talking statue!'

The young churchmouse's angry tones echoed around the rocky cavern. There was a brief silence, then Malkariss spoke again.

'Take them back and lock them away without light, food or water. They are not ready to serve me yet.'

As they were led up the gloomy winding passages, Tess began to weep. 'Oh, I'm sorry I spoke out. I've caused you all to be locked in the dark and starved again.'

'No, you haven't,' Cynthia Bankvole said bravely. 'I'd rather starve than be beaten to death like those poor creatures.'

Auma seconded her. 'Aye, don't worry, Tess. If you hadn't spoken out, I would have.'

'That's it friends, we stick together. Redwallll!' Mattimeo's voice rang out like the Abbey bells.

He was knocked flat with the butt of a spear before they were flung back into their darkened prison.

45

It was mid-afternoon, and Redwall lay quiet under the heat haze. Hardly a leaf stirred in the vastness of Mossflower beyond the north and east walls, and the plains shimmered and danced, making the horizon indistinguishable.

Down below in Cavern Hole depression had set in. It had started when little Rollo and a baby fieldmouse wanted to go out to play. Naturally the Abbot had to forbid any such idea with the birds about, so Ambrose Spike took them to play down in his wine cellar. Cornflower fanned herself with a dockleaf. The heat seemed to have penetrated the stones, even down to Cavern Hole, where it was usually cool.

'Poor Rollo, he did so want to go out to play on the grass. I remember Mattimeo, Tim and Tess used to go out in the orchard. Sam Squirrel would teach them to climb the apple and pear trees, and that sweet chestnut over by the gooseberry patch.'

Abbot Mordalfus mopped his brow with his habbit sleeve. 'Ah yes, he was a scamp, that Sam Squirrel. Mind you, so was I at their age. I used to get sent off to bed for dashing around the top of the outer wall when I was a young one. Haha, old Sister Fern used to say it gave her dizzy spells just watching me. Phew! I don't know about

Rollo, but I could certainly do with a stroll outside in the grounds. It's hot in here.'

Mrs Churchmouse closed her eyes dreamily. 'Mmmm, I'd love to be sitting dabbling my paws in the pond on an afternoon like this.'

Foremole tugged his snout obligingly. 'Burr, if'n you'm laydeez ud loik to wet you'm paws, oi'll take you'm thro' yon tunnel to pond.'

Winifred the Otter sprang up. 'What a good idea! Oh, would you please let us go, Father Abbot? We'll be careful, I promise we will. The first sign of a rook and we'll pop into that hole like moles, pardon the expression.'

Abbot Mordalfus took his spectacles off. Smiling indulgently, he settled back in his chair.

'Well, it's pretty certain I won't get any rest with you chattering creatures about. Of course you may go, but don't stay out too long and be very careful. I'll stop here and take a nap.'

Foremole was first into the tunnel. 'Age afore booty. Foller me, gennelbeasts.'

The Abbot settled back in his chair with a sigh. A ray of sunlight crossing Great Hall penetrated down the stairs across the barricade top and shone in his eyes. He watched the small golden dust flecks dancing in it, his eyes gradually closing as he drifted into his noontide nap.

∽

Cornflower came wriggling back down the tunnel, followed by her companions. She scurried from the entrance and, not bothering to dust herself down, began shaking the sleepy Abbot by the paw.

'Wake up, wake up, Father Abbot, quickly! They're attacking it, the poor thing. Oh, it'll be killed if we don't do something.'

The Abbot blinked and jumped up. 'Eh, what? Attacking what poor thing, where?'

Winifred grabbed his other paw. 'A big rusty-coloured

bird, much bigger than Ironbeak's lot. It's over by the pond and the rooks are attacking it. Oh, I'm sure it isn't an invader. We've got to help it.'

The Abbot leapt into action.

'Find Constance quickly. Get any available moles and bring them here.'

A moment later, Constance rushed in from the kitchens, covered in flour with a bunch of scallions in her paw. She climbed into the tunnel, shouting orders:

'Everybeast stay here except the moles. Send them after me. I'll deal with this!'

<hr />

In front of the pond the great red bird lay. With one final effort she had flown over the outer Abbey wall, landing with a thud on the soft gatehouse garden soil. Seeing the water glint in the afternoon sun, she hauled herself painfully over to drink at the pond. The throat of the great red bird was dry, her tongue parched, spots danced before her eyes. Crazily she staggered and wobbled towards the water. Next instant she was harried by three rooks who descended upon her. They pecked and dragged at the great red bird, lashing out with their clawing talons. Half unconscious and defence-less, she lay at their mercy.

Foremole was awaiting Constance's arrival up the tunnel.

'O'er thurr, stroipmarm,' he said, pointing to the scene of the attack. 'They'm akillen yon burd, they gurt bullies!'

Constance hurtled from the tunnel and was upon the rooks before they knew what was happening.

She bulled the first one straight into the pond and cuffed the next one high into the air with a quick hefty paw. The third rook took off, leaving most of his tailfeathers between the badger's teeth. The attackers flew squawking through the broken dormitory window, terrified to look back lest the big badger was coming after them.

Swiftly Constance began dragging the great red bird to the tunnel. It raised its head feebly and tried to attack the badger. Constance narrowly avoided the fierce curved beak but took several scratches from the powerful talons before she stunned the already half-unconscious bird with a smart tap of her paw between its eyes.

'Sorry, but it's for your own good, you silly great thing. Here, Foremole, which end do you want?'

Foremole scrambled from the tunnel, leaving three of his crew ready to receive the burden.

'You'm leave et t'me, marm. Yurr, Jarge, oi'm asendin' burd in 'ead furst, save reverse feather draggen. Chuck yon rope round they claws. Oi'll tie beak. Gaffer, be you'm ready wi' grease case'n et be too woid in beam.'

⟋⟍

Ironbeak and Mangiz flew through the dormitory window with several rooks. They landed where the attack had taken place. The General looked particularly bad-tempered after being disturbed at his noontide roost.

'*Yakka*! First it is ghost mice, now we have a great disappearing red bird. Where is it, fools?'

'It was right there, General. We pecked it and scratched it—'

'Yes, yes. And what happened then?'

'The big earthcrawler, the stripedog, it tried to slay us.'

'So you turned tail and flew off,' Ironbeak said scornfully.

'Chief, there was nothing else we could do. That stripedog is a wild beast!'

'How long ago did this take place?'

'Only a moment back, Ironbeak. We were at the dormitory window when we saw this big rusty-looking bird come over the wall. It must have been ill because it flapped and flopped about like a new eggchick.'

'So you attacked it?'

'Oh yes, Chief. We gave it a good clawing and beaking—'

'And you killed it!'

'Yes, er, no. I mean, we were going to, when the earthcrawler came.'

'Where did the stripedog come from?'

'Search me!'

Ironbeak buffeted the insolent rook flat. He ground his talons against its beak and pecked it hard upon its leg.

'*Kaah*! Out of my sight, nettlehead, I think the sun in this warm land has addled your brains. First you see a great bird, then you are attacked by the stripedog, and that was only the flick of a feather ago. Now there is no sign of the earthcrawler and the big bird has vanished too. Maybe they are both hiding underwater in that pool. Shall I throw you in so that you can search them out?'

'The stripedog has already done that, by the look of Grubclaw,' Mangiz interrupted.

Ironbeak shook his head sadly. '*Gaah*! You too. You make me sick, all of you. Watch this.'

The raven spread his wings and hopped about cawing aloud, 'Earthcrawler! Rustybird! Come out and fight me. It is I, General Ironbeak, terror of the northlands!'

There was no response. The raven turned to Mangiz and the rooks.

'See? It is the same as the ghost mouse. Get out of my sight, the useless lot of you!'

∽

From the hidden tunnel entrance in the shrubbery by the rushes, Brother Sedge chuckled quietly.

'Oh dear, oh dear, whatever next?'

∽

The great red bird was taken into Ambrose Spike's wine cellar. It was cool and spacious there.

John Churchmouse walked around it awestruck. 'Whew! That *is* a large bird. I've never seen one like it before. What sort of bird do you think it is, Mordalfus?'

The Abbot looked up from the deep scratch he was attending to. 'I don't know, John. This is a very strange bird. It is not a woodlander, nor does it live on the plain, or we would have seen it from the Abbey walls. I wonder what brought it here.'

Sister May worked at the other side of the bird. She laid herbs and dabbed lotions on wounds, bandaging wherever possible.

'Poor thing, she's taken quite a savage beating.'

The bird kicked and tried to raise its head. Sister May leapt up.

'Oh dear. Look out, she's coming round!' she warned.

The huge flecked eyes with their dark irises snapped open.

Constance beckoned the onlookers away. 'Sister May, Abbot, would you carry on with your healing? The rest of you go back to Cavern Hole. I don't want this creature to feel surrounded. Cornflower, pass me those scissors, please.'

She snipped at the beak and leg fastenings. 'We mean you no harm. You are among friends. Lie still,' she said gently. 'You have been hurt.'

The bird groaned and lay back. 'Werra diss?' it asked, in a strange accent.

The Abbot recognized the tongue. 'She speaks like the mountain hawks and eagles. I'm sure she understands us, though. Hello, I am called Abbot, she is Sister May and she is Constance. This place is Redwall. We will make your hurts better. Who are you?'

Sister May worked on a deep gash in the bird's leg. 'This will take a stitch. Be still, please. I want to help you.'

The bird lay patiently watching her. It spoke again: 'I be still please. Diss bird called Stryk Redkite, comin' from allrock allrock.'

The Abbot wiped grease from a neckfeather. 'Ah, a great red kite, a mountain bird. I've read of them in our old records, but I've never seen one until now. Most impressive. Well, Stryk Redkite, lie quiet while we try and heal you.'

'Stryk need waterdrinks.'

'Oh, right. Constance, would you ask Cornflower to bring water for our guest. Tell me, Stryk, is your wing broken?'

Slowly, painfully, the big bird stood. She looked indignantly at the frail old Abbot. 'Stryk Redkite mighty flyer!'

Sister May wagged an admonishing paw at the bird. 'Stryk Redkite mighty fibber. Look at that wing. It's totally useless, and I'll wager you've been making it worse by trying to fly with it.'

The red kite limped sulkily off into a corner and huddled down.

'Rockslip, nestfall, *Phweek*! Who needs fly? Stay now, here with friends, with Habbot, with Sissismay.'

Sister May took the water from Cornflower and held it up to the huge hunting bird.

'That's all very well, but you'd better be on your best behaviour. And my name is Sister May. Say it, Sister . . . May!'

'Sissismay, goodan' very fierce!'

46

With Matthias and Orlando in the vanguard and Basil Stag Hare acting as scout, the depleted shrew army padded silently down the steps to the Kingdom of Malkariss. At first it was quite dark, with the morning brightness filtering down only a short way, but gradually the steps opened out on to a broad torchlit corridor.

They halted while Basil scouted the lie of the land. As they waited, Matthias took in his surroundings. The well-finished stone now coated with moss had once been an upper-storey passage. Tree roots forced their way between the masonry, causing some of the wall to buckle and bend outwards and water dripped from the roof, forming small pools on the well-worn floor.

Basil was back shortly with some information.

'The blinkin' place is worse than a great rabbit warren, with corridors, caves, passages an' tunnels, all slopin' downward too. As for the enemy, well, it's rats again, old lad. They wear a black robe with a hood and their weapon appears to be a short kind o' spear; not the throwin' kind, you understand, more your good old stabber. They don't seem to carry any other type of weapon. In a place this size there must be a lot of the blighters, I'd guess.'

Matthias tried to form a plan in his head as he

discussed the information with his friends.

'We'd best stay together. No sense in splitting the force. Jess, you, Cheek and Jabez guard the rear and watch our backs. Orlando and Log-a-Log, stay in front with me. Guosim, have your javelins, slings and bows ready. If we run into a small bunch, pick them off right away. Don't let them get back to their main force and report that we're down here, or we'll lose the element of surprise. Basil, was there no sign of our young ones?'

'No, 'fraid not. They must be further down this bally maze somewhere. I'll keep my eyes open. Which way d'you suggest, right or left along this passage?'

Orlando placed his axe on the floor and spun it. 'Right is as good as any way. Trust to luck.'

They stole off, right down the broad torchlit corridor.

∽

Nadaz brought Slagar before the idol on the ledge. The masked fox stood tensely, awaiting the decision of Malkariss. From the depths below, the sounds of young slaves toiling drifted upwards. The Sly One watched the statue of the huge white polecat, wondering what sort of creature lived within it. Was it a polecat, or a fox like himself? Slagar liked to think it was a fox. He considered foxes to be the cleverest of animals. The voice issuing from the monolith interrupted his thoughts:

'Nadaz, you will tell the masked one that I have made my decision. He is to be given fourscore rats and left to carry out my commands in the territory above my kingdom. Tell him that he will be watched closely. I have many more blackrobes waiting to carry out my word, more than leaves on an autumn wind. If the fox plays me false, he will be slain, both him and his fourscore fighters. If, on the other paw, he remains loyal to my bidding, by the time the snow falls I will increase his command by ten times and set my slaves to build him a stone fortress above ground, where he can rule all the territory from the cliffs to the south hinterlands. Malkariss has spoken. Go!'

Slagar quivered with excitement. He had heard every word. His silken mask fluttered in and out as he swelled his narrow chest, revelling in the new-found power he had been given.

At a signal from Nadaz's bone sceptre the fourscore rats emerged from the winding causeway and took up their place behind the new commander. Many thoughts ran through Slagar's fertile mind as he marched at their head alongside Nadaz, up the winding passages of old Loamhedge toward the lands that awaited him in the morning sunlight: his territory. Malkariss was no fool, he thought. The fourscore die with me if I prove false, so he was providing himself with extra insurance. The rats in my command will be watching me closely, and no doubt Malkariss has issued them with secret orders to slay me if I try to cross him. I will show him who the Sly One really is. After I am commander of a great horde with my own fortress, I will make Malkariss wish he had never met Slagar. I will trap him down inside his own underground kingdom, and within a season he will either be dead or eating from my paw. As for this one, Nadaz, he is only a servant to the statue. Slagar serves no statue; the Sly One serves only his own ideas.

Slagar's plans had made no provision for what came next. Rounding the bend in a passage, he found himself face to face with Orlando!

The warrior badger gave a roar and swung his axe, but nobeast was quicker than the masked fox in an emergency. He ducked swiftly back into the ranks of his rats, pushing the nearest two in the path of the swirling axehead. Matthias deflected a spear with his sword. Crouching low, he fought his way into the ranks, sword flashing as he went after his enemy. Log-a-Log yelled and the Guosim hurled a rain of stones and arrows at the rats. Nadaz fell flat, then crawled back against the side of the wall. Springing up, he grabbed a torch from its sconce and flung it among the attackers as he yelled; 'Retreat! Back to the ledge!'

Amid the milling confusion, the clang of Orlando's axe rang against the stone walls as he scythed madly at the rats who were trying to turn and run. Matthias had fought his way among the rats but lost sight of Slagar. Turning, he faced the rats who were trying to push past him. Blocking, sweeping and hacking, he battled away until he met Orlando coming from the opposite direction. Log-a-Log passed them both at the head of the Guosim.

'After them!'

They stumbled over the bodies of fallen foes. The passage was dark because Nadaz was taking the torches from their holders as he went. Stumbling and banging against the walls, the woodlanders dashed wildly through the inky blackness, guided by the sounds of the retreating rats ahead of them. Light showed from the back of the column and they made way for Cheek, who had thoughtfully retrieved the torch thrown by Nadaz and swung it back into blazing life. Now they could see where they were going, the attackers ran pell-mell downwards, through winding passages and deserted halls, heedlessly past a heavily locked timber door.

∽

Mattimeo sat up in the darkness. 'Listen, what's that? Something's going on out there!' he said excitedly.

They crowded round the door, banging and shouting.

'In here, in here! Help us, we're Redwallers!'

But they were shouting to an empty corridor. The sounds of the chase died away into the distance.

∽

The hunted rats broke out on to the ledge, with Slagar and Nadaz in the lead. Ignoring ceremony, the purple-robed rat shouted towards the idol, 'Enemies – a badger and a mouse with a band of woodlanders. They are right behind us!'

The voice from the idol rang out:

'This is your doing, fox. You were followed here. I will deal with you later. Nadaz, tell your fighters to surround

369

this statue. Sound the alarm, throw the whole weight of my host against these impudent intruders!'

The rats formed themselves in a cordon around the idol, spears pointing outwards. Nadaz dashed to the far side of the ledge and began pounding on a deep circular drum to sound the alarm. Slagar did not wait for the attackers to arrive, he slunk off quickly down the winding causeway stairs, pointing to the black-robed rats who charged past him on their way up.

'Hurry to the ledge, everybeast. Malkariss wants you!' he told them.

'Redwall! Mossflower! Logalogalogalog!'

The woodlanders came roaring out of the passage on to the ledge. Log-a-Log and the Guosim charged the rats defending the statue, but they were quickly repulsed by the fanatical dedication of the fighters with their stabbing spears.

More rats were already on the platform of the ledge. Matthias gasped with shock. A countless horde was pounding its way up the stairs of the causeway. He had not realized the numbers were so vast. Like seething black ants, they swarmed up from the misty green depths. Without thinking, he threw himself at the foremost group. Orlando and Jess ran to help him, the squirrel armed with a short shrew sword.

'Drive them back, we've got to stop them getting on to this ledge!' Matthias shouted.

A spear thrust nipped Orlando's muzzle and blood sprang to his nosetip.

'Eeeeeuuulaliaaaaa!'

The maddened badger went in like a battering ram. Rats who tried to back out of his way were driven over the edge of the ledge and plunged screaming into the green misted depths. Matthias was filled with battle rage. He tried hard to keep a level head, using all the time-honoured skills of the true warrior swordsmouse. Sweep, slice, cleave, thrust; he worked like a machine, relentlessly battling great odds. Jess was different, she leapt and bounded, stabbing left and right, blood flowing from her tail like a scarlet ribbon. Though the stabbing spears were unwieldy at any great range, they were proving effective at close quarters. None of the blackrobes spoke or shouted. They formed flying wedges, charging individual attackers, often breaking to surround them in a stabbing ring of spearpoints.

Log-a-Log had been driven back twice. At the second attempt he fell, wounded in the throat by a spear. Basil Stag Hare leapt into the breach.

'Righto, Guosim lads. Form three ranks over here. Front and centre now, look lively! Slings and bows only, fire, drop down an' reload. Keep advancin', that's the style. Fire, drop down, reload, but keep movin' to your front. Sharpish now. Good show!'

The rats were forced to break their circle and came round to defend the front of the statue from Basil's strategy. The hare was a veteran at manoeuvres. He gathered a small force of shrews carrying javelins.

'I say, young Cheek, here's your first chance at a command. Take these fellahs to the back of the ledge, work your way round that dirty great statue thing and come up behind those rodents facin' us. Give 'em plenty of the old one-two, and don't forget, m'lad, duck an' weave!'

Cheek saluted smartly, his fear diminished with the heat of battle. 'Righto, Baz old sport!'

Basil watched him go, shaking his head and smiling. Hardnosed young blighter, bit like m'self when I was a nipper, he thought. 'Fire! Now drop down an' reload, shrews. That's the stuff t' give the troops!'

∽

The battle raged back and forth as Nadaz pounded the war alarm. The booming drumbeats echoed around the rocks as arrows flew, slingers hurled and spears stabbed. Matthias looked wildly about amid the melee. His forces were vastly outnumbered and still rats were waiting on the causeway steps in droves. Breaking clear of the fray, the warrior mouse yelled aloud, 'Retreat! Retreat! Take your wounded and get back to the passage we came in by!'

The Guosim carried Log-a-Log as they hacked their way back to the mouth of the passage. Orlando, Jess and Jabez stood side by side with Cheek as Basil fought a fierce rearguard action. Matthias, weaving in and out of them, helped with the wounded.

Finally they gained the passage, the drum stopped pounding and the rats fell back halfway across the ledge, protecting the causeway steps as their comrades swarmed up, spreading across the length and breadth of the rocky plateau. In the midst of it all, Nadaz stood rattling the mouse skull at the top of his sceptre, pointing at the woodlanders as if trying to cast some sort of spell over them.

∽

Orlando cleaned his axe and set about sharpening it against the rock wall.

'Well, we gave them a good fight, even though we were outnumbered,' he said consolingly.

The warrior mouse sat with his back to the wall breathing heavily. 'Aye, if we had the young ones now we could back up and go above ground. Trouble is, I haven't seen them anywhere.'

The badger licked a wounded paw. 'Nor have I, or the fox, for that matter. I'm not leaving here while he still lives, then if I can't find my Auma at least I'll know he won't enslave any more young ones.'

Cheek stood at the mouth of the passage, pulling faces at the ranks of blackrobes gathered a short distance away.

'Yah, tatty ratty! Your silly old statue isn't worth a crushed acorn. It takes a horde of you to face real fighters, doesn't it!' he taunted them.

Basil and Jess were trying to bandage the awful wound in Log-a-Log's neck, which was deep and serious. Basil shook his head.

'Will y' listen to that young rip? Shortly we'll all be slaughtered, and there he is calling names like a vole-maid at a tea party. Haha, the little bucko, good for him! I say, old Log-a-thing, stay still. You'll only make that scratch worse, y'know.'

The shrew leader pawed at the wet bandage around his neck. He was panting hard.

'It's a bad one, mate, I'm out of it,' he said, rasping harshly.

Basil waggled his ears encouragingly. 'Poppycock, old lad. We'll have you as good as new shortly.'

Log-a-Log pushed himself into a standing position and turned to Matthias. 'Where's Flugg? I must see him. Matthias, I've got to go up into the daylight. I don't want to die down here in this dark place.'

Matthias grasped his friend firmly by the paw. 'I understand, Log-a-Log. You go up top and rest. You'll be all right. Flugg, will you and some of the others take Log-a-Log up into the daylight? Easy now, mind his neck.'

'Matthias, look!' Orlando was standing on a pro-truding wall rock, craning his neck. 'They've let a sort of a rope over the side of the ledge and there's a large basket on the end of it. Looks to me as if they're lowering something down. I wonder what it is.'

Matthias shrugged. 'Your guess is as good as mine. Listen, Orlando, pretty soon now they're going to attack. I can feel it. We might hold out for a bit, but we'll end up being overwhelmed. I have an idea that might buy a bit of time for us, then if all fails at least our creatures might make a run for it and escape.'

Standing out from the cave entrance, Matthias pointed his sword at Nadaz.

'You there, rat, I challenge you to single combat!' he shouted.

Nadaz continued chanting and shaking his grisly sceptre. The warrior mouse tried again.

'You're afraid! It's all right when you have your horde

373

with you, but on your own, ha! You're nothing but a coward. Send anybeast out, then. I am Matthias of Redwall, I am a warrior who does not know fear. Are there any among you like me, or are you all spineless scum?'

The black-robed rats turned to look at Nadaz.

'You're not saving my acorns, Warrior,' Orlando whispered fiercely. 'I stay down here with you until the end. I'll fight their champion!'

Matthias smiled, shaking his head. 'Orlando, you are the bravest creature I have ever known. No, my friend, they know you could beat any one of them; that's why I offered to fight. There must be quite a few of them who'd fancy their chances against a warrior my size. But if you must stay, then so be it. When I fall, you can guard the passage and buy our friends a bit of extra time to escape.'

Orlando placed a heavy paw upon Matthias.

'Champion of Redwall, you may be a mouse but your heart is far bigger than mine. Look out, something's happening over there.'

Nadaz was now pointing his sceptre at the causeway. The rats on the steps made way, and they seemed to shrink back against the rock walls in fear. Matthias gripped his sword hilt tighter and his breath caught in his chest.

It was a huge rodent, somewhere between a ferret and a stoat. The beast looked like a primeval throwback; it had no ears and practically no neck. The hulking head perched squat upon its heavy shoulders leered evilly through curved and stained teeth. Sinew and muscle stood out like great cords all over its body, and heavy spiked iron bands ringed its paws and waist. It carried a stabbing spear of fearsome size and a weighted net.

Nadaz made an evil, sniggering noise.

'Matthias of Redwall who fears nobeast, this is your challenger. The Wearet, the slavemaster!'

47

Sister May and Cornflower had tried to feed Stryk with Abbey fare, but the red kite was no vegetarian, so they finally compromised by giving the great hunting bird a net of water shrimp. Stryk had taken to the corner of the wine cellar, and she settled down to sleep on a pile of moss and sacking.

'Stay out of Mr Spike's wine cellar, little one,' Sister May warned baby Rollo. 'Never go down there alone. We can't take chances with a bird like that one.'

'Huh, hope it doesn't get a taste for October ale or elderberry wine, great hulkin' thing like that'd empty my cellar,' Ambrose Spike grumbled into an apple and blackberry pie wedge.

The Abbot looked over the top of his spectacles. 'No quicker than the average cellar-keeper could empty a larder. You're right, Sister May, Stryk is a fine big bird, but she is not used to our ways. Pity about her wing. She's very proud. Did you see the way she got huffy when I remarked that it was broken? I'd like to take a look at it sometime.'

Cornflower stopped Rollo roaming in the direction of the wine cellar and sat the mischievous infant on her lap.

'Poor thing,' Sister May said sympathetically. 'Apparently she built her nest on a piece of branch sticking out from the mountain, then one night the branch rotted and the nest fell. She struck her wing awkwardly on a jagged rock and broke it. Stryk said that she lay in the ruined nest for many days, unable to move. She had no mate to defend her and she was attacked by other birds. Finally she forced herself to fly. Bit by bit she made her way across the western plain, looking for somewhere to shelter, and that was when she saw our Abbey.'

Constance came in mopping her brow. 'Still hot out there. Where's the big bird? Asleep? What a size! I'll bet she could almost lift me. D'you think she'll ever fly again, Abbot?'

'I don't know, Constance. Maybe if we could look at her wing we'd be able to tell. However, big red kites aren't our present worry, it's ravens, crows and rooks I'm concerned with. Cornflower, you must stop this masquerade as Martin the Warrior. I know it annoys Ironbeak, but it isn't getting us anywhere. There's another reason also. That raven is no fool, and sooner or later he'll be a bit quicker than us and he'll catch you. There's too much risk involved, you'll have to give it up.'

Cornflower became indignant. 'But Father Abbot, when I get dressed up as the ghost I know it upsets Ironbeak, and that's why I must continue. It has also started to demoralize his rooks. They're scared, and the crow – wotsisname, Mangiz – he's frightened of me too, I can tell. That crow is a very superstitious bird and the others take notice of him. Let me do it just one more time tonight. Please!'

Mordalfus polished his glasses. 'Cornflower, you're a bigger mischief-maker than your son and a fighter as brave as your husband. Make tonight the last time that you haunt our Abbey.'

Baby Rollo had dozed off, and Cornflower placed the sleeping infant in the Abbot's lap.

'I will, thank you, Father Abbot. Sister May, come on, we have work to do if the ghost is to walk again tonight. Come on, Constance, we need you for the voice of Martin.'

The Abbot stroked Rollo's head. 'And I'm left holding the baby, as usual!'

∽

Ironbeak sat at the broken dormitory window and related his troubles to Mangiz.

'Warrior mouse ghosts, big red birds; what next, my seer? The earthcrawlers are down in that Cavern place where we cannot get at them. I have conquered nearly all this great redstone house from the roof down and I cannot let it slip away from me. If I were forced to leave here, we would have to go back to the northlands. They are cold and hard, Mangiz, and it is all fight and no food. We are getting older and could not face many more winters in the north. Tell me, Mangiz, have your visions come back? Are you seeing anything in the eye of your mind again?'

'My General, you were right,' Mangiz said readily, glad that he was back in favour. 'I see the ghost mouse was only a trick of the earthcrawlers to frighten us from here. As for the great rustybird, *kachah*! It was only the imagination of scared rooks. The heatwaves shimmer and dance in this country, and you could see more strange things than on a dark night in the northlands.'

Ironbeak was heartened. 'Well spoken, Mangiz, my strong right wing. What else do you see? Are the omens good for your General?'

'The omens are good. It all becomes clear as water now. Ironbeak, you and I will live a good and easy life in this redstone house, the food will be plenty and the seasons good, winters cold will not harm us in this place surrounded by tall woodland. When the earthcrawlers get tired of playing their silly little games, we will catch them all out in the open, and that day they will be slain. Then there will be none left to oppose us. This I see truly, my General.'

Ironbeak stood and stretched his wings, and Mangiz ducked to avoid being knocked out of the window.

'*Kachakka*! This is good, Mangiz. I feel good in my

377

feathers too. I think I will fly up and perch awhile on the roof of my big redstone house. Tell the rooks to rest well, and sleep yourself. You look tired and hot.'

Ironbeak launched himself from the sill and spiralled up to the Abbey roof.

Mangiz blew a great sigh of relief and settled down to nap in the hot sun. It was the first time he had lied to Ironbeak about his visions. They were still clouded by the warrior mouse, but the crow was not going to tell Ironbeak that. What the General did not know for the moment would not harm him, and compliments were better received than kicks.

~

When night fell over Redwall and the Mossflower country, Cornflower began buckling on her armour. However, Sister May had a better idea, so she unbuckled it and listened. Constance covered her mouth and shook with suppressed laughter when the ruse was outlined to her.

'Oh yes, let's do it. I wouldn't miss this for a midsummer feast!'

~

The rooks perched in the dormitory, half dozing, half awake, none fully asleep since the General had issued the order for them to have the rest of the day off. Most of them had slept all afternoon, and they found it difficult trying to sleep in the night also. It was hot and airless for birds who had lived their lives in the cold northlands. A full moon beamed down through the dormitory window, bathing the entire room in pale bluish white light.

'Leeeeave oooooour Abbeeeeeeeeey!'

'*Yaak!* What was that?'

'Death is neeeeear!'

The rooks froze on their perches.

'Death waits outside this rooooooom!'

A black shadow cast itself across the beds and the floor. There was something at the window.

The rook Ragwing turned his head slowly and fearfully until he could see the window.

Framed by the broken pane, with cold moonlight surrounding it, was the head of the Warrior, the helmet with no face; pale grey mist hovered in place of the Warrior's features. Ragwing and his companions were in a state of panic bordering on hysteria, and the words of the bodiless phantom were like some dread puzzle: *'Leave our Abbey'*. How could they leave the Abbey, knowing that the ghost had said *'Death waits outside this room'*? There was only the window, and the horrible head was floating about there. Even the bravest rook would not venture out that way. It was more than the terrified birds could stand, so they scrabbled underneath the beds, afraid to look or move.

~

As they stole back to Cavern Hole Constance shook the window pole that had supported the ghostly head at Sister May.

'One more giggle out of you, Sister, and I'll have you put on cooking duties with Ambrose Spike!' she said menacingly.

Cornflower held a kerchief to her face, pretending to blow her nose. She was, in fact, biting the material to stop herself roaring with laughter.

Constance waited until they were out of earshot in the tunnel, then she laughed.

'Heeheehee! I took a quick peek through the window, and the rooks were underneath the beds trying to make themselves invisible.'

Sister May shook her head in mock sympathy. 'It's no wonder. You didn't give them much choice: leave the Abbey, but don't leave the room. Really Constance, what made you think that one up?'

'I don't know. I suppose I just lost my head. Hahaha!'

Cornflower wiped tears from her eyes, realising that the fun had turned to sorrow and longing for her family.

'My Matthias and Mattimeo would have appreciated a

joke like that. Dear me, I can't get them out of my mind night or day. Oh Matthias will be able to take care of himself, no matter where he is, but what about my little Mattimeo, I wonder what he's doing right now, I hope he's safe and well fed. I'm sorry my friends, I'm an old wet rag these days, moping about like I don't know what.' Sister May began weeping herself.

'There there, we understand, don't you worry, your young one will be all right.'

Constance sniffed loudly.

'Of course he will.'

48

A silence had fallen upon the ledge. Friend and foe alike were hushed as Matthias and the Wearet circled about. The warrior mouse, straight backed, moved lightly on his paws, the great sword of Martin held double-pawed against his right cheek. The Wearet crouched low, spear held pointing at his opponent, the loaded net making swift dragging noises as he cast it in small circles continuously. The eyes of the two fighters were locked as each tried to read the other's thoughts, hoping one false move of a paw would give him the advantage.

Matthias attempted to keep his back to the entrance, where Orlando and his friends waited, but the cunning skill of the Wearet forced him round until he could feel the rat horde at his back. The Wearet snarled viciously and shuffled forwards, jabbing at his foe. Matthias was concentrating on the spearpoint and the swirling net; not until too late did he feel the spear butt of a black-robed rat hit him in the back of his legs. The warrior mouse fell backwards. The Wearet hurled himself forward, spear first, but Matthias twisted to one side, caught the end of the net and gave a sharp tug, adding impetus to his enemy's charge.

There was a bubbling scream as the Wearet stumbled in his lunge, and the rat who had tripped Matthias with the spear butt staggered forward, impaled upon the Wearet's stabbing spear. Matthias goaded his foe sharply across his hindquarters with the needlelike swordpoint. The Wearet foamed and screeched as he shook the fallen rat from his spearpoint, casting the weighted net back over his shoulder. The weights struck Matthias on top of his head. Blackness interspersed with coloured stars exploded behind his eyes, and he felt rather than saw the spear jab at his throat as the Wearet attacked on the turn. There was a ringing clang as the Warrior's swordpoint countered the spear blade.

His head clearing, Matthias leapt nimbly forward, clipping the Wearet's slobbering jaw and slicing across his spear paw. Despite the ferocity of the attack, the Wearet kicked Matthias in the stomach and whipped away at his body with the folded net. He drove his opponent back until he was practically at the rock wall of the ledge. Matthias whirled the sword and came forwards, propelling himself forcefully off the rocks.

'Redwaaaaall!'

The fury of the onslaught drove the Wearet back. He took two sharp slashes upon his flanks before clouting Matthias in the face with the flat of his spear blade and throwing the net over the mouse warrior. Matthias knew he was snared. He could not use his sword, and the net weighed heavily upon him as the Wearet stooped to gather the ends and fully entrap him. Seeing a slim chance, Matthias trod on the grounded blade of the spear, causing the Wearet to try and pull the spear free.

It was all the chance Matthias needed. He bulled forward, battering into the Wearet. Shoving hard with head and paws, he sent his foe hurtling back into the ranks of the rats. Matthias dropped his sword and fell flat, keeping his paws tight to his sides. The Wearet stumbled and struggled amid the rats. Holding only one edge of the net, he dragged at it. The net slid from Matthias, who snatched his sword and jumped up, charging straight in among the rats, hacking this way and that in an attempt to get at the Wearet.

'Get out of there, watch your back, Matthias!' Orlando roared from the cave mouth.

Matthias dimly heard Orlando. With the spirit of Martin coursing through his veins, he whirled in a tight warrior's circle. Up, down and at middle height, the great sword was everywhere at once in a glittering circle of steel. Rats fought to get out of its way.

Wearet cut through the rats to Matthias's opposite side and regained the open space. As the warrior mouse came spinning out of the horde, he saw Wearet and carried on his deadly course. Still spinning, his sword sheared into the net, shredding it to a useless mass of cordage as it was swept from his foebeast's paw. The Wearet snatched a fallen stabbing spear, arming himself doubly. Prodding and thrusting, he locked blades with Matthias. The ring of sword upon spears echoed around the ledge as the pair fought madly, backwards and forwards, hacking and slicing, parrying and striking in a hideous ritual of death.

⁓

Mattimeo and his friends had lain miserably in the darkened cell until they lost track of night or day. Several attempts had been made to force the door, each one more futile than the last. Auma's body ached from the number of times she had thrown herself at the heavy unyielding door, and Sam's teeth were numb through trying to gnaw at the timbers. Mattimeo, Tim, Tess, Jube and even Cynthia had tried in one way or another, all resulting in bleeding and splinter-stuck paws. They sat miserably in the darkness. Cynthia began weeping.

'There, there, hush now. We'll get out of here, you'll see,' Tess comforted her.

Auma placed her aching back against the wall. 'I'd like to think we'll get out of here too, but where would we go?'

'Anywhere!' Mattimeo's voice trembled. 'I wouldn't

mind getting out of here just to die fighting those robed rats instead of perishing down here like some insect under the ground. At least it would be better than a life under the whip of a slavekeeper.'

'Ssshhhh!'

'Who said that?'

Sam crawled close to Mattimeo. 'I did. Listen, can you hear anything?'

'No, can you?'

'I'm not sure, but it sounds like a drum pounding far away and the sound of voices.'

Cynthia Bankvole sobbed aloud. 'I knew it. They're having some sort of feast, and we're going to be dragged out of here and eaten. I'm sure of it!'

'Oh, stop being silly, Cynthia!' Tess snapped at her impatiently. 'What a foolish idea. Where are all these drums and voices coming from, Sam? I can't hear a thing.'

Auma stood up. 'I can. Sam's right, it sounds like pounding and chanting and shouting. Whatever it is, you can wager it's not going to be any party for us. Maybe Cynthia's right.'

Tim's voice came out of the gloom. 'Really, Auma, not you too. Voices, drums, chanting. I thought you had a bit more sense than frightening others.'

'Huh, I can't hear anything, but I agree with Auma. Sometimes it's best to expect the worst. That way you're never disappointed,' Jube said philosophically.

'Thanks for cheering us all up, hedgehog,' Tess scoffed. 'Here we are, locked in a cell below ground and manacled without a hope or a weapon between us, and you're chattering on about us being the dinner at some sort of evil ceremony—'

'Hush,' Sam interrupted, 'I can hear paws coming this way and a dragging sound too!'

Cynthia gave a little scream.

Mattimeo stood up, resolute. 'Well, let them come, and we'll make an end of it one way or another. Let's try

384

and do what our parents or Martin the Warrior would do in a corner like this: sell our lives dearly. We have manacles, and they can be turned into weapons. Let whoever beast it is come and try to do their worst.'

∽

Supported by Flugg and two other shrews, Log-a-Log made his way painfully up the tortuous winding passages towards the surface. The shrew leader groaned and lowered himself slowly down, resting his back against a door.

'Log-a-Log, are you all right?' Flugg asked anxiously.

He nodded wearily. 'I must sit here awhile. It's all uphill to the copse. Let me rest and catch my breath.'

The shrews sat with him.

'When we get above ground you must leave me,' he said, turning to Flugg. 'Go back and help our friends. Flugg, you have been my good comrade and brother for many seasons. Listen now. Once you leave me and I am no longer with you, the Guosim must have a new leader. That one is you, Flugg. Forget your name; now you are Log-a-Log of all the Guosim.'

Flugg banged the door angrily with his sword hilt. 'No! Do not talk like that. You must live!'

Log-a-Log held a paw to his throat wound. 'You cannot disobey me. The law and rules of the Guosim say this is the way it must be. If there were a river or a stream here now, I would ride a log on my last journey. Then you would have no choice. Hear me, I have spoken. What was that?'

Some creature was banging on the door from the other side.

Flugg banged in reply. Placing his mouth near the jamb, he called, 'Logalogalogalog!'

There was more thumping in reply, followed by a voice calling, 'Redwaaaall! Mossflowerrr!'

Log-a-Log struggled to his paws. 'I'd know that voice anywhere. It's just like his father's. It's Matthias's young one. Get that door open, Guosim!'

There was a heavy padlock and hasp on the door, but one of the shrews named Gurn produced a small dagger.

'Stand aside. Let me try with this,' Gurn told the others.

Luckily it was a lock of simple and ancient design. Gurn's dagger jiggled and twisted a few times, then there was a click, and he pulled the padlock curve from the hasp ring.

Inside the cell Auma had her ear to the door. She listened carefully.

'Keep quiet. We've given them our challenge, now let's see what they do.'

'Are they shouting flogaloggle or whatever it is?' Jube piped up. 'Daft sort of war cry, if you ask me.'

'We never asked you Jube. Be quiet,' Mattimeo commanded curtly. 'What's happening out there, Auma?'

'I think they're unlocking the door, Mattimeo.'

'Right, this is it. Get your manacles ready and give the best fight you can manage. If we don't meet again, my friends, goodbye.'

Auma's voice was hoarse and urgent.

'They've unlocked the door, wait, it must open outwards. . . .'

Mattimeo felt for his companion's paws in the darkness.

'Why wait? Let's rush them.'

'Chaaaaarge!'

They hit the door. It flew open wide. Mattimeo flung himself upon the first creature in his path. Tim and Sam leapt on another. Even the dim passage light dazzled their eyes, which were accustomed to nothing but complete darkness. Grappling on the floor, the young mouse heard his name called by a deep gruff voice:

'Mattimeo, it's me, Log-a-Log!'

Mattimeo had Flugg by the throat. His paws dropped with a clank of manacles as he yelled out. 'Stop, they're friends!'

Immediately, the fight halted. Mattimeo and his companions stood in the torchlit passage, rubbing their eyes. Gurn shook his head admiringly.

'What a bunch of young warriors. Don't rub your eyes too hard. Let me open those manacles with my dagger.'

Cynthia began sobbing again, but this time it was with happiness.

The friends were smiling at each other. Gradually it was dawning on them that they were no longer the prisoners of Malkariss, Slagar, Nadaz or any other evil creature.

Mattimeo's laughter boomed around the passage walls.

'Hahahaha, free. We're free. It's my father's friends the Guosim!'

'It's certainly your lucky day young 'uns, most of your parents are here. There's Matthias, Orlando, Jabez, Jess, even old Basil Stag Hare. We joined forces with them to search for you. They're down on the big ledge fighting the hordes of Malkariss.'

Mattimeo could hardly believe his ears. His father, the Champion of Redwall . . . here!

Auma let out a great whoop, Sam leapt high into the air, Jube wrinkled his nose knowingly.

'Told you so, I said we wouldn't get far without my old dad catching us up. Do you remem—'

He was seized by Tim and Tess and whirled around, then Cynthia joined in.

'Good old Basil, the Redwallers are here! Hurray!'

Flugg was knocked flat by the whirling dancers, but Mattimeo helped him to his paws. Dusting himself off the shrew grinned broadly.

'By the fur and the claw, and the law, I'm glad we found you lot, though you've got our Log-a-Log to thank for that. If he hadn't decided to rest here awhile we'd have gone right past you and you'd have rotted in there.'

Laughing happily, Mattimeo knelt to shake Log-a-Log by the paw.

'I knew you'd find us. Oh, I just knew it would happen some day. Thank you Log-a-Log. Oh, thank y—'

The Log-a-Log of all the Guosim was smiling, even though his eyes had closed for the last time. He had lived long enough to keep his promise to his friends. He had found their young ones.

~

Matthias was growing tired. The Wearet seemed to have hidden stores of insane energy. The strange beast was wounded in a dozen different places, but his size and mad ferocity seemed to buoy him up. The warrior mouse went into the sword fighter's stance, blade held ready to cut, sweep and thrust, gaining a small respite for breath as the Wearet circled him, looking for an opening. Matthias turned slowly as the Wearet tried to get behind his back.

In the mouth of the tunnel, Orlando stood alongside Basil, watching the gruelling conflict.

'That creature can't get the better of our Warrior, but I think Matthias is looking very tired now. Is that a very deep gash on his brow, d'you think, Basil?'

'Tchah! A mere scratch, old lad. I've done more damage to a salad with a spoon. Don't let the Champion of Redwall fool you, Orlando, oh dear no. In a moment or two he'll decide it's time for lunch and he'll settle old thingummybob's hash, you mark my words!'

Basil was proved right. The moment Matthias saw he had the Wearet with his back to the wall, he came in like a hungry wolf. Sparks flew from the rocks as Matthias smashed home a devastating attack. He seemed to be everywhere at once, roaring, slashing and milling. The confident sneer faded from the Wearet's face as he found himself battling for dear life. The mouse warrior fought with the strength of two and the skill of many seasons. The Wearet pushed himself from the rocks with a gigantic effort and lunged savagely forward with both spears. Matthias darted to one side, and his blade crashed down like summer lightning, shearing through both spear handles in one heroic sweep. The warrior mouse turned a half-circle with the momentum, but the Wearet was swifter than a shadow. He leaped at Matthias's unprotected back. Passing his paws over Matthias's head, he began strangling the warrior mouse with the broken handles of the spears which he had held on to.

Choking for breath Matthias slammed his swordpoint down into the Wearet's footpaw. Grasping the spearhafts with both paws, he crouched deep, leaning forward. The Wearet screamed and shot over Matthias's head, landing with a thud at the end of the ledge. Matthias leapt up and hurled himself on to the Wearet. His foe was waiting. The Wearet thrust all paws straight into the air and Matthias felt himself rise. He struck the very brink of the ledge and rolled over into the void with a shout of dismay.

∽

General Ironbeak fluttered about in the sunwarmed shallows of the Abbey pond. He took a deep drink, throwing his head back as the bright droplets sparkled from his fine dark plumage. Mangiz stood to one side, taking in the scene with disdain. He had often drunk water, but bathing in it was out of the question. The raven General shook himself and swaggered briskly about at the water's edge. Today was a day for great plans. The omens were good and he felt energetic.

'*Chakka*! That was good. Now, my Mangiz, are your visions favouring us? Does your mind's eye see clear still?'

'*Kayah*! All is still well, my General, though my visions say that haste would be unseemly.'

'*Kaah*! Unseemly, what kind of old farmhen's talk is that? Listen to me, my strong right wing, you just keep your visions happy and Ironbeak will do the planning.'

'But, General, I told you yesterday, the visions said that—'

'Silence. *Kraggah*! I have heard enough. Go and bring

389

my magpies to me and all my fighting rooks. I have a plan to put paid to all the nonsense that surrounds this redstone house. A good plan, straightforward, with no trickery or sneaking about like thrushes in a hedgerow. From now on we will fight as we did in the northlands; no creeping around the back, good direct attacking, straight wing-to-beak fighting with no prisoners taken. Now go!'

Mangiz was beset by a dreadful feeling of foreboding, though he knew there was no talking to Ironbeak when he was in conquering mood. The crow withdrew, bowing respectfully.

'General, your wish is my command, I will bring all our birds to you.'

∽

Little Sister May looked a simple soul, but that was because deep down she was a very wise schemer. During the night she had laced Stryk Redkite's drinking water with a huge dose of the drug she had concocted for the magpies in the orchard. Stryk was a thirsty bird, and she had drunk deep. Now the great red kite lay soundly under the influence of Sister May's knockout drops.

Abbot Mordalfus, John Churchmouse, Brother Rufus and Sister May gathered round the unconscious bird, each of them versed in the art of healing as passed down through generations of Redwall Brothers and Sisters.

John Churchmouse donned his spectacles and dusted off a slim volume. 'Hmm. *Old Methusaleh's Index of Bird Ailments and Remedies*. What d'you think, Father Abbot?'

The Abbot looked up from a tome he was studying.

'Aye, that's a good one, John, though there's much to recommend this fine book, *Sister Heartwood's Compleat Category*. It contains nearly five chapters on birds.'

Brother Rufus helped Sister May as she raised Stryk's broken wing. Then she wiped her paws busily upon a clean white apron.

'Oh dear, that is a nasty-looking break. Mr Spike,

would you roll one of those small firkins over here so we can keep this wing in the right position?'

Ambrose grumpily complied with the request. 'It don't do much for the clearness of beetroot portwine to be messin' an' rollin' it about. Here, I 'ope you're not goin' to feed that great feathered lump on my best beetroot portwine.'

'I should say not, Ambrose,' John Churchmouse chuckled. 'Though we may need a drop or two of it ourselves before we're finished here.'

'Then I may's well stay here an' help you,' the hedgehog cellar-keeper grunted.

The broken wing was propped up on the barrel top and weighted securely with books. Abbot Mordalfus inspected the wingtip.

'Look, there's a pinion feather missing. Sister May, will you check the bird's tailfeathers and see if there's one the same size as the final outward pinion on the other wing? Ambrose, would you have a look in the kitchen for any good strong fishbones. Oh, and we'll need fine greased twine and some dried onionskins, and have a scout round for that jar of rivermud compound we use on burns. I have great faith in the healing powers of that stuff.'

They called their requests after Ambrose as he trundled off:

'Fetch the finest sewing needle that Cornflower has got.'

'And don't forget the witch hazel.'

'Some almond oil, too.'

'Then nip into Cavern Hole and pick up my herbal bag, please.'

Ambrose shrugged his spikes moodily. 'I don't suppose you'd like me to fetch your lunch, dinner, tea'n'supper too. Huh!'

'Oh, and Ambrose, would you ask Winifred to fetch our lunch, dinner, tea and supper out here? This is going to be a long job!'

Ironbeak left off tugging a worm from the lawn as Mangiz approached. He saw the crow was alone and glared severely at him.

'*Yakk*! Well?'

'My General, what has happened is none of my doing. If you peck me and claw me you will be doing me a great wrong.'

Ironbeak's bright eyes shifted back and forth between the Abbey and the crow.

'I will peck the tongue from your foolish beak if you do not stop babbling and tell me what is happening.'

'*Kaah*! It is the rooks and the magpie brothers, my General. They have barred themselves within the dormitory room and will not come out.'

'Now what has got into those duckbrained idiots?' Ironbeak snorted.

'They say that the head of the ghost mouse appeared to them last night, and it warned them to stay in the dormitory room.'

The raven leader struck his powerful beak sideways against a stone. The noise it made surprised Mangiz.

'*Kaahagga*! Then I must go and talk to them!'

Mangiz followed the General at a respectable distance. He did not like the way Ironbeak had said the word 'talk'.

The raven perched in the broken window space; his seer crow sat upon the grass, listening intently.

'*Kaah*! So, my fighters, you have been listening to the ghost mouse again. What did it have to say this time?'

Apart from a few muffled caws, there was no clear reply. Ironbeak dug his claws into the woodwork of the window frame.

'*Kraa*! You do not choose to speak to your leader. Then I will come in and speak to you.'

He hopped down and vanished inside the dormitory. Mangiz hunched up, closing his eyes as he listened to the awful sounds of birds screeching and beds being upset. He couldn't see the feathers which flew out of the dormitory window.

'*Yaggah*! Who gives the orders, a mouse's head or Ironbeak? I am in command here. Get out! Out, you worthless rabble!'

Rooks poured out of the window, struggling against each other to get through the enclosed space. Mangiz winced at the savage sounds of his General dealing out fierce punishment. Not for nothing was he known as the most feared fighter in the northlands.

49

The great sword of Redwall disappeared into the green mists of the abyss. Matthias scrabbled furiously as he rolled over the brink of the ledge, his paws grabbing automatically for anything that would check his head-long plunge. It was the rope which the basket had been lowered down on that saved him. He seized it wildly but was unable to grasp it firmly and he began sliding downwards, the rock face of the chasm passing him in a blur. The Wearet leapt up and began immediately hacking at the rope.

Bellowing aloud, Orlando charged at the head of the woodlanders. Rats went down before the great battleaxe like corn to the scythe. With Basil and the others facing outwards, guarding his sides and the rear, the Warrior of the Western Plain fought his way through. Too late. The last strands of the rope twisted and shredded, to snap under the blade of the spear. Matthias was gone.

The Wearet turned to look up. The last thing his eyes beheld was the huge male badger swinging a double-headed axe in his direction. Orlando gave a great howl of rage. Rage against himself for letting Matthias accept such a challenge. Rage at everything in this evil place that had taken his young one from him, and rage fuelling his great fighting spirit so that he wanted to do battle against anybeast that stood in his way.

'I am Orlando of the Axe. Eeeeeulaliaaaaa!'

The woodlanders' war cries rang about the underground Kingdom of Malkariss as Basil, Cheek, Jess and Jabez headed a wild charge into the rat horde. Nadaz stamped and screeched like a mad thing, rattling his sceptre as he chanted death threats against the invaders.

∽

Matthias felt the rope go slack, and he plunged like a falling stone into the green curtain of mist. Racing through his mind were the faces of Cornflower and Mattimeo, certain he would never see them again.

Whump!

The warrior mouse landed on something soft and yielding. It was a large woven grass basket, thickly padded inside with moss and purple cloth. The force of the fall stunned him temporarily. He lay on the ground beside the basket, trying to galvanize himself into movement and collect his thoughts, amazed at the fact that he had lived through such a fall.

The lid of the smashed basket moved.

There was a slobbering, snarling noise from within the basket, then it fell to one side as Malkariss rolled out.

The creature on the floor beside the basket bore little resemblance to the high statue on the ledge. Malkariss was gross! The great white mound of scabrous fur, now broken by the weight that had dropped on it from above, was something out of a bad dream. Short floppy paws with long mottled nails which hung limply reached up to wipe the crusting bleariness from eyes dimmed and half shut with age. The mouth sagged open, revealing blackened stumps of teeth.

Matthias sat up groggily. His senses swam, and he began to doubt whether he was still alive when he saw the broken vision of evil crawling towards him. Surely such a thing never lived above or below ground. When Malkariss spoke, his voice was thin and reedy. Not being projected by the chamber within the statue or echoing around the rock ledge spaces, it was almost a piteous whine.

'You have looked upon Malkariss. You must die.'

Matthias shuddered. The horrible thing had its paw upon his sword, which had fallen close to the basket. As he was about to lever himself upright, a chunk of rock struck Malkariss upon the back and he arched in pain. Another rock hit the white polecat, striking him on the paw. He released the sword with a whimper. More rocks pelted in.

Matthias scrambled away, retrieving his sword as he went. Thin, ravaged creatures, fur welted with lash-marks, their paws manacled, were advancing on Malkariss like a grim army. They hurled rocks at the cringing figure. Dragging slowly forward, pulling slave chains along the ground, they chanted:

'Die, evil one, die!'

'We will bury you with pieces of your own Kingdom!'

Gaunt young hedgehogs, squirrels, mice, moles and otters were picking up big rocks from a pile of debris with both paws. They gathered around the fallen tyrant, heaving the stones on to him with all the force they could muster. Matthias watched in horror as Malkariss was buried beneath a growing mound of rocks. Malkariss could no longer be seen, but still the slaves continued hurling rocks on to the pile.

The Redwall Warrior grabbed a half-starved otter and pulled him to one side.

'Here, hold your chains tight across that rocky slab. Do not be afraid. I am your friend.'

The otter did as he was told, hope shining in his dust-flecked eyes.

'Strike hard, friend!' he cried to Matthias.

The Warrior's sword whistled downward through the air. With a sharp snap it sheared the links of chain like a billhook chopping grass. Nothing could withstand the great sword of Redwall, whose metal had come from a falling star.

Once he had severed the lead dragchain, Matthias set about cleaving the manacles from slaves. Young creatures wept openly, and some cheered and began to dance, with broken chains dangling from their paws. The mouse warrior was freeing them two at a time as quickly as he could, for sounds of battle raging above had reached his ears. A black-robed rat ran up, brandishing a whip, but before he could reach Matthias, a squirrel felled him with a whirling length of chain.

'Well struck, squirrel,' the mouse warrior called out. 'I am Matthias of Redwall. What do they call you?'

Despite his scrawny appearance, the squirrel laughed and swung the chain until it whirred around his head.

'Elmtail. I am called Elmtail. I will buy my freedom with this chain that bound me as a slave!'

'That's the way, Elmtail. When I have freed your friends we will do it together, mate!'

The slaves began cheering, and those already liberated swung their chains aloft.

∽

The battle on the ledge was in full flood. Side by side the woodlanders stood in a tight circle within a circle. The outer ring of shrews, with Jess and Jabez, was stabbing and thrusting with swords and javelins, all the time moving in a clockwise direction. The inner circle fired over their heads. Urged on by Basil and Cheek, they pelted stones and arrows into the tight-packed horde of rats that surrounded the woodlanders on all sides

Commanded by Nadaz, the rats fought back with fanatical vigour, and many a good shrew fell to the stabs of their short spears.

Orlando would stand at the centre of the circle until he regained his breath, then with a mad roar he would charge out to wreak slaughter upon the rat horde, only coming back into the circle to wipe the gore from his axe and lick wounds.

Whenever Basil saw a particularly vicious attack, he too would go vaulting over into the thick of it, his long flailing limbs laying rats senseless, to be trampled under the masses of their own horde.

'Yahooooo! Take that, you blighter! Here, old lad, have some of this harespaw pie and lie down for a bit.'

Thud!

Another rat would stretch his length on the rocky ledge.

More blackrobes pressing up the winding causeway steps piled in to fight, fired on by Nadaz.

'Kill! Kill! Slay the invaders who dare come to the land of Malkariss.'

Jess Squirrel angrily turned a rat's own spear upon him. 'Wait'll I get my paws on that one in the purple robe. I'll make him sing a different tune!'

Cheek flexed his throwing paw and spoke his mind to a nearby shrew archer.

'There's just too many of 'em. If we lose a creature we're one short, but you can knock ten vermin out and twenty spring up in their place.'

The shrew sighted and shot his arrow, nodding with satisfaction at the result.

'Right twixt the eyes. They never come back for more after that. What's that you say, otter? Oh aye, there's no stoppin' 'em, is there? Still, we've signed for the trip so we might as well make the best of it, eh!'

Above the din of the battle, Jess caught a ripple over on the far side of the ledge at the tunnel mouth. She fought her way to Basil.

'Over there, look. It seems we've got some kind of reinforcements.'

Basil did an extra-high leap, taking great care to kick a rat flat on the head as he went.

'Yahaha! Well, blow me old whiskers, Jess, it's the young uns. Hi, Mattimeo. Over here you, young scalla-wag. Redwallll!'

The cry was taken up in answer across the melee:

'Basil, we're coming. Redwallll!'

398

Mattimeo and the former captives were battling their way through the throng. Using flailing manacles and spears from fallen rats, they drove across the platform with their cell door in front of them as a shield. Pushing, shoving, thrusting and whipping out left and right with everything available, the young creatures fought their way to be reunited with their friends. Nadaz danced and screamed louder, urging his rat horde to greater efforts. The inevitable victory he had foreseen began to waver as the tide of battle flowed in favour of the brave wood-landers.

∽

The Father Abbot was delivering a stern lecture to Cornflower concerning her ghostly antics.

'I did not approve of this venture from the first, my child. One false move and the General's birds would slay you and Sister May. Constance could be badly hurt too.'

Cornflower avoided the stern gaze. 'But, Father Abbot, we have got the birds frightened. If the ghost of Martin walks the Abbey by night, we will make the rooks lose heart and they will not enjoy living at Redwall. Maybe they will fly off to their northlands and leave us in peace.'

The old mouse held up a paw for silence. 'We went over this argument once before. At first I thought it might have done some good; perhaps it has. But, Cornflower, you are taking this whole thing too lightly, treating it as a big joke. I feel it in my whiskers, one of you will be badly hurt or captured. The whole charade must stop.'

A rebellious gleam shone in Cornflower's eyes. 'Matthias would have approved of it. I'll bet he and Basil would have kept it up until those birds were scared out of their feathers.'

Mordalfus peered severely over the top of his glasses. 'I am glad you mentioned Matthias. Have you thought of my duty to him as Abbot? What if he came marching back out of the south with our young ones, as I am sure he will do one fine day? How do you think I would feel, having to report that whilst he was gone I allowed you to play foolish tricks until you were killed? You see, Cornflower, I have a responsibility as Father Abbot to you, Matthias and all the creatures within our walls. Now will you please do as I say.'

Cornflower sighed deeply and bowed. 'I will do as you say, Father Abbot,' she said reluctantly.

The kindly old mouse rose stiffly. He patted her head. 'Thank you, Cornflower. Now, Constance, will you take all the warrior's armour to the gatehouse and put it back carefully.'

Constance gathered the armour and climbed into the tunnel.

༄

Ironbeak was stalking the edge of the Abbey pond. The silver glint in the waters told him that there were fish about. He marvelled at the abundance of food the earthcrawlers had within the walls of the redstone place: orchards, gardens, a great storehouse in the area below stairs, even a pond with good water and fish for the taking. Sometime soon it would all belong to him. He looked about in admiration, staring at the strong outer wall that would keep other earthcrawlers out. His quick dark eye caught a movement over by the main gate. The big stripedog had materialized practically out of thin air. It was carrying something. Ironbeak crouched in the reeds and watched intently.

Constance took a quick glance around to check nobeast was observing her. Swiftly she unlocked the gatehouse door and slid inside with the armour. The door closed behind her. Ironbeak could see the key still sticking out of the lock. Seizing his opportunity he rose and glided silently across to the gatehouse. The deed was accomplished in a trice. The raven leader slammed the door. Sticking his beak into the handle ring of the heavy iron key, he gave it a swift turn and withdrew it from the lock. There was a scrambling noise from inside, then the sound of paws pounding against the solid timbers of the door as the badger called out,

'Cornflower, is that you? Stop playing about and open this door. Come on, I know it's you!'

Ironbeak soared off jubilantly with the key looped on his beak. Now that the enemy he feared so much was out of the way, there was nobeast strong enough to withstand a sudden attack. Truly Mangiz's visions were becoming reality.

∽

Inside the gatehouse, Constance had her eye to the keyhole. She could see nothing. Whoever had locked her in was gone, for it was quiet outside. The badger ran to the window. Redwall Abbey was a long distance from the gatehouse. It stood serene and peaceful across the lawns, beyond the pond. The window was too small for a fully grown badger to break and crawl through, so she began exploring the place. Other small windows in each of the bedrooms proved useless. Constance noted the chimney vent in the cosy hearth, but it was out of the question; a badger of her dimensions would be jammed right away. She tried the door again. It was solid, with florin spikes and iron bands fixed to the stout oak timbers.

After exploring every possibility, Constance resigned herself. There was a jug of water and plenty of dried fruits in the cupboard. She sat at the living room window, watching and waiting for help to appear.

∽

'Stryk Redkite wanna fly 'gain. Must fly, Sissimay!'

Sister Mary scrubbed her paws wearily. 'No, no, you naughty bird. You must rest until the wing heals. Now be still, or you get no supper.'

'Don' wan' supper, wanna fly.'

The Abbot and Brother Rufus sat with John Churchmouse, taking their supper at a barrel top. John rubbed the back of his neck. 'Whew, I wish that bird was a sparrow instead of a great red kite. It would have been much easier.'

Abbot Mordalfus took a long draught of October ale. 'It was difficult, John, but I think it was worthwhile. You did a marvellous job putting those new pinion feathers in place. Did you take all your instructions from Methusaleh's book?'

John shrugged modestly. 'Not exactly, Father Abbot. I did invent a little fish glue to reinforce the twine that I tied them with, though I actually did manage to get the feather ends into the cavities of the old ones. They should take and be as good as new by the end of season. What about you Rufus? How did it go with the break?'

Brother Rufus munched wild-cherry flan. 'Mmmff, 'scuse me. We used fishbone and feather quill to repair it. Everything was a bit messy, but quite straightforward when you have our Abbot to help you.'

Sister May dried her paws. 'I've used every kind of ointment and healing nostrum I know to help the operation along. Now we must wait.'

'Wanna fly. Stryk Redkite flyover mountain like sky-clouds,' the big bird wailed.

John folded his spectacles away. 'Huh, now we must wait? Try telling *her* that.'

The great red bird made as if to move. Sister May picked up a wooden ladle.

'Just you dare, m'lady. I'll tan your feathery hide!'

Stryk perched sullenly, her wing still supported by the wine firkin and the books.

'Warra warrior, Sissimay shoulda be Redkite.'

'The very idea of it, you feathery baggage!'

∽

Cornflower had great difficulty keeping baby Rollo away from the wine cellar. He was anxious to see the big bird. At the moment she and Mrs Churchmouse had the infant occupied by the barricade in Cavern Hole, where he and some of his little friends were busy at their self-appointed task of watching for rooks. Rollo crouched down, peering round the edge of the table that lay on its side. After a while he turned to the mousewives, who were busy shelling peas.

'No cooks.'

'He's trying to tell us there's no rooks,' Cornflower explained to Mrs Churchmouse.

'Oh, I thought he was referring to Mr Spike when he said "no cooks". He's no cook at all.'

'Indeed he isn't. Hotroot pepper in the scones! I could have drunk the Abbey pond dry that night. Though our Rollo might have a point. I haven't noticed any birds out there, yesterday or today. They may be up to something. Do you think it's worth telling the Abbot or Constance?'

Mrs Churchmouse rolled a small garden pea over for Rollo to play with. 'No, I shouldn't worry. Ironbeak knows he can't get us out of Cavern Hole. It would make him look bad in front of his birds if he failed in another attempt. I think they're doing the same as us; waiting it out. This weather's too hot to do anything. They're probably idling about in the dormitory, eating and sleeping.'

∽

Ironbeak was not sleeping, nor was Mangiz, or any of the rooks.

They were gathered at the edge of the Abbey pond, listening as the raven General outlined his strategy, the final plan to conquer Redwall Abbey. Ironbeak paced up and down in front of his command.

'Yaggah! Listen well, my fighters. I will not say there is no ghost mouse, what I say is that it is a trick, some silly thing the earthcrawlers have thought up. When we conquer them I will make them tell us how they did it, then we will throw their ghost from the very top of this redstone house. Kaah! See if it comes back to haunt us then. In the past I was like you. One time in the northlands when I was standing nightwatch, I was sleepy, my wings drooped and my eyes began to close. Yarrak! I saw a great green eagle, a fearsome bird. Instead of running away I flew to attack it. Kaah! It was only an odd-shaped green bush. Do you see what I mean? Tired eyes, darkness, even sun shadows when you are dozing,

403

can cause your mind to see strange sights. So let me hear no more of these things. They are like the first sight of lightning to an eggchick.'

The rooks were unconvinced, but dared not speak.

'Tonight we will make ready for our final battle,' the General continued. 'Mangiz sees that the omens are good. I know you are loyal fighters. You have fought under me in the northlands. Now you shall have your reward in this warm country, for we will live together in the redstone house with lots of food, sun and easy times. Here is how we do it. I have not posted guards or sentries for two days now. The weather is hot and the earth-crawlers are resting easy. They have plenty of food and think themselves safe in the Cavern Hole place. *Kayah*! This is good. Let them go on thinking we have forgotten them, then they will relax. They have posted no guards at their barricade for two nights now. I have seen this. In the hour before the sun rises at dawn, Quickbill and his brothers will go down the stairs. If all is quiet, they will signal to us. *Kraa*! Silence is the key to my plan. Without the big stripedog we will have them at our mercy.'

50

The battle beneath the ground raged back and forth. Mattimeo and his friends had joined forces with Orlando and the woodlanders. Heaving masses of rats pressed in from all sides, the double circle continued its deadly function, reinforced by the willing young ones. Jess Squirrel stood alongside her son Sam, but there was little time for happy reunions in the midst of a battle. Orlando and Auma lifted the door bodily between them, using it as a large flattener on the black-robed rats. Nadaz kept up his chant, wailing and screaming as he sent in wave after wave of blackrobes. Shaking his eerie bone sceptre, rattling the mouse skull, he pointed to the woodlanders.

'Die, die, you will all die here. Your bones will rot in the kingdom of Malkariss. The Voice of the Host has spoken!'

Basil Stag Hare and Cheek lifted a rat between them. The wildly struggling creature screeched as he was hefted above the heads of the hare and the otter.

'We're goin' to chuck you over to your boss,' Basil informed him. 'Tell him t' keep the howlin' an' yellin' down. Bad form, y'know. Right, me old Cheek. One, two and away he goes!'

The rat flew through the air. Falling short of Nadaz, he landed on the spearpoints of the horde.

Basil tut-tutted. 'Oh bad shot, sir, what've I told you about holdin' your end up, Cheek? Never mind. Try, try again, that's the spirit. Grab hold of that smelly chap to your left.'

Now Nadaz was standing on the big drum. He pounded it with both paws in a mad dance, and the noise rolled and boomed, encouraging the rats on the causeway steps to press forward on to the ledge.

Jube Hedgehog and Jabez his father were unassailable. They rolled into one tight ball, hurtling madly about, spiking rats over the brink of the ledge, deflecting spearthrusts with their needled armour casing.

But the rats still came forward.

Tess and Tim Churchmouse formed a trio of flailing chains with Mattimeo, and managed to gasp snatches of conversation as they pounded the rats with the swinging slave-chain manacles.

'Watch your back, Matti!'

'Got him, thanks, Tess. Look out!'

'Good shot, Tim. Are you all right?'

'Phew, my paws are getting tired!'

'Aye, there's no end to them. Look down those steps. They're pouring up four abreast!'

∽

Matthias ran farther up the underground workings, dealing with any guards that were left and freeing slaves as he went. Climbing over piles of rubble and dashing through half-finished chambers, the mouse warrior swung his sword like an avenging pendulum, striking the chains of slavery to smithereens and dealing death to the oppressors. With both paws aching, he stopped and took stock of his surroundings: a long passage with a blank wall at one end. Through the semidarkness he glimpsed a vast carving on the rock wall. It was a frieze of woodland creatures chained together, dominated by a prominent relief of the statue on the ledge, surrounded by robed rats. Relaxing his guard, he laid aside the sword and studied the carvings. Obviously it marked the boundary of Malkariss's evil kingdom.

Slagar stepped out from behind the mouse warrior. The Cruel One dealt Matthias a swinging blow with the metal weights of his three-thonged weapon, and the mouse warrior pitched forward, overwhelmed by the striking bolas. Grinning behind the silken mask, Slagar turned his victim over.

'You did well, mouse. I am saved the trouble of slaying Malkariss. When the horde has overcome your woodlanders, I will rule here. But first I must fulfil my oath of vengeance.'

Grabbing Matthias by the throat, the fox reached for the great sword.

'Yaahaa! It's the fox! Kill Slagar!'

Like a hunting pack, the slaves came through the rubble at the masked fox. He looked wildly about for an escape route, and his eye fell upon the carved mural a few paces away. The silken hood sucked back and forth wildly as he snatched up his bolas and leapt over the fallen Warrior. Gripping the outstretched left paw of the polecat image, Slagar twisted and pushed in the same way that Nadaz had done the previous day.

The stone polecat swung inwards. Slagar stepped through into the bottom of a deep well shaft with sunlight pouring in from above. He slammed the exit door back into place and mounted the pawholds to the surface, reciting an old woodland verse in a crazy singsong as he climbed:

'A fox who fights and runs away,
Lives to fight another day.

It is not over yet, Matthias of Redwall. I will live to take your sword, your son, and your life!'

∽

Willing paws helped Matthias up. He shook his head groggily as the slave army packed in about him.

'Where's Slagar? He was here wasn't he?' Matthias asked uncertainly.

Elmtail gave the Warrior back his sword. 'You'll never

believe this. The fox vanished completely into that carved rock wall. We were never allowed up this end of the workings, so the rats must have made that carving themselves. Anyhow, he's gone. What are your orders? Where to next, Matthias?'

The warrior mouse shook off his dizziness. Waving the sword, he began running back up the tunnel.

'To the ledge. Let us finish this thing. Follow me and shout our battle cry so that my friends will know we are coming!'

Like a tidal wave beginning to build out upon the sea, the army grew. Creatures poured out of caves, passages and corridors, running with Matthias towards the causeway steps. They heard his war shout and echoed the wild cry until the caverns of Malkariss's Kingdom rang with their voices.

'Redwaaaaaaaallllll!'

༄

Nobody had really missed Constance. As always, the creatures of Redwall were free to go or come as they pleased, and it was not uncommon for the badger to seek solitude and a place where she could be alone with her thoughts for a day or two. The Abbot was not exactly happy with the situation, for in times of trouble his great badger friend seldom left the Abbey. Mordalfus yawned, settling himself on a makeshift pallet by the tunnel entrance in Cavern Hole. Who could tell what was in a badger's mind? He would probably awake the next morning to find Constance busy cooking breakfast for them all, he thought. He checked that the Redwallers were bedded down safely. Baby Rollo was squeaking in his sleep as he snuggled between Cornflower and Mrs Churchmouse, and a night-light burned dimly in its wall sconce. The old mouse folded his spectacles away into his wide habit sleeve. Closing his eyes gratefully, he composed himself for a restful night's sleep.

The fighting birds of General Ironbeak also slumbered peacefully on their dormitory perches through the warm summer night. Mangiz and the raven leader catnapped on the windowsill, awaiting the hour before dawn.

∽

Inside the gatehouse, Constance had slept fitfully during the early evening. Now she was up and roaming restlessly about. Every aperture she had tried was checked and rechecked. The badger had reached the conclusion she had been locked in by a bird, and that the raven had some plan which he would put into operation quite soon. Picking up a fire iron from the hearth, Constance began working on the hinges of the heavily bracketed door.

∽

As if summoned into wakefulness by some inner alarm, Ironbeak's eyes snapped open wide and he surveyed the sky and the top of the outer ramparts.

It was the hour before dawn.

Rousing Mangiz, he hopped down into the dormitory and began waking his fighters, talking to them in a low voice.

'*Kurrah*! Now is the time. Brightback, take two rooks and your brothers. Mangiz will show you what must be done. Bring the wood. *Akahh*! Careful now, do not drop it. The rest of you, follow me.'

A medium-sized plank of pine wrapped in sheets was picked up by Mangiz and his helpers. They slid it silently along the floor, taking great care not to let it bump against anything. They moved it slowly down the stairs and out into Great Hall. At a signal from the crow, they latched their claws into the sheets. It was hard work, but after a bit of wingspreading and flapping, the plank rose a short way from the floor. With Mangiz holding it steady at the front, they flew low towards the steps of Cavern Hole.

Brightback and Diptail settled the rear end of the cloth-covered wood securely on the third step down, and Mangiz and two rooks placed the front end on top of the barricade at the foot of the stairs, so that it formed a straight walk from the third step to the top of the table that formed the mainstay of the barrier. The crow tested it. Walking the length of the plank quietly, he ducked his head under the arch of Cavern Hole entrance. Ironbeak had worked it out well. A bird could pass into Cavern Hole easily this way.

Mangiz flapped one wing three times from the top of the stairs, and Ironbeak and his rooks materialized out of the shadows to join them. The General's quick bright eye sized up the muffled plank on the third stair.

'Karrah! You have done well. We will pass inside as softly as a feather on the wind. Keep behind me and wait for my signal.'

∽

The Redwallers slept on, oblivious to the feathered head which poked itself into their refuge.

The night-light guttered low as Ironbeak crept in, positioning himself on the inside of the barricade where he could assist his birds. One by one the rooks came through the opening, bobbing their heads as they passed the space between the plank end and the curved entrance arch. Ironbeak silently beckoned them to take up specific places he indicated; the tunnel entrance, the two steps at the far side which led to the kitchens with the larders and wine cellar beyond, and the edges of the barricade to prevent it being moved outwards as an avenue of escape.

Next came the magpies. He stationed them at the top of the barricade to stop any earthcrawler climbing out. Mangiz was last to come through. Together he and Ironbeak slowly climbed down until they stood firmly inside the final bastion of Redwall.

Mangiz could not help but admire his General. Truly Ironbeak was a conqueror. Despite false prophecies and fighters scared near witless, he had stayed in command and fulfilled his own visions. The redstone house would fall to his beak and talon.

410

Constance worked furiously with the bent and battered fire iron. Her hackles stood erect with an unmentionable dread, and some sixth sense drove her to greater efforts as she battered and bludgeoned at the unyielding hinges. Timber splintered and groaned as she struck the door; sparks flew as metal clashed against metal. The stouthearted creature crashed the fire iron into the door again and again, her paws numbed by the stinging vibrations. She had to break the door down, she had to get back to the Abbey with all speed to save her friends from the unknown danger which threatened.

∽

A heavy talon raked the sleeping Abbot's back. He arched into wakefulness with a grunt of pain.

'*Yaggah*! Wake up, my little earthcrawlers, this is the day I make you do the dance of death. Ironbeak has captured this great redstone house. *Karragaaaah*!'

Cavern Hole echoed to the triumphant harshness of the raven General and his fighters, mingled with the confused and terrified cries of shocked creatures.

∽

Tim Churchmouse was wounded in the side by a rat spear. He fell as two of the blackrobes hurled themselves on him. Mattimeo battled his way through with Cynthia Bankvole screaming shrill war cries alongside him, and together they beat off the rats that beset Tim and hauled him upright.

'Tim, you're hurt?' Cynthia asked anxiously.

'Yes. I mean, no. I'm all right. Give me that spear!'

Orlando and Auma stormed through, the big badger practically holding the door as a shield with one paw as he flayed his battleaxe left and right, while Auma was creating havoc with a billet of ashwood she was using as a club.

'Get Tim behind my father. Quick, take that, you robed vermin!' Auma shouted.

Orlando glanced anxiously at the causeway steps. 'Here comes another wave. There's more pressing up from below. Listen, they're chanting something!'

411

Sam Squirrel vaulted across like an acrobat. He leapt to the top of the door as Orlando held it upright.

'It's "Redwall"! They're shouting "Redwall"! Mattimeo, it's your father with an army of slaves!'

Orlando passed his axe to Auma. Grabbing Mattimeo, he lifted him high above his head.

'Tell me, young 'un, is that your father?'

Mattimeo was weeping and laughing aloud as he roared at the top of his lungs:

'Yes! Yes! Redwallllll! No warrior can swing the sword of Martin like him. Father! It's meeeeeee!'

∽

Down below on the causeway stairs, Matthias heard the voice of his son rise clear over the pounding drumbeats and the noise of war. A great wave of shuddering joy swept over him, and he began fighting like a berserker. Rats dissolved in front of him as he battered his way madly up the steps. Nothing could stand in front of the Redwall Champion and his army.

Basil Stag Hare whooped with happiness as he struck out powerfully with his long limbs.

'Hoorah, Cheek old lad. Let's show these rotters what a fight looks like. Right, you wicked bounders, look out. Here comes the hare for the job!'

Tess Churchmouse and Sam Squirrel flung themselves in like twin windmills of spinning chain.

'This is for the beating and the marching and the lashing and the starving.'

Thwack! Swish! Crack! Swoosh!

∽

The woodlanders fought with renewed heart and hope. Blackrobed rats went hurling over the ledge, they fell back down the steps, and for the first time they tried to escape by the tunnel entrance. Orlando hurried through and blocked their exit. He stood with his back against the door, wielding his axe.

'Come to me, come to me, rats. Eeulaliaaaaa!'

The shrews fought like little demons under the leadership of Flugg, their new Log-a-Log. Leaping and stab-bing, twisting and hacking, they were everywhere at once, shouting the Guosim war cry:

'Logalogalogalog!'

∽

Nadaz saw the battle had gone against the creatures of Malkariss. All was lost. The purple-robed rat slipped quietly off the drum. Abandoning his bone sceptre, he weaved between the blackrobes until he was behind the statue of the white polecat. Only Tim Churchmouse saw him enter the statue. He remembered what he had just seen before leaping back into the fray.

∽

Now Matthias and his slave army were near the top of the causeway steps. Behind them they left a trail of slain blackrobes. Others had leapt from the stairs into the void rather than face the creatures they had treated so cruelly, or the hot-eyed warlord who led them.

Basil and Mattimeo fought their way down the causeway until they met Matthias on the stairs. The old hare twirled his ears in the most curious manner.

'What ho, Warrior. I see you've taken steps to help us, wot?'

The light of battle left Matthias's eyes as he gazed upon his long-lost young one. He threw his paws round Mattimeo, hugging him fiercely. Tears sprang to the Warrior's eyes as he pressed his face against his son's ragged habit.

'Matti, you're here, you're alive, by the stones of Redwall!'

Mattimeo clung tightly to his father, sobbing and laughing at the same time.

'I knew you'd find me someday! I knew it!'

Basil nodded back towards the ledge. 'Come on, chaps. There's still a battle t' be finished. Those blighters don't want to give up. Gang of bally fanatics, if you ask me.'

∽

Outside, the small wooded copse lay peaceful. Butterflies fluttered about the business of summer, grass-hoppers chirruped and small insects slept on mossy stones, oblivious to the carnage that raged in the charnel house beneath them.

A short distance from the copse, Slagar lay behind a rocky outcrop, the deadly bolas grasped firmly in his paws. Warm rays of golden sun beat down upon his torn and stained cloak, making the silken harlequin pattern tawdry against the emerald green of the grass. The hood fluttered and moved spasmodically as the Cruel One muttered to himself, his dreams of power shattered by the very creatures he had sworn vengeance upon. But Slagar would never admit defeat after all he had been through. His breath rasped harshly as he made insane promises to himself.

'Slagar will win in the end. Am I not the Lord of light and darkness? I never needed Malkariss or Nadaz, or anybeast. If the blackrobes win then I will rule them. If Nadaz lives I will slay him and say it was he who betrayed Malkariss. If the woodlanders are victorious then I will slay Matthias and take the sword. I know now, the sword of Redwall is magic, and whoever holds it is the leader.'

∽

The defeated woodlanders were huddled against the walls of Cavern Hole. Ironbeak stared at them and wondered how a ragtailed little bunch of earthcrawlers managed to cause him so much trouble.

Under the fierce eye of the raven General, Cornflower drew baby Rollo close and hugged him.

Mangiz strutted up and down, his voice harsh with power. '*Krakkah*! Now, earthcrawlers, you will pay for your defiance. I am the voice of the great General Ironbeak, mightiest fighter in all the northlands. He does not wish to speak with scum like you. Think of all the silly little tricks you have played. You could not fight like real warriors. Filthy grease and dirt, drugging our magpies, stupid mouse ghosts. Who did you think you were dealing with?'

414

'A bunch of puffed-up feather bags!' Ambrose Spike said boldly.

The hedgehog was forced to curl up defensively as he was set upon by vicious rook beaks. Winifred managed to fend them off. She helped Ambrose up, and he shook himself defiantly.

'They couldn't hurt one of the Spikes. I'm all right,' he told the otter.

'Where is your great stripedog now?' Mangiz sneered. 'She has run away in fright.'

Brother Rufus shook his curled up paw at the crow. 'What have you done to our Constance, you villain?'

'Silence, mouse! Worry about your own fate. The great stripedog will meet hers in good time, but you, all of you, this day will be your last. You will die in this place!'

Abbot Mordalfus shuffled forward. 'Let them go. It was none of their doing. I am Abbot here, and I alone am responsible for defying your leader. Take me.'

Ironbeak dashed forward and knocked the Abbot down. '*Yagga*! I am Ironbeak. I say who lives or dies, earthcrawler!'

Before anybeast could stop her, Sister May leapt at the raven leader. She kicked and bit, tearing plumage from the raven's puffed-out breast.

'You big bully. You leave our Abbot alone!' she shouted.

His dignity lost for a moment, Ironbeak hopped about wildly until he had shaken the mouse sister off. As Sister May lay defenceless on the floor, the enraged raven began attacking her.

'*Kraah*! Stupid little earthcrawler, you will be the first to die!'

Cornflower and several other creatures were about to run in and help Sister May, when the thunderbolt struck.

◡

A giant red bird came soaring through from the wine cellar into Cavern Hole and struck Ironbeak like a battering ram.

415

'*Kreeeeeeegh*! I am Stryk Redkite. You hurt Sissimay, I kill. Kill!'

Feared fighter as he was, Ironbeak did not stand a chance against the ferocity of the mountain bird. There was a massive flurry of red and black feathers upon the floor of Cavern Hole. Over and over they rolled, with Stryk always coming out uppermost, her great powerful talons and beaking tearing and rending.

'*Yaak*! Help me!' Ironbeak managed to scream out to his fighters.

∽

The barricade fell with an earsplitting crash, and Constance was in the middle of the rooks like a striped whirlwind.

∽

Cornflower and Mrs Churchmouse managed to grab Rollo and the few little ones, and hurried them into the kitchens. Settling the infants under the kitchen table, they ran to peer round the archway into Cavern Hole and witnessed the liberation of Redwall Abbey.

∽

Stryk Redkite fought Ironbeak across the shattered barricade and up the seven steps into Cavern Hole, where the two birds took to the air.

The raven had no way of escape. He flopped about, bouncing from the walls and windows, relentlessly pursued beak and claw by the red kite. She drove at him with her beak, raked and clawed him with her talons. Ironbeak tried every trick he knew, plunging and dipping. Whichever way he went, the kite was unshakably on top of him, around columns, over galleries, under roofbeams, glorying savagely in her regained gift of flight.

Ironbeak tried one last desperate attempt at escape. He winged straight up to the trapdoor leading to the place in the eaves, and he had actually set his claws into the ring of the wooden door when the kite struck full force.

Stryk Redkite circled the ceiling of Great Hall as the

lifeless carcass of General Ironbeak plummeted down to hit the stone floor below in a ragged heap of raven feathers.

'*Kreeeeeegh*! Stryk Redkite flies!'

⤳

Mangiz tried to flee. He took wing and left the ground, flying for the stairs and the ruined barricade.

Constance was waiting. She stood with one paw swinging strongly upward. As the crow drew level with her, she batted out hard. The seer crow hit the far wall of Cavern Hole like a ripe fruit. Then he slid to the floor, never to rise again.

⤳

The remaining sparrows of Queen Warbeak's command took care of a rook and a magpie between them. Winifred flattened two rooks with a big frying pan, and Brother Rufus and Sister May accounted for a rook between them.

Immediately, the fight went out of the remaining rooks and the two surviving magpies. Without their leader and Mangiz the seer, they lost heart. Constance pointed a blunt paw.

'Into that wine cellar, all of you. One squawk or false move while you're down there and we'll do to you exactly what you planned for us. Now get out of my sight double quick, before I change my mind and let the big red bird loose on all of you!'

⤳

Shepherded by Winifred and Ambrose, the birds fled hurriedly through the kitchens to the wine cellar.

Ambrose, armed with a soup ladle, threatened them, 'Move along there! If one o' you rotten eggspawn so much as looks at my barrels of wine and ale, I'll chop off your tails and pickle the lot of you in a barrel of sourapple vinegar!'

⤳

Constance set the big table back in its former place. 'No real damage done, except to your gatehouse cottage door, Cornflower. I'll help you repair it. There! The old place looks nearly as good as new. Father Abbot, Redwall is yours once again. We await your word.'

The Abbot glanced up into Great Hall. 'Our first problem is how to stop Stryk flying about. She's making me dizzy, soaring and wheeling around the Abbey. John, you can make an addendum to the books on birds, concerning the remarkable healing powers of a great red kite's wing. By the fur, that bird looks as if she wants to spend the rest of her life in the air.'

John Churchmouse, not renowned for his humour, smiled.

'When I was a young un I could never make a kite that flew properly. Funny how you learn as you get older,' he joked.

∽

From the wine cellar, the tiny gruff voice of baby Rollo sang raucously:

'Chop up a rook'n make a soup,
Send him to bed wivout any bread,
Dip his tail in 'tober ale,
An' good ol' magpie pie!'

The sound of happy laughter rang through Redwall Abbey from the wine cellar to the very roofbeams of Great Hall, where the big red bird soared gracefully.

51

Matthias stood with his paw upon Mattimeo's shoulder and gazed around the hushed ledge. Orlando and Auma were with him, Jess Squirrel and her son Sam, Jabez Stump and his son Jubilation, and Basil and Cheek with Tim, Tess and Cynthia. Log-a-Log Flugg and his remaining shrews stood behind Matthias, while before him there was gathered a motley horde of young woodland creatures.

The surviving blackrobe rats had fled down the causeway steps, back to the green misted caves and tunnels that had been the Kingdom of Malkariss. All along the ledge, down the steps of the causeway and across the floor of the bottom workings, lay the ranks of the slain. In the flickering torchlight, eerie shadows danced around the silent rockface.

Mattimeo took the great sword of Redwall from his father as Matthias stood on a rocky knoll with his paws outstretched.

'You are free!' Matthias proclaimed.

A roaring cheer echoed through the underground.

The warrior mouse nodded approvingly. 'All of you who suffered under the cruelty of Malkariss, you who were stolen from your homes to lose many seasons of your young lives chained in dark places, let me tell you

419

something. The world outside is dressed in the colours of summer. Grass, flowers, trees and rivers, they are yours. If you cannot remember where you came from, if you have nowhere to go, come with me and my friends to Redwall Abbey in Mossflower country and live in peace there. For two days we have had to fight the powers of evil. Many were slain in the great battle, and you must never forget them, the good creatures who gave their lives to buy freedom for you.'

Heads were bowed, and tears were shed, for lost youth and lost friends. Matthias stepped down and nodded to Orlando, who took his place on the knoll. The warrior of the western plain raised his battleaxe as his thunderous voice boomed out:

'Let us go up into the sunlight! But first we will destroy the symbol of wickedness that has plagued this place!'

Orlando and Matthias took their weapons to the base of the great white statue which reared from the ledge to the roof of the immense cavern. Orlando spat upon his paws and grasped the axe handle firmly as he swung it back.

'The purple-robed rat, Nadaz, he's in there!' Tim Churchmouse cried out.

A hissing voice came from between the crystal teeth of the monolith:

'Fools, you cannot destroy the Kingdom of Malkariss. Now I am not only the Voice, I am King of the void.'

Matthias walked round the statue until he found the secret door. It was a tight-blocked entrance, cunningly carved so that it appeared as a mere hairline crack on the smooth limestone.

Matthias struck it with the flat of his blade.

'Come out, Nadaz, it is over!' he cried.

'Over?' The Voice of the Host laughed scornfully. 'No, it is just beginning. Malkariss was old and weak. I am Nadaz, I am strong. You cannot get me. The entrance has a secret seal that only I can unlock from the inside. When you are gone I will get more blackrobes, more slavers, and I will follow you and hunt you down like insects.'

Orlando swung the axe, hacking a chunk from the limestone. 'Then go to your kingdom, evil one. Eeeeula-liaaaaaa!'

∽

Woodlanders scattered and began running for the tunnels as pieces of limestone hurtled and flew, shattering against the rocks. Matthias hewed at one side of the statue with his war blade. Orlando pounded at the other side with his battleaxe.

Nadaz screeched and raged inside the head of the great white idol. Steel rang against stone as chunks, splinters, powder and lumps of limestone whizzed in all directions.

The muscles stood out like knotted cords upon the back of Orlando of the Axe as he slashed and hacked.

Coated in white dust, Matthias swung the double-edged blade, biting deep into the base of the statue.

Grunting and sweating, the two warriors battered away at the likeness of Malkariss until the limestone began shuddering under the impact. Cracks started to show, running the length of the limestone column which joined the floor of the ledge to the ceiling of the cave. The warriors continued their onslaught, but now dogged-ness had replaced their former reckless spirit. Still they swung with deadly purpose, ignoring the chips and lumps of stone that flew about them like missiles, directing all the force of their blades against the idol, while Nadaz ranted and screamed.

'You cannot escape. I will hound you across the woodlands, through the seasons, by night and day!'

∽

The rat's tirade was blotted out by a deep rumbling that emanated from base to apex of the statue, and the whole ledge began to tremble. Matthias shouldered his sword. Then realization of what was happening took over, and he jerked at the fur of the badger's back.

Oblivious to everything except the destruction of the evil symbol, Orlando the Axe flung his whole frame against each crashing blow as his weapon bit deeper and deeper into the groaning, splitting stone. Matthias ducked as the double-headed blade swung past him.

'Orlando, stop!' he roared at his companion. 'The whole place is collapsing! We must get out!'

With an explosion like a thunderclap, the statue of Malkariss broke off at its base. Matthias and Orlando ran for the tunnel entrance, hearts pounding, ears ringing, as they raced across the quaking ledge. They had caused the earth to dance, just as Jabez Stump's forebears had witnessed long ago.

The untold weight of the idol dropped, tearing a colossal piece of the cave ceiling with it. A widening rift split the entire ledge into two sections as the statue plunged into the depths, and the rock walls shattered. The two warriors dashed up the tunnel with the entire underground collapsing behind them.

∽

Mattimeo sat in the copse, watching the last of the woodland horde climbing out into the sunlight. Creatures danced and laughed, rolling in the grass, embracing the trees and waving at the great golden eye of the sun above.

Basil winked at him. 'By jingo! That's something worth waitin' to see, wot?'

Tess flung herself down at the young mouse's side.

'Fresh air and freedom, Matti. It tastes better than strawberry wine and new bread!'

The ground beneath their paws started to tremble. They froze, hugging the earth as the whole copse began to shake.

Jube grasped his father's spikes. 'What is it, Pa?' he asked worriedly.

Jabez hugged his young one to him. 'The earth is dancing, just as the cliffs once did!'

Jess and Sam dashed to the flight of steps that ran down to the underworld.

'Matthias, Orlando. Get out of there!' they called.

The steps shuddered violently. Jess peered into the gloom. 'There's somebeast coming. Make way, Sam!'

Little Vitch the rat scampered out as if demons were biting his tail. 'Yaagh! My whole cell began moving and the door fell off. Help me!'

Mattimeo grabbed him by the neck. 'My father and Orlando, did you see them?'

'No, no, I just ran. It's falling in down there. Can't you hear it!'

Basil Stag Hare flung himself upon Auma and dragged her back as she tried to get to the steps.

'Father, my father's in there!' she protested.

A deep rumbling boom exploded from the bowels of the cavern. Trees started to sway crazily and the earth bucked like a tablecloth being shaken free of crumbs.

Mattimeo took hold of Auma's paw, and they lay flat on the ground. 'We don't leave here until our fathers are out!' the mouse declared.

Basil buried his face against the trembling ground. 'Well spoken, young un. I second that proposal.'

There followed a terrific bang.

The entire copse fell, creating a huge valley. From the hole in the ground where the steps started, a whooshing gust of air, white with limestone dust, flew high into the sky like a geyser.

Two round objects shot out like balls from the mouth of a cannon. Matthias landed high in the branches of an elm. Orlando hit the top of a rowan and came crashing to earth in a cloud of twigs and leaves. The axe and the sword stood quivering in the bole of a young beech.

Then the earth stood still.

Basil got slowly to his paws and guffawed. 'Haw, haw, haw! Mattimeo, there's a flyin' white mouse up a tree over there. Looks a bit like your dad's ghost, wot?'

Mattimeo could hardly believe his eyes.

Jabez Stump tapped Auma. 'Your old pa looks like a lump of white dough ready for the oven, I reckon, missie. Hu-huh-huh!'

Jube patted his spikes to make sure they were all there. 'Whew! That big hatchet nearly scalped me!'

Orlando rose, dusting himself off in a dignified manner. 'Be careful how you talk of that weapon, young un. It's a battleaxe, not a hatchet.'

Jess Squirrel and Sam went haring up the beech trunk. 'Stay where you are, Warrior. We'll get you down, but only if you promise to do no more bird imitations.'

Matthias smiled at Sam's impudent remark.

'I promise. Just get me down.'

⌇

That same joyous day, the remnants of General Iron-beak's force were led out on rope leads to the top of the north battlements.

Ambrose Spike and baby Rollo followed them up the north wall steps to the ramparts, the infant bankvole waddling along comically in a passable impression of the bird's gait.

A light, warm breeze stirred the Abbot's robe as he and Constance lined the prisoners up. The inhabitants of Redwall stood about on the broad wall top, glaring at the subdued line of rooks and the two magpies, who blinked in the strong sunlight, huddling nervously together at the sight of Stryk Redkite as she watched them from the wall threshold above the gatehouse.

'Is that all of them, Ambrose?'

'Aye, 'tis, Father Abbot.'

'Good. Mrs Churchmouse, Cornflower, would you put the collars on them, please?'

The two mice emptied iron collars from a sack. Ambrose Spike had made the collars from iron barrel hoops. They were circular and left open in the middle, and slipped easily around the birds' necks.

Ragwing the rook dipped his head cheekily, and the iron collar slipped off and clanged upon the wallstones.

Winifred replaced the collar and whacked the rook with her rudderlike tail.

'Do as you're told, featherbag, or I'll give you something you won't forget in a hurry,' the otter warned.

The Abbot folded his paws into his habit sleeves.

'You birds, listen to me! We have not slain you or treated you badly, but this does not mean we are soft. Your leader and his crow are dead, the siege of Redwall is over. I have granted you the gift of life. You will be spared, but you must go back to your northlands and never return here again. This is my decision. I will not slay or enslave you, as your General would have done to us. However, you will take with you a token to remind you of your visit to our Abbey. The collars will allow you to fly, not too high, though. They will also prove an encumbrance. Forget your warlike ways; from now on, survival will be your main object.'

The Abbot nodded to Constance.

The mighty female badger took the collar of the first rook between her paws. With a small grunt of exertion she bent it so that the open ends of the iron closed about the bird's neck. The collar was now firmly in place, not too tight, but not loose enough to get off.

From bird to bird she went, bending the iron neck rings into place until the operation was completed. The rooks and the magpies pecked at the collars and cawed angrily.

Sister May lifted her paw high. 'Now, you villains, when I drop my paw the bells will ring and you will fly northwards as fast as you can. When the bells have rung three times, my friend Stryk Redkite will be right behind you, and you know what will happen to anybird who tries to stop or fly off in a different direction. So good riddance, birds. I would advise you to fly pretty fast.'

Sister May dropped her paw.

Bong! Boom!

The Methusaleh and the Matthias bells tolled out across Mossflower. General Ironbeak's depleted fighters flew off as fast as the burden of the iron neck collars would allow.

Bong! Boom!

The Abbey creatures watched them winging low over

the treetops, flying north across the summer green fastness of the woodlands.

Bong! *Boom*!

The great red kite took off from the west wall threshold with the graceful soaring motion of a natural hunter.

'*Kreeegah*! Stryk Redkite fly, Sissimay. Look!'

'Yes, I see you, Stryk. But remember your promise. Let them leave our country peacefully.'

⁓

When the birds were lost to view, Cornflower and Mrs Churchmouse took Rollo with them around the walltop to the south edge. The Abbot watched them go.

'Where do you think you're off to?' he asked them.

'Now that the Abbey is safe, Father Abbot, we are going to keep a vigil from the south wall until Matthias comes home with our young ones. With your permission of course,' Cornflower added.

Mordalfus smiled understandingly.

'Permission granted. You are excused all other duties. Keep a good watch with stout hearts. I know in my bones that our Warrior will return with the young ones.'

Cornflower shaded her eyes with her paw, repeating quietly to herself as she gazed south into Mossflower, 'Martin, return our loved ones safe to us.'

Baby Rollo had not quite got the gist of Cornflower's quiet words. However, he placed a chubby paw to his brow as he chanted with her, 'Marto aturnd luv ones safetyus.'

52

The Kingdom of Malkariss was gone. So were the last remnants of old Loamhedge. Sunk deeper beneath the earth, the jumble of stones that had once been planned as an underground realm was blocked for ever to the eyes of everybeast, choked and cemented in its deep grave by rocks, shale, soil and roots.

Matthias looked up to the rim of the crater, where trees leaned at odd angles in the sunken copse, and brown and black soil showed through the riven cracks in the grassy carpet. Wearily he sheathed the sword across his shoulders and turned to his followers.

'Follow me to Redwall!'

They were halfway up the steep hill when Vitch made a bolt. He dashed downhill, crossed the depression and began climbing the other side.

Mattimeo started to pursue him, but his father held him back.

'Let him go, son. He has no place among honest woodlanders.'

They stood for a moment and watched the small rat scramble over a large boulder half embedded in the hillside. Suddenly Vitch screamed and began scrambling back on to the boulder, holding both paws up pleadingly.

'No, no, please. I never told them anything. I wasn't

427

going with them. They found me!'

The silken mask and cloak appeared in view. Then there was a whirling sound as the metal-ended bolas hissed through the air.

Vitch died without a sound.

'Slagar!'

Matthias and Orlando rushed down the hillside, unloosing their weapons as they ran.

The crazed fox stood up. He ran halfway to the fallen Vitch, changed his mind at the sight of the oncoming warriors and began scrambling to the top of the hill.

Foam flecked wildly from Orlando's mouth as he swung the axe, pounding uphill as easily as he would over level ground. Spurred on by the sight of his arch-enemy, Matthias raced alongside the badger, his teeth clenched tightly, brandishing the sword of Redwall. The whole army turned and followed them.

Slagar made it to the top of the hill. He glanced behind, to see the two Warriors halfway up pursuing him. Still looking over his shoulder, the masked fox ran.

But only three paces.

The earth swallowed him up. He fell like a great fluttering moth, down into the one place that had not sunk or collapsed: the old well of Loamhedge Abbey, the secret exit from the Kingdom of Malkariss!

∽

Matthias and Orlando stood with their chests heaving as they gasped in air, staring down at the crumpled mass far below in the deep well. The secret way was no more an avenue of escape, it was merely a deep pit that proved useless except for its final function: the grave of Slagar.

'I swore to slay that silken hooded thief!' Orlando sighed with regret.

Matthias leaned upon his sword. 'So did I, friend. This has saved us any argument. Let's get some rocks, at least we can bury him together.'

The body of Vitch, still with Slagar's bolas wrapped around its skull, was lowered down into the pit. The former slaves filled in the last of the pit with soil.

Orlando tamped the earth with a hefty paw. 'There's an end to him. There are no words you could say over such a creature.'

As Matthias nodded agreement, a poetic voice rang out from above:

'A taker of slaves and a thief,
I know not what master he served,
Cruel Slagar has come to grief,
'twas all that he deserved.'

'Sir Harry!'
The big owl flapped down beside Matthias.

'Yes, it's old Sir Harry the Muse.
I see you won victory,
So I flew back to bring you the news.
Just guess what happened to me.
I chased those vermin south,
I think they're running yet.
When I heard a great noise from afar,
So I said to myself "I'll bet
That's my friends doing battle beneath the ground!"
Then I turned on my wings and flew to see
How a mouse could make such a big sound!'

Basil came ambling up. 'Oh, hullo, it's you, the great flyin' poetic feedbag. How are you, old chap? Hungry, I'll wager. Wot?'

Matthias chuckled as he gave Mattimeo his sword to carry. 'Come on, son, let's go home!'

53

The Summer of the Golden Plain drew to a glorious finish, and the yellow flowers faded and died. Matthias had not returned to Redwall, but still Cornflower did not give up hope. She even pleaded with the Abbot not to name the season. Though Mordalfus had chosen Autumn of the Early Chestnut, he bowed to Cornflower's wishes. Stryk Redkite had returned to her beloved mountains, and the orchard was beginning to get heavy with the rich harvest of fruit and berries.

Cornflower stood on the south wall and faithfully kept up her vigil with Mrs Churchmouse and Rollo.

'See, the woodlands are turning brown and russet. Soon the hazelnut and acorn will be ready for gathering. We'll miss Jess and Sam; nobeast gathers the nuts as well as a squirrel,' she said sadly.

'Aye, beechnuts too,' Mrs Churchmouse added. 'Remember last autumn, when all the young ones went into Mossflower nut-gathering? My Tim and Tess both had long sticks to knock them down from the low branches.'

Cornflower sighed. 'My Matti got into trouble over the nut-gathering. He took his father's sword from the gatehouse to rattle the branches with. Oh, I do wish he and Matthias were back, Mrs Churchmouse.'

'If hopes were honey we'd have a cupboardful,

Cornflower. Ah well, we'd best get indoors. It's way past young master Rollo's bedtime. Who's on supper tonight?' Mrs Churchmouse asked, to change the subject.

'Er, Sister May and Brother Trugg. It should be something nice. Come on, little Rollo, supper and bye-byes.'

The infant took Cornflower's paw as they descended the wallsteps.

'A come t'morrer on wall?' he wanted to know.

'Yes, Rollo. We'll come to the wall tomorrow, and all the tomorrows after that until my Mattimeo comes back. Do you remember Mattimeo?'

Rollo rubbed a tiny paw into his eyes. He was tired. 'A'member 'timeo.'

∽

Supper *was* good: redcurrant fritters and honeybread with hot elderberry cordial. The Abbey had been repaired after the bird damage, food was plentiful and the season was mild, yet a gloom hung over the Abbey without the presence of absent loved ones.

Cornflower sat late at table with Constance and the Abbot. Ambrose Spike had gone to his wine cellar, Mrs Churchmouse and John had carried Rollo off to the dormitory, and all the other Redwallers had gone off to settle down for the night. The only sound was Winifred and Brother Rufus laying the trays out in the kitchen for next morning's baking.

Mordalfus folded up his glasses and yawned. 'Still no sign of them yet, Cornflower?'

'No, Father Abbot. But don't you worry, they'll come home soon.'

'You have great faith, daughter. That is good. But we must learn in this life that the time comes to be realistic. You must see that they've been gone nearly a season's length now. That is a long time in the span of any creature.'

A tear rolled down Cornflower's cheek, and she wiped it away busily.

'Oh dear, my eyes get so watery when I'm tired. Maybe I should get Brother Dan to make me spectacles like yours.'

Constance's heart went out to the brave little mouse, and the badger stood up decisively.

'Right, it's quarter moon tomorrow night. If they're not back by the time the moon is full, then I'm going out to look for them!'

The Abbot nodded his approval. 'An excellent idea, old friend. I'll send the remaining sparrows with you and whoever you choose to take.'

They shook paws across the table. Constance winked cheerily at Cornflower.

'Come on, Cornflower. Off to bed with you, or you'll be too tired to climb those south wall steps tomorrow.'

∽

When Cornflower had gone, Constance shook her head.

'I'm afraid I must agree with you, Mordalfus. A season is a long time, and the longer they're away the less chance they stand of coming back.'

'I know, Constance, but I couldn't say that in front of Cornflower. She keeps her hopes up though she looks so sad these days, and the churchmice too. D'you really suppose they'll come back?'

Constance toyed with some crumbs on the tabletop. 'My heart likes to think so. However, my brain tells me different. At least the hope that we'll be sending a search party out soon should cheer her up. Ah well, come on, young feller, it's past bedtime.'

The two friends shuffled off wearily up the steps into Great Hall.

∽

Shortly before dawn, Cornflower turned restlessly on her pallet in the dormitory. She had decided not to sleep in the gatehouse cottage until her family was reunited. Soft voices rang through her head as grey figures stole across her dreams. 'Matthias, is that you, are you back?' she called out in her sleep. 'No, wait, you're not

432

Matthias. It's Mattimeo. Oh, my little Matti, how you've grown. Is it really you? Come closer and let me look at you.'

The figure loomed closer out of the mists of slumber. It was a warrior mouse, neither Matthias or Mattimeo, but so like them both. The mouse smiled at Cornflower and pointed in the direction of the south wall.

'Martin becomes Matthias becomes Mattimeo, and so it goes. Go now.'

∽

The dream faded as some creature tugged at Cornflower's paw.

She opened her eyes and sat up, as baby Rollo climbed on the pallet.

'Wanna waterdrink, Rollo firstee,' he pleaded.

Cornflower hurriedly threw on a habit over her nightgown. 'Come on, little one, we'll take water and bread up on the wall. Lets have a picnic breakfast. The sun will soon be up.'

Rollo skipped beside her happily. 'Water'n'breads, pickernick on wall.'

∽

The sun rose over Mossflower like a ball of red fire, lighting the treetops, and dispelling the long grey and purple rolls of cloud. The sky was soft pink tinged blue. Birds heralded the day as a light mist rose from the forest.

Cornflower looked out eagerly over the still woodlands. Not a leaf moved or a blade of grass stirred. There was nothing out there. She set Rollo's breakfast out upon the stones. Then, clenching her paws in determination, she waited. Still nothing.

∽

The morning brightened as Redwall Abbey came alive with the sounds of creatures going about their daily chores and pursuits. John Churchmouse sat next to his wife at the breakfast table. He looked up from the maps of Mossflower he was studying.

'No baby Rollo this morning, dear?'

Mrs Churchmouse passed the cheese to Ambrose. 'No, that's strange. Cornflower's missing too. I wonder where they have got to.'

John finished his October ale at a single draught. 'Top of the south wall, of course, where they go with you every day. Come on, I'll take you up there and we'll stand with them for a while.'

~

When they arrived at the south ramparts, Rollo was hurling apple cores over the wall at imaginary rooks.

'Morning, Cornflower. Glad to see you've got a warrior to protect you in case of invasion,' John remarked.

'Oh, good morning to you both. Sorry I didn't give you a call, but we decided to come up here early and bring breakfast with us.'

John chuckled. 'Good job it wasn't porridge, the way that young scamp is chucking stuff about. Here, Rollo, why don't you try throwing a pebble with your little sling. It'll go further.'

Rollo tried, but the pebble kept hitting the top of the wall and bouncing back. Half preoccupied with watching the antics of the little one, Cornflower turned away from her vigil. Constance joined them, and as the mice played with the baby bankvole, she looked out across the south reaches, casually at first.

Then Constance froze as if she had been turned to stone. She remained rigid, staring southwards and slightly west.

Cornflower looked up as she retrieved Rollo's stone. 'Constance, what is it?'

'Dust!'

'Dust? Where from?'

'Seems to be from beyond that bend in the path, behind the trees. I can't tell yet. Wait a moment. . . . Yes, it's dust all right, and it's coming this way!'

The three mice scrambled to the top of a battlement.

Cornflower jumped up and down, and Constance had to catch her apron strings to keep her from falling.

'It's dust! Somebeast is coming up the path, I know it!' Cornflower shouted.

John Churchmouse quickly donned his glasses. 'There must be a great many to send up a dust cloud like that so early on an autumn morning. They'll be round the bend soon. Listen, can you hear voices?'

Constance leaned forward, straining her ears. Faintly she could catch the strains of voices chanting the familiar warriors' cries of Redwall and Mossflower.

Round the bend of the path they came, the paws of the horde raising a cloud of brown dust.

Cornflower could see the leaders as they began to march in double time at the sight of Redwall Abbey.

'It's Matthias and Mattimeo, they've returned!' she shouted.

John Churchmouse and his wife yelled aloud, 'Look, there's our Tess and Tim. . . . Hooray!'

Constance leaned out across the battlements. 'There's Basil, and Jess and Sam. See, they've got young Cynthia with them!'

'I can see two badgers!'

'There's an owl. Look, an owl!'

'Hedgehogs, shrews, woodlanders! By the fur and claw, there's a great army of woodlanders coming this way!'

'Turn out the Abbey, tell the Father Abbot. Sound the bells!'

∽

Matthias marched shoulder to shoulder with his friends, while the horde packed in behind them gazed up in awe at the red sandstone Abbey which reared above the trees ahead.

Mattimeo began laughing. Tim, Tess and Cynthia pounded him on the back as they shouted and cheered wildly:

'Good old Redwall, tell Ambrose to get the barrels open!'

435

'Who's that on the walls? It's your mum. Look, there's ours too. Mum, Mum! D'you think they can hear us?'

∽

The Methusaleh and the Matthias bells began pealing and clanging out across the clear morning air.

Bong! Clang! Boom! Bong! Clang! Boom!

Basil halted the army. 'Right markers, get fell in. Come on, you sloppy lot, we're coming home like a proper army, not a ragamuffin crowd. Ranks of six, chins in, chests out, shoulders back. Step lively there, you at the back, catch up. Come on, come on, laddie buck, you're not on a daisy-chain ramble now, y'know. Quick march!'

'Never gives up, does he?' Jess muttered to Sam from the side of her mouth. 'You watch, he'll be the first to break ranks and charge if anybeast throws a pie over that wall.'

∽

The hot morning sunlight shafted down on the brown dust rising between the green and gold leaves of Mossflower as the main doors of the old red sandstone Abbey burst open.

The Abbot walked out at the head of the Abbey dwellers. They lined the path facing Matthias at the head of his army.

There was complete silence as they stood looking at each other.

The warrior mouse unslung his great sword. Stepping forward, he laid it flat in the dust at the paws of Mordalfus.

'Father Abbot, we have come home.'

There was a mighty cheer which shook the timbers of the main gate frame, then the ranks broke as every creature dashed forward to greet old friends and meet new ones.

So it was the young ones returned to Redwall.

∽

It took the whole of that day in the Abbot's study for the full story to unfold from both sides.

Matthias, Jess, Basil and Orlando, with Mattimeo, Tim, Tess, Sam, Cynthia and Auma, crowded in alongside Cornflower, Constance and Ambrose Spike.

Food was brought in to them as the young ones related all that had happened from the night of the feast to Malkariss's cells. Matthias, Orlando, Jess and Basil related the hunt for the young ones from the same night up to the death of Slagar.

It was late afternoon before they were done. The Abbot had listened intently to the harrowing narrative. He shook his head sadly.

'In the midst of all our joyous reunion we must never forget fallen friends, particularly Queen Warbeak and Log-a-Log. I will hold services for all our fallen friends at the first sunrise of spring, and they will remain dear to our memories for all the seasons to come.'

In the sad silence that followed, Matthias decided to lighten the mood of the proceedings a little. He slapped his paw down on the table.

'Well then, Mordalfus you old twig, I suppose you've been sitting here twiddling your paws while we've been away. Tell me, how did you manage to keep busy?'

The Abbot chuckled. 'Oh, we managed, I suppose. However, I'll let Cornflower tell you about that.'

Cornflower took her paw from around Mattimeo's shoulder for the first time that day. She stood up and grinned mischievously.

'Hmmm, it was as dull as ditchwater without our warriors and young ones about. Then one fine day we had a visit from some birds. Let me tell you about it. . . .'

They listened spellbound, fuming with indignity at the thought of baby Rollo being held hostage, cheering for Sister May and her drugged strawberries, laughing aloud at the warrior ghost mouse and the terror it caused among the rooks, and finally applauding Constance and Stryk Redkite at the final struggle.

Mattimeo picked up his father's sword and offered it to Cornflower.

'Here, Mum, you should be the Champion of Redwall!'

Matthias shook his head in amazement. 'By the claw and the fur! What a brave bunch we have at our Abbey. I would dearly like to meet this Stryk Redkite.'

Constance gazed fondly at Auma as she stroked the young one's headstripes. 'You will, Matthias, you will, someday. Now, we must find quarters for our new friends. Sister May and Brother Rufus will open the infirmary to all, for sore paws and old wounds must be treated. I'm afraid there's no supper tonight. You'll have to go straight to bed. Anyhow, you lot look as if a long rest will do you good.'

Basil's ears flopped with disappointment. 'What, no supper? I say, Constance old fruit, the only thing that's kept B. Stag Hare on his paws for nearly a full season was the hope of a good old scoff at Redwall. I mean, what's a chap to do if he's had the old nosebag cut off, wot, wot? Bad form, old gel, t' say nothin' of rank bad manners to our guests. No supper. I don't believe it!'

Mrs Churchmouse slapped Basil smartly upon the paw. 'Mr Stag Hare, will you kindly give your overworked jaws a rest and be quiet! Thank you. Now let me explain. The reason that we are not cooking supper is that the season is to be named first thing tomorrow: the Autumn of the Warriors' Return. All our Abbey dwellers have volunteered to work through the night, but new arrivals must sleep and keep out of the way. Starting at sunup, we are going to hold a feast in the orchard.'

Basil's ears stood up like two signals. 'A f-feast, y' say, marm. Will it be a big un?'

Cornflower spread her paws. 'The biggest one you've ever sat down to, Basil.'

'Golly! Bigger than the summer feast?'

'Far bigger!'

'An' you're all goin' to cook right through the night?'

'Oh yes, that's why we don't want you under our paws. Otherwise we might not have it ready on time.'

'Got it, marm. All the weary warriors sleep while you sportin' creatures cook up a whackin' beanfeast. Right?'

'Right!'

Basil shot out of the Abbot's study like a rocket, calling over his shoulder as he went, 'Last one in bed and fast asleep's a rotten egg. Yaaaah!'

Foremole entered the study, rubbing his nose. 'Oi jus' bin a-runned over boi a mad creatur'. Hurr.'

Orlando laughed so hard he hurt his jaw.

54

The feast of the Autumn of the Warriors' Return began just after dawn. Mist rose in the orchard as the sun began to mount in the sky, and rosy apples dripped dew on to the heads of the creatures who sat beneath the trees. There were far too many for tables, so the entire party sat on the grass.

Chestnuts were baked and roasted on the fire pit dug by the moles; cheeses were rolled from the larders; fresh fruit lay in heaps between honeycombs and small hillocks of new baked bread.

Ambrose Spike tapped the casks of cider, October ale, berry wines and various fruit cordials which stood on trestles around a thick-boled beech tree.

The liberated slaves sat transfixed. They had never seen such an abundance of fare. Moles called for gangway as they trundled deeper'n'ever pies out on trolleys; long poles slung between otters wobbled under the weight of cauldrons of watershrimp and hotroot soup: hazelnut and acorn scones were laid out in rows to cool by the raspberry canes.

Mrs Churchmouse and Cornflower barely managed to stop baby Rollo diving from a pear tree into a maple and mint cream trifle, while Mattimeo and his friends were recapturing their lost season with other young ones from the slave pits. They dashed about, plucking wild cherries from the tops of iced cakes, and sneaking candied chestnuts from an arrangement which Sister May was making. She scolded them tongue in cheek as the intricate heap fell apart for the umpteenth time.

Jabez Stump and young Jube were discovering the delights of strawberry cordial cold from the cellars. They lay beneath a trickling barrel with their mouths open wide, only stopping to munch celery and young onion flan.

෴

Basil Stag Hare was instructing his protégé young Cheek in the art of trencherbeastship.

'No, no, m'lad. Don't grab it all at once. Watch me. A smidgeon of fruit cake on the plate, a slice to eat now; a pawful of honeyed blackberries for yourself, and one for your plate; a quick swig of elderberry wine, and fill your beaker with beetroot port; now, some of the Abbot's Redwall pie; lots of Brother Trugg's celery and woodland herb dip; compliment the old mole fellers on the deeper'n'ever pie an' they'll give you an extra-large helpin'. Right, tackle that lot, and we'll start again!'

෴

Sir Harry was perched among the sparrows.

'Now listen and mark my words
As I eat this delicious cheese.
You're really quite lucky birds,
To live in surroundings like these,
Woodland nutcrunch, gooseberry pie,
Honeybaked apples too.
Billberry pudding, my, oh my,
Just swallow, don't bother to chew.'

The Abbot looked apologetically over his glasses at Matthias. 'There's a very nice fish baking in the pit, a grayling, like the one we caught together many seasons ago. I'm sorry I didn't wake you up to go fishing, but you were sleeping so peacefully.'

Matthias shook his head regretfully as he watched the

moles take the dockleaves from the steaming white fish which lay on the pit embers.

'Hmm, I've missed our fishing trips, but I forgive you. By the way, who did help you? It's more than a one-mouse job, landing a fish that size.'

Sister May tugged shyly at the Warrior's habit.

'Beg pardon, Matthias, it was me. We hooked it, played it and landed it together, the Abbot and I.'

'Well, I never! Sister May, you're getting a dreadful name around here. Knocking birds out with herbs and cooking pots, helping ghosts to walk, now fishing half the night after grayling on the Abbey pond. What next?'

'Taking my paw to your young Mattimeo's ear, if he keeps upsetting my candied chestnut display. If you'll excuse me,' Sister May said, and hurried off.

~

Baby Rollo had finally succeeded in diving from the pear tree straight into the centre of an oversized sliced apple and wild plum crumble. He sat smiling and eating his way out, a mass of sweet acorn crumbs and sticky fruit.

Basil Stag Hare wagged his ears in admiration. 'Now there's a buck with the right idea. Here, Rollo old messmate, chuck Uncle Basil a helpin', will you? I say, marm, this Mossflower salad is outstanding. Is that fennel you've grated in with the carrot? Excellent. My, my, what a pretty pattern of parsley and cucumber around the edge. Talented gel!'

Sister Agnes blushed at the compliments. 'Oh, Mr Stag Hare, have you tried my orchard fruit cake with the buttercup cream centre?'

'Lead me to it, marm!'

~

Jess and Sam had taken the young squirrel Elmtail in tow. They laughed at his curiosity as he sampled everything put in front of him.

'What's this one called?'

'Blueberry cream tart.'

'Mmmph, great! What's this nice drink?'

'Oh, that's cold mint and apple tea. D'you like it?'

'I'll say I do! Can I have some of that funny-looking pie?'

'Ssshh! Don't let the Abbot hear you, that's his new invention, wild cherry and glazed plum gateau with elderflower cream. He's very proud of it.'

'Mmmm, so he should be, tastes marvellous. D'you use paws or a spoon?'

'Try using your mouth. Hahaha!'

∽

Morning slid into afternoon. A gentle breeze drifted small white clouds across the serene blue expanses of sky, and the autumn sun shone down kindly upon the happy scene as the creatures of Redwall feasted through noontide, across the balmy evening until the night fires and lanterns in trees illuminated the joyous scene below. The half moon came out to watch for the sun. It shed pale light upon baby Rollo, fast asleep on Orlando's lap. The big badger's battleaxe hung from a beech tree nearby. He turned to Matthias, who was drifting off into sleep, holding Cornflower's paw.

'Warrior, I have never seen such a wondrous place as this. Look at the beautiful building, those huge safe walls, the fruit and food growing from the ground; and that pond, it glows like a silver plate in the moonlight. Aaaahhh! These contented old ones, peaceful, wise, and your young ones too, they look so happy and good. Even when I lived out on the Western Plains with my Auma, we never knew such wellbeing as this. Can you explain it to me?'

Matthias let his eyelids droop until they shut.

'Orlando, my good friend, the explanation to it all is merely one simple word: Redwall.'

The badger turned to reply, but Matthias and Cornflower were asleep. He looked down at baby Rollo slumbering on his lap without a care in the world. Settling himself down, Orlando turned his face to the night sky which surrounded Mossflower. He repeated the precious word aloud to the moon:

'Redwall!'

55

Extract from the diary of Tim Churchmouse, Recorder of Redwall Abbey:

It is the summer of the Roschay Willowherb!

Great masses of the pink mauve flowers nod their heads by the sides of our Abbey paths. Seven seasons have passed, counting the Autumn of the Warriors' Return, and this will be my second season as Recorder. John, my father, retired. He is now helping the Abbot to compile a great volume of Mossflower recipes. Strange, when I was young our Father Abbot was an old mouse, yet still he carries on changeless as ever. I think he will outlive us all.

The slaves who were freed from the evil of Malkariss have all settled here. They are our Brothers and Sisters now, and a happier band you could not meet. The Sparra colony is growing and flourishing in our roofspaces, though now it is called Warbeak Loft. Sir Harry the Muse lives up there with them. He was elected Leader and Poetry Instructor. Several times now he has resigned in despair at the Sparra language, though his love of authority always leads him to be re-elected.

Redwall is surely a place of curious happenings, not the least of which is the adoption of Cheek by Basil. There was much amusement three seasons ago when he became officially the hare's young one. Now he calls himself Cheek Stag Otter, and the impudent rascal has also adopted all Basil's manner-isms (and his appetite too).

Stryke Redkite is at present paying us a visit. She has a mate, a huge fellow named Skine, and they have their first eggchick too. Sister May was delighted at their announcement that the young one is to be named after her. However, she insists on the little female being called May and not Sissimay.

Ambrose Spike is revelling in his latest title, High Keeper of Cellar Keys, and the entire family of Jabez Stump – Rosyqueen his wife and their ten hungry daughters – are living in the wine cellar with Jube. Ambrose has put in an order to the Foremole for the cellars to be extended, and it will be attended to immediately after the mole crew finish enlarging and lining the tunnels they dug during Ironbeak's seige. They are a useful underground system, particularly in deep winter snow.

∽

The Guosim marched off into Mossflower again; they were born to wander. Flugg is a strong Log-a-Log, wise too, and he brings them to winter here every fourth season. They are good allies.

Rollo and Cynthia Bankvole are bellringers, just as Tess and I once were. Rollo's latest yearning is to become a squirrel and join the band of Sam and Elmtail to become part of the Mossflower Patrol. That Rollo, he will probably want to be a badger next.

Constance is getting ready to sit out in the sun and take things easy. She is teaching Auma all she knows, and some season soon Auma will become the Mother of Redwall. She is dearly loved by every creature in our Abbey. Orlando is Constance's firm friend and they are seldom apart. His axe hangs in Great Hall. As Lord of the Western Plains he only has to stand on the west battlements to survey his lands.

Last summer the Churchmouse family was united to the Warriors, much to the delight of my mother and Cornflower. Mattimeo and my sister Tess were married. Our parents like to sit out in the sun a lot, my mother and father, Cornflower and Matthias. Like all life, they are growing no younger. They prefer to talk of the old times with friends, and that is good. They deserve a little rest and peace after bringing us up, though Matthias still joins Basil and Orlando to train the defenders.

It is difficult to believe that we have all grown from young scamps into responsible creatures. But I am rambling. I will finish my writings and go outside into the sunlight, to the ceremony and the feast at the main gate. Forgive me for not telling you earlier, but today we have a new Redwall Champion and a naming party. Matthias is to place the great sword in the paws of his son Mattimeo, and he will be our Abbey Warrior from henceforth; there is one scamp who made doubly good. Did I not tell you? Tess and Mattimeo have a little son and I am an uncle! My mother and Cornflower chose the new baby's name; he is to be called Martin.

So the legend of Redwall has come full circle, through Martin to Matthias, from Matthias to Mattimeo, and finally back to the little life we are all so proud of: Martin, Son of the Warrior. The bells are tolling for the ceremony, so you will have to pardon me for hurrying off like this.

May your lives be as full and happy as ours, and may the seasons be kind to you and your friends. The door of our Abbey is always open to any traveller roaming the dusty path between the woodlands and the plains.

Tim Churchmouse (Recorder of Redwall Abbey
in Mossflower country).

BRIAN JACQUES
The Long Patrol

*Y*oung Tammo dreams of joining the Long
Patrol, the army of fighting hares who serve
Lady Cregga Rose Eyes, ruler of Salamandastron.
And with Damug Warfang's mighty Rapscallions
on the rampage, Tammo's dream is about to
become a brutal reality...

They came pounding through the woodlands towards
Tammo, a score or more of snarling savages, brandishing an
ugly and lethal array of weapons.

Foliage rustled overhead and Russa came sailing out of a
tree to land beside him, her jaw set grimly.

'I never figgered on this many, mate. The villains've got us
surrounded. Pity it had to happen yore first time out, Tam.'

Tammo felt no fear, only rage. Drawing his blade he
gritted his teeth and swung the loaded sling like a flexible
club. 'Stand back t'back with me, pal. If we've got to go then
let's give 'em somthin' to jolly well remember us by.
EULALIAAAAAA!'

THE LONG PATROL, A Tale of Redwall by Brian Jacques
Hutchinson hardback, £12.99 ISBN 0 09 176546 3
And coming soon in paperback from Red Fox!